THE SONS OF MIL

THE INNISFAIL CYCLE

BOOK ONE

L.M. RIVIERE

CHAPTERS

PART ONE

VAGABONDS

THE HUNT

n.e. 508
13, dor samna
eire

B en was bored out of his mind. His arse was fast asleep, and he hadn't felt his toes for eons. At this point, he'd be better served drinking himself into a stupor rather than idle here in solitary sobriety. Never mind the blasted weather, which grew increasingly bitter as the sun sank in the west. Twilight crept into the valley. Long shadows stretched between the trees like poured ink. To the east, swift clouds raced through an amethyst sky, awash with rivers of white stars. As evening descended, owls hooted from their hollows, and foxes and voles gave chase in the underbrush.

Prosaic as the scene might have been, comfortable it was not. Ben shrugged his cloak tight, annoyed by its insufficient weight. He would much prefer to watch the seasons change from a nice cozy window, with his hands wrapped firmly around a piping hot tankard of spiced cider. Spending the night high in a tree, in the middle of a damp forest, was *not* his idea of a fine time. Dor Samna batted her lashes at winter, and Ben missed the Ban months more than ever.

What, in the nine hells, was *keeping* them?

Absent the sun, the wind clawing over the Boyne cut deep. Ben blew into his palms. This was absurd. If the temperature dropped much further, he'd be obliged to work on the flask hidden within his

1

vest or risk his extremities to the elements. That would prove a bit counterproductive, considering the reason he was out here in the first place. Alas, a watchman had a duty to remain sober. His job was to guard the Greenmakers' reentry into Eire, and it would be foolish to get whiffing drunk to keep warm. Ben was an accomplished archer, but everyone knew drink and tedium made for poor aim.

Nevertheless, knowing better would not dissuade him for much longer. When his bollocks started to shrink into his torso, wisdom be damned. Perhaps a nip or two now wouldn't hurt anything? He took one, then another, and by the fourth or fifth, decided a lousy shot was better than none.

It was unlike Robin to dally. Ben's mood soured for the interminable waiting. Any Greenmaker worth his salt knew better than to linger over this border. Robin Gramble certainly understood his business as The Quarter's Headman. Hadn't he emphasized the importance of haste this very morning? Ben would be delighted to know what was keeping him. The wilds of Aes Sidhe were not a pleasant place for mortal men to roam, regardless of circumstance. This delay could only mean something was amiss.

Pocketing his flask with a sigh, he scanned the border for the thousandth time. A thick, aberrant mist crowded the river on the opposite shore, impervious to the bracing wind. Ben strained to peer further than the first line of smoking trees that curled toward the embankment. His head throbbed from having been on the lookout all damned day. The mists of Aes Sidhe marked the border between the realm of men and the land of the Immortals to the north. Even from his elevated vantage, visibility was minimal. This effect was by design. The Sidhe did not invite prying eyes into their domain. That pervasive cloud concealed much more than riches or game. Dark things. Horrible things. Most men who dared to trespass never returned. The Greenmakers of Rosweal were likely the only men in the whole of Eire who fully grasped the significance of that warning. Something was wrong. It must be.

They should have been back by now.

2

Brooding over a host of potential perils that might have delayed his comrades, Ben finally caught a hint of silver and ivory in the distance. Winking in and out of the fog, a pale figure dashed alongside the riverbank, something metallic glinting from a clenched fist. Ben inched forward on his bough, hugging the heavy branch with his knees while he unslung his bow. That was no Greenmaker. Ben's crew did not own such flashy gear, nor were any of them half so tall. That shock of white was a Dannan cuirass. A hunter from Bri Leith, no doubt.

Ben muttered a curse. Struggling to nock with half-frozen fingers, he searched for any sign that his friends were on their way and in one piece. He saw nothing at first save mist, the impression of dark trees, and great pools of swirling gloom. Then, he heard shouting and the undeniable ring of steel against steel. Shimmying further out on his limb, Ben spotted several charcoal silhouettes running through the haze, dragging men and dead animals between them. Robin's booming baritone was unmistakable.

"Get over, lads! Go, go!"

The Dannans blew their horns. The chase was on.

Someone must have done something stupid. That was the only explanation that would warrant such a swift martial response. Robin was usually a stalwart professional on a raid. He demanded nothing less from his men. Whatever had happened surely hadn't been his call. Ben spied his friend a hundred or so yards to the northwest. Robin ran pretty fast for a fellow of middling age. Gerrod and Paul splashed through the mud behind him, hauling a six-point stag with a snow-white pelt over their shoulders. They were covered head to toe in the beast's blood.

Ben's ears grew hot at the sight.

Ah... he thought.

Bloody fools!

What idiocy prompted this madness?

Sylvan stags were sacred to the Sidhe. Venerated as vessels of the god Herne, the famed beast was the sigil of the High King's Clan. No *wonder* the Greenmakers had a score of Dannan warriors in pursuit. Robin damned well knew better! What had possessed him to allow such an obvious, careless misstep on his watch? Growing angrier by the second, Ben drew his longbow crosswise. No damned good was going to come of this; he was certain. Seamus' vivid red head emerged from the curtain of mist after Robin, two sable fox tails swinging from his wide belt. In his haste, Seamus slipped into the detritus littering the forest floor. An ivory-fletched arrow missed his ear by a breath. Another zipped past his thigh, making him stumble again.

"For feck's sake!" he cried. "Robin! Keep goin'! They're everywhere!"

While Seamus scrambled to his knees, a Dannan hunter leapt from the woods on his right, twin larks poised to slice through his middle. Seamus raised a useless hand to ward off the attack. He needn't have bothered. The Sidhe scout was thrown backward by one of Ben's arrows. His blond head cracked off the trunk of a nearby birch. The arrow's plain brown fletching protruded from a painful but non-fatal wound in the crook of his shoulder. Seamus wasted no time skittering away on all fours. Slithering down the embankment on his belly, he was halfway across by the time Robin, Gerrod, and Paul plodded into the current. Ben fumed, watching them heave their heavy prize through the water by its rack. Robin shoved them off and stood sentry in the shallows, his crossbow poised to defend their position.

"Nat! Marty! Get yer arses moving!"

Another hunter emerged from the canopy on Robin's right, raising his larks high. Robin sent a quarrel through his gut, felling him on the spot. Gore spewed from the back of the Sidhe's lovely white cuirass. Robin reloaded and shot the next Dannan through the throat. Ben heard a distinct click. He was out of ammunition.

"Ben, Siora, damn ye! Tell me yer out there!"

Ben whistled back in mimic of a common marsh swallow. Signal received with a curt nod; Robin drew his daggers.

"Marty," he roared with new urgency as three more Sidhe hunters darted into his line of sight. "Nat! Where are ye?"

Dropping to a lower limb, Ben nocked and fired twice more. The first target took an arrow to the thigh; the second through the ribs. Neither shot was fatal. Ben made sure. He would not kill a Dannan warrior unless he had no choice. A third hunter tore out of the trees and threw himself at Robin with a snarl. They splashed into the river in a rolling tangle of limbs and steel. Ben didn't have a clear shot.

Robin would have to sort himself.

Instead, Ben focused on a burst of activity in the distance. Red-faced, Marty dragged Nat's flaccid frame by one shoulder. An ivory shaft bloomed from the center of Nat's chest. A thick line of blood dribbled down his dirty green jerkin.

"Ben!" squealed Marty. "They're comin'!"

More Dannan hunters tracked them to the riverbank. Two were mounted on dappled grey horses. Ben was too far removed to nail either one from his vantage.

"Robin!" his voice carried over the river. He slung his bow over his shoulder to descend. "They're not going to make it!"

Aware that he'd given away his position, Ben clambered to the ground like his feet were on fire. The Sidhe were the finest marksmen in Innisfail. He would pay for one wrong move with his life. Sure enough, an arrow sailed into the trunk where his head had been a moment before. Another tore a hunk out of his cheek. Dodging a third missile, his boots bore into the mud below his rowan. Ben returned fire. His arrow struck something solid, but he was already running from another volley by the time he was ready to draw again.

Robin dumped his attacker's corpse face-down in the Little Boyne. The slain Dannan's pale hair churned in the frothing red current. Clutching at a fresh wound in his side and with one dagger remaining, Robin bellowed, "Where are they?"

An arrow ripped through one of Ben's sleeves, very near his ribcage. "Damn it! I'm a little busy here! On your right!"

Robin waded downriver toward his two injured men. Marty attempted to run to him but wobbled forward onto his knees. Robin screamed a warning too late. A razor-thin lark slammed into Marty's back, shoving bits of his heart through the front of his tunic. The Dannan withdrew his blade with a wary green eye on Robin. Marty slumped face-first into the river. There was nothing to be done for him now. Nat, on the other hand, bobbed just shy of Robin's reaching fingers. Waist deep and ducking arrows, Robin snatched at the unconscious lad's cowl, desperate to drag him over. If they could make it across, they might be safe. The Sidhe never trekked into Eire unless expressly ordered to do so. Though, there would hardly be a need if the last two poachers died in an attempted escape. Robin would never make it out alive if Ben didn't start shooting with real intent. He had no desire to kill anyone for this day's idiocy, but he wouldn't let Robin die in front of him either.

At the waterline, Ben dropped to a knee in the sand. Gerrod and Paul heaved the stag's carcass up the beach toward the ridge. Ben had no doubt that hauling it through the river was no small task. The stag must have weighed at least four hundred pounds and was easily six feet or more in length. With a resolute sneer, he refused to acknowledge either poacher while they ran for cover.

Ignorant bastards, Ben mused. If their stupidity got Robin killed, Ben would personally string both of them up by their innards. Meanwhile, Robin side-stroked for shore, dragging Nat by his hair. Ben drew and fired twice, sending more Sidhe hunters to the ground. He had a third arrow nocked and waiting for a decent shot when a Dannan Captain strolled out of the mist, his superior ash and yew longbow trained on Ben. He was taller than the others, his status evident by the six gold chains dangling from his left ear. He wore an immaculate sealskin cloak trimmed in arctic ermine, with a massive silver torc fixed at the collar. His long flaxen hair was unbound, save for a pair of braids at his temples. The leaping stag on his cuirass was crowned by three gold stars. Here was a member of the Ard Ri's personal guard. Ben dropped his elbow a fraction. *Fionn?* The Dannan Captain mirrored Ben's motion. His mint-green eyes narrowed in mutual recognition. Ben noted the disbelieving derision on Fionn's face, the surprise, and silent condemnation. Ben stared, riveted by the cruel irony of the situation.

Of course, it must be Fionn. Ben had shite luck.

"What in the hells are ye doin'?" cried Robin, struggling for the shallows on the Eirean side of the river. The Dannans lined the far shore, their numbers replenished, bows drawn. Ben knew they wouldn't fire for the same reason he could not. Fionn's handsome upper lip curled in disgust. With a sigh, Ben released his bowstring. Robin was nearly over. Gerrod waded in to help him out. Nat trailed in the river behind them, his skin as grey as a winter sky. Ben didn't see them. He stood motionless, staring across the river. The echoes of a former life traced clammy fingers up and down his spine.

"Feckin' snap out of it, will ye?" Robin followed Ben's gaze to the knot of Sidhe hunters gathered at the river's edge. The look between Ben and the Sidhe Captain was not lost on him. "Damn ye, Maeden! Shoot him!"

Fionn shook himself at Robin's voice. Nostrils flaring, he raised his bow.

Ben threw out a hand as if that would stop him. "No! Don't!"

An elegant, ashen shaft hammered through Nat's prone body, straight through the heart. With little time to respond, Robin and Gerrod were obliged to dive underwater to avoid the following volley. When they came up for air, Nat had turned over in the current.

His body bowed under the weight of a dozen or more arrows.

Unable to prevent the lad from washing downstream, Robin snarled abuse at Ben, the Sidhe, and the world at large. Gerrod managed to pull him out of the river, despite the older man's girth and flailing limbs. Robin's screams shook the leaves overhead with heart-rending vehemence. Unperturbed by the drama unfolding before him, Fionn waved at Ben— a flippant gesture dripping with contempt. Shaking his head on a wry laugh, Fionn handed his bow to an aide and climbed into his saddle. He didn't spare Ben a second glance.

Wordless as the wind, the Dannans melted into the trees after him, carrying their dead in silent procession. Ben didn't call out to Fionn as he faded from view. How could he? Slinging his bow back over his shoulder, he tucked his shaking hands into his pockets, where they wouldn't be seen.

Out of nowhere, Robin's fist crashed into his right cheekbone. Ben staggered a bit. Paul and Seamus clawed at Robin's arms to halt a second attack. The veins in his scarred forehead bulged. He spat, red-faced, "What in the hells was that about? Why didn't ye do somethin'?"

Swatting Gerrod's helping hand away, Ben got to his feet under his own steam. "Whose clever plan was it to shoot the stag, Robin? Which of you was arrogant enough to kill one of the High King's deer?"

Robin fought so hard to free himself from Paul's grip that his lips purpled. Saliva trickled over his bleeding chin. "I'll kill ye for this. I'll do it. I swear to Siora. How dare ye attempt to scold anyone? Nat and Marty died today!"

"Nat was dead long before Marty dragged him into the river, Robin."

"It's true, boss," cut in Gerrod, in Ben's defense. "I saw it. One o'them took him right in front o'me. Marty, rest him, shot the stag. I tried to tell him, Ben. I did."

Paul waved his red right hand. That was his way. Insolent and blockheaded. "The hide's worth at least a thousand fainne. Rack, near five thousand, I'd say. The fox-tails on Seamus' belt, maybe two hunnerd'? Three? Who cares about a dead deer?"

"You don't kill white stags, simpleton. They're charmed beasts. You're lucky every Dannan for twenty miles didn't answer the call!" Ben shoved him hard. He couldn't help himself. Someone had to answer for this mess. Why shouldn't it be Paul, who didn't have the sense the Gods gave a goat?

Paul raised his hands in mock surrender. "Tryin' to see the good here, Maeden. That's all."

"The good? Are you mad?"

"That's why ye let Nat die?" seethed Robin. "Because Marty shot a deer? We're bloody Greenmakers, ain't we? It's what we do. Tell me ye didn't take their side, Ben. Tell me yer bollocks don't swing so low."

"Three of you are alive at this very moment *because* of me. If I'd killed him as you asked, we would all be toasting each other in Tech Duinn right now. You know it as well as I do."

Robin towed Seamus and Paul at least three feet in his urgency to get at Ben. Ben threw down his bow and unbuckled his swordbelt, letting his weapons thump into the sand at his feet.

"Let him go!"

Robin barreled into him with a guttural grunt, but it was no use. Ben was twice his size and outweighed him by at least fifty pounds. Ben let him take one or two swipes before he hooked an arm under Robin's shoulder and spun him around. With one blow from his right hand, Robin's arse struck the earth with a solid thud. Dazed, Robin gaped up at him with unfocused malice. Ben leaned in, ready to strike again if he must.

"You deserved that, Robin. Stay down."

"Aye," said Robin, spitting out part of a tooth. "We're done, Ben Maeden. Yer no Greenmaker. We don't choose the Sidhe over one o'our own, do we? Don't think I didn't see ye."

"Have it your way," agreed Ben. "You're too old to learn common sense, aren't you?" He retrieved his weapons, shoved Paul again for good measure, and turned on his heel. He refused to look at the stag where it lay broken against the riverbank; its perfect white coat speckled red and black from the wound in its ribs.

Sacrilege of the first order.

He spared Robin one last withering glare.

"I quit."

Gerrod ran to catch up with him. "Wait, Ben. He don't mean it! We're sorry 'bout the stag, all right? Marty got desperate. Ye weren't over there. Ye don't know what it was like."

Robin threw out a spiteful laugh. "He ain't ever over there, is he? Stays on our side o'the river like a bleedin' coward, he does. Tell us, ye faerie bastard... how many kills have ye made to keep our folk fed and clothed? How many times have ye given over the last coins in your precious purse to help one o'ours? None. Yer a selfish sack of shite, ye are."

Ben ignored him. It wasn't easy. Robin Gramble had been his friend for almost fifteen years. Gerrod's anxious expression bordered on despair. "We'll meet up at Barb's later, yeah? C'mon. Ye can't leave it like this. We'll sort it all out."

Ben paused, for Gerrod's sake if no one else. "Later then."

"Ye'll meet us there?"

9

Ben blew out a protracted breath. His oldest friend had gone to stand by the water's edge, hiding a face full of tears. Nat was his kin, his sister's son. Ben could understand his irrational rage, even if it was unfairly directed. "I'll go and look for the bodies first. They can't have gone far."

"Thank ye, Ben."

Ben faced east. "Don't thank me, Gerry. Robin isn't right… but that doesn't make him wrong." He didn't give Gerrod a chance to process his statement. Ben yanked his hood low over his eyes. He faded into the Greensward like the Sidhe, only minutes before.

⚔ ⚔

THE DEAD WERE LAID OUT SIDE-BY-SIDE. Tallow candles flickered from lanterns tucked into cobweb-laden corners. Though the roof was well-tended, water trickled from one of two boarded windows. Ideally situated between the infamous *Hart and Hare* and Rosweal's high northern wall, The Greenmakers' Guild used this dilapidated stable as a waypoint for their nefarious gains. Long-abandoned stalls overflowed with crates and barrels stuffed with pilfered goods: bows, arrows, daggers, pelts, and the odd cask of peat-rich uishge. In the center aisle, Nat and Marty were stretched out on a broad oak table. Rose took the time to close their vacant eyes while she and Violet washed and prepared their bodies. Usually, the families would bear such a responsibility, but Marty's wife passed three winters before, and Nat's widow had two small children to manage. The task had to be performed in-house, as it were.

Rose met Ben's muted expression over Nat's gaping chest wound. She gave him a weak smile. He looked away. He'd done his part, as he said he would. Bringing both bodies back in one piece hadn't been a simple errand. He owed none of them a bloody thing now. Confident that tonight would be his last here in Rosweal, he saw no point in getting Rose's hopes up. Besides, a clean break was always the least painful sort.

The stag's white pelt dangled from the rafters in the farthest stall. A stinking pile of discarded organs, fat, and bone was all that remained of the magnificent beast. Ben's stomach roiled. Its glorious rack had been

10

taken to the salt-shed outside to dry. To think of it made his skin crawl. That such a holy creature could come to this end was more than he could stomach. Seamus and Paul had no idea what evil they'd invited into their lives. Ben stared at the exit, eager to leave. He didn't have to wait long. From the raucous tavern next door, Colm stepped into the stable, a grim cast to his painfully thin face.

"Apologies for the delay."

"Not coming then, eh?"

Colm rolled a bony shoulder. "Grief's a bitter dose, Ben. He's not hisself right now."

"You know I didn't do what he's accusing me of?"

"Course I do." Colm strode over to stare at his fallen comrades, tugging a bone flask out of his jerkin. He toasted the pair, then took a long pull. "Bad business all around, and for what?"

Ben tugged a thumb behind him. "For that."

Colm shuddered at the sight. "Bloody bad luck, that."

"I said so."

"Barb'll murder the lot when she finds out that thing was here. Anyway," heaving a sigh, Colm jerked a hefty purse from his belt. "All the wages yer due, minus today's mess. Plus, severance."

Ben took it without complaint. "What else?"

"You already know. I'm sorry for it, Ben. This here weren't yer fault, but with Barb away, Robin's word is law. Best to stay clear o'town for a while, yeah? He wants ye gone by mornin.'"

Rose's lip quivered. "Ye can't be serious?"

"Outta my hands, missy."

"But—"

"It's fine, Rose," said Ben, tucking his earnings away. "A dreadful line was crossed today. It's time."

Rose came around the table, reaching for his fingers. Violet made a grab for her but missed. "Barb will sort this out when she gets back. You don't have to leave!"

Ben pried her hands from around his neck. "Some things are best left unsaid." He felt terrible for the hurt in her eyes, but that wouldn't change the outcome of this failed raid, would it? Robin's mind was made up. Staying would only invite more trouble. Ben would sooner avoid another row for everyone's sake.

"Don't go, Ben, please!"

Ignoring her took some effort. He paused in the open door. "Colm?"

"Yeah?"

"Make sure Gerry doesn't touch a spare copper of that stag's take."

"Aye," Colm agreed. There was an appropriate dose of fear in his voice. "It won't be easy to convince any o'them. Fools have gold on the brain."

"Then, I wish them luck. They're going to need it."

"Wait!" Rose cried out, wrenching herself free of Violet's staying hand. "What about Gerry? Seamus? Don't ye want to say goodbye?"

"Tell them for me, won't you? I wish you health and fortune, Rosie," Ben smiled. Without another word, he swept outside.

The night swallowed him whole.

THE KELPIE

n.e. 508
14,ÐOR SAMNA
ÐROSheÐa

A five-hundred-ton galley bobbed alongside the jetty, awaiting passengers, goods, and crew. Una was so close now that she could taste linseed and tar at the back of her throat. She'd been wringing her hands in the queue since first light, eager to get on with it. *The Kelpie* wasn't what she would consider an impressive vessel in her limited reckoning of such things. Years of bad weather in the Straits of Mannanan had taken their toll on the old girl. The ship's rigging sagged from three puny masts. Patched sails were hastily strapped to her creaking crossbeams; bits of frayed rope and sailcloth streamed from the mast like stockings on a clothesline. *The Kelpie*'s starboard side was pocked with poorly tarred holes, some perilously near the waterline.

Una didn't have the luxury of worrying whether the ship was comfortably seaworthy. *The Kelpie* was the only available boat for the next few weeks. As winter tiptoed into Innisfail, the shallow straits between Eire and Cymru would clog with ice. Shipping and transport would dwindle to a trickle for the next month, then halt altogether by the following. Only heavy ice-crushers and barges would dare the Straits of Mannanan in winter. Most of those were unfit for human cargo. This galley was Una's last chance for a clean escape from Eire. If she didn't board now, she would be forced to travel south to the Port at Bethany or

13

west to Ten Bells to book passage at a later date. Neither option was an attractive one. The first would bring her well within her greatest enemies' reach. The latter would require many travel days, costly accommodations, and weeks of potential waiting. Both avenues were too dangerous to incite enthusiasm. She had to leave now, today, before it was too late.

So far, so good.

From here at the Port of Drogheda, the Boyne slogged five miles east to the Straits. The distance was not too great to taste the salt in the air nor smell the decaying seaweed dumped into the river's mouth at each high tide. Unused to the gastric stench of brackish water and vegetative river mud, she covered her mouth and nose with a gloved hand. Dockhands hauled crates and barrels overflowing with salted mackerel, whiting, turnips, cabbages, and leeks up *The Kelpie's* gangplank. The cacophony of competing odors intensified a hundred-fold as her queue wound up the ramp. She could get used to the smell. She might even learn to love it.

She would endure whatever she must to be free.

The crush of people waiting to board was another matter; three score stood on the wharf, herself included. Most of these folks were small-time Merchers, workers, or Agrean Migrants. Una didn't see how this many people could fit inside a ship this small, never-mind comfortably. Few passengers carried much in the way of luggage, but some did have children or small animals in tow. A grizzled, middle-aged man in front of her held a goat leashed to one hand and a wire cage bearing two hens in the other. Beside her, a young mother clung to two unruly children. The boy eyed Una with frank, unblinking curiosity. She wiggled her fingers at him. The child grinned around the drool-slathered fist he'd crammed into his mouth. In the distance, the Citadel loomed stern and oppressive. The Cloister of the Eternal Flame rose from the center of that menacing fortress. Its seamless granite edifice glinted red in the sun. Una shivered at the sight. If she never had to set foot there again, it would be too soon.

A commotion at the inner gate caught her attention. The harbormaster made a beeline for the waiting passengers, holding a wadded document in one meaty hand. He didn't look happy, nor was he alone. The black and gold cuirasses of the Citadel guard dogged his heels. Gasping, Una whipped her head around. There were four of them, she noted with rising panic. They shoved through passengers at the rear line, irrespective of age or disposition. An elderly woman cried out as she was knocked to her knees on the dock. The crowd parted for the guards like a stream diverted by a large stone. Una kept to her place at the rear of the queue, her head down. Willing herself as small and insignificant as possible, she tugged her cowl low over her forehead. The harbormaster stomped past.

Relax, she commanded herself.

If you appear anxious, they will wonder why.

She sent a surge of Spark into her blood to calm her nerves. She wasn't going to panic. Not now. She'd made it this far, hadn't she? Just a bit further... and she would be out of reach. Gone. Free. Safe.

Breathe, she chanted inwardly.

Everything is fine. They have no reason to suspect you if you stay calm. Upon first glance, she was just another Agrean migrant worker awaiting transport to the Colonies. Her papers were in order. Gan had seen to them, along with the coins bulging from the purse strapped to her thigh. An official Union Seal was stamped into her patent of labor. Her boarding pass read 'Kea Folna.' Kea was an average girl from the Midlands, shipping out to seek work in Swansea, like so many others on the wharf this morning. She would make it. She had to. If only *The Kelpie* would start boarding.

One of the guardsmen grabbed a girl at the front of the line. She was forced to remove her cap and tatty cloak. Una's heart skipped a beat. A cold knot of fear hardened in her belly. She watched the girl comply; her face streaked with tears. Her parents were held at arm's length while the forward guardsman searched her. He was not gentle. His gauntleted fists rent the girl's sleeves to the elbows. When nothing but her sun-kissed brown skin was revealed, he shunted her away and reached for another.

The harbormaster paced alongside the crowd. Fat beads of sweat slid down Una's nose. He held up a bit of vellum with its bright red seal: The Red Wyrm of the Union of Commons. Nema's seal. Una would know it anywhere. For a moment, all she could do was stare at the scarlet wax, her pulse louder than any drum.

15

"This here," he bellowed over their heads. "Be a warrant for the arrest of one 'Una Moura.' We'll thank ye lasses for cooperating with our search by rollin' up yer sleeves before ye make yer way up the ramp. If ye resist in any way, one o'these men will arrest ye. Raise yer hands if ye heard me, please."

A host of dirty, shaking fingers floated upward.

Una took a step back. *No, no, no...* she was too close! Gan assured her that no one would come looking for her until her journey was well underway. How did these guards have a warrant already? Why did it bear Nema's seal? Every second that passed made Una's nerves sing with renewed anxiety. Had Gan betrayed her? He must have... but why? Had Aoife discovered their plan and informed Nema? That was entirely possible, likely even. Aoife was a loyal snake: clever and ruthless. Ahead, *The Kelpie*'s sails were rolled down. The ship would sail soon, with or without its passengers. Una might have known. Things had been going too smoothly.

"What's she done then?" asked the matron beside her, hefting her son high on her hip. Her antsy daughter wriggled around her knees. "This girl yer searchin' for?" As she spoke, another woman was jerked from the line and forced to partially strip. A second guardsman moved in from the opposite side, yanking hoods and hats off every female head he approached. It wouldn't be long before it was Una's turn.

She closed her eyes in silent prayer.

So much for her easy escape.

"Raise yer hand please, missus, so I know who's speakin,'" boomed the harbormaster, holding the warrant over his eyes to block the sun.

"I've little'uns here, master," the matron snarked. "I've no free hands to spare. Answer the bleedin' question. What's this dread girl done, requires the manhandlin' o'respectable women like us, hey?"

A murmur of 'ayes' rumbled through the crowd. Women did not expect such treatment in Tairngare. Her neighbor stared straight at Una, her interest plain. Una took a step backward.

"She's a Prima of the Cloister, missus. Them women don't deign to tell us men nothin.' They want her. That's all I know," he replied,

16

signaling the nearest guardsman to follow her voice. Una shot the matron one pleading glance. To her surprise, she winked. The next thing Una knew, she was holding the woman's sticky, squirming son. The little boy blew wet bubbles into her ear while his mother made a grand show of rolling up her sleeves on a dramatic, put-upon sigh.

The guardsman neared. Una was bustled further down the line.

The matron raised her arms, making a grand show of her bare wrists. "When he comes, hand my son back and go, milady," she said over her shoulder. "I'll keep him busy long as I can."

"How did you know?" Una was dumbfounded.

"Yers isn't a face I'd forget."

"Aye," said a nearby man. "Me neither. He's close, milady. Pass the boy, then get behind me. I'll cover for ye."

Una didn't have an opportunity to thank either of them, for as soon as the guardsman approached, the woman wrenched her son out of Una's arms and placed herself firmly between them. The man who'd offered his help swung Una into the mob by the waist, then dove headfirst into the soldier's chest. Her defenders tumbled to the dock with the guardsman, a tangle of curses and fumbling limbs. Una didn't waste a moment of the reprieve they'd bought her. She clawed through the rear of the crowd toward the Drough Gate. A shout went up at her back.

"Long live the Moura! Long live the Queen!" cheered the matron. Some took up her chant; others booed or jeered her for it.

Una was near the arch when the harbormaster singled her out. "The Gate! She's headed for the Market!" Heavy footsteps pounded down the wharf after her. She dumped all the Spark she could spare into her legs and sped on, ignoring the dumbstruck faces in her way. Hands reached out to halt her. She dodged, kicked, or slapped anything in her path. Under the arch, she took a sharp left toward the Market, then another leading her back to the city. She had no choice now but to run for the Ward Gate. The Navan High Road would lead her west to Ten Bells – her next best option. As long as she remained in Eire, anything could happen.

"Stop her! Stop that woman!" barked one of her pursuers. Una barreled through the Market, driving through people and bounding over impediments in her way. A quarter mile up, she cut a second corner at Oisin, then another at Pennyroyal. Thankfully, there weren't many people out this early, save workers and vendors loading their shops and stalls. The streets were mostly clear. Rounding the intersection at Balmoral, she veered left into a narrow alley. Her lungs burned like lamp oil, but she could not stop. The men chasing her had much longer legs, unfortunately. On Aine, a large stone wall abruptly halted her progress toward the Ward Gate. Too late to stop, she ran into the wall, nose first. Her rump struck the cobbles with an uncomfortable crack. Stars swirled before her eyes like multifaceted gems. She groaned and rolled onto her side, tasting blood. Newly cut stones were stacked under the scaffolding above her head. How could she have known they were working on this end of the Citadel? This was the first time she'd set foot outside of the Cloister in years. Groaning, she held a hand under her streaming nostrils.

"There ye are!"

Her ears rang. Shaking her head to clear it, she pushed herself to her feet. Una glared up at two Citadel guards. One of them unwound a bit of rope from his forearm and slunk toward her with an oily grin. He was an odd-looking fellow, with spindly limbs but portly round the middle, like a spider.

"Careful," his companion huffed from the corner. "She'll kill ye if she gets a hand on ye. Don't rush."

Una tilted her head. That wasn't a Tairnganese accent, was it? Come to think of it; these men didn't even look the part. Neither were exceptionally fit, and the Citadel did not tolerate sloth of any variety. The pair wheezed like they hadn't run in a decade or more.

"Who are you?" She wiped her face against her sleeve and slowly removed her gloves. The larger man watched her do it, his expression wary.

"Conor, like that time in Innisport, yeah, but easy. She's got fight in her. I can see it."

"No worries, boss," said the spider. "So do I."

18

Una leered at him. "Your friend was right, Conor. If you touch me, I'm going to kill you."

Another man thudded around the corner behind them. This one was probably the bulkiest person she'd ever seen. Instinctively, she jumped back a pace.

"Boss!" he rasped, holding his quaking ribs. "Guards're comin.'"

"Hold there, Fergus," sighed the balding man. "We got her now. Just make sure they don't come this way."

"Boss," Fergus droned, sparing Una the briefest disinterested glance. He ambled off like a sleepy bear. She heard his heavy, rhythmic steps for quite a while after he'd gone. Conor gave her a sloppy grin. He slung a makeshift lasso toward her. She stepped out of its testing path with a hiss.

"Careful, Conor. I mean it! The Duch don't want her harmed."

Steaming heat filled her cheeks. "The Duch?"

"That's right, missy," the leader told her. "Yer Da wants ye home. Where were ye gonna go in that rickety little dinghy, eh? The Colonies?" He blew a wet stream of air over his lower lip. "Don't think a fine lady like ye would like Swansea much. Everywhere ye go stinks o'shite, and the flies come at ye in clouds. Bethany's a sight better, I can tell ye."

"A damn sight better," Conor chuckled. "Bloody buggers'd gobble all that soft skin o'yers, right up. What a shame that would be, eh?"

"Conor, mind yer manners now," warned his boss. "That there's a princess. She's worth a hunnerd o'any one o'us."

"Patriarchal drivel," Una spat. "That's 'Prima Moura,' to you scum."

The leader pulled a face. "A thousand pardons, milady. Conor, grab her, will ye? We need to get gone."

As he advanced, she kept her eyes on Conor, withdrawing a dagger from her belt.Conor laughed. "I think I like her, Rawly. She's awful cute."

"Yer not gonna think so when she melts the skin from yer bones."

Conor shrugged as if to say, 'sorry, can't play anymore.' He lashed out at her face with his rope. She swerved, then dipped forward to plunge her blade into Conor's reaching hand. She would have connected, too, had she been quicker. He side-swept her clumsy blow, then smashed his elbow into her gut. The breath burst out of her lungs in a rush... but she dug her fingers into the cloth at his elbow anyway. He couldn't shake her off in time.

"Burn," she whispered. Instantly, the fabric sparked and caught fire. Conor spun aside on a howl, slapping at the smoking wool with his free hand.

Rawly, their leader, threw up his hands. "What in the hells did I say, ye bleedin' idiot?"

Una kicked Conor while he was down, in her hurry to leap past him. Grunting in pain, he snatched at her heel. She tripped over him with a cry. Rawly was on her before she could roll aside. He tamped down on her fingers with a booted heel. She heard two distinct snaps and screamed.

Rawly's left hand grasped her hair while Conor twisted her ankle about ninety degrees the wrong way. "Sorry, missy, but orders are orders." Rawly smashed her face into the dirty cobbles, hard. It wasn't stars that crossed her vision this time. Waves rolled out of the dark crevices of her mind like ripples over a silent lakeshore. A tiny, dilapidated galley sailed into that obsidian curtain, its tattered sails billowing over an empty deck. As it passed, all hope of liberation faded to black.

⚔ ⚕

BEN FOUND HIMSELF AT A seedier tavern on the outskirts of town. He had no idea what time it was nor how long he'd been there and couldn't care less. No one would come looking for him. That was the important bit. On this side of the city, no breeze could penetrate the miasma of human filth, refuse, and unwashed flesh that loomed over the slums. The South-End was a hive of ramshackle huts, rotten buildings, and mud-slick streets: the perfect place to hide. This nameless tavern, for example, was one of many unlicensed and unregulated establishments that catered to Rosweal's poor. Northers referred to this sort of hole in the wall as a 'dive.' A reference to a vat of spirits perched on the edge of a dusty wooden bar, laced with dregs from emptied tankards and the odd scrap of meat or bread. Less flush patrons would pay two coppers to take a 'dive' with the dipper chained to its rim. The very meanest among them would wait all night for the vat to be dumped into the muddy sewer.

In the taproom, there were rats and fleas in the rushes. Birds and bats roosted in the rafters. Feral cats lurked in the shadows hunting omnipresent vermin. Several customers were asleep (or perhaps dead) on the pine-strewn floor. Some lay in the damp outside, snoring bubbles into greasy mud. Whores plied their trade in full view of patrons without shame. The sounds of rutting, drunken argument, and fevered gambling rang throughout the structure. The stench alone could drop a boar at ten paces... and the liquor. If one had to guess what might be killing patrons, they wouldn't have to search very hard for the culprit. Ben had had a very good run at a game of Porter for a while but soon became too inebriated to maintain his lead without cheating. He hated to cheat at cards but couldn't very well let these ingrates outwit the last copper from his pocket, either. At one point, he'd considered curling up on the floor with one of the girls. He thought better of that brilliant idea when he realized the floor was *squirming* beneath a reeking layer of urine-stained straw.

In disgrace, as he was, he'd likely be sleeping outdoors. More's the pity. The air outside felt about as soft as a slab of granite. He did have another flop on the other side of town, but realistically, Rosweal was not a large place. His rooms above *The Hart* might as well have been on the moon for all the good they'd do him tonight. Ben was adrift on a lonely, friendless sea for the first time in over a decade. He'd forgotten how miserable solitude could be. He would miss *The Hart*: Rosie, Gerrod, Seamus, and Colm. Hells, he'd even miss Barb, and she was a badger on her best day. Robin, too... though part of Ben wanted to bash in the old codger's brains for his idiocy.

Ben took a long pull from his tankard, all but immune to the sharp bitterness of the raw liquor within. It wasn't the worst he'd ever had. What unaged spirits lacked in flavor, they made up for in efficacy. He couldn't feel his tongue anymore. That was just fine. The more he drank, the less bothered he could be about anything, least of all the life he left behind. Deprived of one's illusions, the mind made spears of the most mundane details. He was going to miss Rosweal, warts and all.

With a sigh, Ben laid his hand down. Four cups and two nails. A concert of groans circled his table. Several inferior hands were tossed into the center in disgust. An opponent dropped two coppers into the pile and got up. The others glared spitefully at Ben over their mugs.

"Another?" the nearest inquired.

Ben rolled a shoulder. "Why not? Who wants to deal?"

"Not ye, ye pretty peacock," snapped a rough fellow on his right.

Ben handed him the deck with a smirk. He wasn't sure which perturbed these men more: that he was winning or that none of them could catch him cheating. He took another sip, accepting his newest hand without comment. One of the girls, emboldened by his winning streak, worked up beside him. She smelled of smoke, onions, and cheap perfume. She did have expert fingers, however. As she worked them into his shoulders, he decided he didn't care what she smelled like. The next hand finished much the same as the last, with Ben emerging the victor, three gems over three bushels, this time. With his masseuse nibbling at his ear, Ben grinned. Two more men got up to leave, their faces red as his dulcet lady's hair. An insistent rapping on the tabletop dragged his attention upward.

The poacher seated across the table, whose name he couldn't recall – Padraig, was it? – flashed a short knife at him.

"That's yer last hand tonight, Ben Maeden. If I were ye, I'd place me fainne on the table and duff outta here afore I gut ye like the cheatin' swine ye are."

Ben blinked slowly, willing his brain to order. He gave Padraig his best if sloppiest, grin. "Relax. I think I've lost as many hands as you have."

He hadn't, of course.

Cursing, Padraig nodded to other unamused players at the table. If Ben were sober, he might find the situation humorous... ousted from two establishments in less than a day. He was on a roll.

"For some reason, that stack o'coins on yer side hasn't lost a shred o' weight. I call that suspicious. Don't ye agree, boys?"

A murmur of general acquiescence rumbled around the table.

Ben spread his hands. His reputation preceded him. "You wouldn't be threatening me, would you, Padraig?"

"Ye might be a dandy with that elven sticker at yer side, but there's more o'us than ye can handle, Ben. Do it now, slow like."

Ben thumbed his pommel. Pointless comfort. He had no desire to waste the effort on weaklings like these. What purpose would it serve? It wouldn't repair his wounded pride nor improve his situation in the least.

"If you say so." He couldn't halt the blatant mockery in his tone. "No need for such bother. I'll be off." He stood up, pleased he didn't waver on his feet as much as he expected to. Leaning over the table, Ben scraped his winnings into the pouch he made of his tunic.

Padraig slid his chair back; knuckles stark against the tabletop. "I said, leave yer coins on the table."

Deliberately, Ben drew his purse-string taut and looped it through his belt. "I believe I left enough to go around. Plenty for you lot. Night, gentlemen," he snickered. Dipping a derisive bow, he shuffled to the door. He'd barely made it two steps before he felt the prick of a blade against his neck. The stink of onions and unwashed skin enveloped him. His lady of the evening also took a shine to his newly fattened purse. Figured. If he hadn't felt overly sorry for himself and hadn't gotten sloshing drunk in this stinking shitehole in the first place, he would never have allowed her anywhere near him. For that matter, he wouldn't have sat in on a game of porter with poachers of Padraig's ilk either. If he hadn't cheated (though he had... just a bit), he still wouldn't have walked out unmolested.

Straight Ben would have known better.

Straight Ben was a much wiser man.

"Sorry, lover," said the woman in his ear. Her breath stung. "I have little un's to feed, meself. Why not hand Padraig yer purse there, and we'll let ye off with no more trouble?"

"Of course, milady," said Ben. "Why don't you reach around my chest and undo the strap? I'd do it for you, but I find I don't fancy a shave just now."

23

"Yer sweet," she purred, pressing close as directed. Her humor dissolved into shock when Ben pulled her across his chest and flung her bodily onto the table. Coins, cards, and tankards flew in every direction at once. In a lunge for Ben's throat, Padraig launched over the screaming bawd. Ben ducked and kicked Padraig's leg out at the knee; audibly, the bone crunched inward. Keening like a girl, Padraig crumpled to the rushes below. In the meantime, Ben wasn't about to let the others have a go. He grabbed the nearest table and heaved it into at least three charging torsos. Two men fell backward. The third tripped over Padraig's thrashing body and crashed into the rushes face-first. Ben didn't linger.

He was out the door and darting through the alley before the proprietor could shout for help. Unfortunately, this nameless juke also had a back door. Five men, including Padraig's two cronies, were fast on his heels.

Ben was usually quite fleet of foot, but he was also drunk as a satyr and severely outnumbered. Looking up as he splashed through the alley, he realized the buildings on either side were too high to scale without a boost. No doubt, the racket his pursuers made would summon the profligate constabulary sooner rather than later. He had two options: get out before he was cornered, or turn and fight. Neither was appealing nor likely in these narrow, malodorous lanes. Slipping and sliding through the slums and back alleys, he made slow progress. After his second dousing stumble, he skidded around a sharp corner on his right. A sheer wall lay ahead: no windows, railings, or bricks to climb. Ben caught his breath on a curse. He heard whistles and shouting from whence he came.

He was out of alternatives. The last thing he needed was to be dragged to gaol in the East End. He would likely be beaten, robbed, and promptly murdered there, not necessarily in that order. Rosweal's gaols were less a punishment for deserving offenders than a venue for blackmail and homicide. That was not an outcome he longed to experience for himself.

Offering a prayer of apology to Danu, he begrudgingly drew his sword. The hum of pure, sylvan steel sang into the night. The first thug tore around the corner with a crude cudgel in his right hand. Before the fellow could register the weapon waiting ahead, the cudgel and the hand

24

that held it followed his head to the cobbles below. Two more pursuers, one carrying a lamp, were not far behind. When they splashed into view, Ben was ready for them. Howling in rage, the largest of the two hurled himself at Ben with his long dagger raised. His head rolled to a stop under an oxcart. His companion with the lamp backpedaled. Ben held his bloodied sword aloft and steady in his right hand. All traces of intoxication faded. His arm did not shake. His eyes, which once seemed a dull blue-grey, flashed silver in the lamplight.

"You have one chance," he said.

The poacher gaped, surrendering every inch that Ben advanced. All color drained from the fellow's ruddy face as he dropped his lantern, throwing spirals of sizzling lamp oil into the muck at Ben's feet. Sucking in a gulping breath, the poacher screamed at the top of his considerable lungs. "Help! We're under attack! There're High Elves here!"

Ben's sword took him through the middle, cutting his exhortation short. The blade had barely exited the fellow's guts when the next round of lamps came bobbing up the alley. Ben belted for the next lane and fumbled at his collar for something missing. He cursed to a new and spectacular degree. The whore's knife must have severed the cord, or perhaps he'd dropped it at the dead end. Without that ogham stone, he wouldn't be able to conceal himself any longer. He had to get out of Rosweal post-haste. He ran with no direction in mind except out. Finally emerging from the web of alleyways, he, at last, came to the Navan Gate. The Gate was closed, but no matter. He could scale the wall here easily enough. Ben was just cresting the top as a cadre of armed men with lanterns emerged from the labyrinthine alleyway. The lamps' glow hit him full in the face for a brief moment.

Thankfully, he was over the wall and deep within the Greensward when the real screaming began.

SOJOURNER

n.e. ꝼ08
ꝼ, ꝺoꞃ samna
ᴄhe ᵹꞃeensᴡaꞃꝺ

D awn arrived before he knew it. Slow to wake, Ben squinted at
a sky the color of ash. A thick layer of hoarfrost crunched in
the underbrush as he worked himself upright. Winter was nigh,
and no mistake. What few animals he spied were as sluggish and maudlin as he. Squirrels, rabbits, and deer hardly flinched at his intrusion of
their domain. They slagged off into the Greensward, more interested
in foraging for food than a wandering drunkard. Even the birds knew
better than to loiter outside their nests on such a wretched morning. His
hangover didn't help, of course. Whatever had been in the uishge last
night must have been equal parts sugar and lamp oil. His head throbbed
so hard that his teeth rattled in their casings. Added to this was dazzling
fatigue, a mouth full of long sour ale, a belly full of cheap meat pie, and
crushing regret. All told, it was the beginning of a rubbish day.

Ben was, by far, the sorriest sad sack in Innisfail. This wouldn't be his
first winter outdoors, but the prospect was infinitely less attractive now
than ever. A decade of relative warmth and comfort had seen to that.
Ben knew he had no one to blame but himself. He should have led the
Greenmakers farther west, into largely vacant territory. He was aware
that Fionn kept close to the border in Dor Samna. Hells, he'd done so
himself when he boasted command of *An Fiach Fian*, hadn't he? The Wild

Hunt's purpose was to safeguard the border between Aes Sidhe and Eire. Not only to defend those who dwelled within the Sidhe realm but also to protect the Milesians in Eire from many of those same inhabitants. Rosweal was the nearest Milesian town to the border. Therefore, her citizens were well advised of the peril such proximity afforded.

Nevertheless, fear of starvation often outweighed common sense. Raiders braved the border every autumn with limited recourse and little reward. Most raids were fruitless and often spent more lives than they benefited. Many Eirean men and women died to bring Aes Sidhe's natural treasures home to their impoverished communities.

When his sojourn in Eire began, Ben had derided the ballsy stupidity of poachers who dared to cross for meat or pelt. Since he'd witnessed firsthand the toll winter could take on whole families in the Greensward. Having watched folk bury their nearest and dearest each year, he could no longer fault them for their audacity. Ben could attest that unfounded bigotry rarely survived the nuance of experience. Coming to Rosweal had taught him the meaning of desperation, a lesson well learned. He could not, however, forgive rampant greed. To kill a sylvan stag was crude iconoclasm. Pure barbarism. Even had he been invited to stay in Rosweal, he wasn't sure he would have. He was disgusted with the Greenmakers, who should have known better. More so himself. Ben sighed.

Dwelling on it wouldn't change anything, would it? In the uishge-addled depths of his overtaxed brain, he couldn't forget the shock on Fionn's face when their eyes met across the Boyne. They'd never had any great love for one another, but the disgust and ire writ in Fionn's eyes had wounded Ben more deeply than any arrow ever could.

How the mighty had fallen...

Of course, Robin had been right about Ben. So what? No one living in the Greensward was whom they wished to be. Some were there to flout the rules of the 'civilized' Southers in Ten Bells or Bethany. Some fled the rigid theocracy in Tairngare. Some sought adventure. Most simply had nowhere else to go. Rosweal was not an illustrious destination, by any reckoning. Its few charms appealed to a tiny fraction of the population.

Despite this (or perhaps because of it), Rosweal had become a second home for Ben somewhere along the way. He shook himself. Hadn't he vowed not to brood?

Feeling lost, he shuffled through a deep gulley choked with thorns and dead leaves. Over a jut of stone encircled by rotting vegetation, the forest fell behind him, opening a vista into the bog at *Bru na Boinne* below. He groaned. Why in the nine hells had he come this way? Did he have some internal inclination to compound his torture? Taking stock of his surroundings, he leaned on his Milesian longbow and scowled down at the river valley. There, just beyond the bog, was an ancient meander in the Boyne's path. The trees were too dense to see much across the border, but he smelled the watchfires burning at *Si an Bhru*. A deep pang squeezed something soft within his chest. Rather than prolong his homesickness, he turned away. Ben's people once called this place *Bron Por*, though the Milesians did not honor that tradition. To them, it was nothing more than a massive, malodorous swamp named Bally Lough. The bog spanned a circumference of no more than three miles, but it was treacherous all the same. It might have been bottomless in some places, for all the hope one had of escaping some of its well-hidden pools.

Opting to maintain a healthy respect for the unfathomable, Ben carefully backtracked uphill toward the Greensward. A nest of twigs snapped beside him. He froze. Never in his long life had he been distracted enough to allow a Milesian to sneak up on him… and in the Greensward no less? He half wished the intruder would just shoot him to alleviate his acute shame.

He heard a familiar giggle, then let out a bit of the breath he'd been holding. "That you, Gerry?"

"Robin, don't keep me on for me looks."

Ben couldn't help but chuckle. Not much in a tussle was Gerrod, but woe to any quarry he meant to track. The fact would chafe if Ben were in a position to be proud. "Planning to shoot me in the back?"

"Nah. Robin would box me ears if I did— angry though he is. Ye really cut his teeth this time, Ben. Three more decent fellas is lyin' dead in town. You coulda picked a better time for it. Summer maybe? When folks ain't like to starve, 'cause we can't provide."

"They tried to rob me."

"We figured. Padraig's a right twat, but he works hard. Robin's got him tucked safely away in gaol now. For disturbin' the peace and all. Only audience there are rats and half-dead drunks."

That was interesting. Robin must not intend to broadcast Ben's identity. Why not? "How many men know?"

"About ye bein' Sidhe?"

"What else?"

Gerrod blew air over his lower lip. "No one with any smarts. Don't worry. Robin sent me ahead to warn ye. We had to make a show of it, at least. Folk wouldn't like it if we let a murderer duff away unscathed, would they? Any reason I shouldn't shoot ye somewhere painful for bein' a dishonest prat?" What he meant was, did Ben have anything to bribe him with? Ben cursed at Gerrod's cheek but wasn't about to kill the lad for a pittance. He was rather fond of Robin's apprentice. Growling, he tossed Gerrod his smaller sack of coins. The lad hefted it with a grin. "So," Gerrod resumed with his usual humor, "an Elf then, eh? Robin's actin' like he ain't the least surprised, but ye could blow me down with a whistle right now. Were ye always so bloody tall?"

Gnashing his teeth at the common racial slur, Ben stuck his hands up and faced him. Gerrod sucked in a sharp breath.

"Yes, Gerry," said Ben. "I have always been this tall."

"*Siora's tits*! Seamus owes me twelve quid for this," hooted Gerrod. "What's yer real name then?"

"I... don't think you want to know."

"Oh, come on! I'm the last fella in the Greensward ye have to worry about right now." Gerrod flung his homely little bow to the ground to prove his point. He waggled his fingers in the air. "See? Now yer name is all I'm askin' for." Gerrod's spotty smirk nearly ground the words from Ben's mouth. Thankfully, before he could answer, voices and popping twigs alerted them of approaching company.

Gerrod glanced furtively over his shoulder. "We don't have much time. A lot o'the boys don't know it was ye in that juke, and they certainly won't know who ye truly are. Robin's keepin' that close to his chest," he said, cracking his bow over his knee and mussing the leaves and foliage below. "Ye'll have to hit me. Come on then. Be quick," he tugged his bare chin in Ben's direction. The distant footsteps moved closer. "Go on then. We're mates, ain't we? Ye'd do it for me." His eyes were full of innocent confidence.

Ben shoved a surge of raw guilt down his gullet. He probably would not do the same for Gerrod, and that thought brought him fresh shame. A figure materialized from the trees on his left.

"I owe you," said Ben, clouting the boy across the temple with the butt of his longbow. Gerrod crumpled. An arrow whizzed past, taking a lock of Ben's pale hair with it. He had no choice but to run and leap over the rise, straight into Bron Por.

HOURS LATER, BEN STOPPED TO rest below the eaves of a great rowan, some miles past the infuriating bog. Every inch of his body felt heavy, sore, and bruised. His once fine boots were sopping wet with mud and algae. His tunic, vest, and trousers weighed an additional forty pounds for all the sulphuric water they'd absorbed. He'd mislaid his cloak, longbow, and two of his daggers somewhere. Doubtless, they'd sunk to the bottom of one of the bog's mercurial pools. When afternoon had melted into evening, Ben struggled to discern the sparse patches of dry ground from deceptively shallow pools of noxious green water. Twice he'd gone under, submerging his head and shoulders in a murky, foul-smelling mire. Both times, he'd managed to claw himself out, but he was lucky. Many who strayed into Bron Por often never made it out again. It took ages to cross in one piece. He was thankful not to have lost his sword or purse. He wasn't sure which deity he owed for that minor miracle but vowed to honor them all in turn, regardless.

Ben's pursuers gave up after the first quarter mile, as expected. Even gutsy Northers like Robin and his Greenmakers knew better than to chase through Bally Lough at dusk. They'd have to travel around for miles and miles to try and reach him from the other side. Since the wind was cold as a tomb in the Riverlands, Ben was sure sane men would prefer the warmth of their beds to drowning or frostbite.

Danu knew *he* would rather be hugging a tankard of ale in a nice fire-lit room right about then. Instead, he dug mud, grass, and reeds out of his ruined boots. An impatient hangover roared like a caged bear in his skull. All the running, tumbling, and dousing had worn him down to the nub. He was cold and starved and right about then, would have paid any amount to return to his rooms in Rosweal whence a warm meal and his soft bed beckoned. His stomach snarled at the thought of something other than rotgut uishge roiling within its hollow, trembling cavity. It would be dark soon. If he didn't find something to eat swift enough, he could be in real trouble. Ben wondered if he would be the first Sidhe to starve to death in the history of his race.

How mortifying…

He might as well have been naked for all the use he'd get from his ruined gear. His sword stuck fast in her scabbard, encased in nearly a foot of cloying bog mud. Without a bow to bring down game, he had no idea how he would feed himself tonight. Perhaps he could build a trap or snare, but that would take too bloody long. Ben jerked a small silver flask from inside his spoilt vest. At least he had more uishge… thank Herne for small favors. He might be buggered about nine different ways, but at least he didn't have to greet his next pathetic dawn sober.

To busy his hands, he cleaned out his scabbard, then his boots, and scrubbed drying filth from his sword with a soggy shirt sleeve. Samn was high in the sky when he realized his hair had frozen stiff to the trunk behind him. Reciting a retraction of formerly grateful prayers, he pried himself loose, donating a patch of scalp in the process. Just as he considered cradling a log in his arms and heaving himself back into the por, the most wonderful, mouth-watering aroma wafted toward him on the breeze. Ben's mouth flooded with saliva at the scent. Though, as quickly as it came, it evaporated. Skittering around the little copse of trees with his nose in the air like a dog, he searched for the source.

Liquor and fatigue barked through his veins, urging him toward a small game trail that led back toward the river. Here, the scent was more pungent. It seemed someone else shared Ben's sojourn... someone with food. An olfactory parade of smoked salmon, charred potato cakes, and roasted venison conquered his thoughts. Whoever they were, they weren't exactly roughing it, were they? Wait... was that ale he smelled? Ben would trade all his silvers for a cup of ale and a quarter-hank of their venison. He rambled down the game trail, intent to buy, beg, or steal anything these fellows might spare. Whatever they might be doing in the woods, in this weather, at such an hour, didn't make the slightest difference to him.

The uishge burning in his gut demanded company, *now*.

It didn't occur to him to consider his appearance, nor what a shock he was bound to give the chef. What decent man camped in the borderlands at night when there were two towns nearby with warm beds? This was a question he might have pondered had he been sober. Instead, he marched downhill with nary a second thought.

SHANE RAWLY WAS TOO OLD for nonsense such as this. Thirty-odd years of smuggling and head-cracking in Duch Donahugh's name had worn his bones brittle. Yet, he was again, in a godforsaken wood along the border, doing the old bastard's dirty work. And for what? For a bit of property in the garden district for his wife and five children. For a lump of coin that wouldn't last a year if the winter went hard. For the privilege of being the fellow Patrick called upon when he needed something reprehensible done right. The things a body must do to climb upward in life: morally defunct and *illegal* things. Rawly knew a man not born to comfort had less choice than experience.

He squinted at the waxing moon and spat out his second wad of bitterroot in under an hour; his nerves jumbled taut. He scratched at his grizzled cheek and glanced sidelong at his young son Gabriel, who was meant to be on watch. The lad struggled to keep both eyes trained on the package they were to deliver to the Duch. With a full belly and a mite too much uishge, Gabriel's chin had already dipped toward his collarbone several times. He was such a scrawny boy, both slight of stature and bearing. Rawly could remember a time not so long ago when it took only one of his burly arms to hoist him high. The lad was nearing seventeen winters now.

By Bethonair law, Gabriel was of age to inherit his father's chosen craft. Wasn't it a shame that Rawly's profession would never earn the respect of their peers? Ah, but such was his lot. The Duch paid better than any lord in the South. His lordship often looked after Rawly's kin when all others would have let them starve in the street. To put a fine point on the matter, Rawly owed the Duch his life, livelihood, and anything else the man might ask of him. Such was the debt he owed for a lifetime in servitude. Rawly was a valuable tool for better men. Though, because of this, he was also an utter failure as a father.

Gabriel looked up for a moment, his blue eyes sparkling. His lopsided grin showed the uneven tooth his sisters constantly teased him about. Thought it was all a merry jig, Gabriel did. This awful business the Duch demanded... the lad had no idea what he was doing. Rawly was his father! No matter what he owed the Duch, a father knew better than to ruin his child to stave off a creditor. Duch Patrick had commanded Rawly to teach the boy his trade. Not having a choice didn't make Rawly feel one whit better about it. This quandary reminded him of his long-suffering mother. She'd been a Kneeler from Cymru in the East and had spent a great deal of effort trying to cure him of his delinquency. It did no good, of course. Rawly's fate had been fairly sealed as soon as he realized it was easier to pick a pocket than earn a coin. Now that he was older and a parent, he recalled her lessons with a twinge of conscience. What was it she had said most often?

The sins of the father...

"Boss?" Fergus's rumbling voice interrupted his musings. Rawly looked up. Fergus was a beast of a man, at least six and a half feet tall and weighing nearly three-hundred pounds. He might have been terrifying were it not for his obvious case of idiocy. Fergus blinked in that slow, stupid way, which made Rawly want to bash his monstrous head in with a rock.

"Fergie, I told ye to keep yer gob shut until we left the river behind," Rawly sneered, contemplating slitting the buffoon's throat before they made it to Ten Bells. He'd always threatened to but never had, despite an ever-present urge. The truth was the lumbering oaf was a handy man to have around. A drooling fool he might be, but easily worth three in a fight.

Fergus' shaggy, straw-colored hair glowed white in the rising moonlight. "I know that boss, I 'member. It's just I think I hear somethin' out there."

Rawly rolled his eyes and stretched to his full height— considerable at six feet but not outstanding when placed beside the likes of Fergus. The way the giant shrank from his approach, Rawly might have been eight feet or more. "Keep yer bloody voice down! We're close enough to Aes Sidhe now; the smallest fart might bring one o'their hunters across the border to slaughter us all where we stand."

An empty threat.

No Sidhe warriors crossed into Eire unless they were on a march. Nevertheless, the warning achieved its desired effect. Fergus's beady eyes widened to their maximum capacity. Perhaps it was cruel to torture a grown man with a mind trapped in childhood? Rawly didn't do so without purpose. Fergus' voice carried very far. Any number of unwelcome visitors might follow its boom into their little camp. Like the Tairnganeah, for instance, on a mission to reclaim the thing Rawly and his fellows had successfully stolen from Drogheda yesterday morn.

"I don't like elves," Fergus pouted. His mountainous shoulders quivered in irrational fear. Rawly adjusted his sword belt with a groan.

"No shite, ye sweet lass. Keep yer bloody comments to yerself until we clear the bog." Gabriel laughed once, then covered his mouth to prevent a further outburst. Rawly set a searing eye on his son. "That means ye too, boyo!" Still grinning, Gabriel turned back to his task.

Their fourth companion stomped through the trees just ahead of them, making Fergus yelp and stumble back several feet. Gabriel giggled into his hand, careful to avoid his father's glare.

"What's all this about then?" wheezed Conor. His trousers were filthy with muck and grime, and he stank of mold so strong, Rawly sneezed. Conor was the exact opposite of Fergus in temperament and appearance. Outwardly, he looked more like a harmless moneylender than a brutish ruffian. Rawly had never known a man more ruthless— save for Duch Patrick. Conor was Rawly's right hand. He was cunning but loyal. On the other hand, Fergus was mere mindless muscle: his purpose was to dissuade fights before they began. His bulk was effective, so long as he didn't speak.

Rawly shook his head. "Nothin' of note. This large girl here has a fear o'elves swoopin' down on him in the night." His expression imparted that he meant to keep the impression solidly in place.

Conor nodded. Message received. "Oh, aye. Terrible close to Elf Land now, ain't we? Ye ever hear about Dumnain Fergie? Them longhaired devils hung each o'the villagers in the square by their entrails. Their leader was the bloody Kneeler's Devil hisself. I was there, ye know? A great white-haired brute he was, with eyes cold as knives...." Conor's rotted teeth looked a bit like fangs in the night.

Fergus deflated. "I don't like that story."

Sensing weakness, Conor's favorite, he leaned closer. "Lasses and babes with their guts strung over clotheslines. The stink was somethin' like Butcher Lane in summer, only worse. Ye ever smell decayin' people, Fergie? Not much difference 'tween us and rottin' meat."

Fergus went green.

Rawly heard his stomach shift. "That's enough now, Conor. What did ye find?"

"Not much but Eire's longest, widest, most vexin' swamp a mile west. We can't cross her in the night, Shane. Some of them ponds are deeper than a man is tall and damned near invisible in the dark. I know ye don't want to hear it, but we should wait till dawn."

Rawly glanced back at his son's expectant, trusting face. "We hafta get movin'. Them witches in Tairngare got outriders fast on our trail by now. I'm not waitin' here with me stones in me hand." He scowled into the forest behind them. If the Tairnganeah caught up with them now, they'd have no choice but to drop their prize and escape into Bally Lough anyway. They'd packed light for the trip to Tairngare and back, and by his reckoning, they still had a week to reach Ten Bells. The Duch would have his head if Rawly failed him… or worse. "We're gettin' through that bog tonight. Make no mistake."

"Not gonna happen, Shane. Ye'll get us all killed and lose the Duch's prize anyway. I like to gamble, but not with me life," said Conor.

"Bogs are bad places, me mam told me," Fergus declared. "Pooka play in them at night, waitin' for folk to wander in," he crossed himself.

"Me own mam told me I was the handsomest dandy in the world. What's yer point?"

Ignoring them, Rawly scratched at his stubble, eyeing the loose branches and boughs littering their clearing. They could make a raft if they had to, using the longer branches as measures.

"I know what yer thinkin', but it won't do no good if we can't see where we're walkin.' Not even if ye marched us single file, tied to the same log, would our footing be sound enough to carry her over all that uneven ground. Yer outta yer bloody mind."

Growling in frustration, Rawly gazed at Gabriel for a long while. No. He wouldn't risk his son in Bally Lough at night any more than he would risk him to Tairngare's city guard. Damn, damn, damn! The Duch wouldn't have hired him if he'd thought this task would be easy. Rawly was sorely disappointed to discover how bloody difficult it was turning out to be.

※ ※

Ben concealed himself in a dense thicket, quickly realizing he'd bitten off a mite more than he wanted to chew. How he'd ever imagined these men might have been out here for pleasure or sport was lost on him.

Probably, he shouldn't have downed the rest of that uishge on an empty stomach. There were four men in this camp. All were armed to the bloody teeth. Ben didn't fancy losing a hand for a meal. He should find somewhere to sleep it off, then head down to Navan in the morning for a flea-ridden bed and a hot bowl of porridge. Of course, that was what he *should* do... but no matter how insistent the thought, his legs would not obey. Uishge whispered courage in his ear. The pickled part of his brain was highly susceptible. He had no doubt he could take them.

Although, Ben knew the difference between common thieves and professional smugglers. From the look of things, these fellows were expecting to be laid upon at any moment. The shivering girl they'd tied to a tree on the opposite side of the fire was the reason they were so well armed and jumpy. Poor thing. She was blindfolded and gagged, wearing only a fine linen tunic and thin woolen trousers. A filthy burlap sack barely covered part of one leg. Likely, she was freezing. Ben's lip curled. *Kidnappers...*

He was so inebriated he'd practically strolled right up to them with his hands out for scraps. Worse, these men were *Souther* mercenaries from Bethany, if he wasn't mistaken. Their costly serrated sabres plainly bore the truth of that. Northers preferred slimmer, more practical weaponry. He figured these men must have been sent here for the girl. Drunk he might be, but Ben knew which end of his arse was up. No Souther mercenary would venture so far into the inhospitable North without the promise of a hefty purse awaiting his return. There were far easier pickings in the South. Ben didn't have to work hard to determine where she must have come from. There were only two wealthy cities in the North, and from the tattoos he spied roaming her exposed clavicle, he could guess which it was. She was Tairnganese. Noble too.

Worth quite a lot of fainne to this lot.

Ben watched the bald man very closely. Clearly, their leader, his steady eye roved the makeshift camp with wary regularity. Of course, shrewd and vigilant as he might be, he was no Sidhe. Ben smirked. If this intelligent man only knew what lurked in the shadows, he might fear the 'elves' across the border as much as his oafish friend Fergus did. The largest of the gang snored in his bedroll, utterly oblivious to the world around him. He was a gentle, simple creature in an overlarge package, nothing more. Ben felt he wouldn't be much trouble. The reptilian creature Conor, however, would be slightly more challenging. He lay prone as if asleep, though his right hand fingered a vicious dagger at his hip. There was another strapped beneath his left leg and a smaller one in his right sleeve. Ben marked him well. He would have to kill Conor quickly. No one who found a need for so many knives loathed their uses.

Beyond him, the youngest of the band perched nearest the fire. He made a grand show of pretending to be awake, but his breathing gave him away. This was the leader's son. Ben would've inferred that at a glance had the boy not already called the man 'Da.' He was a gangly, underfed lad of scant years. What did his father mean by bringing him along on such a job? Ben would have to incapacitate the boy first, to keep him from underfoot while he killed his father... that is if he felt up to getting involved here. They were all nearly in the same profession, weren't they? Ben was hardly an innocent. He'd done many things he wasn't proud of in the past few years for a profit. He didn't know this girl nor particularly care where she came from. Her family must be rather important in the Red City for brutes like these to go to such lengths. Either that or someone in Bethany paid good money to make her his leman. Ben wrinkled his nose.

What did he care? She was nobody to him.

Yet... his feet refused to budge. Did it matter where she came from? If he walked away now, whatever might happen to her would weigh on his conscience. Ben was in a position to do something to help her, and as much as he knew he should, he couldn't bring himself to leave. He was still his father's son, beneath the years of poverty, anonymity, and self-inflicted degradation.

Ben Maeden might be a degenerate criminal, but inside, his father's lessons held firm.

Not like this.

She *was* a tiny little thing, and there *was* quite a lot of meat drying over the fire. Besides, he was too hungry to walk to Navan in the cold and too drunk to bother.

He looked up. The night had matured. The uishge in his ear assured him that his intrusion wasn't merely the right thing to do; it was the best thing to do. Why should these Southers get to keep all that food, all that uishge, and make it out of the Greensward without paying a toll? Besides, he hated the cunts in Bethany. This was the North, and Southermen hadn't been welcome here for almost fifty years. To taunt him with meat and good strong ale... by Herne, he could kill them for the brass alone. With a gurgling gut, Ben waited for his moment. The fact that the scene blurred before his eyes and his head spun a little every time he moved meant less than nothing in the face of such sport.

Heart of Darkness

n.e. ʄ0⸵
ʄ, ðor samna
eire

R awly's eyes snapped open. He'd no idea how he'd managed to fall asleep. At some point, he dreamt a silver wolf stalked him through an impenetrable mist. Just before waking, a feeling of imminent peril dug into his semiconscious brain like a tick. Odd. He rarely dreamt at all. Shifting himself into an upright position, he took stock of his companions. First, he looked to Gabriel to be sure the lad was doing his duty. He wasn't, of course. Gabriel was fast asleep, with his dark head tucked into the crook of his arm. Fergus, too, snored beside the fire's dwindling embers. Conor had stopped thumbing his daggers, which never happened unless he had drifted off. Rawly knew he must rouse these fools before the sun broke. They should be well past Bally Lough by afternoon. It wouldn't be long before the Siorai girl's pursuers discovered their little campsite.

Having rested for half the night had already sawed into Rawly's tight schedule. He got up, did his business against a tree, and glanced over his shoulder at the Duch's prodigal daughter. Either the girl had grown weary of struggling or was blissfully insensate. He didn't much care, either way. It wasn't Rawly's place to question the Duch's orders. If Patrick demanded she be hauled back to Bethany in burlap... so be it. She'd put up a good fight, in any case. Everyone knew the Siorai had strange powers. He'd

41

been duly warned not to touch Lady Donahugh casually. Lord Bishop had been implicit on that score when Rawly was hired. Even so, Rawly hadn't expected her to be such a bloody handful. He'd love to see what the girl could do if the numbers had been in her favor.

To subdue her, they'd been forced to strike her; quite a few times, he was sorry to say. She'd set fire to Conor's sleeve, broken three of Fergus' teeth, burned two heavy ropes, and tried to bite off one of Gabriel's ears. Rawly discovered that the Duch's errant daughter was easiest to handle when sound asleep. They'd divested her of her boots because she'd kicked two of them in the face and burned her cloak to ash in her last attempt to escape her bonds. She was exhausting. 'Twas a pity. She was such a tiny thing, despite her gifts. Rawly could never command such indignities to be inflicted upon one of his daughters. He pitied any man that might ever try. Though, he and his lord were different men. Duch Patrick would sacrifice a hundred daughters to achieve the throne of Eire. That was hardly a secret. Lady Una was merely a means to an end for her ambitious father. Rawly didn't much like Patrick, but he was hardly in a place to give his opinion to a man of Donahugh's stature. Better to serve and serve well, for there were few rewards in innocence or integrity.

After retying his stays, Rawly bent to secure the blade at his ankle, which had worked itself partway from his boot. He heard a faint sound— almost a sigh— from the woods behind him. The dagger was in his palm before his eyes came up. Straining his senses, the only sounds he heard were breathing men and the clamor of his own heart. Focusing his gaze on the trees, he scanned the area for a complete turn. Nothing but black forest all around. He couldn't smell anything but evergreen, moss, dried leaves, and smoldering wood. Did he imagine things? Some trick of an overtaxed mind? After a while, he felt a bit foolish. It was probably a bird or other night creature swooping down on its prey. His nerves were coiled so tight that he counted phantoms.

Rawly shook his head and bent to dissemble the campsite. Time was running out. They needed to get on the road.

Bᴇɴ ʜᴀᴅ sᴛᴏᴏᴅ sᴄᴀɴᴛ ɪɴᴄʜᴇs from Rawly for quite a while and hadn't been spied. A thrill coursed through Ben's veins at the revelation. Perhaps he was sobering up? He bloody well hoped so because as the night wore on, he began to realize what a terrible idea this was. He had only his broadsword and a pair of daggers. Usually, when one attempted to rob a gang of criminals, they had help, or at the very least, better weapons. If he didn't get a move on soon, he'd sober up and talk himself out of this altogether. He was too damned hungry to nitpick the details. Also, he was reasonably sure yon girl would prefer not to be tied to a tree any longer.

He slunk closer, eyes raking the camp for something he could *use*. He grinned when they alighted on a worn yew longbow lying atop one of the mercenaries' packs. See? He knew Herne listened when he prayed! Wraith-like, he slid around the campsite toward the heap of piled packs, careful not to disturb so much as a blade of grass. He might have been a leaf blown about on the wind or a shadow flitting from tree to tree. He was the very soul of stealth. The heart of darkness… nay, its master. The girl snorted from behind her gag. She stared directly at him; her brows knitted together in disdain. Ben froze, fingertips inches from the bow's haft. What witchery had she employed to spy him in the dark, silent as a shade?

"Now, this has got to be the queerest thing I ever did see—" Rawly's voice broke in from just beside him. The blood pounded in Ben's ears. Rawly chuckled. "Never heard o'anyone sneakin' up on a Sidhe before. I'd ask if ye was sober, but from the smell, I'd say I have me answer."

Ben straightened, swaying only slightly. The girl made a rude sound in her throat. He frowned at her. The bloody cow could have warned him! Her answering glare was incredulous as if to say, '*How would I do that, you idiot?*'

"If this is a rescue attempt, it's the worst one I ever heard of." Rawly's laugh inspired another from behind him. Conor, too, was awake.

Fantastic, Ben thought. *Next time sleep it off, hero.*

"Or didya come to rob me, maybe?" Rawly asked, his tone taking the hint of an edge. Rawly's sabre rested inches from Ben's throat. It would take but a single thrust to force it through flesh. Conor struggled to his feet over his bedroll but remained several paces away. Ben thought he might dodge past Rawly and smash in his nose... but then, both the boy and the big man stirred. *Damn.* Whatever he was going to do, he'd have to be quick.

"What's tha— holy Chrissakes!" cried Fergus, rocking up to his knees. "Boss! Ye brung him down on us!" He crossed himself.

Rawly muttered something unintelligible. "This one's not a fine elf-lord out for yer blood, Fergie. Not even sure this fella's a Sidhe a'tall. Fathom a guess; I'd say he came here to steal food and supplies from us. Am I right?"

Ben realized he'd been asked a question a tad late. He was too busy doing sums in his head. Four paces to the woods behind him, nine to that fellow Conor with the sharp daggers. Two to the girl, five to the big man who ogled him in abject fear.

"Think what you like," he said, recounting.

"Well, ye could blow me down with a whistle. I've half a mind to let ye take what ye were aimin' for, poor, sad bugger that ye are."

Ben's nostrils flared. Even in Rosweal, which sprouted men like Rawly by the dozen, he was treated with cool, respectful disdain. Men simply did not speak to him this way. *Not ever.* He met Rawly's eye with a caustic scowl.

"Appearances can deceive, don't you agree?"

Conor swore from Rawly's far end. "Shane, be careful there. That big fella... can't say as how, but I know I've seen him before."

Rawly took Ben's measure. "Doubt it."

Gabriel stirred near the girl. "What's happenin', Da?"

"Nuthin' to worry over, boyo. Ye stay back there."

"But, Da—"

"I said, stay back!" hollered Rawly, taking a firmer grip on his sabre.

Ben knew what was coming. Though he'd made a hilarious botch of his entrance, there would be no talking his way out of the situation now. These men would have to kill him, even if they didn't want to. He'd seen them with the girl. That suited Ben just fine. He came here to pick a fight.

"Conor—" Rawly began, but Ben ducked under his arm, too fast to follow. He rolled for the longbow he spied earlier. Mercifully, its quiver rested just beneath. It wasn't full, but four arrows would be plenty. Rawly lunged forward as expected, sabre raised for a high slash over Ben's shoulders. Ben twisted himself nearly double to avoid it. Shifting his weight onto his heels, he rocked back, using the longbow's butt as a lance. It shot out, taking Rawly first on the chin, which sent him skittering backward, then hard in the center of his chest. Rawly yelped as his spine crunched into hard-packed earth. About five paces from the girl, Ben nocked and knelt low. The bow was taller than his kneeling form and took some extra effort to draw. He flipped it crosswise to level it with his shoulder span. Arrows had a greater impact that way. "Don't move an inch further."

Rawly went still as a stone. Ben crab-walked the last few feet to the girl, keeping his bowstring taut. From the corner of his eye, he watched Conor slide around the fire, his hands hovering near his belt. Fergus, on the other hand, squeaked like a frightened rabbit. Rawly's boy faded into the trees on Ben's left; hands raised high. No matter, Ben must only worry about their leader for now.

"'Spose I should apologize for mockin' ye?" acknowledged Rawly dryly. A thick trickle of blood ran down his chin. Ben didn't answer. "If the girl is yer concern, she's not worth the trouble. She stole some o'the master's silver. Takin' her home for a whippin.'"

"Let's pretend that you and I are both intelligent men. I'll give you one chance to clear out of here. The girl stays."

Conor set his feet; both hands crept toward partially concealed blades. As for Fergus, the look on his face broadcast that he hadn't yet decided if he should run or stand and fight. A good thing too. Fergus was twice as wide as Ben. If he weren't an obvious simpleton, he would be a serious challenge, all by himself.

"There are four of us. Yer alone. That's a sure bet, I'll warrant," said Rawly. The timbre of his voice hinted at a secreted fear. Not only had he not expected something like this to happen, but he was also unprepared for its outcome. "I'll let ye keep that bow and even a few coins if ye walk away now."

45

"Part like old mates?"

"Why not? Stranger things have happened."

"Not in my experience, Southerman." As soon as Ben lowered his bow, that scrawny arachnoid behind Rawly would send one of those thin blades sailing into his throat. That is if Rawly failed to cut him in half with his sabre first.

"Well then," sighed Rawly. "Can't say I didn't try."

Two things happened at once. Rawly shouted an alert to the group, and Conor jerked aside to throw a dagger. Ben snaked his upper body out of its path and twisted around, firing his first arrow into Conor's dominant hand. The spider shrieked like a diving bird. Ben nocked and fired the second arrow into his thigh, right into the knee joint. Yowling, Conor went down beside the firepit. In the meantime, Fergus sprang at Conor as if to shield him. Instead, he tripped over his bedroll. His chin slammed into the ground, hard. Fresh piss clouded the air around him as he whimpered into the dirt.

With an enraged howl, Rawly pitched himself at Ben. Ben side-stepped his first thrust and bent at the waist to tug his nose away from the next slash. Snarling, Rawly hefted his sabre for another wild swing. Too fast for Rawly to track, Ben, reached out and struck him in the face with the butt of his bow. Dark blood spurted from Rawly's busted nose. Grunting, he slashed blindly to keep Ben at a distance while he struggled to wipe his streaming eyes. Rawly's face was a horrible mask of blood and wrath, but he lacked the strength and speed to maintain a proper defense. Ben's third arrow burst through Rawly's skull, directly between the eyes. The arrow's point exploded from the back of his head; bits of brain and bone splashed to the ground beneath him. Rawly's last sight was of the earth rushing toward his face as he fell.

A rustling near the fire spun Ben back around. With a roar, Fergus bounded over on all fours like a lumbering bear. His massive hands stretched up to yank Ben down by his calves, dragging deep runnels in the earth. Knowing he was done for if the big fellow got his arms around him, Ben struck out with the broad haft of the bow, putting everything he had into the stroke. Thankfully, Fergus' windpipe cracked like a reed.

He careened backward, eyes darting around like a frightened rodent. His cheeks went purple from lack of oxygen. He choked to death on his own blood.

Ben felt something whistle past his ear. Several strands of silver hair departed with it. Without looking up, he fired his last arrow into Conor's chest. Twitching, Conor dropped the blade he'd intended to throw next. It splashed uselessly into the dirt. Ben strode over and jerked the arrow from his ribcage. A widening pool of gore spread beneath the man's knees. There was a lascivious cruelty in Conor's eyes that Ben did not care for. Who knew how many innocents Ben might have saved by putting an end to him tonight? A hissing breath rattled out of Conor's closing throat. Ben dug the remaining daggers out of the mercenary's cloak. There were many.

"I suppose you're wondering why I didn't put this arrow between your eyes as I did your boss?"

Speechless, Conor glared defiantly up at his murderer.

"I've seen eyes like yours a thousand times before." Ben spared the girl a glance. Her jaw set, hard. The bruises around her eyes and mouth said it all. "Your boss didn't strike me as the sort to do that to a woman. That's your handiwork, is it not?"

With the hatred on Conor's face— the sadistic tilt to his mouth, the empty vacuum of his eyes; Ben had his answer. Without ado, Ben took the daggers he'd collected and jammed them one by one into Conor's guts. The spider died without much fuss. Before Ben had time to sigh in relief, he heard a shuffling sound behind him. The boy. He turned.

Gabriel trembled, not ten paces away. Strong, cold moonlight shone through the thinning canopy overhead. The lad's features were pale and soft-cheeked. He stared vacantly at his father's remains as if his mind couldn't register any other sight in the world. "Da..."

Something dark rustled in the depths of Ben's limited conscience. This fate was more or less what Rawly would have received at the hands of Tairnganeah or any other pursuant force. Yet, the heartbreak on the lad's face shifted something at Ben's center. Sobbing, Gabriel ran a hand over his tousled hair. He reached into his belt for his dagger. Ben tensed. The arrow he'd reclaimed from Conor's corpse was nocked and waiting.

47

"Don't, boy," he pleaded. "Your father deserved what he got. Don't add your death to his litany of failures. What was wrought here today was the only end he would ever carve out for himself. Do you understand?"

"Dunno about that. Ol' Paddy ordered me Da to get her. He don't leave much choice, ye know," said Gabriel. A bead of sweat slithered down Ben's collarbone. The bodies were already beginning to attract flies from the bog.

"There is always a choice, lad. I know of what I speak."

"Yer awful preachy, for a murderer," he said. "I went to school, ye know? Learned all about you Dannans and yer Fir Bolg cousins. All that gold in yer ear means yer a noble, don't it?"

Smart kid.

"Doesn't matter who I am."

The strange smile again. "Why do ye look like that if yer a noble?"

Too clever by half.

"Go home. Take whatever you need to get there but go. I beg you." The tension in the atmosphere swelled to bursting. Gabriel pulled himself as tall and straight as his meager height would allow. Grasping his dagger, he bared his teeth at Ben.

"Ye should have walked on, ye know?"

Ben's hand moved on the bow of its own accord. "Gabriel, stop. Please, don't make me shoot you."

"Ye know, it's funny. Always wanted to meet one o'yer kind," Gabriel sobbed. "It just... ain't fair." With an adolescent scream that Ben would hear in his sleep for years to come, possibly forever, Gabriel charged.

Ben had no choice but to let fly. The force of the impact sent the boy sailing into the oak behind him. His back hit the trunk with such force that Ben heard something snap inside his chest. He sputtered for a moment but lay still, silent too soon. Ben lowered his bow, unsure of the emotions roiling through him. He'd never killed someone so young before. He tried to tell himself that it was probably for the best. Gabriel's father had been a mercenary with skewed morals. The boy had undoubtedly been headed into the same societal breach. Ben told himself this, though deep down, he believed that each man might choose his destiny. The boy could have made a different choice had their paths not crossed this night. Gabriel's vacant eyes stared up into the moonlit sky, his mouth agape as if in wonder. Ben pried the arrow from his ribcage with a resigned sigh.

He'd done what he must.

For a while, he almost believed himself too.

Having exhausted his last ounce of strength, Ben fell upon the remnants of the mercenaries' meal like a starving wolf. There wasn't much left but thank the Gods; it was still warm. Heedless of the blood and filth coating his fingers, he tore into the charred meat with relish. He didn't even bother to chew. Cramming mouthfuls of muscle, gristle, and tendon down his throat at breakneck speed, he barely noticed the girl grunting at him from her tree. Still swaddled to her waist in burlap, she thrashed about, her eyes, two accusatory white beads.

Ah, he thought.

I nearly forgot about you.

Looking around, he spotted the waterskin across the firepit. Tearing another hank of mouth-watering venison from the bone, he shuffled over to pick it up, still chewing. She kicked out at him as he approached and muttered something unflattering around her gag. He unstoppered the vessel and tossed a fair amount into his overfull mouth with a sigh. Licking his fingers, he leaned over to remove her gag. She drew in a deep breath as if she meant to give him a piece of her mind, but he jammed the waterskin's beak into her mouth instead. Sputtering, she coughed up a good portion before basic human need took over.

When he felt satisfied she'd drunk her fill, he removed the skin from her mouth and replaced its stopper. Again, she sucked in a lungful of air to protest, but he swiftly replaced her gag. She thrashed, bucked, and screeched behind the soiled cloth like a newborn eaglet.

"Wait right there, mistress," he said, swallowing another enormous mouthful of meat. Dodging dead men and their puddles of oozing fluids, he gathered arrows, pocketed daggers, coins, and any other supplies he could stuff into his vest. All the while, the girl vowed bloody murder from behind her gag. Rummaging through what he assumed was Rawly's pack, he threw a glorious oiled sealskin cloak over his shoulders with a relieved sigh. The expensive garment boasted a wool-lined interior and a deep, comfortable cowl. It didn't smell very nice, but then again, neither did he. For the girl, a second, smaller cloak from Gabriel's pack and a quilted blanket to tug up beneath it. From skinny, diminutive Conor's feet, he prized a workable pair of boots. They would serve.

When he dropped his findings at her feet, she muttered invectives that he could scarcely comprehend. She must have realized by now he wasn't interested in anything she meant to shout at him, surely? Kneeling, he wrenched the bag off her lower body. He took a seat on her legs to hold them down. She grimaced dramatically when he tugged each boot over her bare feet. They were a bit big and reeked of dead mercenary, but they were warm, and warm meant she would keep her toes. Next, he tossed the small, fur-lined woolen cloak over her shaking shoulders and tucked the blanket around her legs. She uttered so many foul things behind the obstruction that spittle ran down her chin. He stomped to the fire and stuffed a few more handfuls of meat into his mouth and several more into his pockets. When he returned, he laid two greasy piles on her lap. She gave him a look that should have boiled his guts to broth. Disinterested, he reached behind her to saw at the rope binding her to the elm. Only the topmost layers, mind. She must take responsibility for the latter bit. He slid the handle of one of Conor's daggers into her grasping fist. He pressed her fingers around its grip and laid the waterskin across her knees. She stared up at him in silent accusation.

"Don't look at me like that, mistress," he said, shaking his head. "Shouldn't take you more than an hour to saw through that rope if you get busy." Giving her a mock salute, he moved off. She thrashed around, attempting to shout over her gag. Ignoring her, he discovered one item in his path that he'd nearly overlooked. He whispered a prayer of thanks to every God he knew, as he bent to retrieve the small stone jug of uishge, he spied near the fire. He was grinning again. The girl's mumbled protests faded to a hum behind him.

50

THE SIORAI GIRL

Ben awoke to the forest creaking around him. *Again*. He pulled a face. A blustery wind whistled through the treetops, dispassionate as a scythe through wheat. Not a single bird sang overhead, nor did anything rustle nearby. The animals in this thicket had better sense than he. Perhaps the numb ringing in his ears finally stirred him, or was it the weight of the ice coating his cloak and collar? If neither, then maybe it was the prickling, lumpy bracken he slept upon— who could say? All he knew for sure was how bloody uncomfortable his accommodations were. His back was stiff as a ship's prow. Every move he made was agony. Gods, even the feeble, waxy bit of light peeking through yon heavy silver clouds made his eyes sting. If his gut weren't churning like the sea in a storm, it would be for the noxious fumes seeping from his clothing, hair, skin, and mouth.

Great Herne.

He was a rising corpse. Without a fire, the little lean-to he'd hastily constructed in the night was hardly protection from the weather's searching fingers. Shaking ice chips from his new sealskin cloak, Ben ran a hand over his grimy face. Just how much had he drunk last night?

Gods... *all day?*

"Rough night?" a piercing voice inquired, penetrating his skull like a hammered nail. He spun round to face the speaker, who perched on

51

a nearby rock staring down her grubby nose at him. Head swimming, stomach sloshing, he tripped over his own clumsy feet into the frozen grass below. There she sat, with his dagger dangling nonchalantly from her right hand. The Tairnganese girl had an intense, judgmental sort of disapproval on her face. Ben frowned. What in the hells was *she* doing here? Hadn't he left her tied to a tree some miles in the opposite direction?

"How'd you get here?" he gagged down a greasy surge of bile. Just opening his mouth to speak was risky.

"Walked. Same as you."

"I didn't realize they taught woodcraft in the Cloister?"

"A child could have followed your trail last night," she snorted, rolling her eyes. "You made enough noise to rouse half of Eire. I don't know how far you planned to go, but we're less than half a mile from where you left me."

He watched her tap the flat of the blade against her knee. The scowl on her dirty little mouth would unsettle a troll.

"I see. Come to kill me, then?"

"Thought about it for a bit. You snore, you know? Like a bloody boar. I suppose you dispelled many of my notions concerning the Sidhe last night."

A direct hit.

"Sorry to disillusion you, mistress. Now, is there anything else I can do for you before you slog off?" He would throttle her if she didn't stop tapping that bloody dagger soon. The repetitive racket made his gums throb. All this talking was murder. His voice made the pressure in his head feel like someone was attempting to squeeze his brains through a vice. In no mood for company, he figured now was as good a time as any to get going.

She cocked her head at him. "Don't you want to know whom you killed last night? Who I am?"

"No," Ben grimaced. "Not my bloody business. You should save your breath. I have places to be, so—" he waved her away with his right hand and struggled to his feet. Bones creaked, and joints popped all the way up. Why did he feel like he'd aged a thousand years in a single night?

52

The girl didn't budge. Her eyes were steady: calculating, estimating.

"What, damn you? I have nothing to share. No food, no drink," he swallowed, his throat dry as vellum, "and no interest in your problems. I did you a favor last night because I was drunk, and it seemed like a good idea at the time. The way I see things, we're square."

She considered him for several tense moments while he limped about his little makeshift camp, gathering what few items he had left. "I can pay you."

"You don't know how to get home?" He raised a silver brow at her, pleased to watch her flush. Tairnganese women were notorious for their independence. In fact, their entire society was built on the absurd notion that females were the superior sex. Bollocks and nonsense, of course, but no concern of his. He made it a habit to keep as far away from the Red City as he could manage. He was sure 'Ben Maeden' had a hefty bounty awaiting him there. Danu only knew what the Cohort might do to him if they saw him as he was now. Without his ogham charm, no city along the border would likely roll out the red carpet for him. His best bet was to make it to Ten Bells as fast as possible and buy one from the Sidhe Consulate. Aside from lurking in the Greensward for the foreseeable future, he didn't have many attractive options. Though, there was a man he'd known many years ago who might be able to help him.

Arthur Guinness didn't live far. Ben intended to make for his farmstead first. Failing that, he'd have no choice but to trek down to Ten Bells. As unattractive as the prospect was, he would commit himself to it if necessary. What he was not prepared to do, however, was babysit a Tairnganese brat who should be thankful to be alive. Ungrateful wretch. He didn't appreciate her haughty stare in the least.

"In theory, *yes*," she enunciated. "But I don't know what to expect between here and there. It'd be safer if we traveled together. For both of us, I expect."

"Not interested." He spared her a curt nod. "Pleasant journey, then." He waggled his fingers at her as he ambled onto the path and away from his camp.

"I can pay you your weight in fainne!"

He paused, turning back. "Do you have any of that gold on you now?"

She stammered, gulping air like a goldfish. "Of course, I don't! But—"

"That's too bad." He pointed. "Tairngare is that way, milady. Brida's luck upon you!" Plugging his ears against the litany of curses she spewed behind him, Ben marched toward his purpose with nary a backward glance.

⚞ ⚟

IN NAVAN VILLAGE, TORRENTS OF freezing Dor Samna rain rushed through the muddy lanes at his feet. Ben waited for dusk before entering the town; his cowl pulled low over his face and hair. He was thankful for Rawly's big, shapeless cloak. It would serve so long as no one bothered to peer too deeply into the hood. When the sun disappeared over the Western Hills, he could safely stroll into the inn across the street.

Two days out in the wind and cold were plenty. The sign over the entrance bore two arrows crossed at their hafts, points skyward. *Bowman's Cross*, the sign read: a typically Norther title. Navan wasn't as rough as Rosweal but didn't lack for ne'er-do-wells or questionable characters intent on their privacy. Folk shouldn't be quick to ask questions in a dive like this. He hoped, anyway. He'd had his fill of waking up covered in ice and filth and could do with a dry bed and a hot meal. When thick shadows stretched between buildings, he shrugged his cloak close and splashed into the downpour. He could only pray the *Cross* had more to offer than porridge or gruel. A hearty stew would warm his bones better than a nice dram of uishge. Well, almost. Just as his boot struck the tavern's jamb, a host of fully armored Tairnganeah marched down the opposite intersection. Fat raindrops pattered against their black and gold armor. He watched them trudge past until they disappeared around a far corner. His hand frozen against the door handle, he let out a breath he hadn't realized he'd been holding.

That was somewhat unexpected. Tairngare's martial corps didn't often patrol this far west and rarely within town limits. In Rosweal, soldiers didn't dare march beyond the Navan Gate— the Guild would pick them off from the rooftops like grouse. Rosweal rejected governance of any stripe. Woe to anyone who meant to prove otherwise. Navan might not reside under the Greenmakers' protection, but even so, she was a long way from the Red City. He wondered what Tairnganeah were doing in this insignificant little village on the rim of the Greensward anyway. The only explanation he could surmise was that they searched for that blasted girl. As he thought, she must be some important noblewoman's spawn to warrant such concern. He wished them luck but kept well out of sight.

Pulling his cowl low as it would go, he discovered a renewed appreciation for Navan's poorly lit lanes. There weren't many who could afford tallow candles in Navan, far fewer proper oil lamps. The streets were almost always dark, wet, and treacherous. Most lanes lacked cobbles or even wooden planking to break up the sluicing drainage that plagued each intersection in a downpour. Residents here made do with one-quarter of the luxury Roswellians were accustomed to, which wasn't saying much.

For example, the *Bowman's Cross* didn't boast *The Hart*'s fine glass windows or even a fraction of her light fixtures. There might have been five scrapped candles burning within the whole of the windowless, dank little structure.

Shoving the door open, a blast of poorly ventilated peat smoke, body odor, rotted cabbage, and flat moldering ale rushed into Ben's face. Eyes watering, he coughed his way to the bar, which was essentially four un-sanded boards propped over two rotting ale barrels. As he suspected, the taproom was silent as a kirkyard. Various patrons were scattered around a few rickety tables gathered before the hearth. No one looked up as he entered; all were seemingly as desirous of anonymity as he was, their hands wrapped around wooden tankards, hoods pulled deep, eyes resolutely forward. This was just the sort of establishment he'd hoped for. The innkeeper didn't look up when Ben took a seat and set two coppers down on the bar. He was a large fellow; his pocked cheeks sagged into a grizzled, graying beard, and he had a frown that could cleave stone.

"Ale," Ben said, his tone casual. The silent innkeeper slid the coin into his palm, then turned to fill a clean tankard. The right sort of place for Ben, indeed. Sliding his mug over, Ben placed two more coppers on the bar. "Came to ask where I can buy a horse and supplies? Maybe a room for the night, if ye have vacancy?"

Again, the innkeeper scraped the coins into his palm without investigating their donor. He had the attitude of a man who was used to answering, rather than asking, questions.

"Have a room at the rear o'the buildin', top o'the stairs. Nuthin' fancy. A bed and dry beddin.' Not the cleanest, nor the biggest spread. Six coppers, and it's yers."

Ben reached into his vest for more coin. "A meal, if ye have that as well?"

"Two more coppers," said the innkeeper. "For a silver, ye'll have yer choice of nag from me own stables out back there and two bowls o'porridge with bread and cheese. Ye want more ale or uishge? Pay as ye go. Fair?"

"Fair indeed. Thanks." Ben's stomach grumbled at the promise of hot food and warm ale. He didn't mind that it was bound to be tasteless mash. Anything would do. The proprietor tossed down the cloth he'd been wiping mugs with, then disappeared through a small doorway toward his dimly lit kitchen. Ben sank into his shadowy corner, keeping his back against a mildewed wall.

When the innkeeper returned, he carried a steaming bowl of grey shapeless mush, topped with a massive crust of hard bread and a half-wheel of greenish cheese. He set a wooden spoon beside the bowl, no knives for the bread. In the North, folk ate bread and cheese with their fingers. If meat needed cutting to chew, it was expected that one produce their own cutlery.

Ben laid into this bounty with a blissful sigh. The porridge was surprisingly palatable despite its underwhelming appearance. Bringing out a second helping, the innkeeper was visibly pleased someone appreciated his cooking. Ben was confident he could win a third bowl for a few colorful compliments.

Behind him, at a small table beside the hearth, he overheard two men having a rather heated political debate. One had the look of a constable, or perhaps a lamplighter, even though there weren't many lamps to light in Navan. He was some sort of town official, from the emblem sewn into his coarse woolen coat.

"Ain't what I heard," he was saying. "I heard ole Drem and that Nema woman have come to blows in Parliament over this."

"Nah, we was at market three days ago, and I'm tellin' ye, the Doma's forcin' a bill through. Nema's not got the clout in the Cloister that she do in the Commons. It'll pass," said the other fellow, puffing on a hornpipe.

The town official pursed his lips, blowing air out of his nostrils. "Aye, that's nepotism, that is. Parliament won't stand for it. Lady Nema is second in the Cloister and holds more power with the folk than them grand Mouras in the Citadel. The Merchers will vote it into oblivion."

"Olly, ye know how these things work. Parliament 'tis naught but a dog and pony show for the mob. Drem Moura's been Doma for near a half-century. She didn't bother about the law twenty years ago, and I'm sure she ain't worried 'bout it now."

"Has it been two decades already?"

"More. Closer to thirty years, by me reckonin.'"

Olly, the official, took a long pull from his tankard, a dubious expression on his wind-lined face. "I don't think as ye should count Ole Nema out, Dan. She's been fightin' for us wee folk for as long as I can recall. None o' us want any more religious twiddle-twaddle crammed down our throats. If Parliament can't stop the Doma, the Commons will revolt. I'm sure o' it."

"I think yer underestimatin' how much power the Cloister holds in the Red City. There's been a Moura Doma all me life... nigh a full century, if ye trace it back to my Grandda's time. Ye don't gather such power and just let it go, now do ye? Drem's done it before, and I'm tellin' ye, she'll do it again."

Olly swore a host of foul-mouthed oaths into his tankard. "Just ain't right. Me mam was Siorai, and so is me wife. It ain't that I don't believe, I just don't see as them Moura should run things as they used to. We're an open-minded sort o' folk, ye know? Laws should give all o' us a chance at a better life... not just them ole hags in the Cloister and them toity bitches in Parliament. But what do I know, eh? I'm just a bloody *male*."

"If that ain't the truth," Dan toasted with a self-depreciative smirk. "Still, don't see as it'll affect us much out here in the townships. They can make whichever Moura cunt they want a queen, and it won't make a lick o'difference here, will it? Life don't change for those o'us actually works for a bloody livin'—"

Ben tuned out. He wouldn't trade a tinker's fart for Eirean politics. He didn't care which self-important ass sat in whatever symbolic chair; it was all smoke in the breeze to him. Milesian governments were cyclical and predictable as the tides. When one ruling class rose, another fell, and on it would go, so long as people walked the earth. Power was viciously fought for, imperiously wielded, and jealously guarded. A merry farce, which Ben eschewed at all costs. He preferred to keep well out of the cities so he wouldn't be subjected to this opera of short-sighted, rhetorical fallacy.

There was only one true king in Innisfail. Midhir did not concern himself with the political pantomime in Milesian Eire. These fools may argue over this or that city's social constructs and governing classes until their bones crumbled to ash. Midhir had been Ard Ri for almost a thousand years and would be High King long after their grandchildren's grandchildren faded from memory.

Ben finished his second bowl of porridge, then withdrew his belt knife to work on the bread and cheese. When the innkeeper came to collect his discarded crockery, Ben tossed two more coppers his way.

"More ale, and I'll have a snort o'that uishge ye mentioned before."

"Aye, sir." He warmed to Ben's coin, if not Ben himself. While he poured, Ben leaned closer. "I was wonderin' if ye might know a man used to live round these parts some years back?"

"I 'spose I know most folk who do. What's his name then?"

Ben realized he was breaking his moratorium against asking questions, but he didn't want to waste a day's ride if he didn't have to. "Man, by the name of Guinness. A doctor or was. He's an old friend. Ain't been in these parts for some time and wondered if I should drop by for a visit?"

"Aye, I know him. Ole feller, with that faerie woman," he spat into the rushes. "Friend o'yers, ye say?"

58

Ben cleared his throat. He was thankful his hood hid most of his features from view. Northers didn't care for half-breeds like Arthur's wife. Faeries were Sidhe half-breeds, and often, the blood mixture wasn't ideal. They tended to be off-putting physically or overly weak or aggressive, sometimes mad as a rabid dog. Come to think of it, they weren't well-regarded anywhere in Innisfail but especially not in the North, where they were most common. Poor buggers. They were hardly at fault for the misconceptions of others. Ben curbed the rebuke coiling on his tongue. Without an ogham stone, he would receive no better treatment in a backwater like Navan.

"That's the one," Ben said, taking care to keep his tone light. "Made a tonic for me missus that soothed her nasty cough for a time. I thought to drop in for a second dram. He still got a stall in town?"

The innkeeper relaxed. "Ah, well, no. Keeps to himself o'late. Me Martha thought he was likely ailin' hisself... what with that woman's passin,' some while ago. Still sells potions and other cures from home, though, last I heard. Ye remember how to get there, then?"

"Aye," Ben passed him another copper for his trouble. Innish tradition. "I do, and thank ye. Two more snorts o'that uishge, if ye please, and I'll head up to sleep. Top o'the stairs to the right, ye said?"

"Yep," the barkeep answered, happily supplying Ben with generously poured libations. He probably wasn't used to patrons who didn't haggle over fair prices and was pleased to return the favor. "I'll have me boy set ye up with our best nag in the morn. A goodnight to ye, sir."

Ben polished off his two shots. He gathered his cheese and his tankard in hand. "Many thanks for the food and hospitality." He tipped the edge of his cowl at the grinning innkeeper and made his way upstairs.

🦌 🦌

Ben rose before the sun, well-rested and eager to be on his way. He didn't want to risk being seen in full daylight without the benefit of his ogham charm. Guinness' farmstead was only ten miles or so southwest of Navan. It would take him a couple of hours to get there, no matter which way he went. No need to hurry. He could only hope that Aednat left some of her charms in Arthur's keeping when she passed.

He was sad to hear of it. He hadn't known many faeries before or after his time in Eire began. Aednat was the first of a small few. He was ashamed to acknowledge that both sides of the border suffered from the same cruel preconceptions where half-breeds were concerned. Aednat was a sweet girl, gentle and quick with a smile. She was also one of the most beautiful women he'd ever had the fortune to meet. She'd quite stopped him in his tracks the first time he'd laid eyes upon her. Despite her twisted arm and slightly malformed fingers, she had pure, sky-blue eyes, pale cornsilk hair, and a lovely neck. If Arthur, assigned to one of Ben's units all those years ago, hadn't commanded every corner of her heart, Ben might have stolen her away. She was a good woman. He'd never heard her utter an unkind word to anyone, even when they deserved it.

The air outside held a bite that could leave a mark. Ben jerked his cloak tight over his chest, tucking his ears deep into his wool-lined cowl. Bloody weather. Perhaps once he had a new charm, he'd winter in Ten Bells after all? Ben Maeden could find work anywhere. There were Guilds aplenty in the city. Might he exchange his loathing of cosmopolitan life for fine ale, more refined dining, and warm, properly insulated apartments? He would be free to decide soon enough. Maybe it was time to move past the Greensward for a few years? He wondered why the very idea felt so wrong.

A person he assumed was the proprietor's son stomped into the stable, carrying two large hay bales over each shoulder. He spied Ben waiting by the door.

"Ah, hello, sir. Got yer mount ready for ye here." He led Ben to the second to last stall. A decent middle-aged mare stood inside, awaiting her breakfast with a sloe-eyed glare. The burly, red-cheeked lad set some hay in her trough, then moved along her flanks to check her saddle straps. "This here's Vixen. She's a smart, loyal lass, she is. She don't run so fast no more on account o'her age and all, but she'll get ye where yer headed sure and steady. Just... if ye don't mind me sayin' so, take it easy on her? I'd be much obliged. She were me mam's favorite."

"I will, lad. Ye have me word." Ben meant it; he didn't love many things in this world, but he did hold a soft spot for animals. That was his mother's doing, right enough. Ben stuck out a palm, allowing her to snuffle his fingers.

"See! She likes ye. Well, that's good enough for me, then. She's a picky lass. Me Da chose her for ye cause she's our tallest nag. He did say ye was a big fella, so—" The lad handed Ben a bundle with another hunk of bread and a generous slice of cheese. "That's from me Da, too. He says to thank ye for yer patronage and to come back whenever yer in these parts. He'll give ye half rates at yer next visit."

"Most generous. Thank him for me, will ye boy?"

Nodding, the stable lad patted Vixen's flank. "Will there be anythin' else, sir?"

"Actually," said Ben. "Is there a haberdashery in town or some other shop that sells tack and the like?"

The boy pointed him toward a building two lanes over. Ben thanked him, hitched his pack to Vixen's saddle, and took his leave.

⚹ ⚹

He spent maybe ten minutes in the haberdashery. He bought a second-hand tunic of heavy rough-spun wool, a fur-lined vest, and a new linen undershirt, which he tucked into a pair of thick, sealskin trousers. A good deal warmer than he had been when he entered the shop, he left sporting a newish pair of high, boiled leather riding boots. He also purchased arrows for his empty quiver, a pot and kettle, two pouches of strong black tea, and two heavy blankets— one for himself and one for Vixen, who wasn't used to roughing it outdoors. All told, it was a successful venture. Like the Bowman's Cross proprietor, the shopkeeper was only too pleased for the polite patronage.

Well, Ben did enjoy being appreciated.

This was one thing Navan had over Rosweal. If it weren't for the women, the porter, the uishge, and the company... he could very well mark Navan higher in his esteem. The shopkeeper had seemed so happy to be making a sale of this size that he didn't mind waking at dawn to open his doors. Like most folks Ben encountered in Navan, he did not ask impertinent questions. If Ten Bells weren't his next destination, maybe Navan would be a good place to hang his proverbial hat.

Ben was pleased with himself when he rode out of town. After five miles on the Navan High Road, he would turn south at the tiny village of Keller, then ride on for a further five. The road to Ferndale, where Arthur lived, was narrow and much less traversed. He'd feel more comfortable in broad daylight once he was off the High Road. About two miles outside of Navan, he noticed a peculiar amount of activity through the trees around the next bend. He tugged on Vixen's reins. There were mounted men up ahead, at least six of them. From the color of their cuirasses, there could be no mistaking their identity. Another Tairnganeah patrol. Corsairs, to be precise: Special Light Cavalry. Ben's brows knit together. What now? He moved Vixen into the woods on the North side as quietly as he could manage.

Dismounting, he crept forward on foot, taking care to muffle his steps. Whatever they were doing here, he doubted they'd be pleased to discover a fully armed Sidhe archer on the road. Assured that he couldn't be seen or heard, he crept closer to get a better look. The Corsairs advanced upon a small, unarmed quarry. Their spears at the ready, they backed the figure into the trees. She held a single dagger in a shaking, bleeding fist. Ben cursed long and low under his breath. Of course, it was that bloody, troublesome girl! With her clenched teeth flashing white against the mud crusting her face, she slashed wildly at anything that came near. Ben shook his head, intending to head in the opposite direction, but made the mistake of taking a last glance over his shoulder. He stopped cold. The first rider, most likely the commander, barked a curt order. Two of his men lobbed long spears at the Tairnganese girl as if she were a boar they hunted for sport. She dodged the first. The second sliced through her side on its way past. She cried out, tearing back into the trees. As if she could outrun four mounted Corsairs.

They pursued.

She did not get far.

THE RED CITY

n.e. ꝼ08
16, ꝺoꝛ samna
ꞇaiꝛnᵹaꝛe

A oife grew bored of this sycophantic display: the bowing, the scraping, the affectation of reverence. The endless fog of heady incense turned her stomach. Its cloying stench singed the back of her throat from dawn to dusk each day. Worse, the silence within the microcosmic hive they called the Cloister of the Eternal Flame was smothering. A person could wander its halls for twenty-four hours without hearing a single voice, save for those inside their head. As if the heat, stench, and cavernous silence weren't enough— there was little reprieve from one's thoughts. No escape. No respite. This fortress was a prison, despite the wealth and prestige of its prisoners. No one of her rank and position was free to come and go as they pleased. She must remain behind the Citadel's stifling walls lest she lose the standing she'd striven for.

As a Prima, Aoife could move from the bottom near the Initiates' spartan cells to the sumptuous Eighth floor at will— but no further. She could not depart the Cloister without express permission from on high. Thus, the city piling around the Citadel might have been a thousand miles away for all the distraction it afforded her. To gain the privilege to come and go as Aoife pleased, she must climb literally and figuratively. Only an Alta Prima had total agency over her own body. Therefore, sponsorship from higher castes was the simplest way to rise in the Cloister. Women who passed the Eighth Ordeal could ascend higher than the Primas'

Eighth Floor, but one must prove her worth to do so. Most would fail and return to their families as very wealthy women. Some would rise to the level of Prima, but no higher. Many would never step foot outside the Cloister again. Like the Unknowable Tenth Law, the Tenth Floor was forbidden to all but the Doma herself.

Aoife was fortunate to hold the sponsorship of the great Vanna Nema. Nema was second only to the Doma in power. Differing from most Altas on the Council, she was favored by the people, being the sole representative for Parliament in the Cloister. Aoife was Nema's right hand with all accordant honors, such as they were. Unlike most girls who entered the Cloister at age five or six, Aoife didn't submit to the First Ordeal until she was already an adult. As a result, many in the Cloister viewed her with equal parts suspicious jealousy and respectful fear. Siorai twice her rank, believed she held a singular gift. Because of this, she must always guard her back. The Cloister of the Eternal Flame was not a welcoming place for those with natural talent, especially those who lacked the proper family names.

Nema was herself an outsider to the Tairnganese aristocracy. Her origins were reputed to be common, and her name new to the Citadel's Registry. Nema was an enigma, one that challenged convention at every turn. Despite this, or perhaps because of it, Nema's star was ascendant in the Cloister, whilst the Doma's had been waning for decades. Her influence with the Commons had much to do with this upset to the natural order. Without the support of the masses, the Doma's hold on the reins of power waned by the day.

The government was designed to operate as a theocratic democracy, but that was also changing. Parliament ran the day-to-day affairs of the City, its colonies, and its citizenry via its two warring houses: the Libella and the Union of Commons. The Libella featured only scions of Tairnganese nobility. None without a Patent of Maternas could gain entry into this esteemed collective of noblewomen. On the other hand, the Union was for educated people of the Merchanta and Agrean classes, into which any class was welcomed. Above these, but without direct access to the people, was the Cloister of the Eternal Flame and its

Council of Nine. Parliament wrote and decided whichever laws could be presented to the Holy Order in the Cloister but had limited power to gainsay directives from on High. Nema currently strove to repeal another of Drem's high-handed directives.

Drem intended to put her granddaughter forth as a second puppet Queen. Nema had spent decades stoking foment against the Moura for heretical tyranny since Drem's first attempt at regal dynasty. With the support of the people, Nema was winning her argument too. The merchants, farmers, guildsmen, artisans, and laborers: all adored Vanna Nema. The nobles, however, were a different story.

On her way to the Grand Arcade, where Parliament was about to convene, Aoife dodged courtiers, clerical Secundas, Cloister stewards, servitors, Academians, and Citadel Cohorts in their black and gold breastplates. The halls were stuffed to bursting with people, a far cry from the quiet isolation upstairs in the Cloister. She often had to press herself into the walls to avoid collisions. A multitude of hands reached out to stall her, and voices were raised with incessant and impertinent questions.

One fellow, an overweight Agrean Exciseman, jogged to keep up with her.

"My Lady Sona," he said, his breath short. "When can we expect Alta Nema's address?"

"In due course, Master Birna." She brushed past him. But he was barely shoved aside before another pest took his place. This one, a self-important Judge's clerk dipped in the colors of House Tenma. Aoife wrinkled her nose. The Tenmas were almost as bad as the bloody Mouras.

"My lady! Will she order a purge of the Cohort? Judge San will want to know!" Aoife swerved and turned the next corner, striding swiftly past the gilded floor-to-ceiling windows. An oiled steward with many fat gems winking on each stubby finger caught at her sleeve.

"Do tell Lady Nema that we are expecting an answer to our—"

Aoife shrugged her arm free and continued forward at twice the speed. People oozed from corners, doorways, and alcoves, frantic to impede her progress. So far, every Judge's effort to assuage public outcry was met with raucous jeering from the mob gathering outside. Noblewomen generally did not go missing in the Red City. The fact that both victims in the past quarter century were Dominas of the Moura clan was not lost on anyone. Primas did not wander from the Citadel on their own, and they certainly did not attempt to flee, scions of the powerful Moura family, especially. The whole affair smacked of treason at worst, or at best, rank incompetence.

Prima Moura had been missing for three days. Already, violence had erupted in the markets and gathering places. Several hunting parties were dispatched to find her, but therein lay the crux of the problem. Many factions in Tairngare believed the Moura girl to be a heretic and her grandmother a charlatan and fraud. No one could be certain if she'd been kidnapped and manipulated by unknown agents or if she'd fled growing political instability in the Cloister. Either way, the event spelled trouble for the Moura Clan. Vocal members of the Union of Commons seized upon the opportunity to further their cause: the unequivocal surrender of Drem Moura and the installation of Vanna Nema as the new Doma. Others sought to hamper the Union's cause by accusing its venerated members of collusion and treason. Despite growing unrest in the city and the Citadel, Nema had been expertly feinting all claimants away. She would not take a side.

Not publicly, anyway.

Aoife found it all quite amusing.

She pushed open the heavy iron door leading into the Grand Arcade. Heat and smoke licked at her eyes. Her ears rang for the noise. Commoners shouted from behind a golden gate and could not be silenced. Their volume was tame compared with the aristocracy. Ladies of the Libella screeched down at the panel of Judges on the dais. Their male relatives squawked from the balcony above. Seated below them in the Arcade, Union members howled scorn up at their social betters, some with spittle dappling their livid cheeks. Judges beat their gavels to splinters, to no avail. It was absolute chaos. Smirking, Aoife slid a scrap of parchment from her robe, crept onto the dais from the rear, and tucked it into Vanna Nema's open palm. As always, Nema sat dead center on the dais. Her shrewd green eyes blazed emerald against the crimson of her Alta robes. On her either side sat eight Parliamentary Judges who'd gone hoarse from trying to bring the Arcade to order. Nema appeared nearly fifty or so years old. Though, she would never admit to whatever age she truly was. Her bearing, beautifully braided grey-black hair, and the regal tilt of her head were hard to ignore, regardless. Nema raised a single elegant eyebrow at Aoife's note but did not reply. Aoife kept her head down as she backed away from the dais. Taking her place beside the door, she kept her eyes held sharp on the Arcade.

"This treachery can have no other author!" bellowed a frequent speaker from his seat in the auditorium's center. Mel Carra, former Master of the Academy, now Union Minority Steward. He shook a meaty fist at the Panel on the dais, his face purple. "Who else would dare to infiltrate the Citadel to reclaim her?"

An ear-splitting chorus of protests and base name-calling exploded over the chamber like gunpowder. A woman from the Libellan Balcony smacked her hands on the banister.

"Lies! You slander our greatest ally in Eire! A good, noble man who has always been true to his word!" Pors Yma shrieked. Her fine silk robes were dyed a brilliant vermillion, the color of her House.

Mel Carra snorted theatrically. "We are all aware that House Yma has its interests in Bethany, madam. We are equally cognizant of the importance you place upon nobility."

"How *dare* you? Your family was scrubbing dockside latrines for coppers while mine paid to build your precious Academy! Upstarts like you are nothing without us, Carra. You forget this at your peril."

Carra bowed. "You are quite right, my lady. What would we Merchers do without the nobles? Tell me, how many years' taxes did anyone in your clan pay, before or since your most generous donation?"

Pors' lips nearly puckered into her spine. "I will have you beaten from the Citadel... whipped through streets like the mongrel you are."

"Ladies and gentlemen, please!" cried two of the Judges at once, each banging their gavels with furious futility.

Eva Alvra stood up next. She was a respectable noblewoman whose second husband brought her family great wealth from his vineyards in

Cymru. She once aspired to the title of Alta Prima herself, though she'd failed the Ninth Ordeal. Having retired honorably from the Cloister, she was now the Domina of her House. Her ochre skin and amber eyes were the envy of every woman present save Aoife, who couldn't care less. The Alvras were related by blood to the Mouras. If Aoife had her facts straight, Eva was the Doma's favored niece. This would explain why she tended to take the Doma's side in every Parliamentary meeting.

"I disagree with Lady Yma. One does not require an astronomer to see facts when they are right before their eyes. Of course, Donahugh planned this. Who else benefits more than he? What a coup for him. He's thought of little else since Lady Arrin died!"

The crowd burst into so many banal quarrels that Aoife was obliged to plug her aching ears. Judge Isa Ganon's gavel broke in half. The mob behind the gate all the while called for Drem's word, Siora's Mercy, and justice. Heaving a heavy sigh, Vanna Nema vaulted to her feet. Her red robes painted a blazing exclamation point against her fellow Judges' somber black silk. All eyes gravitated toward her.

Nema fixed the assemblage with a grim smile. "You dishonor yourselves and this Institution with your behavior. Sit down, all of you." Her tone was soft but carried the length and breadth of the chamber. The citizens in the Gallery obeyed first. Most sank to their knees. Aoife rolled her eyes. Nema was second to Drem in the Cloister, but for many of the easily led sheep in the Gallery, she was the most beloved Siorai in Tairngare. "Each of you is the leader of your respective House, Guild, or Establishment. Do you think," her eyes were sharp, "that this infighting and finger-pointing will bring the Doma's grandchild back? Do you suppose petty accusations will allay the people's fear?" She gestured to the myriad faces squeezed into the gate.

Aoife was pleased to watch Pors Yma and Mel Carra resume their seats. Lady Alvra also sat down, her back ramrod straight.

"Now," Nema went on." The Cloister holds this affair as its foremost priority. The Doma commands that you submit to Siora's Word and heed the Judges' decision in this matter."

A murmur passed through the assemblage. A man stood up; he had the look of a merchant from a middling Agrean family. "Begging yer pardon, Lady Nema, but many o'us here have another subject to put before Parliament today."

The silence deepened. Aoife would swear she heard everyone swallow. Alta Nema smiled coldly at the erstwhile speaker. "I know what you would say, Master Hollin. I assure you we will not be discussing such things today."

An outcry issued from behind the gate.

Nema bit her lip, rather than smile, Aoife knew.

"But my Lady!" objected Hollin. "When shall we discuss it, if not now? The people demand to be heard! The Doma reaches too far, and we've—"

Another woman in the Arcade bounced upright. "That is blasphemy!"

Supporters jeered. The women and men in Hollin's camp bawled back.

Hollin finished his statement by raising his voice as many octaves as he could: *"We've had enough o'Moura rule!* This is a democracy, madam! We do not require another puppet Moura Queen! 'Tis sacrilege!"

"Sit down, you!" Mel Carra roared. "Or I will *cut* you down!"

"We'll not be cowed by corrupt nobles nor lickspittle Merchers, what have been in the Moura's pocket for eons. 'Tis time to vote them out. The Doma means to make herself an empress, at OUR expense!" A dozen lawmakers rallied around Hollin for his brave words. Many people tussled on the other side of the gate: Nema's supporters versus the Doma's loyalists. The Libellan nobles in the Arcade threw shoes, papers, and whatever they could find to mark their outrage.

"I SAID BE SEATED!" Alta Nema shouted at the top of her considerable lungs— but it was no use. The mob would not be laid to order. Disgusted, she pulled the red robes of her office tight over her bony shoulders and stormed from the dais. Many gaping, floundering faces surged forward to stop her from leaving. Aoife grinned as she shut the iron door on the lot.

"**Y**OU'RE SURE THIS INFORMATION IS correct?" asked Vanna Nema when they entered her lavish apartments on the Ninth Floor. Long latticed windows, shuttered by white Cmyrian double doors, were gorgeously appointed with five panels of thick mottled glass edged in gold flake. The walls were polished pink granite, as the Cloister was carved from a single slab of rose-hued stone. The city glowed a warm, brilliant red in the light of dawn or sunset. Many referred to Tairngare as the 'Red City' for this phenomenon. In Vanna Nema's chamber on the Ninth Floor, she dressed her share of these walls with many stark tapestries, various paintings and collected artworks, here and there, the odd animal hide. Indeed, the flagstones at their feet were at least four layers deep in gorgeous ornamental carpeting. Her bedchamber was draped everywhere with furs, curtains, and heaped woolen blankets. Vanna Nema did not care for the cold. That was one thing this drafty old fortress had in abundance.

Without knocking, Fawa Gan bowed his way through the door. Aoife hated this little toad more than she hated most everyone else. Holding far too high an opinion of himself, he was rude, snobbish, and greedy. Moreover, Aoife felt sure he'd been skimming Nema's books for years. Not that Nema would mind. There were few people the old witch cared for more than her precious Gan. Aoife had tried many times to get rid of the oily little prick. Each time, Aoife had been the one to suffer for the accusation. Honestly, she had no idea what Nema saw in him. Only women sacred to Siora might ascend higher than Secunda in the Cloister. In Gan's case, males might offer their lifelong service and loyalty to Primas or the Dominas of powerful families. This was the only way a man could rise any higher than the Fifth Floor and therefore install themselves near the fount of power swirling around the Doma. Fawa Gan might expect a seat in Parliament one day for his service.

That is if Aoife couldn't get rid of him first.

"Your Excellency, the Doma has requested your presence at your earliest convenience," Gan whined, in his horrid, nasally drawl. His family had been quite influential in the Libella once upon a time, but they hadn't presented a girl born with any Spark for decades. Therefore, they were underrepresented in the Cloister. The lack of a female heir could have doomed the Gans to exile in the Colonies. Fawa had been their last hope. He was born with just enough Spark to make him appealing to the Novitiate but not enough to propel him to the coveted rank of Secunda. Lucky for them, having hitched himself to Nema almost thirty years before, Gan had risen with her through the ranks. He was an officious, soft-bellied snob, but he got things done. Most of the time, Aoife wanted to spoon his eyeballs out with a spade.

Vanna gave him a long searching look. "She asked that nicely, Gan?"

"Of course not, your Excellency. Her request was peppered with language I shall not repeat, but you gather the gist."

"I do indeed. If you would be so kind, please alert her steward that I will be there before fourth hour is called."

"Yes, your Excellency," he genuflected. "What should I report is the reason for your delay?"

"Do you think 'rampant disinterest' will play well?"

"Sadly, I do not."

Nema rolled a shoulder as if to say, 'well then.' Gan saw himself out without waiting for dismissal. He knew his task better than most. Nema strolled to her banquette and poured herself a tall glass of her favorite Bretagn vintage: a crisp, bubbling white wine that only the Bretagns could produce. Aoife concluded it must be something to do with the soil across the Bretagn Sea. They *did* tend to get more sun and less rain. Nema took a dainty sip of her wine. "You never answered my question. How old is this news?"

"Hours. Less than half a day, at most."

"That damned girl. She has the luck of the Sidhe, I vow," Nema said and popped a dried grape into her mouth. "Do we think she can survive out there alone?"

"She never appeared very resourceful to me. More concerning is who helped her and why."

"The area is rife with poachers and low-born scum of every stripe," sniffed Nema, pouring herself a second glass. "One can only hope this individual is clever enough to sell her back to our agents in Tara or contact us through the usual channels."

71

Aoife looked away, knowing she would pay dearly for her opinion later. "I wouldn't be sure of that, my lady. Whoever killed the Duch's men did so viciously. My informant vows the scene was a bloodbath—grisly but meticulous."

"A random act of violence, perhaps? Someone who happened upon the scene and decided to intervene for the girl?"

"If so, why not take her? I'm told the larger set of footprints were hours older than hers. This individual seems to have come for Rawly and his men, specifically. Killed each of them, rummaged through their supplies, then departed – leaving Prima Moura to free herself. None of it makes an ounce of sense to me."

"Give me your best guess."

Aoife blew a strong breath over pursed lips. "Robbery, maybe? Perhaps Rawly had a fifth companion he didn't report to us? Perhaps they argued, and the fifth man killed them all in a rage? Who knows?"

"I don't appreciate your glib tone, child."

Aoife flushed. "Forgive me, my lady."

"This matter is quite serious, is it not?"

"Of course."

"I would advise you to recall to whom you are speaking."

"I beg your pardon."

"Una Moura should be collecting worms at the bottom of Bally Loch by now. Though, if this interloper abandoned her after the slaughter as your man believes, we may yet have hope." Nema rustled papers on her desk. "Is everything arranged downstairs?"

"It is. Commander Hamma is quite worried that his involvement should be discovered before Parliament can force the vote through."

"As am I," said Nema. "Too much hinges upon this. I will take personal exception to discover the girl has been reclaimed by Donahugh, after all." She pressed a finger to a sensitive spot at her temple. "Perhaps we've been betrayed?"

Aoife felt the skin at the back of her neck crawl. She'd guessed the old hag would somehow attempt to blame her for this. The stripes on her back from last month's displeasure had yet to heal. "From the

72

description of the scene and the random nature of the violence displayed there, I believe this person is an outside agent. My source is a talented tracker. He was as perplexed as we are now."

"Who is this male?"

"Tav. Third Equestrian Corsair, my lady. Head of scouts."

"Hm," Nema sighed. "How long has he been in our service?"

"A year. His family hails from the south side, near the pleasure district. Solid Mercher class. They loathe the Libella more than we do. He has no reason to lie."

"If I discover differently, it will go very badly for you, Aoife. Surely you realize this?" Aoife swallowed. She did. Oh, she did.

"Of course, my lady. I will happily end him should any sign of disloyalty arise."

"I'm afraid I cannot afford to risk this reaching new ears."

Aoife kept her face blank as parchment. "As you command, Excellency. I shall see to it immediately."

"No need," Nema waved her comment away. "It's been managed. I expect you to handle these affairs before I am apprised of them from now on. Understood?" Her stare bore a hole straight through Aoife's ribcage. Of course, Nema knew who her contact had been. She likely knew what Aoife had for breakfast this morning and every expression she wore on her face each hour of the day. Nema trusted no one. How could she? Serving as her right hand held as many perils as benefits. Aoife did not feel anything resembling sympathy for Tav; he was only a male, but he had been a useful tool she would now have to replace.

It took months, sometimes years, to develop reliable sources. Nema, in her usual imperious habit, discarded those hard-won relationships at the slightest provocation. Inwardly, Aoife longed to rip the old woman's throat out for wasting so much of her time, yet again. "You are quite right. I will seek a suitable replacement."

"Well," laughed Nema dryly. "This is disappointing, at any rate. We're too far along to let that blasted girl get in the way. I want it finished, Aoife. Whatever method you must employ, by whatever means you deem necessary. I cannot afford to have that Moura creature back in the Cloister. The people are close now. I can feel it."

Aoife dipped her head. "Yes, Excellency. I have Corsairs loyal to us, searching the roads in all four directions. Surely, if she is out there and alone, she will run straight to them for help?"

"I want you out there. You will handle this personally, am I clear?" Nema gave her a long, meaningful glare. As much as Aoife's heart surged at the prospect of even a few hours' freedom outside these oppressive walls, she also knew that any failure to achieve Nema's commands would be on her head. Nema wouldn't kill her. She'd demonstrated that principle many, many times. It would be worse than that.

It always was.

Aoife bowed low, heart racing. "As you wish, Excellency." She backed out of the room. The faster Nema's goals were achieved, the swifter Aoife's freedom gained. If one spoiled girl had to die to accomplish that... so be it.

⚔ ⚔

IT TOOK A FEW HOURS to pass beyond the Citadel without being noticed. Primas simply did not have the liberty to come and go as they pleased. It might be the beating heart of political power on the Continent, but the Cloister was still a cage, however gilded. Aoife would have been remanded to the Censors at ground level if she'd been discovered attempting to leave. Thankfully, she had a few tricks up her sleeve that most Siorai would never dream possible. She was through the Citadel's portcullis, past the Ward Gate, and onto the Navan Road before sunset. As she walked, the fetters of despotic Cloister life slipped from her shoulders like a discarded cloak. She intended to stroll through the night and enjoy the crisp autumn air— the smell of damp fallen leaves, the bite of the Dor Samna breeze— for as long as she could. Nothing was as sweet as freedom, however temporary. She would locate her quarry before long, she knew. Aoife was drawn by the flash of Una's power. A faint vibration pulsated along the strands of Aoife's Spark like a fly caught in a silken web. A genuine smile tugged her lips upward. She marched forward, content to be asked to do something she would enjoy for once.

THE HIGH ROAD

n.e. ⌐08
16, ÐOR SAMNA
eiRe

Ben couldn't believe his eyes. Breathing hard and bleeding, the young girl he'd encountered twice already clattered through the trees like a hare pursued by hounds. She clutched the dagger he'd left her in a white-knuckled grip. Of the six Corsairs present, four gave chase. They spurred well-trained palfreys into the woods after her, heedless of the uneven terrain. With a piercing cry, she slipped into the leaf-strewn duff and tumbled to a sobbing heap at the base of a slight rise. The nearest horseman charged down the escarpment, his fellows close behind. In a flash, the girl was surrounded on four sides by fully armored men. These were no mercenaries like Rawly and his gang of miscreants from Bethany. No. These were proper soldiers: Tairngare's finest, by all accounts. Ben hadn't seen Corsairs at work for a long time, but he remembered their predecessors well enough. Ben's brow furrowed. She struggled to her feet; his dagger held out before her— like she had any chance of warding off the swords these men drew with such a small blade. What could she possibly have done to prompt this attack? Ben felt a tiny pang of guilt. If he hadn't left her to fend for herself, this might not be happening to her now.

Sidling away from Vixen's flank, he crept closer to get a better view of the scene. Three soldiers dismounted. A fourth remained in his saddle, holding the knot of communal reins. Another hung back, just in case the girl attempted to bolt. While the nearest trio circled her, Ben factored distance and velocity in his head. He had plenty of arrows now, didn't he? Ruthlessly, the Corsairs struck. They took turns working her over with fists, shins, and boots. The iron-sweet tang of fresh blood tainted the air. She managed to land quite a few cracking blows, but his dagger did not. It pinged uselessly from a tree trunk near her head. Ben uttered a foul *Ealig* curse low in his throat.

These pig-fucking sons of whores.

He was many things, but a woman-beating sack of shite, he was *not*. Whatever their excuse for this, he didn't care to hear it. These were dead men.

In the next few moments, as she gasped for air, Ben readied his feet. He no longer worried if they caught sight of him first. He rather hoped they did.

"Stop… please," she choked into the forest floor. "I don't want to h—"

One of them leaned down to wrench her up by the hair. His companion shouted. "Careful there! Don't let her get a hand on your bare skin!"

Ben plucked an arrow from his quiver, counting paces from these men to those waiting on the road above.

Her captor grasped one of her breasts above her tunic. "A shame, that. If she weren't a Siorai witch—"

"Well, she is, and you can be certain you won't live through it," remarked his accomplice. Snarling, he cuffed her hard with one gauntleted fist. A thick line of blood ran down her chin. Her left eye swelled up like a gourd. Gritting his teeth, Ben drew his bowstring taut.

"You 'don't want to' what, heretic slut?"

Moaning, she sagged into the soldier behind her. Ben took that for a cue. His first arrow dove through the bastard's right eye. Before the would-be rapist's back struck the earth, Ben was already nocked and drawn for a second shot. Distracted by the arrow that had killed his friend, the speaker's eyes bulged elsewhere— a fatal mistake. The girl leaned forward. She slammed her palm flat over his unguarded cheek.

"*Reorder*," she hissed. Beneath her fingers, the leader's cheekbones smashed into one another, spurting his eyeballs from their sockets like pressed grapes. He was permitted one loud pitiful shriek. His jaw met his forehead with a sickening crunch. In the split second it took for this horror to manifest, the girl had moved deftly to her left and snatched at the third Corsair's cuirass with one hand. With the other, she swiped a finger across the bridge of his nose. "*Boil*," she whispered. The soldier fell backward. Growling, she tottered with him to the ground. This one's eyes dissolved like cream from a hot spoon. Dark fluids gushed from his open mouth, steaming like a geyser in full vent. He lay there twitching, his throat melting as if he'd swallowed acid.

She struggled to her knees beside his body. Gulping air, she watched the mounted soldier unwind a rope from his saddle. "I said, I don't want to hurt any of you!"

In shock, Ben dropped his elbow. His newest arrow sailed into the bracken, useless. He'd never seen anything like this in all his life. Siorai were forbidden to kill, weren't they? Or so he'd been told once, many years ago. A girl with this one's ability was clearly something special. Ben sincerely regretted not taking the time to learn her name. As his mind raced along a host of interesting possibilities, the fourth horseman slung his rope around her throat. With a single twist of a gauntleted wrist, he jerked her from her feet. Ben heard her wheeze and watched the rider wind the rope around his saddle horn drawing it tighter and tighter. Ben slunk after them, bow drawn. Oblivious to the threat, the Corsair dragged the girl over the ridge behind his horse, shouting an alert to his comrades on the road above.

BEFORE HER CAPTOR RETURNED TO the road, five arrows sailed out of the woods on his right; two burst through his throat, shoving him arse over ankles from his mount. Rope gone slack, the girl, tumbled face-down into the dirt. Ben's next arrow took a second horseman through a gap in his armor between the armpit and ribcage; another propelled him bodily into the nearest trunk. Rearing, his horse thundered off without him. Ben's final arrow pinned the last Corsair's un-gauntleted hand to his thigh where he'd been reaching for a vicious throwing knife. His screams grew shrill when Ben emerged from the trees. Reaching over to grasp the dagger the fool had been trying to draw, Ben plunged it to the hilt into his clavicle. The whole affair was over in moments. Taking stock, Ben sighed.

What a damned mess.

At least this lot had died for a better reason than meat or uishge. With a scowl, he approached the girl gingerly, lest he accidentally touch her. After what he'd seen her do, he wasn't fool enough to try her now. Her eyes spun white as she lay there, scarcely conscious. She had a terrible, oozing gash above her left eye. Blood poured freely from her mouth and nose. The wound on her head was already a fierce blue-black and engorged with fluid. One more strike might have killed her. Crossing his arms, Ben stared down at her.

He didn't have time for this, did he?

He had matters of his own to attend to. If Guinness was no longer alive or unable to help him, he'd many miles to go before he could rest. He desperately needed a new ogham stone. Without one, he'd be cursed to live in this wilderness alone for the next two decades. He wouldn't go back now. He could not. Arthur was a physician or had been, once upon a time. Who better to help the girl than a doctor? Perhaps Ben could kill two birds with one stone? Realizing the direction of his thoughts, he swore aloud.

Gods damn it.

He was obligated now, and he bloody well knew it. If he didn't help her this time, his conscience would nag him to the ends of the earth. Ben was no hero. He didn't suffer romantic delusions of grandeur nor fancy himself a champion for bothersome females astray in the Greensward. Truthfully, if he didn't already feel bad about leaving her tied to that tree the other night, he would probably be long gone.

Not today, the annoying voice in his head assured him. He could be a rotten bastard for the rest of his life, but… *not today, damn you*. Despite his inclination toward self-preservation, he couldn't leave her again. He would never forgive himself for something so foul. Ben unwound the cloak from the nearest dead horseman, tearing strips to bind first her head, then her scraped, bleeding hands. *Just in case*, he thought, while he wrapped the remaining bulk of the fabric around her small, limp body. Hefting her over his shoulder, he tracked back through the trees toward Vixen.

⚚

APPROACHING THE LITTLE FARMSTEAD, BEN stopped to catch his breath. A weather-beaten chimney blew little tufts of silver smoke above the treetops. He recalled Arthur being quite proud of this place when it was newly built. After so many years of service in the militia, Arthur had been happy to have such a fine home to call his own. Seeing the place now, Ben was struck by how small and isolated it was. Arthur was a friendly man. It didn't suit his tastes to live so... alone. Aednat had undoubtedly been the reason for this solitude.

Ben had only visited once when the foundations were freshly laid. The charming couple had received him graciously, as they were able. Until this moment, it had never occurred to him that they might not have been given a choice but to retreat to this backwater. He understood that some folk were bound to be unaccepting of Aednat, particularly in the cities. By the time Ben had made his acquaintance, Arthur had planned to leave his family's small medical practice in Ten Bells to start a life with his new bride. Ben only realized the extent of that decision as he looked over this homely little farm. How preposterous and unfair? Aednat would have been the toast of Ten Bells society were her heritage not an issue for the locals. Well, it had been almost three decades. Who knew what plights the Guinness' had encountered since? The fields suffered from a lack of tending and the outbuildings for want of nails. Perhaps Arthur had gotten too long in the tooth to manage on his own?

The hedges were trimmed, if poorly. A few skinny sheep bleated in a small meadow. A hoary dairy cow chewed cud at Ben as he neared, sparing him a haughty glare. "And to you, missus," he huffed back. The heifer snuffled a curt reply.

He tied Vixen to a short wooden gate near the house and tugged the girl into his arms. She didn't utter a sound, which was a bad sign. Ben stopped shy of a faded yellow door to tuck his cowl tight over his ears. He could attempt a glamour, but without his ogham stone, he wouldn't hold one for very long. He must make do. Besides, if this trip proved fruitless, he'd need his strength for the journey ahead.

The door cracked just as he raised his fist to knock. A lovely, vaguely familiar face materialized at the gap, a cautious look in her cornflower blue eyes. Aednat? But... it couldn't be? This girl was far too young. Even if faeries did not age as Milesians did, Aednat had been well into her third decade when he'd met her. She would have been nearly seventy if his maths served. Ben was sorely disappointed to learn the Innkeeper must have been right about her passing.

"I saw you coming through the trees there," she pointed at the hills behind him. "Is she alive?"

Ben had about a gallon of blood dried into the back of his cloak, so he wasn't laying any odds just yet. "I think so, but I'm not sure how."

Aednat's doppelgänger leaned in to check his ward's pulse. Ben gently intercepted, pushing her hand away. "I wouldn't do that," he warned. "It could be dangerous."

A little crease formed between her delicate blonde brows. Now that he was really looking, she wasn't quite as lovely as Aednat. Her cheeks were too thin, her complexion slightly sallow, and her pinched brow smacked more of shrewishness than beauty.

"How can I treat her if I can't touch her?"

Ben blinked. "Treat her? You? Where's Arthur? It's been a long while, but I was sure this was his home."

She ran a hand through the hair at the nape of her too white, too long, too thin neck. "My father died last autumn, sir. Influenza."

"Aednat?"

She reddened at his impertinence. "Gone more than a decade. Who are you?"

80

Ben fidgeted. This was Arthur and Aednat's daughter? Both parents gone? He honestly didn't know how to respond. He was disappointed, to say the least. Arthur and Aednat were the only two people in Eire that knew who he was and wouldn't find it a detriment. In the second place, he desperately needed another ogham stone. He'd hoped to avoid having to risk the city to get one. Aside from these concerns... he'd liked Arthur a great deal. There was this blasted Siorai girl to deal with, as well.

"I'm very sorry for your loss, lass. He was a decent sort, your Da." He dipped his head with respect.

"You knew my parents?"

"Once upon a time. Not to be indelicate, but would you perhaps know of another physician in the general area? I do think this damn— er, this *girl*— might be in danger if she isn't treated."

Her eyes narrowed to blue slits. "I did say I was capable but since you're after being rude, by all means... take her that way," she gestured up the path, "about fifty miles, and you shall find a proper barber. Good day." Without ado, she shut the door in his face. The hinge came into hard contact with the boot he shoved into the jamb. Grunting, he jerked it open again with his heel. The door bumped her on the shoulder, knocking her into the wall. "Ow!" she cried, rubbing her offended arm. "How *dare*—"

"You did not say. You implied. Since you're so sensitive about your skills, consider yourself hired." He barged past her. An easy feat, considering he was thrice her size and outweighed her by at least a million pounds. "Where do you want her?"

Irritation rumbled in her throat, but she didn't answer him. Instead, she hobbled past a tiny kitchen toward a small door to the left of a stone hearth. Her right foot, twisted about forty degrees the wrong way, impeded her progress. Ben refrained from comment, knowing how she came by it without asking. Many faeries were marked in such ways. She didn't appear embarrassed by its obvious deformity, but he knew better than to open his mouth. He had some manners, thank you. Sourly, she gestured for him to proceed her.

This chamber was much larger than its stunted doorframe portended. He bent almost double to get through the door. On the other side, the ceiling was a good four feet higher than in the foyer: an addition, no doubt. White scrubbed walls were lined with shelves, overstuffed with books of every variety. Arthur hailed from a moderately wealthy Mercher family and had a particular enthusiasm for the written word. There were hundreds of tomes to choose from, most of which was likely more valuable than any of the animals outside. Ben raised a brow. Arthur's girl clearly knew what a treasure she possessed in this little study. What care was lacking outdoors was doubly applied here.

On a wall opposite the library, pine shelves were stacked high with jars, vials, and vessels in various shapes and sizes. Everything was lovingly labeled and arranged according to the Common alphabet. Medicinal tools were laid out in neat rows on a metallic cart: a handsome pair of copper scissors, various pincers, and grips, all honed to a high gleam. Beneath a south-facing window on his left stood an ornately carved desk with snarling hounds for feet. Upon it sat a small painted globe, clearly ancient, as evidenced by the place names the world had not seen for a half millennium or more. The Guinness girl moved some books and scraps of loose paper from a second rolling table. Many were open anatomical volumes, with hasty notes scribbled in their margins. She motioned for him to lay his burden down, so she might make a cursory examination. Noting the seeping lump that had once been her patient's eye, her lip curled.

"*Siora*," she pulled a face. "Did you do this to her?"

"If I had, would I have brought her here?"

"Good point. I'll need your help, then. We have to ascertain whether or not she's bleeding internally. Will you hand me those scissors behind you?"

Ben threw up his hands. "Oh no. I have business of my own to get to. I'll be leaving her in your care."

Her fingers froze over the girl's abdomen. "You what? You're just going to leave her here?"

"Well—"

82

"No," she said, setting her tools back down.

"What? But—"

"No," she repeated more firmly. "You may as well throw her back over your shoulder and duff off. I'm not taking responsibility for your mess."

Beneath his hood, Ben squinted. This was Aednat's daughter? It couldn't be... Aednat had been the sweetest woman alive. She could no more ignore a sick bird in the grass than leave a possibly dying human being right before her eyes. Perhaps some horrible, Otherworld creature had devoured Aednat and went about wearing her face?

"You would refuse to treat an injured woman? Your father never denied a patient, no matter the circumstances."

"Sir, my father was a good honest man. I buried him in burlap. I am not my father, and this is no charity."

"Ah," said Ben, digging around in his cloak for his purse, the very one made heavy by cheating others at porter. "I've coin aplenty if that's your problem. You may have an entire royal fainne. What I lack is time, mistress." He set the heavy gold coin on the injured girl's open, insensate palm. "Do we have an accord?" He watched color bloom in the faerie's thin cheeks and heard her swallow as she gazed down at the gleaming yellow metal. A single gold royal was nearly triple the amount a prolific farmer might hope to earn in two full years. For an orphan living in the middle of nowhere, miles from any reasonably sized town, full of Milesians hostile to her for her heritage... maybe four times the average?

"No," she breathed.

"I got a good look at those scrawny animals on my way in. I know you need the money. With your father gone, I'll wager you don't get many folks ambling up your walk with coin to spend, do you?"

"I decline. Take her and go."

Ben ground his molars over the injustice of his luck. He reached again into his purse to produce another sparkling fainne. His last, as it happened. Its glitter reflected from her large, glassy eyes. This would leave him a mere handful of silver stags and three coppers. If he must pay for the materials he needed to make his ogham stone, he'd be obliged to sit in on another game of porter to earn more coin. Hells, he might resort to base robbery at this rate. He'd almost be better served heading back to Rosweal to search for his own missing stone. That wouldn't be any more troublesome than what awaited him in Ten Bells, the way things were going. When had a bout of conscience ever benefited him in the least?

"Two then, but mark me, it's my final offer."

"Again, no," she said, looking like she might be sick. Two royals were a fortune for a girl like her. She could pack up this dusty old farmstead and head off to a proper life in Tairngare, Ten Bells, or hells, warm Bethany in the South. She could buy herself a shop to run, maybe even find a husband. The possibilities were limitless.

Ben was tempted to snap her delicate little neck. "You're joking? Two fainne are more than you could hope to earn in years out here by yourself with your erm, malady."

Her cheeks burned a brilliant scarlet. She elbowed past him, rummaged about in her tiny kitchen, and stomped back with a fresh rag and a bowl overflowing with strong herbal tea. He moved to let her through the door rather than suffer a second jab to the ribs. Resuming her place at the girl's side, she held up a warning hand when he opened his mouth to speak. Lightly, she dabbed mud, blood, and muck away from the unconscious girl's outstretched arm. The skin beneath all that grime emerged a smooth, golden brown. Emblazoned in blue woad coiled dozens of whirling, entwined serpents. No, not serpents... dragons. Everywhere she moved her cloth, beautifully appointed wyrms were revealed. Ben had no idea what these markings meant, but the solemn expression on the Guinness girl's face did not bode well.

"Do you know who she is?"

"No idea. Do those markings mean something to you?"

"Anyone who's ever spent time in the Red City knows which family flies the Blue Wyrm. Only the women of the Moura Clan are permitted to wear them as decoration. Tattoos of this sort... do you follow?"

Ben sat heavily on the edge of the hound-footed desk. He didn't like where this was headed at all. "I figured her for a noble or an escapee from the Cloister. These markings make her someone from an important clan, I suppose?"

"You could say that. She would have to be Doma Drem herself to be marked like this, or her heir apparent."

He went still. A terrible foreboding slithered into his veins. He couldn't stifle the groan that escaped his throat.

"You're telling me this girl is the Domina of the Moura Clan?" She'd offered her name to him, hadn't she? That morning when she found him in the woods, sleeping on the frozen ground— she'd asked him if he wanted to know who she was. *Damn. Damn. Damn.* He'd stuck his foot in it this time.

Beyond the shock of her identity were the incessant questions her situation posed. Why would a noblewoman of her stature, the future leader of the most powerful family in Eire, be attacked by her own Citadel Corsairs? Furthermore, how was anyone able to infiltrate the deepest sanctum in the Cloister of the Eternal Flame— the most heavily guarded structure in Innisfail— and manage to remove her without bringing an entire Cohort of Tairnganeah down around their ears? The thought of common Souther ruffians from Bethany accomplishing this herculean task unaided was about as likely as the sun rising in the west. Someone must want this little lady out of the way very badly. Someone with enough power and influence to smuggle her out of the Citadel and seduce many Citadel cavalry officers to their cause. Just what in the hells was happening in Tairngare? Ben had spent so long hiding out in Rosweal and other border hovels that he had no idea what went on in greater Eire besides whoring, drinking, and the next card game.

The thought brought a small pang for his loss.

"I'll do my best to help her," Mistress Guinness said, breaking into his reverie, her expression stone serious. "Both royals will be fair payment. Though, you'll take her elsewhere when I'm done. Whoever had the stones to do this to *her* wouldn't think twice about silencing someone like me. What good is gold to me if I'm dead?"

Aoife grew bored of walking a few hours outside Tairngare. She'd bought a pony in Fennick, but riding was just as tedious. By the time evening set in around Slane, she'd been on the go since dawn. There were dozens of Cohort patrols moving up and down the road, stopping to question suspicious individuals or otherwise hassling travelers for the missing Moura Domina. Aoife's disguise dissuaded any interest directed her way. The little stone at her throat guaranteed very few second glances. To fellow merchants, tinkers, and farmers on the High Road, she was merely another old woman, ambling along at her own pace. Once or twice, she spotted Corsairs roving through towns or farmsteads. Some she recognized immediately as loyal servants of Alta Nema. If they found the girl first, they had orders to destroy her on sight. Aoife didn't bother to hail them or alert them to her presence.

Their numbers were a sign that the search was not going well for either interested party. If they'd found Prima Moura, they would have already ridden back to the Citadel to deliver the news. Loyalist Cohorts and Tairnganeah Infantry outnumbered Nema's Corsairs two-to-one. Aoife was not encouraged by the sight. These soldiers were out in their hordes to do the Doma's bidding and bring the Domina home by any means necessary. There was no guarantee that Nema's forces would find her first. If the loyalists managed to drag Una home in one piece, Aoife's mission would end in failure and punishment. She refused to worry just yet. There could be only one reason the girl had yet to be found. Aoife stared straight into it. Vivid autumnal trees thickened beside the road, obscuring the sky overhead. The Greensward stretched hundreds of miles to the west and still further north, into Aes Sidhe. An unwary person who dared step off the road might be lost forever in this teeming ocean of trees. Soldiers could search for months and never find Una, should she choose to hide.

Well, Aoife would see about that, wouldn't she?

When the road curved toward Slane, she dismounted and led her pony through the woods on her left. Trekking southwest, she kept the road on her right but well out of view. Here the forest marched on for days, crowding hills and dells in every visible direction. If Aoife wandered too far, she could quickly lose her bearings. Without the sun to pierce the net of shadows creeping between the trees, one copse looked like another. Best not to linger.

She stopped at a slight rise less than a mile from the road, stripping her right hand free of its warm leather glove. Aoife drew a tiny dagger out of her vest and, without ceremony, drew it across the breadth of her palm. Clenching her fist around the wound with a hiss, she held her arm out in front of her. Bright blood dripped into the black mud at her feet.

"*Come*," she called, tapping deep into her Spark. A sharp wind ripped through the boughs around her, threatening to snap them at their joints. The earth trembled and quaked, and great chasms rent the ground, from which it seemed the very soul of darkness spewed forth. Two sets of glowing eyes slinked into view, growing wide on a pair of monstrous black heads. The world smudged wherever these beasts moved, two pinholes of absolute night. Aoife grinned at her pets as they slunk forward, hungry. "*Go and play*," she commanded and laughed as they eagerly bounded away.

Aednat's Child

L *eave,* Ben thought to himself, for the hundredth time in an hour. *This is not your problem. You owe them nothing.* He wasn't sure why he hadn't laid the girl on the front stoop with a couple silver stags, and then fled back into the Greensward. He wasn't noble or chivalrous. Who were either of these women to him— Milesian women at that? He had troubles of his own. He couldn't continue to wander around undisguised like this. If Ben didn't do something about his appearance soon, it could cost him more than precious anonymity. His was not a face Milesians in Eire would be apt to appreciate. If he couldn't mockup a new ogham charm, he would have to hide again. He was bloody tired of hiding. Ben didn't thrive in solitude, he could admit without shame. He knew he should go, *must* go. Why risk exposure for a girl he didn't have the least connection with?

You should have freed her from the start, you miserable shite, said the other voice. The one from his gut. The one he liked least. *You involved yourself. You are obliged.*

"Bah," Ben grumbled aloud, well into his third dram of Arthur's finest uishge. He was bored of the argument raging inside his head. Having made it as far as the rear stoop of the Guinness cottage, he eyed the looming Greensward with longing. How did he manage to get himself into these things? If only he'd led the Greenmakers further west last week, none of this would be happening. He'd still be in Rosweal, snug in his own bed with Rose, or drinking at *The Hart* with mates. His mournful sigh was bone-deep. Busy wallowing in self-pity, he didn't hear Arthur's daughter limp out onto the stoop until the hem of her skirt brushed his boot.

Drying her freshly scrubbed fingers on a rough linen towel, she reeked of camphor and other medicinal odors.

"Well, she'll live," she exhaled hard, sounding easily as old as his father. "I'm fairly certain she's concussed. I'll have to dose her with a stimulant to prevent her from slipping into a coma. All that aside, most of her wounds look much nastier than they are." She moved closer. "May I have some of that?"

"It *is* yours," he pointed out, passing it up to her. The grimace she pulled after the barest sip earned her a chuckle. She handed it back.

"Siora, that's bloody awful. Tastes like burnt grass and lamp oil." She took a seat beside him, not bothering to wait for an invitation. "I'm surprised you're still here." His shrug was half-hearted.

"Who says I mean to stay?" She watched him sidelong for a moment. Finally, he gave up, and snorted, "When she wakes, we'll decide the safest place to take her, then I'll be on my way. Fair?" He didn't care for the measuring expression on her face. "Gods, what now?"

"Nothing..." her voice trailed off.

For Brida's sake. "Out with it."

"Well, I left that fainne on the table."

"You wish me to take it back?"

"I suppose I'm surprised you haven't tried."

His head swiveled around like an owl; eyes narrowed to slivers. "Ouch."

Demurely folding her hands in her lap, she stared straight ahead as if the trees were suddenly fascinating. "I thought you had something important to get to?"

"Are you giving my money back?"

"Not a chance."

90

"Shut up, then. We made a deal. Despite your rather unsubtle implications, I never break my word once I give it. Satisfied?" Inwardly, he fumed. He took another sip to keep his head cool. "How long before she can be moved?"

"Two days? A week? Who knows? That blow to her head could have killed her. Half her face is swollen black. Not to mention the bruising around her throat or the hemorrhaging around her ribs and kidneys. She needs to rest."

Ben blew a long breath through his nose, cursing whatever unfortunate star he'd been born under. He shifted his attention to the farm around them: the pasture, the hills, and the forest that pressed in from all sides. The Guinness farmstead was remote. He doubted that Arthur and Aednat's young daughter here got around much. There was a good chance anyone searching for the Moura girl would miss the place entirely. If he set some rudimentary wards, he might ensure no one would ever find the place unless they were explicitly determined to do so.

"Look," he began cautiously, "there is something I must see to before I can take her anywhere else. I was on my way when I witnessed her attack."

The second encounter, at any rate.

He didn't feel a need to share the first.

"For an ogham charm, I suppose?" she smirked at Ben's startled expression. "Don't look at me like that. You said you knew my father. It stands to reason you also knew my mother and how she supplemented my father's earnings. My mother's mother came from Aes Sidhe, same as you."

"Right—" Had Arthur been as infuriatingly direct? Ben couldn't remember. Aednat definitely hadn't. He struggled to equate the sweet, biddable mother with the observant, slightly shrewish daughter.

"I knew the second you crossed my mother's wards in the forest, just there." She tugged a thumb toward the front of the house. "Only a trueborn Sidhe could stomp right through them without even noticing they were there. My mother called it her 'peasant magic.' At any rate,

91

they keep the house safe from unwanted visitors. This is the Greensward. The locals here don't much care for my family."

Setting down his bottle, Ben half-promised himself never to pick up another. "*Right...*" he repeated. This week just got better and better.

"You can take off that hood now," she said. "Doesn't fit, anyway. Stole it, I gather?"

A hard-blown sigh was his answer.

"Figured. As it happens, you passed my test. You may both stay until she's well enough to leave. But I warn you; if you get any ideas about breaking our deal, you won't like the consequences." He could tell she resisted the urge to wag a finger at him. She laced her fingers instead. "Can you reinforce my mother's wards? I'm afraid I never learned how."

Ben pursed his lips. "Might. It'll take a bit, though."

"Good. Because it isn't common knowledge that my father passed recently. Many townsfolk will recall he was the only qualified physician in the area, though he stopped practicing a few years ago. They will eventually be directed here if anyone comes looking for her."

Damn, Ben mused. The thought hadn't occurred. It wouldn't take an overly clever tracker to work out that the Moura girl might be injured after that tussle on the Navan Road. He hadn't bothered to hide the bodies, either. He'd stripped their horses and packs of anything useful and dragged them from the road. If anyone clever investigated that scene, they would infer that at least three of the dead Corsairs bore arrow wounds. That someone had come to the girl's rescue should be obvious. Ben swore under his breath.

"I didn't think that far ahead," he removed his hood. "I can't do anything for anyone in Eire like this. I was on my way to remedy this situation when I found her."

She paled. "Where are you from? Connaught? Donegal? The Isles?"

He had no idea which lie she would believe. Therefore, omission was the safer bet. He didn't reply.

"Fine. If you don't want to talk about it, that's all right. I know you came here partly to look for my mother, for obvious reasons. I wouldn't worry too much about it. She taught me how to make charms. Thought it might help me cope with my... erm, peculiarity."

Hope soared anew in his breast. If this was indeed the case, perhaps coming here wasn't such a waste of his precious time after all.

"Please don't say this if you're unsure about your ability."

"It could never be as strong a charm as what I'm sure you're accustomed to, but I've made one before. An old woman on the road alone is less a target than a half-breed. It won't be perfect, but it'll be better than nothing."

Ben had been preparing himself for another, even more, dangerous journey than the one he'd been on for the past few days. Could his luck have changed so suddenly? Why, if she could do what she said, he would be free to roam where and when he willed. Tara maybe, or perhaps Man? The Peninsula was neutral territory, wasn't it, not quite an exclusive Sidhe domain? Hells, if Ben could convince Robin of what an enormous braying ass he'd been for casting him out, perhaps he might return? He could be back in Rosweal in his flat above the Boyne in no time, drinking, dicing, and whoring himself into oblivion. The point being that the stone gave him options he currently lacked. By Herne, maybe he wasn't so unlucky as he thought?

"Aside from that girl, this is what you were hoping to find, yes? For two fainne, new wards, and some light help around this farm while she convalesces. I'll consider this a fair deal. Is this acceptable to you, erm, what's your name?"

"Ben," he said firmly, ignoring her dubious frown. "The name's Ben Maeden. Mistress–?"

"Rian."

Ben stuck his hand out. "Rian, we have an accord, and you— my thanks."

⚜

IN THE MORNING, RIAN GUINNESS roughly nudged him awake with the toe of her boot. Ben lay on the back stoop, curled around the empty uishge bottle as if it were a woman. His collar stuck to the wooden slats beneath his head, and a thick coating of frost crept over his cloak and right cheek. A second prodding jerked him upright. He rubbed at his sore, chapped jaw. *Again?* So much for abstaining from spirits. One would find it difficult to be certain, but it appeared to be midday. The clouds overhead were thick enough to cut with a knife and dark, save for the barest milky smudge in the center. Groaning, Ben ran a frozen hand over his aching eyes. Rian's pinched expression hovered over him.

"You smell like a vagrant." There was a reason why most of Innisfail had outlawed uishge, even if the law was all but ignored. His brain sloshed inside his vibrating skull. *Gods,* Ben thought. *You need to quit drinking, sir.* Rian wrinkled her thin little nose at him. A worn but clean tunic struck him in the face. He refrained from comment.

"There's a stream behind the barn. My father dug out a small pond for the geese, but they've long gone. I think you'll find it's about chest deep. It won't be anywhere near warm, but," she sniffed.

"Wonderful," he grumbled, momentarily praying she'd fall down the steps and break her neck. He couldn't believe she was Aednat's child. "Is there no tub indoors? A pitcher? Hells, a bloody kettle?"

"You're not to set another foot inside this house until you get it over with. I'd get to it if I were you. There's a horse brush and a brick of lye soap there for your... erm, clothing. Here's some lavender soap for the rest of you." A small, fragrant missile thumped from chest like a rock. Ignoring his wince, she said, "It took almost four hours this morning to scrub the mud and muck from my floors. Anyway, I have to head to Ferndale for supplies. I go every week on the same day, so if I fail to show today, it will look suspicious. There's food – just some bread and cheese, mind you, on the block in the kitchen. I've nothing fancier to spare. You're welcome to it when you're as clean and respectable as you can manage. Any questions before I go?"

"No," he croaked, wishing he'd managed to drink himself dead last night.

"Good," she hobbled down the steps but turned when she made it halfway around the porch and marched back. "One last thing, which I'm

94

sure you're smart enough to figure out on your own. Keep an eye on her. Her fever broke last night, but she could dislodge her bandages or hurt herself if she tries to get up too soon. There's a pot of tea loaded with willow bark on the larder in the kitchen. If I'm not back by nightfall, be sure to make her swallow half a cup at dusk."

"How am I supposed to do that?"

"Are you an idiot?'

Ben scowled back.

"Then, figure it out," she spared him a flippant wave over her shoulder and took her leave.

Bᴇɴ ʜᴀᴅ ᴛᴏ ʙʀᴇᴀᴋ ᴀ great deal of thick ice to get into that 'pool' behind the barn. Although he didn't feel the cold as sharply as a Milesian might, jumping into a bowl of ice water, bare-assed, on a frigid day in the Greensward, was far from pleasant. After ripping nearly every hair from his head and grating off swaths of skin with the sandpaper Rian Guinness claimed was soap, he was thankful he wasn't bleeding from head to toe. Once clean, he donned a pair of Arthur's old trousers and a moth-eaten linen tunic. Both were too small for him, but the trousers at least fit into the tops of his boots. Arthur had been quite tall for a Milesian, though Ben had still towered over him at close to seven feet.

He finally ambled back to the house over an hour later, with his wet clothing over one arm. His lips had taken on something of a bluish tinge. All the way up to the house from the barn, he recited the foulest curses he could conjure. He couldn't believe how ridiculous his life had become. Coming through the back door into the cottage, he felt the hearth's intense blast of warmth straight to his toes. Steam curled from his exposed skin like fog. Beside the larder lay the promised trencher of bread and cheese. Rian, bless her contrary soul, had left a cup of homemade mead beside it. Maybe he had been a bit dramatic when he labeled this the worst week of his life. Why, things were looking up already, weren't they? While his fingertips stung and thawed, he laid his wet clothes on the flagstones by the hearth... and froze. There, beside the mantel, stood the Moura girl. She clutched the back of a chair as if it were a lone buoy in a storm, huffing, shaking, and furious. Ben gave her a weak smile. Gods, he really must cease making things worse for himself by entertaining optimistic thoughts.

"*You!*" she hissed, her eyes blazing. "*You bastard.*"

The chair-back she gripped for support cracked. So much for the faint hope that her head wound would take care of her memory. Ben raised his palms, feigning surrender.

"You should be abed, mistress. You've been through somewhat of an ordeal, and I—"

"*Left me.*" Wood splintered under her nails. "You left me there to *die!*" Her one good eye glowed molten amber, bright as any coal in the hearth. A nasty seeping cut over her eyebrow strained against its stitches. Her left eye was a red and blue bubble. Her throat, neck, and collarbone, where she'd been roped and dragged behind that Corsair's horse, were torn to the tissue beneath.

Ben swallowed hard. "Now, that's rather harsh. You're only standing here because I came back for you." A half-truth, but she didn't need to know that. He'd be damned if he'd admit to spending a relaxing evening in Navan Village while she'd most likely spent a sleepless night in the wilderness. Worse – that he'd been spending coins lifted from her captors while she was chased down the High Road by her city guard. No way in nine hells would he tell her any of that now!

She stood up a bit straighter. It did not improve her height. The top of her head would barely crest his ribcage if she stood on her toes.

"You came back for me?" Her voice was as harsh as the sandpaper soap he'd been forced to use. He supposed she meant to sound dubious.

"Of course, I did."

She attempted to snort, but the fluid in her nose prevented anything but the weakest whistle from escaping her nostrils.

"Never-mind. You needn't bother to lie. For whatever reason, you *did* come back," she gnashed her teeth, "so, I suppose I must be grateful for your interfering when you did. I would bow and say the words, but you'll pardon me if I refrain this once, won't you?" Halting like a fawn, she moved around the chair and slowly inched herself onto its seat. Ben resisted the urge to help, instead tucking his hands under his arms. His head still thrummed; his gut roiled with oily, queasy emptiness. A reminder that neither of them was enjoying themselves overmuch in this little cottage, deep in the Eastern Greensward. Though he must concede, listening to her try to breathe, it was obvious which of them was worse for wear. "Would you mind, terribly," she inquired, in a frog's impersonation of a clipped Tairnganese accent, "bringing me something to drink?"

He didn't mind if that meant he wouldn't have to face her for a few moments. Gods, but they'd made a mess of her! Guilty and searching for a means to make amends, he rummaged through Rian's small kitchen like the useless clod he was. There wasn't much to the place save two small cabinets, one wooden countertop, and a stone tub with a hole drilled into its base for drainage. He returned with the tea Rian mentioned before and waited nervously while she tried to tip the cup against her ruined lower lip. She wrinkled the good side of her nose.

"Ugh. Laudanum and willow-bark? Isn't there anything else?"

"No," he lied again. He could go and fetch her water, but she needed to sleep, and, as it happened, so did he. If she was up and about this soon, there was a good chance he wouldn't have to stay here much longer. Gods be merciful. If Rian hurried with that stone, he might be able to... well, he'd worry about that later. Despite her aversion, the Moura girl drained the cup dry. He poured her another cup. That too, she slowly choked down. Afterward, she settled into the cushions with a pained sigh. He poured himself the next dram, filling it almost to the brim.

She raised her right brow at him. "Someone beat the shite out of you too?"

"You could say so." He tossed the noxious liquid back, then poured himself another. "That, and we're out of uishge. You really should sleep. That shrill girl will scold me for letting you out of bed."

"Who is she? And where is this?"

97

Ben wiped his mouth on his too-short sleeve. "An old friend's farmstead. He was a doctor. The girl seems to think she is too. Not that I'm complaining, mind." He indicated her state of semi-upright mobility.

Mute, she frowned at him for several pregnant minutes. When next she spoke, her voice was a little less grating. The opiate had gone to work in her bloodstream. "What happened to those men? The Corsairs?"

"Dead."

"All of them?"

"Yes."

"Siora," her voice bore genuine regret.

"They were trying to kill you, you know? Don't waste your sympathy."

She didn't answer. Ben didn't understand what she could possibly have to feel guilty about. Those Corsairs were scum of the lowest stripe. They'd nearly beaten her to death right in front of him. While he puzzled over her empathy, he noted the way her hands shook in her lap, the tremors that quivered through her shoulders.

A sudden explanation for her behavior dawned.

She's never killed anyone before.

All that terrible power, and she'd never used it on another human being— at least, not as he'd seen her do. She must have walked right up to them, looking for aid. If true, what a horrible shock all of this must be to her.

Ben squirmed. He was a rare shite, indeed.

"You did what you had to do," he meant to reassure her, best he was able. "I did the rest. Do you understand?"

"They were... you're right," she said. He wasn't witness to her internal conflict for long. She drooped like a dying weed. Eager to avoid further questions, he waited for her to fully succumb to Rian's brew. His brains had finally stopped pounding against his skull, so there was that to be thankful for too. "Wait," she struggled against the drug. "Where are we again?"

"Safe."

"There... is no such place." Three heartbeats later, she was gone, leaving him blessedly alone. He watched her sleep for a while, his thoughts all the more confused by this new, burdensome knowledge. If she were an innocent, which his instincts assured him she was, how had this happened to her?

Better yet, why?

❦ ❦

Later, Ben crammed a few bites of bread into his mouth, then stretched out on the floor beside the hearth. His head a riot, he'd wrapped the girl in one of Rian's old, patched cloaks by the door before laying her on the small couch that divided the tiny room. Making sure she got some rest was the very least he could do for her, given everything that had happened in the past three days. He felt increasingly remorseful for his own part in her situation. If only he hadn't seen her shed genuine tears for men who didn't deserve it, he could continue to convince himself that this was all a horrid inconvenience and not a tragedy. How'd she come to this pass?

None of it made any sense. Ben didn't want to consider anyone else's circumstances, needs, or feelings. That way lay trouble, complications he didn't need. He didn't know anything about this girl. The Moura family had been in power for at least six decades that he could recall. He also knew that they could be a little heavy-handed with their policies. That debacle with the 'attempted' queen... what was her name? What a tone-deaf, political fiasco that had been. He didn't know all the particulars but understood that Tairngare's citizens were bound to be displeased about the Doma's daughter being elevated to autocrat overnight. What was worse, Drem claimed the girl— thereby the family— was fated to absolute rule by prophecy. If Ben remembered correctly, this very foolish move had prompted the Duch of Bethany to instigate the war in '84. If Drem Moura hadn't tipped her hand in her quest for power, the North wouldn't yet bear the scars of that ugly conflict.

Ben shook his head at the ceiling, conflicted by unpleasant memories. If this girl was the next Domina of the Moura Clan, it stood to reason that Drem was grooming her for her own position. If such was the case, perhaps there were new players on the board in the Red City who sought to oust the Moura from the Cloister? This may explain why some of the Citadel's Corsairs would label her a 'heretic' (as one of them had called her) and attempt to hunt her down. She couldn't become the next Doma if she were dead, could she?

It was a sound theory if a bit underdeveloped. For one thing, it didn't explain Bethany's involvement. If this were a plot from within the Cloister, why didn't they simply kill her inside the walls? Why pass her off to agents from a hostile city to the south, then send soldiers out to finish her off? One thing of which he was sure— if he hadn't killed Rawly and his mercenaries, someone would have. Ben would wager that whoever planned all of this never had any intention of letting this girl out of the North alive. Which begged the question— why? Why go to so much trouble just to undo it all again?

Ben told himself that he didn't wish to know. He didn't want to be involved. He didn't care about this girl, her problems, or the intrigues that threw them together. This wasn't his business. She was not his business! He had his own life, such as it was, and his own plans. If Rian could make the stone he needed, he should leave. Still... the sight of her fragile shoulders quaking in silent, personal horror tugged at him. She seemed a decent enough person. He was sorry she was caught up in the middle of this, whatever it was. Maybe he could take her as far as Tara or Ten Bells? Leave her silver to book passage to Cymru, Scotia, or even Bretagne? There were plenty of Siorai retreats in the Colonies. One of them would surely give her sanctuary until all of this blew over. Honestly, what else could he do for her? He was nothing. A nobody. He lived at the edge of the Milesian world, in the wilds of the Greensward. He was in no *position* to help someone like her.

Was he?

TALL TALES

n.e. ſ08
17, ꝺoʀ samna
bethany

Martin reclined in the Great Hall, enjoying a well-deserved ale when Cunningham's corpsmen marched in. Cunningham's close-clipped red hair, brilliant blue cuirass, and greaves were liberally caked with reeking black mud. His men rushed to tables situated below the dais. They tore into the bread, ale, and porridge laid out for the guards' luncheon like wolves. The Duch was absent. Martin happened to know Patrick was locked in his chambers with the doctor, who was busy trying to coax the Duch's old bowels into relative usefulness. As he'd been at it for about twelve hours, one could safely assume it was not going so well.

Martin set his tankard down as Cunningham approached – the scowl on the captain's face could have been carved in. "That bad, huh?" asked Martin dryly, needing no response. Before this group of outriders even made it south of Ten Bells, he'd known that their trip had proven fruitless. Patrick's daughter was not among them. Cunningham glared. The Duch's absence could only mean he'd have to accept Martin's assessment of this failure— an inconvenient fact which rankled. Martin felt just a pinch of sympathy. Serving the whims of wealthy men was not always a pleasant occupation. "Report."

"I need to see His Grace. What I have to say is for his ears only."

Martin's grey brows shot upward. "That's a bloody shame for you, Wallace because it's my ears you've got." He took a large, sloppy bite out of an apple. "Either make your excuses here, or you can scream them from the dungeons later. Up to you."

Cunningham's unshaven cheekbones went stark white under all the road grime. It rained bloody sheets outside, and the Corps had ridden through it for almost two days at full clip. Martin knew because he paid to know. In due course, nothing came or went along the Shannon Road that he was not apprised of. He knew the hour Cunningham and his men emerged from the Greensward and precisely when they'd entered Ten Bells to lay over. Martin was also apprised of the meals Cunningham had had each day (dried tack, bread, and hard-boiled eggs), what he whispered to his closest companions, and how many times he took himself in hand every night (twice, which was a bit worrisome for a man of Cunningham's age). Martin probably knew more about him than Cunningham's own mother. What Martin did not know was how such a carefully plotted task could have been bungled to such a degree. Only Cunningham had the answers he required. Martin would have them, one way or another.

"May we retire to someplace more...."

"We may not. Say what you must, Wallace. For your sake, I hope it's worthwhile. The Duch is furious. I think you know how dire that is for you and your men," prompted Martin, chewing. Plenty of men and women dangling from cages over the ramparts outside could attest to the Duch's temperament.

"He will not want this information bandied about."

Oh? Well, that *did* sound intriguing. Martin spat out a seed and waved a hand at the men seated around him. Nearly as one, they rose, carrying their trenchers and ale to tables set against the far wall. The Great Hall was much warmer than most of the castle, with its four imposing fireplaces and tapestry-laden walls. At the end of each table, a bronze brazier radiated slow-releasing heat throughout the communal space. The chamber was vented by narrow rectangular windows set high into the slate walls, just below the dramatically arched timbers overhead.

102

Four massive iron chandeliers hung from the ceiling, providing warm tallow light for at least ten hours a day. Each of the eight tables in the room was hewn from whole-split oak and could seat up to twenty men apiece on long benches at either end. Martin sat highest, just below the dais. That was his place, after all, as Commander at Arms. He was the highest-ranking knight in the Duch's service. Aside from Lord Bishop, of course, who was the Duch's nephew. Martin gingerly patted the bench beside him, encouraging Cunningham to get on with his tale. The Captain of the Steel Corps seated himself somewhat farther away than expected, stiff as a board. Martin chuckled.

"Now you have me all to yourself, Wallace."

Cunningham's expression bordered on dread, propped up by baseless bravado. Well, he had cause to worry. Martin had orders to nail his bollocks to a post in the courtyard if he did not like what the captain had to say.

"Sir–"

"That's 'Commander O'Rearden' or 'milord' to you, Captain. I haven't been a 'Sir' since you were swinging from your mam's tits. Get it right, or I'll drag you outside myself." The Steel Corps liked to imagine themselves apart from the hierarchy of the regular army; they were not. Martin enjoyed knocking them down a few pegs whenever he had the opportunity. Especially Wallace Cunningham and his lot. They were fine warriors, true – the finest if he were being honest. That didn't grant them the privilege to flout their superiors. Martin's family had been Merchers. The Cunninghams were gentry... such was the way of the world. Nevertheless, Martin didn't make third in command by being an insufferable lickspittle. Nor would he let cunts like Wallace forget it. Not *ever*.

Cunningham's Adam's apple bobbed. "They were not at the appointed meeting place, milord— I'm sure you expected to hear that. So, we waited a full day more. Bally Lough claims victims daily. We thought perhaps they were forced into the bog before Navan."

"Go on."

"They were nowhere. We searched the bog, the outlying moors, the woods leading into the Greensward, the roads...."

103

"To the point, Wallace."

"We found them on the third day, at dawn. Dead, to the last man."

"How?"

"I don't know. At first glance, you'd assume it was a raid by poachers or some other ragtag group of ruffians."

"You don't believe that?"

"I don't. The violence was random but efficient."

"Tairnganeah?"

Cunningham squinted. "Possibly. They could have sent one or two men in to do the job and make it look like a raid. I don't think so. In fact, from the sparsity of tracks in the area – I'd say this was one man, maybe two. We didn't find any trace of a large unit of soldiers at the site. We would have to. Citadel Cohort travel shoulder-to-shoulder in groups of six to nine. You know how they work."

Martin dropped his core into the rushes. "I've known Shane Rawly a long time, you know. I fought with him at Dumnain and countless battles besides. There is no bloody way one man could take him and that cunning bastard Conor alone."

"I'm telling you, *milord*." There wasn't an ounce of levity in his tone. "I can read a scene. The tracks don't lie."

"You're saying one fella marches out of the woods, takes Rawly and his men out, then marches back into the trees with our girl? Bollocks."

"Not at all. I'm saying one man wanders out of the Greensward sometime in the night, kills Rawly and his companions, rummages through their supplies, and leaves the bloody girl where he found her."

Now he had Martin's full attention. Cunningham was many things, but a jester, he was not. Martin doubted the man had ever made a joke in his life. Cunningham had risen through the ranks of the Steel Corps very fast for a man as young as he was, mainly because he didn't have much of a sense of humor. He did what he said and said what he did—a proper soldier.

"And?"

"She was tied to a tree. From the look of things, whoever he was did his deed, fed her, then left her a knife. There was blood on the ropes where her hands would have rested. His tracks say he knelt in front of her for a moment, then slagged off. Took a few coins and some food then disappeared. I think she followed him sometime later when she'd finally managed to free herself. Two sets of tracks lead a mile or so away to another campsite. Only those two. There, they diverge. It's as if he wandered into Rawly's campsite to beg or buy food, was rebuffed, and things went south from there. I think she may have followed him to ask for help, and he refused. It's the damnedest thing I've ever seen, Commander."

"Huh," said Martin, supremely confused by this news. "Some vagabond wanders into their camp to beg for food and just happens to get the best of some of the most vicious men I've ever met. A poacher or other Greensward tough?"

"Doubt it."

"You struggle with the point, don't you?"

Cunningham exhaled sharply. "A trained individual, sir... erm, milord. Someone good. Damned good. Better than anyone in that armpit of the world should be. He'd have to be."

"A former soldier then? A deserter, down on his luck?"

"I don't think so. Mostly used a longbow – the lad's, I expect. Only shot four bloody arrows. I only know of one group of fighters that bloody good with a bow."

Martin slapped his hand against his knee and grinned over at Cunningham. "You're tellin' me this fellow is a *High Elf?* Bollocks! What a bloody pillar of shite."

The look on Cunningham's face said he didn't share the Commander's humor. That's precisely what he thought, though he didn't bother to defend his opinion. He crossed his arms over his cuirass; his mailed vambraces scraped against the steel plate embedded in the leather.

"Do what you want with me, O'Rearden. That's my observation. I know I'm right."

Martin stopped laughing, though the smile remained fixed over his mouth. "That's certainly the most inventive story I've heard in ages. You're serious, I take it?"

"Perfectly."

"You want me to tell the Duch that a rogue Sidhe wandered over the border for some unknown reason, killed Rawly and his fellows, robbed their corpses, and left the bloody Princess of Bethany tied to a tree? You must know how this sounds, Wallace?"

"I did say it was the damnedest sight I've ever seen."

"Doesn't explain where she got to after that, does it? Or why you haven't found her already."

"I left men up there, sir. Disguised as tinkers or other backwoods trash. If she walks into any town East of Navan, I will hear of it. But... there's another problem."

"Of course, there is," Martin waved him on.

"Tairnganeah are everywhere now, and not just foot soldiers. There are Citadel Corsairs lurking at every crossroad. I don't think they're working together, either."

"Well, they wouldn't. Half the city has sided with Vanna Nema against the Cloister, last I heard– including the Corsairs. It's in Nema's best interest, Lady Una never be found." Martin didn't like where this information was headed. "The Duch will be incensed to hear this, regardless."

"I thought the Duch made arrangements?" Irony.

Martin had argued that the old hag could never be trusted from the start. "No one but His Grace believed that, honestly," Martin issued a long-suffering sigh. "Is there anything else, Captain?"

Cunningham straightened. "I take full responsibility for our failure to bring Lady Una back. My men are not to blame."

Martin stood, rubbing his palms together. "Ah, well, that's the thing, Wallace. That part was never up to me. I was only granted the final say about you personally," he nodded to men at a nearby table. Six of them, wearing the white and grey cuirasses of the City Guard, dragged the five Steel Corpsmen to their feet, some midbite. Others spilled tankards, hunks of meat, or bread. Their heavy pewter plates clattered to the flagstones.

"O'Rearden, please! They did their duty!"

"Captain Cunningham." Martin injected every ounce of authority he could muster into his voice. Wallace's men were led away, protesting. "By order of Duch Patrick Donahugh, your men are remanded to the stocks for failing to heed their Duch's commands. He loves his Corpsmen so well that he will spare their lives. Are you protesting the justice of the Duch's command?"

"No. I... no."

"Good. Bully for you, Wallace— I don't think you deserve to die today. You are docked a half-year's wages and will be given ten lashes for your incompetence. Do you object?"

Cunningham drew himself to his full height. "No, Commander. I do not."

"I thought not. Remand yourself to barracks."

Cunningham saluted relief (commingled with abject loathing) apparent in his eyes. "*Sir!*" he spat and stalked from the Hall; his spine as rigid as a marble column. Martin didn't bother to correct him again. The lad might be an arrogant peacock, but he was no liar. Martin watched him go, only allowing himself the luxury of distaste for the situation when he was no longer observed. It did not please him to punish good soldiers for events that were not of their own making. Martin may not care for Cunningham or half his corpsmen, but that didn't mean he blamed them for their inability to foresee the unknowable. They were fine soldiers, and things happened. He'd done the best he could for them. Heaving a bone-weary sigh, he took another long pull from his tankard. He must report what he'd learned to the Duch. Patrick would be incensed. Martin could only hope Lord Bishop would receive the news better and intervene on the men's behalf.

≰ ≱

Dᴀᴍᴇᴋ ᴘᴀᴄᴇᴅ ʙᴀᴄᴋ ᴀɴᴅ ꜰᴏʀᴛʜ in the Duch's privy chamber, squeezing a lavender-scented handkerchief over his nose in revulsion. Martin stood just outside the chamber door with his eyes averted. Thankfully, Damek had caught Martin in the stairwell on the way up to the Duch's apartments. Otherwise, he might have missed the exchange, as the Duch would no doubt prefer. As Bethany's Lord Marshal, Damek kept his own spies and likely knew what Martin knew long before he learned it. In fact, Damek had been dancing attendance upon the Duch for the last two days, waiting for the chance to ambush the old prick with something he didn't already know. This argument between them was long overdue. Damek only wished the Duch had the bloody decency to ask for him after his arse vacated his privy.

"Uncle," Damek said, prying the shutters back to let in some fresh air. He didn't wait for permission to continue. "You should have let me go in the first place. This wouldn't have happened if you had, and Una would be home by now."

Duch Patrick Donahugh, his doughy face gone red round the edges, looked up at Damek with an irritated groan. His jowls were wet with perspiration. One hand gripped the hem of his nightshirt while the other clutched the rim of the privy dock. His gut hung well over his privates, blocking anything untoward from view except his knobby knees and overly thin legs.

"Who is Duch here, boy?" His tone lost some of its bite for the strain.

"You are, Uncle— but that hardly invalidates my point. If I don't go and handle this as it needs to be handled, we could lose your daughter before she's of any use to you."

Patrick wiped his damp brow with the back of a greasy hand. "Humph. Do I look like a bloody fool to you, Damek?"

"I'm not sure I take your meaning, My Lord. Please, tell me how stalling me here has helped in any way?"

"It's done wonders for my peace of mind, not handing my greedy, ungrateful nephew the means to supplant me – that's bloody how."

"The Barons won't sponsor me for Duch unless you do, Uncle. I am not so great a fool as you'd paint me."

Patrick's eyes hardened. "No, they won't, boy. Best not forget it. Some might like your look now, but we'll see what they think of you when you've kidnapped and made a whore of my daughter."

"Marrying her is hardly making a whore of her."

"Tell her that," chortling, Patrick tipped his head at Martin, then raised a brow at his nephew. "You are too young to recall my late wife, boy... that Siorai witch. I lost half an ear and a quarter of my tongue getting that worthless girl on her. If you think my Barons will stand by while you attempt the same on a Donahugh, you're dreaming."

"I won't lay a hand on Una until she asks me to."

"Is that what you think? That you'll make an ally of her?" Patrick's laughter boomed throughout the chamber, drawing Damek's molars into one another like a press. "You know what they teach them, don't you? In that red mortuary, they call a Cloister?"

"Yes. Better than you do, Uncle."

"Humph. I'll bet that's what the Bolgish slut would have you believe, but you'd be wrong. They teach them that men like you and me are irrelevant, boy. She'll never give you what you want. I daresay, especially not you. Remind me, Martin – how old was Una when this young jackass attempted to bed her?"

"Thirteen, your grace," Martin spared Damek an uncomfortable frown. Damek bit the inside of his cheek hard enough to make it bleed.

Patrick shook his head. "*Thirteen*. You hope to make her another offer now? You're lucky she didn't kill you. Hells, that I didn't kill you."

"I was young. I loved her, and she loved me."

"Well, she bloody well might have before you forced yourself upon her. You blithering nonce! Do you realize the trouble I've gone to to undo your idiocy?"

"I did *not* rape her, damn you. You'll never comprehend what's between us. I'd die for her."

"You'd die for her inheritance, more like. Boy, who do you think I am?"

"Believe what you like, Uncle. I'm still the best choice for her, and you know it. Who else could match her but me?"

"Reason save me from ambitious gallants," Patrick pinched the bridge of his nose. "It's been years, Damek. To her mind, she doesn't need any man, least of all some snot-nosed upstart who's presumed too much already!"

"It was a misunderstanding! She fled because she believed I betrayed her to *you*, not because I took her without consent. This has always been your doing, old man." Blood filled Damek's face. "I would *never—*"

"That's enough," Patrick waved his defense away. "I don't care that you lust after my daughter, Damek. Nor do I care that you long for the throne. If you didn't want it, I'd have little use for you. What I do care about is that damned girl returning home in one piece, where she can be put to good use. If you continue to please me and make no attempts to thwart my plans, you may get what you want... one day. Until then, obey."

"May. Soon. One day. *Never.* I've heard all this so often, I wonder if your imagination is drying up? What are you so afraid of, Uncle? If I have an heir, it is your heir. A Donahugh heir, through and through. What else did you bother to raise me for, if not this?"

"My point, dear nephew, is that you reach too far, too fast. Every step you take in your effort to force this issue only brings you closer to a very dark precipice, my boy. You will obey me, or I will teach you the lesson you so richly deserve."

Damek wouldn't bother to argue that he didn't seek the throne. He was the only male left in Donahugh's line. That he was the bastard son of Patrick's long-lamented sister made no never-mind to most. By rights, he was the heir apparent. Let none mistake it. The only thing that could make him a more viable Duch than Patrick himself was a Donahugh bride. If he could get Una with child, there'd be no dispute. The people tired of Patrick. He was ruthless, callous, thin-skinned, and despotic. His Barons respected his rule, but the people most certainly did not. They longed for a more sophisticated ruler, someone with respect for the arts, and an eye to improve trade and foreign relations. They wanted Lord Bishop, and Patrick certainly understood this better than anyone. The only thing Damek lacked was legitimacy: all he needed was Una. Patrick kept him from marching North for that very reason. His power waned in Eire. Soon it would be time to pass the torch to the next generation.

110

No benevolent god saw fit to make Patrick Donahugh immortal. He had no intention to take his fist from the reins of power until his cold dead hands unfurled of their own accord. He had a legacy he meant to carve out first, a grand design that would cement his name above all his ancestors. Una was the key to the North. Patrick wouldn't give her to Damek right away. Likely, not for some years. He would use her to gain supporters in the Midlands, thus attracting more able men to his cause here in the South. Only after she'd brought him what he required would Patrick consent to give her to his nephew. However long that took. Damek had no bloody intention of waiting. He'd had a bellyful of that already.

"You have my word, Uncle—"

"Oh, shut your mouth! Go and charm your fawners and bum boys with these meaningless platitudes. I know precisely what you will do if you manage to find her. But I'm telling you that if by some miracle I let you go – a rather large *if*, mind – you'd better resist the urge, or it will be the death of you. I vow it."

Damek glanced at Martin, who tactfully averted his gaze. Patrick could play it off, deny the obvious, speak banalities until he was blue in the face. Hells, it was what he had been doing the past few years in general and the past two days in particular. Look where that tactic got him.

"Fine. Cards on the table?"

"It had better be worth hearing," Patrick cautioned.

"I do intend to disobey you. I will suffer her to belong to no one else— not now, not ever. What harm will it do? I am your heir! You raised me, you taught me, and you certainly intend that it should be me who rules after you. Give her to me. Not later. Now. I can be of greater use to you if you legitimize me."

"You are not the anointed heir, Damek. If you continue to test these waters, you'll drown in them. I will give her to whomever I deem worthy... as many men as it takes until my investment bears fruit. Then, and only then, will I consider giving you what you want."

"The Barons will not allow—"

"My Barons will do whatever I tell them to do!" Patrick blasted spittle down the front of his tunic. He waved a cowering girl over from the corner of the wood-paneled chamber. She dipped her sponge in lemon water, then went to work behind him, her expression impassive. When she'd finished, and Damek thought he might vomit, she patted the Duch's arse with a dry wad of linen. The sponge and bowl she removed. Patrick readjusted his clothing. "As will you, boy. As will you." Chuckling, he strode into his bedchamber. Damek and Martin followed, both mute. "So, those witches in Tairngare mean to outwit me, do they? I would dearly like to know what old Nema thought she would accomplish by betraying me in such a way?" He lit a gilded pipe and marched toward the fireplace on hoary bare feet. "Any ideas, Martin?"

"Your grace, I don't presume to know what goes through any woman's head, especially not one of the conniving witches in the Red City."

"Fair. However, the question demands an answer."

"I would think there's likely a disconnect between our source and Nema herself. Perhaps each hand works a separate thread? Who knows? All I can say for sure is someone knew what we planned and set up a counter-maneuver. Until we glean who that may be, we shouldn't depend upon our original source for information."

Damek, wisely, kept his mouth shut.

"Agreed," growled Patrick. He shook his head at Damek. "That doesn't mean I want them to know we're suspicious of them. Boy, I want you to keep your meetings with that woman. Bring every scrap of information back to me. No detail is to be omitted, or I shall know of it. Do you hear?"

"Of course, Uncle," said Damek, rolling his eyes. "I wasn't born yesterday. Besides, I enjoy our meetings enough that it would pain me to halt them over this unfortunate turn of events."

"I bet you do, lad. Would that I still had your stamina. Nema's pet is quite the piece. Isn't that right, Martin?" Patrick's hoarse laughter grated the very limit of Damek's endurance. Martin found something new to ogle, far above his head. "All right then, Martin, take troops north. As many as need be– I leave it to you."

112

"But, My Lord!" protested Damek.

Duch Patrick shook his fist at his nephew. "You heard me, boy! Do consider yourself duly warned. Disobey me this time, and it won't go well for you. Not at all... do you hear me? Not at all!"

⚔ ⚔

"My Lord," sighed Martin. "I'd be remiss if I didn't advise against this tomfool plan. Your uncle has expressly forbidden—"

"I don't give a tenth of a shite what that sodding old tyrant has to say about anything. I'm going, and that's all there is to it," Damek assured him, adjusting the saddle straps personally. An aging guardsman rounded the corner of the stable, where O'Rearden's men gathered to leave.

"Lord Bishop!" the guardsman huffed, out of breath. "The Duch commands your presence in the—"

Damek grabbed the fellow by his collar and flung him onto his arse. "Do you wish to lose your pension, your home? Have your children sold off to work the mines in Cymru?"

"N-no, milord."

"Then you'd best pretend you never saw me to relay that command. Who do you think will rule here when the Duch finally ceases plaguing us all with his presence?"

The guardsman flushed, his head low. "Very good, milord. S-sorry, milord." He scrambled out of the courtyard so swiftly that the colors of his doublet were but a smear.

"Perhaps that wasn't the wisest course? He will surely rush back to your uncle with news that you've disobeyed him."

"So, what? Let him."

"My Lord—"

"Patrick will fart and wheeze a bit, no doubt. Wax poetic about the myriad ways he'll have my corpse displayed," Damek shrugged. "All meaningless twaddle. He's been vowing to murder me my entire life."

"Damek," Martin used his given name on purpose, "how many times do you think he'll allow you to call his bluff? Publicly or otherwise? My

113

family has served this clan for almost two hundred years. My father once imparted a piece of advice I will now pass on to you: 'never embarrass your betters.' It's saved my life more times than I care to count."

"That dithering old snake is hardly my better."

"At the moment, he is. What's more, his Barons and landsmen believe he is. The Merchers in Ten Bells know he is. As long as they *know* this, they'll never finance another. Least of all, a half-breed lordling, with more bollocks than brains."

Damek's hand paused on his straps. "They sold her out, Martin, and they betrayed us. I must go. I'm all she's got."

"If Patrick disinherits you while you're gone?"

"Don't you realize by now? He can't do a damn thing about it! All he has are threats! If he could have stamped me out by now, don't you think he would have done it? The people love me. The Barons might be loyal to him, but I have the love of literally everyone else. I am the only presence keeping him in power. He needs me now, far more than I need him."

"That may be true, but this wouldn't be the first time Patrick acted against his own interests in a rage. I advise you to be cautious. A defanged bear still has claws," Martin said.

"You know what he will do to her, Martin. He leaves me little recourse. I can't allow him to get his hands on her first. I will not."

"As you say, Lord Bishop. I merely work here. What do I know?"

"Don't be like that, old friend. Your concern is appreciated, as always. But I thought you liked our little princess?"

Martin went quiet. Target struck. He loved every hair on her head as if she were his. Far be it for him to say as much, however. "I do, of course."

"Then don't you think she'd be better off with me than placed on the auctioning block?"

"Yes, I do— but I know your uncle, Damek. He'll find a way to hurt you for this. Hurt you both. I merely caution, not condemn you for your intent."

"I'm going to bring her back. I vow it. Once she's home and safe, I will deal with the treacherous dogs who've betrayed us."

"*All* of them?" Martin's stare was direct.

Damek had the grace to look down. "Most of them, anyway."

"If you will not listen to me about your uncle, Damek, you'd best heed me about that woman. Aoife is the last person you should put your faith in. Has it occurred to you yet, I wonder? For selfish reasons, she might be vested in removing Una from your orbit?"

"It has."

"Well, what do you mean to do about it? She betrayed you. My lady might even now be dead or dying for it."

"I will deal with Aoife, and her mistress, in my own time," Damek said. "For now, let's go find my cousin, shall we? If anyone in Tairngare has harmed her, I'll raze that city to the ground."

Martin's nod managed to appear more like a flinch. "As you say, My Lord. Please consider my council. It's well meant. Caution is always wise, lad. Patrick's rage may be less engulfing than it once was, but it still burns, all the same. He will pay you back for this disloyalty. Never forget it."

"Fair enough," winked Damek, throwing his leg up and over his saddle. Once seated, he shrugged his heavy wolf-skin cloak tight over his shoulders. "I'm sure you're right, Martin. If he lives so long."

From Darkest Dreams

n.e. 508
18, Ðor Samna
Ferndale

At full dark, a blunt object connected with Ben's bruised shoulder. Half-awake, he tried to shove the offensive appendage away. It wouldn't budge. Grumbling into the dusty floorboards, he cracked an eye open. Rian's moon-pale face stared down at him with unspoken urgency.

"Ugh. What? You are a terrible host, you realize?" he said, attempting to roll over and face the opposite wall.

She nudged him again.

"Keep it up, and I'm going to break that foot. What will you do then, hm? Hop?" He jerked his pilfered blanket over his head to ignore her. The laudanum in her tea wasn't strong enough to render someone of his size completely unconscious, but neither did it make him eager to rise. He was snoring again when her toe plowed into him with renewed force. "Ow! Damn it. Didn't I tell you to slog off?"

"*Be quiet*." Kneeling beside him, she clapped a shaking hand over his mouth. He was ready to fling her across the small room when he absorbed her expression. Though the fire had long since burned out, he could see the stark whites of her eyes and the bloodless pallor of her cheeks. She was terrified.

He sat up, wrenching her fingers from his face. "Tell me," he said, blinking himself to full cognitive speed. He might not be able to recite a sonnet, but he could at least string coherent thoughts and words together. That was a start.

"Did you try to reset the wards outside?"

He winced.

"You idiot!"

"What's happening?"

She pointed to the back door. "They're out there...."

"How many men?" he asked, getting to his knees.

"Not men. Something... else."

"What is that supposed to mean?"

Having just been kicked awake after a nice drug-induced nap, it wasn't entirely his fault he wasn't quick-witted enough to immediately grasp her cryptic answer.

"Whatever they are, they're not human."

He looked at her like she'd been at her own tea. Then, suddenly, he heard the barest hint of a scrape: a sharp object dragged faintly over stone. Rian opened her mouth to say more, but his palm mashed over the lower portion of her face. Concentrating hard, he tapped into the deep well of Sidhe gifts he'd been born with but found so little use for of late. Now, he could hear *everything*—the two women breathing, one erratically. Rian's heart thudded cavernously against her ribs. The Moura girl's thumped slowly, evenly, in a happily sedated rhythm. Her breathing, however, was not as reassuring. Sucking thin streams of air through her bruised windpipe, she exhaled in rasps.

Narrowing his focus, he marked the more frantic heartbeats of nearby animals: mice in the cupboards, behind the walls, and beneath the floorboards. Birds nested in the eaves, and voles and rabbits dug burrows below the house. Spiders tapped along their webs in the rafters, jingling strands like silken bells. He reached further, listened harder, and cast a wider net. The cow snored in her stall inside the barn. Cud still clung to her broad, flat teeth. Sheep and chickens, snug in their hay, were oblivious to the owls and other nightbirds calling from the trees beyond the barn. Vixen, however, was not so restful. Whickering, she stamped the earth in her unlocked stall. She was upset about something, though he couldn't immediately sense it himself. Cocking his head, he listened while the old mare reared and pounded out of the barn as if something chased her.

He stood up.

"What?"

Ben held out a hand to halt Rian's questions. Leaves rustled in a mild but insistent breeze. Water trickled in the brook, disrupted only by crackling ice and encroaching frost. A half-mile or so distant, a doe scraped her teeth against a birch.

Too far.

Again, he shifted focus. Reeds and long grasses sighed over the pond; a loose gate creaked to and fro in the wind; a latch rattled against the paddock; a magpie chittered from the front of the house.

Nothing.

"What do you think you saw?"

Rian fumbled closer, her clothes sodden from the rain freezing in the meadow. It seemed she'd been caught out in it. Touching her finger to her lower lip, she gestured to the back door, begging him for silence. *That* was when he heard it again. Not the wind nor the flutter of nighttime wings: a shuffle and thump. Bird sounds ceased. The doe halted mid-scrape, ears no doubt twitching toward the farmstead. She leapt into the forest for safety. Her hoofbeats faded into the night, as had Vixen's. The animals in the barn jolted awake. The cow dropped her cud. Sheep bleated in instinctual alarm. A heavy but nimble body stalked through the grass. Vixen, whose ears were sharpest, sensed the danger early enough to escape. A predator drew near. A bump against the back door.

Ben's head whipped around.

"How many?" he mouthed at her.

She held up two shaking fingers. Ben took a step back. His heel unsettled a loose board. He might have shouted a challenge. An unearthly whine… then a snuffling at the keyhole. The back stoop groaned under the thing's substantial weight. Rian squeaked. The creature let out a trill, such as Ben hadn't heard for a very long time. This wasn't a sound one could forget. "Siora!" Rian whimpered.

"Ghasts—" the blood drained from Ben's face. That was why Rian couldn't describe what she saw. They weren't always visible to the naked eye and were certainly *unlike* any animal she would occasion to see in Eire. "Dor Sidhe…" His voice hadn't been any louder than hers, but the thing outside heard him anyway. It screamed, grating as a knife drawn over glass, and hurled itself at the structure. The cottage shuddered beneath its weight. Rian covered her ears and dashed for the corner at the opposite side of the hearth. Ben spread his feet for balance. The door took another timber-splitting blow.

🦌

UNA'S EYES POPPED OPEN. A thunderous roar shook the house from top to bottom. Something substantial hammered into the back wall like a battering ram. Glass shattered. Crockery burst from their cupboards. Books, utensils, and other bric-a-brac clattered to the floor. She struggled to rise from her couch, only to hear the unseen assailant howl.

A terrible, hair-raising bellow that propelled her heart into her throat. *What was that?* She'd never heard anything like it, nor could conceive of such a sound in her worst nightmares. She sucked in a slow breath, making her one good eye water from the pain. The beast outside shrieked, heaving its bulk repeatedly into the door. Iron hinges bent inward, birthing a deep crack in the lintel above. Una's hand flew to her swollen throat.

"Siora," she croaked, carefully slipping to the floor and moving toward the smoldering hearth on skinned knees. "What is that?" The moment the words left her mouth, she found cause to regret them. A second creature bayed from the front yard. This one flung itself against the house hard enough to bow the heavy oak door inward. The presumed pair took turns barreling into opposite ends of the dwelling with murderous urgency.

She had no idea what was going on. A girl she couldn't quite place cowered in a corner beside the fireplace. In front of her, lowering himself into a defensive crouch, was the enigmatic Sidhe who'd twice saved Una's life. She didn't even know his name. He skimmed her as she approached, his face inscrutable. She didn't know what to make of him. He seemed two different men entirely, depending upon his mood. One, a heartless ruffian with little regard for anything, save his own comfort; the other, someone willing to risk his own life to save a woman he'd previously abandoned. She couldn't puzzle him out. Every one of his actions was contradictory. Her instinct might be to dismiss him as a shiftless scoundrel down on his luck, yet... *nine gold chains* swung from his right ear. Una had the education to wonder: why would a high Sidhe lord prowl the wilds of Eire dressed like a beggar and kill for crumbs? Though she longed to ask, she wasn't afforded the time.

A blood-curdling howl shook the cottage to its foundations. The ceiling's main support timbers shuddered, showering them all with curtains of dust and splinters. Una crept toward them.

"What in the nine hells is *that*?"

Her erstwhile savior's silver eyes flicked her way, then back to the fractured lintel over the rear door. "They're ghasts."

"What?"

"*Ghasts...* Hounds of the Dor Sidhe. They hail from the deepest reaches of the Oiche Ar Fad. Full of insatiable hunger and bloodlust– sound familiar?"

Una's brow furrowed. "You're saying these things come from the Otherworld? Why? How did they get here?"

"Been asking myself the same question," he drawled with pointed cynicism. The creatures circled the dwelling, each searching for any weakness in the structure– a way in. One sword-length claw jabbed through the broken south window, but the opening was too small to garner any purchase. Every wall was reinforced at the casings to prevent buckling. Having been built of weathered Innish oak, it would take some effort to pry loose. Even so, the beast wasn't given much opportunity to try. Some invisible element singed the meat of its obsidian paw, leaving a foul-smelling trace of black smoke in its wake. It yelped in frustrated pain and backed off. Its companion responded in kindred fury. The pair circled twice, then thrice more, growling, snarling, and snapping. On the fourth circuit, they abruptly bounded away. Soon after, a chorus of splintering timbers and baying animals rent the night outside.

The girl in the corner crumpled into herself, sobbing, "*No!* Oh, no... no!"

The vagabond Sidhe laid a hand on the girl's shoulder. "I'm sorry, Rian. Your mother's wards don't extend to the barn."

The girl, Rian, flinched at every pitiful cry.

"Can they get in here?" Each hopeless wail trailed cold fingers down Una's spine.

"I hope not."

"If you're unsure, we have to get out while they're distracted."

"You won't get far."

"*We* won't get far? What about you?"

"I very much doubt they're here for me."

"What's that supposed to mean?"

"I'm sure it will come to you."

She returned his accusatory regard with alacrity. "I've never even heard of such creatures, *My Lord*. They hail from your homeland, not mine."

His head swiveled slowly around. "The name's *Ben*."

"Is it? Nice chains, by the way. You steal those too?"

"Funny." His tone wouldn't melt cream.

"Of the three of us, only one is hunted by her people. Why is that, I wonder?"

"Shut up, both of you!" Rian cut in, with gobs of snot running down her chin. "Who cares why they're here? My animals are out there dying, and we're trapped. What are we going to do about it?"

"We should go," Una repeated, "before they come back."

122

"That's quite a plan. They'll be on you in seconds, no matter which way you run."

"What else are we supposed to do? Sit here and wait?"

"My mother's wards are only good so long as the house stands," Rian said.

"Can you set more?" Una watched the crack in the lintel widen before her eyes. That wall wouldn't take many more strikes. Of that, she was sure.

"My mother spent years on them. Ben, can you?"

"Bit late to try," he said.

Una kicked out at him with her right foot. "If all you're going to do is sit there and make a sarcastic arse of yourself, then get her out of here, and I'll–"

"Do what? Nag them to death?"

"I'm stronger than I look."

Ben grimaced, remembering. "True, but that sort of thing won't work on Dor Sidhe. You'll be dead long before you can get a hand on one of them."

"Fine. I'll lure them away. Take her somewhere safe, at least," she sneered, raising her chin to conceal her shame. *You insufferable bastard.* "I'll buy time."

Whatever sharp retort he'd been saving died on his tongue. He stared at her as if he couldn't decide what sort of specimen she might be. "Don't be stupid, girl. They'll kill you."

"My name's Una, not *girl.* And, you don't know that."

"Yes, *Una.* I do."

"What else are we supposed to do?"

"Not that," he sucked his teeth at her.

"You're annoying. You know that?"

Rian swiped at her nose. "We're wasting time."

The noise outside grew less ghoulish by the second. Una was tired of arguing with him. "Rian, help me up, will you?"

"Only if we're leaving. I'm a healer, not a sadist."

"Just—"

"Stop!" Ben drew himself up to his full, considerable height, cutting her statement short. "Save your breath. *I'm* going. If you run, it would merely sweeten the chase." He had a very petulant tilt to his jaw that Una wanted to clobber with a brick.

"I can help. If we work together—"

"You'll just get in my way."

Fuming, she watched him stomp to the back door. He paused to retrieve a beat-up Souther longbow Una happened to know he'd stolen from Rawly's camp and a heavy broadsword with a leaping silver stag for a pommel. He slung the bow over one shoulder, and its plain leather quiver over the other, cursing in Ealig all the while. Sliding his sword free of its scabbard, he heaved an annoyed sigh. Shooting her one last indignant glower, he kicked open the door. It dangled queerly from its warped hinges.

"Stay inside!"

⚜

Ben didn't have time to fletch more arrows, nor were there any conveniently lying about that he could steal. The few he lifted from the Tairnganeah he'd slain allotted him a whopping three to work with. He must make them count.

Of all the idiotic, pointless things he could have gotten himself into... this was by far the prize.

You just couldn't leave her to die, could you? You see where conscience gets you? You bloody daft lummox. Still mumbling invectives, he slammed Nemain point-first into the ground at his feet. Her hilt vibrated from the impact. Some fifteen feet from the battered cottage, sickening sounds of shredding meat and crunching bone wafted from the barn. Ben was no vegetarian like most of his people, but the horrors he heard and smelt from within that structure might change his mind. The whole farmstead reeked of blood, piss, and putrefying flesh. Wet, smacking mastication accosted his ears. Eyes watering in revulsion, he groaned. The feasting paused. An atonal rumble filled the pasture. The small hairs at his nape stood on end.

Too late to change your mind now...

Two pairs of glowing yellow eyes, set in massive misshapen faces, skulked from either end of the dilapidated barn. Each of their grinning maws poured steaming gobs of gore onto the grass below. Multiple rows of razor-sharp teeth rotated mechanically in their hideous, malformed jaws. Spear-point claws carved great furrows in the soil as they loped forward. Ben's nose twitched at the ozone that crackled along his skin. Everywhere they moved, traces of miasmic void lingered like a charcoal smudge. Like most Dor Sidhe, Ghasts were notoriously rapacious, gluttonous, and difficult to control. Left alone, they would slaughter and feed for weeks. They were insatiable. Whoever summoned these was stark raving mad. One didn't send a lion to hunt a mouse.

He knew of no Sidhe that might have cause to hunt *him* at the moment. Therefore, there was only one person these beasts could be after. He cracked his knuckles, aggravated by the imposition. He'd never heard of Siorai's ability to tap into the Otherworld. Who exactly wanted her dead? Someone with power— serious power. There was more to that blasted girl inside than met the eye. He intended to have it out with her as soon as he finished here. He'd had enough surprises for one week, thank you.

Ri Tuiathe, one of the beasts, snickered, fangs snapping in delight. The second grinned back; a macabre rictus split its garish mouth wide.

Ard Tiarne... it agreed, advancing.

Nocking two arrows at once, Ben droned, "Yeah, yeah. I'm excited to see you too." He widened his stance and worked out the maths. Distance, wind speed, arc, velocity...

Both ghasts stalked around him, cackling. These were creatures crafted from mortal man's darkest dreams. Their bodies were lithe, though ungainly, having the hindquarters of wolves and the grasping forepaws of mountain cats. Their fur was a burning onyx, dark as the gaps between stars, on a moonless night. Sniggering to each other, they were most pleased with the unexpected prey that stood before them. He was the very last Daoine Sidhe they likely imagined they would get the chance to eat. The stench of their fetid breath was so overwhelming that he could taste it. They drew near, taunting, jubilant.

Ard Tiarne! the first chortled with glee.

Ben was unmoved by their elation. "Come and get it then. I'm bloody bored of standing here," he said, taking aim. With twin howls, the ghasts swerved in for the kill. Ben let fly. Two arrows sailed into the nearest beast's open maw. It struck the earth face-first. Its gaping mouth plugged with dirt and rubble. It had scarcely breathed its last before its partner bellowed in rage, a racket to shake the very hills.

⚔

Uɴᴀ ᴡᴀsɴ'ᴛ ᴏɴᴇ ᴛᴏ ʜᴇᴇᴅ orders, even when they were wise. She hobbled to the open doorway to see what was happening in the yard outside. Clutching a rather useless kitchen knife in one shaking hand, she hefted herself up the ruined doorjamb with the other. Despite her best efforts, it took several painful minutes to crawl so far. Now, she *knew* she wouldn't have been the slightest use against these creatures. Breathing hard, she hoped she was not about to witness their reluctant ally being torn in half. What she saw instead, she could scarcely comprehend. A host of armored men would fear to approach monsters like these, even should there be a dozen or more in their company. Ben, however, marched right up to them with only a sword and three arrows left in his quiver. To add weight to the matter, he did so totally *alone*. Watching him work, the swift deaths of seven well-armed men no longer shocked her. Her jaw slack, Una could only stare.

Ben drew and slew the first beast without stopping to watch his arrows land. Two missiles sailed its open craw mid-leap. It slammed to the ground and died long before its body slid to a halt. Ben jumped out of its way; his attention already fixed upon its partner. Enraged by the death of its mate, the creature beat the ground with a mammoth forepaw. His arm drawn back over his last arrow; Ben casually shifted left as a three-foot claw gouged into the earth near his feet. Just as the thing paused to retract its paw for another swing, he released his bowstring. His last arrow plunged through the beast's right eye. Its baleful roar rattled the teeth in Una's gums. The ghast reared, its head taller than the massive oaks towering over the roof. She'd never seen such a horrific sight in all her life.

Ri Tuiathe, it thundered down at Ben, manic with pain. His quiver empty, Ben flung it aside and rolled for his sword. He moved so fast that Una had trouble tracking him in the shadows. She lived in the most heavily guarded fortress in the world. The Citadel was infested with fine preening soldiers– presumed to be the best in Innisfail. None of them had ever moved as lithely or with such sure-footed grace. She was astounded.

"*Siora...*" she breathed in morbid fascination.

Swinging his sword into a high, arcing guard over his left shoulder, Ben waited for the creature's next lunge. As its claws lanced downward, he charged– so unbelievably quick, all she could discern were the metallic flashes of his sword in the moonlight. A slash here, and the beast stumbled. A brilliant streak there and its flailing claws obliterated one-half of the now empty barn. Again and again, his blade whirled around its torso like lightning crackling through a swirling fog. A strike to its rear hamstring and it backpedaled, uprooting two trees in the process. Another, and it came down with a forceful thud, driving a wall of dust and debris toward the house.

Una coughed as the cloud rushed through the open door. She couldn't make out much beyond the bulk of its spasming body for a moment. Its partially decapitated head leaked mellifluous black fluids into the dry, frigid soil. Dying, it glared at Ben with impotent fear as he approached, sword in hand.

Ard Tiarne... Mo Flaith... it whined as if begging for mercy. She strained to hear. Ben spat on the ground near its twitching claws and hefted his longsword for the final stroke.

"You talk too much." He brought the heavy edge down, cleaving its head in a final stroke.

Aoife watched the spectacle from the trees, amazed, her fists balled at her sides. This unwelcome complication boded ill for her carefully laid plans. How was this possible? *How*? The girl should be a gory stain in the grass, her severed head an offering laid at Aoife's feet. What could Aoife do? Myriad scenarios played out in her head, each ending very poorly for her, indeed.

I must report this, she thought.

Her agitation bordered on desperation. Her hands shook with the urge to march into that pasture and slay the interloper where he stood so proudly... so *alive*, poised over his kill with perfect authoritative arrogance.

Why is he here?

This was such a ludicrous coincidence; she had no idea how she would explain it. A dead man stood between Aoife and her prey, wiping her pet's inky blood from his blade with a bored, disgusted pout. If she hadn't just watched him slay her beasts as easily as he would rub his nose, she might imagine he'd done something inane or perfunctory. Aoife burned to destroy him, once and for all. Without a backward glance, he stomped toward the house, mumbling. Much, which rested on this day's effort, now lay in tatters. The Moura Domina was there, a few paltry paces away, just waiting for the justice she so richly deserved. Not today, Aoife surmised with gritted teeth. Now, she had bigger problems. The one person she'd never expected to see again had materialized out of thin air, like smoke. Worse, he was *defending* the bloody girl! This defied all logic. Aoife had to blink a few times to assure herself she was seeing things correctly.

That unmistakable silver hair, the sword with the prancing stag at the pommel, the merciless skill required to wield it— there was no mistake.

Her ghasts, sacred Dor Sidhe hounds bought with blood sacrifice and tremendous energy, were dead. All because one bloody Dannan lordling didn't have the sense or grace to stay dead as he should have.

How are you alive, you Dannan bastard?

Aoife stumbled away in shock. Now was not the time. This was far too inexplicable a coincidence to be believed. Nema would know what to do if Aoife could convince her not to destroy her for her failure. If *he* was here and involved with the heretic… there was a good chance he wasn't alone. Maybe the Ard Ri sent him here for this very purpose? She pursed her lips. Perhaps not? All she knew for sure was that Nema would not take this news well. Aoife could lose more than her standing in the Red City. She could be marching to her doom.

How would she have had the faintest inkling that such a curious, tricky snag would appear at just this moment? Aoife took her time and planned each word she meant to use, each expression, every gesture. Nema would seize upon any hesitation in her description of the night's events to punish her mercilessly. Aoife had only one chance to convince Nema of the truth. Aoife had no friends, no family to protect her. She had only her word and Nema's dubious mercy.

How can this be?

She raged at the night sky, the wind tearing through the trees, the hardening loam beneath her feet, and the very air she breathed. The walk back to Tairngare was sure to be a long one. She made sure to take it slow.

THE PRISONER

Patrick shuffled along the corridor, hands tucked under his arms to avoid touching the moldering walls by accident. There were very few torches lining the way. He found that no matter how many times he underwent this journey, it was best to watch where he stepped. He'd never liked coming down here. The dungeon was endlessly murky, consistently damp– and reeked of piss, vomit, and stale flesh. His father used to bring him here twice a week when he was a child. Duch Michael insisted that to be a strong ruler, one must harden oneself to the pain of others. From a very young age, Patrick was forced to watch as men were interrogated and tortured. His father had been a notorious sadist. He enjoyed the screams, the pleading, the sight and scent of blood. Nothing delighted the old bastard more, in fact. Michael would often take his supper here as if the suffering of men who'd displeased him was mere spectacle for his entertainment.

The first time his father made him watch a man having his teeth scooped out with a speculum, Patrick was ill. Michael had him whipped for that weakness. Patrick was only six. The second event was made grislier by the Duch's express order. A house steward– one who'd practically raised Patrick– had his tongue ripped from his mouth and the skin peeled from the soles of his feet. His father had never given a reason, but Patrick

131

knew it had been a personal punishment, designed to harden him against his squeamishness. He'd learned to swallow his sympathy, strangle any inclination toward empathy, to guard the slightest hint of emotion.

Watching men whipped, bludgeoned, scourged, branded, and flayed before his young eyes, Patrick vowed never to flinch again… and to date, never had. He had very few fond memories of his father. Though, he'd been told his grandfather, Duch Kevin, had been the greatest ruler Eire had seen in a thousand years. Kevin was brave, wise, merciful to the deserving, and exacting when required. Either every tale spun of that great and noble man was false, or Patrick's father had come by his cruelty from some other source.

Sighing at his unpleasant memories, Patrick rounded the next corner. He plodded down the last set of stairs into the dungeon's bleakest bowels. Each of the twenty-six cells on this level was built into the main support arches for the floors above. Every one was a windowless chasm of oblivion– save the farthest alcove, on the right. A flicker of pale sunlight shone from an arrow slit high in the rear wall. Patrick strode toward it with purpose. On his way past each cell, men moaned from somewhere in the deep wet dark they stewed in. None called out to him. Most knew better than to beg the Duch for mercy. Before the rusting iron bars, he snapped his fingers. One of the three guardsmen worked a pronged key through a series of triple locks, then slid the grate wide for his Duch.

"Leave us," Patrick ordered, taking the torch in his right hand. "But remain near." The guards moved a mere six paces from the open door. Patrick hooked his torch into a creaky sconce on the wall inside. It took a moment for his eyes to adjust. Perched on a cot with his back against the seeping wall sat the prisoner he sought. The figure blinked wildly, holding one gnarled hand over his eyes to shield himself from the invasive flame and clutching a bit of chalk in the other. He'd been using it to decorate the walls of his cell with verse. Patrick frowned at the sight. From floor to ceiling were thousands upon thousands of white-etched words and phrases.

A single line was repeated several hundred times: *He knows what lies in the darkness…*

"You know," Patrick's voice carried an added boom in this hollow stone chamber. "I can have these walls scrubbed clean again." Even the ceiling bore evidence of the man's ravings.

The prisoner's blackened fingertips were bundled with bits of filthy cloth. His scrawny arms and legs were bone-white and bare. Nervous, he inched forward until he knelt before Patrick on his cot. The poor bugger reeked of urine and excrement, body odor, and decay. His shaggy grey hair and beard were wild about his face.

"I will only rewrite them." His voice was dry with disuse.

"If I take your chalk away again, what will you do?"

The prisoner held up the dried, bloodied nubs of two bandaged fingers. "One less won't kill me, I'm sure."

"You've gone mad, Brother," said Patrick. He snapped his own arthritic fingers a second time. A guard brought in a tray laden with fresh bread and broth. Patrick gestured for it to be set down upon a moldy carpet.

The starving man, all awkward limbs and animal hunger, leapt upon the tray like a slavering dog. Patrick covered his mouth and nose. The sounds the man-made turned his stomach. The prisoner looked up, mouth wide open, mashing food into his rotting gums.

"If I am, you saw to it yourself."

"You've held the key to your release for years, Henry. Renounce this lunacy, and I shall be lenient."

Henry sat back on his haunches and sucked the last bits of broth from his bread. Despite his obvious cataracts, his eyes hadn't lost their defiant gleam. It pained Patrick to see him like this. Henry had once been a handsome man, far grander to look at than Patrick ever was– that was sure. In their youth, Henry wooed ladies by the dozen. They used to joke that half the Pleasure District was set by just to house Henry of Bethany's mistresses. Now... here sat a scabbed old beggar, decaying from the inside out. He was older than Patrick by some five or so years, but having been bastard-born, he'd spent his life in service to his younger brother. That is until Henry decided *he* should rule in Bethany, despite his illegitimacy.

After Patrick's failure at Dumnain, Henry took it upon himself to rouse the South against him. If Patrick's loyal Barons hadn't betrayed him, their roles today might have been reversed. Escaping his failed coup and Patrick's subsequent wroth, Henry fled to the Outlands of Cymru, a place where folk outside the Colonial Law lived hardscrabble, often brutally short lives at the rim of the Briton Wastes, the soil there too thin and too stony to yield but the weakest crops. The air in the Wastes was noxious with methane vented from beneath the remnants of the Ancients' faded civilization. Only those with no alternative would dare attempt a life there.

When Patrick finally caught word of his brother a decade after his rebellion, he discovered that the once brutal, bastard son of Michael Donahugh had become something of a self-appointed cleric for the Kneelers who subsisted there. Henry would rail long and hard against the injustices of the Eirean city-states and their sacrilegious, immoral peoples. He'd whipped up such fervor among the uncouth frontiersmen–Patrick believed it another of Henry's ploys.

He didn't expect his elder brother to believe the drivel he preached. When arrested, Henry's newfound zeal burned from his eyes like kindling. Henry longed to martyr himself; he craved it like a drowning man craves the press of dry sand. Thus, Patrick had been obliged to toss him into a dank cell: unseen, unheard, and all but forgotten by those above. What satisfaction could be gained from killing a man who lusted for it as Henry did? None that Patrick could stomach.

"Kill me, Brother," goaded Henry, gumming his crust, "and you can keep your walls how you like them."

"If I ever deign to have you executed, I will simply have you strangled down here in the dark and your body tossed out with the rubbish. No one will ever hear what became of you."

That wiped the manic smirk from Henry's toothless face. "Then what have you come here for, little brother? To glower at me? Please yourself by my state? Well, look all you like. You will atone for it in the end." Smirking, he crossed himself.

134

Patrick rolled his eyes. He shifted against the bars and rubbed a clean hand over his balding scalp. "I don't know which is more pathetic, Henry. Your spectacular fall from grace, or this pathetic nugget of theosophical drivel you cling to? Where is this god you claim sees all, hm? It seems he left you here in hell, cloaked in your own filth. I'm the one who will release you... one way or the other, Brother. No one else."

"As you released your lady wife, Patrick? She whom you stole from her people, imprisoned, drugged, and abused? Didn't she drown in the Shannon outside your summer palace?" Bits of moistened bread dribbled into his ragged beard. "So sad that the Duchess had been given no guards that day, don't you agree? The only time you ever permitted her to wander the grounds, absent a half-dozen armed men."

This was not a subject Patrick wished to discuss with Henry FitzDonahugh. "What purpose would it have served to kill Arrin before she bore me the son I needed? You go too far."

"Forcing another's suicide still amounts to murder. Why, just ask Alis about that–"

"I had *nothing* to do with Alis's death, damn you! I loved that girl as much as you!" shouted Patrick, heat rushing into his cheeks. Here it was again: the very same accusation Henry had lobbed at him before the citizens all those years ago. Irrelevant as it was untrue, it had been the bone of contention between them for the past thirty years. Henry blamed Patrick for Alis' death; tragic twist of fate, it was. She went with them to Council in Aes Sidhe before the war. After disappearing from the feast one night, neither brother saw her again. That is, until she reappeared some months later, heavy with child and mad as a tanner. She died shortly after giving birth to Damek.

Patrick gave the boy their mother's surname. The Bishop family were all but extinct from the annals of Bethonair nobility, saving one useless old uncle. It would never make Damek trueborn, but it did help to alleviate some of the stigma associated with his bastardy– a notion Henry should have appreciated more than anyone else. Alis had stopped nursing Damek a week after his birth. For weeks afterward, she haunted the rooftop, 'waiting for her fine 'Sidhe Lord' to take her back. Alis believed he would simply reach down from the sky, like some avenging god, and scoop her into his arms. Patrick would not chain his sister like a dog to stave her madness. Perhaps because of that lapse of judgment, she fell to her death. He didn't have a thing to do with it, but Henry would never forgive him for her loss, all the same.

Henry never let him forget, either.

"I didn't come here to rehash the past, Henry. What you accuse me of, I did not do. You know I didn't. We fought a war against the immortal tyrant who stole our sister, if you recall. A war we very nearly won, if I may be so bold? Now, it's a matter of family I've come here to discuss with you, Brother. Will you listen, or shall I leave you to your ramblings?"

Henry gave him what he assumed was his most condescending stare, stretching his bony back as straight as it would go. "You come to *me* for counsel? That's just... sad, little brother. Run through everyone loyal, have you?"

Patrick refused to take that bait. He turned to the door. "Guard," he said, allowing himself a tinge of pleasure while Henry scrambled backward like a frightened rat. "A chair, if you please? Perhaps a stool, for Lord FitzDonahugh?" When the guard came and went, Patrick seated himself. Henry eyed his brother and the waiting stool with commingled fear and mistrust. Deprived of dignity, men were little more than whipped dogs. Patrick held out a hand. "Please, Henry. Let's have a civilized discussion for once, shall we?"

Henry worried a single black tooth against his swollen lower lip. "It's a trick. You'll have that ape beat me if I try."

"I'll have him beat you if you don't. Stop this. I am not our father." Like a skittish fawn testing thin ice over a streambed, Henry lowered himself to the mildewed carpet, then crept slowly toward the stool. His eyes shifted wildly, as if the guard would burst into the cell with a cudgel at any moment. When no one came after several moments, awkwardly, he lowered his angular rump to its seat. He looked uncomfortable, disused to sitting upright like a human being. That was as well for Patrick. He preferred him disquieted. "I would ask your help with the boy, Henry."

"What boy?"

136

"Alis', of course. The only Donahugh male left in my family."

"What of him? He's a bastard. I thought you'd have him locked in with me by now?"

"I have no sons, Henry. I'm too old to try for more. After twenty-six years, I have only daughters to carry my line. The eldest of these is an ungrateful Siorai witch, like her mother."

"And? Why are you bringing this to me? The Barons will never support a bastard for Duch. Trust me, I know. You'll have to marry him to your girl and pray Wickert or Sibley don't take it into their heads to oust the Donahughs altogether. Recall what happened with Herbert O'Rearden."

"I do," Patrick squeezed through his teeth.

"What then? If you mean him to rule after you, marry him off, legitimize him. I hope the Barons don't interfere. What's the problem?"

"He's too eager for rule. He takes power before it's granted, defies my orders at every turn, and if I can't bring him to heel... the Barons will have his head on a pike. My line will end. Our grandfather's legacy, all of it... gone."

"What does this have to do with me, Patrick?" At last, a trace of the old cunning flickered to life in Henry's eyes. Patrick felt a thrill course through him at the prospect. The game was never any fun without Henry. He'd ever been his only worthy opponent. "I don't give a damn about your legacy," Henry assured him.

"Ah, but you *do* give a damn about your own, don't you?" Acute silence was his answer. Patrick detected a note of resentment in the air. *Good.* "You have an opportunity here," he went on, sensing blood in the proverbial water, "to cement your own."

"I have no legacy to speak of."

"You have two sons, Brother. Born to a Cymrian woman you wedded outside the Briton Wastes. I've taken the liberty to bring them here, to Bethany."

If possible, Henry went even whiter beneath all that hair and grime. "You wouldn't dare."

"Tis already done. They reside within these walls, where they receive regular meals, etiquette lessons, and basic schooling. Really Henry, why would you wish to leave them in that shitehole? They were half-wild, all but illiterate, and crawling with parasites when we found them."

"I wanted them kept safe... from *you*."

"You should have known you can't keep anything from me. As soon as you decided to appoint yourself some nomadic religious leader, they were as good as mine. Your wife is dead, by the way. What was her name?"

Henry heaved a sudden sob, a pathetic, mewling sound that part of Patrick enjoyed very much. He might not be his father, but he did inherit a bit of his sadism. "Bledydd."

"Lucky for you, we found them, Brother. They would have starved or perished from the same wasting sickness that killed her. Most of your flock are dead from famine, and many of the survivors have formed ragtag bands who roam the settlements, raping and pillaging. I've been told there have been atrocities such as the world has not seen for hundreds of years. You should thank me."

Henry swallowed. He was defeated, and they both knew it. His self-inflicted martyrdom deflated before Patrick's eyes. "What do you want from me?"

Patrick leaned back in his chair, folding his hands together. "I would have you back, Henry. Fully endowed. Your lands, your titles... all."

Dumfounded, Henry shook his head voraciously. "You've never forgiven a single offense in your life, Patrick. Least of all, mine."

"Whom should I pardon if not my blood?"

"You mean to use my boys against me."

"Well, I won't allow you access to them until you've proven yourself to me. These boys are Donahughs. Properly born too—if to a tribesman's daughter. No matter, we can concoct a grander origin for her. They belong here. I want them at my side, towing the family line, same as you." Henry was mute for a long while. His mind ticked through the potential benefits and pitfalls of accepting Patrick's offer. Henry was no fool, despite his irritating newfound philosophy. Patrick needed him. He knew he could

138

never be fully trusted again, but if he could maintain proper leverage, Henry could be invaluable to him— in more ways than one.

"Why now?" asked Henry softly. Patrick forced himself not to smile.

"Checks and balances, Brother. Checks and balances. More Donahughs to stand between my Barons and the throne. Simply put, I aim to remind them who rules here in the South. Given your history with Wickert and his ilk, I should think you'd be eager to upset their plans. Besides, with two more Donahugh boys in the line of succession… Alis' son must try much harder to earn the throne he aspires to."

"Ah," said Henry with a wry, grotesque grin. "The point emerges. You mean to remind him that he needs *you*. Threatened by a rising star, Patrick? I see. If he fails as a potential heir, you gain two spares. I can accept that, so long as my boys are kept from the resulting drama. I'll kill you if either of them comes to harm for your ambition."

"You're hardly in a position to make threats, Henry."

"All the same, you have my vow. Micah, for one, will only heed you at my behest. I expect you already knew as much before you bothered to come down here, didn't you? Isaac will follow Micah's example, as always. They have no reason to trust the man who imprisoned their father these past ten years."

"I do not wish to harm them, Henry. I wish to make men of them— Donahugh men. Even if Damek takes the throne, he will have no support from the aristocracy. Our House will have none. Don't you see? Your sons will be lords of Bethany. Proper Southers, no matter how the succession plays out. The Barons will fall all over themselves to support their rise."

Henry *did* see. He *was* easy to read. "You'll protect them."

"I will."

"From our nephew, chiefly."

"Of course."

"You'll take no revenge on my sons for my failures. Not ever, Patrick. Or I will strike at you in any capacity I have left."

"Yes," Patrick growled. "You've said. Again, my plans will be better served with your assistance but do not depend upon it. Remember this while you're making your threats, Henry. I'm offering you the only olive branch you'll ever get. Accept it or die here. It's up to you."

Henry was silent for a long while, absorbing the magnitude of Patrick's uncharacteristic proposal. Patrick felt no fear that he might refuse. Simply put, what choice did he have? Henry would never be the martyr he desired to be if he died in this god-forsaken hole in the ground. Furthermore, that part of him that longed to see his sons grow tall and strong would never be satisfied. He had only this one chance. Despite the duplicity of the source, any opportunity was better than none, wasn't it?

"I accept."

"Excellent." Patrick rose without aplomb. "On your feet. We must make you nominally presentable before you return to Court. I've stricken the 'Fitz' from your boys' surnames in my records. As far as any need be concerned, they were born to a noble Cymrian lady. It's enough to legitimize them."

Henry cursed. "So simply done."

Patrick paused at the door. "Of course. I'm Duch, Brother. I urge you to remember that I didn't make you a bastard nor drag you to your present circumstances. As long as you serve our house and this family well, I will elevate your sons higher than they should ever hope to rise."

"You want me in your debt."

"You *are* in my debt." Patrick took one last look at the crazed scribbling Henry etched all over his cell. The one phrase which repeated itself over and over dragged a curious scowl over his face: *He knows what lies in the darkness...* perhaps Henry was truly mad? Maybe Patrick had waited too long to redeem him? Only time would tell. Damek had to be collared before he ruined everything Patrick had spent the last three decades striving for. Reappointing his brother to Court was no subtle move. He refused to suffer only one reckless choice for heir. His Barons could rail all they liked. Patrick would be damned if he'd be forced from his throne before his life's work was complete. The boy would learn or be replaced. Patrick exited the way he came, leaving the guards to whisk his brother out of the dark and into the land of the living once more.

140

Whℰn thℰ nℰws caught thℰm up from Bethany, Damek and his outriders had just arrived at The Ferryman, within the limits of Ten Bells proper. The ride was almost twelve hours for a single horseman and nearly twenty-seven hours for an armored force. Lord Bishop and his men had made the journey in a tidy sixteen hours. Damek never traveled anywhere without fresh mounts at the rear of his line. He prided himself for the speed his priceless Bretagn thoroughbreds could muster. As always, he kept a steady network of spies and messengers at his back, guaranteeing he never lacked pertinent information on a march. It so happened that the latest message beat him and his impressive speed record by half a day. The ranger who'd brought this news had ridden all the way from Bethany in under eleven hours. He'd half-killed his horse to manage it too.

The ranger, Blane, knelt in the rushes beside Damek's booth, clearly done in. Damek ordered the man a chair, but the ranger refused it.

Blane reported, "Milord, there's no fancy way to put it, so I'll just give it straight. The Duch has released Henry of Bethany, Lord FitzDonahugh, from his long internment."

Damek's spoon paused midway between his mouth and a steaming bowl of rabbit stew. Violet eyes flashed below his coal-black brows. "Say again, Ranger?"

"Lord FitzDonahugh has been freed, milord. He's been granted rooms within the interior Keep and the use of Duch Patrick's personal surgeon. He's ailing, it seems, but is expected to recover in due course."

Martin scratched at his beard, eyes going to the ceiling with a rueful smirk. Damek and his guard weren't alone in *The Ferryman*'s dining room. Dozens of wealthy travelers gathered nearby, eating meat pie and tarts or tugging at their tankards. None were likely to have missed Lord Bishop's colorful reaction, but few dared to eyeball a man accompanied by so many swords. Damek and his officers were seated at the rear-right corner in a well-appointed part of the Inn reserved for gentry and wealthy Merchers. Six high booths were set into the private dining area, divided from common patronage by a slim paneled wall. A stately fireplace dominated the center of their alcove, which blasted comforting warmth between each row. Only Damek's officers were afforded a fine meal with the Lord of Clare. His rear-guard and uniformed regulars occupied rooms in the dormitory next door. There they would take their meals and sleep on cots in the hall. Lord Bishop himself would claim the lavish suite on *The Ferryman*'s top floor– leaving his officers to bunk at the lower levels. As for this ranger, his reward would be a hot bowl of gruel in the stables outside. Such was the messenger's lot in life.

"You're sure of this?" Damek let his bread splash into his broth, rubbing his fingers together to dislodge any crumbs. He gave Martin a long look. Martin smiled without mirth.

"I am, milord. I came as soon as I learned of it. By now, the whole of Bethany must know," Blane replied. He kept his head low, as was proper in such exalted company. Damek had used this man before, he vaguely recalled, looking into his face. The ranger was one of his best riders, and a grand tracker, too, if he wasn't mistaken. Though he was vastly irritated by the news Blane carried, Damek was impressed with the speed by which it arrived.

"Understood. Consider yourself promoted. Speak to my steward at the eleventh bell. He'll register your new rank and pay. First Ranger sounds about right for smashing my speed record. Also, inform him that I wish you to have a proper meal and a bunk downstairs for the night."

Blane couldn't conceal his genuine surprise. Rangers were rarely promoted, remembered even less, and never granted such fine accommodations. His grimy cheeks glowed with renewed admiration for his lord. Damek was well-loved for a reason. That this affection was carefully calculated made no never-mind to men on the receiving end of his generosity.

"Th-thank you, milord."

Damek waved him away. "If that's all?"

"Well, ah…"

Martin stood up, knuckles white against the table. "Speak damn you, boy. What else have you ridden so hard to say?"

The Ranger bowed low again. "The FitzDonahugh, that is, Lord Henry… he has two sons, milord. The Duch announced them to the Court this morning." He withered under Martin's glower. "His grace named them true-born sons of the Donahugh Clan, milord, and he, ah, had their names added to the line of succession."

Martin resumed his seat, mouth twisted. "I suppose he had the exchequer sign and read the document before every courtier in Bethany?"

"Yes, milord," Blane answered with a guilty frown.

"Is there anything *else*?" Damek's tone blew as cold as the wind over a distant mountaintop.

Blane cowered. "No, milord."

"Then go. Do as instructed."

Blane backed out as fast as he could manage.

"Well," Martin said when he'd gone. "The old bear still has claws. I think I said as much. He can still take you out of the running altogether."

"Did you know about these boys, Martin?" Damek inquired, around a mouthful of stew. His typical, slightly bored mask was fixed again upon his face.

"He kept that little tidbit close to his chest. It seems I must have fallen out of favor, somehow. Can't imagine why?"

"Martin, I doubt even *he* knew what he was going to do with them until an opportunity presented itself. He makes much of being some grand strategist, but in truth, he's merely an opportunist with a cruel streak. He never does a damned thing that isn't meant to hurt someone else and waits for these moments with singular pleasure. If I know my uncle, he hung on to the truth of these boys just to spite Henry, personally. If I hadn't displeased him by daring to inspire meager confidence in his Barons, he'd probably have squatted over the knowledge until he died, or Henry dared to before Patrick was done humiliating him."

"Henry rebelled, My Lord. That was quite public."

"Doesn't matter. He locked the man in a stinking cell for almost ten years. There can be only two reasons he didn't have him killed. One, he was waiting for the day Henry might be useful to him again. Two, there's no sport Patrick enjoys more than pitting family against one another. He'll juggle us all like pins. Any who dare falter in rotation will lie where they fall. In truth, I feel for those poor boys. They have no idea what hell they've just been inducted into."

"Aren't you alarmed?"

"Of course I am," Damek said, tearing into his bread with a faraway look in his eyes. "It's Una who will suffer for all of this, you know? If I don't bring her back, he'll supplant me but won't kill me. No. He'll grant me the Henry treatment until I'm needed again. If I bring her home, he means to dangle her in front of all the men in the family– a carrot before the cart."

"Whatever your uncle's intent, I doubt his Barons will support those boys. They had no love for Henry after Dumnain and have even less for him now. You're the obvious choice, no matter how your uncle spins things," said Martin, toying with his tankard. "What will you do?"

"What I set out to do. He's only prompted to act because he fears I'll succeed with Una. We all know his health is failing. It's the worst-kept secret in Innisfail. At best, he has a few years left. Meanwhile, I am young, capable, and best placed to take power. The knowledge must gnaw at his guts every night."

"Here's to the success of our mission then, My Lord. Though I caution you, and you must hear me on this score— Henry of Bethany... now there's a man you must be wary of. Just as Patrick is cunning and manipulative, Henry is cautious and clever. He's trouble, I vow it. He once held the love of the people, much as you do now. Never forget it."

Damek's smile did not reach his eyes. "Never fear, Martin. The Duch isn't the only one who knows how to plan a decent intrigue. The difference between us is our approach. He sees only the rules of the game as he makes it."

"And you, what do you see?"

"There are no rules, Martin," Damek's teeth flashed very white, wolfish. "And I stopped playing his game a long time ago."

Prima Moura

ᴨ.ᴇ. ᴦᴼ8
19, ᴅᴏʀ 걷ᴀᴍᴨᴀ
ꜰᴇʀᴨᴅᴀʟᴇ

"**Y**ou!" Ben dragged the Siorai noblewoman from the doorway and dropped her heavily onto the couch. Rian lurched to her side, but Ben stalled her with an imperious wag of the finger. His gleaming eyes promised he'd do worse to Rian if she interfered. "Stay," he warned and fixed his attention upon his intended target. "Explain this now while I'm asking politely."

"Explain what?" Una's expression teetered between nausea and shock.

"Don't play with me, girl. Why are they after you?"

"I'm... not sure."

Crossing his arms, he pushed his face into hers, eyes narrow. "Oh, *really?*" Rian made a fumble for his elbow. Shrugging her off, he growled at Una. "You're going to tell me what in the hells is going on, or, by Herne, I'll wring what's left of your neck." Ben had never maltreated a woman in his life, but just then, he seriously considered altering that policy. He was owed answers. If he must shake them out of her, so be it. Una met his glare with a deep reservoir of calm. Something slid behind her face— an unseen energy coiled there beneath her skin. Without realizing it, her fingertips came bare centimeters from his jaw. He backed away so fast that he nearly tripped over his own feet. That indefinable

145

sound he'd heard when she touched the first Corsair hovered in the air between them like an afterimage. His skin crawled.

She gave him a slow, smug smile. "Touch me again. I dare you."

"You wouldn't."

"Why don't you try it and find out?"

Bluff called; his nostrils flared. Instead, he scowled down at her with all the masculine derision he could muster. "Three times, I've been obliged to kill to help you."

"Twice, I think you mean? You helped yourself to a hank of venison the first time and left me tied to a bloody tree."

He shrugged. "Still counts."

"You *can't* be serious?" scoffed Una, incredulous.

"You're alive, aren't you? Now, answer the question."

"You're one to talk, *tuaithe*. Why is a Dannan lordling traipsing around the Greensward, dressed as a stinking vagrant and murdering for uishge? Hm? You tell me that– and I'll tell you whatever you want to know."

Ben bared his teeth. "Ladies first."

They stared each other down for quite a while. Having grown uncomfortable at the tension between them, Rian resumed her seat by the hearth. Ben didn't budge. Una looked away first.

"Fine... but I'm not sure where to start."

"Try the beginning."

"All right then. Ah, you might have heard there's been some trouble between the Cloister and Parliament?"

Ben's brows cinched up. "What does that have to do with–"

"Prima Moura, isn't it?" Rian cut in.

"How'd you know?"

She pointed. "Your tattoos."

Una glanced down at her exposed arms. "Oh. *Right.*"

"You're the Domina, aren't you?"

"Not by choice."

"I see."

"*I* don't," rumbled Ben. "Why were you taken from the Cloister, only to be hunted down by your men after? It doesn't make sense to me."

"I wasn't taken. I left of my own accord."

Ben went quiet for a moment. That hadn't occurred to him at all. "Then, how did you end up with Rawly and his lot?"

"I trusted the wrong person," she said. "Rawly caught me on the docks at Drogheda. My escape was foiled, you see?"

"In Brida's name, why were you trying to leave?"

"I meant to start over in Scotia, or perhaps Bretagne. It hardly matters now, does it?"

"All right... let me get this straight. You made arrangements to leave the Cloister but were set upon by mercenaries from Bethany. I'm assuming this person you shouldn't have trusted arranged to have both you and your abductors assassinated on the road. Again, why? Why would someone want you dead?"

"Do you have linen between your ears? I *just told you*. I'm the Moura Domina. Doma Drem is my grandmother."

"That means nothing to me."

"My mother was Arrin, the eldest...." Una said, nodding slowly as if teaching a child how to speak.

Ben ignored her condescending tone. He knew that name but couldn't quite remember why it was important. Something to do with the Doma, and... he'd had a bit too much of Rian's tea tonight.

"This means what, exactly?" Both girls looked at him like he'd asked why water was wet. He bristled, spreading his hands. "Am I not speaking the common tongue? Explain it to me."

"Do you live under a rock? Everyone knows who Arrin Moura was, you fool," said Rian.

Una rolled her eyes at his blank face. "My mother was Queen of Tairngare, inasmuch as anyone can actually rule in the Red City. Nothing more than a figurehead, really. Do you get it now?"

Ah. That *Arrin... great gods... you are a fool.*

Slowly, a deep crease formed between Ben's brows. Drem Moura used Arrin to reach for more power in Tairngare, and it had cost the girl her life. That's what he recalled anyway. Supposedly, the Doma had something new up her sleeve that everyone was incensed over. He'd heard a few snippets of gossip swirling through the North about this more recently but couldn't have cared less if he tried. Milesian politics were as pointless and impermanent as a cloud tracing over the sun. He could never keep the details straight.

"I'm sorry about your mother, but why does this matter? She died years ago, I think."

"My grandmother is determined to repeat her previous mistake by holding me up to Parliament as the next Queen. I assume she believes that by forcing me into this, she can instill a Moura Dynasty. The Commons are unamused, and frankly, so am I."

More silly Tairnganese politics. "Mercenaries from Bethany kidnaped you because your grandmother declared you Queen... and Corsairs from the Citadel want to eliminate you for this reason?"

"Isn't it obvious?" Rian broke in with a huff. She held out a hand to the girl on the couch. "This is Una Moura, daughter of Arrin Moura, granddaughter of Drem Moura... and that makes her father Duch Patrick Donahugh, you dolt. Honestly, you *have* been living under a rock, haven't you? Lady Moura here is the heir apparent to the two greatest cities in Eire."

A sudden, irreversible heat clawed its way into Ben's throat. The room vibrated at the edges of his vision as if every nerve in his body decided to stand up all at once.

"*What?*"

Una Moura *Donahugh* stared back at him, visibly surprised by the venom in his tone. "Patrick tried to use my mother to take Tairngare before I was born. I'm sure you've heard of that, at least. Not long after, your High King was forced to wrestle the North from him." She looked anywhere but at him. His silent glare must have unnerved her. "Anyway, he took her against her will and held her captive until I was born. I fled Bethany when I was thirteen. In the South, I am his property, you see? He means to reclaim me."

I have soiled my hands for a fucking Donahugh?

Clenching and unclenching his fists, he cleared his throat. He couldn't believe his rotten luck.

148

"What were you thinking just now?"

"You don't want to know."

"Fair enough."

He should have left her in the woods… he should have dropped her on this doorstop and walked away… he should have… he grew more incensed by the breath.

"Who helped you escape the Cloister?" He should have walked to Navan that night and drank himself to death in the *Bowman's Cross*. Or walked to Slane, maybe? Hells, he could have gone *anywhere* else. If only he hadn't been drunk, hungry, and curious, he would have avoided this mess from the start. Better yet, if he hadn't pretended to hold some moral superiority over her Souther captors, they might all be alive, and Patrick fucking Donahugh's daughter would have met whatever fate she deserved by association.

He was furious with her. Livid with himself. Positively irate with the Gods. This was a sick, cosmic joke.

It *must* be.

"They're irrelevant—the point: they work at Vanna Nema's behest. Nema offered me a way out. I was desperate and stupid enough to take her at her word. All of this is my fault. My irresponsible cowardice. I'm sorry." Her apparent sincerity didn't assuage Ben's anger in the least.

"What will you do now, my lady?" asked Rian, flinching from Ben's thunderous, disapproving face. He couldn't help it. There wasn't a name in all of Innisfail that he loathed more.

The daughter of Patrick Donahugh, he derided himself. *You've saved your worst enemy's child.*

"I don't know. I haven't exactly had time to think it over," said Una, absently touching the wound at her temple. Her eyes popped at Ben. "Will you please stop glaring at me like that? You're making me nervous."

"Sorry," Ben lied.

"Look, I know how your people feel about the Duch. Just so you know, he's not my favorite person, either. I didn't ask for any of this, and I can't help who my family is."

She was right, but that didn't make him feel any better. Patrick Donahugh was the author of his present circumstances. There wasn't a man on earth Ben loathed more. He let out a long hard breath.

Calm down.

"Well," interrupted Rian, throwing up her hands. "Let's get you back to bed. We can figure out what to do later–"

"No," Ben refused. "We can't stay here."

Rian turned on him. "What? Why not? She should be abed. We might not get the door fixed tonight, but we can at least close it off...."

"No," he repeated. "Whoever sent those beasts is bound to know they've been destroyed. They're unlikely to stop now if they've gone to this much trouble."

"Wait, just a moment–" Una began.

Ben held up a hand, cutting her rebuttal short. "Do I need to spell it out for you? It's not safe here for you, for me, or for anyone around you. We have to go as soon as possible."

"We?"

"*I* can't leave... are you daft? This doesn't have the first thing to do with me. It's you two who should go!" Rian protested, hands on hips.

Ben prayed to Danu for patience. "If you want to wait for Corsairs to follow these beasts, by all means. Do as you like, Mistress. I thought you were smarter than that." He scrubbed a hand over his face. Of all the random encounters in the world, Una just had to be a Donahugh. This was going to get messy. Bound to become a bloody political carnival, no doubt. The thought incensed him. What did he care for Milesian politics? Which temporary body occupied whichever impermanent throne was all the same to him! All he wanted was an ogham stone, to return to his life in the border towns, to drink, dice, and fornicate his miserable way through his remaining time in Eire. Ben wanted to be no one. He'd no wish to involve himself in these pathetic Milesian power struggles. He should leave the girls here to fend for themselves. Hadn't he spilled enough blood already? Yet... something else nibbled at the corners of his mind—something he hadn't considered until now.

150

"Where will we go, hm?" Rian asked. "Where *can* she go, where she would be safe? The colonies? Bretagne? To the High King?" She paused when the color drained from Ben's cheeks. His eyes flew wide as if she'd just imparted the secret to life itself. "Siora," she said. "I was being sarcastic, you know. The High King doesn't involve himself in Eirean politics. Unless someone is marching on the border, why should he care?"

"I'm sorry I got you into this, Mistress... Rian, is it?" Una offered, despite Ben's comments. Rian waved her away. Instead, she watched Ben closely. He said nothing, but he might as well have been shouting.

"You can't be serious? You might cross that border without repercussions, but her? You're deluding yourself. You'll have to apply for a permit at the Sidhe Consulate in Ten Bells and wait for your case to be reviewed. It'll take months to be considered. By then, she could be dead."

"He can't cross on his own either," Una said.

Ben rounded on her. "What do you know about anything?"

"Stop assuming everyone you meet is a fool, *tuaithe*."

"What do you mean he can't cross? The stone? Is that why–" both parties ignored Rian's questions while they glared at one another.

This time, Ben broke eye contact first. The damned girl had far too much sand for her own good. "I must think this over. Get packed. Only the essentials, mind. I'm not a bloody mule! When I return, be ready to leave."

Rian stammered, "Wait just a minute! You can't order me to leave my own home!"

"If you want to live and possibly make something out of this situation, you'll do what I say," he cleared his throat, ignoring Una's suspicious glare. "I'll be back." He needed to get away, outdoors, where the cold air waited. His thoughts were a riotous jumble only the night wind could untangle.

SIMPLE. OBVIOUS. WHY HADN'T HE pieced it together from the first? Ben truly was a blithering dolt. All this time, he'd been trying to avoid involving himself in Milesian troubles... and the answer to *his* had just dropped into his unsuspecting, ungrateful lap.

You're a spectacular fool!

Donahugh's child– indeed. His heart hammered against his ribs. His palms were clammy. Why had it taken him so long to realize the advantage here? He was so determined to avoid any inconveniences that he'd almost wholly missed the glaring point.

Una was a Moura, but she was also a *Donahugh*!

As much as he loathed her father and the Southers in general, the fact that she happened to be Patrick's daughter made her extremely useful to him. Who would most benefit if he removed her from the playing field altogether? If the Moura faced internal conflicts in the Red City, Tairngare's government would be unstable– weakened to advance from the South. This was a flaw Patrick must be salivating to exploit. Whoever sent those Corsairs to 'clean up' after Rawly and his men knew what the Duch would do next.

The girl was fodder for the ambitions of others.

Unless she could escape to the High King's Court... Midhir would want to know about this. He would want to eliminate any claim Duch Donahugh could manipulate to rule over a unified Eire. The Ard Ri did not want another war. He would be happy to intercede in this matter, Ben knew. If only someone could hand the High King complete control over the situation before it came to that. Someone with no inconvenient ties to either faction in Eire. Someone with nothing left to lose... someone like Ben.

The knowledge brought a fresh current of electric anticipation with it. Pacing around the front of the battered cottage toward the North road, his nerves felt like they might burst into flame over his skin. He took a deep breath to still himself. He could go home! Not to Rosweal. Not to Navan. No more border hovels and backwaters. Home. To his own life– his position, his family, his name. The girl was a free pass back to Aes

Sidhe. This was *beautiful*. He mustn't embellish a single detail. He'd saved her life three times without having the first clue who she was or why anyone wished her harm. Better yet, she could readily testify to that. By bringing her to the Bri Leith, he'd prevent another bloody conflict in Eire and stall any future invasions of Aes Sidhe from the South. Ben might be welcomed back into the Ard Ri's court with open arms!

Ben felt like he'd just discovered a pot of gold under a thorn bush. There were, however, a few minor details that needed seeing to before he could make this thrilling new prospect a reality. Item one: he was forbidden to cross the border upon pain of death. A trifle this was *not*. He would either have to take the girl to the Consulate in Ten Bells to await a permit to cross or brave the border alone. If the first, he would likely be turned away at the gate or be forced to wait months for a temporary pardon. Worse, the Ambassador could simply seize the girl and negotiate with Tairngare or Bethany for her release. Odds were, if he took her to the Consulate, Midhir would never hear a word about Una... or of Ben's involvement. That would not do. Not in the least. What was the point to any of this if it didn't benefit him too?

The latter option was far riskier.

Far deadlier.

He'd need help... someone who could get word to Bri Leith and negotiate a temporary reprieve for himself before he attempted to cross with an Eirean fugitive. There was just one individual in Innisfail he knew of that could help him manage this. The only person that might help him, regardless of his current standing in Bri Leith. He had to get word to his uncle, Diarmid. Moreover, Ben needed a place to lie low until he could get in touch with him. Since the girl was bound to be pursued through every town, hamlet, and village in the North, there was only one logical place Ben could go.

He winced at this further complication.

He must return to Rosweal.

153

"I WONDERED HOW LONG IT would take you to figure out how this could work in your favor," mocked Una as he boosted her onto Vixen's back. He shot her a look that should have made her blush. Instead, she blew an exaggerated breath through her pursed lips. "What a shame. I haven't any gold or uishge to pay you with, either."

Shoving her foot viciously into the stirrup, he waited for her answering hiss of pain before he jabbed a finger at her. "Let's get this straight. You simply appeared in my life. I didn't leap into yours, causing trouble and mucking up your plans. Did I?"

Her lip curled. "I suppose not."

"Then shut your mouth, hm? If it's occurred to me that this situation might— just might— have a decent ending for me, then so be it. You'll just have to make peace with that, or I'll slog off, and you can figure out the rest on your own. Ten Bells is that way," he tugged his thumb behind him.

Rian hobbled up to the gate where Vixen was tethered, already huffing from the weight of the pack at her back. Ben had ranged over two miles to find the old nag, and it took him quite a while to calm her down enough to follow him back. Vixen nervously pawed the ground beneath her hooves. She didn't care for the foul stench of the two deceased beasts nearby nor the hostility of the people holding her reins. Rian patted her flank as she walked by.

"What are you two arguing about now?"

"Nothing of import," Ben replied, with a narrow eye on Una. "Only that we should stick to the game trails, far from the roads."

"Surely we can't just stroll across the border," said Rian, crossing her arms. "I'm not taking another step until you explain yourself."

"He's exiled," Una suggested helpfully. He chewed the inside of his cheek at her, but she ignored him. "Seems an important one too. What? I told you I wasn't stupid, *Ard Tiarne*."

"I liked you better when you couldn't talk," he said.

"Ard Tiarne?" Rian choked back a laugh. "Do you know what that means, Lady Moura?"

154

"Given the amount of gold in that right ear, it seems we should be honored," Una made a rude sound. "Means he used to be a big someone in Aes Sidhe, doesn't it? In the past tense, of course."

Ben shouldered his small pack and readjusted his weapons without comment. If he lingered too near her, he might reach up and jerk her into the mud, the ungrateful, waspish, little wench. Maybe he should leave her and be on his way after all? It would cost him his first solid chance to go home in almost three decades, but he just might finish the job the Corsairs started at this rate.

"That makes us quite a pair then, doesn't it? 'Queen Donahugh.'" He watched her grin fade with intense pleasure. "We don't have time to discuss pedigree at the moment, do we?" He gestured up the muddy lane toward the west. "Shall we?"

"Which is it?" Rian prodded. "O'Ruiadh, Bres, O'Donnell... come on, there's only six High Lords in Aes Sidhe. What do they call you–"

"Ben," he said with finality. He grabbed Vixen's bridle and turned up the road, cursing long and loud in his own tongue. Una shifted uncomfortably in the saddle. Rian was forced to stumble up the lane behind them. "My name's Ben Maeden, and that's as good as you're going to get."

PART TWO

EXILES

MISERY, IN COMPANY

n.e. ſ08
2J, ðOR samna
navan

B en, Una, and Rian spent the better part of two days wandering
the Greensward southeast of the Boyne and avoiding the roads.
As expected, the weather was dreadful. After an evening, squalls
had stripped the leaves from nearly every tree. A stark wasteland spread
before their eyes– full of drab browns, dull greys, and mournful blacks.
The only sounds were spattering raindrops, creaking limbs, and the
steady chattering of their teeth. Omnipresent mud ruled all. It seeped
into their boots, dragged at their cloaks, and wormed its clammy way
into their stores to mingle with their swiftly dwindling supplies.

The girls bore up better than he thought they would. Other than a
few questions pertaining to direction or to clarify a plan, he didn't hear
a single word of complaint from either of them. He was both surprised
by their steely-eyed determination and irritated by it. It was rather
embarrassing that they should feel less daunted by the abysmal climate
than he. What sort of Sidhe loathed the wilderness? The shame he felt at
that thought amplified his general insouciance.

Ben would lean into the wind a bit and dream of distant taprooms.
It was easy enough to resist temptation for the first day or so. When
they came too close to a town, the flash of steel winked at them through
the trees. Everywhere they went, Tairnganeah patrolled in force. Rather

than risk being seen, they would press on. In short, order, playing it safe lost its appeal. By late afternoon of the second day, the persistent fog they'd been muddling through graduated to a torrential downpour. They spent a sleepless night under a canopy of hardy pine trees that offered little protection against the elements. Most of the next grim day was spent hacking and sniffling into their soaking wet cowls.

As their third night in the Greensward loomed, they were all sodden, shivering, and despondent. Ben conceded defeat. They must find somewhere to dry out, a place to sleep, and something warm to eat. With few trustworthy options nearby, Ben had to make a decision fast. Navan might be the safest place outside of Rosweal to spend a night. Warmth. Food. Sleep. *Uishge*— siren songs, all, lured them through the trees like a match in a cave. At dusk on the third day, they hesitated outside Navan Village, wretched and desperate. Rian sidled up to him, holding her already soaked hood up against the rain. Her thin face was as blue as her eyes.

"W-will we... be safe in there?"

Ben patted the little river stone resting below the neckline of his tunic to ensure it was snug and secure. He'd strung it through two strips of leather this time, just in case. Rian's arcane skills were no match for the craftsman who'd carved his previous ogham charm, but they would do. He didn't look quite so much like Ben Maeden as he had before. Maybe he was a little too tall, his bones a little too fine, or perhaps his eyes were a mite too bright? No matter. Only those who knew him well would be given real pause. He was satisfied that he could walk around without drawing attention to himself.

"I don't see we have much choice," he said, meeting Una's wary expression over Rian's head. She, too, drowned upright in Vixen's saddle. Una made a reflexive gesture, proposing he make the call. If Ben chose wrong, they might be forced to fight their way out. He was too bloody tired to fight. Too hungry, too wet, too cold... and far too sober, all told. He needed to dry off, eat, and drink himself to sleep– in that order. "Rian, I'll need you to loan me one of those fainne."

"Not blo... ody likely," she argued, her lips purple.

"Do you fancy freezing to death?" She didn't answer immediately, but Ben knew what her response would be. The longer they waited, the colder it would get.

She dug into her pocket with a stern scowl. "Jus...t so you know, I'm keeping tally."

He shifted the coin to his belt. "Course you are. Look, I've been here before. If we pay the innkeeper well, he'll overlook the oddity of our circumstances and say nothing about us to anyone. I'll wager on it." he nodded up at Una. "Cover your face, and whatever you do, don't say a word. That haughty Tairnganese trill is a dead giveaway."

She muttered something unkind under her breath, but he ignored her. Taking Vixen by the bit, he led them downhill. The old mare nickered, excited by the scent of home and the prospect of her cozy stall, no doubt. He felt a genuine pang of pity for the poor creature, being treated as she had been for the last few days. Maybe it would be best to trade her for a more spirited animal? He didn't have time to consider the matter too carefully as they rounded the muddy intersection near the *Bowman's Cross*. Turning down a dark side-alley toward the stable, he was grateful for the poorly lit streets all over again. Tonight, the lamps were lower than they had been upon his first visit, and far less light shone through firmly fastened shutters in the tavern proper.

As they neared the stable, the proprietor's lad looked up from the tack he was polishing. He was so happy to see Vixen that he scarcely glanced at either girl. Ben knew he liked this place. It wasn't Rosweal, but in a pinch, it served. The stables were largely devoid of horses, which suited their purposes quite well. Most folks had better sense than to travel through a Dor Samna deluge. Ben could only pray that any advancing Tairnganeah would eschew humble little Navan altogether. There were undoubtedly much finer inns and more illustrious company, a short march back east. Ben handed the boy an extra two coppers for his tact and care. The proprietor's son slid the coins into his vest and led them inside with nary a word. Enveloped in a blast of heat and smoke, both girls sighed. Ben slid off his gloves and placed his florid fingers on the bar to thaw.

161

The innkeeper took one look at Ben's sealskin cowl and gave him a gap-toothed grin. "Good to see ye again, Master. What'll it be?"

"A single room? For me n'me sisters?"

The proprietor hardly glanced at the girls, but a slight twitch to his lower lip said he was far from stupid. "Very good, sir. The same room is available. I'll have me boy bring ye a cot and some peat for yer hearth. Will ye have hot water and a tub brought up? A rack for yer wet things, perhaps?"

As polite as he was, Ben repressed a groan at the cost this would likely incur. "Aye," he said, sliding Rian's royal fainne across the bar. "I trust ye'll have the means to make change for this?"

Gold sparkled from the innkeeper's dilated pupils. He licked his lips. "Indeed, sir!" he scooped the heavy coin into his palm and shoved it deep in his apron before any wandering eye might catch its gleam. "I'll get that ready for ye, directly. Ye shall have extra blankets, pillows, and all the ale ye wish for on the house. Also, I have some ladies' things set by from me own dear wife. I'll have me lad bring those up as well, shall I?"

"Just the thing. If ye will, the lasses will take their porridge upstairs."

Grinning happily, the proprietor poured Ben a towering tankard of spiced ale and a full pint of uishge to match. Ben plopped down, eying this bounty with a fat lump in his throat.

"If ye'll follow me, ladies," said the innkeeper, coming around the bar with a heavy set of swinging keys. "We'll get ye sorted."

"Wait," stalled Rian, reaching around Ben to grab both his tankard and the glass of uishge. He moved to stop her, but she batted his hands away. Una attempted a hideous wink as they were herded upward.

BEN FELT SOMETHING BRUSH HIS elbow. He'd fallen asleep at the bar; arms wrapped tightly around his tankard. The innkeeper, for once, wasn't wiping anything. He leaned over the bar, arms splayed, palms down.

"And to ye, good sirs." His voice carried a bit further than it should have. "What will ye have?" Ben shook himself. Someone stood near the rear exit, on his right. Several someones, in fact, escorted by the stable lad, with a poorly concealed panic evident on his face. Ben sat up, suddenly alert as a hare. Three men, wearing the black and gold emblazoned cuirasses of the Citadel Corsairs, waited impatiently for service at the opposite end of the bar. Ben dipped his nose into his pint, feigning drunken disinterest. Each bore the typical Citadel-issued rapier sheathed in their belts, and their silver spurs were slung low over their ankles— cavalry officers, no less. Their heavy grey cloaks dripped lakes into the rushes beneath their boots, and due to the warmth from the peat-fed hearth, tendrils of steam curled over their shoulders. Ben took a long pull from his lukewarm ale and observed them from the corner of his eye. One of them spared Ben a cursory sneer. His companions seemed more interested in the innkeeper and his wares.

The tallest of the three, marked out by his golden torc as a captain, dropped a fistful of coppers onto the bar. "For our mounts," he demanded in his nasally Tairnganese drawl. "There's more where that came from if I find they're brushed and clean come morning."

The innkeeper cleared his throat. "O'course, sir. How many beds will ye need? We have only two rooms left, but I can have me lad set cots in the loft, above the stables–"

"That won't be necessary. We'll split the two rooms. There are five of us. Two beds to a room, I hope?"

"Beggin' yer pardon, sir, but no. I have cots aplenty if that will do?"

"I suppose it must, though my men won't thank you for it," the captain said sourly. "We're accustomed to better service."

"Porridge and ale, on the house, sir. Boy, get upstairs and see to them rooms." He handed over his heavy ring of keys. On his way, the lad sent Ben a non-verbal warning. Message received. Ben set his empty tankard down as quietly as he could and relinquished his stool.

With a pointed interest in Ben, the Corsair stepped in front of him as he neared the stairs. "You," he sized Ben up. "You're rather tall."

"So I've been told." Ben tried to step around him. The smaller, stockier soldier pressed a gauntleted fist into Ben's chest. Ben froze.

The look on the proprietor's face was mild, but the tension in his jaw belied his neutrality. He seemed well aware of the danger.

"You a... what're they called?" the Corsair's nose cinched up. "A 'faerie'? That why you look like that? Yana, what do you think?"

The third soldier shrugged; he was more interested in the tankard of ale the innkeeper hastily placed in front of him. "Don't care. Ask him if he's seen our fugitive."

"I hear you're all deformed," laughed the man with his hand on Ben's sternum. "Born without cocks or brains. You have a cock, faerie?"

Ben took a deep, stilling breath. If he killed this man, he'd have to fight all of them at once, alone. He was damned good in an open field, but close quarters like these were nowhere near as promising. Ben held his tongue while the two soldiers laughed at his expense.

Their captain wasn't as amused. He commandeered Ben's discarded stool. "That's enough. You may follow him upstairs for a peep and tickle if that's what you're after, Dara?"

Dara's hand slid away, and his smile faded. "We're looking for a girl. She's about five-and-a-half feet tall, amber eyes, curvy. Loads of tattoos. You see a girl like that, faerie?"

"No," replied Ben, straight-faced.

"If you had a cock, you'd remember her. Warm, brown skin. Sweet, full mouth. Sure you haven't seen her?"

"Sergeant," warned the captain, sipping at his tankard. He twisted to focus on Ben, his face stiff as a stone. The captain was tall for a Milesian and broad through the shoulder. He had an unmistakable, aristocratic tilt to his jaw. The Corsairs of the Citadel— which defended both Parliament and the city gates— were most often selected from the grandest houses in Tairngare. To achieve the rank of captain so young, he must belong to a relatively important family. He wore his hair in traditional, foppish Tairnganese fashion: long braids bedecked with golden beads and unpolished gems. "What's your name?" he asked, his tone casual.

"Ben."

"Just Ben?"

"Maeden."

The captain held his tankard in front of him. "That a Souther name, Ben?"

"No. My folk're from the West, near Fenn."

"Ah, I see," he took another sip while Dara moved around Ben in a slow, calculating circle. Yana attacked a plate of bread the innkeeper placed on the bar, heedless of the interrogation. "Tell me, how'd you come by that fine cloak? Last I checked, there aren't many seals in Fenn, being landlocked and all."

"Bought it off a tinker's cart in Ten Bells. Seemed a good investment at the time. Proved handy this week, sure."

"What brings a half-breed from Fenn to the Greensward?"

"He's got a nice bit of steel in his belt there, Captain. Sidhe make if I'm not mistaken. Real longsword." Dara whistled appreciably.

"Answer the question, Master Maeden," the captain persisted.

"I'm a trader."

Dara slid around Ben to kick open the front door. "Everyone but the two of you," he pointed from the proprietor back to Ben. "Out. Now."

There weren't many patrons, but the few there were rushed from their seats, abandoning tankards, card games, and the odd pipe.

The innkeeper backed away from the bar, raising his palms. "I don't want no trouble, Sirs. I run a respectable establishment."

"Shut it, you," ordered Yana, over a mouthful of bread and cheese. His right hand patted the rapier at his hip. Dara stalked to the stable door, his eyes on Ben. If he called for the men outside, things would get ugly in here, fast.

Ben risked a glance at the innkeeper. "Just came for a bed and some ale, fellas. No need for all this."

"I'll decide that," said the captain. "A villager saw a very large man with two females pass over the High Road some miles back. Told me he paid attention because he found it odd that they would head into the woods rather than make use of the road. The weather being foul as it is...."

Dara moved to push open the back door. *Think, damn you, think!* Just as Ben's fingers flexed over his pommel, a high-pitched voice wafted down the rough wooden stairs. Her hair damp from a bath and wearing an overlarge, misshapen dress that had seen more years than she had, Rian stepped down beside the stable lad, her blue eyes wide.

"Brother, I left ye some bath water. Will ye order me an ale and... oh, what's all this?"

The Corsairs' heads swiveled toward her simultaneously. The captain launched to his feet, still holding his tankard. "You there, come down here!" Rian obeyed, looking every inch the frightened country girl.

"Oh my," she gasped, strolling into the taproom with exaggerated timidity. "What has me brother done, sir?"

Blinking at her pretty face, the captain frowned. "This man is your brother?"

Rian edged around Sergeant Dara to stand at Ben's side. "He is. What's this all about?"

"I'll ask the questions, mistress. Dara?"

"Aye," he drew his dirk and jabbed it at the stable boy. "To her room, now." Watching them head upward, Rian slid her fingers over Ben's forearm, applying light but reassuring pressure.

"Where is she?" the captain's attention honed on Rian.

"Where is who?"

Ben didn't have the first bloody clue what was happening. Rian dug her nails into his wrist, and he took the hint. He allowed her arm to wind through his as if she sought protection from these vicious armed men.

The captain exhaled through his nose. "The other girl. You were seen, mistress. 'A larger than average man, leading two women away from the road.' If you don't tell me where she is, it will go worse for you. Stay right where you are, old man." He didn't turn to watch the innkeeper place his hands back on the bar.

"There's only the two of us, sir," deflected Rian with perfect innocence. Clearly, the innkeeper had sent his son up to warn the girls. Ben found that very interesting and entirely unexpected. Why would someone who balked at Rian's family go out of his way for two supposed 'half-breeds' now and endanger his boy like this? Ben hoped he'd get the chance to ask him.

166

Dara stomped back downstairs, shaking his head at his captain. "Nothing. Unless this one—" he pointed at Ben— "hid her somewhere outside. She isn't here. I searched every room, every window, every cupboard."

"Girl," the captain crossed his arms. "Where are you from?"

Damn it.

"Fenn, sir. Round the Shannon. Why? What's me brother done? Are we in some kind o'trouble?"

"Could be if you don't start telling the truth."

At last, Ben found his voice. "My sister doesn't lie. We're on're way home from a rather successful trip to Tara."

"What is the nature of your business?"

Ben opened his mouth to reply, but Rian beat him to it.

"I'm a midwife, sir. A healer, if ye like. I tend to the ailin,' and me brother sells me remedies at market."

"What remedies?"

"Herbs, tinctures, and the like. For burns, scrapes, head pains… ye see?"

Dara sheathed his dirk. "Got a hitch in her step. Like I said, all faeries are disfigured somehow," he spat into the rushes near her hem. She pulled a genuine face in revulsion.

"You gonna ask her if she has a cock next?" Yana giggled into his tankard. Dara opened his mouth to retort, but the captain cut him off.

"Quiet, both of you! All right, mistress. What would you recommend, for a toothache, say?"

"Willow bark, four times a day with tea. But if there's an infection at the root, ye may want to pull the tooth and apply a poultice of nettle and honey for a week after."

"How about a cough?"

"First ye have to determine a cause. Many agents can lead to infection or irritation in the lungs. Do ye suffer from either? I can examine ye to prescribe an appropriate dosage. For a small fee, I can mix ye–"

"That won't be necessary. You may go." With a bored grunt, the captain turned back to the bar. The innkeeper leapt to pour him another round. Dara and Yana sniggered as two more soggy soldiers came through the stable entrance. They gave Ben and Rian a hard once-over but moved to the bar without comment.

Ben understood a cue when he saw one. He grasped Rian's elbow and steered her toward the stairs like a recalcitrant child. The stable lad led them upward with a weak smile.

"Let me get some fresh hot water for ye, sir. I fear the tub has run cold." The look in his eyes was loaded.

Ben patted him on the shoulder. "Thank ye, lad. I could use a soak."

"Just so we're clear," the captain's voice followed them upward. "I expect you'll let us know if you see a girl fitting the description you were given. I think you'll find there are a great many of us searching for her. You might say hundreds. I imagine you'll see us every step of your way home."

"Of course, sir," said Ben, half-shoving Rian before him. "We'll be sure to report anything we happen to see. Ye have me word on that."

⚔ ⚔

ONCE THE DOOR CLOSED, RIAN leapt to action. She and the stable lad darted to the wall beside the window to remove a large piece of heavy paneling. Una poured out, coughing, and covered in cobwebs. Rian helped her to her feet.

"We have to go!"

Una spat out a mouthful of dust.

"How many?"

"Five," Ben scowled. He moved to the window to glance down at the streets below. It was still pouring out but windless, which allowed a thick fog to creep in from the north. All to the good, if they could get out without incident. "Presumably more on the way."

"Siora," Una shook her head. Ben noticed she'd eschewed the homespun gowns that poured out from an untidy trunk before the hearth. The proprietor's wife had been at least four inches taller than either girl and twice as wide if Rian's dress were any guide. Una opted

168

for a clean nightdress and woolen leggings, which she'd belted together with a wide blue sash. Remnants of another gown lay over the single bed, presumably the source of her new belt.

It seemed that the girls had been busy while he was downstairs enjoying himself at Rian's expense. A wooden tub sat before the hearth. Their attire—boots, cloaks, scarves, and gloves— dried on a rack before the fire. Too bad these newly clean items were destined once more for the tempestuous elements outside. Rian scurried about like a frantic mouse, whipping on her cloak and gloves and helping to shove Una's feet into her boots. The lad twiddled his thumbs at the door, ear pressed against the wood. Ben opened the window and stuck out his head. Ten feet to the ground, maybe less. The wall was too steep to climb, but he was over six and a half feet tall. He could drop to the street without much effort. The girls, on the other hand, might break a bloody leg. He turned.

"I'll have to go first. Rian, hand me your packs."

She passed hers, then Una's. The lad clutched the door handle. "Ah, if ye'll excuse me? Them soldiers have their mounts and hounds stalled with Vixen. I should go tend to them, or it'll look suspicious."

Ben nodded, pulling Una toward the window first. "We'll leave her in your care then, young man. Where we're going, it'll be too dangerous anyway."

The boy was visibly relieved. He reached into his vest for a small leather pouch, which he tossed to Ben. The purse was heavy with coin. Ben gave him an odd look.

"What's this?"

"Yer change. Da charged ye a lil' extra for the trouble, but ye'll find yer remainin' stags and a handful o'coppers in there." Ben didn't need to open the purse to know he'd massively underpaid. There had to be at least seven silver stags in there and another twenty coppers besides. A small fortune. The innkeeper would have been justified to keep the entire royal fainne. Ben was nonplussed.

Una shrugged on her damp cloak, sporting a dubious brow. "Well, isn't that generous?"

"Why would your father do this, boy? He owes us nothing."

169

The boy blushed under his scrutiny. "Da said ye'd ask. Tole me to tell ye he was at Dumnain." The blood drained from Ben's head. "Said to thank ye for what ye done, yer Lordship. Never forgets a face, ye see—even one done up, as yers is now." His red-chapped fingers closed over the doorknob. "We'll keep 'em busy long as we can."

"Wait," asked Una. "How did you know they were looking for me?"

"We didn't, until the Corsairs startin' askin' questions. Ye two girls, and them patrols," he shrugged. "Made sense."

"Thank you," Una said, awed. "Sincerely."

Before the boy slid through a crack in the door, Ben called out. "I will remember this, lad. Tell your father."

"He said ye'd say that too," the boy grinned, taking his leave as quietly as he could. Ben stared at the closed door; his mouth pressed into a firm line. This was… unexpected. He wasn't accustomed to anyone sticking their neck out for him—especially those who remembered him as he used to be.

"What was that all about?" Rian bolted the door behind him. Ben hurried toward the open window.

"No time now. Let's get going."

⚒ ⚒

STRUGGLING THROUGH THE MUD ABOUT three miles outside of town, they paused when they heard the first howls. Una's breath puffed silver, and Rian clutched at her chest; her eyes were two large white pearls in the dark.

"Wolves?" Rian was a long way from her comfortable, warm cottage now. Ben scanned the eerie fog-shrouded forest to the East. He saw nothing but a silver and black smear on the horizon. The howling came again, closer.

He shook his head. "Hounds. They must have realized we've escaped. We must get to the river." Cursing, he drew Nemain with one hand and scooped Una under his arm with the other. She yelped as his rough handling jarred her ribs. Too bad. She'd only slow them down if he didn't carry her.

170

He handed Rian a dagger. She stared at it like it might burn her. "What am I supposed to do with this?"

"Swing it at anything that tries to bite you." He shifted Una onto his back and passed her his pack. He tossed hers, which contained most of their muddied food, into the trees. One last scent for the beasts to track. "Put that on. It'll be better protection than nothing if they get behind us."

The howling inched nearer. Owing to the heavy rain and sluicing mud, the sound held a tin can quality, a haunting, mercurial echo. Distantly, Ben caught the unmistakable jingle of a bridle and the clink of spurs. Horsemen waited on the road to the South. Ben tilted his head in the opposite direction, listening to the telltale rush of the river on his right. Rian tied her skirt over her knees and hugged her pack close. She was terrified, he could tell. The prospect of being torn apart by dogs was not a pleasant one.

"*Run*. Don't stop until you hit the river. Go!"

With a whimper, she shot off as fast as her twisted foot would carry her. Ben followed, keeping her ahead of him. The going was tough. They slipped down steep gullies and struggled up every slick rise. Ben could smell the river and heard its rapid overflow about fifty paces ahead. A snarl on his right-hand side made Rian cry out in fear. She stumbled down the next slope, slashing wildly at a snapping set of jaws. The hound, an ugly, ungainly beast with grizzled fur and wide-set clipped ears, launched to its feet before Rian could regain hers. Ben slid down to her on his knees. Nemain's point sliced through its neck before it could latch its teeth around her ankle. As it died, another burst through the trees, yellow eyes wild, mandibles dripping. Snarling, it sunk its fangs into Ben's right arm. Grunting in pain, he dropped Nemain into the muck and used his free fist to pound at the animal's ears. Terriers did not respond to much else; their eyes and ears were their softest spots. A third hound joined the fray. It tucked into a crouch near Rian's flailing body. She gripped his dagger in a trembling fist when a fourth beast edged around the top of the rise to guard against potential escape.

Una dropped from Ben's back. He was too busy punching the animal biting his arm off to pay much attention. It shook its head back and forth, trying to snap his forearm like a hambone. He kicked out at its ribs with his left heel but lost his footing and went down hard on his right knee. The dog took advantage, using its bulging chest muscles to roll him over onto his side. Ben heard a telltale creak, the herald of an oncoming break. Then, the searing pressure abruptly ceased. The hound whined pitifully as Una's hand came away from its rump. Its spine concaved, nearly folding the animal in half from the wrong direction. Kicking its mangled corpse into the flooded gulley, Una held a hand out to Ben. He took it with a grateful groan. Pulling Nemain out of the mud, he ignored the boiling pain in his right arm.

Rian screamed as the beast she faced sprang at her for a second time. She slashed wildly at its eyes, as instructed, but barely grazed its ear. Ben turned his attention to the one just ahead of him, which growled low in its throat in anticipation. He reached into his belt to pass Una his last dagger.

"Can you help her?" Una took the blade without bothering to answer. "Good," he said. "Kill it, then get to the river."

She hurried to Rian's side. The fourth dog snarled, waiting for Ben to give him an opening. He anticipated it would lunge in whichever direction he moved. As it leapt, he spun right, severing its head. The torn nerves in Ben's arm shrieked in agony. By necessity, he shifted his sword to his left hand. Newborn howls reverberated through the rain-soaked forest to the south. The beast that circled the girls below seemed to derive courage from the imminent support. It snapped at Rian's front left ankle. Una struck out at its nose to distract it. Summoning all the courage she had, Rian jumped forward with a bellow and plunged her dagger through its right eye. She fell backward, gasping. Una helped her up.

"Well done, Rian."

"Can you run?" Ben asked, keeping his eyes on the trees. Una shoved Rian up the rise with renewed urgency. He followed, impressed by the speed they could summon between them, considering one dragged a crippled foot behind her and the other sported a dozen wounds that would keep a man twice her size abed for months. He was not used to being surprised. People tended to irritate rather than astound him. He caught a growl on his right. He lashed out with Nemain from his left, gratified by the beast's answering shriek. "Keep going!" he shouted.

They cleared the last copse of trees. Una's breath rattled from her chest as she pounded through the thin ice on the riverbank. With gritted teeth, Una dragged Rian upstream. Ben pointed north-west.

"Keep to the river! When you get to the second bend, there'll be a cliff with heavy overhanging trees and a wide beach. Wait for me there!"

Una looked back; lips already blue. "Where are you going?"

He wiped Nemain's blade clean with his cloak and faced the wailing forest behind him. "To pay our new friends a visit."

ARD TIARNE

D ara rubbed his hands together and blew into them, hoping to still the prickling numbness that leeched warmth from each digit. His thin leather gloves were all but useless out here. Excited as he was for the hunt, he couldn't get over the cold. As if this stinking, primitive strip of Innisfail needed any help being less pleasant or inviting. He couldn't wait to get back inside that warm publican. He was going to plant himself beside the hearth and sip warm liquids until he set down roots. While he mused, the howling muted in the distance. Relief struck like a dart.

"Bloody finally! My bollocks are crawling into my chest."

Yana snorted, taking yet another pull from his flask. "It's cold as Siora's tits out here. When we get back to the Citadel, I'll be lucky if I have any bollocks left."

"What I hear, you never had much, to begin with."

"Your wife begs to differ, Dara."

"If I had one. Your wife, on the other hand, never stops raving about mine."

Yana sniggered. "Everyone knows it's the tackle that counts."

"Quiet," the captain snapped, leaning low over his saddle. "I don't hear the hounds anymore." He nudged his charger forward with his knees, reaching into his cloak for a small silver whistle. After blowing into it several times, without answering yips or barks in response, he frowned. "I don't like this."

The captain didn't like anything in Dara's experience. He was another Tenma by-blow, and because he had the right name, he'd practically been handed his commission in the Corsairs. Dara's mother was an Agrean administrator, long retired. Any wealth his family might have had evaporated the minute she bore a son rather than a coveted daughter. Dara's family scraped together enough for him to enter the Citadel guard. He worked his way up without sponsorship or recommendation. It didn't bother him that most of the elite guardsmen in the Corsairs earned their way via intimidation and bribery, but he would be damned if he would take any shite from those that did.

"Perhaps they're out of range?" He offered, not caring a whit for the captain's bloody terriers. He'd like to see the heretic Moura bitch get what was coming to her as much as anyone, but preferably *after* it stopped fucking raining.

"Their ears can detect sounds some miles distant," said Yana.

Dara rolled his eyes, but that wouldn't stop Yana from reciting meaningless facts, as usual.

"Did you know they can discern the nuances in a human sigh? No, they can. They're smart."

"There's a lifelong mystery solved."

Yana gave a mock salute. "That bastard did have a fairly savage longsword. You don't think–?"

"Impossible," Dara blew a puff of air over his lower lip. "Eight vicious coursers against one man with a sword, him with two girls clinging to his trousers? Not bloody likely. Those mutts probably can't track through this Siora cursed downpour. It's a bloody swamp out there."

"I said, quiet!" the captain shouted, shifting uncomfortably in his saddle. His charger's ears twitched sideways. Dara's mount nickered, prancing nervously from one leg to the other. The rain came down in a steady drizzle, blighting all but stark shadows between the trees. Something made the horses nervous. The captain drew his rapier. Instinctively, Yana and Dara followed suit. A slight rustling ahead; faint splashes on their right. Raindrops or footsteps? The captain struggled to urge his charger forward, but the beast fought his lead.

"Sir," urged Dara. "We should regroup."

The captain growled. "Dara, I bloody well told you—" his head suddenly tilted forward at an unnatural angle, down his collarbone, chest… then over his knees. With horrific finality, it bounced from his horse's flank and rolled into the mud under Yana's stirrups. Dara's eyes bulged. The captain's horse reared, dislodging his headless body, in its hurry to gallop away. Yana shouted a belated alarm and swung his mount around to guard against an unseen assailant. His arm came down with a grunt; steel met steel. Dara couldn't get there fast enough. Yana suddenly spewed blood as the business end of a sylvan longsword sprouted from the middle of his chest like a pillar. Yana gurgled; his expression peppered with shock. His mouth opened as if he were about to ask Dara a useless question, but the blade retracted, and his body drooped sideways. Yana's horse trampled him in its rush to chase the captain's up the road.

Dara turned in his saddle, rapier high in his right hand, his long dirk clenched tight in his left. The tall half-breed from the tavern stood less than six paces away, watching him. He held his vicious longsword in an impossible arc over his right shoulder. That bloody sword must have weighed thirty pounds or more. Furiously blinking rainwater from his eyes, Dara sputtered, "There are more of us coming up the road. Two more, at least."

"No, there aren't." The specter tossed two bloodied daggers atop Yana's steaming corpse. "I prefer to be thorough."

"You… but how did you get there so fast? In this?" Dara waved his dagger, indicating the atrocious weather. "On foot, no less?"

"Let's just say, you boys are out of your depth."

Dara couldn't argue that. "All the same. I'm going to kill you, you pretty bastard," he snarled, stilling his jittery mount with his spurs.

The tall stranger chuckled, unfazed by Dara's bravado. "You'll try."

Dara dug his heels into his charger's ribs. The horse bolted forward, pounding through the mud toward his assailant. Dara's rapier was poised to take the leering bastard through the eye, but the figure jerked aside too quickly to track. Something hard connected with his right leg. Unseated, he toppled backward over his horse's rump. His spine slammed into the mud below, sucking the wind from his lungs. The half-breed kicked his rapier from his twitching fingers and knelt over his left hand, grinding his wrist under one knee.

Dara gasped for air. White-hot flashes of searing pain burst behind his eyes. He couldn't feel his toes anymore. He couldn't feel his foot… why couldn't he feel anything below the fire in his thigh? *Where is it?*

"Now," his tormentor said. "In these last few minutes you have, there are some things I would like to ask you. Every time you refuse to answer, I will hurt you. Do you understand?" Dara shuddered beneath him. "What?" In the dim mist-ridden light, the figure's teeth gleamed white as a Prima's robes. "Ready?"

🦌 🦌

UNA AND RIAN HUDDLED UNDER Rian's heavier cloak on a small beach choked with fallen boughs and heavy stones. When they emerged from the river at the place Ben described, they found a wide cut bank tucked into a low limestone cliff. Its chalky face was overgrown with moss and bracken and partially obscured by an impressive ancient oak. The tree's mammoth boughs stretched far over the river, cutting rolling rapids through its overflowing current. Nearer the cliff, they discovered a little copse tucked into a nest of low-lying limbs, dried shrubs, and furrowed trunk. At the rear hid a small, barely discernible cavity. Rian moved some branches and fallen twigs away to get a better look. The depression seemed to be a small tunnel that widened as it went on, shielded from the elements by the weight of the mighty roots twisting overhead. They wasted little time crawling into that hollow with mutual cries of relief. The air within held a stale, musty flavor. There were odd shapes ahead, and her breath echoed queerly in her ears. Una inhaled sharply. This had to be a cave! She scrabbled to the end, heedless of the sharp roots that tore at her face and hair. When she stopped, Rian came up beside her, squinting.

"W-what is all th… is?"

"Sh-shelter, I think." Scant, murky moonlight filtered in from the entrance and trickled through myriad holes below the root wall. After a few moments of intense concentration, details emerged from the dark. The cave was much larger than it should be— wide enough to accommodate a half-dozen people lying side by side. They no longer needed to crouch as the tangled roof hovered four or five handspans overhead. Rian tripped over a pile of long-dried sticks bundled in a slight depression at the center.

Una knelt to run her stiff fingers over a hand-dug pit. Firewood was stacked neatly in the middle as if waiting for their arrival. "S-someone lived here." Frowning, she took in the indistinguishable lumps scattered all over. Feeling her way around, Una brushed against a low shelf containing dozens of dusty items she couldn't identify without a lamp. A cot stood against the rear wall with two moldy blankets piled on top and a few things stacked beside it that she thought felt like armor or something similar. Her eyes had trouble adjusting to the dark.

"There's kindling in h-here already," shivered Rian. "Prima, erm?"

"It's Una, please."

"Right." Una could barely make out Rian's narrow shoulders while she hunched beside the pit. "C-can you reach into m-my pack there? There should be a leather pouch toward the bottom."

Una retrieved the pouch, then fumbled back to Rian, taking care not to trip. Rian set to work straightaway, layering the little stone circle with flammable fodder and stacking twigs upright over the top.

"Break up the bigger pieces first. Good. L-like that. Can you find any more?"

Una found quite a few, actually. Rian struck the flint she'd removed from her little bag, and a fire sprang to life within the pit after a few minutes. Una felt like crying. She held her shaking hands over the little blaze while Rian stacked larger twigs around the rim. Now lit, the chamber's mysteries fleshed out. One intriguing fact that leaped out at them was the obvious sign of tool marks carved into the soft limestone of the far wall. This cave was probably formed by roots pressing mercilessly into the pliable stone, but it took a human hand to expand the depth of this chamber to such a degree. There were two homely little tables, the larger shelf Una discovered earlier, and several oddments scattered over each. A few parchments, grown yellow and green with age; a silver box, etched with intricate curling vines; a few gleaming bits of gold— jewelry perhaps; a carefully folded, if slightly mildewed white tunic; gloves of soft kid; and a dagger with a silver hilt, which was covered in cobwebs and a thick patina of grime. Opposite the shelf, what she guessed correctly to be armor, leaned against the wall; a cuirass of once brilliant white leather embossed with metallic shapes too dusty to read. An impressive, unstrung longbow arched over one shoulder, half-covered in a filthy bit of tarpaulin.

Pursing her lips, Una looked over the cot with its long-forgotten blankets, the parchments stuffed below one of the homemade tables, and the pewter candle holder with a burnt nub protruding from its taper. Her brows drew together over the scene. Clearly, this was no mistake. The rushing river outside, and the tangle of roots, tree limbs, and boughs provided the perfect cover. The beach could only be accessed from the river, and the limestone cliff-face would prevent any but the most determined climber from attempting a descent.

How much time had Ben spent here?

He'd gone to considerable trouble to make it somewhat comfortable, hadn't he? Why? She didn't have the chance to seriously ponder what she was seeing before Rian jerked her upward by the elbow.

"All right, get these things off. There are blankets in that crate there." She pointed with her right hand and unbuttoned her own vest with the other. "A fever would end our little adventure on the lowest possible note."

Una rifled through the crate. Eschewing the topmost coverlet for its abhorrent layer of black mildew, she dug for better fare. She discovered one partially clean woolen mantle, another heavy tarpaulin, and a moth-eaten, fur-lined cloak in some fabric that felt very much like velvet. She wasted no time stripping off her sodden clothing to her thin, wet underthings. Handing Rian the warmer blanket, she threw the cloak over her puckered skin inside-out. Its soft fur tore a heavy sigh from somewhere deep inside her chest. She dragged the tarpaulin over to their little fire and spread it over the flattest portion she could find.

180

Meanwhile, Rian busied herself by hauling soiled textiles from the cot and cramming them into the roots over the entrance: a makeshift door to block the elements searching through the gap. In moments, the small space filled with reassuring warmth. Una buried her face in the smelly cloak.

"Siora, but this is wonderful."

Rian adjusted herself beneath her blanket, tucking in her bare toes. "I've never been so cold in my life."

"You said that yesterday," said Una, her voice muffled by fur. Her extremities stung as they thawed. A more welcome pain, she couldn't fathom.

"Consider this the new standard," laughed Rian, reaching out to teepee two more branches over the fire. She looked around, her smile fading slightly. "Where are we?"

"His hiding place, I expect." Una snuggled further into the cloak. "He spent some time here too, I'd say."

"You know who he is?"

"I'm pretty sure I do now."

"What tipped you off?"

Una nodded at the shelf. "That cuirass. It's filthy but take a good look at it. I suspected before, with the garish amount of gold swinging from his ears."

Rian got up and bunched the blanket around her knees to squat before it. With her bare hand, she wiped the dust away in a single brown-grey crease. The white leather under her palm bore heavy silver embossing: a leaping silver stag adorned by three gold stars. Rian sucked in a breath.

"*An Fiach Fian!* This is the standard of the High King's elite guard."

"That's the one."

Brow furrowed, Rian reached for the covered bow and removed its protective covering. The most beautiful, intricately carved longbow Una had ever seen emerged into the firelight. The bow was easily seven feet long, hewn from a single piece of gorgeous white yew, and tipped at each end with heavy silver plating. Its staggering beauty and exquisite craftsmanship drew appropriate sighs of admiration from each girl.

Such a thing was unheard of in Eire. It would be so costly that none but the wealthiest Lord could afford it. The artistry was superb. A stag, a boar, a fox, a raven, and a bear chased each other around its haft. Rian ran her fingers lightly over some Ealig wording carved into the underside of the arch.

"*Sinnair*," she read in apparent awe.

"What does that mean?" Una spoke only Eirean and Bretagn. Ealig was not highly prioritized in the Red City since only council members had ever been invited into Aes Sidhe.

"'King killer.'"

"You're joking?"

Rian shook her head, folding her hands beneath her blanket. "That's what the inscription reads."

"Confirmation then?"

"Certainly makes a strong argument. If this is the weapon I've read about, this bow is quite famous. It was made especially for—"

"Someone unworthy of it," said Ben from the entrance.

Rian nearly jumped out of her skin. "Don't bleedin' do that! You almost gave me a heart attack!"

Unlike the two girls, he'd had to crawl through on all fours. Soaking wet and scowling, he dragged himself through Rian's homemade doorway.

"My apologies, Mistress." He gave no warning before divesting himself of his sodden outer garments and depositing them in an unceremonious heap by the door.

"Are you all right?" Una winced at the state he was in.

Ben wasn't as clean as they were, so he must not have come via the river. He must have climbed down. His tunic was shredded, and his boots were spattered with something darker and thicker than mud. He spared her a dismissive smirk.

"I'll live." He unlaced his sopping jerkin with his left hand; his right was a tad worse for wear, though he'd wrapped it with a torn shred of cloth, which was a suspicious black with gold threading. Una recognized it instantly. She opened her mouth to ask him about it, but he turned

182

away. Without a shred of modesty, he peeled off his inner vest, tunic, shirt, and boots. Una flushed as a broad expanse of scarred flesh was revealed. Her eyes drifted to the roots curling above their heads. She struggled to affect an intense fascination with the smoke curling upward from their fire.

Rian was not as shy. "How'd that happen to you?" she gestured to the swirling mounds of scar-tissue tracing over his pectoral muscles. They were long healed but ragged and must have been debilitating when inflicted.

He grabbed the mildewed blanket Una discarded from the knotty floor. "A mistake, long forgotten."

Once he was appropriately covered, Una cleared her throat. She wasn't a prude, mind. She'd just never seen someone like him before. Come to think of it; he might be the very first Sidhe she'd ever met.

"Will they follow?"

"No." He met her eyes firmly.

"I see." She couldn't say she wasn't grateful to be alive nor that he'd gone to such obvious trouble to ensure their safety… but the ease with which he took life unnerved her.

"You'd mourn these men too, I gather."

"No," she lied. "I'm not accustomed to so much death. All right?"

"Some ruler you'd make."

"I don't want to 'rule,' damn you. Besides, why shouldn't I despise killing? Civilized people do."

He rolled his eyes. "Don't delude yourself, princess. Those men meant to kill all three of us. How civil were they?"

"I didn't say you were wrong, only that it's such a simple matter for you. Life and death. I'll kill if I must, but I will never find your ease with it."

"It's lucky for you that I am the more efficient killer, don't you think?"

"You *enjoy* it."

"You have an odd way of showing thanks."

"*Listen—*"

"Where's your stone then?" Rian interjected. She was eager to prevent yet another pointless spat between her companions. They'd had dozens in the past two days already. Una just couldn't stop herself from rising to the occasion every time. Rian seemed to handle him better, though Una couldn't imagine why. He was insufferable.

Ben raised a silver-blond brow. "In my pocket. Don't worry."

"Why bother to take it off?"

"Didn't want to lose it on the way here."

"Well," she sniffed. "So long as you have it."

"Was the river too cold for you?" Una quipped, half-angry, half-relieved. He settled beside her, sparing her a rue twist of his upper lip.

"Obviously, it wouldn't be prudent to come from the same direction."

Una glared at him in silence for some time. He pretended to ignore her.

Rian bustled around, retrieving things from her pack, then taking a seat on his opposite side. "Arm, please?"

"Why?" Ben jerked away, suspicious.

"I need to wrap it, you infant. We're in a bloody cave. Now give it."

While their heads bowed together over his wound, Una couldn't help but be struck by their fair beauty. They were quite something, the two of them. Both had the same luminescent skin... like sunlight glinting over a pearl. Though, in Ben's case, the effect was startling. He seemed to carry that light inside as if a candle burned within. His eyes, a true silver, flashed her way more than once in suspicion. She pretended her heart didn't skip the tiniest bit each time. He was too lovely to be male, yet there could never be a doubt of his gender. She knew dozens of warriors in both Tairngare and Bethany who would gnash their teeth in envy at Ben's physique. It seemed a shame he was so... disagreeable. Her mind wandered for quite a while until she was forced to bite the inside of her swollen lip hard enough to make her eyes water. Why was she thinking about such useless drivel now?

"What?" he asked, brimming with ready irritation.

"Nothing." Una sat up a bit straighter.

She pulled the cloak closer to hide her burning face. She'd sooner be raked over hot coals than admit to her train of thoughts. Instead, she chewed the interior of her good cheek. Rian poked at Ben's arm while he glared down at Una. The soiled, stolen scrap he'd haphazardly wound around the wound, Rian threw into the fire. Flames hissed and popped around the sopping wad of black fabric. His flesh was torn wide near the wrist in a couple of places, but he didn't seem to bleed as badly as Una expected he should. Rian cut away the free-swinging pieces of skin with a tiny pair of scissors, then slathered it liberally with a healthy dollop of the honey and nettle mixture she'd used on Una's face.

Once properly bound, she folded her tools back inside her pack. "There." She handed his arm back.

He mumbled something incoherent, which Una assumed were thanks.

Rian blew her drying hair out of her eyes and settled again into her blanket. "You killed them then? The dogs?"

He considered Una pointedly. "Yes. All of them."

Rian blew out a deep breath. "Good." She slid a somewhat guilty look Una's way.

Una wouldn't argue that the death wrought tonight wasn't necessary. She just wished it wasn't. Siora, she was tired. Tired of running, tired of being in pain, and tired of being afraid. That aside, Ben had killed more people in a handful of days than anyone she'd ever heard of. He made her nervous. His lack of empathy, his disdain for life— all of it. Could she ever call someone like him an ally? Did she want to?

He leaned in. "You truly believe I enjoy this?"

"I'm trying to figure that out."

Ben grunted. "Don't bother. Whatever you think of me, I don't kill for pleasure. I won't shed tears over any of those men, and neither should you. Get some rest. No one will find us here." He motioned to Rian, whose chin had already dipped toward her collarbone. The day's events seemed to have caught up to her all at once. Chuckling, he gently nudged her onto her side so that she wouldn't tumble headfirst into the fire. "To be clear, I didn't ask for any of this, but I'm making do."

Una acknowledged the justice of that statement with a cold smile. "Fine. That's fair. I didn't mean to imply that you're a base murderer. I'm struck by how easy it is for you to take life."

185

"Let me put it this way: I kill when I have to. The men hunting you kill because they're ordered to, and they obey those commands because they choose to. You've taken life recently, haven't you?"

Target struck. She flinched. "I suppose I lack your comfort with it."

"You should start getting comfortable, my lady. In my experience, it is better to be sorry than dead."

Kicking him wouldn't make him less right. "I haven't known many soldiers, personally. Far fewer with your, erm... talent for it. I have only one basis for comparison."

Ben sneered. "I am nothing like your father, girl."

He wasn't. Patrick wouldn't bother to feign offense; he was proud to be a megalomaniacal beast. On the other hand, Ben didn't seem overly pleased by any of this, but neither did he hesitate. It unnerved her. He struck her as the sort to avoid conflict not because he feared its outcome but because he knew how events would play out if forced to act. Given what she suspected of him, it made sense. He *would* wish to avoid trouble for one reason alone. Her eye slid to the cuirass against the wall. He saw.

"Go ahead and ask."

"Are you... really...?" She was embarrassed by the wonder in her tone.

"I used to be." The fire cast shadows over his profile, enhancing the sharp planes of his face. "Makes how we met all the more absurd, doesn't it?"

She swallowed. She was coming to understand why Eirean women tended to disappear over the border fairly regularly.

"Who else knows?"

"Does she know?" He jerked a thumb at Rian.

"I'm not asleep." Rian pulled her blanket over her head. "And yes, I do."

He held up two fingers. "There you have it."

Una wasn't sure what to say. She'd wandered into a bedtime story and become entangled with one of its most iconic characters. "What, ah, should I call you then?"

"Ben. It suits me fine."

She didn't believe that for a moment. "What happened?"

186

"It's irrelevant. We have more pressing matters to discuss."

He leaned backward to tug his rumpled, soggy cloak from the entrance. Reaching inside an interior pocket, he lobbed her a sheaf of damp papers tied with a red leather strap. A warrant from the Citadel, she knew without having to unravel the wad. She'd seen them before, hadn't she?

"Someone named Alta Nema has ordered your arrest on the grounds of heresy and usury."

"I know, and it isn't legal. Nema holds no such power in Parliament."

"Most common folk won't know that, will they? The Corsair I questioned said Parliament voted to rescind your status as Domina of the Moura Clan three days ago. Some claim you're the victim of attempted regicide. Others, namely this Nema's supporters in the Commons, label you a heretic and escaped criminal."

"Nema, and her cronies in Parliament, arranged all this in the first place. She's manipulating the Commons against my family."

"I'm sure, but it hardly makes a difference if half the city is howling for your blood, does it?"

She stared down at the wet bundle as if it were a nest of spiders she'd accidentally set her hand in. She threw them onto the fire. "If that's the case, then perhaps I should return to Tairngare as soon as possible."

"You won't make it five miles down the Navan High Road before a patrol picks you up, or worse, drags you into the Greensward to finish the job the first batch started. Use your head."

"But… how can I trust you to help me when you aren't permitted over the border yourself?" She felt a bit bad watching him wince, but the question was warranted, nonetheless. "Look, I know this was thrust upon you, and you hope I can help you get home, but how do you propose that's going to happen? There's no guarantee the High King will even see me."

"He'll see you," Ben smiled, melting her ready retort like butter from her tongue. "Trust me. Midhir is the finest king in this or any land. He won't allow either faction to harm you. I vow it."

"Easy to say," she let out a long breath. She would get a hold of herself, *by Siora*, one way or another. "But will he see *you*? I don't fancy fleeing across the river, only to run straight into a Sidhe arrow for the gall. Nor do I love the idea of being carted to Bri Leith in chains."

"I'm asking you to trust me. You can, or you can't. It's that simple."

Did she trust him? Could she? She didn't know. She was unused to depending upon others, and Ben didn't make anything easy. Still... he'd saved her life many times— whether he found this inconvenient or not, it didn't cheapen his effort. He was offering to help. True, he hoped to benefit from the arrangement, but that didn't mean she couldn't or shouldn't trust him. He was a sour, sarcastic drunkard with a talent for death and an acute disdain for people... but he was also brave. He was also capable. Simply put, what choice did she have?

None. Absolutely none.

"I do trust you."

He seemed as shocked by her acquiescence as she, more, perhaps.

"Don't tell me you were expecting me to say something else?"

"I was," he admitted freely, without sarcasm.

She rolled a shoulder under her stinky moth-eaten covering. "I suppose we're stuck with each other, for now. So, let's do this the right way, shall we?" she unwound her arm and extended her hand. "I'm Una. Pleased to make your acquaintance... Ben."

Hesitantly, he wrapped her fingers in his own massive, clammy hand. "And I, yours... Una."

"There now. Friends?" Ben said nothing. He expected he would have to prove his case and was somewhat off-guard now that he did not. It was written all over his face.

"If you like?"

"'The true mystery of the world is the visible, not the invisible,'" she mumbled, tucking her cloak carefully around her knees with a sigh.

"What was that?"

"Oh, just something I read once. I never understood the quote until now." He stared back, silent and inscrutable. "I'm glad you found me, Ben... and thank you for everything." With that, she took Rian's cue and hunkered before the fire to get some sleep. She could feel his eyes boring holes into her back for quite a while until slumber finally hushed the hammer of her pulse.

ETHICS OF CRUELTY

n.e. ʃʊ8
22, ꝺOꞃ samna
ꞇaiꞃnᵹaꞃe

A oife wept silent, bitter tears. Her ears and nose bled. Her fingers scratched uselessly against the heavy, cold granite, tearing out several nails. She gasped for air, helpless against the monstrous pressure that smashed her in place. Her robes were torn open at the back, and the skin there was corrugated like a plowed field. Her arms and legs were twisted at awkward angles. Mortifying pain flashed behind her eyes each time she tried to move. Aoife would do anything to make it stop, but she was far past begging. All she could do was struggle to breathe and pray.

"She's bleeding all over your favorite rug, Excellency," Fawa Gan said from somewhere below Aoife's navel.

"Then you'll buy me a new one," Vanna Nema replied from further away. She was at her desk, signing papers and shuffling parchments—scratching away with a knife-slashing quill that made Aoife twitch.

Gan whined, "This rug dates from before the Transition, Excellency. There *isn't* another to be found." Aoife could practically see the pernicious little toad setting doughy fists on his wide girlish hips. She might spit on him if her mouth weren't smashed into a wide crack on the ceiling.

"Fawa, do you fancy a place beside her?"

"If you want to start braiding your own hair and mixing your own tea, by all means. I'd adore a lie-down, thanks."

Nema's quill paused long enough to glare over her desk at him. Aoife had seen the same false threat a thousand times before. Truth be told, Gan got away with bloody murder. Aoife hated him for it. In Nema's eyes, Gan was irreplaceable. He had a talent for ingratiating self-promotion that Aoife could never lower herself to match. As much as she longed to watch him drown in a pool of his own fluids, replacing him would be a nightmare. Who else could keep the old hag happy? Run her errands, keep her books, and order her appointments? He was too damned good at his job. This was the only thing that kept Aoife from shoving him off the Citadel's highest parapet. *She* certainly had no desire to take his place. Head bootlicker was not a position to which Aoife aspired.

"You're here for a reason, I presume?"

"I am Excellency. Did you happen to hear that racket outside?" He referred to the mob gathered before the Citadel's gates. Thousands of angry, riotous citizens descended upon the Grand Arcade. They pounded on the walls, gates, and windows, desperate to lure lawmakers into the streets to face the mob's justice. The outcry began before Aoife had returned from the Greensward three days before, and the violence grew worse by the hour.

Riots broke out in the Spice District, the Docks, and the Merchanta Ward. Homes and shops in residential areas were looted and burned. Merchants and civil servants were attacked and bloodied in the streets. The mayhem grew to such a fevered pitch that the Council was forced to summon troops from the Academy to clear the city thoroughfares. Citadel Corsairs trampled at least a dozen people during midday prayers, and by sunset the previous day, the city had been placed under strict martial law. Guards stood four men deep at every gate. Commerce in the Red City ground to a screeching halt. Brothels in the Pleasure District emptied, taverns and publicans ceased pouring libations, and markets shuttered. Even Parliament refused to convene, though the people cried out for deliberation. Judges and Libellan representatives preferred to cower behind scores of armed Tairnganeah rather than face the wroth of the Commons. In one week, Tairngare's government had been pushed to the brink of collapse. Vanna Nema certainly wasn't displeased by the violence and fury outside. She was its architect, after all.

"I have." Aoife heard Nema's lips slide over her gums in an audible grin. "How calamitous. I do hope the matter is cleared up soon. Every day this unrest persists is another the Citadel loses revenue. It's most perplexing."

"Oh, of course, Excellency. Most dreadful, indeed. However, I've just been informed that Judge Zelda San has proposed you undergo the Tenth Ordeal."

The scratching stopped altogether. "Already?"

"Seems so. As you said, the longer this goes on the more coin hemorrhages from the Citadel's treasury. I was informed you're summoned to a private interview with the Judge's Panel in chambers, Excellency."

"When?"

"Tomorrow, or the day after. Perhaps sooner, if the guards are forced to shoot any more citizens from the Ward Gate."

Aoife heard Nema's chair creak. "I should have had that girl dragged from the Citadel years ago." She gave an uncharacteristic giggle. "Wonderful news. Please extend my humble apologies to Judge San's staff. Of course, I am but a servant in the Cloister of the Eternal Flame. These are ecclesiastical matters that must be decided in Council."

"You mean to refuse again?"

"Absolutely." Aoife could picture Nema moving to the windows to admire her handiwork, though Aoife would have to skin her nose to see it for herself. Nema laughed. "Caesar refused the title of Imperator before the public three times, did he not? I will continue to decline until the people tear the gates down around Parliament's ears. Now is not the time for haste, Gan dear. We must be patient."

"You've been patient, Excellency. Folks are ready to burn us out of here as it is. Don't you think it would be wise to give them what they want before we're all out there, begging in the street?"

"Not at all. I won't accept half a victory. There must be such a clamor in the air that those who oppose me fear to speak out. No change can be permanent unless it is unanimously craved. My detractors must see me reject power as often as it takes."

"Until when?"

Aoife heard her tap a long nail against the glass. "Come to think of it; I should probably request Parliament to convene on the issue. Publicly decry this rebellion. Show the people how reluctant I am to seize power."

"Ah, I see," Gan chuckled. "A grand gesture. If only they knew how many years you've waited for this."

"Coups are fallible, my dear. They ignite, consume, then burn out just like that." She snapped her fingers. "I mean to remake this city from the ground up. To do that, the people must be willing to bleed for it."

"Oh, I think they're bleeding well enough. I urge you to remember what happened to your Caesar, Excellency, but I concede the point. When should I send your summons?"

"Tonight, but we won't convene until the day after tomorrow. Let them stew in their failure for a while."

"Very good. And the girl?"

"I have fresh warrants signed and sealed. I want them nailed to every wall in town." Nema moved back toward her desk, shuffling papers into piles. "Here, have these copied and distributed quickly. I can't allow that creature to stir false hope in any Libellan breasts."

"No, not that girl. That one." He looked up at Aoife. Aoife whimpered in mortified loathing.

"Ignore her. Better you serve those amended warrants as soon as possible. I want it clear that we mean to get to the bottom of this debacle as swiftly as possible. Was the girl abducted, or did she escape? This is the question I want on every citizen's mind for the next few days."

"What if the opposition apprehends her?"

"Then she'll be treated to a very nasty, public trial," Nema said. "I'd prefer she didn't return at all... but I'll make sure we take the win, regardless."

192

"As you command, Excellency." Aoife heard Gan's joints creak under one of his flamboyant bows. "Still, I wonder that you don't need her," he was referring to Aoife again. "She does have her talents, doesn't she?"

"Come now, Gan. You loathe one another. Don't tell me you're speaking up for her after all this time. She failed me."

Gan ignored her barb. "Did she? I'd say the information she bore tends to exonerate her. If she's right, perhaps she may still be of use?" Nema went silent for a while. Aoife fumed that such a slimy little creature as Fawa Gan would dare to contradict Alta Vanna Nema on her account. This was so completely out of character for him; his ploy couldn't be more vivid. He hoped to gain leverage over Aoife. That was the only reason he'd speak on her behalf. Aoife wouldn't trust Gan to agree that water was wet.

"Perhaps you're right," Nema sighed. At once, the immense pressure at Aoife's back subsided. She cried out as her torn belly flopped onto the hard floor. "Tell me again, girl," Nema ordered, strolling back to the window to observe the crowd.

Aoife sucked in as much air as she could and rolled slowly, painfully, to her side. Her ribs were broken. One jabbed into her left lung, which made each breath burn like inhaled vinegar. "I swear... was... h... him."

"Preposterous. That man is dead. Condemned by the Ard Ri, himself."

Aoife tried to shake her head. Her brain sloshed queerly against her skull, and she gagged. Gan sat beside her to dab a silken cloth soaked with wine against her parched lips. Mistrustful, she tried to turn away, but he persisted until her body's needs betrayed her. The first few drops seared her throat like molten iron.

"Leave her."

Gan dipped the handkerchief into the pitcher at his knee, defiant as only he could be. "If she can't speak, how can she tell you anything?"

After a few minutes, Aoife pushed his hand away and struggled up to her elbows. She met Nema's imperious glare with trembling sincerity.

"I s-saw him with my own eyes, Excellency. He has the girl in hand."

193

"I don't believe it. How? How could the most infamous Dannan in Innisfail simply appear in Eire, twenty-odd years after his death? And at such a time—?"

"It was him; I swear it."

Nema threw up her hands and resumed her pacing. "All those Dannan pigs look much the same: big, blond, and thick as a lump of stones. He was probably a half-breed. There are hundreds of these crazed, disfigured creatures in the Greensward. You're making excuses to save your skin."

Aoife leaned forward. Blood streamed down her jaw. "He was Kaer Yin Adair. N-no faerie wears nine gold chains in his right ear, n-nor carries a Dannan broadsword. I'm not a fool."

Nema clenched her fist. Aoife was lifted into the air again. This time, she crashed into the wall nearest the blazing hearth. She spat up something darker than blood. Nema loomed, the green in her eyes predatory.

"You dare to speak to me in that manner? I made you, Aoife Sona. I will unmake you as easily."

"Your Excellency!" cried Gan, trying to intervene. Nema extended a single finger, and he was flung to the carpet himself. He squealed like a girl half his age. Nema leaned close to Aoife's breathless face. She smelled of ink, woodsmoke, and crisp linen— and power, always that.

Aoife could only glare back, vulnerable in her defiance. "I s-speak true, Excellency. He was the Adair."

"How can you be sure?"

"He used a Dannan longsword with a silver stag for a pommel."

Nema cursed. Aoife suddenly crumpled to the floor in a choking, boneless heap.

"Impossible! Why now? Why here?" Nema clawed at the edge of her desk. "Did you confront him?"

Aoife paled. "Of course not! He would have killed me."

"If you're telling the truth, this is an infuriating complication."

"Why?" Gan struggled to his feet. "Who is he?"

Nema sneered at him. "He is a Sidhe lord, Gan. Not some garden gnome. You would do well to forget that common racial slur."

"Who?"

"He's someone who shouldn't be alive. That's who he is." Aoife wiped the blood from her nose. "Someone that doesn't belong in Eire, and even less, in our way. Your Excellency, he must be dealt with."

"Distribute those warrants as ordered. Also, I want to triple the Corsairs on the High Road."

"But—"

"Do it!" With the put-upon grace only he could manage, Gan bowed his way out of the chamber with the stack of leather-bound documents in hand.

When he was gone, Nema whirled on Aoife. "Tell me everything. Leave nothing... not a single detail out."

"I have, my lady."

Nema shook her head. "Oh, not yet you haven't. How did he seem? I want to know what he looked like, down to the buttons on his vest. Every action, every mannerism. Most of all, I want to know if he was truly *alone*...."

🦌 🦌

FAWA DID NOT HURRY. As a rule, he never rushed anywhere, even when he had cause. As the great Vanna Nema's personal steward, he must always reflect a serene mask of control. Rumors, he found, often started with the servants.

He held his sheaf of warrants tight against his chest and sauntered down the South Hall. He held his head high, despite its not being overly handsome or of any great height. He was calm, composed, and well-dressed as usual. He wore a tunic of Bretagn silk in Nema's brilliant scarlet, belted by a bright vermillion sash, interwoven with solid gold threading. His slippers were the finest kidskin, dyed a regal red. Gan thought himself rather dashing today. How others saw him was a matter of perspective. Those in the Cloister viewed him with grudging respect. In the Citadel, Union members treated him with a shade of the fear they felt for his mistress. Nobles in the Libella, however, would sooner see him dead than pass by him in the hall. Gan didn't care what they thought of him.

Today, even less than usual.

He came to the last turn at the far end of the Hall and veered left, down the long Southern windows, then up a half-flight of stairs toward the Eastern Wing. Here, he cut right through a door set into the wainscoting on the other side. The next chamber was supported by a long row of arches, lit only by oil sconces mounted on either stone wall. He sailed past these, conscious of the subtle footsteps behind him. He smiled to himself. What fools. He'd been dodging spies in this fortress for almost forty years. He wasn't about to let one catch him now.

After a complicated network of turns and descents, he shut the last door softly behind him. In a painfully dark antechamber, straddled between two rear halls, Gan pressed his ear against the moldering oak door and withdrew a delicate little dagger from his golden sash. The spy was light on her feet. Very carefully, he tiptoed to the far entry. When it opened, he held a finger to his plump lips. His expected guest froze. Gan slid back to the door he came through. The door swung inward after several breaths. Gan reached out quick as a serpent and yanked the little spy inside. She was only a Nova, perhaps no more than twelve. She squealed when Gan's hand clamped over the lower half of her face. His guest, robed entirely in black, waited into the darkest corner, silent as death.

"There you are, you little shite. How long have you been following me?"

The girl shook her head, frantic, her dark eyes pleading.

"She must die," said his contact in a low, muffled tone.

Gan didn't like it, but there was too much at stake. "Tell me who sent you, girl? Tenma, Carra, Nema? Who?"

The spy squeaked and kicked her slippered feet, while clawing at his hand.

"Do it."

Gan wasn't to blame for this girl, was he? Whoever had forced her to spy for them held that honor. He turned, so he wouldn't have to watch the life leave her eyes and twisted as hard as he could. A sickening crunch reverberated around the small, windowless chamber. He let her little body flutter to the dusty stone floor. "You owe me for that."

196

"I owe you nothing. You're lucky I haven't killed you already."

Gan trembled. "I risk *everything* for you!"

"You risk everything for *coin*. Don't confuse things."

Gan wiped his mouth with his guilty right hand. "I have new information."

"How much are you asking this time, Gan? I can't come down here every time Vanna Nema kills an underling or writes a speech she never gives."

"This information is worth more than anything I've ever given you. The Doma will want to know— to plan. I mean it. This changes everything."

The figure considered him in silence for a long while.

"Fine. Tell me."

"Oh no! Not this time." Gan fidgeted a bit. He'd just murdered a child, and his nerves were already catching fire in his body. "I want what you promised. Now. *Today*. After this, you and I are done."

"Very well," the figure replied and turned to exit through the far door. Gan slapped his palms flat against the jamb.

"No! We had a deal! My freedom for Vanna. You promised me."

A strong hand shot out from beneath the cloak and wrapped itself around Gan's throat. Gurgling, he stumbled backward. "I do not take orders from traitors, you delusional insect." The hand squeezed. "Maybe I will kill you after all? Or let slip to Nema, whom you really work for? Wouldn't that be fun?"

Gan wheezed. "She'll kill me," his chins quivered.

"As will I if you continue to waste my time. You know? I'll never understand how you managed to elude the Judges all this while. Perhaps you hold more Spark than the average male? Is that it? Is that how you've fooled Nema for over thirty years?"

"I... serve her well. She needs me."

"I'm sure she'll be delighted to know that her trusted steward is a thief and a liar. Does she know about your little harem on the Third Floor? What you've made her party to?"

Gan's eyes bulged a bit. "Please... you promised."

"A vow given to a pimp is hardly worth the effort used to speak."

"He... is... alive..." he choked.

"*Who* is alive?"

"Kaer Yin A-Adair."

The figure released him. He crumpled down the door, landing heavily on his rump. "... You lie."

He held his stinging throat with a free hand. It would probably be bruised now, and he'd have to invent some story to explain it. Nema would notice. Nema noticed just about everything. Well, perhaps not everything.

"No. I'm not. The Sona girl recognized him. Said he has gold chains in his ear and uses a sword with some kind of prancing deer. I remember that part very clearly."

"It can't be. After Dumnain—"

"Aoife is Fir Bolg or at least half-breed. I told you this a long time ago. She would know. They hate him almost as much as they loathe Duch Donahugh."

"If I find out you're lying—"

"I'm not. And that's not all. *He* has your girl."

"*What?*"

"Siora's Truth. He killed two creatures Aoife summoned to finish her. Ghasts, I think she said? He's protecting her."

"Is that all?"

"What do you mean, is that all? I've just given you the juiciest gossip in Innisfail, not to mention the Moura Domina's whereabouts. That's quite enough, I'd say. Now, you promised me an escape. I have done everything you've ever asked of me."

"For which, you have been paid a fortune."

"All the same!"

"The Doma will consider it. It's out of my hands."

Gan fumbled to his feet. "You swore! You SWORE you'd help me!"

"If you remain useful, the Doma will honor her word. You are in no position to make demands of anyone."

Gan swallowed the lump in his throat. It wouldn't be long before his myriad deceptions unraveled around his ears. Nema would forgive him many offenses, but not this. By allowing the Mouras to gain leverage over him, he'd forfeited his safety long ago. The only hope he had now was escape. The figure tossed him a small purse as if that would assuage his terror.

"Go back to Nema. I will triple this amount if you can discover what she plans to do with this information. I must verify all of this. I'll contact you in the usual way in a matter of days. Do not ignore my summons if you value your life." The cloak fluttered as the figure spun to leave.

"Wait!" Gan pleaded. "What should I do with her?" He was referring to the young girl stashed in the corner.

"Leave her. No one will notice."

⚔ ⚒

W HEN NIGHT DREW DEEP OVER Tairngare, three women climbed the highest set of stairs in the Cloister. The youngest of them held a thick black cloak over her right arm. Straight-backed, she led the way up the tenth and final flight of steps. At the top, she nodded to the guards with their heavy black shields. She led the others through an opulent hall, hewn of pure polished obsidian; its peerless black surface showed no veins, no tool marks, nor crevices of any kind. At the end of this oblique tunnel, past two wide doors, waited a room decorated entirely in burnished gold and gems. The women strolled into this lavish space with scarcely an upward glance. The ceiling here was easily twenty feet high. Gold panels bedecked with fistfuls of amber adorned each of the four interior walls. An opulent hearth, molded from one gigantic amber core, yawned cavernously beneath a diamond-studded mosaic; its polished curves cast sensuous light, like warm honey, over the walls. A lapis lazuli dragon with amber chips for eyes dominated the ceiling, dripping expensive beeswax candles from each of its four-inch talons.

The eldest woman paused to sneer at this pretentious display, as always. The scene never failed to vex her, no matter how many times she'd glimpsed it. However, the women weren't there to admire the craftsmanship of an unknown architect. The youngest craned her neck to peer within two smaller chambers set at either end of the towering northern wall. Candlelight winked from a garnet room on the left, but she saw no one inside. Moonlight gleamed through the window in the Doma's office on the right, which Drem referred to as her 'silver box' for evident reasons. It, like the parlor, was done entirely in leaf, only this, in unalloyed silver. A shadow passed before the window. The women walked toward it. Within, a small, slightly rotund old woman stared down at the burning city below. She was wrapped in a white sealskin coverlet, her arms folded over her ample bosom, her rich brown skin still taut and fresh despite her age. Wild silver curls sprang around her face like an angry cloud. Doma Drem Moura slid an almond-shaped, honey-brown eye over each of her visitors.

"What took you so long?"

"She's asking you, Eva." The eldest crossed her bony arms.

"I believe she's asking all of us, Mother," sighed the middle-aged lady.

Drem glared at the eldest of them with thin lips. They were old rivals, she and the Dowager Domina. "I don't like your tone, Basa."

"Since when have I given the slightest shite about what you like or don't, Drem?" retorted Basa, as her porcelain denture clacked awkwardly in her weak jaw. "You made me climb up here. Now I expect you to get to the bloody point."

"Mother, please?"

"Enough, the pair of you," Eva – the youngest – chided, shaking her head. "I'm sorry, Auntie Drem. My nona isn't used to answering summons so late at night. Mother and I apologize on her behalf."

"Humph." Basa took a seat without asking.

"You're not old enough to pretend senility, Basa. Just because we share blood doesn't mean that I won't fuse your arse to that chair," Drem warned with a curl in her lip.

"Humph," Basa repeated.

Drem considered the trio in silence for several moments. "Ana, do you share your mother's reluctance?"

"No," Ana replied. She flushed under that imperious glare. "I'm ready to do my duty to the Ancestor, my lady. As are we all."

200

Drem stared at Basa pointedly.

The older woman threw up a hand. "Would I bloody be here if I wasn't? Tell her what you learned, girl."

Eva cleared her throat. "I had to ascertain a few facts before I felt my information was sound."

"Oh?" Drem's velveteen voice betrayed no emotion whatsoever. "Was Nema's little pet telling the truth?"

"I'm not sure. I don't believe he could invent such a fiction alone. He's not very bright nor brave enough to lie to me. My talents are insufficient here. Too much noise for me to 'hear' properly."

"That isn't good enough."

"I know, and I'm sorry, Auntie."

Drem exhaled through her nose. "I want to know where my granddaughter is, and I want to know why she'd be traveling with a rogue Sidhe lord. I never believed he was dead, you know?" she scoffed, "… Always did find it hard to believe that Midhir would execute him, despite his crime."

Ana nodded. "I struggled with that too. Truth be told, If I'd been in the Adair's position that day at Dumnain, I'd like to think I'd have done the same. Many think him a hero."

"Most think him a monster," snorted Basa.

Ana patted her mother's shoulder. "Perhaps, but I'll contend that if he is alive and takes Una under his protection, there's hardly a safer place she could be. He'll surely take her to Bri Leith if he can."

Drem pursed her lips, thinking hard. "If this person is *the* Adair, he wouldn't be in Eire unless he had no choice, would he? I don't believe he can cross that border unaided. No matter how I picture the encounter that supposedly brought him and Una together, I can't figure he'd be wandering the Greensward looking for damsels to rescue."

"Likely not," Basa conceded.

"Must have been pure coincidence or Siora's love for my girl."

"Must have," Ana laid her hand over her heart.

"Midhir's a just ruler, but his punishments are cruel poetry. If he's not dead, he's been exiled. I'll wager my title on it."

"How do you suppose?" asked Basa.

"Knowing the Grand Marshal as I did once, banishment here would be the worst sort of hell for him. He always was arrogant as the day is long." Drem said. "If it *is* him, you may take his protecting her as confirmation of my granddaughter's worth. Ana's right. He'll take her to Midhir. The trouble with that will be either smuggling Una into Aes Sidhe without getting shot or procuring a special warrant to cross with her, legally. I'm betting he plans on the former."

"And Nema?" Ana cut in before her mother could argue.

Drem traced the iron latticework on the windowpane. "She's done her work well. I'll say that for her."

"She'll ensnare herself in her own net," said Eva.

"It pleases me that you are such an optimist, child, but I fear we're caught in that net, just the same."

Ana folded her long brown fingers together. She always did have such beautiful hands. She'd been quite the lutist when Drem had chosen her for her only son. But that was many years ago, and her Kaya long dead. Ana never remarried, and Drem loved her for it.

"The Corsairs may be loyal to Nema, my lady, but they alone cannot hope to hold the city against Souther forces. Nor, dare I speak it, forces from Aes Sidhe. Nema's coup can never be a success so long as Arrin's daughter lives. She knows it as well as we do."

"I don't believe she intends to hold this city against any army, my dear."

That was something Eva hadn't expected to hear. "How so?"

Drem shot her a wan smile. "You're too young to have witnessed Nema's ascent through the Cloister, but we did." Every woman present, save Eva, could attest. "No one is that gifted from birth. It takes training, as you well know, but also blood. Our great families were made great by breeding. Selectivity is the key to power. *Genes.* Manipulation is a discipline founded on genetic inheritance. It's not a calling."

"Perhaps Nema is an exception to that rule?"

"And her follower— that creature Aoife?"

"I could accept Nema as a genetic fluke but not her little helper too. Genetic variances resulting in Manipulative Ability are so rare that they might as well be pebbles on a lakeshore. Aptitude is a by-product of selective breeding, Eva. I don't believe in lucky coincidences."

Basa grunted. "That's the red truth. No Patent of Maternas. No family. No children. Nema appeared out of thin air." She twisted her nose. "Though I hate to admit it, however she came by her gifts, they're *formidable*. We must acknowledge her power, Drem. I could almost respect her for her brass if she weren't trying to eradicate the Libella."

Eva leaned in. "Auntie, do you believe she somehow stole her powers from another? Broke the Ninth Law?"

"No, I'm saying she isn't who she says she is," answered Drem. Eva digested this statement with a perplexed frown. "I know it, though I've never been able to procure any evidence of this. Believe me, I've tried. There was something else about her. Something… *more*. It's been in her eyes for almost four decades. I suppose I've been expecting her little coup for years."

Basa said, "I told you to kill her long ago, Drem. You disobeyed my order. Now look what your sympathy bought." Drem made a face. Forty years before, Drem had won the right to the Tenth Ordeal before her cousin Basa, who'd once been her superior on the Council of Nine. When Drem donned the Doma's robes and ascended to the Tenth Floor, Basa vowed never to forgive her. All water under a dusty bridge now, but the embers of that old enmity still smoldered in Basa's eyes.

"Our only hope is to raise an army in Swansea and pray the High King will heed my request for aid. The rabble in the street will pull the Cloister down, brick by brick, unless we stop them. Without Una… without a sure, stable future— Nema will have her way. Is everything prepared?"

Ana, the senior Alvra Judge, bobbed her head once.

"Good. We have very little time to waste, it would seem. I expect that mob outside to have the gate down in days, maybe less. Have you made your arrangements?"

"House Alvra will not be in residence when this debacle gets heated, of course," said Basa sternly. "I don't like you, Cousin, but I'd fain see my family suffer for your abysmal mishandling of this office."

"I'm so pleased for your support," Drem growled.

"You should be. Our House is only doing this for the Ancestor's Heir. Nema is your mess. Now she's grown too tall to hack down, hasn't she?" the older woman chuckled. "Consider yourself fortunate we like your granddaughter better than you."

"My mother means," Ana smiled nervously, "that we are eager to help. Isn't that right, Mother? For Siora's sake."

"Humph," granted Basa.

"All right then. Eva, my dear, how many have sided with us?"

"All, save Houses Yma, Hamma, and Ganon."

"None of which bear surprise."

"Jumped up Merchers, the lot," added Basa. "As bad as Hollin and his band of lowborn lickspittles."

"Nema wants war with the Libella, so we shall oblige her. She may have the people's love now, but let's see how much they adore her when the markets dry up. They'll run out of food in a month— less if Siora is merciful."

"I like my estate in Bretagne this time of year," Basa noted. "Lord Gaelin is a particular favorite of mine. He'll be pleased to see me."

"Let's hope he'll be even more enamored of our terms," Drem said dryly. For Ana, she softened her regard. "Kernow is not quite as civilized nor pleasant this time of year, I'm afraid."

"I enjoy the sea air, Eminence."

"Excellent." Drem turned to Eva. "How fast can you get to the Sidhe Consulate in Ten Bells?"

Eva's smile flashed white in the dimly lit chamber. "I'm bringing Mel Carra. I have yet to see him lose an inch to bad weather. If Una is in Eire, we will find her. I swear it."

Drem tucked herself deep into her sealskin mantle. "And I shall await you all in Swansea, around Imbolg. May the Ancestor hold us in her wisdom."

"*In Her Eyes, In Her Heart, In Her Spine,*" they chanted in unison.

As her visitors bowed to leave, Drem turned back to the window to watch the rain patter against the panes. At the very least, the weather would slow the burning and chaos in the streets for a while.

"Let's see how you win a rebellion without fainne, Nema. Let's see how the people love you when their children are starving."

204

Rosweal

"I don't see why I must be dragged all the way to Rosweal. I could as soon walk to Tara or even Ten Bells. They're not looking for me," Rian grumbled from behind Ben. Her twisted foot wasn't helping her move any faster, and having to evade the roads at all costs took its toll. Ben was heartily sick of the woods. He wanted to drink himself to sleep in Barb's bathhouse, wake up to one of Rose's famous massages, and dive headfirst into one of Colm's salmon stews. Above all, he longed for a warm mug full of honey-gold uishge.

Gods... just imagining any one of these luxuries was its own relief.

They were arriving a bit later in the evening than he would have preferred, but they'd made it. That was something. Each of them was exhausted. Several miserable days in the Greensward would do that to anyone. Even Ben, usually a light sleeper, didn't crack an eye until last evening, and only then to stuff his mouth with dried tack. They'd spent most of the previous day camping and consuming the remainder of Rian's stores. Finally departing at first light this morning, they were hungry, despondent, and reeked of mildew. Illness and fever would inevitably follow. After another full day trudging through abominable terrain, Ben caught the familiar scent of civilization on the air. At last, emerging from a high thicket of elms, they looked down on a large, wooded valley. Three gently sloping hills intersected at a bend in the rapidly flowing Blackwater. Nestled into this natural bowl sat a large walled hamlet he was avidly familiar with. How many days had it been? Ten? A hundred? He couldn't tell.

Rosweal looked just the same: little squares and warbled rectangles, mashed together in a stinking, impersonal jumble. Twisting lanes wound their muddy way in every direction. Hundreds of chimneys puffed greenish peat-smoke into a coral and grey sky. Rooftops were dusted white with sparkling frost. All around the shale exterior walls, the Greensward pressed in. Even fallow fields to the south were threatened by hungry trees. From their vantage, they could clearly see the smoking mists that curled over the river. Rosweal was the last Milesian settlement of any size along the border, the wildest, most lawless region in Innisfail. Ben couldn't think of a better place to hide. He glared at Rian.

"We've been over this."

Una huffed in his ear, and he readjusted his grip on her knees so she could breathe easier. She'd walked most of the way on her own, but her broken ribs eventually caught her out. Without Vixen to share her weight, Ben had been obliged to carry her himself. *Reduced to a bloody pack mule, indeed.*

Rian pulled up short, noting the scowl on his face— a look she definitely deserved.

"What? I'm just saying there's a good chance we will have to head south anyway. What if your brilliant plan doesn't work, huh? It's not like you've told us how you're going to—"

"Rian," interrupted Una. "If you go home, you could be arrested or worse. You heard what those soldiers said. There are possibly hundreds of them on the road, searching for us."

"For *you*," sulked Rian.

"Say you head south? They've been to your farm, and into town looking for its owner. I guarantee it. The townsfolk will surely tell them all about the unwelcome faerie girl living in Arthur Guinness' house," added Ben, dryly. "They're looking for you as well. Believe it. Whoever sent those creatures for Una knows you were there. You're safer with us."

Rian swore under her breath. Something about 'trouble' and 'fault;' Ben ignored her. Una gripped his shoulder with silent pressure.

"I'm sorry you were dragged into this, Rian. I vow, I'll repay you one way or the other, and so will he. Won't you, Ben?"

He sucked his teeth and tilted his head, so she could see the likelihood of *that* happening. Bloody women and their need for useless platitudes. How in the hells was he supposed to know what was going to happen? He was making this up as he went along. He needed a drink, is what he needed.

He hadn't been sober so long in *decades*.

"But," argued Rian. "I can't eat promises, can I?"

"Then go. Take your chances, what do I care?"

"Ben…" Una warned.

"None of us is happy about any of this. We're coping, best we can. Life isn't fair, Rian. You'd better get used to that."

Rian wiped at her damp eyes with the back of a filthy hand and pretended to ignore him. He understood that she just wanted to go home, but what could he do? Staying alive was the priority, not comfort.

Una shook her head at him. "You're an ass, you know."

"So I've been told," Ben said. "Look Rian, I know this isn't a holiday but for better or worse, we're alive, and none of us are alone. All right? Let's try to make the best of this."

After a while, Rian bobbed her head. "Fine."

"Necessity provides all the faith one needs, right?"

She marked his point with a clenched jaw.

Good. A silent fury would suit his taxed nerves much better. Gazing down on the city, he thumbed the crude ogham charm below the hem of his tunic. Most folks he'd spent any amount of time with wouldn't immediately notice the difference between this Ben Maeden and the one they remembered, but he had to admit a select few most certainly would. His reflection that morning in the river was very similar to the one he'd worn for over a decade… though not quite. Rian, being only one-quarter Sidhe, couldn't hope to produce the same strong glamour his previous stone held. He and the old Ben Maeden shared the same height, weight, and build. His hair was Ben's— shaggy and yellow. He wore the same rough patches on his hands and stubble on his chin. However, the similarities stopped there. Rian's stone couldn't alter the translucent sheen of his skin, nor obscure the shape or depth of his silver-blue irises. He *was* Ben Maeden again... and distinctly, not. At least Gerrod and Robin already knew. He only hoped he'd be given a chance to explain himself before Robin had him shot in the street like a dog.

Well, he thought to himself.

No point worrying over it now.

He'd figure something out. He always did.

"Listen," he cleared his throat. "Rosweal's not a pleasant place. Everything you've heard about it is true. There are very many bad, desperate people behind those unkempt walls."

Rian leaned against a birch to catch her breath. "Can't you get in touch with whoever you need to somewhere *safer?*"

"Rosweal's the last place in Eire that anyone would think to look for Prima Moura. No one from the Red City will wander in here on a hunch."

"You'd better be right," Rian said. "Because if we're murdered down there, I will curse you to the blackest depths of the lowest hell in Tech Duinn, *tuiathe*."

Ben thought about pitching her over the hill. Una's blasted fingernails were going to give Ben a rash at this rate. He tried to slap them away.

"Damn it, woman, stop that!"

"We're in this together, like Ben said," Una sighed. "Can we move past this now? We can claw each other's eyes out when we're dry."

"Siora, help us," Rian pined. "At this point, I'd hand over every coin in my purse for a bath and a warm meal."

"Gods, *uisghe*," moaned Ben.

Una, for once, agreed. "Or the tallest mug of spiced cider in Innisfail."

"Uishge *in* the mug of spiced cider."

"Don't tease me. They do that here?"

"Hells yes, they do," Ben assured her. "I intend to drown myself in a cask at the first opportunity."

Rian wrinkled her nose. "Don't look at me when you're both puking your guts out."

"It'll be nice to have *something* in there to throw up," Una said.

"I'd better get something grand out of this. A house, a new farm, or better yet, my own peerage. *Lady Rian Guinness* has a nice ring, don't you think?"

⚚ ⚚

They approached the Navan Gate from the riverside. The sky had faded to a dull charcoal overhead. Ben pointed to a small, homely gap in the low city wall overgrown with weeds and piled high with discarded refuse.

"Best to avoid the gate, for now. We'll head through there." Both girls gaped at his proposed entrance with mirrored horror. The 'wall' was constructed of crudely stacked shale without a hint of mortar. This was the old Innish way to build, unchanged from the dawn of time. Perhaps it wasn't beautiful, but it would stand for centuries, so long as no one bothered to knock it down. Ben would tell them this if he thought either would hold the slightest interest.

Behind the section they crept toward stood hundreds of dilapidated huts, crammed one on top of the other. Weak lamplight flickered from flooded rivulets carved into each lane by heavy wagon wheels and overburdened horse carts. Dor Samna rains had left their ugly brown mark everywhere the eye rested. Rosweal often took the brunt of any storm, as it was perched at the crux of three steep hills. Here in the low east-end of town, where the poorest souls made their homes, folk trudged through ankle-deep filth just to get to their front doors. After so long spent in the relatively fresh air in the Greensward, the stench was overpowering.

"Dear, sweet, Siora," Rian gagged.

Una buried her face in her tunic.

Ben smirked. "Welcome to Rosweal, ladies."

"We're not staying *here*, I hope?" pleaded Una, her face scrunched up like she'd swallowed a lemon whole.

"We'll take the alley past the Hunter's Quarter to the other side of town. Those buildings on the hill, facing the river. See them?"

He felt her nod at his back. Rian hitched her skirts as high as she could and still managed to keep hold of her walking stick. It wouldn't help. Even with the boards hammered into the middle of each lane, there was no escaping the sludge below. They would likely have to burn their garments when all was said and done. Ben didn't frequent this end of town. He did have standards... well, he once had them, anyway. He shifted Una forward a bit so he could step carefully onto one of these semi-useful boards.

"I have a place overlooking the river. It's not much, but I doubt anyone will be expecting me."

"You sure?" inquired Rian, with a suspicious scowl.

"... We'll worry about that later."

"Oh, great," said Una. "I suppose you owe someone money?"

"No need to be rude."

Rian squeaked when a dead rat floated over her boot. "Who'd want to live here?"

"Not everyone's father was a successful physician," said Ben.

"How magnanimous of you, your lordship," jeered Una.

Ben bristled. "I've lived here for years, *princess*. Be careful not to stare too long into the light you're attempting to shine upon me."

"I'm *not* a princess. How about you? Did you grow up on a farm like Rian, I wonder?"

"No, but I've been here longer than both of you are old. So, shut up."

"Siora!" Rian snapped. "Will you two *please* stop bickering?"

"We're not bickering," Una sniffed. "We're merely—"

"Didn't you just get on my case about arguing with him?"

That did the trick. Una's mouth clapped shut over her retort.

"A plan, Ben. Do we have one or not?" Rian demanded, forced to grab onto the back of his tunic to keep her footing on the way uphill.

"I'm working on it."

She grumbled several unflattering things beneath her breath. "Right. Why plan ahead? It's more fun this way, isn't it?"

"Do you fancy a bath and clean clothes, or not?" He was slightly mollified by the intense, hopeful longing that chased her sarcastic

210

expression away. "Well, they're this way. You can come along or make your own plans. Got it?"

Una patted him like he was a faithful pony. Because, clearly, she knew it irritated him. Grumbling, he led them through the complicated patchwork of lanes through the slums and the hilltop perched above.

THEY PASSED EVERY SORT OF low establishment imaginable. What Rosweal lacked in size and grandeur, it made up for in squalid, belching, screeching, raucous humanity. People everywhere were hanging from doorways, shouting drunkenly at their neighbors, or shuffling aimlessly down mellifluous lanes. Women cackled, spat, scolded, and catcalled from various misshapen windows and rickety awnings. The rain didn't dissuade any of Rosweal's citizens from wandering outdoors to seek their various entertainments. Men gathered outside run-down shops and taverns, smoking, arguing, fighting, or generally carousing. Ragged, half-starved sticks Una assumed were children ran hither and thither through foul streets, dodging grasping hands, abandoned carts, and the odd animal carcass. As Ben and company ambled up a narrow lane crushed between two leaning wooden tenements, an overhead shutter slammed open. Without a word of warning, a bucket full of human waste splashed downward in a reeking brown cascade. Rian shrieked, almost knocking all three of them into the muck to avoid it. Ben hauled her upright by the collar.

"Don't draw attention to yourself."

"I don't think we could if we tried," said Una with a dismayed glare.

"Oh, you *can*. I mean it, don't make eye contact and keep your voice down." His eyes darted around. "You don't want to appeal to anyone here."

From the shanty town, with its flooded streets and violent surging mortality, they ascended a steep hill, which leveled out around a much more stoic neighborhood. Everything seemed quieter here, less cluttered and congested. The air was a bit cleaner too, but not by much. Una turned to marvel at the bobbing lights and ramshackle roofs whence they came.

"How many people live down there?"

"Hundreds, maybe more. Who cares?"

"Awful," said Rian. "Did you see those poor children?"

Ben shrugged. "Half of those kids likely have no relatives left to depend upon. People starve out here in the wilds come winter. The smart ones will live. The rest... well. As you can see."

"Their parents and guardians could make their lives better if they wanted to," she argued. "Besides, what does a nobleman like you know about poverty, *tuiathe*?"

"I know who I am, Rian, but I also know them," he paused to jerk his chin downhill. "This *is* a rough place, but I'm telling you, these people make do. While I might not always understand them, I know how hard these folks work to survive, and I'll not fault them for their efforts."

"Then why don't you live down there with them?"

"I said I respect them, not that I envy them. We each must make our way, heedless of circumstance or consequence."

"That's rather poignant for a debauch like yourself."

Una said nothing for a moment. It surprised her that Ben found some measure of camaraderie with the outcasts in Rosweal. Everything she'd ever been told about him suddenly seemed somewhat biased. Perhaps he didn't despise 'Milesians' as much as everyone believed he did? Or maybe he'd been here long enough to develop an appreciation for those he once considered inferior? One thing she knew for sure: solitude courted strange bedfellows. She probably knew this better than most. The Cloister of the Eternal Flame was not a place of communal harmony. To dwell within that sumptuous prison, one must accept that they are well and truly alone. She wondered if Ben might have been brought up to feel the same way. She folded that kernel away for later examination.

"I think if more people knew of the suffering here, they might seek to lend a hand," she said.

He craned his neck to give her a dubious glare. "Some things are easier said than done, princess."

"I won't forget those children if I ever make it home."

212

"You may want to remember the ones in Tairngare first," Ben chuckled. "Poverty is not a novelty anywhere in your Milesian societies. As soon as people figured out it was easier to exploit others than work for themselves, it's been much the same throughout your history. Be careful not to applaud yourself for your condescension."

Rian stumbled up the rise. "No child deserves a life like that. Besides, grand lords and ladies, like yourselves, should ask what can be done. Don't you think?"

Una decided just then that she liked Rian Guinness very much. She smiled over at her. "Well said."

Rolling his eyes, Ben led them through two more alleys connected with the first, then up a crudely carved set of stairs to a semi-cobbled lane. Again, the streets got cleaner the higher they climbed; the air more tolerable. Ben took them below an arch down the wide main street, then cut right into another alley. This row was easily the best of the lot. The buildings here had sturdy stone foundations and high stucco walls painted in various cheerful shades. Almost every window had two sets of shutters: some even fine latticed glass. Almost every cross-street featured tall lantern poles, which poured muted lamplight onto the cobbles. There were more people out on this side of town than there had been in the last two neighborhoods— though nowhere near as many as the mob in the slums. There were one or two publicans with heavy creaking signs. Random knots of nominally well-dressed individuals gathered in front of each. Ben paused at the sight and gently tried to steer the girls into the next lane. One fellow leaned out, waving.

"Ho there! Ben Maeden? Is that ye? Well, I'll be blustered. Ole Gerry said ye left town. Where ye headed?"

Ben cursed as the caller trotted down the street toward them, two others close on his heels. Ben shoved Rian against a dark wall, prodding Una to slide down to her feet.

The short, dark-haired fellow who'd called out to them slowed about five paces away. "Oh. Who's that ye got there, huh?"

"Looks like girls, to me," remarked one of his more brilliant friends.

"Don't look like any'o Matt's goods. Maybe Barb's got some new stock?"

"Oh, aye. One's quite fair, ye ask me. The other looks like she's been done for. Who beat the shite outta ye, lovey?"

The first's easy smile faded when he saw Ben's fingers close over his sword pommel. He slid his hands up. "Whoa, Ben. Just came to greet ye. No need for that."

"You've never greeted me in your life, Vincent. What do you want?" The erstwhile Vincent backed up a step. His mates were still arguing about what establishment Una and Rian might have been prized from. Una ground her teeth. She was not used to treatment like this *at all*.

"It's just Vick, Ben. Sayin' hallo, s'all." Despite his harmless grin, Vick kept his hands up, but he wasn't leaving. Ben's reaction made Una nervous. These lads didn't look dangerous, and their clothes weren't fine by anyone's standards— but they were cleaner and better tailored than anything they wore, saving Ben's stolen sealskin cloak. Rian seemed to anticipate the trouble they might be in. She clasped Una's fingers in hers to propel them both backward along the wall.

"You've said it, now slag off."

Vick didn't stop smiling his affable smile. "Yer on the wrong side o'town, ain't ye, Ben? Ole Lon, at the *Juke*, said ye roughed up some o'his customers few nights back. Been mighty noisy 'bout it too."

"Guess how much he'll pay for yer corpse," sniggered the taller of Vick's companions. "Offerin' a full stag, what I hear. Said he'd pay Matt double, jus' for signin' off."

Ben gave them a cold smile. "Crossing me didn't work out so well for them, did it?"

Vick's smirk flickered. "Them were friends o'mine, Ben Maeden."

"*Were*, being the operative word."

The three louts didn't appear eager to leave. Ben slid back until his right heel connected with the toe of Una's boot. "Three up, one over. Understand?"

"What?"

"Will ye listen to that voice? Gave me a chill, that did," said the tall one.

"Long as ye don't have to look at her face!" laughed his friend.

"*I* do." Rian drew the little dagger Ben gave her from her belt. She yanked Una away from the wall. From then on, Una couldn't say what happened because all she could hear was shouting, shuffling, and steel striking steel. She and Rian ran until Una's broken ribs felt like they might pierce her lungs. When Rian jerked her around the corner three lanes up, they discovered a sad little park of sorts. The space was set into a wide cul-de-sac down the end, overgrown with weeds and littered with debris— not much to look at, save for a low stone bench and the remnants of a fountain. A playful howl echoed from the buildings around them. The taller youth swaggered into the slanted moonlight, his face a ghoulish leer.

"There ye are. Thought there'd be a bit more chase in ye's."

Rian raised her dagger. "Oh, there is."

He clapped his hands together like a giddy child. "Good! I hate it when there's no dash in me ladies, ye know? Dull, that way."

Una inched forward, but Rian stopped her. "No. You'll just hurt yourself worse."

"But—"

Without warning, the boy sprang at Rian with a skeletal grin. Rian moved left to slash at him with her right, but he was faster. He grabbed her around the waist and swung her to the ground, yowling with excitement. Rian thrashed, but he struck her once, hard. She went limp for a split-second too long, and he took advantage. Wrenching her forward by her vest, he climbed up her torso to snatch at the front of her dress.

The dagger skittered away, out of reach. With a snarl, Una lunged at him. He tumbled backward, smacking the base of his skull against jagged paving stones. Grunting, he grabbed a fistful of the hair at Una's nape and tugged her head back. White stars traced across her eyes at the pain. One meaty fist smashed into the right side of her face, from her ears to her chin. Una blinked and clenched her jaw against the chorus of bells in her ears. Blood ran down her cheek from her already swollen eye. She shoved her knee into his solar plexus to keep the boy from dislodging her and brought her elbow into his nose. He screamed as the cartilage gave way to the bone. She hit him again, and several of his front teeth cracked and splintered. Una wasn't given time to enjoy the sounds. He drove both fists into her face, then bucked her aside with his legs.

He got to his knees. "I'm gonna cut yer tits off!"

Una spat out a mouthful of blood. "Thought you liked a woman with fight?" He caught her ankle, intending to drag her within reach, but wasn't watching Rian.

Wiping the blood from her nose, Rian gripped Ben's dagger in a white-knuckled fist. Before the boy could speak or make another move, Rian drove the dagger hilt-deep into his neck. He gurgled in surprise and crumpled forward. His eyes bulged when he hit the ground.

"So happy we could oblige you. You piece of shite." She didn't wait to watch him die as he deserved. She pulled Una to her feet. "Siora, I think he broke your cheekbone. Can you walk?"

"Quick, before he's gone. I need to...."

"What are you talking about?"

"Just take me to him!"

Visibly confused, Rian lowered Una beside their scrawny, would-be rapist's dying body. Una didn't have time to explain. He was moments from death. She could not waste him. She shot Rian an apologetic glance and placed her right hand over his gore-slick face. He choked as her palm covered what was left of his mouth. Una took a deep, stilling breath. She let her Spark reach for him... *into* him. Life flowed back into her body, streams, and streams of pure raw energy. She tapped, molded, and sent it where it was most needed. Her heart beat clearer and stronger. She felt her lungs expand; her air passages widen. The blood replenished itself in her veins, cells divided with the speed of a rushing river. Her ribs and throat burned. The bones in her face glowed hot as coals under her skin. Una shuddered when those same molten bones fused; fractures mended on each breath.

Then it was done.

Incomplete. Her Spark retreated, stilted and unsatisfied. Una collapsed on her haunches, gasping. Her burning palms slid over her partially mended ribs.

Rian gaped at her like Una had just helped herself to the man's brains. "What in the *nine hells*... did you just do?"

216

"He intended to use us. I used him instead."

"Hallowed *Siora*. I've never seen anything like that before."

"Nor will you. It's forbidden."

"I can bloody see why!"

"Rian, I'm sorry. Truly. But I didn't have the time to explain myself. My injuries were going to get me killed. Can we leave it for later?"

"… You tried to save my life just now."

"And you certainly saved mine."

After a while, Rian exhaled. "Give us some warning next time, is all I ask."

Una smiled. She held out a hand to be helped up. When they were face to face, she patted Rian on the shoulder. "Deal."

A scrape behind them, and they both turned, alarmed.

This time, it was only Ben. He stood at the edge of the cul-de-sac, taking in the shriveled dead man and the bloodied girls standing over him. Ben didn't seem the worse for wear himself if slightly winded… the bastard.

"What in blazes happened here?"

Rian wiped her hands on her skirt. "You know, more *fun*."

He crept toward them, eyes wide. "We should go. Right now. This isn't Guild territory, and we've killed *two* men."

"Is that supposed to mean anything to us?"

"We're on the wrong side of town."

"Does that imply there's a right side?" Rian asked Una, who shrugged.

"Doubt it."

"I've lost Vick but killed his mouthy friend. They'll be looking for us. Let's go, please. *Now*."

Una sidestepped the corpse toward Ben. Rian stooped to retrieve her dagger, making a disgusted snort while she scrubbed the blade clean on the dead boy's tunic.

Ben's fingers caught Una's elbow before she could walk past him. He stared. "What happened to your face?"

"Fast healer, remember?"

"Right," he frowned.

"Won't they just follow us to your preferred end of Rosweal?" Rian asked, coming to stand beside them.

Ben couldn't seem to stop scowling at Una's face. Una purposefully ignored him. He gestured for them to follow him to the north end of the park, where another alley twisted along the wall, then angled westward.

"Not at all. They know better than to enter the Greenmakers' Quarter."

"Oh, so we'll be safe there?"

"Well, in a manner of speaking," said Ben, still staring at Una in morbid fascination.

"Wonderful," she breathed. She wasn't sure why, but the prospect of danger didn't seem to frighten her as badly as it might have a few days before. Either she was getting used to this chaos, or she was beginning to trust her new comrades. For Una, this was uncharted territory. She'd spent the past ten years in her apartments, reading, writing, and honing her Manipulation. Monthly training sessions with Mel Carra in her private courtyard on the Ninth Floor had been her sole means of physical exercise. That Una seemed so far away from her now, they might have been staring across a vast ocean at each other. It had been less than two weeks since she'd been taken from Drogheda, but already, she felt like a completely different person. Though she hated killing, she was learning the value of her life. She wasn't afraid of herself any longer. Her revelation felt surreal— odd.

Optimistic was too solid and preposterous a word for the situation. Wasn't it? *Foolhardy* seemed a far more appropriate term.

Twelve Steps

n.e. 508
23, ƀor samna
ꝼernƀale

Damek left the wooden gate swinging free in the strong, northerly breeze. He circled the partially destroyed cottage with a wary eye on its damaged façade. Frowning, he traced a gloved finger over the huge claw marks that bisected the north wall. Deep, gaping slashes cut through the siding and mortar to the stone beneath. Several shingles had pried themselves loose on the roof, exposing the roof's supporting timbers to the elements. After a few days of steady rain, huge sagging holes already coalesced there. The roof would eventually cave in without someone to shore up the damage. Damek tread around the rear corner and raised his eyebrows at the damage done to the back of the house. The doorway leaned haphazardly sideways, its lintel having fallen and smashed against the stoop. He took a few steps back to admire the scale of the destruction. One more heavy rain and the house might crumble like stacked kindling. Holding his breath, he faced the mutilated barn. There were shredded piles of livestock rotting all over the place. Flies choked the air in dense, buzzing clouds. A ribcage discarded like so much dross lay over the splintered remnants of what once must have been the door; bones glinted white in the morning sun.

A thick coating of frost did little to hide the carnage he cataloged in that yard. The barn's roof had been smashed to splinters. What animals made it out before the collapse were ripped in half and only partially consumed as if they were killed merely for sport. Whatever did this must not have been able to do the same to the house. Otherwise, it might have been Una he found lying here, half-eaten, in the mud and frost. Perhaps there was some rule associated with Otherworld creatures like these? Could they not enter a person's home without invitation? The owner was rumored to be a faerie girl. Did she know some charm that could have prevented these beasts from leaving her home in the same state as the barn? He had no idea. He'd never encountered anything like this before. Damek drifted toward Martin, and his men, careful not to step in any of the gory remains littering the pasture. His knights were gathered around the monsters' carcasses, jabbing sabres and spear shafts at the still-smoking hides. From the state of things, all of this must have happened days before— yet the creatures in question did not desiccate. Why? Who would send beasts like these after Una? Who could?

Damek had only one suspect in mind.

Martin, he noted, arrived at the same conclusion. Their eyes met over a steaming foreleg. Damek knew Una had escaped the smugglers he'd hired, and he'd heard there were six dead Corsairs back east, rotting in a wooded dell beside the High Road. He was certain Una had also survived that encounter because two men bore sure signs of her handiwork. One man's brains had been boiled out of his open orifices, and the other's face had been crushed from inside his skull. He knew of no one, save Una, with the macabre ability to mangle flesh and bone from within. What had happened to her after was less certain. Why did Corsairs hunt her in the first place? Were they not armored knights from Tairngare's Citadel? Hadn't Damek paid a small fortune to smuggle her from the city in one piece? His connection assured him that nothing would serve their purposes better than to have the Moura Domina out of the way. Apparently not. Either the Citadel Corsairs were engaged in a coup, or Damek's contact had lied about her intentions through her pretty white teeth.

Damek did not believe in coincidence or bad luck. He'd been betrayed, likely from the very first. It seemed his blasted uncle had a point, after all. Their contact in the Cloister was a double agent. There could be little doubt now. Damek wasn't sure which angered him more: that someone he held a modicum of affection for was a traitor or that Patrick had been right about Aoife from the start? She was not the only complication plaguing his overtaxed mind, however. He'd already paid a visit to the campsite a mile north of Bally Lough, where Rawly and his men had been viciously slain. It took almost three days to backtrack from their appointed rendezvous to the site. Everything was precisely as Cunningham had said it would be. Though badly decomposed in the harsh elements, the evidence was plain; Rawly's crew had been slain by someone exceptionally skilled with bow and blade. Damek doubted that archery was a prized subject of study in the Cloister. Therefore, this ruled out Una having taken matters into her own hands.

According to the rumor about the six Corsairs who were found beside the High Road, they'd been observed chasing a small woman about twenty miles west of the village of Slane. Witnesses didn't see what happened to the woman in question. They could only point to the place the Corsairs' corpses had been found. Again, all were slain by an experienced hand.

It seemed Una *had* found herself a reluctant protector.

While Damek was relieved to learn that Una wasn't out here alone, he was annoyed that some unknown agent had intervened. Furthermore, he was incredibly apprehensive of this mysterious individual's intentions. First, Una should be in Bethany now and safe in her father's house. None of this incessant backtracking should have been necessary in the least. If Rawly had made their rendezvous, she would have passed into Damek's company in Ten Bells, grumpy, no doubt, but otherwise, none the worse for wear. Secondly, whoever interfered to save her was taking her farther west rather than back to Tairngare to presumed safety. That could only mean the rumor about the Corsairs chasing a woman into the Greensward bore truth, and Damek must infer that someone had pursued Una from the Citadel. He was having a hard time denying the obvious. Nema had no intention of honoring her arrangement with Bethany. Clearly, she and Aoife played a side game that didn't include him. Well, he would just see about that, wouldn't he?

221

He knelt beside a decapitated head larger than his torso.

"Martin. Call for Cunningham."

"Aye, My Lord." Martin barked orders to the men behind him. It took a few minutes to wrangle Cunningham from the back of the line, bound to his horse as he had been. The disgraced Captain of the Steel Corps scowled down at his liege lord, infuriated by his inhospitable treatment. Damek couldn't blame him, but he had to be sure of the man's absolute loyalty.

Damek nodded at the Corps Lieutenant. "Hisk. His bonds, if you please?" Cunningham's eyes burned with mistrust. Martin's fingers curled over his pommel in response. Hisk unlocked his manacles, and Cunningham shoved him backward, hard. "Now now, Captain. Behave yourself."

"Fuck you, O'Rearden."

Damek laughed. "Charming, don't you think, Martin?"

"I wonder how adorable he'll be without a tongue?"

Cunningham stood as straight as he was able. "I've taken all the shite I mean to for telling the truth."

"You got a complaint you'd like to lodge now? Formally?" Martin's steel sang a bit as it slid partway from its sheath. Cunningham swallowed audibly.

"No, *Commander*."

"Very good, Captain." Martin's blade snapped home with a sharp click. "Now, you may address your lord. Respectfully, remember."

"Why was any of this necessary?"

"You're not a stupid man, Wallace. I've been fed one line of horseshite after another. I wanted to be sure of you. As you can plainly see," Damek gestured to the general nightmarish absurdity of the scene, "we're in uncharted waters here. It doesn't appear that my fair cousin has merely been abducted, does it?"

"No," Cunningham agreed with a semi-shrug. "Forgive my tone, but I believe I said so in my initial report?"

"Watch yourself," Martin droned.

Cunningham raked a frustrated hand over his scalp. "Lieutenant Hisk can attest to my observational ability, My Lord. I'll swear to it

222

again if that's what you want. She was taken by your man and his crew, as ordered. Someone in the Citadel must have observed their leaving or knew their general escape route, for they were soon chased into Bally Lough by scores of Corsairs and Tairnganeah Regulars. There, they were slain to a man by someone who came from the *wrong* end of the woods. Someone too good to be considered incidental, yet, all the physical evidence left at the scene would argue the contrary. I can't put it any plainer than that."

Damek shot Martin a twisted lower lip. "A High Elf, I believe you said?"

Cunningham absorbed the laughter that echoed around him with a rigid spine. "That is my assessment. I have no reason to invent such an odd tale, nor do I enjoy a fable. I stand by my report."

"Very well." Damek waved Hisk and his men back. They took Cunningham's manacles with them. Cunningham looked around, guarded and uncertain. "Your ability is quite clear, Major. You've exceeded my expectations. Now, would you be so kind as to examine this scene and report your conclusions?"

Cunningham gawped from Damek to Martin and back, his mouth opening and closing. "M-My Lord?"

"I asked you to examine these beasts, *Major* Cunningham— and tell me if it is your opinion that the same hand which slew Rawly and his men also did this. Was that clear enough? I do hate to repeat myself. You could as easily be retied to your horse. Your choice."

Cunningham flushed crimson to the roots of his red hair while he fumbled a salute. "Right away, sir, erm, My Lord!"

Damek winked at Martin, who shook his head. He veered away from the bestial corpses and headed back toward the house. Martin followed.

"Well," he said, clasping his hands behind his back as they walked. "I doubt a field commission is what young Wallace Cunningham expected back there."

"The man earned it. He was right."

"You agree with his assessment then?" Damek saw the lesions on the larger beast's carcass. Arrowheads, he was certain, though said arrows were long absent. Any self-respecting archer would do his utmost to preserve his supply, so Damek was not surprised to find them gone. He didn't need them to confirm the sheer artistry of each wound. They were too clean to be hurried and loosed from too far away to be directed on the fly. Given the scene, each shot should have been practically impossible. Distance, velocity, angle, inertia: all of these were imperatives in a bowman's arsenal. What was evident here was a haphazard disregard for basic calculations. The hand that drew down on these creatures did so too quickly to guarantee aim yet hit each target without a second glance.

How did Damek know this? The tracks.

The beasts' prints were everywhere, hard to miss for their size and irregular gait. Of the archer, there were only two well-defined sets. This person had walked, rather than ran, in a straight line from the cottage; the tracks there were too narrow and shallow for a dash. There was a slight impression upon the right heel at the end of the line, which indicated the bowman had tilted back to draw, but that was all. He didn't hurry. Damek wasn't as skilled a tracker as Cunningham, but he saw the wounds on each creature's bodies. The archer took a couple of shots from this position, which dropped the first beast with little ado. From there, the second beast seemed to rise on its hind legs. The fellow had emptied his meager quiver, then took up a sword or axe to finish the job. Damek followed the mess of tracks in the earth around the headless beast's body.

Whoever this person was, he had slain both of these unnatural beasts in about twelve steps. The whole affair had probably lasted less than five minutes. If Damek didn't already have Cunningham's previous testimony, he wouldn't have needed it to make an educated guess. "I concur with the Major. No one is this good. We can't be sure who he is, but I'd wager my arse against his heritage."

"You rather *are* making that bet."

Damek made a face. "I suppose I am, aren't I?"

"At least one mystery has been solved."

"Yes," Damek's expression darkened.

"I suppose your girl had other plans, then, eh?"

"I'll be damned if I know why." Damek ducked under the leaning doorjamb, careful not to touch it. The last thing he needed was to trap himself inside a crumbling building. He motioned for Martin to wait shy of the jamb. Martin was almost twice as wide as Damek and therefore couldn't hope to squeeze through that gap unmolested.

Martin crossed his corded arms. "You'll forgive me for saying so; I daresay she's been leading you by the nose."

Damek laughed without mirth and picked his way through the largely undamaged interior. Whoever built this little cottage had known what he was about. Aside from puddles collecting beneath holes in the roof and the imminent threat of collapse, the foundations were strong. If the outer walls could be repaired in time, perhaps the roof could be mended. Though, what did it matter? The owner was long gone. Damek stepped over to a little couch beside a homely fireplace to retrieve a bloodied shawl draped over its arm. This was one of the few items strewn about the cottage which wasn't soaking wet with moldering rainwater. He held it briefly beneath his nose. Whatever alchemical mixture of components caused human scents to leave an indelible scar upon one's memory assured him that Una had been wrapped in this garment. The scent was faint and hampered by the coppery sick sweetness of drying blood, but present, nonetheless. A carefully concealed fury surged through his veins. She was injured— badly, it would seem. Was that Aoife's doing, or Nema's, working independently of her right hand? To *whom* should he direct his rage?

"I've known Aoife for most of my life, Martin. This entire plan was her idea, to begin with."

"My point exactly."

Damek looked up. "I won't argue her treachery or complicity. No point to that now. I simply can't help but wonder what she thought she'd gain. Why spend a decade planning this, only to betray me before I could see it to fruition?"

"Why indeed, your lordship?" Martin toed a loose clod of earth with his boot. "Perhaps something went wrong on her end? We have reports that Tairngare is in chaos. Rioting, and the like. Maybe, she worried that

Lady Donahugh would return to Tairngare and ally with the opposition? We know how much the Alta Prima loves the Mouras."

Oh, Damek knew. He knew better than Martin, that was sure. But this was not information he intended to share with anyone, even his most trusted friend.

"It's possible." Damek tossed the soiled garment back on the couch. "There's a deeper game here that I'm not seeing."

"If you'll pardon me? I, for one, am not in the least surprised by this double-cross. I think you've been played for a fool here, and the Duch with you from the very first."

"It suits Nema's interests to have Una out of the way, and it suits mine to take her to wife before Patrick can get his hooks into her. They were to cede Tara and Malahide to me, and I would use them to hold the Midlands against the Duch until the Barons fell in line. This was a win-win."

Martin gave him a smile that told Damek he knew more than he let on but was willing to keep his peace. "I know how you like to second-guess your conclusions, My Lord. I think you arrived at the answer long before I did, and I doubt it shocked you any more than it does me. In no scenario can I figure does Una being married to a powerful Souther lord bode well for Nema's new government. You must realize, as much as your piece might please you, that her loyalty has always lain with her mistress. With Una out of the way, Nema can cry foul and retract her support for Patrick's siege."

"This will only goad Patrick to hostility, and without me to intervene, how does she propose to block him?"

"I gather she *wants* Patrick to attack. Unrest in the Red City, Una's abduction, enemies marching through the North— sounds like she's makin' her bid for the Tenth Floor. All this," Martin waggled three fingers at Damek, "helps her cause, don't you think? If her main argument is that the Mouras are unfit for leadership, everything that's happening now can only encourage the people to see things her way. Honestly? What does she need you for, begging your pardon, My Lord— other than to serve as a distraction?"

That gave Damek pause.

He must assume any additional promises made to him on a more personal level were equally nullified. It didn't seem likely that Nema would attempt to set Damek on such a wild goose chase unless… she intended to divide him from the bulk of Bethany's forces in the first place. Nema wouldn't have to concern herself over invading nobles from Ten Bells, Tara, or Malahide if Damek was busily revenging himself upon them for Una's loss. Wasn't this fascinating? Either Nema believed Damek could still be manipulated after showing her hand so baldly this way, or she had no further use for him at all. If she didn't fear reprisals from any Souther lord, what else had she been keeping from him for so many years? Nema was not one to act in a hurry. Plans within plans, Nema had— like a fat spider at the center of a web.

It seemed everyone in Innisfail had a mind to use Damek to achieve their own ends and discard him after. He'd be pleased to disappoint them all, wouldn't he? Before now, he could never hope to hold onto the Northern cities without backing from the Souther Barons. He knew it, and Nema had surely counted on it. She perhaps hadn't realized before she stuck the knife into his back that she was handing Damek an invaluable gift: *cause*. The Barons would fall all over themselves to accommodate him now. The Cloister had not only kept their future Duchess from her true home in Bethany all these years, but now they'd attempted to murder her too. The irony was beautiful. Perhaps if Nema had managed to kill Una as planned, she might have pulled off her little coup without a hitch. Damek *would* have burned the North to cinders in a fury for his lost chance at legitimacy, and Patrick *would* have had him killed or imprisoned for his failure to hold it. But… Una had defied the old bitch and her shoddy plans, hadn't she? She was alive. All Damek had to do was find her, and his chips would fall into place on their own.

Perhaps he should write Nema a 'thank you' note? She could remove it from Aoife's conniving mouth after Damek strangled her and sent her body back to Tairngare in burlap. Musing over how he'd make the women in his life pay for underestimating him, he ducked into a parlor with books strewn about the floor. A handsome desk held several broken jars of herbs, foul-smelling fluids, and pungent powders. On a table along the right wall lay a bowl and cloth stained with dried blood, all of which alluded to Una's state when she'd arrived. She was alive, but for how long? He had no time to waste. Damek strode outside to find Martin sitting on the stoop, cleaning his nails with the tip of his dagger.

"Anything of note?"

"Una was here. She's injured. If I may hazard a guess, I'd say our strong fellow carried her here to see the good doctor Guinness before they were attacked by these Otherworld... things."

"Townsfolk in Ferndale say the doctor died some while back. Must mean his daughter has some skill with the needle herself?"

"Must do," agreed Damek. "I found no trace of human remains in that barn or anywhere nearby. The owner left with them or fled elsewhere."

"I would have if those beasts came to blow down my house and eat up all my pets. Wouldn't you?"

"Hm," Damek marched past his forward guard as they set up cookfires for mid-morning luncheon. The majority of his forces waited in town, about five miles south. His officers saluted him as he strolled past. He approached the larger of the two dead beasts, where Cunningham knelt. All Damek needed now was confirmation of his assertions before deciding what to do next. "Martin?"

"My Lord," said O'Rearden from behind him. As faithful a shadow as there ever had been.

"You've fought them before, the Daoine Sidhe?" This was more a statement of fact than a question, as everyone knew very well what a hero Martin O'Rearden had been at Dumnain. Bethany may have lost that battle and ultimately the war against Aes Sidhe, but Martin had famously made them pay for every inch the Sidhe gained. No one in the South would ever forget it. "Do they fight with such weapons? Broadswords, I mean?"

"Not generally. They prefer the lark—a long slender blade made from an alloy we've never been able to duplicate. Most of their foot soldiers carry two of these larks; built for speed, not bone-cleaving strength."

"What do you make of this, then?"

"Could be Sidhe, sure. Though I haven't seen many elves use a weapon heavier than the lark outside of pitched battle. Don't need anything heavier, you ask me. Bastards are bloody quick and strong enough without the added weight."

"Cunningham?"

"My Lord?"

"What's your verdict?"

Cunningham looked flabbergasted. "It's the same blade, or I'm daft."

"You're sure?"

"I am. Damned strong steel, if I'm any judge. Two-hander, likely twenty-five to thirty pounds, as the Commander said. And another thing." Cunningham gestured to the earth around each corpse. "He's very, very good. I saw the same at Rawly's campsite."

Damek scowled to hear his own opinions restated. "You're positive this is a Sidhe warrior?"

Cunningham didn't bat an eye. "I would count on it."

Absolutely fucking wonderful.

If Aes Sidhe knew what was afoot in Eire, Damek might already be too late. "All right then. It's unlikely that we're all misreading this scene."

"The Duch will gnash his teeth over this." Martin scratched at his scar.

"So too, will Nema," said Damek with a quirk to his lower lip. "But I'm sure her agents arrived at our conclusions days ago… *and* they have a head-start. As for the Duch, I don't give a damn about him right now. We have to find Una fast. I can't spare any men to keep him apprised."

"You know I love you, lad, but be careful now. You know what Patrick will think of that."

"What d'you think he'll make of his daughter being spirited over the border while I waste time penning messages and waiting for orders?"

"I empathize, My Lord. But you need him as much as he needs you. Don't make a mistake that could cost you everything later."

Damek cursed. He hated that Martin was always bloody right. "Reason, damn it. Fine. *Hisk!*"

The lieutenant saluted again. "My Lord?"

"Find someone willing to go home and face my uncle's wroth for me. One horse only, do you hear?"

"Aye, My Lord."

"Lord Bishop…" Martin attempted.

Damek ignored him. "I need every available man on the hunt. Send outriders to every town, village, and way-house for twenty miles. Una's injured, on the run… and in the company of at least two others. One, it seems, is likely a Sidhe agent. He'll be taller than the average man, likely fair of skin, and armed with a thirty-pound longsword. They cannot be far if they haven't crossed the border already."

Martin said, "We don't know all the details yet. He could be some nobody who happened by. Let's not leap to judgment."

"What self-respecting Sidhe have you ever heard of that would willingly loiter around this shitehole, Martin?"

"I can't say, but you never know. Wallace here said himself. He thought the individual that killed Rawly and his band wandered in from nowhere. Wasn't that what you told me?" He glanced at Cunningham.

"I did. My Lord, it was as if this person drifted into Rawly's camp to steal supplies. I don't think he set out to capture the girl at all. He left her tied to a tree that first eve."

Damek wanted to hit something. "Then how do you explain the rest of it? The dead Corsairs? *This* horror? If you're telling me he's some kind of Sidhe sneakthief and murderer, why didn't he leave her to die when he encountered her next? It doesn't add up."

Cunningham lifted a shoulder. "Maybe he realized who she was and decided she was worth the effort, or maybe he carried her away for himself? Who knows?"

Damek ground his molars with no small amount of personal bitterness. "Even injured, I doubt she'd let him touch her unless she had reason to trust him. He's offering her something. I can feel it in my marrow. The only thing I can imagine is sanctuary."

"Whatever the reason," interrupted Martin, sensing the circular nature of this debate. "I agree. We'd better find her. The longer she's out here, the less likely she'll make it home in one piece."

230

Annoyed, Damek nodded. "Major Cunningham, alert the men as instructed. If they find her, they're not to approach. Observe and report. Understood?"

"Aye, Lord Marshal."

Damek clapped Martin on the back. "Let's go, old friend."

"Where to?"

Damek tugged his gloves on, while his squire held his mount steady. "West, Martin. And wherever that leads."

Martin paled. "That leads to Rosweal."

Damek drew himself up into his saddle and took the reins. "If they're still in Eire, there are few options left to them. If I were in this bastard's place, it's what I would do. Where else would he hope to hide her from me and Corsairs from Tairngare?"

"But... Rosweal's a stinking charnel house for fur trappers and poachers."

"Exactly," Damek said, kicking his mount to motion.

TENEMENT BLUES

Una was surprised to learn Ben's tenement had a bathhouse at its lowest level. She didn't expect such luxury could exist in rugged, unpretentious Rosweal. Ben explained that the foundations dated to a time before the Transition when many buildings in the area had similar accommodations. The ancient Eireans had placed this structure directly over a natural spring that funneled mineral-rich water from deep underground. When the most recent owner purchased the building, she'd had the baths renovated. Stone stoves were carved into the outer walls from which copper and clay pipes ran between two large, tiled pools. For a price, the stoves could be loaded with slow-burning peat and peppered with dried lumber to retain heat. These step-down pools were separated by a low stone wall, one for either sex.

The baths were tended by a stern-faced old matron, who spoke very little and pretended to observe even less. She had two little boys waiting to bring in towels, harsh soaps, and oil of lavender upon request. Ben warned Una and Rian not to help themselves to everything in these baskets, but as usual, both girls ignored him. Eschewing Ben's miserly advice, Una and Rian took the longest, most satisfying soak of their lives. The women's chamber was some ten feet wide and eight feet long, covered from floor to ceiling in white rectangular tiles, saving those in the pool, which were blue faience. The polished glass felt wonderful against Una's bare, blistered toes. Their cerulean pool was deep enough to completely immerse oneself when sitting over the drain at the bottom. Seats carved into the edges kept the midsection warm while one washed their hair or reclined in a soak. Rian floated on her back in the middle with a satiated sigh.

"Dear Siora, I never want to step outside this room again."

"Agreed," said Una, scrubbing the mud and muck from her tangled curls with a wad of honey soap. Ben's edict be damned; she was going to use every drop of oil, every cream, and every salve in that bloody basket. "Who'd believe such a place was possible in a town like this?"

Rian submerged herself and popped back up. She hugged her knees underwater. "The Greenmakers are quite famous, you know? It may not look it, but a lot of coin gets shuffled from hand to hand 'round here. The tavern next door is infamous throughout Innisfail."

"How so?"

Rian's pale hair floated around her head in a slippery flaxen cloud. "You've never heard of *The Hart and Hare?*"

"Should I have?"

"It's only the most notorious brothel in the North," Rian laughed.

Una made a face. "Oh."

"You don't have brothels in Tairngare?"

Una cursed. She tried and failed to untangle a particularly fastidious knot. "Of course, we do, but they're different. Clients are selected and must apply to the Voluptatus to ascertain health, wealth, and temperament before their patronage can be approved."

"That's rather complex, given the clientele."

"It's meant to be. Siora forbids sexual predation."

"Then who may... erm, imbibe?"

"There are various sects in the Voluptatus, but the law is designed to protect the women whom they most affect. For example, every Red House pays a yearly stipend— a pension of sorts— for women who retire, have children, or are unable to work due to illness or infirmity. Men are welcome to patronize any of these establishments, but they must adhere to the law to do so. They learn to regret it if they abuse any of these women."

"And this works? Men don't try to get around the law?"

"Sometimes, but they pay dearly for the error."

"They're fined?"

"Castrated," said Una, matter-of-factly. "We don't suffer brutes in Tairngare. Unlike Bethany, or other less civilized points beyond." Una didn't care for most external policies regarding women, especially among the lower classes. Often, a girl was taken while extremely young and roughly used until her youth and desirability waned. Eventually, she would be cast out, forced to try to sell herself for scraps. Sex workers of this sort were beaten, diseased, reviled, and ignored. Such was the fate of thousands of women living outside Siora's grace. The Ancestor herself had been such a woman. The Cloister of the Eternal Flame was founded by souls she'd liberated from sexual bondage, after all.

In Her Heart, In Her Blood, In Her Spine, Una thought to herself. If it weren't for Siora, what a terrible place the world would still be.Rian waded over to borrow Una's soap. "Well, prepare yourself. Rosweal is *not* known for its fair treatment of women, least of all its 'entertainers.' I don't think you will like this place much, My Lady."

"Rian, please. I gathered as much, despite this gorgeous bathing chamber. It's a shame, really." Indeed, when Ben led them through the complicated twists and turns of Wanderer's Alley, she became aware of that fact rather swiftly. This neighborhood wasn't as refined as the one they'd passed on the Hilltop, nor as clean— but it did boast randomly placed street lanterns and sturdy brick buildings, though none were in good repair. The Greemakers' Quarter, as Ben called it, was cut into a large wedge by two wide lanes, which led to opposing corners against a high stone wall. This wall was easily twenty feet higher than the low-shale barriers that encircled the town on three sides. Evidently, the wall had once been the parapet of some long-forgotten fortress facing the border.

Outside the Western Gate, a wide stone jetty sliced rudely into the river's rapid flow. Many wooden boats and nets were moored to its covered docks; even at night, the boatyard teemed with people. Some were loading or unloading merchandise to be shipped downriver past the confluence. Some directed wagons and carts laden with lumber, dry goods, and furs, no doubt intended for markets in Tara, Slane, or Ten Bells. Una hadn't realized Rosweal was capable of such bustling trade. She'd stared a bit until Ben scolded her. He reminded her that Rosweal's citizens didn't care for prying eyes, then none-too-gently nudged her toward the building where they were now accommodated. Before she followed him into the darkened rear entrance, Una had spied several haggard women poised beneath sparse streetlights catcalling workers as they shuffled past. Una averted her eyes, having noted one or two of those girls being used quite casually, in full view of anyone who happened by.

It turned her stomach.

Ben tried to explain that in Rosweal, most 'respectable' women wouldn't brave the harsh Greensward winters to live such paltry, complicated lives. The men of Rosweal weren't grand tradesmen, farmers, or fishermen. They scraped together a meager living through smuggling, poaching, and scavenging. This was not a lifestyle most women would prefer for their children, excluding those with no choice. Ben seemed acutely embarrassed by her questions on the subject but spared her no answers. He elaborated that many of the brothel girls were bought from finer establishments down south and worked until the debt was repaid or until they were banished to the streets— whichever came first.

It made Una's blood boil to think of their suffering. That any woman should be forced to sell herself to eat was abhorrent to her. In Tairngare, the Voluptatus refused girls that made the choice under duress. Girls of that sort were remanded to the Agrea, where they'd be housed, fed, and clothed. There, they were taught various agricultural skills and given a base living upon which to build. Education at the Libellum was offered freely to every class, and every woman had the opportunity to improve themselves if they so desired. No one should be forced to debase themselves to survive. Tairngare had many flaws, as any society must, but in this matter, she was superior to every city in the world. Una wondered how different this horrible little town would look if it adhered to the Cloister's laws.

Done scrubbing her monstrously neglected hair, Una sank into the deep warm tub to her eyeballs. Rian dunked herself once more and stepped from the pool to dry off. Her skin was as red as an apple.

"You know," she said, wrapping herself in a long towel. "I think the housekeeper launders clothing too."

"Such extravagance," Una chuckled, wincing when it jogged one of her ribs. She still had plenty of wounds to contend with, even if they were far less painful or visible than the day before. Rian hadn't said anything concerning this since Una had used her Spark on that street thug, but Una caught her stealing glances at times, and they weren't always flattering.

"I think Ben is waiting for us in the next chamber. He said he didn't want us walking around alone in here. Said it was dangerous for us even to use these baths."

"Hang Ben," Una said. "This was *his* bloody idea. Besides, he told me he has another hiding place he means to take us to tomorrow."

"I don't know why he's being so bloody secretive. It's not like we don't realize he's playing all of this by ear," Rian frowned, observing her soiled clothing. "I'm not putting any of that back on."

Meanwhile, Una dug through the perfumed basket, pleased to find a pair of linen robes at the bottom. "We'll use these. Siora, this is bloody fantastic service."

"Yeah, but it costs. Ben said—"

"Since when do you care what Ben says?"

Rian thought about that for a moment. "I don't. I just don't want him to whine about the spent coin later."

"It's your coin, Rian."

"I can hear everything you two are saying, you realize?" growled Ben from behind the wall. A thin grate in the ceiling allowed light in from the window on the men's side. The girls heard a splash and a curse. "Don't spend all your money on linens and oil, Rian."

"You shut your mouth," she called, defiantly ringing a small bell beside the door. Almost immediately, a little redhead popped into the crack.

"Missus?"

She handed him the pile of discarded clothing. "Take this to your Mistress for laundering, if you please?"

"O'course, Missus. Will ye be needin' anythin' else, some food? Mam told me to tell ye we have salmon stews, black bread, and boiled turnips. Will ye have some?"

"No!" Ben roared from his side of the wall.

"*Shut up!*" Una shouted back.

Rian tucked some coppers into the boy's little palm, smiling as his face brightened. "We'd love some supper... breakfast in the morning, too. If available?"

"'Tis, Missus!"

Ben's curses grew in volume.

"Excellent," Rian patted the boy's unkempt curls. "You know where to bring everything?"

"I do, Missus. Ben Maeden's room, right?"

"That's right," smiled Rian, while Ben thumped around in the next chamber. "Run along now, and don't forget to bring Ben the bill."

THAT NIGHT, LONG AFTER RIAN had gone to sleep in Ben's Spartan apartment, Una was still wide awake, tucked into a (thankfully, clean) woolen blanket she found in Ben's solitary wardrobe. Inside, she was pleased to discover a few tunics, some worn leggings, and several pairs of woolen socks. She helped herself, of course. Since it was clearly Ben's intention to dump the two of them here while he went out to do, Siora knew what, she was going to make herself as comfortable as possible. Ben didn't have much in the way of amenities, but a thick pair of warm, dry socks could be luxurious when one has spent days in a frigid, wet wilderness.

There had been moments in the Greensward when she'd almost wished someone would put her out of her misery. Una craved long summer days with a high cheerful sun dancing overhead, and long warm nights with the sweet scent of flowers and herbs on the air. She was told

Bretagne boasted an entire third month of summer. Watching frost creep across the mottled glass in Ben's window, she rather hoped she'd have a chance to experience it for herself one day soon. Una was exasperated with the cold and the damp, and it wasn't even Dor Oras yet. Sighing, she snuggled deep into her pilfered blanket and gazed outside. She could just make out the river snaking through those dark, foreboding hills. The north side, as always, was obscured by a dense, obfuscating mist. To the far northern horizon, Aes Sidhe was shielded from mortal eyes.

Una wondered why Northers accepted the presence of the Sidhe so readily yet never bothered to complain of their exclusion from Sidhe society. Indeed, Una couldn't recall ever having met one before Ben. They didn't mingle much with Eireans nor Cymrians, as far as she'd gleaned from her studies. They kept their own company and never involved themselves in Eirean affairs unless any upstart 'Milesians' dared to breach their firm Natural Law.

The High King allowed each city and province to self-govern but forbade them to mine, divert rivers, or otherwise tamper with the lay of the land. The Southers, for one, chafed under Aes Sidhe's detached edicts and made no secret of their contention at every Five-Year Council. Bethany, for example, believed this heavy-handed ruling prevented them from achieving true economic prosperity. Hence, the enmity between Bethany and her neighbors over colonial resources and the many failed revolts instigated by the Donahugh Clan to throw off the High King's yoke. Tairngare, on the other hand, was not hampered economically by the Law. Thus, they had less need to be offended by it. Shipping and trade with the wealthy colonies lined the Red City's treasury with fainne, and her thriving Mercher class kept the economic wheels turning.

Bethany was hardly land-locked, but it lacked the lumber to build ships or the Cymrian mining rights to purchase them. In many ways, Bethany was at the mercy of both Aes Sidhe and Tairngare due to basic geography and the lack of a meticulous central government. At its core, Bethany was a feudal patriarchy, dependent upon fiefdom and the eternal servitude of the poor. There, the common folk existed simply to prop up the landowners... and women had it worst. They could neither own property nor inherit their wealth. In many ways, Bethany was not all that dissimilar from Rosweal. It seemed to Una that Tairngare possessed the only thriving society in Innisfail, given its wealth, influence, and social privilege. Perhaps if Bethany empowered their women and working classes, might they not share in some of Tairngare's success?

Thinking of the Sidhe, she wondered how they treated their women. One did not hear much about them if anything at all. Were matrons autonomous, like the women in Tairngare? Or were they subservient, like those in Bethany? Even in the Colonies, women could own property and have a hand in their own governance. Cymrian women oversaw the rearing and education of their children and administered their individual unions. Was it the same in Aes Sidhe? Una honestly had no idea, and her lack of knowledge on that score vexed her. Civic Law had been a favorite subject of hers, after all. Why did she know almost nothing about the Sidhe? She determined she would ask Ben when they had time. For instance, why did they not allow Eireans into Aes Sidhe, as a rule? Why did the Sidhe refer to her people as 'Milesian' when that ancient tribal king, Mil, had little to do with modern Eire?

She had so many questions that she scarcely knew where to begin. Not that she expected Ben would be forthcoming on this topic. Far from it. An irritated smile crept over her mouth at the thought. Secretly, she found she didn't mind his dry wit as much as she had from the start. She supposed he was growing on her. If she was honest with herself, his bravery and frank practicality might have softened her regard. Though she would rather be raked over a bed of hot coals than admit it out loud to anyone, least of all Ben... he wasn't very hard to look at, either. Perhaps it was just the novelty of his height or his fine Sidhe bones that struck her? The sharpness of his smooth brow, maybe the angle of his sculpted jaw? She couldn't say for sure.

Una did not lack a solid foundation for comparison. Tairngare was filled with bronzed, dark-haired, bright-eyed specimens of every stripe—but Ben was something else altogether. If his manners weren't atrocious, Una might be forced to concede that he was the most beautiful person she'd ever met, male or female. She shook herself. Perhaps this was the reason the Sidhe kept to themselves? She could only imagine the chaos that having such unspeakable creatures underfoot would reap through the female population of Eire. If Ben was so, Siora only knew what the women were like. She bit back a chuckle so as not to disturb Rian, who snored lightly into the mattress behind her.

As if summoned by her train of thought, a thump against the short iron balcony outside the window made her jump. Ben cursed through the glass and fumbled unsubtly for the latch. Shaking her head, Una got up and pried it open herself. He tumbled inside, almost taking her with him on his way to the floor.

"Herne!" he giggled into the floorboards. Una fanned the air around her face and shut the window behind him. He reeked of uishge, witchroot smoke, and cheap perfume. Maybe he *wasn't* attractive, after all?

"Where've you been?" she whispered, covering her nose. "You stink to the nine hells."

"Had to clear up some things," he bellowed. Rian groaned and buried her head, mumbling something colorful into the mattress.

Una nudged him with a toe. "Keep your voice down. What things? What're you on about?"

"Robin's not here. Thank Lug."

He was still too bloody loud. She nudged him again. He caught her foot in one absurdly large hand and held it with a satisfied smirk. She couldn't dislodge it nor use it to prod him again. "Means we have a tentative run of the place, so long as we keep a low profile."

"How does getting stinking drunk, scaling balconies, and raising your voice in the middle of the night even approach a 'low profile?' Let go."

He grinned at her. "No one saw me," he at least attempted to whisper.

"Fine. Let go of my leg, please."

"Nope. Gonna keep it." He grinned like an idiot for several uncomfortable moments while she tried to tug herself free. The moon finally broke through the cloudbank, which flooded their corner of the room with light. His steady stare made her nervous.

Una vowed she would not blush. Not today.

Not ever.

"Should I kick you with the other foot?"

"I'd say I hold the advantage in a wrestling match, but you're welcome to try. I'll go easy on you."

Una fixed a glower on him that should have singed his hair. "You're drunk, and I'm going to hurt you if you don't stop messing about."

Ben didn't let go. Neither did he cease giving her that churlish smirk. "You know," he whisper-shouted. "You're looking a lot better. Were you always so… you know?"

Her eyes narrowed until they were barely wide enough to see his flushed cheeks. "I am not some tavern wench, you clumsy sot." She brought her free heel down hard into his midsection.

His breath came out in a rush. Her foot came free. "Ouch! Damn it, woman. I'm trying to compliment you."

"I don't need your bloody compliments."

"I was only going to tell you how the moon—"

Una rolled her eyes hard enough to crack her brow. "*Insufferable!* Did you learn anything of value on this excursion, or was it merely to have one off that you bothered at all?"

Blinking himself semi-straight, he cleared his throat. "I did need to find out if Robin was in town because that could be a problem."

"Who in the hells is Robin?"

Pursing his lips, he waved her query away. "No one, no one. Nothing to worry about. I thought I'd pop 'round *Solomon's*, to be sure. All is clear, for now, it seems."

"Did you discover how you will get us across the river at the bottom of your tankard, your lordship?" Una's mouth wouldn't melt butter. Ben sank onto his elbows. His irritatingly long legs stretched out before him while he ogled her. His vest was unbuttoned, and his tunic unlaced. Noting the direction of her attention, he grinned wider. She averted her eyes, cheeks flaming. She took back every positive thought about him in the last hour.

"I did. I figured I'd please myself with a good strong drink while it was available. Did you wait up for me?"

She chewed the interior of her cheek. "*No.* What have you decided?"

"Later," he hiccupped. "I'd rather talk about you. For example, I didn't realize you were so… under all that grime. It's distracting, you know. You're quite–"

She muttered a vicious oath that had something to do with melting eyeballs and disintegrating tongues. "I'm going to sleep. You're obviously in no fit shape for an adult conversation."

"Please, Siora!" roared Rian from her tunnel of pillows.

Una darted past Ben's legs to leap into the bed beside her. Una wound herself in her woolen blanket, even though she was warm already from her pilfered socks. Like a worm, Ben wriggled up to the side of the bed. Una clenched a fist.

"What now?"

"That's my bed, you know?"

"*And?*"

He propped himself up on his elbow and fidgeted with the mattress' exposed threading. "It's pretty cold down here."

"Ben?"

He beamed. "Yes, Una?"

"Does this boorish, suggestive attitude ever actually work with women?"

"What do you think?" He gave her a wolfish, white grin.

"Go to sleep, or I'll punch you in the throat."

With an exaggerated groan, he flopped to the floor. "You're quite right. 'Tis the cold boards for me, missus. I've only saved both of your bloody lives a thousand times so far. Only carried you on my back for twenty-odd miles. Only brought you to my home, given you my bed and all my bloody pillows. I *adore* the floor. Really. A gentleman does not complain."

"When I see one, I'll ask him if you're right," Una snarled and folded herself into the fetal position below her warm blanket. After several minutes of listening to the blood rush through her ears, she cracked an eye to find he was still watching her, with the oddest expression on his face. He had his hands folded behind his head, with only the rough rag-woven rug beneath him and his sealskin cloak for a blanket. He looked almost... pathetic. With a long breath, she struck him full in the face with her pillow.

"Ow! What in the hells did you do that for?"

She pulled her blanket up over her ears. "You're welcome?"

He rattled off some very unflattering curses, but Una ignored him. She drifted off to sleep with a smile, despite the thumping, cursing fool on the floor.

THE WATERHORSE

n.e. ꝼ08
2ꝼ, ꝺoꞃ samna
ꞃoswea1

Ben was in a terrible state. He woke before dawn with a splitting headache and an oily stomach. His right arm was numb, and his back was a network of shooting pains. Unwinding himself from the cocoon he'd made of his cloak, he glared over at the two happily sleeping traitors tucked into his bed. Una, having pilfered one of his tunics, lay belly-down on the mattress, the blanket scrunched up around her shoulders. Like darkest honey, a riot of sable curls floated around her face and back. Ben caught himself staring again and scrubbed at his eyes with a groan. He didn't have time to be distracted by ridiculous notions. When he finished his task for the day, he'd apologize to her for his behavior last night and make himself scarce for the next. Mollified by this solution, he scraped himself from the floor as quietly as he could manage. He wasn't overly enthused about his plans for the day, but after a night's drinking and ruminating over the matter, he couldn't argue it was the swiftest possible course. Ben didn't remember removing his swordbelt and boots. While he fumbled to put them back on, he caught one of Una's large uishge colored eyes on him. She yawned into the back of a tattooed hand.

"Morning, Ben dearest," her voice was husky with sleep, her tone teasing. "How fares your head?"

He looked away. "Ah... I must apologize for uh, well, you know." He focused on his boots. "I was drunk, and—"

"No need." After stretching like a cat, she propped herself up on her elbow. "You aren't the first man I've met, you know." Her laughter irritated him. He didn't know why. "Where're you going?"

He wasn't sure how to answer. "I'll fill you in later." Daring a second glance at her, he wished he hadn't. His cursed tunic, much too large for her, displayed a swath of unnecessary skin from the deep 'V' at her neckline. He struggled not to gawp at the corded brown column of her throat or the hollow above her intricately tattooed clavicle. Unselfconsciously, she gathered up her floating cloud of soft springing curls and piled them high atop her head. Ben's throat dried up. What was *wrong* with him? He buttoned his vest as fast as possible. Escape was his only course.

"Listen." He was proud of the even timbre of his voice. "You should be careful of the people in this building. There could be trouble if my return is advertised. Keep to the room, for now. All right? And don't open that door for anyone except me."

"The boy will be bringing us food later."

"Fine but be sure it's him before you open the door. If the Housekeeper herself comes up, don't answer any question she asks. She'll take everything she hears to Barb."

Una gestured for him to keep his voice down. "Who's Barb?" The only evidence Rian even existed was the spill of cornsilk hair dipping over the opposite side of the mattress.

"Barb is the proprietor. She owns the entire block. The brewery two doors down, the livery across the street, the haberdashery, the mill at the north corner, and *The Hart and Hare* next door. She's the Boss around here."

Una's pert nose wrinkled. "Oh, the madam."

Ben looked anywhere but at her while he adjusted his swordbelt. "You have brothels in Tairngare, remember."

She sniffed. "Hardly the same thing."

"Barb's not such a bad sort if you don't have something she wants or try to take what's hers. I think you'd find her girls are better cared for than most in the North… erm, but that's beside the point. I'd very much like to avoid her, if possible."

"How long?"

"What?" He stalked to the windowpane. It'd be safest to come and go from the balcony, so long as it wasn't too late or too early for most residents to notice a tall figure scaling the wall. He'd rather not get hung up at the door downstairs.

"How long will you be?"

"I've no idea, but don't expect me." He had no intention of returning until he could make more comfortable arrangements. This situation was going to get him into trouble. "We can't go to the other place I told you about until I've ascertained the consequences from Vick or his boss."

Una paled a bit. "The boy we killed?"

"I killed one of them too, so try not to punish yourself overmuch. Matt is bound to be livid. The Hilltop isn't in Greenmaker territory. So, I'd prefer to be sure of the consequences before I make a move."

She wasn't satisfied with this excuse in the least. That was obvious. Still, there was little he could do about it now, was there? Though they hadn't had much choice at the time, two more dead men in Rosweal were sure to cause problems. He could only deal with one crisis at a time. The girls would just have to make do until he found the help he needed. Opening the window allowed a much-needed blast of frosty air into the over-warm room. He paused, daring a look over his shoulder.

"Just in case I'm not back until tomorrow, will you do me a favor?"

"What's that?"

"Put on your own clothes. That," he pointed, "doesn't fit." He shut the window on her bemused expression and swung himself into the alley below.

Ben brooded over his circumstances as he walked out of town. He was beginning to wish he'd spent more time thinking things through. If this plan didn't work out, he'd be forced to try the border through the mountains to the west—a far more dangerous and unpleasant path, by far. Conditions were already becoming needlessly complex. Necessity, combined with proximity, made a muddle of relationships. Hells, he was even viewing Rian with a begrudging sort of affection, and he'd encountered badgers with better temperaments. Ben didn't want to form close ties with anyone, whether it be a civil acquaintance with Rian Guinness… or whatever nonsense burgeoned in his blood for Una. He had no idea what God he'd offended, but they were having a good laugh at his expense right now.

Ben should never have taken her hand in that cave. When she said she trusted him, he'd been relieved. Worse, he realized he *cared* what she thought of him. That wouldn't do. Not at all. As soon as her tiny fingers wrapped around his, he knew… she was trouble he didn't need. Not now. Not *ever*. Una Moura Donahugh was a means to an end, nothing more. He would deposit her safely in Midhir's court, then return to his own life. Anything else was pointless.

Ben sighed as he pushed through reeds and half-frozen cattails on the riverbank. He supposed he could charm Rosie into taking him in for a few days. She wouldn't ask many questions. She never had. Her shift ended an hour past midnight. Maybe he would finish up here, have a few drinks at *Solomon's*, and head back to look for her? She'd be happy to see him, though part of him would feel bad about imposing upon her hospitality; worse, considering he did so merely to avoid another woman. What else could he do?

Ben had already made a fool of himself once… damned if it should happen again. He did have a larger place absolutely no one knew about on the Hilltop. Unfortunately, the encounter with Vick meant they'd run afoul of the only non-Greenmaker of real consequence in Rosweal. The Hilltop was Matt's territory, and though he and the Greenmakers held a long-standing truce, that didn't mean Gilcannon would appreciate more of his subordinates lying dead in the street. He'd be even less pleased to learn it was Robin's right-hand man he could thank for both transgressions.

Matt considered himself something of a tosh, with the enormous profits reaped from his illegal distillery in Rosweal. Owing to Gilcannon's bootlegging operation, Rosweal had access to Cymrian wine, silks from Bretagne, lamp oil from Scotia, and produce from Ten Bells. The Greenmakers, who traded only in poached fur, timber, meat, and female flesh, owed many of their connections to Matt. However, that wasn't to say he was well-liked in the Quarter. Barb Dormer, the Guildmistress herself, probably despised him more than anyone alive. She'd been searching for a means to get rid of him longer than Ben had been in Robin's employ.

As yet, unsuccessfully.

Matt was a bad enemy to make, but Ben knew it wasn't Gilcannon he should worry about. Robin Gramble would be his greatest challenge. Barb Dormer might be the queen of Taverner's Alley, but Robin ran the men. If Ben intended to get over the border with the most significant bounty in Innisfail, he needed to patch things with Robin soon. Without the Greenmakers' backing, Ben was a marked man, and neither girl would be safe in Rosweal.

So much was plaguing his mind that he was having trouble focusing on the task at hand. Beneath the sparse autumnal umbrella of a sheltering oak, he stopped just shy of the waterline. In reality, the Blackwater posed no great challenge for those who wished to cross. The river was not especially wide nor deep. What was in it, however… Ben drew his shoulders back and took a deep, thoughtful breath.

Well, you made up your mind.

Get it over with.

Looking around to be sure he had no witnesses; Ben unlaced his boots and placed them in a dry spot beneath the oak. Next went his vest, trousers, stockings, and tunic. Once clad only in his woolen leggings, he took care to tuck Rian's ogham stone beneath a loose blanket of moss for safekeeping. Unarmed and undisguised, Ben waded in. He hadn't done this in a *very* long time. Come to think of it, the last attempt hadn't worked out so well for him, either; two very deep scars ran down his left arm, and another curled over his chest— ever-present reminders of his former hubris.

At first, nothing happened. River mud squeezed between his toes, and ribbons of slimy river grass snaked around his torso. When the water reached his collarbone, the riverbed shuddered. The current shifted around him, flowing in reverse. A heavy fog crept toward him from the far bank like milk poured over mottled glass. He dug his heels in and waited. Silent as silk, a large misshapen head slid from the water. Its black eyes burned with ravenous hunger. Ben repressed a shudder. Amorphous and changeable as the river, its features rippled through simultaneous aspects. First, a smallish humanlike skull with gleaming liquid eyes. Then, the shape of a monstrous stallion. Streaming rivulets of dark water articulated its impressive mane and thick muscular neck.

Ard Tiarne... it gave him the barest hint of a nod, its tone amused but dry. *You are forbidden, as you well know...*

"I'm aware."

It considered him intently. *Do you tempt fate again?*

"No," Ben said, keeping his voice flat. There weren't many creatures Ben feared, but he'd developed a healthy respect for the pooka over the years. Should it wish to try, it might feasibly drag Ben into the darkest depths of the Oiche Ar Fad, never to be seen or heard from again. It wasn't often that the pooka could snare higher Sidhe like himself, but given the slightest opportunity, it wouldn't hesitate. Ben's immortal body— his bones, skin, hair, and blood— the pooka craved above all other prizes. Such a rare feast would be a victory of untold proportions to this prince of the Dor Sidhe. The pooka were formless monsters from an endless, fluid void. One mistake while bargaining with such a creature could prove fatal. Ben knew from experience how troublesome an opponent one could be. This one, in fact. If Ben held his birthright, title, and name, the pooka would never dare to cast aspersions on his person. Exiled as he was from Aes Sidhe, and absent the Ard Ri's good graces, however... *best not to overthink.* Ben willed his clanging heart still. "I have a request to make of you."

A queer gurgling sent tiny waves of greenish brown water into Ben's chin. He ground his teeth. He'd give this thing something to crow over soon enough. "You find that humorous, *isesaeligh?*"

The pooka stopped laughing; the mud between Ben's toes vibrated with its ire. *Insults now? You are very foolish or very brave.*

250

Ben didn't blink. "You watch your filthy mouth. I am still a high lord, you realize?"

The pooka sniggered. *You were Daoine Sidhe... once. Now, you reek of spirits, mortal stink, and fear. How sad you seem, tuiathe. How feeble.*

Ben ignored that as if he wasn't the least intimidated. He was going to bluff his way through this. To do so, he must play his part well. A pooka would exploit any weakness he dared reveal. Ben lifted an eyebrow as haughtily as he could.

"This isn't a social call. I said I've a request to make of you." Water flowed over the stallion's head until Ben stared into an odd three-dimensional reflection of his own face. Minus the ill-fitting, elongated fangs protruding from the mouth, it was a fair mimic. With a sour taste on his tongue, Ben feigned disinterest. "Handsome enough, I suppose."

The figure's grotesque grin turned his stomach. *It will be an honor to peel the skin from your skull, Ard Tiarne. I shall wear it with pride.*

"You would try, pooka."

Hm, so I might, it cackled.

"Enough of this. Your rudeness may deprive you of the gift I meant to offer in exchange for your aid."

You've tried to trick me before. I do not forget.

"That was ages ago when I was desperate to regain my status. Now, I merely wish to protect those I care for."

The pooka considered him. *You are much reduced... Ard Tiarne. A shame. You were a challenge... before.*

"If you persist with these invectives, I'll find another to put my request to and keep her for myself."

As expected, the pooka's mercurial fangs lengthened, catching the sunlight in a horrifying leer. *Her?*

The lecherous old bastard.

"Of course," said Ben, rubbing his chin. "I *should* keep her, after all. She is still so young. Far too sweet to part with so casually. Perhaps I'll ask another—"

Wait. The pooka inched closer; its solidifying teeth snapped in its watery, Ben-shaped jaws. *Tell me more of this sssweet young girl.*

251

So bloody easy, Ben scoffed inwardly. He turned away as if to abandon his purpose. "I shouldn't have mentioned her. Forget what I said. She's too precious to part with, considering her heritage… I must find another way…"

Now, the creature was almost upon him. The current swirled. As it grew, gallons of brown water sucked up and into the pooka's body. The river barely crested Ben's thighs as the beast towered over him; tiny fish, clumping mud, and reeds swam through its massive, translucent torso.

Nooo! it cried, suddenly eager to hear what Ben wished to say. Nothing tempted a pooka more than the promise of a young, beautiful plaything. Never mind that nearly every girl one snatched drowned in the first few minutes or expired from sheer fright. On Samhain, when the pooka took corporeal form, many unwary females were dragged to the bottom of wells or lured into bogs and ponds. Once captured, they'd be ruthlessly ravaged, broken, then savagely devoured. Never satisfied by the flimsy human flesh the pooka hunted most often, they wanted more, something they could not break easily. They craved women of Sidhe blood, perhaps more than they longed for Sidhe bones to shuck.

Is she not mortal? salivated the pooka.

Ben feigned abashed shame. "Well, her father was."

A gurgle of pure excitement. *She is Ban Sidhe?*

"Half, but I haven't agreed that you should have her… yet. You would abuse her horribly, no doubt. I couldn't allow that. She is precious to me."

No, no, no! I would never, it lied. The riverbed thrummed with its shameless glee. *All sweet girls are safe with meee. I would treasssure herrr.*

"I don't believe you." Ben crossed his arms.

What mussst I do, Ard Tiarne?

"I need you to deliver a message for me." Ben looked up into his own maniacal face and repressed a shudder. "To Diarmid Adair."

The pooka recoiled with a hiss. *Fiachra Ri? You trick me! He will desstroy meee!* It shrank down to Ben's size, its fingers lengthening into monstrous claws and its fangs growing long as walrus tusks. Though opaque, its eyes took on a serpentine shape, even more terrible than the enormous teeth protruding from its impression of Ben's face.

252

Thisss iss your purpossse? You mean to lure me out of the way, ssso you may crosss into Aess Ssidhee! One of its dagger-like claws stretched out. It stopped mere centimeters from Ben's nose.

Ben did not flinch. "No. I mean to speak to my uncle before Samhain, and if I do not, I will lose a legitimate chance to cross. I mean to make a deal with you because, frankly, I have no choice. Aes Sidhe is threatened by the South, again. I do not trust the Consulate in Ten Bells, and Fiachra Ri may be my only hope. I am Daoine Sidhe. It is my responsibility to try."

The pooka thought this over for some time. When it spoke, it seemed to have collected itself. *You do not lie, Ard Tiarne. I would taste it, did you dare. Perhaps, we can come to an arrangement… but it will cossst you more than the girl if you deccceive me.* Ben could hear the rank covetousness in its voice. It would do anything he asked for such a prize. A Sidhe girl, even a faerie, was worth twenty mortal women to a degenerate pooka. Herne only knew what it would do to her. Ben forced himself not to overthink it.

"Well," he asked, lining his tone with regal impatience. "Do we have a deal, or not?"

Iss sshe beautifulll?

"Hair like winter wheat, skin like milk, eyes of bluest sky."

Squealing in delight, the pooka leapt below the surface with a hearty splash that doused Ben to the roots of his hair. When its head popped up, it was Ben's features it wore, free of animalistic embellishments. It smiled.

We have an accord, Ard Tiarne. I shall tell the Fiachra Ri, you wish to meet by Samhain. But by the Hallowed Hour, you shall bring my prize to me? Yess?

"Of course," Ben agreed. "But if he fails to show, you get nothing. Remember that."

As you wish, tuiathe, as you wish… If you fail to bring the girl to me, I shall find you on Samhain. The pooka's predatory grin seemed almost harmless by comparison to the horrors it had exhibited previously. *And it shall be your bones I embrace her with.*

HAVING SURVIVED THE FIRST ORDEAL of his three-stage plan, Ben decided to soothe his nerves with the drink he'd promised himself that morning. Hells, perhaps he'd have five after that nightmare on the riverbank? Pulling his hood down close, he sauntered back through the West Gate and down the far end of the Greenmakers' Quarter without looking up. Until he found the time and the means to speak to Robin personally, he'd rather not press his luck.

Solomon's was a sliver of a building, crammed between two larger stone structures: one, a three-story warehouse that had once been a factory of sorts; the other, a long-vacated tenement, which was only safe at its lowest level. Solomon used it to store his ill-gotten gains and often loaned it out to Greenmakers seeking a layover from points beyond. Both buildings were boarded and crumbling. There were gaping holes in their roofs which sometimes poured sheets of mellifluous rainwater down descending floors. The warehouse's few remaining tenants were either of the avian or rodent variety.

Consequently, Solomon's relatively tidy two-story brick edifice crawled with unwanted pests. The patrons didn't seem to mind, as Ben certainly would not. Sol had the best ale in town, with or without the rats, bats, and beetles— or perhaps because of them, who could say for sure?

Solomon made each batch of spiced ale per an old family recipe and, by Herne, if it was not the finest in Eire. Barb herself had been after Sol for years to hand it over, but the old codger would not be swayed by threat or by coin. He paid his tithes to remain in the Guild and always kept ragged men on hand to aid in whichever Greenmaker venture had need. Sol remained free to operate as he saw fit, so long as he didn't venture into any more lucrative avenues reserved for the Guild's upper echelons, namely courtesans, furs, and uishge. Still, women of a certain stripe often congregated outside the brewery, seeking to throw themselves on the mercy of any stray coppers that might come their way.

Those that couldn't cut *The Hart* were too squeamish for life at *The Corset* or unable to procure a personal patron, made do in the streets. That was the law. Rosweal had a way of chewing the good out of everyone and spitting the remnants into the dirt. Several haggard girls, trying their best to look appealing, pawed at Ben on his way inside. Without provocation, he recalled Una's comments to Rian on the subject. The sudden thought made him squirm—gods damn that bloody meddling woman and her sanctimonious morals. Looking around now, he couldn't get her disdain out of his head. He wasn't about to apologize to Una for every man in the North, damn it. These women had choices, no matter what Lady Moura believed. They chose to take their chances out here in rough Rosweal, and there wasn't a thing he could do about it.

Was there?

Scowling at his newfound guilt, he tossed a few extra coppers their way. He supposed they needed it more than he ever would. One of them, a woman he remembered from *The Hart* a few seasons back— Daisy, was it?— gave him a weak, embarrassed smile. Feeling like the worst shite in the world thanks to Una and her big mouth, Ben slipped a few extra into her open palm without saying a word.

"Thank ye, love. I can—"

He waved her away as he opened the door. "No need, Daisy." He paused as real tears formed at the corner of her green eyes. "What's your given name?"

She straightened, despite the underfed sag in her shoulders. From her expression, he was ashamed to realize no one had ever asked her for her name before. "Sara. Sara Crover."

"Well, Sara, a pleasure. Buy something warm. It's cold out here."

Her fingers dragged at his sleeve. "*Wait.* Vick and his lot was here, lookin' for ye. Ye should know. Sol told 'em ye'd been here."

Of course, he did. Bloody opportunistic coward. "Thank you, Sara." He reached deeper into his vest with a wary eye on the six other faces gleaming with open hunger and handed her something heavier. "Appreciated, love." Ben went inside. He wouldn't worry about Sara Crover. Assuming she was under his protection, the others would leave her well alone. Ben had his own reputation in Rosweal. Folks knew better than to cross someone he favored. Maybe he would talk to Barb's housekeeper? See if she needed an extra pair of hands in the laundry. Sara would likely reject such an offer, but he could try, all the same.

THE SONS OF MIL

She'd always been a nice enough girl. Mind wandering again to Una; he clenched his teeth. This was bloody *intolerable*. He did NOT crave her approval, gods damn it. Her opinion meant absolutely nothing to him. Less than nothing. He bit the inside of his cheek to keep from muttering to himself like a lunatic.

Sol gave him an exaggerated, gap-toothed grin when he took a seat in the far corner. As always, Ben preferred to face the door. He noticed the tap was nigh empty, save for two harmless-looking fellows at the back, half-asleep in their ale. That was good. Ben shoved a free hand into his unbuttoned vest. Sol came over with his pint, a steaming mile-high horn filled to overflowing with the spiced Roswellian favorite. Solomon managed to be portly in a town full of half-starved sticks. Ben had always suspected he fermented his ale with animal fat. Sol set the horn down, and Ben slid it over. He looked up slowly, watching the smile flicker from Sol's dimpled brown face.

"What's it then, Ben?"

"You know."

The old man laughed. "Sure, I don't?"

"Really?" Ben picked up his horn with his left hand, leaving his right below his vest, near his belt. He flexed his fingers with exaggerated sloth.

Solomon didn't miss it. He dropped his rag and backed up. "Now Ben, ye know I ain't got the clout to argue with Vick. Gramble ain't here, and I ain't on Barb's shortlist neither. They asked if ye was here. That's all. I swear."

"I don't care, Sol. They're not Greenmakers, and they don't belong in the Quarter. Do you think Robin would approve? I'll give you a hint— that was rhetorical."

"Robin Gramble ain't me boss, Ben. Nor are ye, last I checked. Get out."

"No."

"What was that?"

"You heard me."

Without ado, Solomon tried to dart through the curtain behind the bar, which led through his kitchen to the rooms above. Ben was faster. He

256

leaned forward, grasped Sol by the collar, and slammed his face down onto the bar. Ben's horn spun over the rail, slinging ale every which way. Solomon briefly attempted to struggle, but he was no match for Ben. He threw his hands wide.

"All right, Ben! All right. Ye don't have to make such a fuss."

"Don't I?"

"No!"

Ben pressed his elbow down. "I want to know everything you told them, Sol. If your answers are satisfactory, I won't kill you. How's that sound?"

"But Ben. I didn't—"

"Furthermore, I want to know what they told you, who they've spoken with, and what you told Barb about my visit here last night. If these answers satisfy me, I won't tell Robin that you've been stuffing your pockets with Hilltop crumbs. How's that for fair?"

"I didn't... I don't... I mean—"

Ben nudged him with the butt of his dagger. "Start talking, Sol." Solomon stared over at the two men near the fire with pleading eyes. They turned away, content to sip their pints unmolested. Ben Maeden had never been bested in a fight. Everyone in Rosweal knew that. Besides, hadn't he killed two men for calling him a cheat some weeks back? Ben wasn't worried anyone would intervene to help a rat like Solomon Trant.

"Fine, let me up."

"I think I like you as an armrest, Sol. Very soft."

"I'm not tough like ye! They come 'round, askin' questions, and to get them to leave me alone, I'll tell 'em what they wanna hear from time to time. We all have to live here, Ben. Matt's a scary fellow."

"And Robin's not? What do you think he'd do to you if he heard any of this? I'm not going to ask you again." Ben pressed the flat of his blade against the old brewer's fleshy cheek.

"Ye won't... kill me?"

"Who knows? I've had a rough time of late."

Sol swallowed so hard that his Adam's apple thumped against the bar. "Matt's ordered ye be brung to him. Says ye owe him. Vick is 'sposed to come in tonight, then nab ye."

"And?"

"They was gonna cut me half on my next six barrels of uishge and get me ale to Matt's suppliers in Ten Bells. That's all, I swear. They didn't tell me anythin' else. Why would they?"

That was a fair point, but Ben wasn't swayed. He tugged Solomon up by the back of his tunic and pressed his dagger's tip deep into Solomon's quivering chins. The blade drew a tiny trickle of blood.

"I can respect self-preservation, Sol, but here's what you forget— Matt Gilcannon might have a fellow slit your throat in your sleep. I'll happily do it here, right now. Perhaps in the street? The market? In full view of anyone. There won't be a single person who can stop me, either. Have I made myself clear?"

"Y… yes. I'm sorry, Ben. Please don't."

Ben put his dagger away, and Solomon sagged against the bar. Heady beads of sweat slid down his nose. "No harm done, then." He patted the brewer's shoulder. "How about a pint then, hey? Then we'll sit and wait for Vick together, like the old pals we are."

Ben resumed his seat while Solomon shuffled sluggishly around his taps. Hands shaking, he dropped the first two mugs he groped for. Ben chuckled to watch the old crook try to gather the remnants of his dignity. When Solomon turned around to set a new pint in front of him, he froze. Ben slid a silver stag across the bar, allowing its gleam to hold the dim lantern light overhead.

"Now. Let's make a new arrangement, shall we? One that I think will suit us both much better…."

DOMINA

Una stared through the window, deep in reverie. *Can you trust him?* Despite her every effort, the longer she spent locked within these four walls, the more anxiously her thoughts churned. She resumed her pacing. She'd been at it for hours already, and still no Ben. When he left that morning, she'd assumed he'd be back before dark to take them to that place he'd mentioned— a house or another apartment he knew of somewhere in the middle of the city. Surely, they'd be much safer far from prying eyes? That is if they weren't to cross into Aes Sidhe tomorrow, the following day, or even within the week? She didn't have the first bloody clue what Ben was up to. Aside from a muttered 'soon' or 'I'm working on it,' he'd yet to be forthcoming. How could they trust him if he refused to share his plans? He was out doing Siora knew what, while they languished here, out of sight and out of his hair? The nerve of the bastard!

Just where in the bloody, stinking nine hells *was he?*

"Will you stop that? You're driving me mad," hissed Rian from behind her book. A dusty little number, one of a whopping two stacked on Ben's nightstand: *A History of Eire* by Jonathon Grathin and *Seasons of Transition: Climate and Culture in Pre-Transition Innisfail* by Dominic Callaghan. Rian held the latter of the two, which Una had read during her first year as a Secunda in the Cloister. *Seasons of Transition* was probably the most boring book she'd ever been forced to endure but loaded with fascinating details if one could bear the droning, monotonous text. "He's not going to come back any faster just because you're wearing grooves into his floorboards." Rian held the book under her nose, pretending to read, though she'd scarcely turned two pages. The book was in Old Angleish. Una doubted Rian understood a single word.

Una ran a hand through her hopelessly tangled hair. Today, Rian was trying very hard to be contrary and sullen. Una wasn't surprised. The girl seemed to struggle with her emotions quite often. Una recalled that the very term 'faerie' in old Innish meant *'fey-touched'*: literally, 'doomed.' Faeries rarely, if ever, led happy lives. Whether that ascribed to Rian's case or not remained to be seen. At the moment, Una couldn't tell if she was *'fey-touched'* or just a genuinely disagreeable person. She had a rotten temper. That much was plain. Still, if she hadn't risked so much by opening her door to them, Una would likely be dead. As if sensing the temperature of Una's thoughts, Rian's expression darkened.

"I don't like it any more than you do, you know?" She tossed the offensive Callaghan across the room, where it bounced off the wardrobe and slipped under the bed in a flurry of ruffling pages. She rubbed at her temples. "We could still go south. We don't need his permission, Una."

"We wait."

"Siora's mercy, why?"

"Because he's right. The safest place for any of us is over that border."

"… Never mind that he's playing for time with our lives in the balance?" Rian sat up, tucking her bare feet beneath her. "I'm not saying he hasn't proved himself a strong ally, and I'm not forgetting that he's saved both of our lives more than once. All I'm saying is, if we try to cross with an exiled lord, we might be killed anyway. Have you considered that? You know who he really is, Una."

"I don't believe what he was accused of. Nor, I believe, do you."

Rian mulled that over for a moment. "All right. I'm not as sure as you sound, but if he was guilty, I don't think he would have been merely exiled for the crime."

260

"Exactly."

"Just don't forget that he was banished here. He might not have done as much as they say, but he's guilty of *something*."

"I'm not daft, Rian. I'm not arguing that he's a Kneeler's saint. Only that I think there's more to him than we know. Give him a chance."

Rian's eyes slivered. "'*Give him a chance*?' Ugh. You fancy him, don't you?"

"Why on *earth* would you say such a thing?"

"All that nonsense last night." Rian made a face. "You sounded like a pair of rare idiots."

Una cleared her throat. "I *do not* fancy him. You're after being clever and forget that we're all in a heap of trouble. We need each other. All of us. All right?"

"I don't trust that great lummox, even if you *do* fancy him," Rian said. "He'll let you down. They all do that."

Now there was a statement that resonated. Intrigued, Una cocked her head. "All of whom?"

"He's Sidhe. Trust me, I know."

Ah.

"Is that what happened? With your grandmother, I mean. Is that why—"

"Oh, forget it. Just remember what I said, okay? You're Milesian. *Impermanent.* Keep him distant."

Una affected a weak smile. "Well, we gave him our word, Rian. In return, he has given his. We have to trust each other." Una might have hoped to convince herself, perhaps more than Rian. In this case, actions spoke louder than words. Ben might be many things— a criminal, a thief, a vagabond— but a liar, she knew to her bones, he was not. If he said he would get them across, she chose to believe him. "It's not just crossing the border he worries over. It's getting us all safely to Bri Leith under the High King's protection. That is a far trickier task than simply wading across a river."

"Right. How long have we been here, and what's he doing while we rot in this room? I could appreciate his efforts more if he bothered to share them with us."

Una took a seat on the edge of the bed. "Maybe he's scouting the border? Could be connecting with associates? Gambling, whoring— who knows? We told him we'd wait, so we wait."

"I heard you tell him you left Tairngare on your own before you were taken. Is that true?"

"It is."

"Why?"

"If you heard me tell him, then you already know."

"You told him what you wanted him to hear. I want to know the truth. Why would you leave Tairngare while your grandmother worked so hard to make you a queen? Where were you planning to go?"

Una blew air over her lower lip. "What does it matter? I won't get there with so many people out to kill or use me, will I?"

"I don't trust Ben, Una, but I *may* trust you," Rian paused to emphasize her point. "If you give me an honest answer."

That was fair. She thought quietly for several minutes, avoiding Rian's eyes until she could bear her unblinking judgment no longer. "I wished to take a ship to Swansea and, from there, travel to Alba. There is a place there, beyond the Wastes, I want to go. After that, I thought I might sail to Bretagne."

"Why Alba?" spat Rian, incredulous. "It's dead for hundreds of miles. Hills stripped of every tree, nothing green to see to the horizon. Just hills, rocks, and stale water."

"You know this for sure how?"

"Everyone knows it. It's common knowledge. 'After the Flood, the land was stained by salt and fire.' Why would you go there?"

Una shrugged. "Siora came from there, didn't she? Anyway, I told you it wasn't important. Not now. I won't be going anywhere without the High King's leave. If I try to backtrack to Ten Bells now, I'll probably run into agents from Bethany, if Corsairs don't kill me on the road. Ben's plan is the only one that makes an ounce of sense."

What she wouldn't say burned on her tongue like acid. Some things Una would keep to herself... indefinitely. For instance, how many times had she broken the Ninth Law in the past month? Too many to pretend devotion to Siora's strictures. She was a heretic, and Vanna Nema knew it. So too did Una's grandmother. Una squeezed her jaws tight, hoping Rian wouldn't press her any further on the topic.

After a few tense moments, Rian shrugged. "All right. I believe you. You're not telling me the whole truth, but you're not lying either. I can accept that for a while."

"Thanks?"

"Still, I do find it very interesting."

"What?"

"Your face *has* healed remarkably well."

"What of it?"

"It's monstrous."

Una deserved that, though it didn't hurt her any less to hear it. "That's why it's forbidden." She chewed her lip. "I need my strength, and that scum deserved his fate."

"I'm not judging you. I've just never seen anything like it before. It is rather incredible." Rian set her chin against her knuckles. "How are the ribs? Improved since yesterday?"

"A bit. I've always marveled that the healing should hurt worse than the actual wound. Siorai are taught to control their bodies before any other skill. A girl who can't focus her Spark this way never makes it past Nova in the Cloister."

"Is it so dangerous? The Cloister, I mean?"

"I often wonder if it isn't the most dangerous place in the world," said Una. A shadow crossed her brow. Even in this shoddy room, in this ramshackle hovel at the edge of civilization, Una was freer than she'd been nearly all her life. She should never have trusted Fawa Gan. Had she used better judgment, she might even now be strolling off the dock at Swansea. Anonymous. Unimportant. No one. She refused to dwell on it.

"I admit, I'm impressed. You don't spend your whole life brewing remedies and setting bones without developing at least a mild interest in your subject," Rian said. "I've never met a girl above the Grey before. Can you tell me about it?"

Una lay back against the mattress, letting her arms flop heavily to either side. Siora, but she was tired of this room. She didn't feel up to sharing her experiences with Rian, but what else would they talk about? Ben? *Not bloody likely.*

"I was born in Bethany, I'm sure you know? It's a long story, how I left. No, I don't want to discuss that before you ask." Una squinted up at the ceiling. "Let's see, my mother was made an Alta Prima at age twenty, but not because my grandmother shoved her through the Cloister ranks. Far from it. A girl without the Spark to progress through each level would never survive each Ordeal."

"What's an Ordeal? Like a test?"

"If that test was potentially lethal and the worst torture imaginable."

"How so?"

Una raised her hands over her face. She felt the sure crackle of an invisible energy lurking just below the skin. "The Spark isn't passive energy. We're each born with the aptitude to tame it, mold it— as it were, but only a select few can *force* the change. Every person reacts to the particles around them according to their arrangement; wood is solid, water is wet... and so on. Siorai are born with a gene... an, erm... inheritable trait that gives the particles in their bodies a sort of gravitas; a pull. We do so from within when we wish to alter an object's particles. It's not just asking your cells to obey you. You're commanding them to remake themselves according to your design."

"I don't understand."

Una closed her fist, and the air around it popped and fizzed as if she were stoking a small fire. "We're altering the chemical composition of our own cells to attract or repel particles around us. We call this Manipulation. Essentially, we rearrange those particles at the sub-atomic level, using energy from inside our cells."

Rian puffed out her cheeks. "How?"

"Everything in this world is composed of a set number of particles. The arrangement changes according to its... how do I say this? Its *program*? Siorai study these particles and learn how to harness and rejoin them as we see fit."

"Magic, you mean?"

"No." Una wiggled her fingers, and the energy dissipated. "Not really. Vibration and electric impulse cause particles to either attract or repel one another. We like to think of ourselves— our bodies— as conduits for these forces. Frequency and pitch are what we study most. For example, would it change shape if you were to take one of those pillows and smash it between your hands as hard as you can?"

Rian looked down. "Yes?"

"Manipulation is the same, only at the most fundamental level. Our Spark gives us the ability to push and pull on these particles. To use our life energy as an anchor. The level to which a girl may do so determines her value in the Cloister. Does that make any sense?"

"Not really. Sorry."

Una considered how she might better explain the process. "Okay. How'd you do it when you made that ogham stone for Ben?"

"I carved the correct symbol into a bit of river quartz and repeated the words my mother taught me to say."

"There you have it. You *Manipulated* the stone's particles, using energy from your own body to do so. Spark."

"If that's true, how did it know what form to take if I have no idea how that works? Sidhe magic is different. It's memorizing words, knowing which items can be brought together to... *oh.*"

Una tilted her head back to grin at her. "Exactly. I daresay you've achieved more with one little stone than you believe. You could likely wear the Grey yourself if you'd a mind to."

"Would I pass the Ordeal, do you think?"

Una's smile wavered. "Well, perhaps. Perhaps not. There's no way to know until one has tried. The First Ordeal is about focus."

"How many Ordeals are there?"

"Ten."

"How many have you passed?"

"Eight." Una repressed a shudder.

"Humph." Rian smashed her pillow with all her might, and Una laughed. "There. I'll take my pension now, My Lady."

Una opened her mouth to answer, but a scrape outside the door clapped it shut. She sat up. Rian's eyes flew wide. The handle was tried first, followed by a thump, a shuffle, and a muffled curse from the hallway. A heavy scuffing, like a boot sliding back. Una flung her hand out to Rian just as the door burst inward on its hinges. Bits of splintered wood and flaking green paint blasted into the room. Screeching, Rian darted from the bed to the corner. Una froze. She perched near the headboard on all fours. A very large man stood in the ruined doorway, with hands like anvils. He blinked at the two unarmed women inside and stepped back, a slow, childlike wonder in his beady eyes. A heavy-set, middle-aged woman stepped from the hallway behind him. She must have been attractive once, with her high clear brow, auburn hair, and delicately arched brows. Those days, however, were long gone. She wore so much rouge; her bulbous cheeks were twin bullseyes in a sagging sea of white talcum. Two dangling jowls swung free of a square jaw as she swatted at the giant's shoulder. The blow held all the ferocity of a kitten batting at a feather, but he flinched like she'd struck him with a stave.

"Damn it, Dabney! I bleedin' told ye to watch yer strength! I said a slight nudge— a nudge, damn ye. Not a feckin' jackhammer."

"Sorry, Barb. I din' mean to."

"Ye never do! For feck's sake! Ye better believe that bloody door's comin' outta yer pay." Stepping past him, she started to discover the room occupied. Una glared back at her from the bed. "What's this then? I told that no good, lecherous dog there be NO bleedin' talent on this side o'the buildin'! I've bloody respectable tenants in here!"

Una's nostrils flared. "*I beg your pardon?*"

Barb wagged an imperious manicured finger at her. "Oh no. I'll have no sass from the likes o'ye, girlie," she gave Una the once over. "Yer one o'Matt's girls then? Feckin' savage, lets his gents do as they please, don't he? Too bad. Ye'd be pretty enough, wit'out all that," she waved a hand at Una's healing bruises. "I'll never understand why ye girls let his boys do that to ye."

Rian held up her bookend like a shield. "Una, is she—?"

"*Yes,*" Una hissed.

Barb ignored them both. "Dabney!"

"Missus?"

She jerked her thumb at them. "Get these two gashes outta here."

"Missus," he said, stepping into the room.

Una flounced from the bed and parked herself in front of Rian. "I wouldn't do that if I were you."

Barb was already moving around the room, presumably taking inventory. "Ye tell that good for naught Ben Maeden, that this ain't no bleedin' toy box to keep his trash in. Owes me half a stag for the room this month, and that don't count what he's racked up this week, neither. Booze and girls cost money in this joint. For now, I'll be takin' everythin' in here."

Dabney moved to grab Una's arm. She swatted his hand away. "Madam, I assure you, you're mistaken."

"What's he got in here then, hey?" Barb disregarded her. "Haven't seen the bastard in nigh two weeks, and he has the brass to come back here lookin' for a flop? I won't have it, I tell ye." She dug around in the wardrobe, sucking her teeth at its poor selection of items: a few tunics, an extra pair of boots, and two pairs of moth-eaten leggings. There were no coins, no weapons, and no valuables of any kind. The girls' packs, they'd stashed under the bed. Una didn't doubt it would take the madam long to find them at this rate. The last of Rian's coin and all her medicines were in those packs. They couldn't afford to lose them now.

"We're not, erm, working girls, Mistress," said Rian, keeping a wary eye on the big man's reaching sausage fingers.

Una slapped them away again.

His lip jutted out like a pouting toddler. "Ow."

Barb laughed. "None o'us ever are, dearie. Hurry it up, Dabney! I wanna surprise that sack o'shite when he deigns to show up. Bleedin' show pony has coin to bathe and take meals in here like I run a bloody hotel for degenerate gamblers and thieves. Bringin' girls in off the streets when he ain't paid his tab next door in months!"

Una seethed.

She'd never been spoken to like this before.

267

Not ever.

Dabney leaned forward to hook her around the shoulder. Grabbing the bedpost for support, she kicked out with both legs. He staggered, bleating like an injured lamb. He looked back at her with a trembling chin.

"Why'd ye hit me?"

"I don't think he's right in the head, Una," opined Rian.

"I don't care. You try to grab me again, Dabney, and I'll put you down. That's all the warning you're going to get."

He fidgeted while Barb made a tidy pile of useless junk at the far end of the bed. "Missus? She hit me."

Barb stopped, exasperated. "So, hit her back, ye bleedin' bairn! Honestly, what should I do with ye, hm? Lettin' a little slut like that push ye about. Yer three times her size! Get on with it."

"We are *not* sluts, you *ham-fisted cunt*," Una growled.

Dabney covered his mouth in shock. Una watched Barb's head come up. "What did'ye just say?"

Undeterred, Una glared back. "Oh, I think you heard me. We're not prostitutes, and Ben's debts have nothing to do with us. Now *get out before I put you out*. Was that clear enough?"

Barb drew herself up to her full height. "Second thought, Dabs. I want ye to knock that gash's teeth out. Now."

The giant lunged, but Una was faster. Like a shot, she leapt up. Her hand slipped over Dabney's eyes, her fingers digging into his brow bone.

"*Down*," she rasped. He hit the floor so hard that his head pounded through the floorboards. The impact rattled the window and sent a spray of splinters into the air around his prostrate body.

"Siora!" Rian squished herself into the corner as far as she could go.

All color but the overdone rouge leached from Barb's face. Mouth agape, she stared at Una— who hid her sudden exhaustion— as if seeing her for the first time. Barb's eyes now marked the exposed tattoos at Una's collarbone, her hands, and along her arms. She let out a slight wheeze.

"Of course, ye aren't, *milady*. Forgive me poor manners." Barb traced the ghost of a clumsy curtsy.

Una didn't reply.

Tossing Ben's things back into the wardrobe in an inelegant pile, Barb was at a sudden loss for words.

"He'll be fine in a while," Una told her as she observed Dabney snoring into the dusty underfloor. "I did warn him."

"Well, he ain't the brightest gem in the box, ye know?" Barb patted her dyed hair with a shaking hand.

"Now then, perhaps I shoulda led with this, but would ye two *ladies* care for a stiff drink? Siora knows I could use one meself about now."

Ben TWISTED THE DAGGER, AND on cue, Vick screamed behind his palm. The boy muttered something nonsensical, but Ben didn't care to hear it. He stiffened his forearm, then smashed the back of Vick's skull into the wall. Solomon hovered nearby, alternating between handwringing and complaining of the mess. Astride Vick's knees, Ben leaned in close.

"I warned you not to come into the Quarter, Vincent." Ben removed his hand. Vick stole the opportunity to suck down as much air as possible. His brown eyes boiled with hate and pain. "I hope it was worth it?"

Vick spat at him, but Ben dodged the bloody mess. Cursing, he set his knee down hard over Vick's bleeding thigh. Vick cried out, uselessly trying to shove him off. Ben outweighed him by at least fifty pounds and was twice as tall. Vick didn't have the slightest hope in a wrestling match. Solomon stepped gingerly over Vick's unconscious friend, mindful not to slip in the gathering pool of blood.

"Is that necessary?"

Ben ignored him. "I asked you a question, Vincent. I expect an answer."

"Feck yerself, Ben Maeden. When Matt's done, ye won't be able to piss upright. I promise."

Ben gave him the kind of smile that made the younger man swallow. "I'm sure he'd like you to believe that, but without boys like you to do his dirty work for him, he's just a bootlegger with a paunch. Your boss is a coward."

"Whatta I care?" Vick snorted wetly, "I just work for the man. He says he wants to see ye, so I come to get ye. Simple."

"Funny, isn't it? That he waits for Robin to leave before making a move like this?"

"I dunno what yer talkin' about."

"Sure, you do. Matt heard Robin and I were on the outs, so maybe he figured he'd intimidate me into taking his side, using your two dead pals as leverage. Or maybe this is all about Robin? For Matt's brother, all those years ago. Both, maybe?" Ben jerked the dagger out of his leg. Vick yelped, mumbling nonsense under his breath. Bloody spittle ran down his collar. Ben jabbed the blade point first into the floorboards between them. He watched Vick pretend not to consider trying for it. "Go ahead, if you think you can get to it before I shove it into your eye socket."

"Feck ye."

"I heard you the first time." Ben shifted onto his haunches. "I have to say I'm flattered, but Matt overvalues me. I have neither the influence nor interest to assist in his coup. But you knew I'd say that, didn't you? You brought all this extra steel in vain."

Vick coughed. "Why ask me? Ye've killed friends o'mine, Ben Maeden. I won't forget that, no matter what Matt says. I was hopin' ye'd refuse him, and ye did."

"How's that working out for you?"

"Just kill me. If it keeps that poncey mouth o'yers from waggin', I'm ready."

"Matt surely couldn't have pinned all his hopes on me. He doesn't have the numbers. What else does he have planned, Vincent?"

"Stop callin' me that! Me own mam don't call me that! It's Vick!"

"Cute nickname."

The boy groaned. "Sol, can ye please hand over somethin' to cut me own throat with? This is like arguin' with me bloody granddda."

Shaking his head, Solomon went back to polishing the horn mugs he'd already polished half a dozen times in twenty minutes. No help there.

270

"You know, I don't make a habit of killing men unless they make the mistake of drawing down first," Ben pointed at him. "The other night, too, was on you. Both events were in self-defense. End of tale."

Vick had to think it over for a while, but his tone was less acerbic when he answered. "Don't change the fact that they was friends o'mine."

"You ever hear that you should choose your battles with care?" Vick chewed the inside of his cheek but refrained from comment. "That end of Wanderer's Alley is almost Greenmaker territory. You shouldn't have been there anyway. What *were* you doing there?"

"You'll have to ask Matt yerself. We done here? If yer not gonna kill me, there's lots o'things I'd rather be doin' than bleedin' all over Sol's floors and listenin' to ye prattle on."

"I'm not going to kill you, Vincent."

Vick couldn't repress a gory grin.

"I'm going to take you to *The Hart* and let Barb sort you out." Ben was amused by the speed at which that arrogant grin vanished. Vick shifted. He tried like hell to buck Ben and get to the waiting dagger, wildly lashing out at Ben's face and hands with everything he had. Ben grabbed one slim wrist, then twisted until he heard a definite crack. Vick didn't scream this time, only sniveled like a beat dog. "I can hurt you all night, or you can plead your case to Barb. Your choice."

"She'll kill me!"

"I doubt it. She's a bit less bloodthirsty than Robin or Colm. She'll probably trade you for something she wants."

Vick blew air and bloody sputum over his lower lip. "Good luck with that. Matt don't make trades, and he don't bargain, neither. Ye may as well kill me."

"If Matt's so ruthless, why do you support him?" Plainly, no one had ever asked Vick that question before. He seemed, finally, at a loss for words. Ben stood up. "Stay. If you flutter an eyelid, I'll break that leg. Clear?"

Vick dipped his head at the ogling, traitorous brewer. "Ye know Matt will make ye pay for this, don't ye?" Sol dropped the mug he'd been working on with a startled look on his face. "Whatever this lout promised ye, don't matter. Yer a dead man."

Ben administered a swift kick to Vick's lower ribs. "I thought I told you to shut up. Sol, you can disregard that threat. Matt won't do any such thing."

"I don't like this, Ben," whimpered Solomon.

Vick threw his head back and attempted to laugh. "He'll send more knives when I don't come back. Yer a fool to trust Robin's errand boy here!"

"Ignore him, Sol," Ben sighed.

"How's that? Ye think Barb is gonna trouble herself to protect me? Ye should strangle this whelp and dump his carcass in the river."

"That won't stop him, old man," Vick said. "None o' ye can stop him. He's got means, ye know? And time. Robin's days is numbered, and everybody knows it."

Ben took a long pull from a half-empty mug of ale and set the vessel on a nearby table. Any patrons had cleared out as soon as the fighting broke out. Ben sniffed, using one of Sol's rags to wipe the blood from his hands.

"It'll be rather hard for him to threaten anyone if he's dead. Don't you agree?"

Vick snorted. "Yer sure enough now. It'd be war."

"That's where we'll have to disagree, Vincent. I doubt a single person on the Hilltop would mind in the least. You know why?"

"Yer mad, or stupid. Can't tell which."

"No one will mind because Matt Gilcannon isn't the only boss in town. Barb runs a tighter ship, and no Greenmaker is ever knifed in the dark for aging out. I daresay that removing Matt from the equation solves everybody's problems."

"Yer gonna kill Gilcannon?" Solomon asked dubiously.

"After I drop this cretin in Barb's cellar, yes."

"Yer a crazy bastard, Ben Maeden! He'll kill ye... he'll kill all o'ye..." screeched Vick in frustrated disbelief.

Solomon shook his head at the boy and turned back to Ben. "Ye'll let Barb know I helped ye, won't ye? Do that, and ye can keep yer coins. If she's willin,' all I want is a share."

He filled two mugs, then passed one to Ben. Ben raised his. "I'll go one better and tell her the whole thing was your idea, Sol."

"I'll drink to that," Solomon tapped his mug against Ben's while Vick sputtered vitriol from the floor.

"*...and yer mother's... and all ye cunts....*"

Solomon frowned. "Ye sure ye need him alive?"

"Barb will want him."

"Can ye do it?"

Ben gave him a lazy smile. "What do you think?"

"*...feckin' tear yer throats out with me bare hands... I'll feck yer corpses... ye feckin' dogs... bugger ye with my knife... I'll...*"

"I think ye'd better get to work."

"Keep the stag, Sol. For the mess. I'll see you soon."

Ben set his mug down, grabbed Vick by his collar, and dragged him to the door. Vick kicked and howled like a rat in a boiling pot, but Ben had no trouble hauling him to his feet. He clamped a free hand over the lad's mouth to keep the noise down. Sol took stock of the bodies on the floor.

"Wait! Yer dagger. And what do I do with all o'them?"

"Leave them," called Ben over his shoulder. "I'd send a message to Matt. Tell him I attacked you and the boys in your bar. Do it within the hour before someone beats you to it."

"You want me to betray you?"

"Why do you think you're still alive, Sol?" Ben kicked the door open, smashing Vick's temple into the jam. The boy deflated slightly, making it easier to keep hold of him. "I trust you to tell him everything in *detail*."

Sol sputtered, "But I—"

"Word for word. I'd rather Matt knew I was coming for him."

"Siora, *why*?"

"It's more fun that way, isn't it?"

THE MADAM

n.e. ƒ08
2ƒ, ðor samna
Rosweal

B arb excused herself from the parlor. The Siorai girl watched her leave, though her companion was too engaged in chatter with Rose to notice. Barb didn't have to worry about her girls. No one was immune to innocent, polite flattery... especially when it came from one's social inferiors. Barb's girls would simper, flatter, and charm their way into the Moura Prima's ease. That was precisely what Barb paid them for, wasn't it?

Gently closing the door behind her, she bustled down the hall to the staircase overlooking the taproom. *The Hart and Hare* never officially closed for the day, but there was a distinct deficit of patrons until after sunset every evening. Only one or two stragglers warmed themselves beside her two infamous hearths. Barb ran her hand along the polished birch balustrade on her way to the top landing. She tapped her nails on the railing. Downstairs, a thin man with a face full of scars stopped wiping tables to blanch up at her excitable posture.

"Colm! I need the fellas," she whisper-shouted at him, bosom heaving. "Gerry, Rich, Seamus, and Paul. Anyone ye can find. Have 'em wait down here. I want Paul standin' guard at the back door."

Colm's triangular chin pulled downward. "What for?"

"Don't ask me what for. Just bloody do it!"

Colm tossed his rag onto a partially clean round-top and stomped toward the kitchen door, grumbling the whole way. Barb whirled on one of her guards, who was busy chewing on an apple core from his chair on the first landing. He was there to prevent patrons from wandering upstairs without paying for the privilege and often to keep her girls from ducking out of a shift. He was easily twice Colm's size but possessed half of his acumen. He reminded her of a fatted calf chewing cud. She twisted her nose at him.

"Which are ye?"

Apple-tainted spittle clung to his sparse, unruly beard. "Dean, Missus."

"Dean, I don't keep men that chew with their mouths open."

He forced himself to swallow. "Sorry, Missus."

"*Siora's mercy*," she prayed, brows skyward. "Dean, when Colm gets back, I want ye to send two men to the walkway. Gerry should guard that door there."

"What door, Missus?"

"The one I just bloody came out of."

"Oh right." His brow scrunched up. "But if yer in there, why d'ye want it guarded? I can see it from here."

Barb pinched the bridge of her nose. "Dean?"

"Missus?"

"If ye wanna keep yer job, don't talk back. *Ever.* Understood? Just do what I tell ye."

She watched him struggle to respond until she felt her brain might leak from her ears if she stared too long. Colm came through the kitchen door with two filthy men of similarly lean statures. She inclined further over the balustrade.

"Where's Gerry and Paul?"

"Sleepin'. They only got back from a raid this mornin'. Robin says let 'em be," Colm sighed with a put-upon air. He'd been around so long hthat e didn't worry much over Barb's temper.

She swore under her breath. She'd fix him soon enough, the insolent worm. She shoved past Dean on her way to the landing, her lips pressed into a grim line.

276

"Colm, get yer *bony* arse up here. And ye two," she pointed to Seamus and Rich. "I want one o'ye guardin' the walkway and the other the alley. Don't ye dare look to Skinny! I pay yer feckin wages, don't I?"

"Yes'm," both mumbled and slouched off to do her bidding. Seamus slid by her, careful not to bump into her elbow, which jutted from her hip at a ninety-degree angle. She didn't budge to accommodate him; he was forced to squeeze himself along the banister on his way up. She didn't waste much attention on him. Her ire was reserved for the man who surely knew better than to back-talk her in front of subordinates.

Colm, none too eager for the boxing he was about to receive, inched up each step sideways, a sullen mope tugging at his cheeks. "Barb?" he squirmed under her scrutiny.

"Ye wanna head back out with Robin to earn yer bread, Colm? Because that can be arranged."

He went a shade paler than his typical fish-belly white. "No, Barb."

"Then ye'd better start mindin' yer mouth, don't ye think? Ye work for me, not the other way 'round. Ye could be back over that river in a flash, dodgin' Sidhe arrows, and fey beasties. Am I clear?"

"Yeah."

"*And?*"

"Sorry, Barb."

"Now then," she gestured behind her. "I've got the shock o'me life waitin' in that office up there, and I need to be sure it don't stroll outta here unfettered. I daresay, Robin needs to be apprised o'this."

"I thought ye was interviewin' new girls?"

Barb grinned. "In a manner o'speakin'... one o' them is more'n a common crofter's daughter, that's for sure."

"How's that? Where'd they come from anyway? I saw 'em stroll into yer office, but they didn't come through here."

She almost giggled; she was so pleased with her good fortune. "From the rents next door. A gift from bloody Ben Maeden hisself, can ye believe it? Me an' Dabs were bowled to find them in his room." Her smile flickered. "Now I mention it. Someone might wanna check on the poor lamb. He was out cold, last I saw him."

"Wait, what? What about Ben? Why would Dabs need helpin'? Yer pardon, Barb, but yer makin' as much sense as a cloud does to a fish."

She took a breath, then patted her thudding heart. "Listen, I don't have time to explain. The girl's not stupid, and she's got power. *Loads*, I reckon. We'll have to overwhelm and be quick about it."

"Who? What power're ye talkin' about?"

"She's got to know I put nightshade in her tea with the uishge. I don't expect it'll be long afore—"

"Barb! Slow down! *Who?*"

Barb blinked back. "The Moura girl! She's upstairs in me office."

"What the feck is a 'Moura'?"

"Yer havin' me on, Colm? The fecking Mouras... the richest family in Tairngare? Hells, likely the whole bloody continent. *That Moura*."

"Oh," said Colm, as it sunk in. Then his eyes bulged. "OH! It can't be, can it? What would a girl like that be doin' here?"

"I bloody well grew up in Tairngare, didn't I?" Barb sniffed, "I think I'd know a fecking Moura when I see her. She's covered in blue dragons, ye dolt."

"Dragons?" Colm threw up his hands. "I ain't ever been to Tairngare, Barb. I don't know what that means."

"Siora, preserve me." She squeezed his shoulder. "Just go get Robin and tell him what I told ye. Got it? I don't have time for all this. She'll be gettin' antsy." She paused on her way back upstairs, worrying her nails. "One last thing. Make sure ye tell Robin that it was Ben brung her here. That's very important."

"Why? They're still hot at each other, ain't they?"

"Just do it, Colm," Barb snapped. "Make sure ye keep an eye out for that lanky, blond bastard too. We don't want him buttin' his nose in, do we?"

Colm blew a gust of air out of his gut. "Whatever ye say, Barb, but I'm tellin' ye, Robin ain't gonna be happy. He's knackered."

"Oh, I dunno about that, Colm. I think he'll be plenty happy once ye tell him 'bout our guest."

For once, Ben was marginally pleased with himself. He'd managed to catch his first clean break in weeks. He'd stashed Vick in the cellar of an abandoned tenement two lanes east of *The Hart*, where he could be certain no one would find him. Ben should send Matt a gift for attempting to interfere in Greenmaker business just when Ben needed him to. With Matt's bid to oust Robin from the Guild, Ben had a genuine opportunity not only to earn Robin's trust once again but his gratitude as well. Yes, things were looking up, thank Herne. Finally, he could relax a bit. Maybe let the girls out? Take a few pints with folks he generally mixed with? Why not? By sunset tomorrow, he'd be a hero to half the Quarter and likely, achieve a proper escort over the border for the girls if all else failed. Ben was in a good mood. The first, after so many days on the run, bleeding, fighting, chasing, and hiding. All he needed now was for Diarmid to respond to his message. If his uncle agreed to help him, Ben might not require the Greenmakers' help at all.

Gods be kind.

Diarmid Adair possessed the authority and power to break Ben's geis without a proper hearing at Court or an impossible personal trial. As the Ard Ri's Brehon, Diarmid was allotted powers no other individual in Innisfail could boast of. *Fiachra Ri*, the Sidhe, called him: Raven King. Though Ben had no doubt the pooka would deliver his message as promised, there was no guarantee Diarmid would respond. Ben hadn't seen his uncle in years, and quite possibly, the old bastard had no further interest in involving himself in his problems. Diarmid had spoken up for Ben once before, which hadn't worked out in the Raven King's favor; Ben had heard Diarmid was anathema at Court to this day. If he did show up, he would probably demand some absurd payment for his aid, no matter how limited his involvement. Ben was prepared for all of this, just in case.

Thanks to Una, there was a real need for an audience with Midhir. Diarmid was no fool. He would understand how important this was. At the very least, he could carry the news Ben bore to Bri Leith and let the Ard Ri himself make the decision Ben knew he would. There was no way Midhir would allow Bethany to conquer Tairngare, not while he drew breath. Ben wasn't prepared to depend on Diarmid alone, however. That would be foolish. Diarmid Adair was a great lord but also mercurial, duplicitous, and irresponsible. He was hardly the most charitable or honest fellow in Aes Sidhe. Diarmid ruled over many but dwelt with none. He was rarely invited to festivals or encouraged in Council, nor did he often feast in any rath. The Raven King was unpredictable and intemperate as lightning. Ben prayed for Diarmid's help but would make alternate plans regardless. Ben, too, was no fool. Thanks to Vick and his boss, things might just work out.

Drawing his cowl up, Ben rounded the corner at the rear of his tenement. Leaping to the second-floor balcony without much effort, he was barely halfway through the window when the sight of his room brought him up short. The door wasn't simply ajar; it had been smashed inward and dangled precariously from its splintered jamb. The armoire lay on its side, with its drawers crushed beneath it. The floorboards at the foot of the bed were bashed in, gaping cavernously at the ceiling above. Neither girl was anywhere to be seen.

Panic traced a slow burn from Ben's gut to his throat. What in the *nine hells* had happened in here? Where were they? He darted around the scene to glean clues until he caught a muted gag from the hall. Quick as an adder, Ben ducked through the ruined doorway. He discovered Dabney, Barb's boulder of a bodyguard, crawling toward the walkway on his hands and knees. There was a foul-smelling trail of sick marking his glacial progress. The big tough blubbered the whole way like a whipped child. Ben turned him over with his left foot, sword drawn.

"What in the name of Herne is going on, Dabs?"

Dabney's face was streaked with tears, bloody snot, and rubbed in vomit. He put his hands up in a pathetic, defensive posture. "Don't hurt me no more, Ben! I didn't do nothin' to her, I swear!"

Ben backed up as a fresh puddle of gelatinous fluid burst from the fellow's swollen nose. "*What's* that, Dabs?"

"The girl! She was so lil'... but she hurt me!"

Una. Only one tiny woman he knew of could make a grown man of this size cry like a baby. Ben slid Nemain back into her sheath and eyed the walkway with a furrowed brow.

"Where is she then?"

"I dunno." Dabney wiped at his streaming eyeballs with the back of his knuckles. "She broke me, and I woke up here. She's scary, Ben."

"Dabs, you have *no* idea. You came here with Barb, I presume?"

"Uh-huh."

Damn it. "What happened before she hurt you?"

Dabs blubbered. "Barb told me to grab them two girls and throw 'em out. The scary one called Barb a bad name, so Barb told me to hit her. I wasn't gonna. She was so lil'. Then she… she… that's all I 'member, Ben. Swear."

"Danu's tits! These bloody girls are going to get me killed!" Ben roared in frustration. Cursing, he inched around Dabs' sniveling bulk to get a good look at the walkway. Thankfully, he didn't see anyone at the other end, but that could quickly change. If Barb had Una and Rian, it wouldn't be long before she'd send someone out to inquire about a missing Siorai Prima. Everyone knew Barb had more than one or two bones to pick with the Cloister in Tairngare. If he didn't get to them soon, all the trouble he'd gone to today might amount to nothing.

"You won't tell Barb I was cryin,' will ye, Ben?"

"No, Dabs. I won't tell her."

The oaf gave him a relieved, toothless grin. Ben drew up his cowl and cut around the corner toward *The Hart and Hare*. This was not how he was hoping to end his day. He prayed that both girls were unharmed because he wanted the pleasure of listening to their neckbones snap when he throttled the life from them both.

"THERE'S SOMETHING IN THE TEA," Rian whispered behind her hand. Una took a dainty sip, a false smile mortared to her mouth. Barb's girls worked very hard to maintain a pleasant, harmless façade. Rose was dark-haired with smooth dark skin; Violet was fair and pale as soft cream. Rose was clearly Tairnganese, with her coloring and high cheekbones. Violet must hail from the South, or perhaps she was a Cymrian or

Kernese transplant? One did not come by such fair skin in the North unless they were from some far-flung backwater. Only faeries and trueborn Sidhe, like Ben, had the bones to pull off 'wan'— but perhaps Una was biased? There weren't many fair-skinned girls in Tairngare.

She supposed the girl was pretty enough, in her way.

Una might even feel bad for having such catty thoughts about her if the pasty-faced trollop weren't trying to poison them. "I know," she murmured back. "Work your throat when you pretend to swallow."

Barb's girls prattled on about Tairnganese fashions and bombarded Una with inane questions about this or that city custom. They were so animated that it would have been hard for the unwary to detect the authentic current of nerves bubbling just below the surface of each expression. Una refused to feel sorry for them, Madam's orders or no. Rose seemed wiser and more watchful than her pastoral accomplice. Her gorgeous black eyes were careful not to linger on Una too long. She knew to which house Una belonged, there was no doubt. The lowest girl in Tairngare would never mistake Una for anyone else, with such a wealth of blue-limned skin exposed. Una took another tiny sip of her drugged refreshment. Of course, the Madam knew. She was Tairnganese, too, if from an Agrean or Merchantan household. Una detected the barest smidge of Spark in Barb, as she did with many women who had the misfortune to be rejected by the Cloister. Barb did not possess nearly enough to challenge Una directly, however. She felt sure the old madam was downstairs at this moment, preparing her guards.

Una knew she didn't have much time to decide on a course of action. Rose leaned in to pour more tea into Una's half-finished cup. If she was confused by the fact that the tea didn't seem to have the slightest effect on her, she was careful to conceal it. Rose smelled like mint and something sweeter. Her fingers were long, thin, and elegantly tapered. Her hair was ironed flat, though, at her temples, many natural curls refused to be tamed. Una could admit to a slight pang of envy there. Her own wild hair wouldn't take the iron, no matter how many attempts were made.

"My Lady," Rose simpered, her voice sweet and deep. "Ye have the most beautiful skin (horseshite, if Una had ever heard any before). How d'ye care for it? Oil, balms? Many girls would weep for yer secret." Her accent was softer than anyone she'd met outside of Tairngare, saving Rian. Una returned Rose's ingratiating smile but didn't seem to have a firm grip on her cup. A hot line of black tea laced with nightshade dribbled down the front of her tunic. "Oh no!" cried Rose, hastily setting the pot back on the larder.

She wadded up her shawl to pat Una's lap dry.

Una flushed. "I'm sorry. How clumsy of me."

Clucking, Rose shook her head with reassuring denial. "The fault was mine, My Lady. There's nothin' to forgive."

Una's fingers wound over Rose's own.

"Not for that. *For this*."

A sound like rushing bees filled the parlor.

On cue, Rian launched herself at Violet, who didn't have time to cry out as the taller girl's hand clamped over her lower jaw. "Don't kill her!" Rian hissed, using her body weight to hold Violet down. "You don't have to."

Rose whimpered in a half-faint.

Una frowned. "We have to get out of here."

"Fat chance of that. That woman went to get help."

"Make her drink that tea."

Violet's struggles gained intensity, but Rian knocked the back of her head against the floor, and she went limp. Rian's resilience floored Una. Just a smattering of days before, hadn't the faerie girl seemed to be the weakest member of their trio? Now, Una wasn't sure if Rian wasn't the strongest... Ben included. Her ability to adapt to circumstances, however unpleasant, was impressive. Rian retrieved her cup, then tilted the girl's head back to pour the substance down her throat. Violet sputtered, but enough trickled down that Una was satisfied she'd present no further trouble. Una tucked Rose into her own abandoned chair. Rian watched the door with wary eyes.

"Now what?"

"Get behind me." Una jumped over the fallen teapot to lace her fingers through Violet's. The sound came again.

Rian covered her ears. "Why're you doing that? They're already incapacitated."

Una closed her eyes as her Spark surged inside her. Putting that hulk of a man down had cost her heaps of energy. She'd already expended so much in the past few days. She needed what little she could muster to heal and keep moving. A slow burn could potentially get them both out of this mess in one piece.

Consequently, if she hadn't depleted herself, she'd never have allowed that abhorrent woman to lure them into this situation in the first place. Una's strength had to be replenished— that was all there was to it. They must get out of here before that old whore sold her to the first group that came looking. Siora only knew what she would do to Rian. Una knelt and slid her palms along either side of Rose's face. Rose blinked languidly as if fighting sleep.

"Is there another way out of here?"

"Just the walkway or the door downstairs."

"I don't believe that for a second."

"The truth."

"Siora. Guess it's back the way we came, Rian."

"Then what?" Rian fidgeted, looking around for anything she could use as a weapon. "Where will we go?"

Una shook Rose hard. "Which way? Where can we run?"

"She'll have me flogged."

"*I'll* do much worse if you don't help us. I can make it look like you tried to stop us, or I can break every bone in your pretty face with a thought. Your choice."

"The alley, just behind the laundry. Second stair after the walkway, on yer right." She reached out and clutched Una's arm, her pupils dilated. "Don't stop for anyone. She'll sell ye if she catches ye. If ye see Ben, warn him Robin's back."

Una chewed her lip to conceal her surprise. "I don't know what that means."

"Just tell him, please? I think ye'll have to strike me."

284

"No need." Una pressed her thumb into the girl's forehead. Rose's chin sagged until she bent nearly double. Una scowled down at her for a moment, confused by her sudden concern. Then, her attention snagged on a scrape in the hall. Someone was coming. She grabbed Rian by the elbow. "Ready?"

"No," snarked Rian, wielding a pewter candlestick like a club. Una opened the door on Barb's surprised face. Without a word, she ducked low and rammed her shoulder into the older woman's gut.

Barb's breath burst out in a gush on her way to the floor. "What—oof!" she exclaimed.

Una didn't wait around for Barb's next shout. Two men were racing up the stairs on one end, and another peeking around the corner from where they needed to go.

"Go, Rian! Don't stop!"

They ran. Barb screeched orders, but that didn't deter either girl. Thudding steps behind them made Rian turn only long enough to chuck her candlestick into a pursuer's knees. He crashed into the floor with a yelp, taking one of his companions down with him like pins in a bowler's game. As Una and Rian rounded the corner, they came to the darkened hallway they'd been brought through earlier. Faint, sickly light shone through the sole window in the walkway. The scrape of a booted foot in the passage made Una's blood burn with determined rage. A tall shadow emerged from the light. With an animalistic grunt, she heaved herself at the figure, hoping to offset his balance with her weight as she'd done to Barb.

She might have been a feather for all the effect she managed. Bouncing off a broad chest, her arse thumped soundly into the floorboards. She barely had time to curse her bad luck before a pair of large hands clamped over her shoulders and hauled her upright. He slammed her into the wall one-handed while fending off Rian's feeble blows with the other. Una's ribs still cracked, making their displeasure known.

She gnashed her teeth. "Rian! Go for his legs!"

The figure let go.

"Una? What in the *hells* are you doing?" Ben dragged her into the walkway, tugging Rian behind him by the back of her neck. She slapped at him until he released her. He pressed Una against the windowsill. Breathing hard, she frowned at his bemused expression.

"They're coming!" huffed Rian. "We have to go!"

Una had quite a lot she wanted to say to this bastard, but it would have to wait. "Get us out of here!"

Ben's mouth twisted. "Told you to stay put, didn't I?"

She bared her teeth at him like a badger. "Oh, we're going to have a long talk, you and I. Very soon."

"Can we please get out of here first?" urged Rian.

BEN SHOVED BOTH GIRLS AHEAD of him into the walkway as several stomping feet thundered up the hall behind them. From beneath the alcove came Barb, followed by a new tough Ben had never seen before. Seamus and Colm brought up the rear. Barb clutched at her side, her bosom heaving. She set a hand against the wall under the last red lamplight. Her graying hair was wild about her ruddy face.

"Wasted a full bottle o'me best uishge, and this is the thanks I'm due?"

"Bad manners, that," came a familiar voice from the opposite end of the walkway. Ben shut his eyes with a silent curse. He turned. Robin walked into the light, followed by Paul and Gerrod, effectively blocking their exit. Dabney slumped in a corner and tried not to look at anyone. Gerrod flashed Ben a warning with his eyes, but Ben didn't need it. He already knew what Robin was going to say. His scarred mouth set a grim line. "Ben. I thought I told ye, ye weren't welcome in Rosweal?"

"What? Ye didn't tell *me* anythin' like that," interjected Barb.

"Wasn't yer business, Barb," Robin boomed, never taking his eyes from Ben's face. "It's *ours*. Ain't that right, Ben?"

Barb sputtered. "That's some brass ye got, Robin Gramble. Tellin' me, what pays ye lot, what I oughtta know or not."

286

"This is men's business."

Barb's chin said she'd make him pay for that comment sooner or later. Ben knew them both very well.

Una's fingers tightened on Ben's shoulder. "Who is he?"

"Robin," Ben nodded, ignoring her. "I came to see you, for the record."

Robin cocked his head. "Is that right?"

"I have a proposition for you— for both of you," Ben tugged his chin at Barb. Rian's belly squeezed into the window casing while she searched for the latch. Ben found himself moving out front to block the girls from view. "Something you both want."

"Don't bet on it." Robin drew his sabre.

With a groan, Ben mirrored him. "I'm serious, Robin."

"Love, I dunno what ye two are on about, and I don't care," Barb pointed. "But them two girls're worth a bloody fortune. I want 'em back. Unharmed."

Rian sucked in a sudden breath. Scratching at the glass, she jerked Una around to help. Ben set Nemain's point against the floorboards. "Will you listen to me? We have to talk!"

"I don't care to hear anythin' ye'd say, Ben."

"There's much you don't know, Robin. It's not all black and white."

"Yeah, it bloody well is. Ye lied to me for years, Ben. Nothin' ye could say to me now would change that."

"This is boring the shite outta me." Barb snapped her fingers, "Dean, Seamus. Bring those girls back to me office. Don't scratch 'em up neither! They're worth more than any o'ye."

Parties advanced warily from both sides for fear of Ben's vicious two-handed longsword. Ben reached for the nearest lantern on the wall.

"Una," he said. "Get ready to run right through them."

Rian pushed the window open, letting in a gust of damp, chill air. Without ado, she climbed over the sill. Ben didn't have time to process her intent because Dean lunged clumsily from his left, and Robin took a testing jab from his right. Ben parried Robin's blow and knocked him into Gerrod, who broke Robin's fall with a shaky right arm. Then Ben whirled, grabbed Dean by the back of the neck, and smashed the bulky fellow's nose into his knee. Dean went down, howling. Before Robin could rush back in from Ben's right side, Ben tossed the lantern onto the floor. It shattered into a million glittering pieces. Barb shouted something unintelligible and ducked behind Dabney. Ben had the brief satisfaction of watching every opponent scramble for cover as burning oil splashed throughout the hall, flinging spurting lines of flame over the ancient wooden floorboards. Ben caught only the briefest glimpse of Robin's furious face before Una pulled hard at his elbow. They tipped through the open window together. Smoke and curses filled the void they left behind.

No Quarter

n.e. ᚱ08
2ᚱ, ðoꝛ samna
ꝛoswᴇal

They didn't fall far enough. Two bolts struck the canvas nearest Ben's head. Rian managed to drop them into the alley between the two buildings, where Barb's housekeeper ran *The Hart and Hare*'s profitable laundry. There were dozens of carts and crates piled high with dirty sheets, tunics, linen, and hose. Lines between each brick wall were crowded with drying bedding, gowns, and curtains. Rian clawed her way out of a crate of soiled linens and limped over to help Una and Ben out of theirs. The drop wasn't more than eight feet, which made the landing relatively soft— if unsanitary. Eight feet wasn't quite far enough to escape the hail of quarrels that followed. Ben dodged another missile and another. The air filled with smoke. He got to his feet and dragged Una upright beside him.

Rian led them around a flimsy wall of drying sheets. "Which way?"

Barb trilled orders from the burning walkway. Ben knew they had seconds before Paul, Seamus, and Gerrod dogged their heels. "To the docks! Follow me!"

They fled as fast as their feet would carry them, over slick cobbles and down partially flooded lanes. At the end of an alley, Ben took a sharp left. On a dime, he stopped and kicked down the door to a short, squat warehouse. The girls moved to enter, but he drove them toward the docks instead. Rian, with her bad foot, had trouble keeping up. Ben was obliged to hook an arm under hers and half-carry, half-drag her along with him. Despite this, they made swift progress toward the West Gate. Here he turned again, circling abruptly back around to the east. Ben kicked open another door, shoved both girls inside, and slammed it shut after them. They stood in the unkempt back garden of a small, vacant house. Rosweal had plenty of abandoned spaces for the nefarious to utilize, thank Herne. He pressed his ear against the rotting garden door, waiting for the tell-tale splash of footsteps to come pounding up the alley.

"We're not going to the docks?" huffed Una, near his ear.

"They'll expect us to, won't they?" Rian held her ribs. Ben met her eyes over Una's head. He had to admit that Arthur's daughter had sharp wits and keen instincts. Once again, if not for her quick thinking, their situation could have been much worse.

"Right," he peeked over the retaining wall. No one followed. Yet. "We have to get to the Hilltop. If it hadn't been for Vick and his little helpers, I would have taken you there from the first."

"How far is that?" Rian asked as if doing sums in her head.

"Not far. But we'll have to be quick and quiet. Robin's a keen hunter, and with Barb's promised payday," he pointed at Una, "he'll be getting serious about now. What happened back there?"

Una shrugged. "The madam was a Novitiate in the Cloister."

"How'd you know that?" Rian gestured for both of them to whisper. "She didn't look very refined."

"Not all of them are. I'll wager she came from an Agrean household. Folks often try to improve their lot by offering a girl in service to one of the great houses. Happens all the time. Most of these girls don't make it past the First Ordeal. Anyway, she knows who I am."

"Damn it," Ben groused. "I told you not to open the door to anyone."

"We didn't," snorted Rian. "They kicked it in, looking for you, you ingrate. Apparently, you owe the madam a good deal of money. She took us for courtesans and tried to maltreat us. Una put a stop to that. Then she invited us to tea and promptly tried to drug us. You weren't there."

"I assume she's already made plans to sell me. Tairnganeah patrol the Navan High Road. It won't take long for them to get here."

Ben kept his eyes on the alley behind them. Maybe they were searching the warehouse or the docks? He still smelled smoke. Possibly the Greenmakers got caught up putting out the fire? No matter what was happening, it was better luck than he expected. He had more weapons stashed at his house. They just needed to get there. He ducked away from the door, pulling the girls further into the garden. Behind a hedge, he shook his head at Una,

"No. She wouldn't."

"What do you mean, 'no?' She was going to sell me— both of us."

"I know her. She wouldn't sell you to the first patrol that came looking. Not Barb. She'd send people to find out if there were any other interested parties and how great any rewards might be. Then she'd auction you off to the highest bidder. Very clever and patient is Barb."

"*Wonderful*," Rian grumbled. "Me, I assume, she'd simply put to work?"

"No. She'd sell you to Matt Gilcannon," Ben said. "But that's neither here nor there. We need to get moving. The sooner you two are safe, the quicker I can get back to work and get us out of here."

"Where to?"

"There's a house up the hill, nine lanes up and two over. That's our destination. Move when I move, where I move, and how I move. Whatever you do, keep quiet. Understood?"

"I thought it was too dangerous to go there?" Una looked around with a dubious cast to her amber eyes.

"It is, but after tomorrow that won't matter. We must get moving. Remember what I said?"

Both girls nodded.

"Good. Let's go."

☘ ☘

It took eons to slink around each corner, turn, and rise, strafing from shadow to shadow through gardens, empty alleyways, and across busy thoroughfares. On one residential street, they passed dirty children playing with sticks and balls while matrons eyed them suspiciously from open windows and front stoops. Trying to appear as nonchalant as possible, they crept over garden walls, through yards littered with rusted tools, and lots choked with weeds. Up and up, they climbed, passing shuttered shops, empty taverns, and crumbling tenements. The sun was long gone by the time they rounded the last turn at the hill's apex. The houses here weren't caked black and brown with soot, nor were the lanes six inches deep in stinking, malodorous mud.

This was Gilcannon's territory, and the difference was stark. The Greenmakers might have more money, men, and connections than Matt, but they weren't as concerned with appearances as he was. The underlying rot and social debauchery on the Hilltop far exceeded the vices approved in the Quarter. Ben should know; he was technically a resident of both districts. He'd won this property in a game of porter many years ago but kept it to himself. At one time, he considered taking up regular residence. All things considered, he found he preferred the noise and up-front chicanery in the Quarter.

Since Gilcannon had bought the distillery on the North End, Ben could count the number of times he'd visited the neighborhood on one hand. The characters that flocked to Matt's standard weren't Ben's preferred sort of scum. He took a few switch-back turns from Fulcrum Lane to Goddard, then down Heritage, until he approached an iron gate tucked into a stately brick wall. The back of the house was dark and silent, as always. Ben couldn't recall if he'd ever used the front door.

The lack of street lanterns here certainly held sweetened its appeal. He didn't have the gate key on hand, and there was no time to delay. Looking around to be sure no one was watching, he leapt up to straddle the wall, then stretched a hand down to hoist each girl up. He pulled Rian over first because she looked like she might drop dead at any moment from exhaustion. Of the three, Rian was the most disused to running and the least likely to ask for help. Una came up almost entirely on her own. She just needed a hand back down due to her diminutive stature. He raised an eyebrow at her, but she looked away before he could catch her out. Whatever Siorai tricks she'd been using, they worked all too well. Una had a definite spring in her step that hadn't been there the day before, and the more he looked at her face, the more obvious was her blooming health. He could only guess what she'd done to accelerate the healing process, but it would keep, for now.

They had bigger problems.

Rian flopped onto a stone bench, strangled by creeping vines. Chewing her lower lip, Una stared over the gate on her tiptoes. No one seemed to be following them. Ben wasn't so sure. They were either very lucky, or something must have distracted Robin. He'd been known to hunt a single stag for three days at a stretch. He'd never let them get away so easily. Maybe the fire got out of hand, or Ben lost him back in the warehouses? Whatever happened, it wasn't over. They must lie low until Ben could regroup. He dug around in his dead flower beds for the wide, flat bit of shale he'd stashed his key under. Finally finding what he sought, he fumbled with the lock until he heard a withered metallic click; the door swung inward on its rusty hinges. He waited for the girls to head inside, then shut it behind them all as quietly as he could manage so as not to alert the neighbors to their presence. In the silent musty darkness of a small but effectively appointed kitchen, the trio let out a collective sigh of relief.

"*Siora*," breathed Una. "Let's not do that again."

"Agreed," Rian said. "Ben, do you think anyone followed us here?" Looking through a greasy window facing the back gate, Ben opened his mouth to say no, but a scrape and flash further inside whipped his head around.

Robin Gramble set a lit match to his pipe bowl. Its dim glow illuminated his crooked grin. "No need. We knew where ye was goin' the whole time." He gave Ben a mock salute.

Una tucked into Ben's side. Rian didn't move. "Took ye long enough too. Almost forgot which house was yers."

"Of course, you knew about this place. What was I thinking?" laughed Ben.

"Dunno, but ye was never as clever as ye thought."

Rian inched toward the exit. She jumped when Robin glanced directly at her. "I wouldn't do that, missy," he dropped a heavy crossbow on the table. Its clattering bulk made her squeak. "I'd hate to have to shoot ye in yer good leg. That's right, hands way up there. That's good."

Ben cursed long and colorfully. "You wouldn't happen to be alone, would you, old friend?"

"Am I ever?" A nervous cough issued from the front room. Gerrod emerged from the shadows, taking his place behind Robin's chair. He wouldn't meet Ben's eyes.

"How many more did you bring?"

"Enough."

"I doubt it," smirked Ben.

With a chuckle, Robin shifted his crossbow a half-inch to the right—directly at Una's heart. Ben froze, as Robin knew he would.

"Oh, I dunno about that, Ben. I'd say I brung plenty. Ladies? If ye'd be so kind, would ye take a seat in yon parlor there? Where I can see ye if ye please? Ye'll find me friend Seamus by the door. He'll be happy to build ye's a fire."

Una shot Ben a long, wary frown. "Go ahead," he told her. He was unsure which angered him most: that Robin had outfoxed him or that he had the brass to order him about in his own house?

"Seamus won't hurt either o' ye. Lad wouldn't know what to do with one o'ye if he tried. Paul and Dean, on the other hand, aren't as nice. Best stick with Seamus. Go on now."

With an uncomfortable pout, Gerrod moved aside to make room for them. He was Robin's man, through and through. Ben couldn't fault the lad for his loyalty, though he wished he wasn't involved. When the fighting broke out, he'd rather not have to hurt him for Robin's stubbornness. Una stepped near. Gerrod crushed himself against the wall to let her pass. Robin's smug grin faded slightly when she got close.

"Siora, Ben, did ye do that to her face?"

Una answered for him. "No. He saved my life and hers," she waved a hand at Rian. "More than once."

"Bah," Robin scoffed. "I know him. He ain't no bloody hero."

Una didn't respond. Instead, she lifted her chin and bristled as if to sweep between them into the parlor. Suddenly, she stumbled, the toe of her boot having snagged upon some unseen impediment. Gerrod's hands instinctively darted out to catch her around her waist. She beamed up at him. He only had a heartbeat to wonder at her curious expression when a sound Ben had only heard twice before surged through the room. Perhaps it was less a sound than a feeling, like the vibration of a thousand bees buzzing through a hive or the flapping of wings against a pane of glass.

Rian cried out. "No!" but it was no use.

Una's left hand clapped over Gerrod's bare wrist. "*Down*," she said. Down is where he went.

Aʟʟ ʜᴇʟʟ ʙʀᴏᴋᴇ ʟᴏᴏꜱᴇ ᴀᴛ once. Gasping for air, Una toppled with Gerrod into the rushes. The lad's head lolled against the wall as she dived chin first into his chest. Robin flew out of his chair. He reached to snatch Una off Gerrod by her hair. Ben got there first. His fist cracked into Robin's nose, forcing him to stumble backward into the corner of the fireplace. Seamus cried out with a cracking voice and flung himself into Ben. They tumbled to the floor.

Meanwhile, Paul dashed from the parlor into the kitchen. He grasped for Rian with an excitable leer. Screaming as he wrenched her into his arms, she kicked, bit, and scratched like a demon. Rian pummeled him with her knees, heels, forearms— anything that she could. Paul was wiry, but he had a strong grip. He trundled her against the counter and pressed his fingers around her slender throat. Ben smashed Seamus' head against the floor, once, twice… until his eyes rolled back in his head, and his legs stopped twitching.

"Rian!" Ben shouted, trying to scramble to her side.

Robin bashed him over the head with his crossbow. "I think you broke me feckin' nose!" Ben ducked under his arm, using Robin's own body mass as ballast. He came at him from the opposite side, then struck a hard blow with his left fist. Robin spat blood, but he didn't fall. Instead, he drew a dagger, and opened a wet line across Ben's chest. Ben backpedaled into the front parlor, careening into the covered furniture. Meanwhile, Una got to her hands and knees over Gerrod's prone body.

"Una! Rian!" Ben tried to point, but Robin slapped his hand away. Nodding, Una crawled toward Paul and Rian.

Robin wiped a trickle of blood from his nose with the back of his hand. "Where're ye lookin' then?"

With a grimace, Ben skimmed a hand over his seeping ribs. "Leave the women out of it, Robin!"

"Yer the fool who brung 'em here," said Robin, swapping his blade from hand to hand. "If Gerry don't get back up again soon, I'll string that Siorai cunt from the Navan Gate by her guts." Robin jerked right but flipped his dagger to his left hand to drag its point over Ben's thigh. Ben grunted, then hammered his elbow into Robin's reaching arm at the joint. Something hard crunched within. Robin hissed in pain. His dagger clattered to the floor. Ben kicked it away and shoved him back so he could draw his sword. Robin watched the light play over Ben's sylvan blade with a bloody grin. Pushing himself back up, he drew his Souther sabre. "It's to be that sort o'business, eh? Good. Was startin' to think ye'd gone soft."

Ben couldn't see what was happening in the kitchen. He heard Rian screaming and... something else, but it was lower this time, subtler. Una's power seemed to hold a different pitch now, like the sigh of a wave over a sandy shore.

"Una!" Ben called. No one answered.

Robin's blade thrust forward, testing. "That big Sidhe bitch of a blade just for show then, or d'ye aim to use it?"

"If I wanted to kill you, Robin, you'd be dead."

"Prove it." Robin sprang forward just as the back door flew inward. Dean, Barb's newest meat, rushed into the kitchen with his cudgel raised high. Ben didn't have time to react. Robin's attack was swift and brutal. Ben parried with a twist of his wrist. Then Robin's fist cracked into Ben's jaw like a cannon shot. "Ye'd better start takin' this seriously, shouldn't ye?"

Robin struck out again, and again, and again. His head thrumming, his ears ringing— Ben had no choice but to slide his right foot behind him. He hefted Nemain over his shoulder in a high *Neithana* guard. Blood poured from his abdomen, his thighs, and his mouth.

Robin bared his teeth. "That's more like it, ye Dannan bastard. *Come on.*"

🦌 🦌

WHILE BEN AND ROBIN WERE making each other bleed in the front parlor, Paul bent Rian over the counter by her throat and tugged her skirts up with his free hand. Her bloodied hands flailed around. She snatched at anything she could to turn herself out of his grip. Various domestic items clanged together or clattered to the floor. Finally, she managed to grasp a small black pot. Backhanded, she landed a glancing blow to his temple. He staggered a bit, then came back, bleeding and furious. Paul struck her twice. She withered, and he held her down while he fumbled with his laces. Ben shouted Una's name. Rian kicked and thrashed with all her might.

Una dragged herself upward. Red-faced, Paul fought to hold Rian still so he could wrench her underskirt out of his way. Una gritted her teeth on a ragged breath and hauled herself forward on her hands and knees.

"Hold still, ye faerie bitch!" Paul barked down at Rian while he tried to jerk himself forward. Una's fingers slid under the loose leg of his threadbare breeches. She dug her nails into his calf muscle. Surprised, he let go of Rian, who fell into a rasping heap on the floor. His beady eyes bulged. "What?"

"*Splinter*," Una snarled. The bones below her hand burst to pieces within his flesh. His forehead banged off the dusty iron stove on the way down.

Screeching like an owl, he scratched at his leg like it was on fire. "You *witch*! What did ye do to me?"

Una clawed herself up his prone body while he tried to shove her off. Grinding a knee into his naked groin, her hand latched over his face, ramming it into the floorboards with audible force.

"I'm going to eat you, little man. Every last drop."

He whimpered in confused, impotent pain. Una drew down deep. She gave her Spark liberty to dip its thousand greedy fingers into every one of his cells, to sap every morsel of energy his thin, repulsive body contained. She shuddered against him. Any remaining wounds she bore stitched themselves together in moments. Her bones realigned and snapped into place; nerves and joints popped, stretched, and fused. The energy drained from Paul reinvigorated her blood like a pitcher beneath a tap. She pulled and pulled until his skin sagged inward and his tongue dried up in his gaping jaws. Paul's heart shriveled like a prune in his desiccated chest. Crackling with a new and electric vitality, Una finally felt something like herself again.

Completely whole for the first time in nearly two weeks, she stood over Paul's mummified corpse and spat. Una wound her arms around her choking, shaking friend. "It's all right now, Rian. He's dead. He can't hurt you anymore."

Suddenly, the back door blew inward on its hinges. The dark-haired guard from *The Hart* stepped in, bearing a mean-looking cudgel in his grubby fists. Rian gave a short hoarse scream as he took in the scene. Paul's corpse did not escape his notice. His wide eyes traveled from Paul's remains to the fight in the parlor, and back toward the girls. His cheeks went a bit green at the edges. Someone else stepped in behind him. This one was smaller and skinny as a rail.

"What in the hells happened in here?"

Una put herself between them and Rian. The larger man, Dean, she thought she'd heard Barb call him, pointed his cudgel at her.

"Did *ye* do this?"

"Your friend liked to touch ladies without permission."

"Dean..." his friend eyed Una warily.

Dean shrugged him off. "I'm gonna tear yer head off yer shoulders, ye fecking witch!"

"Kill them, Una!" Rian raged, adjusting her clothing. Una shrugged her shirt over her head, leaving only a thin chemise above great swaths of exposed skin. The swirling blue dragons emblazoned on her arms and chest seemed to glow silver in the moonlight.

"By all means, boys, who wants to touch me first?"

↯ ↯

Bᴇɴ ᴡᴀs ʟᴏsɪɴɢ. Dᴇꜰᴇɴsɪᴠᴇ ᴛᴀᴄᴛɪᴄs were all but useless in such close quarters. If he couldn't reason with Robin, he would have no choice but to engage him seriously. He parried another blow, which drove Robin's sabre into the wooden paneling in the upstairs hallway. Robin jerked his arm forward to dislodge it with a tired grunt, but Ben's fist hammered into his chin.

Robin backpedaled into the alcove. Deprived of his sabre, he slipped two more daggers from his belt. Sweating, Ben leaned on his sword for a breath. Nemain was too heavy for such a claustrophobic space, but she still held the advantage over Robin's thin daggers. Both men were aware of this fact, though only Ben seemed reluctant to exploit it.

"Come on then," Robin croaked. A nasty bruise welled over his right eye and another over his jaw. His nose gushed blood from both nostrils. Ben wasn't in much better shape, truth be told. The cut to his ribs burned like a brand. So much blood was in his boots that his toes squished against their soles. Robin might not be able to beat him if Ben were serious, but neither was he a slouch. Every moment Ben wasted trying not to harm Robin further wore him down. This had to stop.

"Robin, I didn't come here for this," Ben panted. He held his left palm out. "I need your help."

Robin couldn't have looked more surprised if Ben had jammed Nemain through his heart. "Yer havin' me on? *My help*? What in the *nine hells* made ye think I'd help ye?"

"Because we've been mates for almost fifteen bloody years." Ben wavered a bit on his feet. "Do you think I'd be here if I didn't know I could trust you?"

"Ye have the bollocks to ask me for favors? After Nat? Are ye out of yer feckin' skull?" Robin launched himself at Ben, whirling high and

299

low. Each blade came a hair's breadth from vital areas. Ben retreated, unable to get his sword up in time to deflect. He took a deep slash to his battered forearm, which cost him the half-second Robin needed to kick his sword out of the way. Next, the butt of Robin's dagger caught him in his temple. Ben crashed through the bedroom door and tumbled head over arse into the far wall. With a shriek, Robin hefted his blade to slam it to the hilt into Ben's shoulder. Ben jerked his knee up just in time— catching Robin solidly in the pelvic bone. Robin sucked in a sharp breath and doubled over, retching. Face gone chartreuse; his daggers clattered to the floor beside him.

Ben's fingers closed over the gash in his side. He was losing an alarming amount of blood. Robin sank to the floor on his rump. Ben winced.

"You didn't leave me much choice."

Speechless, Robin glared silent murder at him.

Ben hauled himself partway up the wall. Now was as good a time as he was likely to get.

"Robin, I'm serious. I need your help. It isn't just Ben Maeden asking, either. Put aside your anger for just a moment." Ben swallowed, trying to find the right words. "That Siorai girl downstairs? She was smuggled out of Tairngare by a gang of thugs from Bethany. Robin… she's Patrick Donahugh's daughter."

Finally, able to breathe, Robin's eyes narrowed. "Ye lie, as usual. Why in the bloody hells would the Duch kidnap his own girl?"

"Because he means to march on Tairngare— the North, obviously. Overplaying her hand, the Doma set Una forth as some kind of prophesied ruler. Don't look at me like that. I'm dead serious. There's been some sort of coup in Parliament over this."

"What's that have to do with the bloody Duch?"

"With the turmoil in the Red City, Drem's just granted Patrick a viable excuse to annex Tairngare beneath his own rule."

"No," laughed Robin. "The High King would stop him. Hells, the whole o' the bloody North would stop him. He tried that tack before, remember? Our naughty Crown Prince put an end to all that at Dumnain."

Robin spat out part of a tooth and cradled his sore crotch like a basket of eggs. "Besides, Drem would never allow that Souther cunt access to her prize fortress. It would take—"

"… a faction of people inside the Cloister, who believe by allying themselves with the Duch, he'll support the Union's rise to power in Parliament. But that's just one layer. Someone paid a rogue faction of Citadel Corsairs to eliminate her before she could be exchanged."

"Yer barkin'."

"I saw it with my own eyes, Robin. If I hadn't intervened, they'd have beaten Una to death right in front of me. What's more, they're patrolling every road from here to Tairngare in hopes of finishing the job."

Robin fell silent.

"It's only a matter of time before Donahugh discovers he's been betrayed if he hasn't already. What do you think is going to happen then?"

"War… but the High King—"

"He *doesn't know*, Robin. There hasn't been a High Council in almost five years. From what I hear, Midhir didn't even attend the last one. Only one Sidhe consulate operates in Eire, and I doubt they're apprised of the situation. The Sidhe are too absorbed with defending their borders to notice what's brewing behind closed doors down here. Tairngare has been a historically reliable and capable ally. No one expected Drem to make such a huge blunder, nor did anyone suspect Patrick might have the resources for another campaign. Now is the *perfect* time to strike."

Robin wiped his nose on his sleeve. "So, what? Ye expect me to help ye avoid another war? How'm I to do that then, eh? Rosweal ain't no fortress. We'd be better off sellin' the girl to whoever will pay the most for her."

"You do that, and Patrick will own the North, one way or the other. Even with half the standing army he had twenty-plus years ago, he still has thrice the soldiers and siege weapons Tairngare has. They're too busy bickering in Parliament over the ruling class to withstand a protracted siege. Their only hope is to kill Una before Patrick can get his hands on her. If they fail, he will line the North with Souther troops."

"If all that's true...."

"*It is.*"

"If so, what d'ye expect me to do about it?"

Ben held his eye. "I must get her over the border, Robin. Midhir must intervene before it's too late."

Robin threw back his head. He laughed until gobs of snot mingled with the blood on his chin. "Oh, that's *rich*, that is! Ye want *me* to organize a raid for ye? That's a golden apple that is!"

"Robin." Ben got to his feet. It wasn't easy; every inch of him was cut or bruised. "I'm forbidden to cross the border. I didn't let Nat die... I *couldn't* save him. You'll have to forgive me for that."

Robin reached for one of his daggers, drawing it point first along the floorboards. His eyes sparked like two burning coals. "'Forbidden' ye say? Why's that then? Why'd me nephew die, Ben? Tell me."

Una appeared in the doorway. The determination on her face dissolved in shock at each man's state. "What—?"

Ben threw up a hand. "Stay there!"

"But—" He spared her a glare, too preoccupied to notice the sudden health she wore.

She scowled. "If you don't want to kill him, *I* will."

"Lovely lass," Robin spat.

"Your friend Paul thought so. Now he's dead," said Una with a ghoulish smirk.

"Una!" warned Ben. "Stay out of this. I'm begging you."

Robin gave her a long side-eye. "Hurt one o'ye?"

"Tried to."

"Siora sorts 'em," he shrugged. "Bit of a blockheaded cunt he was, ye ask me. No great loss."

She opened and closed her mouth. She clearly expected her news would have a greater impact. She crossed her arms. "Well, yeah."

"Now, ye'd better start talkin' Ben, or I'm gonna jam this to the hilt through yer bloody eye."

Ben was unarmed. That hardly mattered now. Deep down, he had to trust that Robin was the man Ben thought he was.

Now or never.

"The river isn't just a border for me. It's a curse. A *geis*."

"Horseshite!"

Ben shook his head. "It's not. I swear it, by Danu."

"Ben, just show him," Una attempted.

"*Shut up!*" they shouted back.

She threw up her hands.

Ben clutched the charm at his throat, feeling more exposed than he'd ever felt. Robin waited impatiently, a furious sort of curiosity in his expression.

"You were at Dumnain, Robin."

"Everyone knows I was. What's yer point?"

"What I'm about to show you... don't make me regret it."

"I'm makin' ye no promises, ye—"

Ben tugged the strap from his throat.

Robin's insult puffed into the air like smoke.

PART THREE

PRINCES

Hierophant

N.E. 508
25, Dor Samna
Bethany

Henry limped through brilliantly tapestried halls on his way through the Duch's throne room. He was fully cognizant of the whispers he earned as he passed. Not that he wished to mingle with this crowd. He lacked the words to describe the withering contempt he held for every familiar face he encountered in Patrick's Court. Time and age may have dulled his recollection of events, but certainly not his memory of their many betrayals. Hadn't Lord Corrigan sworn Henry absolute fealty after the disaster at Dumnain? Corrigan was fatter now and missing several of his front teeth, but Henry remembered his bulbous, upturned nose. Wasn't it Lord Murphy who vowed to cut Patrick in half if he marched against them at Bantry? Murphy looked much the same as he had all those years ago: thin, overdressed, and boss-eyed. Henry's worthless uncle, Lord Thomas Bishop, had railed loudest against Patrick at their clandestine meetings. Bishop had been the first to swear fealty to Henry. His dedication to Henry's rebellion had been the fiercest. Now, Bishop was an ancient white-haired puppet in piss-stained robes, begging Henry's pardon with insincere, liver-spotted lips.

Twenty-six years had slithered by. Henry might have spent a decade in the dark but did not forget a single name. These men were responsible for his disgrace, capture, and subsequent imprisonment. He marked every simpering, duplicitous face. Now that Patrick had set him free, these treacherous dogs fell all over themselves to curry Henry's friendship. The great Henry FitzDonahugh was home at last! This false exuberance did little to disguise their collective condescension.

Behind their hands, the courtiers scorned his eccentric appearance. They mocked his life in Cymru— his deceased wife, religion, missionary work, and bumpkin children. They spread tales of madness, uncontrolled self-abuse, and the myriad inhuman habits Henry supposedly enjoyed in his cell. Simultaneously, he was a figure of fun and pity. Henry stared past their smug, self-serving smiles to the raw fear lurking beneath. The veneer wouldn't bear scrutiny.

Truth be told, they were *terrified* of him. Henry had nearly over-thrown Patrick— his own brother. By all accounts, Henry should be a sack of bones rotting in a pauper's grave. The nobles turned themselves inside out to fathom Patrick's intent. Why would the most powerful lord in Eire publicly forgive a traitor such as Henry? Why now, after nearly thirty years? Seeing the creature Henry had become was perhaps even more shocking than his abrupt return to the Duchal Court. Henry wasn't the same man they'd betrayed. He retained enough pride to own his reduction in stature. Henry FitzDonahugh had once been a tall, barrel-chested youth with a handsome face and a wealth of curls: the envy of every man in the South. Now, Henry was a half-starved phantom with bleeding gums and carrion breath. His spine was bent from years of deprivation and enforced isolation. What hair he had left must be shorn, for the bare patches of greying scalp were far too numerous to ignore. The wooden teeth in his sunken cheeks did little to recall the boisterous, endearing grin his former followers recalled. It seemed the best parts of him had been melted away from the knobbed wick below.

Henry FitzDonahugh was a grotesque shadow of his former self. Though, perversely, he enjoyed the Court's disdain. He was happy to revile them, these perfumed, overfed whores. He understood what they did not. Patrick never did anything without a thousand-fold purpose, and pardoning Henry wasn't an exception to this rule. Foremost, Henry was a reminder. Behold, this once towering warrior! See him now. Look how low the Duch's retribution had laid him. If Patrick could destroy his only brother… imagine what might become of them? Henry did not care what nonsense the nobles cooked up to explain his presence, nor for their feeble attempts to mollify him. He had no use for any of them. Useless, feckless, faithless dogs, the lot. Soon. Very soon, Henry would prove their folly. They should never have betrayed him. Patrick may have inherited their grandsire's scheming mind, but Henry had their father's patience, his hard stomach, and his single-minded determination. In every way that mattered, Henry was more Donahugh than his foppish little brother had ever dared dream. Patrick had his reasons, but Henry had his purpose. All he must do now was wait.

His boys were *here*, within reach.

Henry would never get such a chance again.

Patrick's oily steward attempted to head Henry off at the second-floor library, but Henry ducked through the Chamberlain's Hall to the rear staircase and the armory on the first floor. Patrick's Court was far from a Spartan affair. The Donahugh Clan conquered, scavenged, thieved, cajoled, and bribed their way to half the Continent's treasures for centuries. If it gleamed or glittered, their forefather would drown whole villages to possess it.

Vibrant tapestries hung from every scrubbed wall. Rich carpets, dyed a thousand different shades, covered polished slate floors. Huge, gilded frames bearing priceless works of art lined every hall. Above the Grand Stair, hundreds of portraits were arranged in descending rank, beginning with the first Duch Donahugh Mather, who died in battle after the Transition. Henry's likeness had resumed its former place way down the line. Henry was immune to such overreaching egoism. He was insulated from it all, safe in the might and wealth of the soul. He would be damned if he would allow this riot of color and wealth to seduce him again. He would keep his innocent sons clear of corrosive idolatry and extricate his family from this nest of devils, even if it killed him. Henry knew God would protect his innocent sons.

Dipping through a door to the right of the Great Hall, he sped below an arch that reeked of linseed. The unlit armory was quiet this time of day. Its cavernous length stretched through far-flung shadows like a mountain tunnel. Micah saw him first. He darted from behind a cask with a muffled cry, dropping his torch against the flagstones. Henry embraced his son for the first time in nearly twelve years. His heart overflowed with joy. When had the lad gotten so tall? His shoulders so broad? Why the last time Henry saw his eldest son, he'd been whittling wooden horses for him. Trembling, Micah clung to him like a buoy. "There now, lad." Henry could hardly trust his voice. "No need for all this. Let's have a look at you."

Micah wouldn't be set off so easily. "I missed ye, Da."

Henry was obliged to pry Micah's too-large hands from his shoulders. The size of him! He was nearly of a height with Henry now. Had so much time truly passed? Henry swallowed a burning lump of ash in his throat.

"Tis pronounced, 'you,' Micah. You must maintain your diction."

Micah's sun-kissed cheeks screwed up in a half-smile. "I ain't seen ye in near on twelve-year, Da. And yer fussin' bout me accent?"

Henry patted his son's golden head with a scarred hand. "Aye, so I shall every time we meet. Remember where you are now, lad. These vipers will make you suffer for every mistake you make. Don't forget that for an instant."

Micah crushed himself into Henry's far leaner chest once more. "Now yer free, can we go home?"

Henry sighed into his son's meaty shoulder, vowing he would not weep. Weeping would not keep Micah safe. Henry would invite no weakness now. "God knows, I wish we could, my boy. Alas, He's brought us here for His purpose, and we'd do well to honor His command. Don't you agree?"

Micah swiped at his runny nose and stepped back a pace. "I 'spose so. Uncle won't allow Isaac and me to speak o'Him. We may pray only in private. When Isaac forgets, Master Holden swipes his knuckles with a stick."

"Never mind that now. I don't know how much time I have with you, and we have much to discuss. How does Isaac fare?"

"Well as a boy o'thirteen can, I 'spose. He went from learnin' how to mind Aunt Tilda's fields to bein' the nephew o'a fancy Dutch in a matter o'weeks. We're bushed and boggled, sir. If I'm honest."

"I am sorry for it, son. I did not think Patrick would ever reach so far for any of us. And it's pronounced 'Duch,' lad. Are they not tutoring you properly?"

Micah flushed. "Yes... *Father*, they are. I just thought ye know."

"Well, *you* thought wrong. I want you to master this, and I want you to do so with all the dedication you brought to your Bible studies. I mean it, Micah. You mustn't give anyone the least advantage over you. Do you understand me?"

"Yes, Father."

"You will need to help your brother too. You are allies now. The only ones you will have here. Do not be fooled by their sweet words, sumptuous clothes, or false smiles— these people are the Devil's own. Do not be swayed."

Henry didn't like the way his son's eye darted discreetly sideways. "I won't, Father. Ye... *you* have my word."

"Much depends upon you now, lad."

"That is what I don't understand, Father. Why do ye... *you* wish me to play the lord if ye despise all these folks? Why can't we just leave? If they're evil, shouldn't we go?"

"Not all of them are evil, son. Some are lost. Some are hopeless. Some have simply been deprived of His grace for far too long. We can change that, Micah. *You* can change that. You *will*."

"How? Uncle says we are important to him. He treats us well enough, but I gather he don't mean it. Looks at us like wild goats he pulled outta pasture."

Henry placed both hands on Micah's shoulders. Micah was uncomfortable, Henry could tell. Henry was also not the same healthy, happy bear of a man he'd been for his son either. He allowed himself one long pang for all his sons had lost on Patrick's account.

"Micah, how old are you now?"

311

The boy straightened. "I'll be twenty-one, Father."

Perhaps two pangs then? For all Henry had lost too.

"That's old enough to be wise. Why do you think your uncle brought you here? Why go to so much trouble to have you primped and educated as a lord?"

"He said he don't have a son o'his own to pass the title to."

Henry nodded slowly. "Tis true he lacks a male heir. We must be ready."

"Ready how? We're nobodies, Father. We've only spoken with a handful of folks since we've been here. Who'd support us against a great lord like him?"

"I will, for one. If I know my brother, so will he... if you prove worthy. The key to all of this is Una. Win her, and you win the throne."

"They say she's a witch. I don't wanna marry a witch, Father."

Henry glared at him. "You'll do what you must to keep your brother safe, won't you? I don't care if she's the Devil's mistress... you'll marry the slut and get her with child as soon as possible. I'll brook no refusal."

"What about my cousin? Everyone says he's a right unholy enemy."

"You were enemies the moment Patrick set you up in his household. No matter what you do now, Damek will seek the first opportunity to destroy you and your brother. He means to be Duch, and no son of mine or anyone else will set him off that goal. You'd better start taking this seriously, son. You're both in this race now, whether you want to be or not."

Visibly shaken, Micah hugged himself. Henry was sorry for these tidings. Sorrier than he'd ever been about anything in his life. However, Henry was desperate for this second chance God was granting him. His sons might be at risk, but they were also being given a gift. If only Henry could make Micah see it in time.

"What do I, Da?"

"Soon, Damek will return with your intended bride. I want you ready long before they arrive."

"My uncle says they should be here within the month! How will I be ready to fight my cousin in time?"

312

"You're not going to fight him with fists or blade. You, my sweet son, could not hope to defeat an experienced soldier like him with martial might. No. Instead, you'll beat him by being *better* at everything else. You will outshine him in every way. You're a legitimate Donahugh heir. You're handsome, kind, soft-spoken, and intelligent. Those qualities should be enough to tempt your uncle and certainly his daughter. For what you don't know is that Una despises Damek. Can't bear the sight of him, from what I've learned. Show your uncle, his Barons, and his people that you are the better candidate for her hand. Can you do this, Micah? For your family?"

"Won't this only make my cousin hate us more?"

Henry pulled his son in for one more embrace. "It won't matter. I have a way to deal with him. The only requirements are that you study diligently, speak as your tutor instructs you, and stay within your uncle's good graces for the love of God. Can you do this?"

"I think so."

"You're a good boy, Micah. God loves a dutiful child."

"By His Word, Father. I swear to work my hardest. What if she don't... *doesn't* care for me? What if our uncle—"

"Micah, focus on your studies. Spend as much time with your uncle as possible, and don't shame yourself by speaking as a savage. You must hold your head high at table, watch your manners, and smile only faintly. You'll answer no questions and ask none of anyone... and *never* let slip that you intend to succeed your uncle to the throne. Watch my brother and learn from him, but don't try to ingratiate yourself to him. Simply be the empty vessel he requires you to be. Show him you are forthright, clever, and eager to learn. That is all you must do, my son. Be silent and learn."

"But Da... *Father*, these people, they aren't godly folk. D'ye... *you* mean me to break His Commandments?"

Henry's answering smile was calculating. "We must render unto Caesar, my son. Sometimes, the shepherd must brave the lion's den to secure his flock...."

"So," PATRICK'S VOICE INTERRUPTED HENRY'S prayers. Henry dropped his wooden cross in surprise. He hadn't heard his brother enter because the door was still firmly latched. As if he'd been caught stealing, Henry shot upward. Patrick leaned against the window casing, wrapped head-to-toe in white bear fur, looking as diminished as his haggard brother. "How did you find my nephew this afternoon, Henry?"

Eyes narrowing, Henry lowered himself to his fur-lined cot. His knees popped mechanically along the way. He might have known Patrick would never place him in a room with any true privacy. He scanned the room again yet found no hint of a hidden door.

"Where did you come from, Patrick?"

The Duch chuckled. "This chamber is just beneath my own. Quite convenient, really. The better for us to reacquaint ourselves, don't you find?" The better to spy on Henry, he meant.

"Of course," his response rang hollow. "What do you want?"

"I want to know what it was like to see your son again, Henry."

"Your steward disclosed my whereabouts?"

"The chambermaid. You needn't bother about the glow of murder I see in your eyes. I'll simply replace her before you can harm her. Honestly. You used to be so much better at this."

It didn't matter where Patrick put her; Henry would find her. Patrick knew that too. "I suppose I'm long out of practice. I wished to hold my son. If you were any kind of father, you might understand that need."

Patrick blew a stream of air over his chapped bottom lip. "My daughter would as soon spear me as embrace me. But that's hardly important. She'll bend to my will, regardless. Just as your sons shall, Henry."

"They're good boys. I daresay, you've seen as much yourself?"

"Spare me the false sycophancy. You needn't pull the lad from his studies to warn him to mind himself. I have it all in hand."

That was precisely what kept Henry awake at night. So much hinged on this pathetic man's fickle attentions. "I have a care for my son, little brother. I wish him not to shame himself before this nest of vultures. They'll tear him apart for the smallest breach of decorum. It's unfair to throw him to the wolves so unprepared."

"I am preparing him, Henry. Or didn't he tell you?"

"He said you've been most kind. I thank you for that."

"I don't require your thanks."

"You have them, all the same."

With a snort, Patrick rubbed his balding pate. "By Reason, you are so fucking boring now. *Are* you actually in there, I wonder?"

"Do you wish me to caper for you? I warned Micah to behave himself. Now, how will you punish me for it?"

"I'm not going to punish you, Henry. I don't need to ask what you discussed either. The lad willingly shared everything with me, as a good boy will," Patrick grinned.

Again, Henry ignored the barb. "Micah knows the Lord loathes a liar."

Patrick's smile disintegrated. He got up and poured himself a glass of wine from a decanter on the larder. The fire in the hearth hissed a greeting as Patrick moved near, drink in hand.

"Enough of this. Micah impresses me, Henry, as I'm sure you longed to hear, but it won't be enough. Damek is more than thrice the Micahs of this world. If your son has a prayer of remaining impressive to me, he must defeat that dragon first."

"Didn't you cart them over here to bring Damek to heel?"

Henry didn't like Patrick's answering smirk. "*Perhaps.* Perhaps, I merely enjoy having more boys from which to choose? Damek does grow a bit large for his boots. He could do with the competition; a bit of sport to sharpen the teeth, don't you agree?"

Henry laughed. "Patrick, you must think I'm a fool. You'd never have brought my sons here unless you intended to make one of them Duch. Let's not pretend you truly support Alis' son for your heir. He's a bloody half-breed and a bastard to boot. What sort of legacy do you mean to lay by with an heir named 'Bishop,' hm?

What's more, your Barons won't have him without Una's consent, and I hear she won't have him, either way. You *need* Micah. We both know it. It must irk you to no end that one of my sons will follow you to the throne. It must gnaw your guts to splinters, to have no choice."

With a growl, Patrick dashed his wine into the hearth. A steaming, fragrant puff of smoke billowed upward. "If you imagine your son is so much better than the outstanding soldier and statesman I raised, you are worse than a fool, Henry. Your sons are here to remind my nephew to behave himself. Nothing more. If Damek should fail me, Micah may serve as a suitable replacement. One day. *That* is why they are here."

He was lying. Henry could always tell. Even when he was little, Patrick had had a spoiled little tilt to the tip of his nose that always gave him away. What's more, he was afraid. Henry could smell it, like wine seeping from his pores. Wisely, Henry kept this knowledge to himself.

"So you say, Brother. I don't think Micah, sweet soul that he is would care for the job anyway. Still, I would appreciate it if you would keep your precious nephew from cutting into either of my boys the moment he arrives. Both of my boys will do credit to the Donahugh name if you allow them to."

"Damek won't lay a hand on them. They're under my protection." Another lie. *Interesting.* Henry understood now. Patrick was afraid of their sister's son. That's why they were all here now. He was losing control.

Very interesting, indeed.

"I pray that you're right, Patrick."

Patrick sniffed and shrugged his heavy fur closer to his shivering chest. "Anyway, this isn't what I came down here to discuss with you. I have changed my mind, you see." Henry felt a flash of cold dread. He could not— would not return to that dungeon. He would chew out his tongue. Claw out his own throat. Stab out his own eyes… "I don't mind so much anymore. About your absurd religion, that is."

For the second time, Patrick had managed to shock Henry to numb silence. Patrick scoffed. "You look like a fish, with your mouth agape that way."

"I may wear my cross openly?"

"For now, yes. I'd hate to deprive you of your comforts, Brother. So long as you vow to remain apart from these boys, I will grant you free use of the small chapel in the North Wing. I'll have Carne bring you whatever Kneeler's tomes our grandsire kept in the library. Of course, you'll need

316

a servant or two to help you clear the place of dust and vermin. We don't hold enthusiasm for such things in the South."

Henry's heart hammered in his chest. There was a deeper game here that he could sense but was far too elated to see with any clarity. Patrick would never give this to him, never. "You mean to let me worship publicly?"

"I'll go one better. I mean to let you use the chapel as you see fit. You may preach empty words to empty pews to your heart's content. I care not. So long as you keep out of the affairs of the succession, I may relent further and let you seek followers one day. If you are tactful about it, of course, and behave as a Donahugh— with dignity."

"All this, for the price of two sons?"

Patrick gave him a smug, confident grin. "Perhaps; when you've proven your devotion to our family's legacy when Micah proves himself a successor, worthy of the Donahugh name. When Isaac is safely fostered in Lord Corrigan's household, learning to squire. When Una is safely home and ready to do her duty, perhaps, when all of these things are as I desire them… perhaps then you may have your family *and* your faith too. Peace. 'Tis the last hand I'll extend your way."

"… This is another ploy."

"Of course it is! I'm no fool, Henry. I won't suffer a second betrayal. This will be the last offer you will ever receive from me. You'll give me those boys and stand apart from their education. Devote yourself to your god and keep out of my way. Do anything else, and I'll hang the three of you from the North tower by your innards. By Reason, I'll smile as they slit you open like a fatted sow. I'll place your sons' heads on pikes beside your rotting corpse and leave their bones for the crows. Do you doubt me in the slightest?"

Henry said nothing. He knew better.

"What is your answer?"

For God… and for *Duch Micah Donahugh*, Henry answered in the only way open to him. "I accept, Brother."

Patrick opened the inner door in the far corner. Within, two knights stood at the ready, decked in full mail. Henry had no idea he went to sleep every night with that passage waiting just beyond an old moth-eaten tapestry.

"Very well. Should you attempt to grow bold, just remember, there is not a man or woman in this city who would hide you from me. Your sons will be Donahugh men, Brother— not bare-footed zealots. You don't have to thank me. You'll come around to it, eventually."

With that, the passage swallowed Henry's brother with nary a sound. Once alone, Henry seethed, cried for joy, and wept for misery all at once. He didn't notice when the hearth burned out nor the depth of the moonless night beyond his windowpanes. Darkness wrapped itself around him, as it always had. Patient. Sympathetic. Vengeful.

He knows what lies in the darkness...

Tonight, it was Henry himself.

He would wait.

When the time was right, he would be ready.

Enemy of My Enemy

n.e. 508
26, ðor samna
rosweal

Vick staggered down the alley, with Ben shoving him from behind. Bound and reeking of stale effluence, Vick muttered to himself the while. Robin walked slightly ahead, which left Ben to suffer close proximity. Their motley group moved through Taverner's Alley toward *The Hart and Hare*, silent and unsure of one another. Una and Rian shot nervous glances around each corner as if they might be set upon at any moment. Seamus half-dragged, half-carried Gerrod, who was still too woozy to walk under his own steam. Following at a sedate pace, Dean twitched like a hare every time Una so much as breathed. Colm had yet to meet her eye even once. Rightly so, if Ben were any judge.

He saw what was left of Paul before Seamus dragged his corpse into the back garden. So far, each Greenmaker seemed eager to grant her a wide berth.

Ben hadn't had time to ask her what had happened in that kitchen, but from the bald hostility she displayed whenever anyone had the stones to look at her... he could guess.

To make matters worse, she'd somehow managed to heal herself at Paul's expense. The effects were obvious... and disturbing. Ben was far

319

from an expert in the New Religion, but he felt sure he'd never heard of such horrific marvels. To grant her the benefit of the doubt, Ben didn't believe she'd do such a thing unless she felt she had no choice. Although, the fact that she *could* unnerved him. Busy explaining himself to Robin for most of the night, Ben hadn't had much chance to pull her aside. She'd been keeping this information from him; he wanted to know why. What else hadn't she told him? Rian didn't seem surprised by her appearance, which told Ben Una had trusted *her*.

Why not him?

Una's ability to sap another person of life was a rather large piece of information she should have imparted to him. Wasn't it? He shot her a glance over his shoulder. She wouldn't even look at him. Perhaps that was just as well? Her beauty was both startling... and macabre. He wasn't sure if he was angry with her or hurt.

Either thought cast a pall over his morning.

At dawn, Robin had insisted everyone regroup at *The Hart*. He had a point. With all the activity at Ben's Hilltop residence, there was no way Gilcannon's boys hadn't learned of their whereabouts. Robin didn't believe any of them were up for a serious fight outside of their territory just then, and Ben could hardly argue. On the way, they'd made only one stop. Vick didn't bother to struggle. After a full day in a hot empty warehouse alone, he seemed eager to get on with it.

"Are you sure about this, Ben?"

This was only the fourth or fifth time Una had asked. Should he be upset that she'd kept such a secret from him? He hadn't told her about... well, many things. He ground his molars. He didn't share his plans for her own good! She didn't need to know everything. *Neither do you*, remarked the irritating voice from his gut. *How do you think she will react when she learns the truth of your geis, Ard Tiarne?* Ben shoved Vick out of pure frustration. The lad took one look at his stony face and bit his tongue.

"Ye gonna ask every five minutes then?" sighed Robin.

"I might," Una retorted, her eyes thin as razors.

"Well, forgive *me*, milady."

320

Ben took a measured breath. With his ogham stone safely around his neck once more, none of the others were any wiser about what was really going on. All save Una, of course, and she was not entirely satisfied with his decision to trust Robin Gramble again. Ben's revelation had been for Robin's eyes only. As yet, no one else need be informed. He could count on Robin to keep it quiet, but the dynamic had shifted between them. The cessation of hostilities between them must appear to depend upon the information Ben possessed against Gilcannon. Hence, the need for Vick to back up Ben's story. If everyone knew what Robin did— things would get complicated fairly quickly. "Una, we don't have a choice," Ben begged her for patience with his eyes.

She sucked her teeth at him. "You can't honestly believe that old whore will bargain with you for one skinny wimp?"

Robin poked Vick. "That's ye, I expect, Vincent."

"Name's not bloody Vincent! It's Vick!"

"Oh aye, 'cept ye was Vincent to us, afore ye went off and changed teams. How's Matt's pay? What's the goin' rate for a back-alley stabbin' nowadays?"

"Feck yerself. Matt feeds us year-round. That's a damned sight better than the pittance ye shitty Greenmakers offer." Vick squared his bony shoulders.

"We do just fine without earnin' our bread on the backs o'little girls," Seamus spat. "Ye chose the wrong side, ye puny gobshite."

"What's he talking about?" asked Una.

Seamus wouldn't look directly at her. "Gilcannon runs girls, erm... missus. Not like Barb's girls neither, what have a say in it."

"He means they're slaves, Una." Rian's voice was rough as sandpaper.

"To my mind, all sex work is a form of slavery," sniffed Una disdainfully. "Brothel-keepers, male or female, turn profits from the hopeless and desperate— even in Tairngare, where the industry is regulated with an iron fist. Your Barb isn't a lick better."

Robin said, "Oh, but she is, milady. I'll thank ye to keep yer personal feelings outta things ye don't understand."

"She tried to sell us only yesterday!"

"I didn't say she were a Kneeler's saint, nor one o'the Ancestor's Faithful, but Barb don't sell lil' girls an' boys. She don't chain 'em, nor force 'em to serve at the expense o'their families neither."

"Gilcannon sells... *children?*"

"Oh, aye. Worse than that, believe me. Barb's been lookin' for any means to oust Matt from Rosweal for years. So far, the bastard has kept it too civil to make a justifiable move. All our businesses depend upon one another, ye see? He has contacts and supporters who could ruin some folk here if Barb moved against him without good reason."

"The children aren't reason enough?" scowled Rian.

"The world's a dark place, missus."

The alley widened a bit, and a row of familiar buildings rose ahead. *The Hart and Hare*'s sign creaked back in forth in the early morning breeze. Taverner's Alley was mostly deserted, save a few determined streetwalkers who scattered at first sight of them. The odd inebriate snored into the muddy cobbles.

"To answer yer charge," said Robin to Una, nodding at the sign. "Barb wants Gilcannon more than she wants ye or the missy there. Ben's bringin' her a means. She'll be pleased as a kitten in cream, I vow."

"And you?"

"What of me?"

"You were set to kill Ben... and both of us," she gestured to Rian, "only hours ago. How can we trust you?"

Robin sized Ben up out of the corner of his eye. Ben said nothing. "Far as I'm concerned, we're square as we're gonna get."

⚹ ⚹

"Well," growled Barb, leaning against the bar. Her pudgy elbows peeked from the excessively voluminous sleeves of a fluffy pink dressing gown. Her graying auburn braid dangled over one shoulder, and her unpainted lips were pulled low in an unamused pout. To Una's mind, she looked much younger than her first estimate suggested— barely middle-aged. Without the overdone cosmetics, Barb might even be called handsome. This observation didn't improve Una's opinion of her, but it did serve to humanize her a bit. She could almost imagine the bright young pupil Barb must have been in the Cloister before life sunk its fangs into her. Almost. "Ye got me outta bed at this disgraceful hour. Someone better start talkin'."

Ben cleared his throat. Barb's finger caught his statement cold. "Not ye, ye fancy twat. Someone who don't owe me a bleedin' mountain of fainne."

Ben shut his mouth again, tight.

Robin crooned, "Barb, love…."

"There'll be none o'that neither. Ye were 'sposed to bring me that girl," Barb jabbed a red nail at Una, then Ben, "and see this lanky vagrant made good his debts to me. Can ye imagine my surprise at yer sittin' together, all companionable again?" Her hazel eyes fell on Vick, who sat stuffed between the corners of the bar and Dean's oppressive bulk.

"What's he doin' here then?"

"If ye'd shut yer trap, I'd be happy to tell ye," Robin grumbled.

Ben took a breath, but Barb cut him off. "I told ye, not a word! If ye've any idea how much rebuildin' that walkway's gonna cost me, ye'd better keep quiet, Maeden. Robin, me sweet darlin' man. Go on... but I warn ye, make it fast. I'm peppered enough to throttle the pair o'ye, together."

Robin tapped the bar with a bloodied fist. Barb threw up a hand when Dabney moved to respond. The hulk's nose was wrapped tight in linen bandages, and the hollows of his eyes were nearly black with bruises.

"No pints, no food, no nothin', if ye don't explain yerself this instant."

Robin, his own nose stuffed with bloodied bits of shredded rags, threw his arms up. "The short? Matt was tryin' to bribe Ben to have me killed!"

"He's been tryin' to kill ye for fifteen years, Robin. What else is new?"

"Aye, but this time, he made his move *after* he bought a bunch of our accounts in Ten Bells and Tara. Our contracts won't be renewed as long as Matt's running uishge outta that stinking distillery. It's not me he's after. Long as he can claim to have no hand in it, that was a grudge between old friends like Ben and me... he's free to strip the legs right outta the Greenmakers' operation."

"That all? We've been playin' this game with him since ye retired from the Cohort. He takes territory. We take it back. Matt's an upstart— hasn't got the clout to replace our contracts with the Guilds."

"He does now." Ben ignored her sharp stare. "I had it from Sol himself. Matt offered them better terms than they'll ever get with the Greenmakers, Barb. Those Matt can't turn for shares in his distillery, he threatens or removes. They've all but issued him his own bloody charter. No, it's true. With Robin and me out of the picture, preferably dead at each other's hands— you'd be all alone. He doesn't just want *The Hart*, Barb. He wants Rosweal."

"I 'spose yer fallin' out gave him the opportunity?"

"The cleanest he could manage. According to Vincent there, he's been skimming from the bottom of your earnings for years, and now that his uishge has started filling *The Butterfly*'s cellars in Bethany, he's got the means to bump you out altogether. He waited for a good clean shot before aiming at you personally."

Barb got up, poured herself a tall pint, and sat back down. "Right," she said after a long drink. "Ye found all o'this out in just two days, Ben?"

"Vincent let some things slip on my way back into town," Ben grinned at the filthy little rat-faced urchin, who attempted to shrink into his corner. "I followed my nose to the rest. There'd be no reason for Matt to attempt to abduct me unless he meant to use me. Until now, his business has depended upon the Greenmakers' contacts in larger cities. It didn't take long to figure out he's long outbid you."

"If Ben hadn't come back, Gilcannon woulda bided a bit longer to make his move against us. I'm sure he figured what few holdouts we had wouldn't pose much trouble if he took advantage of our internal strife," Robin said. "Bastard's got finesse. I'll say that for him."

"I take it ye two made nice again when Ben told ye what he learned? That's just dandy, that is. How's that help me? If what ye say is true, it's a matter of finance, and Matt's holdin' a monopoly on that score. We can sell home scratch as well as any honest bootlegger, but he's got the market fair cornered for properly distilled spirits. We can't compete with him. He's out-earnin' us!" she raised a brow at Una. "Sale o'this piece here might square us up, though.

"Got half o'the Citadel's Corsairs out there lookin' for her. What's more, two full cavalry units from Bethany, led by one Lord Damek Bishop hisself, are movin' up the Taran High Road for her as we speak. Oh," she laughed when Una stiffened. "Ye didn't know? Well, one o'them sorts'd pay a king's ransom for ye. I'm bettin' on the latter, meself. Seems most keen to have ye back if what I'm told holds water."

"Barb," interrupted Robin.

"What?"

"We're not sellin' the girl to the Duch, and we're not handin' her over to the Corsairs neither."

"Oh, we're *not*, are we?" The temperature dropped by a few thousand degrees. Una couldn't repress a shiver.

"No, we're not." Robin's jaw clenched.

"Barb," Ben leaned in diplomatically. "She's worth more to you, to all of us, as an ally. I'm asking you for your help."

Barb threw back her head and laughed so long, she was quite out of breath when she finally settled down. "Yer outta yer mind if ye think I'm gonna help anyone for nothin', Ben Maeden. Ye owe me plenty already. What possible help could I be to someone like her anyway? I've got bloody problems o'me own, as we've all just learned. The competition is edgin' me outta me own bloody business... and I promise ye, it's occurred to her hunters where they might look next."

"I'm aware," Ben shot Una a meaningful look. "I'm not asking you to do anything for free. I'm offering you an exchange."

"Oh, this should be rich," Barb waved him on.

"Una, and that girl's safety," he gestured to Rian, "and your discretion, in exchange for what you want most in all the world."

"What's that then?"

"I'll give you Rosweal. Matt's distillery included."

She considered Ben silently for a long while. "Ye can't just kill him, ye know? Never leaves that gaudy pink mansion o'his, from what I hear. Has a bloody army of knife-wieldin' imps at his beck and call too. It ain't just a matter of beheadin' the dragon, as it were. I need his contacts, his signatories, and his recipes. He ain't likely to hand those over, neither."

Ben winked at Vick, who shriveled under his attention. "I know where he keeps those documents. I know when his guards rotate shifts, and I even know where he sleeps. If you give me your word, Barb— your utmost, to the bloody letter *vow*— to keep faith with me... everything Matt has is yours. His contacts and the names of those who've turned coat."

"Yer serious? Ye think ye can do this?"

"He can," Robin answered for him with surprising confidence. "He won't be goin' alone anyway. I, for one, think ye'd be a fool to refuse."

"No one bloody asked ye, love." Barb took another drink, then toyed with her tankard. Her eyes slid from Robin to Una, Rian, Colm and finally rested again on Ben. He didn't look away. "I just wanna know one thing before I give ye my answer. Why go to so much trouble for her, Ben? What do ye get outta any o'this? Ye in love with her? The other one, maybe? *Both*? What can she offer ye but trouble, deposed and pursued as she is?"

Ben swallowed. "I can't tell you now, Barb."

"That's not gonna work, dearie. I'll send bits o'that girl to that fine Souther lord what marches this way and dispatch Matt in me own good time with the proceeds. Ye tell me what I want to know, or ye have my word she'll suffer for it."

Una bobbed her head at him.

He cursed. "Fine, but not here. The four of us will talk about this upstairs. *Privately*."

"No, ye'll give it to me now, as I—"

"*Barb*," Robin interjected, getting to his feet. His face was solemn as a Merchanta exchequer. "It's for the best."

The feeling that she was being ganged up on won out. She stomped around the bar to the stairs, snarling, "So help me, if this's a waste o'time, or yer stallin'—" Barb's grumbles lost volume as she made her

326

way upward. Una patted Ben's shoulder as she passed. He followed like a man marching to his execution. In a way, he was.

"SIORA'S TITS!" BARB CAREENED BACKWARD into her chair. Ben slipped his charm back over his head, and the startling effect vanished. Barb's left hand flew to her heart while the other rummaged through her desk for a silver flask. After several sips, she sat up straighter and folded her shaking hands together. "All right. What's this mean then?"

Robin pulled a chair over. "What d'ye think it means, love?"

Una sank into the only other seat in the room. She rubbed at her healing face with the heel of a dirty palm. The hollows of her eyes looked etched in. Ben sent her a long, sympathetic frown from where he leaned casually against the closed door. He, too, was covered in seeping scratches and bruises. Robin looked worse than the pair of them together.

"That... yer," Barb flushed, "not Ben, then?"

"I'm the same man you've known all this time, just somewhat more than he appeared."

"Oh, for feck's sake. Yer... one *o'them*."

"Yes."

She wagged a finger at Robin. "Ye said he was a faerie, didn't ye? Some Sidhe lord's by-blow, like the piece downstairs."

"Not quite," Robin laughed mirthlessly.

A sudden thought occurred to her. "Is the faerie down there—?"

Ben made a face. "*No.* Gods, what a misfortune that would be. I did know her father, all the same. He served under my banner during the war."

"*Under yer banner*, ye say?" She took another drink from her flask. Her hand shook. "Right. Can only be one war, ye mention. Who are ye then, Ben? Which o'the Ard Ri's servants are ye?"

"Barb, we don't have much time," Robin attempted to help. The look on Barb's face shut him up. Ben shifted from one foot to the other like a recalcitrant child caught stealing from the larder.

"Ye didn't ask him this question, Robin?"

"Not exactly..."

"I told him," Ben held Una's encouraging stare. "Because I owed it to him, same as I owe it to you. Ask your question, Barb."

"*Who are ye?*"

To speak the name for the second time in less than twenty-four hours wouldn't make its recitation any easier than the first. Ben had become used to concealing himself, grown comfortable in anonymity. It wouldn't do any longer. There was no point in hiding anymore. Ben needed them. Without the Greenmakers, there was no way to guarantee he could get Una safely over the border if he should fail to break his geis. What's more, they were, for all intents and purposes, his friends. They deserved to know.

Ben lifted his charm and dangled the stone, with its crudely carved little figure, before his nose. He smiled ruefully.

"If the Gods had been kind, I'd never have needed a stone like this. I'd be in my proper place, serving my people, as I was born to. It's funny that one's gifts should be so entangled with failings. Why make a man brave if he can't resist arrogance? Why make him a great leader if he can't command with compassion? Why grant him lands, titles, honors, and nobility— if he can't appreciate them until they're taken away?" He let the little stone thump against his tunic. "I think you know who I am, Barb. You're too quick by half."

"But," she stammered, searching for the right words. "*He's dead*. He died after Dumnain. Everyone said so. Robin, ye were there! Ye said they held a funeral for him and all! Didn't they?"

"Aye," Robin admitted. "On the hill, overlookin' the valley. The Sidhe under-commander... that red-haired fellow—"

"Tam Lin O'Ruiadh, Prince of Connaught," Ben nodded.

"Aye, that one. He lit the pyre hisself. Said some words, then we was all sent home. Those that could walk that is."

"Tam Lin's my cousin. His father is Bov Dearg, the Red King of Connaught. Son of Crom Dagda, brother to the Ard Ri of the Tuatha De Dannan. The Adair are my tribe, you might say."

"*Your tribe…*" Barb breathed.

Ben shrugged. "It wasn't a funeral, but a ceremony. The Ard Ri, mortified by my actions at Dumnain, ordered a geis be placed upon me. I'm not to cross into Aes Sidhe, under pain of death, for a period lasting no less than fifty years. In a way, to your kind— I suppose it *was* a funeral, after all. By the time the geis runs its course, most everyone who knew their Crown Prince, or fought under him, would be long dead."

Barb covered her mouth with quivering, pudgy fingers. "That's rather cruel."

"I deserved it."

"No, ye didn't," Robin crossed his arms. "A great many innocents lost their lives that day, Ben. Lots more didn't that would have. I speak from experience. We was pinned down in the bog, surrounded and outmatched. Souther spearmen and archers were pickin' us off from higher ground. If the horns hadn't blown from Dumnain Village, every man o'us would be dead. I might add that there were half a thousand men— good Norther men— who lived 'cause ye did what needed doing."

"I made war on non-combatants, Robin. Women and children died."

"Aye, innocents die in every war that's ever besmirched the face of the bloody world. By takin' on the garrison, ye freed the town from Souther troops. Ye ended the bloody war that day, no matter what the scribes in Ten Bells say about it. Sure, the chronicles claim that yer countryman, Fionn or other, did it by avengin' the death o'that dark elf prince."

"Falan."

"Aye, Falan. Son o'the king o'Ulster, right? Got killed by a green lad, so they say. Cuz o that, the Sidhe rallied and took the field."

"That did happen, yes. But I wasn't there. I spent the day in chains."

"I was." Robin got up and took the flask from Barb. Ben had never heard Robin speak of his time in the war. "It weren't a proper battle o'any sort. The Southers didn't have much left after what ye did to 'em at Dumnain. That fine lord Fionn chased mere stragglers and a handful o' light infantry across the valley. 'Twas over 'fore it even started— didn't draw me bow once. That 'great battle' lasted a mere fifteen minutes, by my count. Why? Because the bloody Crown Prince o'Innisfail slaughtered half the Souther troops in one vicious night, that's why," Robin took a long sip and passed the flask to Ben. "Maybe in fancy Aes Sidhe, or down south among perfumed Souther lordlings, ye might seem a bit of a bastard. Who knows? I can say, in the North, yer a bloody hero. Whatever yer folk believe won't change that neither. Mark me."

Ben was speechless.

No one had said as much to him before. He'd spent the last two decades avoiding his name for fear it would see him hunted across Eire like a dog. That anyone might consider his sin a blessing was a thought he could scarcely comprehend. Una cleared her throat, helpfully pulling the tension toward her. Ben appreciated her effort.

"Mistress Dormer. This isn't about any erm, feelings between Ben and me. Nor personal reward for my bounty, for that matter. Ben is taking me to the High King to prevent another war, a war that my father has been eager to make since long before my birth. He considers it a family legacy. Patrick won't stop until all of you are kneeling to him as King. With my inheritance in hand, given the unrest in Tairngare... he's got his chance. Don't you see?"

"Aye," croaked Barb. "I do. But if yer, erm what d'ye call it?"

"*Geis*," Ben offered.

"Right. If it don't end for another twenty-four years, how can ye hope to get her over the border yerself? Ye have a proxy, or someone ye mean to pass her off to?"

"I mean to break the geis myself, as is my right— on Samhain. This is the swiftest possible way. If I don't take her to my father personally, I can't vouch for her safety. So much rests upon this; I have no choice but to try."

Una's face tightened in distrust. "You didn't mention *anything* about Samhain."

"I am *now*. It's a long story. One I didn't have time to explain. You'll just have to trust me."

"Humph," she sat back, eyes narrow. "More blind faith?"

"I'm not the only one keeping secrets, am I?"

Point taken, she frowned into the hearth fire.

Barb stood up. She reached into a cupboard behind her desk, which held row after row of raw hooch. As soon as she opened the cabinet the sweet, starchy smell nearly overpowered the room. Una held a hand over her nose. Barb popped a jug and sat back down, grasping a small clay cup at the corner of the desk. She filled then emptied the cup twice before she managed to look up at Ben without a quiver to her lips.

"Not Ben Maeden after all, are ye?"

His mouth twitched. "Sorry for it, Barb."

"Bleedin' sneaky bastard, ye are. All this feckin' time, and the Ard Ri's brat in this bloody house drinkin' me swill, and swithin' me girls. Ye owe me a king's ransom for all that too," she guffawed and poured another cup. "What should we call ye then? Yer highness? Yer royal... arseness?"

"Ben will do."

"Oh aye, 'spose ye'd not want the rest o'the lads to know, would ye?"

"Not yet."

"Right," she made a face after a particularly long gulp. "Ye don't know this, but me Da fought at Dumnain with Robin."

Ben's head snapped around to meet his friend's scarred face. "Oh?"

"He lived, cuz o'ye. Same as me man there," she pointed at Robin. "Look, ye don't owe me nothin'... yer highness. I'll sort Gilcannon. I'll not have a prince dirty his hands on our account."

"Barb—" Robin tried to cut in.

She splayed her fingers. "What would ye have me do, love? He's not a bleedin' assassin, is he? He's the Crown feckin' Prince!"

Ben knew the sprout of an argument when he heard one. "No, Barb. I'll keep my word. It'll be trouble if you suddenly agreed to help me without any profit. I'll do this, and gladly. I've been waiting for an opportunity to gut that malicious pederast for years."

"But—"

"No 'buts.'" Leaning over her desk, he gave her one of Ben Maeden's most persuasive grins. "Besides, it's still me in here, Barb. Don't tell me you'd treat me differently just because you found out my Da is rich?"

Her answering grin was slow but dramatic. "All right then... Ben. Do yer worst. I'll keep yer girls safe until you get back... if ye come back, that is."

"That's more like it." Ben jerked his chin at Robin, "Shall we? I'd hate to think Matt's feeling safe and secure in that gauche pink fortress of his."

Una got to her feet, aiming to follow them to the door.

Ben held up a hand. "*No.* You stay here."

She bristled. Her lovely cheeks burned a dusky rose. "If you think you're leaving me behind, you're a fool." The top of her head barely grazed his sternum, but the look in her eyes might have made her ten feet tall or more.

Ben forced himself to look away. "You'll get in the way."

"I'm worth ten of your Greenmakers, and you know it."

"Hey now!" Robin wagged a finger at her. "That's rude."

"Nonetheless, true."

Ben shoved him through the door into the hall before he could return sally. Noting Una's furious glare, Ben paused in the narrow opening.

"Una... just this once, please don't be a pain in the arse."

She drew in a breath to berate him, but his fingers caught at a loose coil of her dark golden hair, halting her argument in its tracks. Her hair was dark at the root, like rich molasses, but golden at the ends, like burnished gold. When contrasted with her dark skin and bright eyes, she was so beautiful that it made his teeth ache. Ben repressed a groan.

"Get some sleep while I'm gone. A bath, some food, and a drink, maybe? You look... like shite." He shot her a wink before shutting the door on her furious retort.

Ben followed Robin downstairs and into the tap below, chuckling to himself.

THE HART
AND HARE

п.е. ʃ08
27, ðoʀ samna
ʀosweal

They'd been gone a long time. Una struggled to hide her concern, to little avail. Rian was far too astute to miss her evident disquiet over the matter. Una had nothing new to reassure the girl with, save her word, and that had worn thin hours ago. After another restless, sleepless evening in Ben's old apartment, Una strode through the charred walkway at first light to seek news. She found *The Hart* deserted but for the skeletal Colm wiping tankards behind the bar and a smattering of workers who darted about with brooms or rags.

Colm scowled at her approach. "Bit early for ale, missus." He sucked a browning tooth at her. Una flexed her fingers with exaggerated effort. He jerked into the shelves behind the bar. Tankards and bottles clanked together ominously.

Batting her lashes, she said, "I'm looking for Barb, not ale."

Colm's Adam's apple bobbed. "She don't usually come down afore noon. We keep late hours round here."

Una failed to curb a sneer. "Undoubtedly. Where might I find her then?"

"Oh, missus. Ye don't wanna poke that bear."

"Do you imagine I'm afraid of your boss?"

"If ye was smart, ye would be. Anyway, I imagine ye mean to ask her about yer man, Robin, and Gerry?"

"He's *not* my man. Mister ah—"

"Colm."

"Right. How do you know what I meant to ask?"

He rolled a bony shoulder, then carefully placed another glass on the shelf. "I run this place, don't I? The day-to-day that is. Ain't much goes down in here that I don't know about. To answer ye, before Barb graces us all with her presence— no, there ain't been word."

"Do you know where they've gone?"

"Aye, but I'm the only one down here that does, and I'd keep it to yerself, I was ye. Barb don't want it bandied about."

"I should say not." Una sank onto a stool with a groan. She watched as kitchen hands scrubbed the flagstones in both mammoth stone hearths. Looking around, Una must admit that *The Hart and Hare* was the best-appointed tavern she'd ever been in. Not that she'd had occasion to visit many, given her seclusion within the Cloister. She supposed vice had a way with profit that reputable ventures might envy. "How long have you worked here?"

He squinted. "Used to scrub pots and pans when I was a mite. Me Mam came up with Barb, ye know. A bit older'n her, but she were one o'Barb's Da's best girls."

"Your mother was a... erm."

"Oh aye, she were a right smart businesswoman in her day. Set by enough for me to have a bit o'letterin' and pay me dues to the Guild. We lived better'n most, I must say."

"You're proud of her?"

He gave her an odd look. "Why *not?* Thanks to her, I had schoolin', food in me belly, a roof over me head, and a job set up. Me mam was a fine woman."

"But she had to... don't you think that's a terrible fate?"

334

Colm leaned close, his expression inscrutable. "Cuz yer a lady who comes from a far fancier set of folks than us, I'm inclined to let that insult pass."

"I didn't mean—"

"I know what ye meant. Maybe in the Red City, lasses have better odds and more choices? In Rosweal, they make do. Though, I daresay they have it easier than them poor Souther ladies. At least here, they have a choice."

"I assume you're equating respectable matrons with women desperate enough to sell themselves for food. I don't buy that."

"Them that marry for position, wealth, or title— how is that so different?"

"I can't speak to Souther ethics, but in Tairngare, women are not required to sell themselves to men for any reason. They're edified, encouraged, and empowered to decide their paths. Survival shouldn't cost one's dignity."

"Aye, in bloody grand Tairngare where the Parliament is so corrupt, a Union Charter may only be purchased by sacrificing one's daughters to the Cloister. How is that different from a father sellin' his girls to a brothel?"

"That is a gross misrepresentation. Novas are given to the Cloister to be educated. To learn to hone their Spark, to study the mysteries."

"No," Colm held up a finger. "They're *sold* to the Cloister to serve the uppity womenfolk what run the city from behind those heavy walls, all so the family can sit back fancy on her stipend. Why don't ye ask Barb about that, love? Her mam's family sold her for that purpose. Later, she was tossed out on her ear for mentionin' the unfairness of the arrangement. Girls what don't have the right name languish in service so their families can use their earnin's to climb the ranks. If that ain't prostitution, I don't know what is."

Una's cheeks burned hot. "That's not a fair comparison *in the least*."

"Name me one common girl, ever made the rank o'Prima, wasn't sponsored by one of the great families?"

Una couldn't, as he knew she couldn't. He took a peek at her stymied expression and poured her a tall tankard of cider. "No disrespect intended, missus. Just see ye judge fair. Society o'any sort makes whores of us *all*."

It took Una quite a while to find her voice again. "I apologize if I gave your mother insult, Colm."

"None needed, milady. There's more'n one sort o'education, I spose."

Una hadn't come down here intending to offend anyone, yet she had. Almost immediately at that. Wasn't she above classist drivel? Apparently not. She sipped at her cider in silent shame. Colm went about his work as if the stool she sat upon remained unoccupied. She'd never been upbraided like that before. The fact that she'd earned it only made her embarrassment more acute. While she mulled over her ideological arrogance, a few shadows passed before the mottled windows. The heavy oak door rattled under the weight of several fists.

"Siora's cunny!" Colm slammed his rag down on the counter. "Feck off! We're bloody closed!"

"Who'd come out at this hour?"

"No one that means to let me get on with me work," Colm scowled at her. Una flushed anew, knowing she deserved that comment too.

Something heavier than a fist struck the door from outside. Colm's expression darkened. "Mickey!" he called, reaching below the bar for a vicious wired cudgel. "Get Dean and Dabs, and someone better wake Barb. Don't take yer time, neither!"

"What's happening?"

"Ye should get upstairs, missus."

Una watched the custodians scramble into the kitchens with real panic on their faces. "Does this sort of thing happen often?"

"Nope. Must've been waitin' for the all-clear."

"Gilcannon?"

"Aye." An object rammed into the glass full force, and they both jumped. "I bleedin' *told* Barb we needed more men down here today."

"They were waiting for Robin to leave?"

336

"Takin' third o'our forces with him too, yeah. I told Barb as much last night. If I were Matt, it's what I'd do, sure."

"How can I help?"

He gave her a long, appraising look. "Ye ain't gonna run?"

"And leave you here alone? No. I can handle myself."

The door bent inward on its hinges. A large crack split the main window down its center. Colm nodded at her. "Aye, I'll say that much for ye, at least. Come 'round here. There's a sticker in me boot."

Una hopped over the bar as the door splintered. A bevy of laughter shook the window casings. There must have been dozens of them out there. Una knelt behind the bar to retrieve Colm's dagger, then slipped behind him, ready. The window took a second impact and the door another.

"I dunno what ye did to Paul, but I hope ye got more o'that in ye."

The window crashed inward before Una could formulate a reply.

LYING FLAT ON THE ROOFTOP, Robin passed his glass back to Ben. "There's somethin' happenin' down there. Somethin' wrong. Have a look."

Ben took a drink from his water skin, then replaced the stopper with a grunt. His back was to the wall, beside the gap. He waved the glass away. "No need. They know we're here."

"Feckin' Hilltop cunts. Why'd we spend all that time sneakin' round them sewers, anyway?"

"So they wouldn't know *where* we are, at least." Ben snuck a glance through the crevice. Matt's house gleamed a vivid pink in the early morning sunlight. No one was about, which was highly irregular. Gilcannon might as well have hung a sign on the front door with 'TRAP' written in bold red script.

"I don't like it, Ben. There's no tellin' how many fellas he's got down there."

"Doesn't matter."

"Yer sure enough now?" snorted Robin.

"See that row of windows on the second floor?"

"Aye, so?"

"That's Matt's office."

"How d'ye know?"

"Even if Vincent hadn't filled me in, it's obvious. It's the only room in the house with open shutters. I might add that candles in the window were a fairly desperate touch."

"He wants us to attack from the front?"

"Doubt he cares either way, so long as we believe that's where he's held up."

"So, what's yer plan then?"

"I think surprise has lost its luster," Ben sighed. "Call Gerry back. We'll have to come at this another way."

Robin signaled to Seamus on the opposite end of the rooftop, who whistled back in a perfect imitation of a marsh swallow, common as grass in this part of Eire. One whistle in return meant that Gerrod understood. Two that he was moving shop.

"Wait." Ben paused. He caught the barest hint of something in the courtyard: a dark flash, which was out of place against Matt's vivid color selection. Ben jerked the glass from Robin. In the courtyard, a bit of fabric flapped in the wind— black on gold. The cloth was tucked tight against the rear of the building. The wearer tried very hard to remain out of sight. Ben had only managed to detect it by focusing hard on the outer edges of the house. He cursed long and low in his mother tongue.

"What's that mean then?"

"Something fucking uncouth." Ben took a second peek through the glass. All of a sudden, it was gone. Ben handed Robin's spyglass back. "Call Gerry to our side of the street. We need to regroup. Now."

"Why? What'd ye see?"

"*Tairnganeah.* Gilcannon invited the Corsairs to Rosweal."

Una was a bit rusty at this. She might have been somewhat proficient with a rapier or even moderately adequate with a crossbow once upon a time—long before she submitted to the Eighth Ordeal at age twenty. For the past six years, she'd been getting fairly soft in the library while she crammed for the Ninth Ordeal. To say she was out of practice was an understatement. Long daggers were never her forte. Colm's was easily the entire length of her forearm.She leapt over the prone bodies of the two boys Colm put down, then swung around to intercept a knife reaching for his kidney.

There were too many of them.

Una and Colm were squeezed back-to-back to ward off a boiling tide of elbows, knees, and sharp objects. Youths clambered behind the bar with whatever weapons they could muster. Some ran for the stairs and met with considerable resistance from above. Dabney's roar filled the tavern to the rafters. He swung left and right with his cudgel, sending men flying from their feet and over the railing. Dean protected Dabney's flanks with a pair of daggers, just like Una was attempting to do for Colm. A blow to her midsection sent her scraping backward. A line of blood opened up at her collarbone. Una grunted and ducked low. She brought the flat of her blade up into the crook of one boy's knee. He went down with a screech. Almost simultaneously, someone grabbed her by her nape and dragged her from Colm's side.

With her head jerked back, her attacker was able to hook an arm around her throat. The youth smashed her into the bar, and the air whooshed out of her in a rush. Her dagger skittered away. As his humid, stale breath assaulted her face, her attacker's hands fumbled at the collar of her tunic. Una dug her fingertips into his forehead.

"*Boil*," she hissed. Going limp, he crashed to the rushes in a wailing fit. She didn't wait to watch the fluids burst from his nose and eye sockets. Another set of hands reached for her. Una smacked them into the wooden bar with both palms. "*Break*," she commanded. Every one of this lad's finger bones snapped beneath his skin, bending each digit at an unnatural angle. He bolted from the tavern, screaming. When the next boy hacked at her with a short cleaver, Una jumped onto the bar to avoid its path. She grabbed her assailant from behind, crammed her nails into the fellow's neck, and crushed his face against the bar with her left hand. Taking a deep breath, she reached out with her Spark, drawing deep into the boy's core. A river of stolen vitality flowed into her blood, which she put to immediate use.

Una's right palm slid over the bar, heedless of the shriveling creature she held captive against it. Anyone that had been thinking about making a grab for her took a wary step back. The wood below her hand warped and rippled— as if billeted by an unseen wind. The lacquered surface became a puddle at first, then a roiling stream into which various hands and feet sank. Panic set in. Those who could not get away fast enough called out to their comrades for aid. Instantly, the fight fizzled out of half a dozen young men. They looked on in horror as their companions descended into the oak surface: two to their elbows, one to his thigh. The last, having been knocked onto the bar by Colm's cudgel, plunged in face first. Una removed her hand, and the bar smoothed over, solid once more… except for the various figures trapped within the wood. Those that could, bellowed frantically at the top of their lungs. As suddenly as the fight started, it stopped. Every combatant in *The Hart* paused to gawp at this terrible marvel, as if their eyes somehow deceived them.

"Witch!" cried one of Gilcannon's boys. A leader of sorts, he held out an arm to keep any of his foolhardier companions from rushing at her. Colm threw another unconscious boy to the floor. For a wiry fellow, Colm didn't lack strength. The speaker's cheeks purpled. "Ye feckin' witch! *What did ye do?*"

"What I'll do to all of you, if you don't leave," she promised, wiping at the seeping wound on her collarbone. She was sick of being cut, struck, shoved, pulled, or otherwise manhandled. The Greenmakers, having rallied on the second floor, had dumped most of their foes over the balustrade. *The Hart's* Hilltop assailants had lost their advantage. Eyes agog, Colm crept around the bar, careful not to disturb the bodies trapped within its glossy oak facade. As for the victim stuck to the thigh, his snivels degenerated into full shrieks. With a sardonic smirk, Una tapped her nails near his left elbow. His remaining comrades didn't wait around to witness further horrors visited upon one of their own. They darted for the busted door as if their trousers were on fire. "Do you want out, boy?" asked Una.

Her victim's nostrils flared. Chest heaving, he looked around for anyone at all who might help him. No one moved a muscle, save Dabney, who moaned his way back up to the second landing. He was petrified of Una, and that fear was catching. *The Hart*'s defenders stared at her like men possessed.

"Ple... ase," the boy cried. Gobs of snot bubbled down his chin. His friend beside him wept openly; his arms were quick to the biceps in unyielding wood. Another dangled awkwardly from his fists, in a stone-dead faint. The last, who'd fallen in to the shoulder, would never move again.

None of them had seen a day over sixteen winters.

"I want you to tell me why you're here, lad. You should hurry before I lose the remainder of my patience. I may decide you should drown in that bar, like your friend there."

Barb shoved her way through the line of Greenmakers into the taproom. "What in the *bloody hells* is all this then? *Siora*," her eyes bugged out of her skull. "Milady... what in the name of the sweet Ancestor have ye *done*?"

The boy blubbered. Ignoring everyone, Una focused on him with a purposefully cruel grin. "Tell me what I want to know, this instant, and I'll let you go."

"M-Matt sent us."

"Why?"

"To distract ye."

"From?"

"Them soldiers needed time to... missus, please! *It hurts*! Hurts so bad!"

Barb stepped over the corpse of the first assailant Una put down; the gases and fluids in his skull still burbled into the rushes. Barb paid him no mind. "What soldiers? Where?"

"You'd better answer her question lad." Una flexed her fingers by his jaw. He jerked, battling desperately to get out of the wood as a rabbit fights a snare. After only a few moments, he gave up. All the blood drained from his cheeks.

Barb slapped him awake. "Answer the feckin' question, boy! What bloody soldiers?"

"Tairnganeah, missus," said the other, who was probably younger than his compatriot. Fat tears rolled clean streaks down his otherwise grimy jowls. He set fearful, hateful green eyes on Una. "They came for the witch."

🦌 🦌

NO BLOODY WONDER, BEN THOUGHT, tracking the train of Hilltop thugs and Tairnganese soldiers through the Quarter.

This was a clever trap.

As it turned out, Matt wasn't in residence at all. If Ben hadn't caught that hint of fabric flapping on the breeze, they'd have walked right into a nest of fully armed Corsairs. *Very clever, indeed.* Slinking along rooftops on their way back to Taverner's Alley, the full scope of the Greenmakers' near-miss dawned. There were easily one hundred soldiers winding toward *The Hart*, spears aloft, rapiers and crossbows strapped to their wide gold belts. Gerrod signaled from the row of roofs on his left, and Ben whistled a response. Robin, who breathed hard from the effort required to descend over slick shingles and rain-soaked gutters, looked up at Ben with a heavy frown.

"I see him, just there," Robin pointed. "Not at the front exactly, but close enough. Yellow cloak, the bloody dandy. Ye see him?"

"Yes," Ben growled. He handed the glass back to Robin. "There's Sol Trant, sitting beside him."

"I hope ye didn't expect that he'd honor any deal ye mighta made? That weasel would sell his mam if he thought there'd be profit for hisself in it."

342

Ben rather liked Sol. A shame the old man wouldn't live to see nightfall. "No matter. Obviously, Matt took a deal of his information from Sol, but I doubt he's the only turncoat we need to manage today."

"Oh, aye." Robin squinted into the eyepiece. "Sam's there too, with his Souther sabre. Ye can count on him followin' his brother's lead. Two Trants means the brewery must be hurtin' for profits."

"I imagine Barb will love having a distillery *and* the best brewery in the North."

"Yer daft. We're outnumbered over three to one."

Ben slid forward on his belly, then shimmied down a tin gutter to get a peek out the drainage hole. In a long line, soldiers were wedged in the alleyways below, perhaps three abreast.

"We've got vantage and arrows aplenty. Tairnganese crossbows aren't worth shite, and their spears are too long to avail them much use. Seems they've just made it easier for us."

"Wonderful. Gonna take the thirty o'us against that lot of professional murderers down there?"

"Don't tell me you'd rather there were more?"

"Course I do," Robin scoffed. "I worry for my reputation, ye know? We'll take many of 'em from up top, but not all."

"Well, it wouldn't be any fun if we could, would it?"

Robin pulled an arrow out of its quiver, jerking his longbow over his head. "'Spose not. Singles or doubles?"

Ben drew down. He counted the nearest dozen men as they milled between tightly packed buildings. "Doubles."

Robin gave the signal with a dramatic roll of eyes. "Had to make it more interestin?'"

"Nah, just cheap. Why waste ammunition when they've made it this easy for us?"

❧ ❦

"Send the heretic out," the voice outside boomed, "*and we won't press our advantage.*" Una thought the speaker looked slightly familiar, with his long braids and handsome dark eyes. Then again, she'd seen most of these men before, hadn't she? A Tairnganeah Cohort with gold cuirasses and long hazel spears gathered behind mounted Corsairs. The Regulars were lined up in neat little rows, awaiting orders. There must have been at least thirty Corsairs out there, all told. She couldn't even begin to count the Cohort. Sixty, maybe? More? Rian clutched at Una's arm, seemingly frightened. Una knew better. She was attempting to steady her.

"Siora," Rian mused. "How'd they get this many in here so fast?"

"Thanks to that pompous lecher standin' below a sign what reads 'Solomon's,' down the lane there," Barb jeered from the bar. She carefully sidestepped a greasy puddle of blood where one of Matt's boys had met a grisly end to pour herself a healthy portion of cider. She didn't bother looking through the broken windowpanes as Dabs and Dean were busy piling tables, chairs, and anything else they could find into the gap. "See him?"

Rian peeked through the barricaded door. "Bright yellow cloak, a bit of a paunch?"

"That's the one," Barb nodded into her pint. "As I said, yer men out there weren't makin' it no secret they was searchin' for ye. Out in bloody force for it too, ye ask me. Matt's an opportunist, same as the rest o' us."

Una scowled over her shoulder. "Well, here's your big chance. See what terms you can make for me."

Rian squeezed her bicep somewhat hard. "No, Una. They'll kill you."

"They'll kill all of you if I don't." Una unwound Rian's fingers from her bruised flesh. "Barb knows it as well as I do."

"Can ye do to them what ye did to this lot here?" Barb gestured to the pile of mangled bodies stacked by the stairs. Una had released her victims from the bar, but what remained of their limbs was a corrugated mess of shredded skin and torn muscles. The lad who'd been stuck fast to the thigh would surely lose the leg now— if he ever woke up again, that is.

"Not all of them. I could probably take any that laid hands on me, but en masse, they'd have the better of me, and they know it."

"Then, we wait for the boys. We ain't exactly defenseless in here, are we?" More Greenmakers filtered through the upstairs walkway. Some had been sent out on the rooftop to tuck themselves against the shingles, short bows drawn. Others gathered at the windows or guarded the walls shy of the door, waiting for anyone to try the barricade. They had perhaps fifteen men downstairs and ten more upstairs, guarding the walkway and alley. Barb sent Colm up on the roof with the archers, which rounded the bulk of their forces to twenty-two. Spread over two large rooftops, the archers were the single best line of defense they had.

"We're outnumbered," Una said flatly. She stepped away from the crack in the window so the Greenmakers could finish their rudimentary barricade. Dean moved aside for her with an ugly scowl on his face. He didn't speak to or look at her, and she sensed a deep hostility within him. Well, that was to be expected. Aside from the day's events, she'd drained his friend and would-be rapist dry as toast— as Paul had deserved. Nonetheless, she understood the unfairness of the situation for everyone else. This wasn't their fight. The tense, tight-lipped malice she detected on scores of faces didn't escape her notice either. Una realized they were afraid of her. She'd seen and done things these simple folks would barely comprehend, not all of it good. Una was well aware of the disparity between them. Why should they suffer for her? A Siorai priestess? A disgraced noblewoman from a corrupt, power-hungry family? She couldn't blame them for their distaste, nor for their reaction to the situation she'd brought down upon them.

"There is no point to this. I will go out."

"Do that, and they'll burn this place down anyway." Rian's fair cheeks flamed scarlet. "You're not a fool, so don't pretend to be one."

"You don't know that, Rian."

"Yes, I do! *You* didn't cause the problem here. You're merely a convenient scapegoat. That fat man at the end of the lane there is using these soldiers to settle a personal grudge. She knows it too!" Rian waved at Barb but didn't stop there. Folding her thin arms over her chest, she narrowed her cornflower eyes at the gathering. "You *all* know it. If Una steps outside that door, you're dead. That Gilcannon character will have beaten you. Is that what you want?"

"They won't get us all," Dean argued in his rich baritone. "Seems to me, with *her* outta the way, our archers up top'll keep 'em honest."

A half-hearted round of 'ayes' followed this statement.

Rose, sans cosmetics and looking much older than she'd first appeared, sighed from her seat on the stairs. She wore a simple brown homespun tunic. Her unironed hair floated about her shoulders in a lustrous black cloud. "No offense, little miss, but we ain't all fighters in here. Some o'us have little-uns or elderly folks to look after. We can't afford to take the chance."

"*... or face the might of the Citadel Corsairs,*" the voice outside continued. "*The Heretic, one Una Moura Donahugh, has been judged by the Common Collective Alliance in Parliament, and by the people of Tairngare, as an imperialist fraud and treasonous defiler of Siora's Sacred Laws. For these offenses, she is condemned to....*"

"I have a little daughter," added Violet from beside Rose. "She'll starve without me."

"Aye," said another girl from the balcony. "We all have someone."

"*... immediately, or we will be forced to burn this establishment to the ground and execute any who attempt to flee....*"

"I don't mean to die for ye today, or any day, missus," Dean curled his lip at Una. "Even if ye was the Queen of bloody Innisfail, as yer bloody grandmam vows, I'd still not die for ye. Yer naught but trouble, I say. Maeden shoulda never brung ye here."

"Now, now." Barb set her pint down. "Watch yer manners, me lad. Trouble or no, the faerie girl has the right o'things. Matt's done this, not this lass. I don't like her neither, but that's not the point. No offense, girl."

"Feeling's mutual," Una shrugged.

"She's just an excuse for Matt to snatch *The Hart*. To have done with the Greenmakers, all at once. If I wasn't so bleedin' furious at his brass, I'd be impressed by the neat little stack he's made o'things here."

Dean held out a hand to the tangle of fearful, angry expressions. "We coulda handled Matt if this gash hadn't brought the Red City's troubles into Rosweal."

346

"If you call me that again," Una drifted close, "you won't live long enough to finish your rant."

Dean went three shades lighter and dropped his hand. Rose was made of more potent stuff. She stood up; her fingers wound tightly through Violet's.

"I have nothin' against ye, milady, please believe that, but I have to think on my family. We all do."

Una's smile was rueful. "I'm very sorry for the trouble I've caused you. All of you. I will do whatever is necessary to keep anything worse from happening. I vow it."

Rian growled into her hands. "*No.* You're all missing the point. They don't care whether you send her out or not. They can't march in here unscathed just yet, and they know it. They don't know how many people are in here or that you have archers on the roof. If you send her out, they'll throw torches through the cracks in the windows. They'll burn the entire block, just to be sure. They could set fire to the place now, but that wouldn't guarantee they'd killed the one they were after. Do any of you follow?"

Barb folded her hands. "Aye, I believe yer makin' a case for keepin' them windows shuttered and waitin' till they march them foot soldiers in here."

"Yes," Rian agreed. "Have your archers shoot the Corsairs from their saddles. Funnel the remnants through the walkway. You could pick them off like rats."

Dean gave a harsh, biting laugh. "Why should we bother? We could sooner run out thatta way, ourselves."

"Because, ye bloody half-wit," Barb balked, "they'll burn me livelihood to the ground. Matt feckin' Gilcannon will be yer new boss, by default. Next time Dean opens his mouth, Dabs, knock his feckin' teeth down his throat."

Sloe-eyed, Dabney nodded. "Missus."

"*... not comply in a reasonable order, we will....*"

Rian pressed her advantage. "I know this is hard; believe me, I empathize. If you give her up, they'd have no reason to leave your

Quarter intact. If you give her to them, they'll burn you out for spite, or because that Gilcannon character has paid them handsomely to do so. Either way, our only chance is to let them know they have no choice but to fight for her."

"Maran?" said Barb.

"Missus?" a kitchen hand called back.

"Head up and tell Colm to kill that loudmouth on the grey first." Barb dumped her empty tankard into the stone sink behind the bar. "And I want Missy, Ronald, and Beal up along that walkway."

"Aye," said the lad. He squeezed past the girls on his way upstairs.

"... *respond? If not, we will....*"

"Dean, ye gonna fight, or do ye want me to send ye out to offer yerself to Matt now?"

Dean sent Una a nasty look, which she roundly ignored. "But, Missus—"

"Choose now." Dabney stepped closer to Dean; his bulky fists prepared to deliver the blow Barb ordered. "I'll not have a half-hearted sissy in my employ. Yer either a Greenmaker, or yer buggered."

He stretched to his full height. "I'm a Greenmaker, Barb. I swear it."

"Good. Ye'll stand at the windows with Dabs, Ned, and Hal. Anythin' tries to get through, I want it to lose a limb. Ye hear me?"

"Yeah."

Stalking around the bar, she waved at Una and Rian. "Ye two, upstairs with the girls and me. Whatever tables we have left, I want 'em stacked up at the second landin'. One thing we got plenty of is arrows. Yancy, George? I want ye to gather up every bow, crossbow, arrow, and cudgel ye can pull up from the cellar— and be quick about it."

"They'll throw torches in the windows, eventually," Una said. "Once they start losing men, they'll fall back on the dependable."

"Well." Barb patted her shoulder almost affectionately. "Let's hope we kill enough o'em that it don't happen too fast, eh?"

BEST LAID PLANS

T he Greenmakers took their time advancing along the Tairnganeah's rear line. Careful to make as little noise as possible, Ben
and company inched from rooftop to rooftop on the balls of
their feet, hiding behind chimneys, trestles, and windbreakers. Gerrod's
group claimed the first victims on the south side of the alley. Foot soldiers at the back with little protection from overhead attacks pitched
soundlessly to the muddy cobbles, unbeknownst to their comrades in
the forward line.

Stealth and speed were the Greenmakers' allies. For a while, anyway.
Fifteen men fell under their arrows at the first flash, then eighteen,
twenty, and nearly twenty-two. The Greenmakers' luck was not to last,
however. A dead soldier rolled into the group ahead, where the alley
spilled downhill into the Quarter. One of Robin's arrows protruded from
his right eye. In a panic, soldiers jostled for cover. They stumbled into
one another like pins in a bowler's game. Commands were shouted, and
easily thirty-five pairs of eyes marked the two groups of archers taking
aim from above. Gold shields came up, and crossbows were hastily
loaded. Despite the ensuing crush in the narrow lane below, several bolts
hammered into the wall near Ben's head. He threw his arm around a
weathervane to keep himself from incidentally tumbling down the drain.

"Shite!" Wincing, he jammed a boot into a jagged crevice to take some of gravity's punishment. "Robin, I might have underestimated those crossbows a bit."

"Ye think?" Robin took a glancing blow along the crown of his shoulder. The man behind him took one through the throat. With a curse, Robin retrieved the fellow's quiver before the body tumbled into the alley. Ben dodged one quarrel, then another. "Suppose our presence has been noted. A shame because I was rather enjoying myself for a bit there."

Seamus' chin hit the tin roof with a loud bang as he dipped beneath the next volley. "Feckin' tits! Tell me one o'ye had a backup plan?"

"I don't appreciate yer tone, whelp." Robin struggled to nock his short bow. "O'course, we got a plan. Erm, don't we, Ben?"

Having scooted to the edge of the wall, Ben lobbed fallen bricks, tiles, pots... whatever he could summon to hand. "We'll have to backtrack. Cross over to the south side with Gerry and the others."

Seamus muttered something rude into the soot-stained puddle beneath his chin. A torch fizzled past the lip in the wall, and they watched it turn over in the air. It skidded to a sputtering stop by Robin's knee. "Feckin' idiots. Don't they know it's too bloody damp for that? They should toss them inside. What sort of soldier don't know that?"

Seamus dragged the hissing missile toward him. "Grab any o'them ye can before they fizzle out."

As he spoke, a second torch sailed over the wall. Ben shimmied toward it on his backside and kicked it over with the toe of his boot. "You got an idea?"

"Might do." Seamus ducked under the next volley of quarrels and wormed a little brown leather pouch out of his waistband.

Robin raised his brows sky-high at the sight. "Feckin' hell! Ye've been keeping bloody *gunpowder* in yer trousers?"

"Got plenty of saltpeter left after slaughterin' that bull last month. Figured 'twas a shame to waste the leavins. Hand me that torch, Ben, thanks."

"How long you been carryin' that around?"

350

"For a bit. Me and Colm thought to give it a go for winter. We had the peter, and a stock o'sulfur we nicked from that tinker last spring. This here's a test batch. Didn't think 'bout it till now."

"Yer a mad bastard, Seamus." Robin shook his head. A bolt passed through his sleeve. He snatched his arm back from the wall. "Whatever ye aim to do, make it quick, will ye? I don't fancy bein' shot or blown to the nine hells."

Seamus accepted the flask of rotgut spirits Donell passed over to him. Next, he tore a shred from his tunic, soaked it in raw uishge, and dropped a tiny pile of powder into the rag.

"Ye'll wanna back off, just in case I muck this up."

Everyone squeezed as far away from him as gravity or ammunition would allow. When the next volley launched over the wall, Seamus stood up. Quick as an adder, he slapped the wad into the hissing flame, and dropped the torch before the rag made contact. "Get down!"

The resulting boom wasn't overly dramatic, but the answering cries from the unfortunate soldiers below were. A cheer went up from the opposite rooftop. Ben grinned from ear to half-deafened ear. Robin threw back his head and laughed. "Don't think they were expectin' that!"

Seamus shredded two more strips from his shirt. "Hand me that second torch…"

$$\text{\reflectbox{Y} \, Y}$$

DESPITE THE TAIRNGANEAH'S IMPRESSIVE TURNOUT, there wasn't much wiggle room through Rosweal's winding, illogical alleyways. Matt figured as much when he opened the Navan Gate for the Corsairs only yesterday. These mounted dandies cut fine figures, with their gleaming armor embossed with coiling blue dragons. Quite handsome, indeed. All were rather large men, well-muscled, and scrupulously clean. No simple feat for fellas who'd been in the saddle for the better part of a month, hunting an escaped heretic. Matt supposed he might have been temporarily dazzled by their initial presentation. The second sons of aristocratic families were often wealthy enough for the smartest kits.

Too fine, however, by half. In Matt's experience, *real* soldiers didn't make a habit of style. Once upon a time, Corsairs from the Red City did not prance and preen. There was no need. They were worthy of the fear that the blue dragons inspired. Times had changed. This new batch dressed the part, but that was all they had on offer.

Matt was seated at a short round table under a wide awning outside Solomon's, and sipping the finest ale in the North, Matt had a front-row seat to a miserable show. Rosweal was a tricky beast to tame. He understood this better than most. Though, the Tairnganeah he recalled from his youth were a far cry from the foppish showmen who were failing him now. Matt folded hoary hands over his well-fed belly. His mouth curled up slightly at the left corner, twisting his manicured mustache into a semicolon. This was hardly worth watching at all, was it?

Sol, who hovered like an agitated bee, wiped nervous hands up and down his spotless apron for the dozenth time in the last thirty minutes. The Tairnganeah had broken *The Hart*'s windows. That was good. Then, the Corsairs' captain made his demands. That was good too… but not long after, the situation soured. Sol wasn't taking the spectacle as impassively as Matt. Sol's fat brother Sam was preoccupied with stuffing his swollen jowls with cold ham. Sol's fidgeting seemed to target Matt exclusively.

"Matt?"

"Don't ask again, Sol."

The meek little brewer wasn't as eager a convert as Matt wished him to be, and the fact rankled Matt's already taxed nerves. Sol crossed his skinny arms as if to buoy himself in the gale of Matt's glare.

"What if—?"

"We'll burn 'em out ourselves, won't we?" Sam offered pork smacking odiously over his brown teeth. He tugged a greasy thumb at Matt. "He's got it all worked out, Sol. These shites will soften 'em up for us, and we'll take it to the finish after. Easy."

Sol wasn't convinced. He claimed to have heard several loud booms when he'd made his rounds through the brewery an hour earlier. Matt hadn't heard any such thing for the racket outside *The Hart and Hare*. Sam had only stopped stuffing his face long enough to drop into a periodical upright doze. Of the Hilltop Boys that hadn't fled back to the slums for fear of the Siorai witch inside, only a few answered his summons. Matt had been told what had transpired inside was a horrific scene, the likes of which he'd only read about. Still, he noted the ones who stayed. He would reward them with extra rations once this ugly business was properly sorted. These few remaining boys stalked the alley, forward and aft, providing a bit of useful human fodder between himself and any stray arrows which managed to make it this far down the lane.

"All I'm sayin' is, shouldn't we prepare for things to turn the other way? Ye don't know Ben Maeden as I do, Matt. Ye can't hang yer cap on the hope that ye've outwitted him. He's a canny bastard, and I daresay, a better fighter than this lot." Sol gestured toward the dead Corsairs lying face-down in the mud outside *The Hart* spotted with arrows, glass, wood shards, and anything else the Greenmakers could call to hand. Their archers started shooting before the final demands left the fine young captain's mouth, then immediately went to work on any fellow not wise enough to dismount and flee or ride up to higher ground.

Matt lit his prized ivory pipe with a sneer. "What *is* this horseshite anyway? Ye can't steal a ribbon in any town along the border without hearin' tales o'what the Tairnganeah do to thieves and traders what don't pay their respects to the Merchanta." He spat into the muddy cobbles. "What a load of tripe! Look at these bleedin' pansies. There can't be more than forty men and women inside or up top. The way they're chargin' straight forward with them useless spears, ye'd think there was five hunnerd."

Blessedly done gnawing on ripe hunks of meat, Sam Trant let out a long odiferous belch. "Aye, they do turn out rather bad, don't they? Spears're only good for open ground. Why'd they bring 'em here, where ye can leap from one door to another without getting yer feet wet, I'd be buggered to know?"

Matt couldn't believe what he was seeing. He remembered an entirely different sort of soldiery, some twenty years past. He'd been in the fight for Eirean freedom on the fields at Dumnain. He recalled the discipline, the hip-to-shoulder lines the Tairnganeah made, marching down the lists. His youthful admiration of the Tairnganese infantry had impressed upon him for most of his life. Either Matt had simply been enchanted by the vibrant colors snapping in the breeze or the flash of gold on their cuirasses because *these* were not the same glorious warriors he'd imagined all those years before.

"Please. Ye don't know. I heard—" Sol buzzed in his ear.

Matt and Sam ignored him.

"Ye know." Sam sat up straighter, pushing the table out with his girth. Matt was hardly slim any more than Sam was, but he at least was conscious of himself. He took pride in his presentation and bearing. Sam Trant was a butcher and cheesemaker of little repute— when he wasn't financing cutpurses from the slums to harry Merchers on the road, that is. Sam had been a disgusting slob as long as Matt had known him, but a clever one, all the same. "I don't think this lot has seen a fight in near thirty years, so I reckon. Not that that's a bad bit, but it don't serve to make 'em shine in a scuffle." He shook his meaty head.

Matt sniffed. "I think it's more to do with politics. The Libella's losing control— power like that just don't last. The upper classes are so wealthy that they've gone soft. I hear a rich family on the climb can purchase commissions in the Citadel for a song now that Drem's star has waned over the past ten years. That new Alta Prima, Nema, I think... she's been in control o'the office o'the Union Registry all that time and been sellin' Patents of Maternas cheap to families that would never've dared to try and ascend to the nobles' ranks. Ye got wine merchants from Cymru, sons o'tanners, and Agrean small landowners. Most o'these boys never held a sword 'fore their parents bought their commissions, I'll wager. Ain't the same anymore, I 'spose."

"Bad business, all 'round."

"Whole place is bound for the midden, ye ask me. Just look at 'em." Matt waved a bejeweled hand at the soldiers that scampered away from *The Hart*. "They shoulda trained them up from nappies like I do. Get 'em young, and show 'em how to handle themselves properly. This just shows that money doesn't make the man... or the family, it seems."

Sol removed Matt's empty tankard with a furtive, trembling insecurity on his heavily lined face. "Matt, please…"

Matt's fist struck the tabletop, rattling the crockery. The boys around them fidgeted. They were well acquainted with Matt's infamous temper. Two large black holes peered up at Sol from below Matt's browbone.

"Solomon, *I heard ye*. We should all be scairt o'this Ben bloody Maeden. Well, I've done for him, ye can rest assured. Him and that scum-slug Gramble, both. Now, quit yer keenin.' Bring me another red ale. Any o'that stew ye have left over from last night, too. Sharpish." He waved his empty tankard back and forth for emphasis. Sol struggled with it; Matt could tell plain as his nose. But like any weasel, Sol was quick to retreat when an easy victory wasn't in the offing. With one last pleading glance at his indifferent elder brother, Solomon slunk back into the taproom to do Matt's bidding. Frowning, Matt watched him go. He cut his eyes sideways at Sam. "Ye think he'd be happier with the arrangement. Was half his bloody idea."

Sam blew his nose on a woolen sleeve. "Aye? Not even me own mam could make him happy, lo she did try. Poor lass. Died in a Tairnganese lock-up for plyin' her trade in the streets rather than pay homage to the Voluptatus. Worked herself ragged to feed and clothe us best she was able. That one—" Sam tilted an ear at the tavern door. "Never did care for what he had. Always thought hisself a bit better'n the fatherless whelp he was." His deep-throated chuckle shook the table braced against his gut.

"Always, ye say?"

Sam gulped his warm tankard and fixed a cool glare on Matt. "I can hear the cogs whirlin' in that pretty head o'yers, Matt. Don't fish around in mine for an excuse to increase yer shares."

Matt feigned perfect outrage. "I would never—"

"Ye needn't bother to lie, neither. Know this, ye make a move against Sol, after what he just done for ye, I'll shove yer own cock up yer arsehole."

"*Now see here….*"

Sam leaned over, taking most of the table with him. Matt sat back on an expelled breath. The butcher reeked of onions, sour ale, and decaying meat. "Oh, I do see, Gilcannon. We're sittin' here with ye outta necessity, not loyalty. Ye'd do best to remember that. The second I suspect ye mean to double-cross one o'us, yer a dead man. Ye think on that the next time ye plan to open that perfumed mouth o'yers."

He turned back to the petering skirmish down the lane, guffawing at the scrambling Tairnganeah. The folk inside *The Hart* gave a merry little cheer as the soldiers fled. Matt seethed in silence. The thud of his heart bore the only indication that he still breathed. Sam was not as easy as his brother. If he said he'd have Matt killed, he certainly believed he could do it. All evidence implied that he had a point. The pair of strongmen standing guard at Sam's right hand weren't known for their cultured opinions. Altxhough, Matt was hardly the man to be put in his place by the lord of pickpockets and sham men. Matt could buy and sell Samuel Trant four times over. How *dare* this jumped-up thug speak to *him* that way? Behind Matt, one of his boys tapped a fingernail against the pommel of his dagger. Matt held up a hand to still his impatient fingers.

"I'll forget ye made that threat, Sam. Today. Our work isn't finished just yet, and there's no sense to be makin' enemies o'ourselves. I have not, nor would I harm sweet Sol for bein' cautious." He'd be sure to stuff Sol's bollocks into his brother's gaping craw as soon as this was all over... but he didn't bother to broach that topic just yet. "Seems our brave soldiers've had enough."

An unhorsed Corsair dashed down the lane toward them, followed closely by three attendants. The lieutenant, a young man with dark hair twisted into the typical Tairnganese nest of complicated braids, came to a huffing halt three paces from Matt's guards. The angry, frustrated pride on the man's handsome face tickled something high in Matt's throat.

"Let me pass!" the lieutenant growled, a bloody hand on his rapier for emphasis. Matt's boys didn't blink. Some were half the size of this fellow, but their bearing made them nine feet taller, to all impressions. You can always spot a killer. A *true* killer, those who possess real menace— from the smallest street rat to the most hardened veteran. It is something in their eyes, a surety. As if they measure each individual they encounter by the effort they might spend to bring him down. Matt's boys were barely adults, but they had what this poor fancy sod did not.

What's more, the Corsair knew it instantly, like a rabbit scenting a fox. Matt observed the immediate change in the lieutenant's demeanor. He stepped back a pace and licked his lips. Fabian, a lad of thirteen, glared back with amused malice.

"Master Gilcannon, you swore to give us your aid!"

Matt splayed his hands. "What the sweet feck do ye call this, then? I opened the bloody gates for ye lot, didn't I? Gave ye shelter, ale, food, and women for the night. All but rolled out the purple feckin' carpet for ye."

"They have trained fighters in there!" protested the lieutenant, "Our men weren't prepared for this sort of pitched engagement."

Sam laughed so hard that the little wads of ham stuck to his teeth sprayed all over his tunic, the tankard, and the table. Repulsed, Matt twitched back. "What did ye say? Weren't yer men 'prepared' for a fight? Yer trained feckin' soldiers, are ye not?"

The lieutenant shifted from one foot to the other. "Yes, but on open ground. Not crammed into tight, filthy corridors... like these."

"I see," Matt nodded. Sam turned a queer shade of magenta, he laughed so hard at their expense. "This isn't the sort o'civilized engagement yer used to, is it? All that bluster on the provin' grounds and not much to back it up."

The Corsair held out a bloody torn arm to keep the men behind him in place. As if their bravado could scare Matt now.

"These people are savages. They fight like beasts, dirty like vermin. They burned two of my men alive, and what they can't catch inside, they shoot from above, like cowards."

"Well, that was yer first mistake, lad." Sam wiped his eyes. "Ye came to bloody Rosweal expectin' a fair fight. Only a fool would make that sort o'blunder, I reckon."

"I believe I sent my boys in first if ye recall?" Matt reminded him. "That witch did unspeakable things to four or more. Here, we thought

357

ye'd have done better?" Sam laughed again, earning him a withering glare full of aristocratic loathing.

"We're leaving. As far as I'm concerned, this city has earned the blaze our army will set upon our return."

"Send in yer reserves. Ye left enough men uphill. I doubt ye'd have much trouble overwhelmin' 'em with—"

The lieutenant blanched. "*What men?* Before they killed him, my captain summoned the reserves stationed several streets away. Many more were sent to circle the tavern, to staunch escape. They're all gone."

Sam's smile flickered, then faded. "What was that?"

The lieutenant tossed him a soot-smeared spear-shaft. Sam fumbled the object a bit before dropping it on the table under his gut. It was broken and burnt black at the butt as if someone had used it to stoke a stubborn brazier.

"Of the fifty men we left in your odious slum a mile or so back, only ten managed to flee whence they came. The rest are piled up at the end of the alley."

Matt shot to his feet. "You lie. That ain't bloody possible."

"Isn't it? I wouldn't put it past scum like you to lure us in here for an ambush. Though, given the state of the area around my dead comrades, I'd say you lost quite a bit on this gamble yourself."

Another soldier approached from the rear. He held his shield above his head for safety while he brought the remaining officer his mount. The lieutenant slid his hands inside his gloves, spat, and spun on his heel.

"Wait! What do ye mean, 'the state o'the area?'"

"Can't you smell the smoke? The natives set fire to their hovels, it seems."

They were upwind. The Hilltop was at their back, to the east. Matt could see nothing in that direction save eaves and close-pitched roofs. "*Fabian.*"

"Aye, boss." Fabian sheathed his dagger for the run south toward the slums. From there, he would double-back and head up the Hill to the east. That was the fastest route.

358

The lieutenant smiled without mirth. "My family name is Hamma, Gilcannon. You'll be hearing it again soon." He pulled himself artfully into his saddle, then kicked his mount forward.

Matt was forced to stumble out of his way, almost into Sam's overflowing lap. "Wait! Ye can't just leave. The heretic is still in there, ain't she?"

"If she manages to survive the animals in this pen, she'll spend the rest of her days a hunted traitor with no people. I wish you all joy of her." Lieutenant Hamma waved a rude gesture over his shoulder. He and his train of spiteful soldiers filed southward down the alley.

Perplexed, Matt watched them go. Of course, he'd meant to double-cross them, but not until he'd exhausted them to extinction on *The Hart*. The girl wasn't what Matt was after, but her bounty wouldn't hurt his coffers either. He'd arranged things just so, and now… suddenly, the street felt far too quiet. Matt's boys chattered amongst themselves. They were all hardened souls, to be sure, but if the Hilltop was aflame, the slums might be next. The families they worked so hard for were in danger. Matt couldn't smell any smoke. Couldn't hear any crackling timber. Only laughter, whistles, and jeers from *The Hart*, as the Greenmakers watched the Tairnganeah march away in defeat.

Sam used the window casing to help himself upright. He had a strange tilt to his mouth that alarmed Matt more than the retreating Tairnganeah or their lieutenant's cryptic warning.

"What?"

Sam waddled toward the open black chasm of a doorway. The day was bright, despite the periodic rainclouds that raced overhead like silver cannonballs. It had drizzled off and on all afternoon, broken by intermittent sunshine. Just now, the sky gave them a bit of both.

"Sol! Where ye got to, then? Ye hear what's goin' on out here?"

Nothing. Not even a whisper in return.

Sam shot Matt a startled round eye. "Solomon? Quit feckin' about!"

Silence. The open door took on the appearance of something much more sinister than a simple tavern entrance. Matt shoved two or three of his boys in front of him. Strong light made for long shadows in tight spaces. That yawning black maw beckoned ominously. Hadn't it only been a doorway mere moments ago? No sound rustled within save the 'drip, drip, drip' of a poorly shuttered tap. Matt's palm wound over the small, stiff muscles of Lance Shoren's shoulder. The boy didn't wince, though Matt's fingertips ground into bone. Sam drew the Bethonair sabre he kept strapped to his side. His stone-faced guards flanked the beckoning entrance. "Solomon Trant! If yer not dead or dyin' in there, ye'd better bloody well speak up now!"

Not a peep at first, then… as if barreling through a mountain tunnel into the cold light of day, something small and silver rolled over the slate paving stones at the stoop, clinking as it sped toward Sam's feet. It was a coin: a whole silver stag. The coin sank into the muck near Sam's right toe. Sam didn't bend down to examine it (as if he could, the pig). He exhaled a rattling breath. Three more coins rolled into the street from the fathomless darkness within. Matt paled. These were the very coins he'd given Sol to betray the Greenmakers Guild, a small fortune in this sad, desperate part of the Continent.

The last silver to find a home at Sam's feet was stained red— presumably with its owner's blood. Sam gave a wheezing sort of half-scream, half-roar. Matt propelled himself backward into the lane, safe behind his boys' bony, startled backs.

"Greetings," sang an elegant, slightly accented voice from inside. It sent shivers down Matt's spine and tore a guttural curse from Sam Trant's chest. "Sol won't be needing this wealth where he's off to. Please, help yourselves."

One of Sam's men took a step toward the door. A thin arrow-shaft burst from the back of his skull. His companion dodged left to avoid the next shot, though Sam was far too bulky to move as quickly. He took one through the quadriceps, near his groin. His answering scream rattled every awning for a mile in each direction. Matt didn't wait around to see more. He shoved two of his boys toward Sam, desperate to escape the brewery. He looked back only once. A tall blond figure emerged from Solomon's taproom. He wore at least a quart of blood and a maniacal grin. The fair-haired fellow whirled about with a two-handed broadsword, painting the stoop a garish red. Matt didn't dawdle. He'd only seen fighting like that once before at Dumnain and wasn't about to hang around in awe.

Those of his boys who didn't stay behind to fight Ben Maeden, Gramble, and others who entered the alley from the darkened tavern, fled south toward Haymaker's Lane with Matt. Some outpaced him, though he'd had quite a head start. Nothing could halt the sounds that traveled up to them: the laughter, Sam's bleating cries, the hacking, pleading, metallurgic sounds of slaughter. Matt rounded the first bend, past old Barnaby's shut-up haberdashery. An arrow thwacked into the brick façade just shy of his kidney. Whimpering, he ran on. That same voice came again, higher and louder, dogging Matt's slip-shod progress over mud-slick cobbles.

"See you soon, Gilcannon!"

Matt could hear the mocking superiority in the speaker's tone, could *feel* the triumph. Terrified, he rounded the next corner, which faced south by east. The air here was thick with smoke. It stung his eyes, burned his sinuses, and seared his throat. The further south he sprinted, the more overpowering it became. Despite the weather, half of the bloody city must have been on fire. Wet rooftops meant squat if interior walls, floors, and joists were dry.

Only minutes ago, he'd been sure of his victory. The Greenmakers were beaten. The Tairnganeah had left of their own accord. It would have been a simple matter to have both Sam and Sol knifed on their way home. In a flash, this day warped into something else: something unforeseen. The Greenmakers hadn't fallen into his trap. Matt had barreled into one of theirs.

That was all right… he would live.

He had another plan.

Hot smoke singed his lungs, but Matt ran until he thought his aging heart would implode. At the crest of the Hilltop, he followed his boys right toward the slums. The Taran Gate loomed ahead. His next chance waited five miles to the south. He could make it. He had to. The low-end of the Hilltop was ablaze, but it was too damp to hold for long. Surely only the low-end near the quarter would have been damaged when he returned tomorrow? Whichever way it played out didn't matter. He only needed to get out alive. He would come back and take what was rightfully his.

He put everything he had into his two feeble legs, pleased to note that despite years of relative comfort, they could still perform their first occupation. Matt Gilcannon fled as if a lad of ten once more, shirking the justice he so richly deserved.

Quid Pro Quo

n.e. ſ08
27, ðorsamna
rosweal

R ian was exhausted hours before the Tairnganeah stopped lob-
bing flaming darts through their barricades or throwing men
with ridiculously long spears at the cracks in the door. When
a chill afternoon rain put out the soldiers' torches and diminished their
chances of burning *The Hart* down with everyone inside, the worst of the
fighting petered out. At the close, over two-score dead Tairnganese soldiers piled up in Taverner's Alley. Rian was bone tired. Fatigue sapped
every ounce of energy she had to spare by the time the remaining Corsairs called for a retreat.

The fight had been nearly comical in its seeming one-sided advantage.
The Tairnganeah had the numbers. They had the weapons: expensive
spears, crossbows, and shields. They had mounted commanders,
vantage, supplies, and an organized line. Yet, nothing worked out the
way anyone (save perhaps Barb) had expected. If one were to judge by
the smug humor on the madam's face, she'd never had a single doubt
about the Corsairs' ability to bungle a skirmish. Rian, however, knew
nothing about battle. Until recently, she'd never even been in a fight.
Hostility, mistrust, and veiled accusations, yes. She'd experienced plenty
of that. But an actual physical altercation? Never.

In Ferndale, she was treated with restrained tolerance. The townsfolk preferred to pretend she didn't exist, even when forced to interact with her. They would lower their eyes when she approached or squeeze their mouths together in a solemn line. Few had any kind words for Rian, less the thanks she deserved for treating so many of their women and children for whatever pittance they could muster. Rian understood subtle enmity, sarcasm, bigotry, and disgust— but real violence? No. Not until Ben dragged Una to her door had Rian witnessed barbarity like this. She'd read about such things. She wasn't a fool. The histories her father lined his treasured shelves with detailed the horrific depths of human depravity. To witness it firsthand, however... Rian was at a loss. Each day away from home was a new trial. Her quiet life had not prepared her for the horrors she'd seen since. The Greenmakers stacked dozens of bodies beneath *The Hart*'s shattered windows. Colm swept glass, wood splinters, and puddles of quarrels from red-stained floors. He scowled over the mess, covered head-to-toe in welts, scrapes, and seeping cuts.

"Bleedin' savages. Just feckin' mopped, didn't I?"

Rian was running out of room and supplies. In her little makeshift clinic at the top of the stairs, she did not lack for patients: men and boys with cuts, broken bones, severed digits, or limbs. She treated dislodged teeth, burns, countless contusions, and colorful abrasions. Almost since the fighting broke out, she'd been on her knees in these halls, tending to casualties. So many, in fact, *The Hart* ran out of bed linens by sunset. Rian sent several of Barb's girls running back and forth from the laundry, hauling clean linens, skirts, chemises, and curtains back to the hall. The girls foraged for anything that could be torn or shredded to meet the ever-increasing demand for bandages. Some scoured both buildings for whatever needles, thread, and small blades they could scavenge. Others hauled bucketloads of sulphuric water from the baths below the tenement. The girls scrubbed floors, walls, or human skin on demand.

Rian wasn't even sure how she came to treat the first few injuries. The fighting commenced, and there she was: staunching, wrapping, sewing, and soothing. Not every fighter's wounds were shallow, either—many required sedatives... or worse. At a critical point, someone had handed her a tincture of belladonna. It wasn't until much later that Rian realized the donor had been Rose. It turned out that Rose had been beside her the whole time, her sleeves rolled up and her forearms wet to the elbows in blood. Unbeknownst to Rian, they moved in concert through each new emergency. Rian mended those that could be mended, and Rose helped make comfortable those who couldn't. Six men died. They lay in the hall, with scraps of linen covering their blank, staring eyes. Two more would likely not recover. Of these, the big man, Dean, took a quarrel through the gut. His cries were weakening but meaningful all the same. Rian could do nothing for him but pour a dollop of belladonna into a uishge decanter and send him off to sleep forever. Such wounds were terrible, degenerative, and far beyond her ability to heal. Dean's last hours would have stretched on in agony. She spared him that, at least.

Thankfully, most fighters bore superficial wounds: a broken finger, a gash on the arm, a blow to the head, a cracked rib, or a cut that simply needed stitching. These would return to action before Rose could tie off their bandages. Some would take a second or third wound, then return to the landing, impatiently awaiting their next treatment so they could return to the barricades. The noise had been deafening: metal clanging, manic laughter, screams, shouts, curses, cries, and moans. Barb's taproom was a riot of foul odors, raucous sounds, and chaotic activity. The smell was overpowering, too: smoke on damp wood, rain against the mud outside, the sickly stench of blood and vomit, an acidic tang of urine, sweat, and stale ale from broken taps.

Several times the Tairnganeah broke through the Greenmakers' line at the front of the tavern but were beaten back with a relish that would surely shame the survivors for years to come. Not a man made it through that wasn't immediately put down, forcibly ejected over the heads of their fellows, or tossed face down into the muck outside. For every Greenmaker felled by Tairnganese bolt or slash, three Tairnganeah either left their guts in the effluent stew that used to serve as common rushes or were shoved back into the street from whence they came. If Rian hadn't been so preoccupied, she might have paid more attention to Barb, who stood framed against the balustrade shouting orders and laughing like a harpy. With her best remaining archers on the roof shooting anything in black and gold with abandon, Barb might have had reason to find humor in all of this. Rian was up to her elbows in blood and excrement and did not share the sentiment. What joy could one derive from such senseless bloodletting?

When the noise died down and the horde of patients thinned along the landing, Rian felt a gentle touch on her shoulder. She was busy stitching a jagged cut over another nameless lad's forearm. He blubbered and teared up as if *she'd* been the one slashing at him with a rapier rather than attempting to staunch a slippery wound he most certainly earned.

"Wait your turn, please." She didn't look up. The needle was too small for this sort of work, a lace needle, no doubt. She struggled to keep it between her thumb and forefinger through each pass.

"Here now, lass," cooed Barb's voice. Rian made a face. The needle sailed through its last damp layer of flesh. She held her left index finger over the exit while she made her loop.

"Ye should take a break," the madam persisted. "It's well and over."

Rian noted four or five boys waiting near the stairs to be seen. Each wore varying stages of triumph or wounded pride on their filthy features. "When I'm done, I'll stop."

"I respect that, I *do*— but yer done, nonetheless. Let Rose take over. She knows how to tie a tourniquet and sew a scratch back together."

Done with the fidgety lad, Rian spared Barb an annoyed glance. She waved the next one over. "I'd rather not have to check someone else's work later when I can do it right the first time."

An elderly gentleman who smelled of uishge and rank cabbages took the lad's place by the wall. He pulled his shirt up with a sheepish, toothless smile for Barb. He had a mean gash down his skeletal ribcage. It wasn't life-threatening but would cost him several weeks of healing, regardless. Rian frowned.

"Violet?"

"Missus?"

"I need more of that nettle stew you brought me before. Mix in at least two cups of the strongest spirits you can find. We're going to need more bandages." She didn't look up to watch Violet rush down the hall. Instead, she patted the old man's hand encouragingly. "I'm going to see those others over there for a bit, but when Violet returns with my supplies, we'll take care of this. All right?"

"Yer a saint, missus," he cackled back.

A Kneeler. Rian hadn't met one in some time. She gave him a reassuring smile and waved the next one over, ignoring Barb and her crossed arms. This fellow had a nasty burn. His eye was swollen shut and seeping pus. She'd need a salve and a thin, scrupulously clean blade to—

"Are ye bloody well deaf, girl? Yer wavin' where ye kneel. Dabs!"

Rian opened her mouth to argue, but a giant meat hook looped around her waist. Dabney hoisted her aloft without much effort. Rian's teeth clacked together over her trite retort. Indeed, she was too tired to squeal. Instead, she settled for silent but sanctimonious reproach. Barb snorted.

"No use givin' me that face, missy. I've seen a great deal more'n ye to be frightened of today. Bring her into me office, Dabs but be careful with her. Rose!" Barb hollered, still glaring down at Rian. "Ye know what to do with this lot?"

"Yeah," Rose droned, easily as tired as Rian. "His eye needs lancin', and that burn needs greasin'. When Violet gets back with the brew, the old man's ribs need disinfectin' and a handy stitchin.' Am I right, missus?"

She was asking Rian, who was impressed, despite being held under the crook of Dabney's arm with her backside high in the air. Rian sniffed. "Yes. Do you—?"

"Oh, fer feck's sake! She'll bloody manage. Siora, but ye'd think none o'us ever coddled a man afore. On the couch with ye. Get some broth and cheese down that scrawny gullet."

Rian was carted into Barb's well-appointed office. There, upon the settee, lay Una... wounded yet again. Una did her level best to pretend such things barely affected her. Sweating, she held a damp cloth against her temple. The rag was tainted a rusty crimson from the purpling laceration Rian saw winding its way along her upper ear. Rian wriggled out of Dabney's grasp and was by her side in a flash. She slapped her defensive fingers away.

"I swear! Do you *know* how to duck? It looks worse than it is, but I'll need to—"

"Rian, it's all right." Una gently shoved Rian into the seat beside her. "Your hands are trembling. Are you hurt?"

"No," Barb barked from the doorway. "But she's been in the thick o'it the whole bloody time. Needs to get some food into her."

"Una," Rian growled. "That could fester if I don't see to it."

"It'll heal."

"But—"

"*It will heal*, Rian," Una's tone was firm, but her eyes were soft. Rian rolled her bottom lip and looked away. Una nodded at the table, which was set with tea, bread, broth, and cheese. Rian couldn't begin to guess how someone managed to get into the kitchens to unearth such treasure. The tavern was a disaster, from the broken windows to the smashed-in doors. Rian fell on the food like a starving rat.

"There now, poor mite. Get somethin' hot into ye." Barb had Dabney pour the tea. He was black and blue as everyone else, save for his dripping hair and clean fingers. Barb noticed Rian's attention. "Keeps everyone in high morale if a fella as large as Dabs here looks no worse for wear. If ye saw what he looked like afore..." She gave a mock shudder and helped herself to some tea. "Anyway, I want ye to know, what ye did for me lads out there, girl— I'll not be forgettin' anytime soon. I mean that."

"S'aright," Rian squeezed out, behind a hunk of muenster cheese with a bit of browning apple. Una, she couldn't fail to see, was having none. She watched Rian silently, with the most peculiar look on her face. A momentary panic crept up the veins of Rian's neck. She looked down at the food, suspicious.

"Oh, not this time, lass. Ye needn't fear," laughed Barb.

"Then... why are you being so nice to me? To us?"

"Pish and posh, girl. All water under a dusty bridge that is." Rian didn't like Barb's smile. It reminded her of the way a hawk eyes small prey. "I owe ye that much, at least." Barb reached inside her vest and

368

pulled out a small bone flask, which she upended into her own spot of tea. "Now, that's not to say we don't have somewhat to discuss before the menfolk return, to pretend they have a say in anything.'"

"Ah," said Rian, as if she had the first clue what the old bat was hinting at.

Barb dragged her chair over. She offered her flask to Una, who, for once, needed no prompting. She dumped a fair amount down her throat and handed it back with a grateful sigh. "I'm not gonna forget how you fought down there, milady. Ye took that wound for Colm, who'd be dead now thrice over if ye hadn't stuck at his back. That's more'n bravery. As the boys say, that took *bollocks*."

"I owed him. Those bastards would never have come here if—"

"If Matt fucking Gilcannon hadn't found out about ye. Don't bother to blame yerself. If it wasn't ye, it'd be somethin' else. I'm not gonna claim to like ye overmuch, but I can lay all this 'pon ye, neither. Yer an opportunity for Matt, same as ye are for those lads to the South, and that old prune what leads the Union o'Commons in Parliament. Bad luck for ye, all around, I 'spose."

"Right. Now, where're you going with this?"

Barb's smile held even less warmth than the previous one. "To the point then? Dabs, close the door behind ye," she said, pouring them a round of tea each and making sure to dollop healthy doses of uishge in each cup. She settled herself against a worn magenta cushion and winced when one of her sleeves brushed against her burned forearm. She'd applied some sweet-smelling salve, which Rian believed to be honey and mint.

"I've got news I feel sure yer not gonna care for, but I'm bound to tell ye anyway." Without the cosmetics, the bluster, or the hordes of male hangers-on, Barb looked almost normal and harmless. What might her life have been like if she hadn't been called to sell herself and others for profit? Rian had little experience with the world. Therefore, she couldn't begin to comprehend the motivation or self-effacement required to make such a decision. Una thought Barb's choices displayed a weakness of character. Rian suspected something different altogether. Only the very strong had the grit to survive at any cost to their dignity. Rian knew this as surely as she knew the length of her nose. Why? Because she understood such strength was not one of her gifts. Rian could *never* do it. The weight of that choice.... the cost would be far more than she could bear. To not only endure but *thrive*, as Barb had— said something for her. She wasn't sure that something was flattering, but it intimated a particular strength of character, regardless.

Rian was less tainted by the Siorai faith than Una. She could see what Una could not. Barb wasn't evil, cruel, or wanton; she was a survivor. She was also someone in a position to help others survive. What's more, she was good enough at both to keep herself and her tiny ignoble corner of the world in relative comfort. Una could barely look at the woman without a curl to her upper lip, but that was her rearing. Rian hadn't been raised to believe herself superior to anyone else. As kind as Una was, Rian believed she had no idea she held such bias. This revelation wasn't something that could be taught, however. Una would come round to it on her own, or not at all.

Una set her compress down. "Bethonair Knights? When you mentioned them before, I gathered they were closer than I'd like them to be."

"Too bleedin' right, ye are. Less than ten miles, last report. Probably much closer than that even. They're setting up a supply camp in Vale, just down the Taran High Road."

Rian gasped. "That's just seven miles away."

"Wonderful." Una pinched the bridge of her nose with blackened fingers. "I suppose he'll send his demands soon enough?"

"No need. We all know what he wants. Them Tairnganese wimps beatin' a hasty retreat from the city walls would've made it obvious to the Southers yer here." Barb eyed her speculatively. "Ye know what I'm getting at here, doncha?"

"Yes."

"I don't." Rian wanted to hear Barb say it aloud. She pushed the bread and cheese away. "Why does it matter?"

"She's asking me to leave, Rian."

"Politely too, I might add." Barb didn't look thrilled about it, nor did she seem sorry. "I've had it from Seamus, who got back about an hour ago— Ben and Robin have split their men into two forces. One to pursue Matt, who's fled through the Taran Gate with whatever Hilltop Boys remain loyal. Another to raid his home and warehouses. I don't expect 'em back for ages. Now, I'll ask ye missy... please don't make me break me word to... Ben. If ye left of yer own accord, ye'd be sparin' these folks more pain on yer account."

Rian inhaled. "You gave your word to Ben, didn't you? To keep her safe while he went out to do your dirty work for you."

Barb gave her a tight-lipped smile. "I bloody well have, haven't I? She's still breathin'. Moreover, there are good folks in the hall who ain't. What just happened ain't nothin' to what the Southers can muster. Yer too young to realize this, girl, but them Corsairs ain't like Bethonair Knights. Them are *real* soldiers. They've plate armor, mail, and siege weapons— keepin' her here is like wavin' a red flag under a bull's nose. If they coulda been kept in the dark about it, that woulda been one thing, but Matt's fled straight to 'em. He'll be hopin' to bribe yer cousin with yer whereabouts. Rosweal be damned." Rian watched Barb's hand shake a bit against her teacup, a barely discernible tic she was likely unaware of.

She was afraid.

Really afraid.

Rian sat back.

"Ye've never seen a city sacked before, have ye?"

"No, but I'm no dolt. I can guess what happens."

"No," Una interrupted. "What *will* happen. I understand, Mistress Dormer. I do. I'll not ask any of you— any more of you— to endure that on my account. I'll go."

Barb breathed a sigh of relief. "Thank ye, milady. There's a good deal spoken in yer favor. I'll say that. But there's hundreds o'families in this town, despite appearances. They do the best they can. No matter what his lordship asks o'me, I owe me first duty to them."

371

"His *lordship* will be furious about this." Rian snarled. "Una, we're in this together, remember? What about the promise you made him? The one you keep reminding *me* of. You can't go."

"He made a bargain with Barb too, which she must honor because she has no choice. Whereas I have made no such bargain with Barb. Damek will raze this town to the ground if she tries to keep me from him."

"You can't run off on your own without a word. What was the point of all this if you do? Besides, they'll catch you if you run south or east. There's nothing in the west but miles of empty Greensward and barren hills beyond. There's nowhere else *to* go."

Una's answering sigh was half a groan. "I'm aware."

"Then what in the hells are you agreeing to here? Wait for Ben, Una."

"Look," interjected Barb. "I'm not askin' ye to hanker off into the wilderness with naught but yer skin and good intentions to keep ye warm. I ain't so cruel as all that. I know a place ye can go, and I'll send fellas with ye— good fellas I trust. They'll keep ye fed and safe, till yer able to cross with... Ben. Or at least until this first emergency is sorted. I just can't have ye here when they ride in. Ye know I can't. They'll take our protectin' ye as an act o'war. If I can prove ye've been and gone that's another matter. That might buy us a reprieve."

"Una, you can't trust her. She'll have one of her men knife you the minute you're out of town. Worse, she'll tell Ben you left on your own, and hand you over to your cousin for the reward money. Don't do it."

Barb slammed her cup into its saucer, chipping the delicate white porcelain. "I don't appreciate the picture yer attemptin' to paint of me, little lady. I may be an old swindler, but I give me word only rarely, for a reason. If I say she'll come to no harm, she bloody well won't."

"That doesn't mean you can't subtly subvert that word. Work around it in some way as you're doing now, with the promise you made to Ben." Rian laughed dryly. "I know that Una's family is a problem for everyone. Believe me. I've lost both my house and my livelihood to help her."

Fresh guilt flickered over Una's brow. "I'm sorry for it."

"I know you are! It's infuriating, really. I'm here with you because you saved my life, Una. Both of you. I'm here because I understand what's happening is larger than me, you, or Ben. It's bigger than Rosweal, Bethany, or even Tairngare. I'm here because we're all caught up in this together. Bethany will make its war, with or without you. It's just easier with you. Tairngare will have its revolution, with or without you. It's just more convenient if you're a suitable scapegoat. Don't you see? *This isn't about you!* It isn't because of you. *It just is.* If you run away now, that won't stop anyone from dying. You won't guarantee that this city or any other will survive intact. It's war, Una. The more cities the Duch burns, the stronger his message will be in Bri Leith. That's what this is all about. What it's always been about. You're just a pawn and have been since you were born."

Una absorbed every word, silent as a stone well.

Barb cleared her throat. "I won't argue ye don't have a point, missy. Ye do, but yer fergettin' some things in that fine speech. These're folks' lives we're talkin' about here. *Folks I know.* Folks I'm responsible for. Ye may say we have no control over what these fine lords have in store for us, but I'll be damned if I sit back while he slaughters folks I care for to get at her— never mind if it's her fault or not. Now, I could sell her and avoid a fight altogether. I could profit for havin' her in my keepin'. I could do that, and no soldier's boot will cross the Taran Gate again. It's not as if the Tairnganeah have siege weapons at their disposal. I'll wager they learned their lesson here today." Her chuckle was mirthless. "I could sell her, and it will save lives, time, effort, and supplies, for what promises to be a rough starvin' season. By rights, it's what I bloody well *should* do. I'm offerin' ye a compromise. I think, given the state o'me livelihood downstairs, ye'd best accept."

"Una," Rian protested. "Wait for Ben…"

Barb scoffed. "For what? If he was standin' here now, I'd give 'em both the boot without an afterthought. Ben's no fool. Once he realizes what's squatting down the High Road like a fat vulture waitin' to spring, he'll come to the same conclusion."

373

"Why not wait for him, and put the question to him too? We'll leave together, and you'd still get what you want." Rian narrowed her eyes to blue slits. Barb said nothing. "I notice you don't leap to respond. Let me help you. You can't wait because you know he'll have another plan. It'll be something that you won't like, and you'll be forced to accept it. He's the Crown Prince, isn't he? That makes this *his* land, and you *his* vassal. You don't like that, do you? Exiled or not, he's our liege-lord. You'd like to retain command of this situation for as long as you're able. Isn't that right?"

"Rian, calm down." Una swatted her leg.

"I won't! This isn't about Rosweal, or Barb, or you, or anyone else! This is about Bethany, and Aes Sidhe. The only hope any of us have to stop this war before it gets started is to get you to Ben's father. Stick to the plan, Una."

"Now see here, ye mouthy little—" Barb hissed, but Una launched to her feet.

"That's enough! *Siora*. I know what's at stake here. Thank you both very much for your opinions on the matter." She chewed her lower lip. "You're both right, but in the end, neither of you knows my cousin as I do. Damek's not going to bargain with anyone. While it may be true that this war isn't my fault, any more than it is either of yours… it will be me he uses as an excuse to sow the seeds of my father's war. If I'm here, he'll take me if he can, and burn you all out for spite. If I'm not here, and you make it seem as if I escaped from your clutches before I could be traded… it'll go better for all involved. Barb, I accept your terms. May I caution you to take your plans a step further?"

Clearly not expecting Una to acquiesce so easily, Barb stared up at her, mouth slightly agape. "How so?"

"You'll have to tell him where I've gone. You'll have to point him in a reasonable direction, and you'll have to be honest about it. Rian, you don't know him!" She held out a hand to stay the rebuttal burning on Rian's tongue. "He'll do worse than burn this place down if he smells a lie, and I warn you, *he will*. He has a nose for deception."

"If I do that, I'd be breakin' me word to Ben. Ye may not realize this, either o'ye… but we Northers fear the Ard Ri far more'n we dread a Souther army. There's a reason yer Da's family ain't ever won against the Sidhe."

"I've seen Ben fight. I know what you mean, but it's beside the point. He can't fault you for this if it was my idea."

"Una!" Rian smacked her palm against the table.

Barb cocked her head. "Ye'd do that? For us?"

"Damek can't kill me. I can't say the same for any of you. I just need a head start, and hopefully enough distance."

"Oh, it has that. In the hills to the west. A high valley hedged on all sides by the bloody Greensward. He'll waste a day're more searchin' for ye. Even with directions. Used to be my Da's village, afore the war. It's completely overgrown and well hidden. Odds are, Ben finds ye long afore he does."

Rian spread her arms. "Lord Bishop is supposed to believe that you didn't send her there? *Come on*! Una, you have to see how stupid this is."

"It's the only place one could reasonably go from here. I'll tell him... I dunno how many men ye have with ye, nor how long a start ye have. The Greensward grows thick and tall there. In some places, there's not a foot between the trees. I'll send Ben after ye as soon as I'm able, and with luck, ye'll be over that border before the Marshal gets a mile after ye."

"I'll leave immediately. Thank you."

"Wait! Una—"

"Thanks?" Barb's brows knit together. "That's just—"

"Aside from Rian and Ben, that's the most anyone's bothered to offer me these last few weeks. What's more, it's fair. I'll get out of your hair, Mistress Dormer. Remember, give Damek whatever he asks for, within mortal reasoning. If I'm ever set right again," Una paused, a sad acceptance of the immutable in her expression, "I'll see Tairngare grants you whatever contracts you require. I swear it, by the blood of the Ancestor."

Barb held out her hand. Una took it. "It's Barb to ye, milady."

"Una. Please."

Barb clasped Una's hand between both of hers. "I'll tell ye somewhat else. Maybe I do like ye just a bit, after all."

The Everyman

n.e. ꝼ08
28, ꝺor samna
taran hiᵹh road

T he road behind gaped dark and silent as an open tomb. A marching bitterness kissed the earth from above, spinning whirlpools of silver mist through stark trees and searing exposed flesh like acid. It would soon snow. The night air was nearly electric with ozone—a warning all warm-blooded creatures must heed. Drifts could drive upwards of three feet in an hour this far north. No one wanted to be caught in a whiteout without the appropriate gear: fur, gloves, and sealskin boots. A numbing gust burst through the northwest trees and straight into Ben's face. He bit back a sharp curse. Whistling, Robin squinted at the treetops, snapping overhead.

"Don't bode well for us, Ben."

Ben pulled his cloak tight. "Dor Oras is impatient to arrive, it seems."

Gerrod wore a deal less than either of them: only a quilted vest over a long-sleeved woolen tunic, and damp woolen trousers. Ben heard his teeth clacking together, even when he'd stood far down the line.

"Fellas, I hate Matt more'n the rest o'ye combined for what he done to me mam all them years ago… but he ain't worth freezin' to death over." His dark eyes were owlish against his saffron cheeks. "Besides, what're we 'sposed to do about *that*?"

He referred to the Bethonair occupation of Vale, about a mile south. A queer orange halo hovered over the village in stark contrast with the snow-bright sky above. Ben, having commandeered Robin's spyglass, counted some three dozen fires just shy of the low town wall. There were so many tents, they might have been whitecaps on a rolling sea. Ben lost count after he reached sixty. Robin nudged his shoulder.

"How many then?"

"Four hundred, give or take. Who knows how many more are hidden in town, or camped at the southern end of the High Road?"

"Siora," shivered Gerrod with a distinct note of dread.

Robin said, "I think we mighta bitten off a bit more'n we can swallow here, Ben."

"Aye," Gerrod agreed, "a *damn sight* more! The Greenmakers don't have a quarter that number in all o'Rosweal. Matt's done for us all, I say."

"Don't be so bloody dramatic, Gerry. Even if he rode back home on the back of this Souther cunt's saddle... one o'us will do for him. If he don't know it, he will soon enough."

"We don't stand a chance against that, boss."

"Gerry, you're right," said Ben. He compressed the spyglass, then handed it back to Robin. They exchanged a knowing look. "I wouldn't dream of raiding that camp in the night. When they'd least expect it. Just before the first snowstorm of the season."

"I'm not hearin' this. It's bloody *mad*."

"It's an opportunity..."

"Them're mounted knights! They've armor, sabres, and pikes half as long as a man. Ye know who their commander is?"

Robin took a speculative peek through the remaining foliage. "They ain't on them horses now, are they?"

Gerrod closed his eyes, as if in prayer. "Oh, that's *brilliant*. Say we make it out alive, then what? They'll just say, 'ah well, bad luck, fellas', and go home? Yer barkin', both o'ye. This lord," he jerked his chin toward Vale, "is the most lauded commander in the South. Ye hear the things they say about him?"

378

Ben shrugged. "He's a boy. Overeager, arrogant, and, if I'm not mistaken, disobeying orders to march on the North, prematurely."

"Quite a lot of men to capture one girl," Robin added.

"*Indeed.* My guess? Lord Bishop is betting everything he has on this. Donahugh's sole claim to Tairngare runs through Una— paltry though that may be. If Bishop can collect her now, he's in a position to make demands of his uncle."

"That's Heir-Apparent Bishop, to likes o'us."

"He has to take her first." Ben's sneer carved deep.

Gerrod waved his hands over his head. "Makes no bloody difference why he's here. He's *here.* He's got more men, more horses, and better weapons than any o'us."

Ben tapped Nemain's pommel. "Speak for yourself, lad."

"If ye pick a fight with him tonight, he's gonna know why, and where ye came from. Me sisters're only four and six. Remember what men like that do to folks like us."

That gave Ben pause.

Robin shook his head. "Gerry, all the bloody towns along the border are ripe for the pluckin.' Ye see? If we can cut some weight outta his purse, he'll have less to spend on any o'us."

"If I'm right, and he's not sanctioned by the Duch in this matter, then this..." Ben gestured toward the multitudinous campfires, "is likely all he could muster. We break his supply line, and his men will lose enthusiasm."

"Ben, that's *four hunnerd men.* Cavalry. Armor. We're less'n *twenty,* all told. No boots, furs, nothin'. Can't ye see what the sky promises for tomorrow? We ain't been home in near three days."

"Don't ye worry 'bout Barb and the boys, Gerry. They beat 'em back fair."

"Ye don't know that for sure, boss. Even if the Tairnganeah retreated, don't mean *The Hart* is in good shape. We coulda lost heaps of folks in there! Don't ye care?"

Robin's smile faded. "Course I care, but we vowed to bring Matt back to Barb. That's what we're bloody well tryin' to do."

Frustrated, Gerrod tried a different tack. "Ben, yer lady is in there. What if she's been hurt? Siora's sake, what if she's been killed? Or Barb?" He turned back to Robin. "Or anyone else? Don't ye think they need us?"

Ben coughed. "She's not *my* lady. Besides, you've seen what she can do, Gerry. If ever there was a woman that could take care of herself, it's her."

"I won't say she ain't tough... and well, scary—but she ain't immune to steel, is she? Can happen to anyone, no matter how tough they are. Even you." Ben mulled that over. The boy had a point. There was a good chance that they were needed at *The Hart*. They'd been too focused on the task at hand to consider it. A full day's scouting, a second fighting Tairnganeah in the streets, and another in pursuit; they were stretched as thin as they could be. There were no rations left in any of their packs, save the odd flask of uishge. The weather was turning savage, as only Innish weather could. Soon, fatigue would spread through their ranks like the pox. The Greenmakers were hungry, tired, cold, and concerned for their families back home.

Ben could hardly blame them for wanting to leave. Yet if they stayed... they could put a solid brake on Damek Bishop's expeditionary force. A host of this size required a constant stream of wagons loaded with grain, ale, meat, and women. Without them, the Southers would be forced to scavenge for meals and entertainment. While that might be bad for the towns and farmsteads nearby, it would also finish them faster than plague. Soldiers who aren't fed, won't fight. Discipline depended upon order; without a steady supply of food and drink, there could be none.

"Lad's not wrong, Ben," Robin said.

"Not everyone needs to stay."

"That ain't gonna happen."

"Look, it isn't about Gilcannon anymore, is it? I won't ask everyone to stay. Gerry's right about *The Hart*. I didn't get a good look at the place from *Sol's*, but I could tell they'd been through it."

"It ain't a good idea to split our men up. Don't be daft."

"Robin, we may not get another chance."

"O'course we will," he chuckled. "Rosweal's uphill. With the weather, I'd say they might be good and buggered anyway."

Ben cursed. Bishop was so close. Gilcannon too. He didn't like that he was near enough to smell the meat roasting over their fires but lacked the men to relieve them of their comforts. Perhaps if he went alone— slipped past their sentries, and snuck into town from the western rim? Could he not guess which building Bishop had appropriated by the number of guards? Ben knew his own strength. He had no fear of these men. Milesian soldiers, Souther or no, were no match for him in close combat. He'd cut through them like curd.

"I know what yer thinkin,' Ben. So you're aware, *over me own bloated corpse,*" Robin growled. "We stay or leave together. Seein' as I'm the boss round here, yer bound to obey me."

Ben's eyes slivered. "Is that an order?"

"Why shouldn't it be? Ye work for me, *Ben Maeden.*"

Ben thought about knocking the grin off Robin's face. "Robin—"

"Home then, shall we?" Robin ignored him. "Me bollocks have crawled into my arsehole. It's so bloody cold out here. I agree that it should be done, but *not tonight.* We need more men. That's all there is to it. Truth be told, I could do with a hot meal and a bed. So could ye."

"But—"

Robin gripped his shoulder, hard. "Another thing to consider. Barb knows this lot are out here by now. I'll wager she knew afore we did. I love the ole girl more'n me own life, but she do have a way of bendin' her word to suit an occasion, don't she?"

It took a moment, but Ben drew himself up to his full height. "She wouldn't *dare.* Not now."

"Rosweal means more to her than any one o'us, Ben. She'll do whatever she thinks she has to."

⚔ ⚔

Sɴᴏᴡꜰʟᴀᴋᴇs ᴅᴜsᴛᴇᴅ ʜᴇʀ ᴇʏᴇʟᴀsʜᴇs ᴀs Una's small retinue shuffled into the hills beyond the city. A fellow named Keeley took the lead. He

381

was a man of few words. His heavily lined face and gruff demeanor hardly endeared him to either girl. His companion, a boy a few years younger than Rian, guided them along the riverbank, then uphill. The boy had the same hard-eyed focus as his leader. Una supposed the pair might be related but was unable to entice them to confirm or deny the notion. In fact, both males ignored her as much as possible, and deigned to acknowledge her only when she stepped outside the imaginary line they kept in the underbrush. After the riverside, where sluggish currents churned swollen brown headwaters, the group hooked left into the forest. From there they climbed up, up, and up. Weighed down by a pack she insisted on bringing, Rian huffed behind Una, her cornflower eyes forward, watchful. Una didn't like Rian being here. What Una felt sure was about to happen would only be another trial for the girl to needlessly endure. Though, the look on Rian's face said she didn't need to be told what was afoot. Una vowed: she'd repay the girl for her unwavering loyalty if it was the last thing she did.

The moment she'd clasped hands with Barb, Una knew the truth. There was no deserted village in the hills. Merely a ring of shacks, some ten miles out of town; a hovel in which Una was to be kept until the Bethonair threat passed. She imagined, once they arrived at their destination, the boy would be sent back to ascertain the state of things in town. If all went well, Una could expect him to lead her cousin right to her for the reward money. If it went badly, he would return with more men... to kill her. If she'd refused Barb, as Rian advised (wisdom, under different circumstances), Una wouldn't have survived the night. She saw Barb's intentions in her Spark, clear as day. It wasn't out of malice or spite that Barb intended her violence, either. Barb felt she had no choice.

When she'd taken Una's hand, Barb held a clear memory of the North after Dumnain in her mind's eye— on purpose, no doubt. Una smelt the smoke, watched the bodies piled high along the roadside. She heard Barb's keening for her younger sisters. Spite hadn't encouraged this betrayal. Barb was *afraid* of Una, and through her, the war brewing outside her gates. The lives she might be forced to waste in her defense. Una was angry (who wouldn't be?) but that didn't mean she couldn't

382

understand the old bawd's motivation. Whether that made the pill more or less bitter to swallow, Una couldn't say. Barb was responsible for hundreds of people. She wouldn't risk her friends and neighbors for one girl, no matter who she was. The moment Ben left them in *The Hart*, Barb had laid her plans. She would doubtless concoct some story about Una taking it upon herself to flee into the wild, as Rian predicted. That would prove a very convenient lie when Bethonair cavalry followed Barb's breadcrumbs in the snow. Better still if Una was never heard from again. Barb was a shrewd woman, and no mistake.

While Una climbed, she felt eyes on her from the trees. How many men had Barb sent to ensure the girls couldn't escape? Una had no idea. It didn't matter. She would fight them if she had to. She'd be damned if she was going to let Rian die out here, in the middle of nowhere. The prickling, eerie sensation of being watched from an unknown vantage was only trumped by the urgent holes Rian bored into her back. She had something to tell Una, but they couldn't stop to converse and let their captors know they were on to them. Nor could Una be sure they could fight off a number of professional woodsmen, so exposed. She was waiting for the right moment. A hairpin turn, perhaps? An escarpment or perilous drop? She'd seize the first opportunity she could muster. She feared for Rian, but perhaps selfishly, was glad for the extra pair of hands. They needed each other now if they were to get out of this in one piece.

Over her shoulder, she sent the younger girl the briefest of apologetic smiles. Rian returned something more. Something important. Una shook her head. *Not now*, she signaled with her eyes. *Soon.* They wound up, rise after rise. Trees grew thick and dense here, leaving spare room between their twisting roots to navigate. Rian stumbled more than once. Their rigid guides showed little interest in slowing down to accommodate her, either. Una decided if she was only able to kill two of their captors, it would be those two— for their cruelty.

Their guides plowed ahead, never stopping, never slowing. Aside from the occasional turn to check the girls' positions, neither man showed any concern for Una or Rian at all. Several times, Una thought about feigning an injury of some sort, just to see what they'd do. If they made her angry enough, she might do it for the sheer pleasure it would give her to make them acknowledge one of them for two bloody seconds. *Bastards.*

Finally, the invisible trail they were on curved into the mountain, which placed a sheer granite wall on their left and a deep ravine on their right. All but the tips of the mightiest conifers were hidden from view in the fog. Ahead, the wall ascended a few hundred feet, then cut around the cliff face in a sharp bow. Whoever was following them would have to take a higher path toward the summit or risk exposure. Una had a pretty good idea they'd been dogging their steps from the south side of the Greensward, which would place the bulk of the hill between them. Once this ugly business was over, she and Rian could make it back to the river in under an hour. With luck, their pursuers might have gone too far out of the way to catch them up. Praying to Siora to lend her strength, she decided this was as good a place as any.

They neared the dome, and wet granite scraped at Una's boots. She risked another glance over her shoulder to find Rian's tiny white fist wrapped around the hilt of a dagger. Una took a deep breath and cracked her fingers. The boy was nearest. His hand traced the cliff face for support while his feet danced up the trail as if by thought alone. He'd been here before. That could mean Ben had too... in case they failed to escape now. Una shook herself. She'd got them into this mess. She would get them out, one way or the other.

The trail thinned, and the cliff face loomed overhead. Una and Rian mimicked their guides, sliding along with their backs against the wet stone. This was challenging, when one considered the drop twelve inches to their north. Rian made a startled sound when the toe of her bad foot slid too near the ledge. Una tugged her into the wall by her tunic. The boy glanced at them, dispassionately as ever. Una ground her teeth. If either girl fell, it would likely save their guides the trouble of killing one or both of them later. With renewed determination, she pulled herself along the wall, and seethed. The boy's fingertips splayed against the face for balance. All Una had to do was reach. She stretched out her arm until the tip of her nail scraped against his knuckle. Just a bit further... and she would have him. All of a sudden, he came to an abrupt stop. Una faltered, and almost lost her footing. Rian cried out, and clawed Una upright by her cloak. Both gasping, Una and Rian clung to the cliff face for dear life, arms akimbo.

The boy bore a blade in his own hand by the time the girls righted themselves, but he wasn't looking at them. A few paces up the trail, Keeley stared down a dark-hooded figure who'd simply appeared around the next bend. Una couldn't get a good look at him from her vantage, but neither of their guides were pleased. The figure raised his hand, as if in harmless greeting. Keeley growled a curt response.

"What's happening?" Rian whispered into her back.

"Dunno. There's someone ahead of us."

"*Up here?* This isn't even a trail," Rian swallowed, her breathing ragged. "Maybe it's one of the others, come 'round the opposite side?"

"I don't think they know him. They've got their daggers out."

"Who then?"

Una couldn't say, for the man had materialized out of the clouds. One minute there'd been nothing ahead but rock, moss, and treetops... next, he was there. Keeley shouted something unintelligible. The figure didn't budge. Though the newcomer's face was largely concealed within his cowl, Una could just make out a glint of white when he smiled. Her heart leapt into her throat on a brief, piercing hope. That smile reminded her of Ben, however unlikely that might be. As soon as that hope arose, she shoved it down deep. Ben wasn't here. Whoever this was, he wasn't here to help them. She and Rian were on their own. Slowly, so as not to rouse the boy's notice, she nudged Rian backward. "Una, I have to tell you—"

"Later."

Rian's hand squeezed hers. "I left word. Ben will come."

Not soon enough.

"That's good, Rian. Stay here."

"Don't. You don't have to."

"You know I do."

Rian slid the dagger into Una's nearest hand. "Be careful."

Una slunk cautiously into position behind the boy. "What's the hold-up?" she asked him. He jumped to find her so close. Keeley's skinny back straightened as he ordered the figure out of their way. The mysterious stranger held both hands aloft, as if to say, 'look how harmless I am, friend.'

"Some wild man, or other," the boy grunted. "Don't worry, milady. Keeley can handle him."

Una rested her hand casually over his. He scarcely had time to suck in a surprised breath. "Oh, I'm not worried a bit." She unfurled her Spark like a net. The boy gave a soft helpless sort of squeak. His dagger scraped against stone as he slid nose-first down the wall. Una tried to catch him, and the noise snapped Keeley's head around like a top.

"Breccan!" Keeley's grey-brown eyes burned with fear. "What have ye done to Breccan, ye feckin' *witch*?"

"Rian, get back!" Una steadied herself against the rock. Keeley didn't even stop to examine the boy. He leapt over Breccan's prone form to slash at her from higher ground. Backpedaling with caution, Una managed to put a wide boulder between them. Cursing, he climbed over the impediment with the ease of a mountain goat. His next swing opened a four-inch seam along her exposed forearm. Hissing, she dropped onto her backside. Her other arm dangled over the infinite. Vertigo struck with sickening urgency.

"Una!" Rian cried, from further down.

"Rian, get away!" Una called as Keeley hunched over her, his dagger high. Kicking out at his legs, she braced herself against the boulder. He came at her twice as quick as the last time. He was certainly more experienced with the slim Eirean dagger than she was. She parried one blow, then another, but jerked to a halt when her heel clipped the edge. If she got up now, she'd fall. He was on her again, shoving his dagger into hers until it scraped the underside of her chin. With bared teeth, she pushed up with all her might. For a sack of bones and loose skin, Keeley was stronger than she'd hoped he'd be. If her arm gave out, he'd drive his knife straight through her clavicle. His hot, fetid breath moistened her cheeks.

"I'll kill ye, ye Siorai bitch!"

Gagging, she rammed her free heel into his spine. Her attack accomplished nothing. Sharp metal dipped through the first two layers of her skin, and she cried out. Summoning every ounce of Spark she could spare, she sent a current of electricity down the shaft of her dagger where it connected with his. The resulting jolt caused him to drop his blade in howling pain. He rolled aside to clasp at his arm. Una's boot slammed into his knee. Keeley's pathetic scream availed him nothing. He tumbled over the side of the mountain, into the ravine. Out of breath and bleeding, Una bit her lip, and pulled herself up the wall. Rian stood a mere four or five feet down the trail, her face ashen, her eyes large white bulbs.

"Una, look out!"

Una hadn't heard him approach over the moss-ridden shale. Like a puff of smoke, the hooded figure was suddenly there, standing beside her with a curious tilt to his head. Rearing back, she reached for a dagger which wasn't there. The toe of her boot ground against its pommel, where it lay uselessly against the ledge. She cursed.

"Stay back!" She couldn't fight fairly this time. The newcomer was tall. Taller than any man she'd ever laid eyes on before, save Ben. Though his clothing was shapeless, rumpled, and clearly worn, she could tell he was a bit broader through the shoulder too. Without a weapon, Una could only hope he made the mistake of laying hands on her bare skin. Otherwise, he could snap her wrists like kindling, and toss her from this precipice like a ragdoll.

"No need to be afraid, little one." Unbidden, his voice summoned all sorts of irrational, unrelated images to her mind: the far-away rumble of thunder in the rush of an oncoming summer storm; waves lapping at her favorite childhood beach in Bethany; her mother's quiet laughter; the bells chiming in her grandmother's chapel; her first kiss— and the wind billowing over the silk curtains in Una's bedchamber. The small hairs on Una's arms and nape stood on end. Why did she recall such things at a time like this? He inched closer. Had she ever seen teeth so white? So neat? "I mean you no harm. I vow it."

Rian was only half a step behind her now. She clutched at Una's wrist. "*Get back!*" she spat. "You're not welcome here."

Una allowed herself to be handled. She puzzled over the power in the figure's voice. Why did it summon the most comforting images she could conceive of? She felt she could wear that voice like a cloak— bundle up in it, as if it were the safest, warmest, most beloved garment she owned...

"Am I not?" he asked, pushing his cowl back. A middle-aged man, with a broad plain face, smiled back. He was so ordinary, so positively *average*, without a single memorable feature to focus on. Una blinked, and the spell evaporated in an instant. "I only meant to see if ye two were all right," his voice now bland as unsalted butter.

Had she imagined it? Blood loss, maybe? Her arm *was* bleeding rather badly. Rian forced herself ahead of Una, using her lithe form as a bony shield.

"What do you want?"

Una shook herself.

"Rian, there's no need."

"*Shut up, Una!*"

The man frowned, with a face like a whipped puppy. "I came to help ye. That's all."

"I don't believe you!"

"Rian, what is the matter with you?" She'd never seen Rian so disturbed before, and they'd almost been eaten twice in one week. The man seemed unperturbed, if slightly crestfallen. He was just a woodsman. Even the bow slung across his back proclaimed his ineffectual normalcy. He must have been as stunned by the outrageous scene he'd wandered into as Keeley had been to discover him around that bend. After a lengthy pause, the newcomer laughed. This time, a ghost of Una's first impression shone through his ever-so-ordinary veneer. Una grabbed Rian's arm, without thinking.

His smile unwavering, he tilted his head at something above them, as if tracking sounds neither of them could hear. Dull brown eyes fell upon them with a sardonic gleam.

"Very well." That voice again! Una shuddered against the onslaught of images that raced through her mind. "Seems we've no time for games, fun though they might have been." His laughter was like the trickle of water in a fountain or the chill of snow on the tip of her tongue. With a gasp, she sent a short burst of Spark into her blood to purge these illogical thoughts.

How was he doing this?

"I *am* here to help. I don't require your belief, or permission. You've many enemies up there," he gestured to the ridge above. "They've heard Keeley's shouts. Even if you make it back to the river, they will follow."

"Why would you want to help us?"

"Because my nephew would want me to."

Una opened her mouth to speak, but Rian's elbow jabbed into her ribs. Una's jaws snapped shut over an 'oof.'

"You won't make it to safety before they're upon you," he added. "I think you are aware what they mean to do with you both? Why kill that knobby old man, otherwise?"

Rian said something in a language Una would only recognize as *Ealig* much later. Its musical quality was simultaneously soothing and alarming. The tall stranger answered in kind, and Una felt the muscles in Rian's back relax slightly under her hand. The scuffing along the upper portion of the trail grew louder.

"Well?" he asked, adjusting a dusty, moth-eaten sleeve as if it were the most delicate lace. "Are you satisfied, or will I have to take you out of harm's way by force?"

Una looked from one to the other, completely befuddled. Rocks slid down the trail from on high. Rian shook her once, hard. "Una!"

"*Yes?*"

All at once, the world rushed by her ears, as if drained through a funnel centered in the core of her brain. Falling upward, racing down, spinning through… all these feelings occurred to her at once. She felt her spine lengthen and shorten; her skin stretched taut to tearing, then clenched tight again, as if rolled into a wad. Her bones disconnected, scrambled, then rearranged themselves of their own accord. She heard

Rian scream from a great distance, its timbre as deafening as it was difficult to discern. Then... the vortex abruptly abated. Una skidded over a grooved wooden floor. Her head struck a wall with a hard crack. The smell of pine was ubiquitous, like the sawdust rushes swept into her open mouth. With a groan, Una choked the offensive offal out of her throat. Rian lay on her back beside her, huffing up at the bare timbers on the ceiling. Una tried to still her roiling guts when the stranger's bland face bent down to grin at them.

"There now! All better, yes?"

Una hacked up another mouthful of dirt, as he stood framed in the open door of this seemingly abandoned cabin. "Who are you?"

His grin was swift and dull as dry toast. "Give it time. I'm sure it'll come to you."

TURNCOAT

n.e. ʃ08
28, ðor samna
vale

D amek leaned against the slanted window box, his arms crossed over his chest. Outside, snow fell in a steady rhythm. He'd taken to wearing his cloak at all hours of the day. If it didn't warm up come morning, he'd also start sleeping in it. He had many reasons to dislike the North, but her early, ruthless winters were perhaps his foremost complaint. Frowning, he watched millions of swirling specks dance on the wind. If this got any worse, he would be forced to march on Rosweal a day earlier than planned. Damek had business in Rosweal. Weather be damned.

Martin caught his eye over their informant's bowed head. Gilcannon blubbered nonsensically. Dawes' expert fists had left huge red welts on the planes of his formerly pleasant face. Damek had very little use for men of this sort, especially one as arrogant as this preening little prick. The bootlegger had tried to make demands of *him* as if the Lord of Clare was some lice-ridden street creature awaiting orders. Martin begged permission to kill the fool for his arrogance hours ago, but Damek thought better of it. The man may be a jumped-up pimp looking to profit at their expense, but he knew things they needed to know. Gilcannon wheezed, and a blood bubble ballooned from one of his nostrils. Damek watched his reflection twitch in the windowpane.

"This would be much simpler if you'd tell me what I wish to know."

Gilcannon flinched from Damek's clipped voice. A thick trickle of pink spittle swung from his trembling chin. "I told ye everything already, yer lordship."

Martin reclined beside him with his legs thrown over a nearby chair. He prodded the bound informant with the toe of his boot. "The world hates a liar, Master Gilcannon."

Dawes delivered another swift open-handed cuff that snapped Gilcannon's head sideways. He sniveled like a whipped girl. Damek waved Dawes away.

"You expect me to believe that you've known this man for over ten years, and you can't properly describe him? That's rather remarkable, I think."

Gilcannon sucked a long stream of air through his open, seeping mouth. "I ain't never met him afore today. Just know of him, don't I? He's Gramble's boy. I told ye what I saw," he shuddered. "What more do ye want from me?"

"You watch your mouth," growled Martin. "Your life's worth less than a wet fart to us, Gilcannon. You'd do well to remember to whom you are speaking."

"I swear it on me mam's teats. I only saw him for a moment. He *killed* me friends, I think. *All o'em.*"

Damek faced the scene again, arms still crossed. "Did you notice anything about him that struck you as strange— aside from this 'bloodthirsty leer,' you went on about at length? You said he was tall? How tall? You said he was fair-haired? Brown, blond? Give us something to go on."

"He's t... taller than most men by a mile, I'd say. Taller than ye, milord."

"And me?" Martin, the bloody tower, pointed a thumb at his own throat. "He's taller than me?"

"Aye, sir. A bit."

Damek circled Gilcannon's chair. "Is his hair a blond so pale, it looks like spun spider-silk, or merely yellow, like hay?"

"Milord, some water, *please*."

"Answer the question."

"Seemed common to me, sir."

Damek paused, mid-circuit. The floor was smeared red with blood and piss. He was careful to avoid the effluent stream. "That doesn't fit the picture Wallace has painted."

"No, My Lord," agreed Martin. "But as I said before, these faeries can be quite formidable. Perhaps he is half-breed after all?"

Ignoring that, Damek focused on Gilcannon's quivering face. "You said he had a sword. What did it look like?"

"Water..."

Damek waved Dawes over with the dipper. When the slurping and racking coughs ceased, Damek leaned in close. "Now, tell me about the sword."

"It were a big bastard, milord. Not like the ones ye all carry nor what we had in the war— beggin' yer pardon. 'Twas a broadsword, I think, but it were different like..." he struggled to find the right words. "Thinner and curved a bit at the point. Sidhe-make, maybe. Never seen one quite like it afore."

"Different how?"

"Well, it were a fine piece, but... it looked old. Worn and beaten, like. 'Cept for the pommel."

"What do you mean? A gem or device of some sort?"

He shook his head. "An animal. A deer, I think. I weren't close enough to get a good look afore I ran. Solid silver too, I 'member that. All the way down the handle, to the guards."

"Could it have been a stag?" Damek held his breath.

"Aye, it coulda been that, yeah."

Martin slid his feet under him, bracing his elbows against his knees. "My Lord, that doesn't mean anything. He could have stolen the sword or bought it. A number of explanations are possible."

"Too much is adding up to the same conclusion, Martin. Our man is a Dannan lord." Damek pinched the bridge of his nose to still the headache brewing behind his eyes.

"You don't know that."

Damek snorted, "A silver stag for a pommel?"

"He could be a thief, a collector, or a wealthy faerie. There are many possibilities. You heard the pimp's description. You're jumping to conclusions again."

"We all saw what he did to those beasts."

"I'll not argue that he has training. Doesn't make him Sidhe, and certainly doesn't make him a lord."

"He's Sidhe, Martin. *I can feel it.* Our men are some of the best-trained soldiers in the world, but I doubt an entire contingent could have killed one of those creatures as easily as Una's mysterious savior killed *two*. Three arrows and twelve steps— that's all it took. He's carrying a Dannan longsword with an Adair device at the pommel."

"My Lord, don't you think we should—"

"Martin, follow me." Damek didn't wait for Martin to get up. He strode into the hall and waited at the upstairs landing. Scowling, he observed his officers in the Greatroom below. Busy drinking, eating, and carousing— they'd demolished Vale's winter stores in only three days. Twice now, Damek had sent raiding parties into neighboring villages to replenish their dwindling supplies, an order he would likely have to repeat tomorrow. Armies were never self-contained for long. Men signed up to plunder. They may soldier for whichever lord swore to feed and house them, but without swift reward, that lord was often hostage to their whims.

Point in fact: the sight Damek beheld downstairs. Here was one act of disobedience that spelled trouble; however he reacted to it. Once boredom set in, insubordination was never far behind. What few prostitutes the farming hamlet boasted were here now, entertaining his officers against his express command. Worse, not all of the women he saw here tonight were professionals. One of them was the Headman's daughter. Damek's jaw set when he heard Martin's step behind him.

"Who allowed them to take these girls out of confinement?"

He heard the air whistle through Martin's nose. "I did, My Lord. They were making trouble in the farms again. Two families done to

394

death for ale and women. I had to string up four good men, including two officers."

"Why wasn't this information relayed to me immediately?"

"You have many concerns to trouble you just now, My Lord. It's my duty as Commander to manage the troops. I made sure only women who volunteered were taken."

"And the ale?"

"That too."

"I don't like it, Martin."

"I knew you wouldn't, but it's this, or I hang more of them tomorrow. They're bored. No damned good ever came from armed men who're idle."

Damek gripped the railing. "That one there," he nodded at the girl in the corner with Killian and his friends. She was pushed, pulled, and prodded from nearly every direction. Damek could see the tears on her cheeks from here. "She's the Headman's get. She can't be more than fifteen. I want her out of here, Martin. Now."

"The Headman's dead, My Lord. Not to put too fine a point on it, but you're the one fucking his widow in their marriage bed every night." Martin clapped a hand on his shoulder. "The girl was given ten silver stags, which she accepted eagerly. That's more coin than she might earn in three years otherwise. Perhaps when we leave, they'll have a new Headwoman?"

"I'm not laughing, Martin."

"The lads may be loyal to you, Damek, but they didn't ride north to sit in camp and make love to their fists. They came to raid. They know the Duch hasn't sanctioned this. No reinforcements will be marching up from Ten Bells, either. These boys are all you have. Let them have their fun, or I swear they'll take it, with or without your permission."

Damek considered the scene before him with a curl in his lip. "We need to get on with it. Every rape and every farm they burn for coppers reflects upon me, Martin. No more paying local girls to whore for them either. I mean it. Tonight's concession is the last I'll make. They'll save it for Rosweal or hang by the roadside, *sans cocks*. Their choice."

"As you will, Lord Bishop," Martin sighed. "Better a drunken fumble than a bloody struggle, I always say. It's a long, cold slog back home, isn't it? Just remember, keepin' these boys happy is your responsibility."

Damek cursed. Bloody savages, the lot. He'd lost more decent fighters to mischief on campaign than flux or combat combined. "Is it true that Sidhe armies don't raid or rape?"

"I hear they raid each other's *raths* in Aes Sidhe twice a year for a laugh. On a march, however, they don't rape or pillage, and they never kill unless ordered. Bastards have steel in their blood, you ask me."

"No finer fighters in the world, I'm told."

Martin raised his brows high. "Aye. If our men had half their patience and skill, we'd give His Majesty real cause for concern."

"Alas, we do not," Damek gestured to the scene below. "If only I knew their secret."

"Immortality, My Lord. I assume patience of that nature can only be earned. Neithana, for example, is the pursuit of many lifetimes."

"I know. The Adair is a master."

"*Was*," Martin corrected.

"It's him, Martin. I know it's him."

"No, you don't."

"I've seen that sword before. It's emblazoned in the glass over my uncle's dais. An elven longsword: four feet long, curved at the tip, and crowned with a leaping silver stag. The man wielding it was nearly seven feet tall. He was said to cut through men as the wind cleaves waves."

"He wasn't the only Dannan with a sword like that. I've seen others. His red-haired cousin, for one, and their champion Fionn. That pretty bastard carried one almost six feet long."

"You're making my point for me. It's a Dannan sword— an *Adair* sword. The Bolg don't carry them, and Northers could never afford one."

"My Lord, we don't know—"

"A *silver stag* for a pommel, Martin."

"It could have been stolen. It could have been made to mimic the others. Don't shake your head. You know it's possible."

396

"Stolen from an Adair lord? Not likely. Purchased? A forgery? *No*. I don't believe any of that. You saw for yourself. There's no way someone just happens to discover a talent for swinging around a thirty-pound longsword. He's the Adair, or I'm buggered. I grew up listening to nothing but tales of his sack of Bethany. Of what he did to my grand-uncle Kevin and the defeats he dealt his predecessors. I've always wanted to see him fight. The man's a legend."

"All right then, My Lord. For whatever unholy reason, if Kaer Yin Adair is alive and seeks to help your cousin across the river to his father, why? That's the last question I'll ask you. Why would he fake his own death, hide in Northern Eire as a lowly woodsman, and creep around rescuing damsels by accident?"

"You said it yourself: 'by accident.' I don't think he planned any of this. As Cunningham said, Una wasn't his objective from the first. The Crown Prince did some very naughty things at Dumnain, didn't he? I'll bet he means to use her to barter his return. He must have taken her to Rosweal to buy himself time to procure a warrant."

"There's still a chance it isn't him."

Damek didn't belabor the point. They would discover the truth in due course. He said, "Anyway, we've gathered all the intelligence we're going to. Rosweal's just ejected a host of Tairnganeah from their walls," he returned Martin's barking laugh, "and I'm sure they're preparing for us next."

"A fat lot of good it'll do them. Our men are so pent-up that they could chew their way through the walls. When do we march?"

"Dawn. We'll discuss tactics in the morning, but I want it finished by sunrise the following day. We've been here too long, as it is."

"Very good, My Lord. What do you want me to do with the bootlegger?"

"You can make him a nice home somewhere along the baggage train. If Rosweal decides to negotiate for Una, we may need him. I'll be in my quarters. Any man who disturbs me will regret it."

"Aye, My Lord," Martin smirked. "Understood."

THE HEADMAN'S WIFE WAS FAR too young for the mealy old miser Damek had cut down days before. It took his men less than a half-hour to sack the village, all told. By the end of the day, the majority of Vale's men were either dead or imprisoned, and the women were confined to the Millhouse under guard. The Headman's wife proved most eager to co-operate with him. He was hardly one to deny an attractive woman the occasional parlay. Damek was pleased to note she didn't bemoan her newfound widowhood, either. With his hands full of her rich brown hair, he lay back against the headboard while she went to work against his pelvic bone. Her tongue slipped out to test his length, and he sighed. Things were just getting interesting when a delicate cough broke his concentration. His eyes flew open. A dark cowled figure stood in the shadows of the farthest corner of the room. In the dim lantern light, Aoife's pale bronze skin gleamed copper. Her eyes, however, glowed a murderous violet.

Sitting up with a start, he shoved the widow from the bed. She tumbled to the wooden floor, a screeching tangle of sheets and flailing limbs.

"Get out," he snapped. "Tell no one what you've seen, or I'll kill you. Do you understand?"

She bobbed her head and scrambled from the room with the ghost of her dignity held before her ashen face. Damek swiftly drew the coverlet over his nudity. With a sneer, Aoife pulled her hood back.

"I should've let you finish, Lord Bishop. I would've liked to see that girl's blood mingle with your fluids."

"Too late for you to feign jealousy now, cousin."

Aoife manufactured a pretty pout and ran her fingers along the furs at the edge of his mattress. "Are you still angry about your little heretic?"

"I need her more than I need you."

"That so?" She unbuttoned her cloak, revealing the simple white robes she wore beneath. Her hair, a midnight mass of glossy black waves, had been clumsily shorn to the tips of her delicate ears. Damek hated seeing her in this Siorai getup, could never get used to it. Forcing a starling to waddle with chickens was cruel. Though, he refused to be swayed by her distracting beauty. She sat at the end of the bed and folded her hands demurely in her lap. "Who'll make you King of Eire if not me?"

"You betrayed me. I should kill you."

Her laugh was like a brush of velvet over his chest. "I didn't betray you, Damek. Vanna Nema gave an order, and I had no choice but to obey. You know that. She holds my geis, as she will one day hold yours."

"*Never.* I'll never swear to that manipulative old hag."

Aoife pursed her lips. "You speak so of your grandmother?"

"I'm not her puppet, nor her plaything. If she desires the house of Donahugh under Armagh's rule, she will cease dangling legitimacy before my nose like a carrot. Una is *mine.* An attempt upon her life is an affront to me."

"That girl is worthless, Damek. She's the heretic spawn of a spent lineage. Her own family has given her up for dead. The Duch's barons didn't love her mother enough to stop Patrick from killing her, and they won't lift a finger to see her daughter crowned Duchess. You don't need her. Our grandmother has striven all your life to ensure that Tairngare is divided and weak. The time to strike is nigh. Be patient, my love."

He leaned toward her, drawing his legs up under the coverlet. "You don't understand a gods-damned thing, do you? The barons may not love her, but they'll fight for her because she holds the right bloody *name.* You might get half of Tairngare to consume itself against the Moura, but the other half— indeed, the whole fucking North— will back Drem if it comes to civil war. You may take the city, but you'll lose Tara, Ten Bells, and all the towns east of the Shannon. If by some miracle I'm wrong... you'll never hold them. Names have meaning. The old alliances have meaning. Una has the name Aoife. Both names. Patrick didn't marry her mother for her cooking."

"*Might* has meaning. How do you imagine these grand names of yours ever managed to craft those alliances in the first place? Not by standing in a field, with only their banners to declare their intentions." She tucked her head in the crook of her arm to watch him. "They took their alliances at the point of a sword. Forged those names through blood and cunning."

"You've been peddling this old chestnut for so long; the tree should be twenty feet tall by now." He rolled his eyes.

"The Bolg will come, Damek. You're Falan Mac Nemed's son."

"I don't need them. I'll have Una Donahugh." He made sure she couldn't miss the deadly sincerity in his eyes. "Next time one of you makes an attempt on her life, I'll take it personally. I don't intend to conquer here for Liadan's pleasure. I mean to rule, and rule well."

Aoife flounced onto her back. "You just want to fuck her."

"That's not your business."

"Isn't it? I would make a much better queen than that dwarf. Have you seen her once in all these years? She's not as beautiful as everyone says she is. She's too masculine, too introverted, and too short. Besides, she isn't Fir Bolg. Our lowest serving women outshine her in every way. Wouldn't you rather have a Bolg queen, Your Grace?"

Damek gave her a knowing smile. He slid down the coverlet on his elbows until his face hovered over hers and drew her full red mouth close. "You'd make a beautiful queen, cousin. Though, you're not free to entice me. Nor do I think I'd enjoy having my throat cut in my sleep."

"Wait for me. I won't belong to Nema forever, Damek."

"I believe it," he smiled and crushed his mouth to hers. Her fingers wound into the hair at his nape. He forgot how angry he was with her for some time. Moaning into his mouth, she rolled atop him. Any further thoughts he might have had departed like vapor. Lifting the hem of her robe, he pressed himself upward. Her skin felt like heated silk against his. He was partway inside of her when she broke off with a gasp. "What?" he blinked.

"I almost forgot to tell you what I came to say!"

His fingers splayed over her bare round hips. The damp hollow between her thighs beckoned. "It can wait."

"No, it can't. Something... odd has happened. Your precious princess has got herself a very interesting ally. I'm not sure how, exactly."

Damek's mood clouded. He bucked her off his lap.

"You already know she isn't alone?"

"Who is he?"

400

"Someone who should be dead."

"Stop playing games, Aoife."

She snickered. "You can't imagine. I saw him myself. Sudden as thunder, there he was: silver hair swirling in the wind. To think of it gives me shivers!"

"So, it is him— the Adair?"

She smacked his arm playfully. "You did know! How clever of you."

"Don't patronize me, Aoife. I thought he was dead."

"After what he did to those villagers, we all thought Bov Dearg slew him upon the tor. They even burned his effigy," she shook her head. "He shouldn't be alive, but he is. I saw him, plain as I'm seeing you now. Gods, what a sight. He's so beautiful. It's almost terrible. Well, I suppose all the bloody Dannans are beautiful if you've a taste for bloodless ferocity."

"He protected Una?"

"What is it about that girl, Damek? She's some kind of trophy, always waiting for the next hand to hold her. It's pathetic."

"You're trying to kill her. In a way, I owe him a debt."

"This is worse for you, Damek dear. If Midhir's son means to keep her, all of our plans will have to be amended. No King of Eire can exist so long as the Prince of Innisfail lives. Surely you know that?"

He did. Only too well. "I have them cornered in Rosweal. I don't think he can cross without a warrant for her. I believe he's playing for time."

"No. I know what he's planning to do. If he's not dead, he can't cross the border."

"A geis?"

She shrugged. "Why else would he stay in this impoverished wasteland? A prince of the Tuatha De Dannan? He's been exiled. I can feel it."

"He must have an ogham charm." Damek toyed with the cool sliver of rubbed quartz at his own throat. "Our captive said he was abnormally tall but unremarkable, with hay blond hair and rough features."

"Not when I saw him, *trust me.*"

Damek ignored this paltry attempt to induce him to jealousy. "He's going by the name 'Ben Maeden,' according to Gilcannon."

"Who's this?"

"A base flesh peddler who incited a trade war between the guilds in Rosweal. Thought he could use me to further his own ends."

"More fool he."

"Do you think he means to pass her off at the border? He could be waiting for someone. A messenger from Bri Leith, or a proxy perhaps?"

"No. What good is a trophy if you can't carry it home yourself? I believe he means to break his geis. All Sidhe have the right to challenge their fates, but some challenges are unequal, even to our gifts."

"What does that mean?"

Aoife propped her head on her elbow, squeezing her warmth into his side. Her eyes were luminous. "There are dread creatures between this plane and the *Oiche Ar Fad*, Damek. You know that well enough. One guards the gates of Aes Sidhe and rules the waterways between realms."

Damek's breath hitched. "Pooka? Gods... they can't be killed." He repressed a shudder. Pooka were shape-shifting monsters from the darkest tales. They assumed the guise of whatever the victim most longed for or feared.

"They can, but only once a year, when the veil thins between realms." She traced little circles on the flesh of his stomach with her fingernail.

"On Samhain, you mean? That's less than three days from now. That doesn't give me much time. If he kills that thing, he'll spirit Una over the border." His stomach knotted in anxious fear... *never to be seen again.*

"Don't be so sure. There is a good chance the pooka will destroy him. Kaer Yin must be desperate for an opportunity to return to his father's good graces. Whoever has the girl holds Eire— as you said. Midhir will reward his errant son for risking so much to avoid another war. That must be his motivation."

Damek scrubbed his face with his open palms and groaned through his fingers. "That *must* not happen."

"Relax," her lips brushed his ribs. "I'm here to help you."

He stared at the top of her head; eyes narrowed to slits. He didn't need to guess that this was part of some grander scheme to eliminate Una before she made it to Aes Sidhe. The destruction of an old enemy

402

before he could return to power was surely an added perk. Damek wasn't a child. He couldn't trust Aoife, and he certainly couldn't trust Vanna Nema. Nema would use him for as long as he served a purpose. When she could find no longer find one, she would eliminate him. This had been the fate of uncounted illegitimate children descended from her rapacious bloodline: pawns, all. He and Aoife were no exception. Though, of the two of them, Damek was the only one who understood this, deep down. Aoife believed in Nema. One day, it would be the death of her.

"Stop. I am no longer in the mood."

Her mouth closed over him, and he gritted his teeth. She smiled on her way back up. "You lie. You must be disappointed I scared off your little conquest."

His smile was cold. "*Not at all*. I'll save it for my wedding night."

She raked her sharp nails over his thigh on her way off the bed, bringing a triumphant chuckle to his throat. "You've become a bore, Damek. I wonder if you realize?"

"I don't care." He stood up and padded to the Headman's wardrobe which held his clothing and boots. On the chair beside it lay his cuirass, mail, and fox-lined cloak. He tugged on his leggings and trousers first, so there could be no confusing his intentions. "I have much to do, Aoife. Unless you have something useful to offer, I suggest you leave before Martin sees you. He's never killed a woman before. In your case, I imagine he'd make an exception."

"I'm not your servant, Damek," she purred. "I came to warn you about the Crown Prince, not to help you trap your little Milesian cousin into matrimony. The prince must be destroyed. I'll do it myself, if I must."

Damek gave her a crooked grin. "Will it be so simple?"

"You may make your jokes, but he is the most celebrated swordsman in Innisfail. He's not a foe to take lightly."

He knew that too. For Damek, who was covetous of the title, Aoife's barb had the opposite effect from the one she desired. A wide grin tugged both of his ears up high. "I can't wait to meet him."

403

LESSER EVIL

A s soon as the Greenmakers crossed the Taran Gate, they were
called upon to alert every person in the slums of the approaching
army. The south-facing neighborhood was low-slung, crowded,
and terminally flammable. If one shack caught flame, so would all the
others. With Lord Bishop's troops dragging a massive trebuchet behind
their lines, Ben doubted this end of town would remain upright through
the first shot. Thus, Ben and company roamed from dwelling to dwelling, shoving men, women, and children from their beds. Gerrod and
Jimmy took charge of directing the excitable citizenry to the northern
end of the city, where every structure was built from solid stone with
roofs of tin or tile. It would take quite a bit of effort to raze that end of
town, catapult or none.

Bearing tidings of a larger incoming force did not buy the
Greenmakers copious affection. After all, Rosweal had just fought off
one onslaught, hadn't they? These were the poorest folk in Eire and
were acutely cognizant that they didn't have many places to flee. Indeed,
many would sleep outside in the Greensward until the threat passed or
be forced to beg in the streets of some neighboring village. With more
bad weather coming on and a decided lack of supplies to travel with,
many would die from exposure long before they starved. In light of these

realities, most preferred to remain behind their useless city walls rather than brave the elements for a conflict they had no hand in starting. Ben couldn't blame them. Wasn't he the one who brought this reckoning upon them? If he hadn't returned to Rosweal, would either group of soldiers have bothered to march this far northwest? He didn't need to hear the answer. All of this was on his conscience and his alone.

Rather than wallow in pointless guilt, Ben opted to save as many people and homes as possible. The Greenmakers worked through the night, carting people and belongings up and downhill to the Quarter. At some point, he managed to cram something halfway edible into his mouth but couldn't recall when or what it was. The snow stopped sometime after dawn. Ben took a break to watch the sunrise. The next thing he knew, Gerrod's toe prodded his heel. Startled, Ben lurched to his feet, hand flying to his sword-pommel. Gerrod's palms shot out.

"Whoa! Whoa. I been lookin' everywhere for ye."

Shaking himself awake, Ben leaned against a rickety timber post for support. He hadn't slept in days and must have collapsed after clearing the area. "What's happening?"

Gerrod looked uncomfortable. "Well, I'm not sure how to tell ye this, so I'll just say it. Robin was right about Barb's intentions. Says the girl left Rosweal of her own accord, but—"

Ben scrubbed filthy fingers over his aching eyes. "Gods *damn* that scheming bawd! When? *How long have I been here, Gerry?*"

"Ye've been here an hour or so, all told. Colm says she was long gone afore we got back. I know yer sore about it, but Ben, please try to see it from her side. None o'the folk here asked for this trouble. We lost good men yesterday. She did what anyone in her position would."

Ben glared a hole through Gerrod's flushing face. "I know that, Gerry. I'm not planning to gut her. Well, likely not, anyway. I need to know where Una is before this gets any worse."

Gerrod visibly relaxed. He chewed his chapped lower lip. "Them ole loggers' huts, in the hills some miles west. Barb only said as much 'cos Robin ordered her to. I expect he'll be around shortly to give ye the news hisself. I just thought rather than waste more time... ye'd like to know, quick as possible." He shuffled his feet. "I know ye didn't mean for this to happen, and it's hardly yer fault that yer lady's hunted, but Rosweal can't bear the brunt for her— beggin' yer pardon. Four hunnerd men takes piss right outta us."

Ben adjusted his sword belt and slapped himself, alert. "I know you all believe that, but I'm afraid you'll have to accept that one way or the other, Rosweal would have been drawn in. Both sides mean to make war, Gerry. Una's just a convenient excuse."

"I do feel bad for her. Ye can't choose yer parents, believe me, I know."

Ben gently pushed past Gerrod. About six steps ahead, he stopped. "When did Barb send her message to Lord Bishop?"

Gerrod's cheeks burned scarlet; he didn't want to be the one to tell Ben about it. "Dawn, I expect. I don't know more than that, Ben. I'm sorry."

Ben nodded once. "Right. Where's Robin then?"

"At *The Hart*, helpin' with the cleanup. It's a right mess. We lost six fellas to them Corsairs. Lots more took bad wounds— dozens, really. We couldn't stand a fight now, even if we wanted to."

Ben exhaled through his nose. "Gerry, here's a free lesson for you— a fight is never fair. The powerful don't make deals with those they consider insignificant. Whether or not you could marshal a defense against this Souther commander makes no difference to him. Bishop's men came here to support him, inasmuch as they are allowed to sack and pillage at will. All Barb has managed to do is buy time."

"But—"

"They didn't come here to make peace! The sooner you realize this, the better prepared you'll be for what follows," Ben pointed to the buildings around them. "Una or no Una, they'll take what they want and burn the leavings. You know why? Because they *can*. Pray to your Siora that I get to her before Bishop does. This is only the beginning. The Sidhe are the North's only hope now." Ben didn't wait for a reply.

Gerrod's voice called after him. "Ye can't mean to try and fight alone? He has hunnerds o'men. Ye'll get yerself killed!"

Ben held up a hand as he stalked away. "He won't send hundreds of men onto uneven ground, Gerry. He'll leave them here with orders to launch an assault come nightfall. He'll take a handful of experienced trackers into the hills for Una."

"How do ye know that?"

Ben raised a shoulder. "That's what I would do."

Ben's RIGHT FOOT BARRELED INTO the heavy oak door, blasting it inward on its hinges. He ignored the sharp tremor that sang along his shin, his eyes ablaze. With a shriek, Barb leaped out of her chair. Robin had been leaning against her desk with his arms crossed over his chest, no doubt berating her for her impetuous meddling. Robin's hand instinctively twitched toward his belt. Behind Ben, Dabney melted into the darkened hallway like a frightened child.

"*You!*" Ben strode into Barb's office with murderous ferocity.

Slipping between them, Robin placed a firm hand against Ben's heaving chest. His feet slid back a few centimeters. Ben was nearly twice Robin's size.

"Now, Ben," Robin grunted with the effort to hold him in place. "Let's not be rash."

"*Rash?* What in the *bloody nine hells* do you think is happening here?"

Barb craned her neck in defiance. "I did what I had to, Ben! She tole me to give the bastard everythin' he asked for! I swear it!"

Ben shouldered Robin aside. "Oh, she *did*, did she? Tell me, did you happen to mention the reward money you asked for?"

"Well, no, but—"

"You're not this stupid, Barb. Bishop will never pay the likes of you for anything. His men will mutiny if they aren't free to raid. *Why did you do this?*"

Barb licked her lips. She looked to Robin to save her from Ben's wroth. Robin wasn't fool enough to speak for her now.

"His man gave his word! These are my people, Ben. This is my home. Our home. I won't risk the lives o'so many for a spoiled Moura bitch. They're welcome to her, as far as I'm concerned."

"You broke your word, Barb. You took my hand, looked me square in the eyes, and *lied*. If you think that was wise, perhaps you are not as smart as I thought." Ben kicked her chair away from her. She fled toward the windows. Robin leaned nearly horizontal with the floor, trying to drag Ben away. Without another word, Ben reached up and yanked the ogham charm from his throat. His glamour fluttered, then faded. Several answering gasps from the busted doorway only fanned his temper the more. *"Just whom do you think you've betrayed?"*

"Ben, I don't think now's the time to—" Robin attempted.

Ben's silver hair swung wild over his shoulders. "The name isn't Ben, is it?"

Robin cleared his throat. "No, milord. It isn't."

Barb paled. "Ben, please! Ye have to see—"

"My *name* is Kaer Yin Mac Midhir Adair, Mistress Dormer. *Ard Tiarne* of Aes Sidhe, Lord Marshal of *An Fiach Fian*, High Commander of the Doaine Sidhe, and Champion of the Tuatha De Dannan. I am Lord of Meath, Dowth, Knowth, Muenster, and Man. I am the Crown Prince of Innisfail, and this is my land. Everything you own, the earth you live on, the very air you breathe— *belongs to me.* You and everyone you know owe allegiance to me, not to the Lord of Clare, the Duch, or the Citadel. Rosweal isn't yours to bargain with, Barb. Rosweal is *mine*."

Murmurs escalated to raucous volume behind Ben's back. He didn't care. He was done cowering behind a meaningless face and a worthless name. Hiding had brought him to this pass. Because he'd been too cowardly, too ashamed to confront his past, Aes Sidhe was now closer to war than it had been for nearly three decades. As long as he'd been trying to remain anonymous, events in Eire had been on a slow crawl to ruin.

No longer.

Ben was done with secrets and done with shame. Rosweal owed fealty to his father. They owed allegiance to *him*. He would not allow Barb Dormer to drag them all into war for her pigheadedness.

"I am your liege lord, Mistress. You broke faith with the wrong man."

Fat tears rolled down Barb's livid cheekbones. "Ben, it woulda been a war. Don't you see?"

"It will be war *because of what you have done!*" His bellicose shout rang throughout the building. "What do you think Bishop means to do with her, hm? Head to Bethany and live quietly as a private citizen?" he snorted. "Una means nothing to these people, save for a legal means to march on the North! How could you honestly believe handing her over would be better for all involved? Unless..." His silver eyes thinned over a new, unpleasant thought. Barb sank to her knees, head low. "You didn't mean to exchange her at all, *did you?*"

"Ben, please..."

A rage he couldn't quantify surged through Ben's gut. Watching her grovel, he willed his lungs to pump clean, level oxygen into his blood. "You will use my title from this day forth, Mistress. I assure you, if your plan has any success— *in either direction*— you will pay for it with your life. Do you understand me?"

"Y... yes, Be... milord. *Your Highness,*" she blubbered. A consummate actress to the end. Her tears didn't move him an inch. Ben shot Robin a scowl, then whirled on the watchers gathered on the other side of the door. He felt slightly bad about misleading so many of those shocked, familiar faces. Though, he couldn't alter the past any more than he could inflict his will on the present. A choice had to be made, and he'd made it. There was no going back.

"I don't have time to explain this to any of you, and I'm sorry for that. Truly. Given what is marching up the Taran Road as we stand here arguing amongst ourselves, events will soon spin out of our control entirely. I'll be happy to answer questions as soon as this matter is settled. Agreed?" The stunned, noncommittal response he received would have to do for now. He pointed to Gerrod's wide-eyed face. "We don't have much time to prepare. I assume the Southers will arrive by nightfall. You'll need to get all the women and children who remain in town over the river as soon as possible."

410

Rose gasped. "Ye can't be serious, Ben... I mean, milord." She shook her head at the unfamiliar phrase. "We can't cross into Sidhe territory!"

Ben tossed her his ogham stone. She caught it instinctively, rolling the crudely cut quartzite over her long fingers. "Most things won't touch you if you hold that close. When the Sidhe come, plead sanctuary. Tell them who sent you and what's happening here. You'll surely be detained, but it's the best I can do for now. Can you manage?"

It took some time. Conflicting emotions chased over her features. Rose dipped her head and wiped a stray tear from her cheek. "Aye. I can, milord."

Ben gave her an apologetic smile. He owed her a much longer apology, but she'd have to wait for it. He couldn't spare the time as much as it pained him.

"Good. Running to Navan or Slane won't do. Your best bet is to cross and brave the consequences. A marauding Souther army trumps the Law. I vow it. Leave no women here for the Southers to find."

He waited for her awkward curtsy before turning to Colm, Seamus, and Dabney.

"You lot. Gather up any valuables that won't rush downstream immediately and sink them just shy of the docks."

"Now, wait just a minute!" Barb launched to her feet.

Ben wagged a warning finger at her. She bit her lip hard enough to make it bleed. He swung back to the gathered audience.

"Did I stammer? Do it!"

Hesitantly, those to whom he'd given orders floundered off in separate directions, appropriately stunned. "As for the rest of you, I wouldn't bother trying to defend the city from within. You'd do better to harry them from Greensward once they've burned and looted to their hearts' content. You stand no chance against fully armed, heavy infantry— not head-on, at any rate. Those that can't fight or track send over the river with the women. Those that can move east through the pines, then head south. The Souther's supply trains are a wonderful place to start. You all know how to raid. I won't explain your business to you. It's more important that none of you are here waiting for the axe to fall. Are we agreed?"

Mouths agape, they looked to Robin. Clearing his throat, he clapped his hands hard.

"Ye heard yer prince! Go, go, go!"

Gerrod didn't move a muscle even as Robin rushed past him, chasing men downstairs like a demon sent to harry them from the Otherworld. The lad spared Ben a small, sarcastic smile.

"What will ye have me do, erm, milord?

"I've sent word ahead to Aes Sidhe. I'm not sure how long it'll be before a response is mustered, but it's coming, I assure you. It may take a few days, maybe a month, but I expect Dannan troops will cross the Blackwater soon. If any of these fools hoped to rampage through Eire unsullied, they'll be sorely disappointed."

Barb sucked in a sharp breath. "Why didn't ye tell me that to begin with!"

"Because I clearly couldn't trust *you* with the information!" Ben roared back. Her teary-eyed pretense melted into something far less feminine.

"Well, that's just bloody perfect, ain't it! We'll exchange one occupyin' force for another!"

"For your sake, Barb," Ben said evenly. "You'd better hope it's sooner rather than later. After I retrieve Una from the snare you've placed her in, I expect the Southers will be none too pleased to leave empty-handed."

🦌🦌

By MIDDAY, BEN'S ORDERS HAD been carried out with a fierce dedication he might find humbling if he were inclined to believe any of it was out of respect. He couldn't afford to be shy about his identity now. Whether he liked it or not, he'd made a decision he must live with. Perhaps stripping away his glamour in a temper wasn't the wisest course, but it was too late to change his mind. The deed was done. It felt odd to walk around such a familiar haunt as Rosweal in his own skin. He'd spent so long pretending to be one of them that he'd forgotten how to be at ease with himself. He felt vulnerable, exposed.

The stares he received as he sauntered toward the docks burned hotter than any brand. Not only had many of these people never seen a full-blooded Sidhe so close before, but many of them were also visibly disturbed to have shared pints, the odd game of porter, and countless skins of uishge preceding various raids into his *own father's lands*. The Roswellians' shock and mistrust prickled along his spine like a thousand needles. Ben had effectively given it up by casting off his disguise in a fit of justifiable anger. Many of these folks had been his friends. His comrades. His rivals. Gone were the days when he could share a companionable meal, or pint of ale, with any of them. They would not invite him to share their fires nor slap his shoulder in mirth or maudlin. It would never be the same again.

Deep down, Ben realized this is what he'd been waiting for these twenty-six years— to reclaim his heritage, his place in the world... his home. He couldn't allow himself to mourn a disguise any more than he could lament being born a Dannan prince. These things simply *were*. No matter how many layers of sediment piled atop that fact, the truth, as the adage declared, will out. He wasn't sorry to leave Ben the Poacher behind in Barb's office. Instead, he would miss the camaraderie he found amongst the rough men and women of Rosweal.

Decades ago, this little backwater had been the last possible place he'd ever expected to spend so much time in the years since he'd come to admire the people here more than he could say. He ignored the frightened glances, the whispers, and glares and made his way toward the Greenmakers on the dock. Ben kept his back straight and squared his shoulders. He was not ashamed.Seamus saw Ben first. Choking on his own saliva he threw a fist into Robin's shoulder. Robin stopped barking orders at the men threading counterweights over heavy chests of non-perishable goods and rounded on him with a snarl.

"Ye bleedin' nonce! I've got a wound in me arm there, ye know!" Robin noticed Ben striding up the gangplank. "What in the *hells* are ye wearin,' then?"

Ben concealed a relieved smile. Well, maybe he hadn't lost everyone after all. He crossed his arms over his white cuirass. Its sigil was a leaping silver stag crowned by three golden stars. Above that, he wore a white and silver sealskin cloak clasped at the throat with a massive silver torc, capped with a gold pin bearing an emerald as large as an eye. A peerlessly crafted longbow of white ash and blond yew was slung around his shoulders, expertly traced everywhere with cavorting woodland creatures. This bow was a masterpiece. Every experienced archer's eyes glittered in awe.

Ben's scabbard drew an appreciable glare from Robin, who swore into his open palm. Whittled from one long piece of bone, the knotwork and etchings along its face were the product of a hundred years of loving toil. Such an object was unheard of in humble Rosweal. The blade beneath shone brilliantly through the knots, like the sea after a storm. The leaping stag on its pommel took on new meaning for those glimpsing it in its proper context for the first time. Ben drew the sword and leaned against its newly polished blade.

"Nemain," he explained. He flicked it broadside. "Named for the goddess of the springs and rivers. She, who spilled her blood to poison the enemies of Lug." Ben slid the dread, infamous blade back into her magnificent sheath. "Only the bones of her beloved, Bronn, can assuage her thirst for retribution."

Seamus shook his head, astounded. "I've seen that bloody sword half a hunnerd times. Who could believe this?"

"And that," Gerrod pointed to the longbow on his back, "is—"

Ben nodded. He'd tied his hair back from his face, allowing the gold chains in his ears to chime free as he moved.

"*Sinnair.* 'King-killer,'" in our tongue."

"Yer tellin' me, that's the bow what slew ole Kevin Donahugh? Can I hold it, Ben… erm, milord?" Gerrod breathed. Seamus punched him next, for good measure.

"It's the bow that unhorsed him, yes, but Nemain took his life." He tapped a forefinger against the sword's pommel. "The sword was given to me as a boy long ago."

Everyone in Innisfail knew that tale, whether they believed it or not. The silence stretched between them as the Greenmakers gawped in

414

bewildered silence. Robin broke the spell. Coughing, he shoved Gerrod toward the ropes.

"Yes, yes. His Royal Arseness is a fine, shiny new fellow. Stop moonin' already." Sighing, he sidled up to Ben. "Well then. I'm pleased to see ye had time to go and fancy yerself up while we've been here, sacrificin' all our gold and uishge to yer goddess."

Ben shrugged. "I do like to make an entrance."

"Just where do ye think yer off to then, all done up like a princess?"

"Had to make certain everything still fit, didn't I?"

Robin sucked his teeth. "I think it's a tad snug 'round the middle."

"Nothing soft over here but your head, Robin."

"The girls'll scratch yer eyes out for that pin."

"Lasses are free to fight over my jewels any time."

"Answer the feckin' question."

"Got some work to do out west."

Robin retrieved his pipe from a hidden pocket in his tunic. He struck one of Seamus' well-made matches against a post to light it.

"Ben, if ye think I'm lettin' ye hie off into the wild on yer own, yer out o'yer gourd."

"Robin, dearest," Ben grinned. "That's not my name, and I don't recall asking your permission."

Robin blew a wad of smoke in Ben's face. "Don't be ridiculous. Ye'll get one or two 'milords' outta me now and then, but ye'll always be Ben bloody Maeden to me. Boys, what do ye say to that?"

"I think ye owe me twelve fainne, milord. I'm adding loads o'interest," said Seamus, whom Ben had once carried over his shoulders for over two miles to escape a team of competing bandits. Colm waved him away like an overgrown child. Gerrod made a crude noise.

"See? Yer a feckin' Greenmaker, same as the rest o'us. Ye mighta been born a poncey lord, sneerin' down at folk like us all yer long life, but yer a bit more'n that now, ain't ye?" said Robin.

Ben had no idea what to say. He'd merely come down here to make his goodbyes and wish them well. He hadn't expected this at all.

"Robin, you *can't* come with me."

"It's adorable ye think ye can stop me. Ye don't get to go off on yer own and have all the fun."

"I appreciate the sentiment... beyond words, but you must help your people to safety."

"Buggers'll be bloody fine. They got Barb and this skinny ole codger to help them," Robin jerked a thumb at Colm. "I don't know if it's occurred to ye yet, but this cunt Bishop probably wants ye to come out on yer own. We may be lots o'things in Rosweal, but we're loyalists to a man. No Souther lord is gonna raid the North unimpeded, by Herne. Not today, not ever."

Ben said nothing.

Robin groaned. "Colm?"

"What?" Colm snarled. He was busy helping Gerrod and four others lower the next basket laden with goods into the river's sluggish current. These containers held nearly all the gold, silver, brass, or glass in Rosweal, four baskets full of uishge pilfered from Matt's stores, trunks containing heavy pewter plates, antique silver utensils, and dry casks stuffed to bursting with costly furs, imported textiles, and fine linen. The Greenmakers would leave nothing to the Southers— not even a pair of dusty curtains. Dragging the haul back up again would be a chore of no mean size, but Ben doubted he'd be around to witness it, either way.

"I want ye to lead the raids on their supply train. I want that blasted catapult in ashes before it can be dragged in range o'the walls. I want ye to kill every man o'them ye can manage without makin' yer presence known till it's too late to stop ye. Can ye do all that?"

Colm snorted, then went back to work.

"See? Everyone knows what to do."

"Robin, you don't understand. It's almost Samhain," Ben lowered his voice to a whisper. "There's going to be more in those woods than a handful of Bethonair troopers. Worse, in fact. *Much*, much worse."

"Aye, I heard ye the first time. Here's the thing, milord. Lord Bishop gets the girl and his war if you die on us. None o'us will stand for that. I vowed to help ye, and that's what I'll do. If ye can't get her over the

416

border, we'll damned sure try in yer stead. Besides," Robin spat, "if ye do cock it up and die, I've called dibs on that shiny bow on yer back."

Ben found Rose by the river, helping little girls and old women into small boats shored along the eastern cutbank. She flinched a little when she saw him approach. She was lovely in the low afternoon light. The long dark column of her throat was cast copper in the fading sunlight. She looked away from him, embarrassed. He caught one of her hands, threading her slender fingers through his. How many times had those fingers held his? Ben couldn't feasibly count. Despite all, Rose had been special to him for quite a long time. He would even go so far as to say he cared for her in his way.

"Rosie, you don't have to be afraid of me."

He could feel the pulse ticking furiously in her palm, like a highly wound clock. "I'm not afraid of ye, Ben... yer highness. I'm afraid of myself. What ye must think of me...."

He pulled her close and brushed her full lips with his. She whimpered, her eyes downcast. "I think highly of you, Rose. Never forget it." He pressed something heavy and metallic into her hand before releasing her fingers from his grip. She looked down at the object with a gasp. "What's this?"

"My father's ring. I want you to keep it safe, along with the stone I gave you. Do you have it?"

She touched the cord slung around her neck. "I do. I remember what ye told me. I won't fail ye if I can help it."

"There's more I would tell you, so listen closely." He nudged her chin up with his knuckle so she couldn't look away. "Don't stay near the river— not for any reason. This is very important, Rose. Any girl that strays could be lost to more than the current. There's a road a half-mile or so from the water's edge. Stay on it, and take it northeast, only northeast. Don't wander. No matter what you hear or what you might see. Do you understand?"

She nodded.

"Good. There'll be a small stone structure astride the road. It won't be far, but don't hurry to find it. The roads in Aes Sidhe sometimes have a mind of their own. When you get there, get everyone inside, and answer the door for no one. A creature that begs entrance to that place is not welcome by nature. Any trueborn Sidhe may enter of their own will. When one does, you give them that ring and tell them what I told you. You tell them their Ard Tiarne has sent you over for your safety. Do you need me to repeat any of this?"

"No, Be... milord," she smiled sadly. "It'll be as you say. I swear."

He brought the top of her head in for a kiss. "Take care, Rosie. I wish you well in the future."

Brushing her fingers along his jaw, she jerked his head down to hers for one last, lingering kiss. Ben could taste a hint of salt on her lips. When she pulled away, her eyes were wet.

"No goodbyes, Ben. Ye do what ye must. Maybe I won't be as jealous o'her as I thought?"

Despite his perplexed frown, she turned away. She grabbed Violet's child and settled her over her hip while she waited her turn to board. She didn't look back. Barb, he noticed, sat sulking in the prow of the next boat, avidly avoiding his eyes. That was as well. Ben wouldn't soon forget what she'd done, and Barb wouldn't forgive him for chastising her publicly, as she so richly deserved. Nonetheless, that wasn't to say he wouldn't miss her, just a bit. Ben cupped his palm around his mouth as they shoved off and called out to her.

"Oi, Barb!"

She looked up; her lips pinched in anger. "I'm not speakin' to ye, yer *high royal arse*!"

"You think you'll still run girls, now that you're the Governess of Rosweal?" he asked.

She blinked at him like an owl for several pregnant moments until she threw back her head and howled with laughter. Leaning over the side, she spared him an obscene gesture.

"Hells yes, I'll run girls! The finest, juiciest, randiest whores in all Innisfail! Ye just wait and see."

418

Surfeit of Will

Una twisted her wild hair into an inelegant knot. Most days, she quite liked her spongy golden-brown curls. Today, however, she could yank every strand from her scalp without a second thought. She was sweating, sore, and exhausted. Her damp tunic and leggings chafed her already abraded skin. She was pretty sure one of her molars was loose, and her right wrist was probably sprained. On her second trip down, she'd jarred something in her hip that made her right knee ache to an infernal degree. To make matters worse, the gash Keeley cut into her forearm had gone a suspiciously puckered purple. Una didn't need Rian to tell her it was likely infected. Bent double and huffing into the floorboards, she reached her limit.

Rian scoffed from her place beside the window. "You're wearing yourself down for nothing."

Una shot her a withering glare. Wordless, she got to her feet, rolled up her sleeves, and dashed once more for the open doorway. The trees outside were so close that she should have launched herself smack into the nearest trunk. She smelled soggy pine needles in the duff on the hillside, fresh ozone, and verdant moss. She tasted an incoming rainstorm and heard the trickle of water as the season's first snowfall melted into the earth.

Her heel sunk into the dissipating slush outside the door, and she grinned triumphantly. That hadn't happened before! Maybe this time she had it? Slipping her left foot past her right, Una prayed gravity would propel her forward and move her out. It did not. Like the first time, she incurred the same gut-wrenching feeling of falling upward, of being sucked through a too-small container, then poured out again at breakneck speed. She screamed. The floor inside the cottage rushed up to meet her face again. Groaning in exhaustion, Una turned herself over onto her aching back. Her arms flopped to either side. She'd sell one of her limbs for a bit of that cool water she heard running down the hill outside.

"Una, stop thinking about it," Rian said. "And stop looking at it."

Una couldn't help it. On a table beneath the far window sat a beautiful silver tray embossed with elegant filigree. It hadn't been there during her second attempt to escape, but just as her exertions prompted thirst, this bounty materialized to taunt her. Two crystalline glasses full of sweet, lemon-scented water beckoned mercilessly. Both tumblers were dusted with condensation from the ice chiming within— ice that retained its shape and size, regardless of time or temperature.

One fat teardrop slithered down the nearest glass, fashioning a shiny little pool on the tray below. Una licked her cracked lips. An overflowing water pitcher sat beside them, accompanied by three plump apple slices and a hunk of creamy white cheese. The more she stared, the greater her longing.

"I said, stop thinking about it." Rian removed the stopper from her water skin and shoved it none-too-gently in Una's face. She drained as much of the stale, unappealing liquid as she dared. They only had this one skin. If the day's events were any indication of what was to come, they'd need to make it last. Hugging her knees, Rian gave Una a tired look. "If you'd stop trying to muscle your way out of this, you wouldn't be so thirsty."

Una wiped her mouth. "I have to try."

"You've tried. It's not working." Rian passed half a stale biscuit over. "Eat that. Slowly. The longer you savor it, the harder your brain will work to convince itself you're satisfied."

The ice clinked together. Una stifled a moan. "How can you be sure he means to poison us? You can't know that the food and drink are bad."

"Don't you know anything about the Otherworld? If you drink or eat anything in the Oiche Ar Fad, you'll be trapped here indefinitely. They don't teach anything about the birth of magic in the Cloister?"

"You don't know that's where we are. It could be... well, it could be—"

"Una, we're in the Otherworld. I guarantee you. Don't you realize who that character was?"

"He said he was Ben's uncle," Una frowned.

"*Yes.* That leaves two individuals, doesn't it? One wouldn't bother, and the other is infamous for toying with mortals. Which one do you imagine he could be?"

"He helped us, didn't he? Without his intervention, I doubt we'd have made it down that hill." *Although*, Una stole a glance at the tempting delights displayed on that silver tray. She wondered why they appeared only when she seemed most desperate for them. Perhaps, whatever enchantment that held this place together was designed to meet the basic needs of those it confined? It wouldn't serve Una's argument, but she must concede that one glaring detail favored Rian's assertion over hers.... *we cannot leave.* No matter how many times she tried to run, the result was always the same. If he meant them no harm, why trap them in this place? This was a question she couldn't logically ignore.

"Okay then. We'll suppose you're right."

"I *am* right."

"*Fine.* It would be wise to assume that you are even if you aren't. I'll accept that. What are we going to do about it?"

"I don't know."

"How much food did you bring in that satchel? A day's worth?"

"Probably less. I was in a hurry when I packed. I hoped we'd be well south by now, at least as far as Vale. I hadn't realized Barb would send so many men to, erm, escort us." That point was moot. Of course, Barb had sent several men. She'd seen what Una was capable of firsthand. Barb wouldn't send her favorite or most trusted lugs, but she'd be sure to send plenty. Una had been actively trying to forget the double-crossing old whore for hours.

"Wonderful. We have about half a day's worth of water, too." She squinted at the sunlit scene outside. "We look to be in the same hills we were in yesterday."

"We probably are. The enchantment could be restricted to this structure only. Maybe a pocket or a sliver in time. Do you understand what I mean?"

"Not really."

Rian padded to the open doorway. The wind howled eerily over the hilltop, but not a single hair on her head stirred in sympathy. She held her palms out to press them through the opening. Una watched her arms quiver under an invisible strain. With a curse, Rian snatched her hands back, rubbing them furiously against her thighs.

"That's awful."

"Tell me about it."

"We can figure this out. There's always a way. We just have to keep trying."

"How do you figure that?"

"Everyone knows. It's the way of things."

"I hope you're right." Una set the precious water skin against the wall. "Because I can't promise not to help myself to whatever refreshments are offered when this skin runs dry. I don't think my throat has ever been so raw."

"That's by design. All that running around surely made it worse."

"Point taken, Rian!" Una snapped. Shivering, she rolled into a ball. "I'm sorry. I'm out of my depth in here."

Rian didn't respond. She took a second turn around the cabin, then a third. By the fifth pass, she stopped short. Her hand flew to her heart. An overlarge shadow flitted across the glass. Then another. Rian backpedaled. Someone squished their nose into the pane from the outside.

A man they had seen before at *The Hart* screwed his eyes up to peer inside. He seemed to stare straight at them. Neither girl so much as breathed. Una's fingers clenched Rian's so hard that Rian winced.

422

The figure in the window shook his head and retreated. He mumbled something to a companion, who took his turn at the window. The girls heard only muffled, discordant grunts or the odd scrape and rustle as heavy boots disturbed the foliage under the casings. Askance, Una stared at Rian. Couldn't they see them? The girls should have been spotted from the first. Perhaps they *were* in the Otherworld?

If these were Barb's men, then Rian's instinct might have been on the mark. Una dragged herself up the wall, and Rian squeezed as far into her side as she could. One of the woodsmen loitered in the doorway for quite a while, considering the shadows in each corner. Without ado, he stomped inside, sopping boots leaving muddy imprints wherever he walked. For a moment, his nose passed so close to Una's that she could have planted a kiss directly on his cheek. Burly brows knit together, he glared at the wall as if something mocked him from within. One of Rian's long blond hairs brushed against his shoulder, and *still,* he did not see them. Fascinated, Una held her fingers just shy of his face. She meant to trace the ridge of his grizzled brow.

She never got the chance to test her physicality. With a disgruntled sigh, the intruder slid his dagger back into its sheath and exited the cabin. Una released the breath she'd been holding in a torrent. Rian found her feet and raced to the window. Her cheeks were white as the snow outside.

"Una, come look! The farther away they move, the slower they go."

Of course, Una wasted no time trying to follow them out the door. She prayed that whatever magic held them here had faded from the woodsman's intrusion. Again, it did not. The next time she struck the floor, she smacked her nose hard enough to make it bleed.

"Owwww!" Her eyes welled with tears.

"What'd you do that for?" Rian mashed a torn bit of her dress against Una's face. "If they couldn't see us, then we're not really in here. Don't you get it?"

Una kept her stinging rebuttal to herself. "Seemed like a good time to try again," she said, batting Rian's fingers away. "Rian, what are we going to do?"

"Our captor could come back and deliver his terms. Maybe he'll hand us over to Ben, wherever he may be?" She blew her hair out of her eyes. "Or we could succumb to thirst and hunger and be stuck here forever."

"I thought you said there's always a way out of situations like these?"

"There is, but the heroine doesn't always see the key until it's too late. Sometimes, these tales are told to warn their listener to beware the Sidhe. To keep well out of their way."

"Don't tell me that *now*! I don't want to hear anything but how we will get out of here."

"All right, all right. We're going to get out of here, Una."

"How?"

"I'm not sure, but we'd better think of something soon. Time moves differently here."

"I swear, you live to give me bad news."

"I'm serious," Rian said. "Running out of food will be the least of our problems if we fail."

🦌

THE SOUTHERS HAD ALREADY STRETCHED their forces between the Navan and Taran Gates at Rosweal when the last boat carrying the women and children reached Aes Sidhe's shore. Colm and his group of twenty reasonably fit raiders were the first to exit through the Ward Gate, intent to track around the Southers' left flank. Colm knew his business. As soon as the forward troops advanced, he'd do everything he could to cripple Bishop's rear line. With his supplies and reserves under attack, the Lord of Clare's assault on the city wouldn't last long.

An hour or so after the Greenmakers split up to manage their various tasks, Ben immediately tried to ditch his retinue. He did not get far; as usual, Robin outfoxed him. He caught up with him just beyond the Ward Gate. Heaving an annoyed sigh, Ben didn't bother to protest a second time. No one told Robin Gramble where he might go, not even a prince— defamed, exiled, and unloved as Ben was.

Gerrod and Seamus, it seemed, shared Robin's pigheaded determination. Thus, the four of them headed into the wild, moving up the trail at a steady clip. These hills weren't especially high, though they were deceptively steep. No simple task, to establish one's footing over moss-slick granite and crumbling shale. A wide variety of trees crowded close: strong Innish pine, squat rowans, slender birches, and oaks as wide as houses. Hordes of roots dove in and out of the stony earth, like sea serpents undulating through dark green waves. Their path was the swiftest to their destination but also the most difficult. After they'd slogged two miles into the teeming Greensward, Ben caught a slight rustle on the wind: the rattle of spurs or the jingle of a harness.

He stopped dead in his tracks. Trying to pinpoint the source of the sound, he leaned into the wind to detect it again. Gerrod, who had pretty good ears for a Milesian, had heard it too. Absentmindedly, he tugged Robin's spyglass out of his pack without permission. Snatching it back, Robin spared the sheepish lad a filthy glare, then set it against his eye. Ben pointed, and he trained the glass on the southeastern terrain. There, the land rolled a bit more than it did at this height. A team of horses would never make it up such a mess of tumble-down rocks and claustrophobic flora. Riders would be obliged to utilize the thin remnant of a pre-Transition road, a mile or so to the south.

"How many?" Ben whispered. Sound tended to travel in these barren hills, bouncing from rock to rock like an amphitheater.

Robin handed him the spyglass with a snort. "Lemme put it this way. If it comes to a fight, we're properly buggered."

It took a moment to place the flashes of blue and grey through the trees. As soon as he did, Ben wished he hadn't. He beheld quite a line of soldiers, winding slowly upward. Many Southers walked their stalwart mounts rather than punish the beasts with this climb. They'd cover twice the ground when the road leveled out higher up. Ben lowered the glass.

"Shite."

"What? How many?" Seamus whispered.

"Fifty, maybe less. Can't be sure."

"*Fifty?*" Gerrod exclaimed.

Seamus held a finger to his lips with one hand and socked Gerrod in the side with the other. "Keep yer voice down, idiot."

"Sorry… but fifty?" Gerrod rubbed his ribs. "Why'd they bring so many into these mad hills?"

"The fucker's got plenty to spare, don't he?" Robin said. "Best we beat 'em there, ain't it?"

Ben didn't like this at all. Armed men climbed the road below, two missing girls ahead, and behind…something *worse* would come calling from the river's murky depths.

"You should go back," Ben said, clutching Robin's arm so he couldn't look away. "I'll have none of your deaths on my conscience. I mean it, Robin. Once they burn through the slums, which they will, and soon, Colm will need your help to divide their forces. You must go."

Robin drew his craggy brows up. "Tellin' me what to do again, are ye? We sunk anythin' o'value in town. Girls and old folks're all gone off to get arrested by yer kin. No booze left anywhere in sight. Far as I'm concerned, they're welcome to burn that shitehole down. Make room for a proper market town once yer daddy rewards us for bein' such loyal pals to his poncey son."

"*Robin—*"

"We're wastin' time jabberin', ain't we? I'll make ye a deal. Ye kill yer beastie when it comes for ye, and we'll get yer girls clear. Fair? I promise I won't lift a fingernail to help ye." Robin covered his heart in mock oath.

"Gods damn you, Gramble," Ben grumbled, getting to his feet. Glowering, he readjusted his weapons. "If you die, I'll visit you in Tech Duinn twice a week to remind you what a useless, bullheaded moron you are."

Robin shoved him forward with a grin. "Can't wait. Now let's see how fast ye fancy Sidhe bastards can really move."

🦌 🦌

Rian's waterskin belched its last drop shortly after their visit from Barb's henchman. Neither girl could ascertain how much time had passed, but they felt its effects all the same. The environment beyond the cabin offered few clues. Nothing moved as it should. Rain clouds that Una watched gather in the west days before had yet to crest the summit of their nearest snow-dappled peak. The sun inched across the sky on such a slow track that it scarcely seemed to move. The wind moaned over the roof like the lowest note in a wood flute: eerie, discordant, and monotonous. When twilight finally deigned to descend upon their valley, sluggish shadows oozed between the trees like tar.

Rian believed a day inside took just under three-quarters of an hour outside. She'd spent indeterminable spans watching the sunlight trace over the floorboards and marking measurements in the dust beneath the window. Una couldn't gainsay her— she didn't have the education nor strength to argue with Rian's observations. Whatever the truth, both of them were miserable. They were parched, starved, and afraid. The unbearable scent of cool water on the tray by the window was exquisite torture. Though they ignored it as much as possible, their throats burned with need by the end of Rian's reckoned third day. Una imagined a desert with hot blowing sands and a merciless sun blazing overhead. Searing winds stripped the parchment of her flesh to insubstantial bone. Her tongue leaden, blood boiling, she wandered alone, burning and desolate.

She couldn't shake herself free of this waking nightmare. Every breath she took, the ice within those glasses would clink together, and chill droplets would slide down the pitcher like a drumbeat. The scent of apples and warm summer cheese twisted her guts to frayed chords. Una tasted nothing save the barren, brittle acid of her sunken cheeks. Her lips were rough as raisins. Each blink pierced her eyes with a hundred needles. The ice would clang. The pitcher would *drip, drip, drip…* until she thought she might run mad. Rian gripped her fingers, and Una would find the strength to resist for a while longer. Then again… and again… and again: *drip, drip, drip…*

Una might weep, but she had nothing wet left in her eyes. Only salt, only burning, only despair. In their wretched state, the girls' surroundings lost meaning. Time and its importance became less vital from breath to haggard breath. When they still needed to relieve themselves, they'd move toward a pair of buckets that appeared in the corner as needed. When they slept, they unrolled mats and fluffed pillows that would disappear as soon as they woke. When they were at their lowest possible humor, a chorus of sighing bells would echo in the rafters, only to fade as they raised their eyes to mark them. They were haunted, supervised by unseen magic, or otherwise ignored.

Once, Una thought about the copper tub in her apartment on the Eighth Floor. She closed her stinging eyes and dreamed of immersing herself in that sumptuous, splendid warmth how she would idle there for hours on end, reading or dozing. She heard Rian gasp; sure enough, this very tub appeared in the corner, steam rising from its fragrant, oil-scented interior. Una cried out, and the vision melted away, same as the rest.

It seemed they could only enjoy these luxuries if they accepted them without question. If either girl spent too long in consideration or spoke of them aloud, these visions would evaporate like smoke. All save the tray and its siren song... that bit of perfidy was as steady as the floor beneath them. Nourishment had a sound. Satiation had a melody. Relief, a chant. It went *drip, clink, drip*. The sun went down. Five full days had passed, by Rian's whispered estimation. They couldn't speak much anymore for lack of lubricant in their throats and could hardly move for the empty void within their bellies. Una and Rian lay side-by-side, fingers woven together and trembled with hunger and dehydration.

Una must have fallen asleep. In her dream, a great *nothing* hunted her through the spaces between lucidity and wakefulness. The thing cackled in her mind, bearing a formless menace as insubstantial as vapor, yet painfully near. It clawed at the fringes of her subconscious. A louder, stronger burst of wind thundered into their valley. On its heels came the glacially slow patter of rain on the shingled roof. Una felt every drop slither down the exterior walls with a lust that made her gums ache. The simmering storm provided somber background music to this torment. Una's nightmares merged. A sinuous creature folded the girls within its ravenous embrace. It whispered things through the rain... horrible things; greedy, wanton things. The pitcher toppled, pouring reeking fluids into a

428

deep black well. This fathomless pool contained a substance fouler and thicker than water.

The *drip, clink, drip…* now talons climbed out of that abyss, up sweating walls slick with blood, ether, spittle, and death.

She felt Rian shudder as if she shared her fear. Una's eyes snapped open. A surge of adrenaline jolted through her heart. She could swallow. There was moisture in her mouth. She was still hungry but no longer starving. Her blood flowed through her veins at regular speed. Her eyes were no longer crusted over with dried salt. Una licked her lips, feeling the weight of her own wet tongue. With a cry, she released Rian's cold fingers like they'd scalded her. Sobbing, Una scrambled to her knees. She pulled Rian into her lap by the shoulders. Her flesh felt waxen, hollow. Her bones were light and fragile as a bundle of twigs. Una pressed her thumb to the hollow of Rian's throat. She was barely able to see Rian's face, for the stolen tears flooding her eyes. Rian had a pulse, but it was very weak— erratic as the wingbeats of a dying hummingbird.

Una screamed at the top of her taxed lungs. In her sleep, her Spark roused itself, searching for the sustenance it needed to keep her alive. Una might have *killed* her friend! She buried her face in her hands: guilt, shame, and rage filtered through her every fiber.

She'd done it again— unwittingly harmed another human being— broken the Ninth Law. Her Spark had a mind of its own. It had prioritized her survival over basic human decency. Revolting. Horrible. *Vampiric.* A hot stream of bile bubbled below her collarbone, promising to surge upward if she dared to breathe. *Drip, clink, drip,* called the tray; ice tinkled its cheerful taunt; wind and rain buffeted the roof with exaggerated stealth. Una held Rian close, willing whatever mechanism that enabled her to leech life away to reverse itself through Rian's skin. The spectral image from her nightmare resurfaced in the depths of her conscience. *Una* was that abhorrent aberration, wasn't she? Crippling self-loathing, fear, and guilt must have leaked into her dreams as ink soaks into a sponge.

What could she do? How could she undo the damage she'd done? Letting Rian's head slip gently to the floor, she resumed her pacing. It was time to *solve* this puzzle. Rian was already so weak and malnourished... if Una failed, she might die. Chewing at her jagged cuticles, Una prowled the confines of their wooden prison like a caged animal. She could figure this out; she *must*. The room attempted to appease her frustration by tapping into her desires. Random thoughts she had flashed briefly in the various corners of the room. An axe appeared and disappeared. A saw, a spear— then a torch, a hammer... she gritted her teeth, willing herself to focus. *Drip, clink, drip,* chanted the tray, and she wailed into her palm... *drip, clink, scrape...*

Her feet skidded to a halt.

Drip, drip, drip, went the pitcher. *Clink, clink...* went the ice. Drumming raindrops struck the roof, and Una shuddered at their lethargic downward progression. *Scrape...* went another sound from the north wall. She whirled. A huge yellow eye bulged at her from the window. Its pupil was a sword-slash vertical slit, which contracted at her answering gasp. On recoil, Una's spine slammed into the back wall.

The eye quivered as the thing laughed. *"There, there, little birdssss...."* Its voice was sweet and corrosive as acid. Una felt every word pound into her eardrums like a bodhran drum. She covered her ears. The thing cackled, an oily, lascivious sound that turned her stomach. The creature slid around to the open door. A formless black shape shifted through a dozen figures at once: a bear, an ox, a raven... then a man. It settled on a perverse, alien amalgamation of Ben's handsome face. Mammoth obsidian talons caressed the barrier between them, curling Ben's hands into unnaturally large, gnarled hooks. Huge tusks sprouted from its mouth as it peered in at Una with unadulterated hunger. *"You're sssso, sssso thirsssty, aren't you, little one? Do not fear. Where I will take you, you'll never thirssst again...."*

THE VEIL

As night descended, Ben felt a change in the atmosphere. A subtle tremor rumbled through his bones, raising gooseflesh over his arms. His nostrils twitched at the faint alchemical shift in his environs. Serpentine mists seeped from the earth, soft and seductive as satin. Ben paused to take stock. He rolled that indescribable *something* over his tongue, like bittersweet toffee. Did the rain smell a bit sweeter than usual, the soil a bit richer? Disjointed whispers rose and fell with each gust of wind. Boughs creaked and groaned in mournful chorus through the valley below. Water trickled from somewhere higher up. Did Ben spy faces moving through each hollow— eyes of various luminance, glittering from the deep dark spaces within? Samhain was at hand. Soon, the veil between the corporeal world and the Oiche Ar Fad would vanish. Many things that should remain forever apart from this realm would seep through like blood through silk.

Ephemeral spirits always came first: phantom wisps and vapors, bearing little intellect or self-awareness. They were as lanterns over still waters, flitting here and there with no purpose save to be. Ben caught a few ghostly flickers on the hillside, winking in and out of sight among the trees. Lu Sidhe would come next: sylphs, undines, piskies, gnomes, and mad faeries. Some delighted in mischief. Some merely wished to troop through this strange literal world that most perceived only once a year. They would band together: a parade of prancing tricksters, pests, and pantomimes. Though… it wasn't the inconsequential Lu Sidhe who were responsible for the cold dread coursing through Ben's heart.

Dor Sidhe would follow their lesser counterparts— malignant, bloodthirsty monsters of man's blackest dreams. They were manhunters, all: avartagh, ghasts, dullahan, bogarts, wraiths, kelpies, goblins… and pooka. Unleashed from the Oiche Ar Fad only on Samhain, Dor Sidhe craved flesh as a starving man craves bread. Ranging far afield, these unnatural beasts stalked human prey in every corner of Innisfail, from deep mountain lakes to the deceptive comfort of one's own home. On Samhain, whence Dor Sidhe roamed, mortals dared not tread. However, once the underworld gates swung wide, these horrid creatures were merely its penultimate terror.

The last of Samhain's gifts was by far its worst. Dor Sidhe were harbingers of the dead. The Sluagh were tortured souls, released from Tech Duinn in search of lost loved ones… or the heat of living blood. Sluagh could not comprehend that they no longer belonged to this plane. In ancient times, many thousands of years before the Transition, Milesian tribes held ritual sacrifices the length and breadth of Eire. Druids burned massive wicker effigies stuffed with willing human sacrifices to appease Donn, the god of death. To honor Samn, goddess of the moon, those sacrificed remains were scattered over fallow fields to guard against pestilence and famine for the following year.

On Samhain, countless fires once dotted the Eirean landscape. Dancers in masks adorned with blood and ash would sketch a living wall between burning men and the dead. The Sluagh were ever near. Empty eyes watched from silent shadows, waiting for a break in that bright mortal line. In modern times, people refrained from burning their neighbors alive, but lamplighters still worked overtime to ensure each town remained lit through the night. Perhaps, if men saw the world as Ben did, they might revive the old ways in a hurry.

An hour after sunset, heavy rainclouds blew in from the west. Hard rain brought their upward mobility to a veritable crawl. Mossy stones, slick with sluicing rainwater, carved treacherous little canyons beneath their unsteady boots. Between the bracing wind and the wet, the Greenmakers might have been attempting to scale a waterfall. Hours passed while they struggled to maintain their footing up the melting tor. The evening was already fully mature before they emerged from the wooded slope. Halfway to the summit, they discovered a rocky outcrop jutting from the hillside, like the keel of an overturned boat. Ben eyed the path that curved along its face. Just shy of the ledge, a copse of bare treetops were snapped as if something substantial dove into them from higher up the trail. Ben crouched near the precipice, dripping brows drawn together. Squat bushes that traced the slope were crushed or uprooted, indicating whatever had gone over had fought hard to remain upright.

"Shrubbery over here's been bothered with," Robin shouted over the wind. Ben got up to see for himself. Robin gestured to his left. "Body was laid up here, ye ask me. A bit of a struggle over that pile o'big stones ahead."

"There are broken branches over the ridge there," Ben pointed. A crack of lightning illuminated the frown on his face. "Someone was thrown off."

"Couldn't be either lass," Gerrod added, his voice holding a note of hopeful urgency. Ben might find that intriguing later on. "Neither o'em weighs more than a bushel o'apples. Whoever it was, wasn't slight."

"There's blood on the rocks here," Ben dipped a gloved finger and inhaled. "Una's, I think."

Robin scratched his wet pate. "What I know o'her, Ben, she got the better o'em. My fainne's on Keeley. He and his grandson are the only two trackers Barb sent. Not enough prints to suggest t'others were on this trail. Too narrow."

"You think they took the high pass?"

"Not enough room for many more than four up here." Seamus ran a hand along a scratch in the granite face. "I think Robin's got the right o'things. The trail tapers ahead. Too many feet would increase the chances o'dislodgin' the dirt holdin' the path against these stones. My guess? Breccan and Keeley were down here with 'em, and I gather Keeley went over. Breccan's just a mite and no fighter."

Ben nodded. "That's as it may be, but the prints end just ahead here." He hoisted himself over the last set of stones in the trail. No fauna was disturbed, and the scent of blood dissipated. Perplexed, Ben ranged ahead several paces, detecting no evidence of either girl's footprints. Robin and Seamus combed the cliff edge, looking for signs that perhaps they'd gone over too, while Gerrod tracked downhill to ascertain if he'd missed a sign of them retreating from whence they came. No such thing, he announced with a confused shrug. He indicated that there were only two sets of tracks: the four they'd followed to this point and their own. The girls might have floated away on the wind.

"Ye don't think they'd have climbed down *that*," Gerrod grimaced into the gorge, with its plump, deceptively gradient slope. One might believe the decline relatively gentle if not for the impressive oaks and elms peeking over the rim. "I'd be buggered to try that bitch, myself."

Robin mashed his lips together. "Mhm, no way. We'd have some sign o'em amblin' near them rocks and bushes. Siora, this is odd. If they didn't slide down, fall, or retreat... where in the hells did they go?"

Ben picked his way back to the spot stained with Una's blood. He flung his senses outward. Concentrating on the immediate vicinity, he marked wet earth, fallen leaves, soaked bark, saturated minerals, and crackling ozone from the storm above. He sensed the clod of hooves and the chime of bridles on the opposite side of the hill— though these were too far away to warrant immediate concern. Ben did find those amorphous shapes and flashing pulses that he'd noted before had increased in frequency. Bright eyes were seemingly everywhere, dipping in and out of sight like fireflies in a summer's gloaming. Tittering chatter, murmurs, and tinkling laughter trilled through the Greensward, buzzing like angry bees. Of the Greenmakers' quarry, there was no sign.

Frustrated, Ben groaned, "I have no idea."

Gerrod jerked, hand on his dagger. "Did ye hear that?"

"Aye," Seamus clutched the sprig of mistletoe dangling from his neck. The Lu Sidhe did not care for mistletoe, all Eireans knew. One could reasonably hope that the sacred plant would guard them against harm. Ben did not have the heart to tell Seamus that on this night of all nights, peasant charms were useless out here in the dark. "Tis Samhain, ain't it? Bloody Greensward'll be filled with randy beasties tonight."

"Superstitious sot," said Robin, tugging his chin at Ben. "We got us our own good luck, don't we? None o'the Folk would dare step wrong with him."

Ben ignored them. Removing his glove, he ran his fingers over Una's fading blood stain. The faintest trace of indelible energy brushed against his skin. There was something else here: less a scent or a sound than a feeling. Crouching in the scree, he held his palm out as if to absorb that something through his skin. A trace of power— dark power— lingered in the damp, like an afterimage. Ben hadn't felt anything like it in a very long time.

"What is it?" Robin knelt beside him.

"Something *took* them from here."

"What, and leaped over the cliff?" Seamus snorted.

"No," Ben struggled to find the right words. "The erm…veil. The fabric between worlds is thinnest on Samhain. We all know that, but here—" He rubbed his hands together to offset their discomfort. "Here, it was cut."

"What's that mean then?"

"Dor Sidhe, or something else. I can't be sure, but I can feel it." Ben scrubbed his hands against his soaked trousers as if to remove a taint. "Una and Rian didn't fall over. They were taken… somewhere *else*.…"

"Ben, ye know we don't speak that gibberish. What in the hells is a 'doo-er shee'?" asked Gerrod, slapping Seamus' hand from the weed at his throat.

Seamus glowered back. "Dor Sidhe, ye nonce. Randy beasties, what eat little girls, and skinny lads like ye."

"Shut yer hole, Seamus, or I'll bash yer good teeth in too."

"Both of ye shut up!" Robin barked. "Ben, if something already had at yer girls, what can we do about it?"

"I don't think this was violence. This feels more like a clinical slice than a tear. All magic leaves a trace. Even this." Ben stared up the trail. "Two girls, both mortal. He can't have taken them far. Not before midnight tonight, anyway. It'd be exhausting to try."

"He?"

"I misspoke," Ben said. He focused on a faint glimmer, guiding his steps ahead. "This isn't Dor Sidhe magic at all."

"What do you mean?"

"It's worse— one of *my* kind. We must go."

Ben heaved himself up the next level of mud-slick rocks without another word. He didn't bother to wait and see if the men behind him could keep up.

❧ ❧

DAMEK ALMOST REGRETTED THE DECISION to lead this expeditionary force himself. The weather made every inch an agony. Their progress couldn't have been slower if they had forged ahead on their knees. Mud sluiced downward at breakneck speed, making an arduous chore of each step. After three miles, Damek and his men were forced to walk their mounts. The following rise led to the base of another punishing slope. Damek repressed a groan. These hills were hardly high, yet they might have been sky-scraping mountains for their tortuous, slick gradients. The Head-woman's lackey hadn't given him a precise distance, but Damek felt sure this hell had to end sooner rather than later. They'd been trudging up this bloody road for hours already. If Una wasn't trussed and waiting for him at the end of this journey, Damek would gleefully order every house in Roswealth burned, every stone smashed to powder, and every man, woman, and child piled in the ashes. He'd endured about all of the North he could stomach, thank you.

Having left Martin and the bulk of his forces behind to guard the city, Damek's impatience crouched in his gut like lead. If that Sidhe bastard managed to spirit Una over the border... Damek wouldn't merely condone a slaughter; he'd *initiate* one with relish. Every moment that passed in this godsforsaken wilderness at the edge of the civilized world only served to quicken his ire. So much depended upon Una, he doubted even she knew the extent of her worth. Marrying her meant he'd be his own man— exercise his own power. He'd be owed allegiances rather than beggar them. With a Donahugh bride, he was half a flight of steps nearer his ultimate goal. Without... well... he wasn't going to entertain that notion. Damek would not fail. He must not fail. No one would get in his way now: not the High King, not his bastard son, not Vanna Nema, not the Doma Drem— not even Una herself. He would lock her away for the rest of her life if need be.

Ages ago, he'd pitied her. She'd always been a forlorn and solitary creature, forever hostage to her name. Once, he'd even imagined that he might become her protector. No longer. Now, she was merely a rather palpable means to an end. Damek's determination, however, did little to take the edge off Martin's intense distrust of this little adventure. Indeed, Martin had vehemently argued that the risk should fall upon his shoulders. Damek wouldn't hear of it. One did not send underlings to claim a queen.

This wasn't to say that he was a fool. Escorted by sixty battle-hardened knights and infantrymen, Damek was the best-guarded man in Innisfail. The weather, however, remained unimpressed by his numbers or the martial might at his back. It wasn't raining hard, but by Reason, the deluge was *relentless*. They were forced to stop and slide wooden planks into the mud every few hundred yards to lead their mounts and wagons upward. Each impediment cost him precious time he did not have. To make matters worse, many of Damek's soldiers were reprimanded for spooking their comrades with tales of eyes following them from the trees. He ordered a pikeman clipped soundly across the jaw for making such an outrageous claim when yet another roadblock halted their progress ahead.

Gritting his teeth, Damek leaned into his saddlehorn. "What now? Just shove the limb over the slope and be done with it! We don't have time for this!"

One of his scouts jogged back to the forward line, eyes huge in the lantern light. "Milord! Beggin' yer pardon, but there's men on the road ahead. They're... they're..."

"Out with it, man!" snarled Cunningham from his dappled charger. "Or you'll dine on your teeth."

The scout wrung his sopping hands. "They're in pieces, milord. In pieces! *Reason*... I ain't ever seen anythin' like it."

Killian and Hamish strode over first. The men at their rear reached for their weapons.

"In pieces?" Damek craned his neck to peer over the fellow's head. There wasn't much to see save a downed tree limb and scattered foliage billeted by the occasional violent gust of wind. Damek dismounted. "Show me."

The scout's face bleached white as a whale's underbelly. "No, milord! No! You *shouldn't* go that way. We should turn around. They're not... they're not—"

"Killian, restrain that man." The scout's answering yelp caused Damek to raise a hand. "No, don't hurt him. Hamish, you're with me."

"Milord," the scout cried as they dragged him to the rear of the line. "They're not dead!"

Hamish drew his sabre; his left hand gripped his dagger's hilt. Damek slogged up the road to the downed limb. He couldn't make much out at first except mud, rocks, thinning trees on his right— and the deep black chasm on his left. Damek heard them before he saw them. The scout's lantern lay smashed beside one of their heads, its candle long extinguished by dauntless rain. The smell struck him next. Damek lurched sideways, smashing his hand over his mouth and nose. Hamish made a weak, mewling sound.

"Major! Lieutenant Killian! *We need more men up here!*"

One of the poor souls in the road attempted to crawl toward Damek, his mangled fingers grasping pitiably as if toward a parent. "C... cold...", he moaned, towing his half-eaten torso behind him like toppled rigging. "So... cold." Damek had to blink a few thousand times to be sure he was seeing what he thought he was. The dead man's skin was blue and grey, but what spilled from his center was black, putrid, and oily as pitch. Though, this wasn't even the most horrifying part of the scene. The boy behind him stared ut the sky, no doubt heaving his final wasted breaths. He had quite a hole in his guts, and his arms had been gnawed to the bone. Meanwhile, the crawling corpse's mouth spilled open over each pathetic whine, pouring gobs of fresh gore down its half-eaten jaw. One eye hung from its socket, asif pecked out by carrion. Chewed fingertips grazed the top of Damek's boot. He recoiled.

Hamish wasted no time. His sabre sang out, severing the thing's head from the root. The head spun over the drop and disappeared into the night. The body sank soundlessly into the mud. Cunningham loped to their side, holding a fresh lantern aloft.

"Dear Reason... *what* in the hells is happening?"

Damek righted himself as best he was able. "He... it... *ate* the other fellow," he gestured to the young man dying against the downed limb. The victim gurgled helplessly. His fingers twitched from a shredded forearm. That appendage resembled a desiccated chicken wing, neatly stripped of every ounce of flesh save the stubborn bits clinging to the cartilage beneath. Damek was careful not to step in his steaming viscera. Lips trembling, the lad tried to speak. Damek had to get close to hear. "What's your name, boy?"

Hamish knelt astride the limb and gently lifted the boy's head. The victim couldn't have been more than seventeen years old, if that. "Bre... ccan."

"What happened to you, Breccan?"

"C... old. I'm so..." The blue-white flesh around Breccan's mouth split wide as if in a maniacal grin. Damek saw what was happening too late to stop it. Breccan's mandibles clamped over the meat at Hamish's wrist; his fleshless arms lashed out, drawing Hamish close with supernatural speed. Breccan's teeth tore into the muscle and tendons below the skin. Scrambling to shove the boy away, Hamish howled in shocked pain. It took Damek, Cunningham, and Killian all pulling at once to separate them. Snapping like a dog, Breccan flopped onto his side. He tried to snare anything his teeth could connect with. Damek kicked him hard in the chin, breaking the boy's jaw with a sickening crunch. Unfazed by such a sseverewound, Breccan gnawed at the ground with his top incisors. His gray tongue lapped at the spill of his own blood. Cunningham stepped onto his back, driving him into the mud with his boot. With a furious cry, he shoved his sabre through the rear of Breccan's skull—

its point protruded from the boy's gaping, grisly mouth. His eyes rolled back to the pearls. Cunningham retracted his blade but brimmediately brought itown from the broadside to sever Breccan's head.

Hamish's shrieks pierced the night around them, despite every effort to keep him calm. His wrist looked like it had been caught in a grinder; blood spurted from the artery, which had all but been scraped away by the lad's ragged teeth. Damek could spy flashes of ivory bone peeking through the mash. Hamish fell on his rump, face stricken. His lips turned blue. He looked up at Damek with eyes full of fear.

"*He bit me...* I can't... can you believe it?" A line of spittle dribbled onto Hamish's stained cuirass. "I don't feel so good..."

Damek sighed, eying Cunningham in silent appeal. Wallace shook his head. Damek's fingertips brushed his pommel. "We'll get you fixed up, Hamish."

Hamish's head bobbed around like a top. "It's just a bite, right? Could you help me to my horse, Wally? I have a blanket in my saddlebag. It's... freezing all of a sudden, isn't it?"

An alarming shudder ran through the large knight that Damek had known all his life. Hamish's cheeks waxed ashen.

"It's... I'm... *cold...*" the whites of his eyes spun toward Damek, same as Breccan's had as if drawn to the warmth radiating from his lord's body. Damek swallowed the solid lump in his throat and brought his sabre down, just as Cunnigham shoved Hamish forward. Headless, the knight's body slumped sideways. Neither Damek nor Cunningham said a word. They merely watched the rain patter over Hamish's breastplate for some time. Only then did Damek notice the sounds coming from the trees around them: plodding footfalls, moans, and muttering from the dark. Damek slid his sabre back into its sheath with a curse.

Cunningham was visibly alarmed beside him. "We should turn back, My Lord. There're more of those... things...out there."

"Every man with a lantern or a torch, get them lit, right now!" Damek bellowed to his horrified troops. "We've enough pitch to last three nights! Let me see no man without a light on his person! Answer if you understand!"

440

He waited for the appropriate bevy of hesitant but dutiful 'ayes.'

Cunningham gripped his shoulder. "My Lord, if those things come for us—"

"They won't. They crave warmth... but the warmth of flesh and blood, Wallace— the life spark inside the living. Fire, on the other hand, they fear. They won't come into the light. I promise you."

"How can you be sure?"

"Don't you know what today is, Major?"

"But... that's ridiculous, lord. Peasant talk. It's just a day for festivals and the like."

Damek gestured to the moaning treeline. "Tell that to *them*. It's Samhain. In the North, we'd best heed that 'peasant talk' to the letter." He stalked back to his horse, taking the hissing torch Killian handed over when he remounted.

"Lord Bishop, ought we not to wait for daylight then?"

Damek waited for his infantrymen, armed with fresh torches and lanterns, to shove the tree limb out of his path. He nudged his horse forward, sparing Cunningham a determined glare.

"You'd leave Lady Una Donahugh to Hamish's fate, Major?"

Cunningham snarled, "Hells no."

"Then get on your fucking horse, Wallace. Pray we get there first."

🦌 🦌

SHAMBLING SOULS, LURED BY THE spray of blood in the road, shied from her approach. Shielding cavernous eyes and horrid rictus grins behind rotting fingers, they moaned in fright. Aoife pitied these creatures half as much as she reviled them. Careful to conceal her disgust, she pushed her hood back. Her amethyst ogham charm swung from her fist by a thin gold rope. She whispered a small incantation, etching an illuminating circle of dry air around the crown of her obsidian hair. Her violet eyes blazed through the misted gloom. Suddenly, as entranced as they were afraid, the dead scrambled away from their kill— weeping in pathetic awe of her might.

The wind rustled through the four silver chains in her right ear, making a music that was at once soothing and terrible, for the dead did not belong in this realm. Only those of high Sidhe blood like Aoife could release them from the torment of their cravings. She could send them back to the peace of Tech Duinn. However, some did not wish to return. These souls hissed at her approach. They were resentful of her power to thwart their revenge upon the living. She smiled back at them. They'd do.

"Don't be afraid." Easily beguiled, they crept forward, dragging bits of themselves behind them. She reached inside her grey cloak and removed a tiny brass bell from an inner pocket. "It is warmth you crave? I shall give it to you."

Movement from her peripherals made her smile the wider. An army of Sluagh ambled toward the shining beacon she presented. All helplessly drawn toward the cool, radiant light in her blood. She tipped the little bell in her fingers once, twice, each stroke eliciting a convulsive response from her growing audience. Like a putrid wave, they swarmed the road from every conceivable direction, macabre features rapt.

"Come," she sang, shaking her bell. "I've all the warmth you can hold... just ahead. Follow me."

THE THING OUTSIDE

n.e. 508
30, ðor samna
the greensward

Ben might have been flying up that craggy hillside. His boots danced over the stone and scree beneath their soles. The rain had let up a bit. The sky overhead bloomed deepest cobalt in the reach of cloud-swept stars. Clear, silver moonlight illuminated their path: a metaphor painted on the evening air. Ben and company dashed upward as fast as they could until the trail banked sluggishly left at the summit. Soon, they arrived in a high valley billeted by bare oaks and fully resplendent conifers. Focusing on the outer rim, Ben discerned a small group of huts and cabins gathered at the opposite end. He pointed at a cabin perched at a distance from the others, which faced the northern slope.

"There," he said. "That's where they are. I can see the traces, but—" He squinted at a peculiar smudge that lurked around its perimeter. Panic struck a resonant chord within his mind.

Robin noted his sudden silence. "What?"

Ben dragged his frown sideways. "You know."

"Already?"

A curt nod was the best Ben could muster.

"Right. Don't 'spose there's any way to kill it from a distance, like?"

"*You* shouldn't get anywhere near it. I mean it, Gramble. That thing will rip through each of you like parchment. Keep to the east of the cabin, on the low trail there. Downwind. I'll draw it off."

"What then?"

"If I can distract it and move it upwind, get the girls down that trail as fast as you can." Ben hacked off a lock of his hair and handed it to Gerrod. "Take that. It won't stop them all, but it'll be better than nothing."

A sharp laugh issued from the cauldron of pines on their right. Ben's head whipped around. An average-sized man with a wan, flat face materialized from the dark. He was eating an apple... ripe and red as no fruit to be found in all of Eire.

"Grand plan you've got there."

Each man went for their nearest weapon, save Ben, who growled deep in his chest. "What are you doing here?"

The mysterious woodsman smirked while he chewed. "You invited me, remember? Or, as I recall, begged me for aid. So here I am." He waved a hand like a shabby magician showing off a dubious trick.

"Ben... is that...?" Robin bristled.

The figure cocked his head. "Do I *look* like a pooka to you?"

"Never seen one, but I'd say yer ugly enough."

Seamus, by far the most superstitious of the lot, turned away. He squeezed his sprig of mistletoe until his fingertips went white.

The newcomer took another bite out of his apple. "That won't work on me, boy."

"What does?"

Their visitor shrugged. "Not a damned thing."

Ben moved between them. "If you've bothered to come all the way up here and interfere, please tell me you've done as I asked?"

Sighing, the newcomer tossed his apple core behind him as if bored already. "Perhaps I have, perhaps I haven't. I am not yours to command, Kaer Yin."

"I wonder then, Uncle, why you bothered to come at all... if my request for aid was so far beneath your regard?"

"Uncle?" Robin's face screwed up. "I heard yer Uncle Bov was a fine lord. Red-headed, like Seamus here."

Seamus drew Gerrod against him like a shield. "Not that uncle, Robin. *The other one…*"

"Yer tellin' me this is the Lord of Tech Duinn? Bah, I have more impressive boots."

"You shouldn't insult him." Seamus looked like he might faint.

"That's the 'King of Tech Duinn' to you, friend," the fellow sneered. "But in this guise, you may call me Faris. It's a wonder you don't remember Faris, Robin Gramble. You've met him many times."

"Can't say I do. Ben, if he ain't here to help, let's go. We've a date with yon beastie, don't we?"

Faris shot Ben a sidelong glare. "Kaer Yin, your friend is extremely rude." The air around him shimmered with tangible malice. Robin did back up a pace then. Seamus prayed aloud to Siora, and Gerrod stared at Ben with his hand on his dagger.

Ben didn't have time for this. "It's why we get along. Answer the question or get out of the way."

"As tedious as ever, I swear. Fine." Faris gave Ben's shoulder a condescending pat. "I gave word days ago."

"To whom?"

"I wonder…"

"Diarmid—"

"Don't you want to know what I've done with your lovely princess and her clever friend?"

Ben went still as a stone. "Maybe I'll just kill you?"

"I'd love to watch you try, Nephew."

Ben tapped Nemain's pommel. "Don't count on it."

"Now, now, gents," Robin interjected. "Surely we can work this out afore that thing down there gets its supper?"

"*Kaer Yin Adair,*" a wholly different voice emerged from Faris' lips. Ben cursed under his breath. "I offer you a choice."

"I refuse. This is neither the time nor place, Uncle."

"Then, I will take both girls home with me. Surely a far preferable fate to the one you've set upon them. No?"

Ben winced. He deserved that. Robin spared him a raised brow, which he roundly ignored. "You don't have the right to challenge me."

"I couldn't allow such a delicate flower to be consumed by Dor Sidhe scum simply because you offered it bait. Could I?"

"I forbid—"

"You don't have a thing to say about it, Ard Tiarne. It's done. Those girls would be dead twice over if I hadn't interceded." Faris crossed his arms over his chest. "Wouldn't my keeping Una achieve the very same you strive for? Presumably, her removal from Eirean politics, for the cessation of hostilities in Eire. Your father will be pleased with you, either way. You'll be lauded in Bri Leith as a hero and be back to preening in your silver spurs in no time. Why should it matter how this end is achieved, hm?"

A slow grin spread over Faris' irritating face. "Unless... but it *couldn't be*, could it? A Milesian woman, Yin?"

Ben fumed in silence. He neither wished to confirm nor deny a Herne-damned thing. Behind him, Seamus muttered a curse and slapped a pair of coppers into Gerrod's open palm. Robin, too, begrudgingly passed the lad his coins. Smirking, Gerrod found something very interesting on the ground to stare at.

"Gods damn you, Diarmid..." glared Ben.

Faris chuckled, "You may take them back before the third hour past midnight. To do so, you must give up your scheme to break your geis. I'll personally send the beast back whence it came, and neither girl shall know how close they came to the most horrid of fates."

"Or?"

"Or, my dear nephew, you may cross into Aes Sidhe this very night. A free man. You shall have your name, titles, and all that you were born to possess... but the girl will go with me. Choose wisely."

Ben launched himself forward. His fist caught nothing but air. When Faris reappeared, some distance away, he laughed at his nephew's pathetic display.

"If you lay a hand on her—"

"Tsk, tsk, Yin," Faris mocked and faded. "Time's running out." With a giggle, he vanished altogether.

Gerrod leaned close to Ben's ear. "What happens in," he looked up at the moon to mark its movement, "three-quarters of an hour?"

"The veil will diminish entirely. The pooka will be freed."

"Ye gonna accept his offer, then?" Robin eyed him closely.

Ben scoffed. "He was stalling."

"For what?"

"He's trying to keep me from getting there too soon and spoiling his fun."

"What does he want with them?"

Ben sighed. "You've seen what Una can do?"

"Aye, so?"

"I imagine he has, too."

🦌 🦌

Una FELT EACH IMPACT AGAINST the cabin in her molars. The creature leered at her from every opening it could squeeze its eyes into. Cackling, it scraped the walls with claws easily as long as Una was tall. It whispered horrible things into the cracks, promising violence she'd never imagined possible. It yearned to shred her insides with its teeth, slather its tongue over the soft core of her still-beating heart, and shuck her bones to the marrow. It vowed to treasure her screams above any prize. It pleaded undying love and devotion. It swore to wear Ben's face for her if she came willingly How it longed to hear both girls weep, to taste their skin, their blood! Perhaps it would be gentle? If they came out sooner, it promised to kill Una long before it ate her. If only she'd allow it to embrace her first. Maybe, let it chew on her a bit before it stopped her heart in its teeth? She would like that, wouldn't she? Wouldn't that be better than fading into Tech Duinn with the Sluagh?

Drip, drip, drip, taunted the water from the tray. Una mashed her hands against her ears to keep either racket from burrowing into her skull. She begged the creature to stop, but that only excited it more. She

447

heard its rows of teeth gnashing all around her. Its lewd suggestions turned her stomach in gleefully described detail. The more excited the thing became— the higher its keening howls.

Water sang *drip, drip, drip*, down the pitcher. Rian's uneven breathing grew weaker by the moment. The ice clinked together in the glass. The wind tore over the roof in an unending cadence. *Drip* went the water. *Clink* went the ice.

I will peel your skin back with my fangs, promised the voice outside. *How you will writhe beneath me.*

Una could bear it no longer. She buried her face in her hands, folding into herself like a child. She screamed until her shrill voice drowned out every other sound. There was no tray of enchanted refreshments. No hollow spaces between worlds to be trapped within. No beasts from deepest abysses vowing to maul, rape, and eat her. There was no wind outside. No time. No battles raging in Rosweal. Nothing. There was *nothing*. Just her own harsh vocal cords, and the beat of blood in her ears. She wailed until she thought her lungs might explode. For a moment, as she drew in her next breath, she heard nothing save the thud of her own heart in her palms. Then, the litany began again…

Drip, drip, drip…

Clink, chime.

…your skin… your bones…

She stumbled into the wall, weeping. Beside her, the silver tray beckoned. Tantalizing beads of cool sweat ran down each glass. The fruit perfumed the air with luscious, irresistible sweetness. She turned her face away on a sob. Her body wracked with fatigue, hunger, thirst, and fear, she pressed her hot cheek to the clapboards, wishing for someone, *anyone*, to make it stop.

A hand slid down the wall, covering her own with reassuring warmth. She cracked a stinging eye to follow that hand to its owner. Tapered fingers bearing simple silver rings engraved with unreadable symbols; an arm wrapped in a linen sleeve, dyed a flat black; silver-white hair brushing the curve of a large shoulder; sympathetic eyes in a green so vibrant she could almost smell the river-slick moss within them.

Ben! She mouthed his name, desperate for comfort, for reprieve. Those inexplicably green eyes held hers long enough to stop her breath.

No... she was wrong.

The planes of this fellow's face were similar but decidedly sharper— symmetrical to the point of perfection. His lips bordered on the feminine. His arched brows were a shade too dark for his impossibly fair hair. They wound together over those beautiful green eyes. Ben's eyes were silver. Una jerked away from the wall, but her visitor did not release her hand.

"Don't be afraid," he said. It was the same voice that had brought her to this pass in the first place. That voice brushed over her arms like velvet, raising gooseflesh along her spine. He was taller than Ben, and there was something else to him, something indefinable that made him feel taller than the pines outside. If she were not terrorized, starving, and dying of thirst, she'd have been staggered by the excruciating beauty of his face. A light, like a candle flame, seemed secreted within his skin. This light illuminated the small cabin to an almost blinding degree. Ten gold chains swung from the arch of his perfect right ear. "I won't harm you, Una."

The sound of her name from his lips sent a shudder thrice as disturbing as anything the lascivious creature outside suggested through her. She wrenched her fingers free and rubbed them against her filthy trousers like he'd stolen their warmth.

"*Who are you?*" she croaked, placing herself between him and Rian, who was still unconscious on the wooden floor. Una realized she couldn't hear the creature anymore nor see its eyes squeezing against the glass to look in on them. Where was it? Had it gone? Were they free? Her visitor took another step toward her as if approaching an unbroken mare. She cleared her blistered throat. "Why have you done this to us?"

"I've saved you, as I said I would." He tugged a sculpted chin toward the serving vessels. "Why haven't you eaten anything I provided? Have you taken one sip of water? You poor things! Had I known, I—"

"*Shut up!* You're a lying bastard!" The effort required to shout was gargantuan. She slipped to the floor, huffing. "Does that... thing out there belong to you too?"

449

"No. The pooka has come for your friend here. I'm sorry to say."
Slowly, keeping his hands visible all the while, he pressed two fingers to
Rian's jaw. "She's alive, but barely. How did this happen?"

Una ignored the greasy feeling in her gut. "You first."

"Una, you both must take refreshment. Only a little will do for now."

"Don't you dare call me by my name!"

"Ben pledged to get you to safety in Aes Sidhe, did he not? Well,
here I am," he said, splaying his beautiful fingers— a lutist's fingers... or
a weaver's, maybe?

She recalled how lovely her father's bard's fingers had been. How
fast they flew over the strings. How deft and skillful they were. Admiring
him, as only a child of six might do, she wanted nothing more than to
possess the same beauty and skill in her own hands one day. She felt
herself smiling. Her eyes flew wide.

"Stop that!"

Her visitor knelt beside her. "Your hands *are* beautiful, Una. Will
you share what the markings mean?" He ran the tip of an index finger
along one long blue whorl. "Especially this bit. I can hear it singing to
me from beneath your skin. How does it do that? Will you teach me?"

She snatched her hands back, then shoved them beneath her arms.
"Don't touch me. Don't touch Rian either. *Get out!*"

Here, his smile lost some of its charm. "If I leave, Yin's pet comes
in."

"What do you mean, *his* pet?"

"Why, you're bait. I thought you'd have put this together by now.
More appropriately, she's the bait," he pointed to Rian. "I'm sure the
pooka is more than pleased to take the pair of you, though, in exchange
for summoning me."

Una opened her mouth for a sharp retort, but despite the cruel
delivery, she detected no lie in his words. If what he said was true... no.
She wouldn't think of it now. There'd be plenty of time to kill Ben later.
"You said, before, he was your nephew? That makes you—"

"Fiachra Ri, at your service, My Lady." His smile was warm as honey
again. "Take some refreshment, Una. We'll leave this place, the three of

us. I shall give you sanctuary. There'd be no war, death, or struggle—no one to use you for their gain. I know you crave peace above all else. Who'd dare to challenge the King of Tech Duinn to reclaim you?"

"In exchange for what?" Una avoided the magnetism in the swirling emerald depths of his eyes. He was too near. He smelled like pine needles in a rain-swollen meadow or the white lilies that bloomed over her mother's fountain in Bethany. She could almost feel that cool water beneath her searching fingers; hear her mother's throaty laughter. She gasped, "Stop!"

"I'm not doing anything, Una. These are your thoughts and feelings, not mine. Everyone responds to my voice differently, but that doesn't mean the images you see are harmful to you. They simply are." He reached out, holding a perfect white lily in his palm. She recoiled. She could hear her mother's voice, almost see her reflected in the translucent pearl of each petal. "What else do you see?"

Una had that strange sensation of falling upward again, but this time through chill clear water choked with lilies. Her bare toes scraped against the bottom of her mother's fountain. Pushing herself upward, she emerged dripping into warm summer sunlight. Una wore a gown of purest white as if it had been made from the petals she waded through. The air was sweet with their scent and dusky with sun-soaked earth. Her wet hair clung to her back, already curling from the heat baking into her skin. She pulled herself over the stone rim, wringing her hair out behind her. A pleasant, half-dreamy smile pulled her cheeks wide. Someone approached her from behind and pressed something smooth and dry against her damp skin. His arms wrapped around her waist. She snuggled into him with a contented sigh. A lock of his silver hair coiled over her shoulder as he bent to whisper against her nape.

Distantly, shock infused the joy in the scene. The image was a feeling… a desire she wasn't aware she had: those warm hands, the familiar, comfortable weight of that body against hers. Her dream self laughed at something he said. She spun in his arms to press her mouth to his. Then Una fell again, back into her body: cold, starved, and afraid. Her cheeks burned with morbid embarrassment. This was something she hadn't known she wanted. She'd been forced to share its realization, with *him*. She squeezed her eyes shut. Her breath caught in her throat. *Ben*, her heart wept for stunted need. No... *Kaer Yin*. The ache was worse for the numbing lucidity the name inspired. It could never be. Hidden longing made a fool of her. He was the future Ard Ri. She'd age and die in mere decades, while he would live on, safe and powerful, in the might of his immortal Sidhe blood.

The King of the Underworld's voice was silk and sinew, spice and balm. "I cannot give you the man, but I can give you everything else." He prodded her chin up with his knuckle. "I know your fears, your pain, and your joys. I sympathize. In Tech Duinn, you'll never age, yearn, or feel pain again. You've had a hard life, Una. Very hard. Born to be a pawn for all who claim you as kin. I can take all of that away. Midhir will only use you in his own game— another endless, painful play for power. As will they all. I will not. Won't you let me give you that fountain, that endless summer's day? Perhaps, even in time..."

"*No.*" Una swiped at her eyes with her wrist. "It wouldn't be real. What you're offering isn't real. What's more, you mean to use me, too."

He watched her for some time in silence. When next he spoke, his voice rang clear. It was only a voice, and he was just a man. His features cut a harder edge, as if he grew more corporeal by the instant.

"I'm in earnest, nonetheless. I'll give you what I know you want most, Una. Solitude. A world without ambition, without war. No one to abuse you for your gifts. A place to hone your skills, to study, to learn. Isn't that what you want? More than anything?"

Somehow, his tone was more seductive without the enchantment. Her Spark flared bright in her blood. A warning. No, more than that. Encouragement. Self-assurance. *Clarity*. This man, this *thing*; whatever he truly was or had been many thousands of years ago was trying to manipulate her— expertly too, there was no point denying. He was the most beautiful creature she'd ever set eyes upon and somehow, fouler than the beast waiting outside to devour her. This wasn't about Una at all. Hidden within his voice, she caught a different note: discordant, patient, and *ambitious*. He didn't want to save her from the world. He wished to mold her, sap her of will and agency, remake her for himself. There was no mercy or peace. The King of Tech Duinn would take her power and use it toward his own ends. All he needed was her consent. There were rules in the Oiche Ar Fad, weren't there? Rules by which even he must abide. Her silence must have impressed upon him some faltering weakness. He snapped a finger. One of the glasses from the tray appeared in his hand. He held it out to her, features pulled into the most perfect mask of tender concern she'd ever seen.

"Take my hand, Una. Free yourself."

Una's fingers wound through Rian's of their own accord. Rian grew colder, her breathing more irregular. Staring into the gratifying liquid tempting her from the glass, Una reached inside herself to a place she hadn't known she possessed. Her Spark flared at the touch. It purred like a cat ready to spring.

Yes, it sang along her nerves, be free. She took the glass, her hand steady. *Be free*! Without a word, she poured its contents down her throat. Her tormentor's smile lit up the whole world. He took the empty glass from her, then tossed it into a darkened corner. It never connected with the ground. The water sloshed around inside her empty belly. She concentrated for only a few seconds; her brows knit together as if she was grateful for the relief the cordial proffered. His hand slithered over hers.

"You've made the right choice, my dear."

She squeezed his fingers back. "*Oh, I know.*" Without mercy, she unfurled her Spark from that secret place at her center. His eyes bulged in surprise. She clamped down hard, wrenching him forward. His power funneled from his body into hers, like a burst dam. Relentless, she pulled until she thought she might overflow. Teeth flashing, he fought to free his fingers from the ever-increasing strength in her grip. "It's called Manipulation, My Lord. I'm only sorry it didn't occur to me sooner… I'm *better* at it than you."

"Let go, you *witch*!"

The walls of the cabin hardened in her vision. The storm finally kept time with their prison inside. The beast's claws penetrated real wood. Her stomach churned a bit at the glee in its poisonous chants. She must be ready for that wall to come down. It wouldn't be long now. The cornices creaked under the pooka's solidifying weight.

"Let me go!" the King of Tech Duinn cried in horror. Such strength he had! Una had never felt anything like it before. It couldn't be all that dissimilar from sucking down the wind at the center of a gale, or swallowing lightning from thin air. She felt the depths of his power boiling straight through the mountain's core, the river snaking through the valley below, and the impenetrable mists of the border beyond. The Veil was apparent to her now— a gossamer thread separating each realm, ready to snap free at any moment.

She sensed riders coursing up the road on the far side of the summit. Their horses were lathered, their eyes bright with lantern light and quaking fear. Next was the dull static of the dead, clambering after them by their hordes. The impression they left upon her psyche made her gasp. She shivered in empathetic alarm. There was more.

Living beings. *Thousands* of them. Some diaphanous as cobwebs, others filled with low cunning, mischief, or unabashed abandon. In this pulsing haze, she discovered men on this side of the hill: four of them. Men she *knew*.

In her relief, she let go. Una positively thrummed with Diarmid Adair's stolen power. He gave her one last withering glare, folded in on himself, and blasted through the rear wall like a cannon shot. Shrieking in anticipation, the pooka rushed toward the opening. Grabbing Rian by the arm, Una dragged her to her side. Una's hand shot out: her best defense. The creature slithered into view... teeth snapping, claws tapping together in delight.

"*Kaer Yin!*" she screamed into the night, just as it launched itself inside.

THE RAVEN KING

n.e. ꟻ08
31, ꝺoꞃ samna
samhain

S ave for the prowling, amorphous creature outside, the rundown
cabin appeared empty. No light glinted from either dirty window,
nor could Ben hear anyone moving inside. If it weren't for the
pooka's frantic attentions, one could reasonably assume the girls were
long gone… but Ben knew better. His intuition told him both girls were
trapped within, and they were not alone. The dwelling hummed with
Diarmid's dark influence. Ben might have known his uncle would pull
something like this.

Inwardly, he kicked himself for his lack of foresight.

Una possessed a deep well of unfathomable gifts, which a Brehon
of Diarmid's talent would find irresistible. The knowledge stuck in Ben's
throat like a burr. If he'd had the time to ask someone else, *anyone* else, for
aid, they wouldn't be in this bloody mess in the first place. Diarmid was a
much-beloved family member. Equally, he was the least trustworthy man
Ben knew. Beggars, as they say, cannot be choosers.

Whatever was happening inside those walls, there wasn't a damned
thing Ben could do about it now. He had to trust Una and Rian to resist
whatever his manipulative uncle threw at them for a while longer. Due
to the wailing westerly wind and the racket the pooka made trying to rip
its way through Diarmid's enchantment, Ben and company were all but

invisible, creeping along the hillside. They tucked in among a thicket of tangled alders to take stock. Robin patted Ben's shoulder.

"Well, what're we doin'?"

"What we came here to do."

Each of them ogled Ben, brows raised.

"What?" he scoffed. "None of you *believed* that tripe, did you?"

"He said he'd let that thing eat 'em, Ben," said Gerrod. "Ye don't think he meant it? Or what he said about—"

"Gerry, here's a free lesson in Sidhe wisdom... *never* trust the King of Tech Duinn. Of course we're not going to let him do either thing he bloody well promised to do. Diarmid can shove his demands up his arrogant arse."

"We're going to get them out?"

"Same plan, same goal."

Slapping Seamus' bicep, Gerrod held out his hand. Grumbling, Seamus dug another coin out of his tunic and slammed it indelicately into Gerrod's waiting palm.

"Bleedin' me dry, ye half-grown weed."

Ben glared. "You boys have something you'd like to ask me?"

Robin cleared his throat, "Just a bit o'nonsense, that. Anyway, I don't think yer, erm, uncle meant to put ye off at all. Seems to me he was testin' yer intent."

"How so?"

"Sounded almost fatherly, ye ask me. 'Son, ye can keep that pup ye brought home, but ye'll have to give up somewhat to keep it.' Like that."

"... Ridiculous."

"What I took from it."

"He's hoping to take advantage."

"Maybe, that too. Point is, I think he was needlin' ye to see how serious ye were about goin' home... and the girls, o'course. One in particular." Robin tactfully avoided Ben's burning gaze.

"It *isn't* bloody like that."

"Sure it ain't." Robin's mouth twitched. Seamus tapped his shoulder before Ben could articulate an appropriate insult. He pointed to the bushes ahead. Something large and misshapen passed before them. "Remember what he said about the time? If we can see that…thing, does that mean the girls're where it can get to 'em?"

Ben peered hard into the small clearing. As the pooka gained strength and substance, it shifted through shapes with rapacious enthusiasm: here, a great black stallion, there a bird of prey, searching for weak spots in the roof. The damage it inflicted increased by the moment. The Veil was fading. While they watched this monstrous display, a small light flickered to life in the nearest window. Ben could see the top of Una's golden head. A dark-clothed figure with fair hair bent over her. Ben was on his feet before he realized his intent. His uncle smiled smugly, his hand over Una's. Ben watched her drink something Diarmid offered. Then, his uncle drew her into his arms.

"Una!" Ben bellowed, heedless of discovery. "Don't!"

"Ben!" Robin shouted. "Watch yerself!"

The pooka loped around the window, momentarily impeding Ben's view. Dragging massive claws along the outer wall, it sought to obliterate all remaining impediments to its feast. Ben ducked, but he needn't have bothered. The beast was so concerned with demolishing the cabin that it didn't even glance up at Ben's shout. On a frustrated growl, it melted into a shape halfway between man and winged serpent. Skittering onto the roof, its claws began to gain purchase.

Ben made a beeline for the window. Inside the cabin, the atmosphere had changed. All of a sudden, Diarmid cried out and fell to his knees. Una held his hand in a death grip, her nails scraping bloody lines over his bare knuckles. Ben was near to the cabin wall when she let Diarmid go. She staggered to the floor beside Rian. His uncle tore through the back wall, smashing it outward in a blast of splinters, dust, and limping magic. Ben barely had time to absorb what had happened when the wall came crashing into the dirt behind the cabin, bits and pieces scattered over the hillside.

Shrieking in delight, the pooka oozed toward the opening. In the wreckage, Una pulled Rian close. She held out a hand, as if that could slow the creature down.

"*Kaer Yin!*" she screamed as the beast lurched through the breach.

"Robin, now!" Ben shouted. Sword drawn, he dove head-first through the open window.

🦌 🦌

Ben's blade slid under the pooka's foremost claw just as the beast attempted to plunge it through Una's chest. Rolling upright, he wrenched the talon painfully aside with the broad side of his blade. Shunting forward with all his body weight, he forced the beast back half a pace.

Its answering hiss blew the hair out of Ben's eyes. The chains in his ear chimed in the malodorous cloud.

"*Ard Tiarne... you betray meeee?*"

"Your fault for being such a gullible, greedy piece of shite." Clutching at its wounded claw, it wriggled outside. It flashed through an assortment of shapes in a clicking, keening rage.

While it vented its anger on nearby trees and buildings, Una's trembling fingers dug into Ben's forearm. "Kaer Yin, *how* did you get here?"

He flinched to hear her speak his name. Without warning, he jerked her into an embrace. "Are you all right?"

"I think so. That *thing*—"

"I know. I don't have time to explain. Rian?"

"She will be, I think. It's my fault, I—"

"Una... it doesn't matter. It's going to come back." Pressing her close for a moment, he lightly brushed the top of her head with his lips. Ignoring her indrawn breath, he shoved her toward the far exit. To know she and Rian were alive was enough for now. "Get out of here quick as you can. Robin is waiting."

"Why did that sound like 'goodbye?'" Her voice quivered.

"In case it is," he stared through the hole in the wall, keeping his back to her. "I'm no good at this... Una. I want you to know, *I* don't care what your name is. My uncle was right, this is purely selfish. I think it has been, all the while."

458

"What? I… don't understand."

"Yes, you do," he gave her a last, lingering look, wishing he had more time to explain. She blinked at him in befuddled embarrassment. If he lived through this, he wondered how she'd react. Ben didn't stick around to make sure she made it out. Head high, he stepped through the back wall. The pooka found another form it liked better than the stallion, the bird, or the lizard. It wore Ben's relative features again, only taller, broader. "Come on then." Ben swung Nemain into a high guard. "Come and see how *reduced* I am now, *isesaeligh*."

With an ear-splitting roar, the pooka charged him, talons unfurling like hooks. Vaulting in from below, it took a testing jab which Ben easily slashed away. Melting left on the next breath, it came at Ben's kidneys from the rear. Ben dipped under its reach, then drove Nemain's tip behind him, slicing a chunk out of its left arm. Howling, the pooka charged again. It hacked wildly from both sides at once. Ben swiveled through each thrust, inching toward its center of gravity. It tried to shove him against the cabin, but he rotated his blade high into a forward guard. Using his own momentum, he whirled Nemain's edge around him in cyclonic fashion. The pooka's talons could find no gaps in his defenses. Orbiting the creature in a dizzying, infuriatingly complex series of dips and turns, Ben got near its core three times before his sword finally bit into its flank. Shrieking, the pooka flailed on the ground like a frightened goat. Ben wasn't even winded.

Smiling, he hefted Nemain over his shoulder.

"That all you got?"

"*LIAR! DECIEVER! I WILL WEAR YOUR BONESS LIKE ARMOR! I WILL RAPE YOUR WOMEN CLOAKED IN YOUR OWN HIDE!*" Into the earth below its morphing body seeped something oily and malodorous. Grasping at the new hole in its side, the pooka's yowling rage shook the hillside like thunder. Now in the form of a great black bear, it took a swipe at Ben's head. On a backslash, Ben cut a deep vertical slit into its unsteady foreleg. A small victory. Before he could get out of the way again, it swatted him into a pine with a gigantic forepaw. His spine struck the trunk with a bone-cracking snap. Also grievously injured, the pooka collapsed against the crumbling cabin, hissing, snapping, and snarling.

Momentarily disoriented, Ben didn't see it melt into the shape of something much smaller, with the head and hindquarters of a boar. Sluggish, Ben reached for his fallen sword. One of his ribs was broken, and his breathing wasn't what it had been moments before. Using Nemain for balance, he struggled to his feet. He hadn't quite made it fully upright when Una screamed his name from somewhere nearby. Ramming into Ben headfirst, the pooka drove one of its tusks straight through his ribcage, piercing his lung. Ben's knees buckled. Grunting, they rolled together through the damp leaves along the slope. He managed to throw a hand out, catching the ledge just in time to stop himself from careening over the first drop. The pooka took advantage. Its claw burrowed deep into his chest cavity, ironically, the very place he'd been wounded the last time he'd tangled with this beast. Ben might find it funny, if the wound wasn't sure to kill him.

With every ounce of strength he had left, Ben heaved the pooka up with his knees and hammered Nemain through its middle to the hilt. Viscous black fluid filled his eyes and mouth. Ben turned his face away.

"*Son of Midhir... I cursssseee youu... you shall never...*" Its reeking heart's blood poured down Ben's sword arm. He spat out a wad of the putrid malfeasance, reached into his tunic, and rammed his dagger into the pooka's brain from the ear. Whatever it meant to utter next died on its slackening tongue.

"I'll hear no more of your curses, *isesaeligh*." Ben drove it off his sword and over the precipice. After hacking up everything in his throat, he dragged himself part way uphill, using his sword as an awkward lever. He was sorry to admit that he left a fair amount of his own blood on that slope. Reaching the woods on more level ground, he flopped onto his back to wheeze at the sky. An unhealthy gurgling caught more blood than air in his throat. Footsteps pounded through the foliage close by, but... someone *else* stood closer, breathing almost as harshly as he did. Diarmid met his eyes from the trees beside him. Ben tried to smile as if to say, '*you too, huh?*'

Diarmid crawled to him, his face as pale as milk. With the skeletal smudges beneath his eyes, Diarmid looked easily a thousand years old.

"Yin... no." He laid a shaking hand over the gaping wound in Ben's chest. Ben wanted to sneer at him, but only blood gurgled from his mouth. This was half the old bastard's fault for being such an opportunistic arse. Though, Ben wasn't really angry with him. There wasn't any point now, was there? It figured Ben's plan would end in such a disappointing defeat— that had been the story of Ben's life, hadn't it? Each defeat bore a lesson, and every victory its fair share of shame. No bloody *wonder* he had to cheat at cards.

Then, Una was there. She pulled his head into her lap.

"Kaer Yin!" Her beautiful, filthy cheeks were flooded with tears. He reached up to touch one. How strange. A *Milesian* woman should mourn him, after everything he'd done? He was amazed. She twisted a glare at Diarmid. "Do something!"

Diarmid flinched from her voice. What had Una done to his mighty uncle to make him fear her so? Ben could only guess. In all likelihood, Ben would never find out.

"What can I do? He took a terrible wound."

Una swiped at her eyes with shaking hands. Furious, she said, "I know you can do something! I know it! He's your nephew, isn't he?"

"Una..." Ben wanted to tell her it was going to be all right, that he was happy it wasn't for nothing, but she cut him off.

"Shut your idiot mouth! *You're not going to die.* I won't allow it." She turned back to his uncle. "I'll give you whatever you want in return. I swear it. Save him!"

Diarmid stared at her and those gathered in mutual shock, with wide green eyes. "Yin, do you see what's happening here?"

Ben couldn't answer. His vision clouded over. A dry humming echoed in his ears. He was dying. It didn't hurt much, which surprised him more than the doing. Una squeezed his hand.

"Yin, these are human voices begging for your life."

Ben was just as mystified as his uncle.

THE SONS OF MIL

"I'll do as you ask, lady… not because you bargain for it, but because I believe he broke his *true* geis long before tonight. Do you hear me Kaer Yin?"

He did, but had absolutely no idea what Diarmid was talking about.

"I can't heal him." Diarmid's weight shifted over his chest. "But I can save his life. When it's done, get indoors as fast as you can. Light fires in every window. I won't be here to stop them."

"Stop who?" Robin's voice sounded odd, weak.

"Sluagh," answered Seamus from farther off. "It's Samhain."

"You'll owe me for this, little princeling," Diarmid whispered into his ear. Next thing Ben knew, the worst pain he'd ever experienced filled his ribs with molten steel. Scorching white flames licked over his eyes. When had Ben swallowed all nine hells? His back bowed. His arms and legs thrashed in the duff. Diarmid screamed with him. For a while, he couldn't discern his own voice from his uncle's… until, suddenly, Diarmid was gone. Searing pain blew the world and all its newfound oddities out of his mind— like a candle smothered in the dark.

🦌

UNA GATHERED HER WITS FIRST. Anxious, she tugged Ben's inert torso up by the shoulders.

"Quick! You heard his uncle! We have to get inside!" As if shaken out of a daze, Robin leaned down to grab Ben by the ankles, while Seamus helped Una lift his top half. As for Gerrod, he tossed Rian's wilted frame over one shoulder, making sure to leave his dagger hand free. With what she'd stolen from the Raven King thrumming through her veins, Una could feel those thousands of frigid empty vessels moving in from every direction. The dead were coming, and they were not alone. Sylphs, sprites, and phantoms zipped from bough to bough overhead. Mad faeries unblessed with Rian's Ban Sidhe blood wandered the wilderness, laughing or aimlessly chattering to themselves. These were Lu Sidhe… *lesser Sidhe.* They were no threat, so long as they were ignored. Marveling at the breadth and depth of her newfound strength, Una reached further still. In the distance, she caught traces of greater creatures in search of sport and slaughter: Dor Sidhe, like the pooka. Some were worse than that lascivious, revolting beast— so much *worse*... she nearly tripped over her own feet at their discovery.

"Ye all right?" Robin regarded her with a concerned eye.

Blood drained from her cheeks. "There are so many... so... *many*."

Robin clearly had no idea what she was babbling about. "Milady, if ye need to rest, set him down, and I'll—"

Her head snapped around at a sudden hum from the east road. "Quiet," she said, tilting her head toward the sound. "Do you hear that?"

Robin frowned. Una could guess what she looked like to him. Her unkempt hair was in wild knots that she would likely have to shear. Dark bruises pooled beneath both of her eyes, and her cheeks were sunken around bones too sharp for her bloodless flesh. She was covered head to toe in grime; days spent in a dusty cabin in the middle of nowhere without food and water had taken their toll. Her tunic and leggings were caked with a dozen species of stain.

Hearing things on the wind no mortal could ever hope to detect must not have helped her case.

"Lady I think..." he began, lowering his voice to as gentle a croon as he could manage. Several snaps from the woods snagged his attention before he could complete his thought. He squinted into the dark; the wind made it even harder to peer through the blowing, waving fauna. A flash of lighting cracked overhead, and in that brief moment of illumination... Robin's eyes widened to the pearls. "Siora's tits!"

He pulled Ben's heels up so high, the motion almost knocked Una off her feet again. "Move, move, *move*! Get inside! *Get inside!*"

Another crackle of light, and Una saw them too: faces...*hundreds* of faces... shambled up the road. There were so many of them, in varying stages of decrepitude, they might have sprung from the earth like weeds. With renewed urgency, Una and Robin managed to half-pull, half-drag everyone toward the abandoned cottages. The dead were so close, Una could smell them. That sweet, rank scent of overturned earth and corrupted flesh. She gagged, nearly dropping Ben in the process. Why was he so blasted heavy?

Seamus whizzed past her, kicking in the nearest door. He yanked something sour smelling from a chord round his throat. Nodding to him, Gerrod laid Rian down just shy of the open doorway, then helped Seamus break off all the shingles and dried bits of wood the cabin could spare. Kneeling on the stoop, they used whatever they could pilfer to start a small fire. Mere paces away, the dead flinched from this tiny, burgeoning light. Seamus wasted no time. He handed burning shingles to Robin and Gerrod to toss into the nearest cabins, setting their long vacant interiors alight. With each new fire that bloomed before them, the dead slunk back, shielding what remained of their eyes. Una labored to drag Ben through the door, while the Greenmakers went to work starting as many fires as they could manage.

Rian, now somewhat sensate, reached out in an attempt to help Una heave Ben's torso through the opening.

"What happened to him?" she whispered sluggishly, as if fighting upward through a drugged haze.

Her little white face seemed needle-thin to Una's guilty eyes. "Long story, can you help me get his feet inside?"

"Where?" Rian yawned, still half-heartedly trying to pull at Ben's bloody shirt. Una moved her hands back into her lap.

"Never mind, love. Why don't you rest there? Set your head against the wall. That's good. Ben's going to use your knee as a pillow, is that all right?" A single snore was her answer.

Out of kindling, Robin paused to help force Ben's boots inside. Gritting her teeth, Una tugged until the crown of his head rested against Rian, where she slumped against a crumbling wall. Even with both of them pushing and pulling, the big Sidhe bastard weighed too bloody much. Una had to think up a new plan. They didn't have time for this. Sweating, she scowled down the ridiculous length of Ben's inert legs. "Go, Robin. Burn everything that will catch, then get back here."

"What about ye?"

464

The dead corralled themselves further down the north-facing slope to come at them from the shadows on the opposite side. The second road cut through the trees on her left, a broad avenue filled with rotting corpses. Unseen by Una's companions, Lu Sidhe clapped encouragement from the sidelines, gloriously entertained. She swallowed, then leaned against the side of the cabin for support. Taking a deep breath, Una drew power out of her belly and into her mouth. She wasn't sure how she knew which words to use, only what she intended. Her voice filled with an incomprehensible charge. Under her fingers, the wall burst into flame so bright and pure that it shone like a star in the darkness. The blaze licked around her hand: spreading, searching, reaching— until the whole building was wreathed in brilliant orange flames.

"They'll burn!"

Una caught Robin's arm before he could dart inside.

"*No*, they won't."

Under protest, she held his hand over the fire. She knew the wood beneath his fingers would be cool as spring water to the touch. Beguiled, Robin unhooked his arm from hers.

"How'd ye do that?"

"I have *no* idea. Go get the others. These cottages are too wet to burn long, and more are coming."

"How many more?"

Una stared off into space. She heard a seductive, corrupt chiming in the distance. There were so many dead souls in the woods, they seemed a wave crashing up the hillside. Whoever the bell-ringer was, they were not alone. Dozens of soldiers preceded that cruel siren's song.

"Many." Una held onto Robin's sleeve, her eyes too far away to notice his instinctive recoil. "Riders too. Damek is coming, with an entire corps of soldiers."

"Feckin' figures! How many?"

That bell rang over and over again, seemingly filling the valley. She heard a voice calling over that beautiful, melodious charm.

Follow, follow, follow… it sang over the wind …*all the warmth you crave is just ahead.*

They were everywhere. All around. She gasped with the incredible, overwhelming power in that bell... the hungry, pathetic emptiness enticed by its peal.

"Get inside!" she screamed over the wind. "ALL OF YOU! Get inside now!"

Robin did not argue. Snagging Gerrod by the collar, he hauled him toward the house.

"Seamus! Get yer bony arse away from that—"

As Seamus turned to look at him, a crawling thing caught his ankles from a black gap between the houses. He gave a sharp cry and dropped his makeshift torch into the sucking mud. Una had only a single breath to witness the startled, petrified look in his eyes before the thing bit deep into the back of his thigh. Screeching, Seamus scrambled to regain his footing. Ceaselessly, he punched, kicked, or cut at the dead man's bare skull. Undeterred, it buried its decayed face in his blood. Helpless, his friends watched in white-knuckled horror as Seamus' assailant tore great hunks of flesh out of his leg.

"Help me!" he wept, grasping for purchase anywhere he could find it.

Gerrod tried to lurch to his side, but Robin locked his arm around the lad's thrashing arms. The fire Seamus had lit already sputtered out. There were far too many wet holes in that sagging roof.

The fresh scent of blood emboldened the dead.

"SEAMUS!" Gerrod roared over and over. Whimpering, Seamus was drawn into the grass beside the cottage. A second pair of hands snatched at Seamus' writhing arms, then a third, and a fourth. His shrieks were dulled by wet, smacking, gnawing sounds. Bones were wrenched open by greedy fingers; flesh and organs spilled into the moaning maws of several nightmarish creatures. In mere moments, Seamus' cries ceased. All that was left of him was the revolting feast.

Una shoved Robin and Gerrod through the doorway. Bleary-eyed, Robin held Gerrod's weeping body in a vice grip.

"Get inside! Do it!" she sobbed.

466

They'd only partly obeyed her when the nearest hoofbeats sounded behind her. Mounted soldiers galloped up the road. Three men rode abreast, holding torches aloft in each free fist. Damek reined his mount between them. His horse spun to a stop before her and he gaped as if he was surprised to find her so easily.

"Una?" his voice was much deeper than she remembered.

Before he could get another word out, she launched herself at his saddle. Squeezing his reins, her eyes were wild with fear.

"Damek! The dead! They're everywhere!"

His Adam's apple bobbed. He didn't appear surprised by this insane news in the least. Glancing around, he took in the burning building (occupied somehow by still breathing faces), the blood on Una's clothes, the dark smear against the grass, and the things creeping along the ridge. Without warning, he kicked her over. She fell on her rump, just shy of the door. Robin jerked her back by the waist. Tossing his torch down, Damek drew his sword.

"Shield wall! Torches at the front!"

His men moved with practiced efficiency. They formed a tight semicircle in the road between Una's enchanted flames and the dead. Rotted fingers sought every nook and cranny below the light, desperate to get at the warm, living blood on display. A single misplaced step, or an opening in an otherwise solid line was an invitation waiting to be exploited.

Queen of the Night

n.e. ſ08
3], ðor samna
samhain

Damek's men fanned out, locking shields on either side of the road. Pikemen jabbed torches into the gaps while the shield-men pressed the flats of their curved sabres point-first overtop. The dead encircled their phalanx in an oozing throng so tight that torches were as nothing before the horde. Una slipped out of Robin's grip and ran into the road. There, Damek and his officers belched orders over the ever-widening circle of steel and torches.

"Damek!" she shouted at the top of her lungs. "The flames won't be enough!" Either he didn't hear, or he ignored her altogether.

A wooden-faced redhead spurred his mount between them, his sabre slapping time against his charger's flank. He spared Una a single, authoritative glare.

"Get back, My Lady. The Lord Marshal has it well in hand."

Her lip curled. "I'm telling you—" The bell chimed from somewhere beyond the trees opposite. Singsong chanting rose and fell with it, like the gentle lapping of waves on a wide sandy shore. The rider heard it too. He cocked his head, his brows weaving together like twin caterpillars

469

mating. She pointed toward the sound. "There! Can't you hear it? The dead are *lured* here."

Disinterested, he kicked his mount down the line and away from her exclamations. Una tried to wade through the men guarding their makeshift perimeter, only to be shoved back by another firm hand. Then another, and another— until she walked in circles, babbling to no one. The soldiers were preoccupied with the slinking things creeping toward them from the woods. They didn't have time to entertain the notions of a bedraggled, half-starved madwoman. Rationally, Una understood this, but she knew what she knew. She held the King of Tech Duinn's power in her belly— a tumultuous cauldron, which threatened to burst from her mouth and over the hillside like a river in flood. As her bones rattled with the overflow, a sudden thought occurred to her. She raced back to the burning house. Damek barked a command, and his men went to work, slashing and burning as a unit. At the door, Una stumbled over Ben's gangly legs. Robin's eyes met hers with apparent concern.

"I don't think they're listenin' to ye, missus."

"*Hang them*! You have to get out of here." She hauled Ben up by his collar. No simple task— he outweighed her by a ton, at least. "One way or the other, Damek's men won't leave anything alive on this hillside," she huffed. Ben's wound was no longer seeping, nor was it half so deep as it had been, but his gore-spattered cuirass sported a new hole about four-inches wide. She wiped the drying blood from his mouth and cheeks with a tattered sleeve. To observe his beautiful, infuriating face so marred struck some deep chord in her heart that she had no wish to contemplate.

"We can't just leave," Gerrod sniffled, still teary-eyed from witnessing Seamus' grotesque end. "Them things're everywhere. This is cause o'the High King's stag, Robin! It's me fault! Seamus, he'd never have killed a white stag if I hadn't..."

"Quiet, boy." Robin trained a wary eye on the door. "There's somethin' happenin' out there now. D'ye hear that bell?"

Shivering, Una gulped down the surge of molten iron in her throat. "I do. Listen, I can't get you home, but *he* can. The dead won't dare touch him. The Lu Sidhe will go out of their way to avoid him."

"The *what?*"

"Never mind. Damek's men don't know what I do. The dead were lured here by that bell. Someone powerful and cunning is behind this. I think... I'm the only one who can stop them."

"Slow down, missus." Robin placed a warm hand on her shoulder. "What're ye gonna do?"

She let out a long breath. "I'm going to break her enchantment. You'll know it when it happens. Get out that rear window and up over the ridge when I do. Do you hear me?"

"Aye, but it'll be hard to clamber down the slope luggin' this big bastard over me shoulder while Gerry's occupied with yer skinny friend there."

Una took Ben's head in her hands. "You're not going to drag him anywhere. I'm going to give him back to you." Again, she didn't know how she could do such a thing, only that she *could*. She could taste a static, a thunderstorm on the root of her tongue— could feel it laying heavy in the pit of her womb. There was so much of it... too much for one person to carry alone... yet, she could. Una had no idea how any of this was possible. "When he wakes up, tell him I'm sorry. I never meant for any of this to happen, not to any of you. Tell him I said 'thank you,' and I did what I could to make it right. Whatever that's worth. Tell him... I'm glad it was him."

"Yer comin' with us," Robin growled. "I won't leave ye behind."

"You must," she smiled sadly. "If I don't stay, none of you will leave here alive." The bell intensified in volume, and screaming followed in earnest. The valley rang with shouts, horses shrieking in terror, and the sickening crunch of steel hacking into meat and bone. Above all, a woman's sonorous voice lilted in a wicked, melodious chant.

... take your warmth... it is within your grasp.

Una closed her eyes and concentrated on the simmering furnace at her core. She shut out every sound, save the magic rushing through her veins like a bottled inferno. Una drew Ben's mouth to hers. Cupping either side of his face, she poured her altered Spark into him with tender violence. In moments, his body convulsed. Renewed vitality coursed through his limbs as a newborn flame rushes through kindling. Each breath brought quickening light and color into his skin. His eyes snapped open just as she broke contact. He stared up at her, bewildered. Una's heart beat a mournful tattoo. It could never be. Brows drawn together, she pressed her lips to his one last time. Her cheek came away wet. Too late, Ben reached for her, his twitching fingers catching nothing but air. On her feet, Una gave him a sad smile.

"Goodbye, Kaer Yin. Thank you for everything."

He slumped sideways in the entrance while she slipped outside. "U... Una!" he croaked. She didn't look back. Her shoulders squared, she disappeared into the chaos beyond the glowing doorway. He couldn't heal fast enough to stop her.

$$\text{\small ⚕}$$

THE CHANTING GREW LOUDER WITH every step Una took. The soldiers were busy slashing, gouging, and burning through the dead. Even so, she was surprised they could not hear it. The bell was *deafening*, a melodic, hammering thrum that shook the earth beneath her feet. The semi-circle of shields and spears shrank back to the middle of the road, making it difficult for Damek's cavalrymen to ride up and down their line. His men worked hard. Torchmen pushed fire through every gap from shoulder to eye level. Shieldmen held the line in a tight phalanx while pikemen jabbed at anything wriggling on the ground.

Despite the practiced effort, the Southers were hardly winning. The dead were too numerous to fend off with might alone. Rotting fingers and gnashing teeth exploited every undefended chink in their steel wall. Some men were dragged below their shields to meet violent ends in a mess of shredded meat and exposed viscera. Others would take bites then were unceremoniously slain by their companions.

Noting the rapid loss of at least a dozen men, Damek bayed a command. The Corps changed tactics. The second tier of infantrymen threw their smaller shields over the heavier ones at the bottom. A third tier moved in to stab through the low gaps with pikes. This heightened bulwark of steel, wood, sword, and sabre braced itself against the tide of dead faces. Decomposing limbs and snapping jaws scraped against that wall as it moved forward, inch by brutal inch. A breach opened up after one soldier's wrist was caught. He was dragged over his shield. The men behind him closed ranks over his body, swiftly stabbing downward to silence his frantic cries. The skeletal thing that had been consuming him alive was ground to dust beneath their shields.

The gap, however, wasn't easily sealed. Too many arms, teeth, and weapons clashed on either side. Una raised a hand crackling with power. It kept the shields apart long enough for her to glide through. Several soldiers tried to top her, but she ignored them. One mounted officer called a panicked halt as she moved past. She had no fear of the Sluagh. Soon, the Southers saw why. Bearing the King of Tech Duinn's power in her core like boiling quicksilver, the dead shied away from Una as if she were a walking bonfire. She walked straight through their center, unmolested. The afflicted scattered at her approach; her every footfall quaked through their ranks like thunder.

Behind her, Damek bellowed, "Una! What the devil do you think you're doing out there? Get back here!"

Disregarding him, Una scanned the wooded slope, feeling anguish and hunger for life all around her. So many tragedies. The Sluagh fled from her with pleading eyes or covered frightened faces with shaking desiccated hands. Their stories swirled in the air around her: a mother stolen from her children by a fever, a son caught in the river during a flash flood, a daughter murdered by a jealous lover, a father who'd fallen under the plow while striving to feed his family… on and on it went. The Sluagh didn't know they were dead; those lives over. They could only feel the bottomless cold beneath their feet as if the earth were an open maw waiting to swallow them whole. Longing for heat and comfort, they sought to hold living warmth inside their mouths, cradle and nurture it within their vacant bellies. Anything to feel alive once more. In their midst, the unseen enchantress' spell wound around them like a coiling chain. The bell pealed steadily.

… *feed, take your warmth.*

Una felt the pull of that bell, anchored somewhere in the distance. Her hands balled into fists. Focusing hard on the trilling music, she sensed the spellcaster on the ridge above.

There you are.

"UNA! What are you doing?" Damek screamed. "Someone get her back!"

... come... the feast is near...

"No," Una breathed. Unfurling her magnified Spark, she didn't so much sever that chord as set it ablaze in the caster's hand. She heard a gasp; felt her opponent stagger in the dark. Una smiled. *Got you, bitch.* Without the bell to urge them forward, the dead hesitated— lulled by the vibrant pillar of Una's presence. Damek's men breathed a communal sigh of relief as the Sluagh ambled away, moaning in desperate longing. Una drew them close. Without fear, she smoothed withered cheeks, patted shrunken heads, and caressed withered fingers, humming a simple tune she couldn't say she'd ever heard. They crowded around, enraptured by the light raging within her.

Kneeling, she cleared away a smattering of dead leaves to place her bare hand against raw earth and stone. Here, Una unleashed the unbridled power grinding through her bones. A torrent of wild energy roared through her palms, channeling the Sluagh's need through her own body and into the ground where it belonged.

Here is the warmth you seek... the peace you crave.

Hunger no longer.

A thin network of glowing blue lines traced over the hillside like a spider's web. The dead sighed. A gentle burst of wind blew their mangled, unnatural figures to dust. Hundreds of wandering souls vanished beneath the soil at once. Una's spell shimmered in the air for a heartbeat before fading below her web.

She gasped for air, astonished at the ease with which it was accomplished. Her might felt herculean, her power infinite. Though, once the floodgates were opened, they were difficult to shutter. The soil softened under her knees, melted, and merged, intending to drink her down like rain. A splintering shock of cold flowed up her arm and into her head, bleaching the hair at her temple white as a cloud. Her right eye burned as if pierced by a sliver of ice. Una snatched her hand back with a cry to avoid being sucked in. Scrabbling backward, she clutched her hand to her chest to stymie the searing cold singing through her nerves. The world went a queer, milky sort of gray. She fell into that fog with a relieved sigh.

⚹ ⚹

AOIFE SPAT BLOOD INTO THE moss at her feet. She reeled as if skewered by lightning. She fell. Her listless body drifted toward the trail's edge and the waiting chasm below. Throwing an arm out, she caught herself against a granite boulder just shy of the precipice. She tore out most of her fingernails in the process. Writhing with the unimaginable pain in her chest, she crawled up the slope on her belly, gulping air like a drowning man. Aoife fumbled at her bosom, searching for a wound that should have split her in half. There wasn't anything to find. Nothing marred her formerly pristine tunic but mud and sweat. The damage was internal as if the hand of Donn had shot out of the night and ripped out her heart. Vibrant hate coursed through her veins, bright and lethal as mercury.

Una. Una did this to you…

Aoife could smell the Moura bitch in the ether— feel her presence at the back of her throat like a budding sore. Whatever Una had done, it was built to last. Dark energy pulsed in the rocks and soil, the wind buffeting the hillside, and the river snaking through the valley like a silver snake in the moonlight. Ubiquitous. Unalterable. Unfathomable. How Una did such an inconceivable thing was as enigmatic as it was infuriating. Even Vanna Nema could not strike her enemies from the heavens.

Full of bottomless pain and quivering outrage, Aoife summoned every particle of Spark she had left to locate the source of her ills. It took a while for her limping magic to snag upon the object of her ire. She found Una amidst the smattering of fearful men and horses. They beat a hasty retreat on the far side of the tor. Her heart beat sluggishly in Damek's proximity— unconscious but very much alive.Aoife gnashed her teeth. No mortal woman should have been able to harness a god's power and live. That damned pest had more lives than a lynx! Well, Aoife would just see about that, wouldn't she? Straining with the effort, she propped herself against a large rock out of the wind. Una had managed to chase away the Sluagh and a handful of sneaking Lu Sidhe. So, what? More than a few terrors were running wild on Samhain, weren't there? The Oiche Ar Fad was wide open. Pookas were not the only Dor Sidhe stalking the night in search of mortal prey.

Aoife smiled. She recast her net toward one such pack of beasts that lurked along the eastern riverbank. The leader lifted its head. Its opalescent eyes narrowed as if it could see her smirking down on it from above. With the last of her strength, Aoife dangled a thread… to show it the way.

Come… she called, weaving images of a hillside road dotted with terrified men on horseback. Men who bore a morsel more delicious than anything they'd ever tasted.

Come… come and feast.

The creature reared its misshapen head, baring its fangs in a macabre grin. The hunt was on.

❦

THE SOUTHERS WERE LEAVING. FROM above, Ben watched the infantrymen hastily gather their undamaged supplies and toss them into one of the two wagons they'd brought along for this excursion. One wagon held pikes, ropes, bloodied sabres, piles of unlit lanterns, and flasks stinking of paraffin. The second was burdened with textiles: tents, tent poles, stakes, and the like. Lord Bishop's men came prepared.

Ben would say that for them, at least.

The second wagon must be his target. At the rate the drivers were moving, they'd scarcely notice the added weight. Ben slunk carefully along the last roof, closest to the back road. Lord Bishop and his officers were already well down the slope by now, outpacing his supply train by a full five minutes. Ben had ground his molars when the Souther lordrode past. Tucked into the crook of his arm and swaddled in Bishop's own cloak, Una looked small and frail, despite the incredible magic she'd performed for all and sundry. That such a tiny vessel could hold such terrible power seemed improbable as a fire kindled under the sea. Walking through a wall of ravening dead unscathed was feat enough—drawing them back into the earth with a touch was quite another. Ben caught the shock of white at Una's temple as they passed by, and worried she may have done serious damage to herself in the process. If she had, he vowed to slay every one of these Southers to a man. He swore it, by the Horns of Herne.

Robin perched behind him on the rooftop, carefully avoiding the burned or sopping bits that would surely dump them into the cottage below. He'd ordered Gerrod to stay safe within the flaming cabin until dawn. The boy didn't protest. This night had already robbed him of his closest friend, and poor Rian was scarcely cognizant. There was no reason for either of them to suffer any further on Ben's account. With Una's enchantment wreathing the place in a protective light, they would both be safe.

Ben tried to make Robin stay with them, but Robin threatened to cram his dagger into Ben's arsehole if he uttered another word about it… and Ben tactfully dropped the subject. Now, the two of them waited for an opportunity to creep into the supply wagon before it lurched down the road. Ben wasn't as quick as he had been at the start of the evening, but he would be damned if he'd hand Una to that Souther fop. Not while he had two working legs, two functional arms, and a semi-operational torso.

Ben wasn't exactly sure what happened after he slid into catalepsy on the slope, but he recalled every moment inside that burning cabin. Una had pressed her lips, her hope, and her Spark into his mouth like a prayer. He could still taste her tears. She'd thought she was going to die. Nevertheless, she'd stood apart to face it alone. For them. For *him*.

The kiss lasted all of a moment, but its effect was permanent. Had he ever met anyone so infuriating, nonsensical, condescending, or rash? No. Then again, he'd never known anyone as brave, passionate, or full of raw *hope* either. Una was a whole new world for Kaer Yin Adair. She'd dragged a selfish, useless scoundrel from the wild, and shook him out of his own self-imposed exile. Ben could never have imagined a woman like her.

The Grand Marshal of the Wild Hunt... that fading fantasy of yesteryear could never deserve her. Ben Maeden might breathe his last here tonight, but Kaer Yin Adair could be reborn. He wanted to be the man he saw reflected in Una's eyes at that moment. Maybe then, he'd be worthy of her?

Robin patted his shoulder. A silent understanding passed between them. "We'll get her back."

"If I must burn them all down."

Robin chuckled low in his throat. "Very good, yer Arseness. Ready?"

Ben stood, pulling his cowl over the golden chains chiming in his ear. "Eager, you might say. How about you?"

"I'm always ready," Robin assured him, drawing his daggers.

"Prove it." Kaer Yin Adair leapt from the roof into the wagon, swift and silent as death itself.

🦌 🦌

THE ARMAMENTS WAGON HAD A loose wheel, which impeded the speed of the Southers' exit. The driver was forced to stop, climb out, and kick the hub back into its axle every few yards. The stops were so frequent that most of the skittish rear-guardsmen left the driver behind to deal with the hindrance alone. No man wanted to remain on that haunted hillside a moment longer than necessary. They'd left over thirty of their own in the dirt already. What was one or two more? Marching doggedly forward, most survivors were so traumatized by all they'd seen that they hardly spoke to one another.

The only sounds were the creaking of the wagon wheel, the driver's frustrated rants, and the trudge of their boots through the ankle-deep mud.

This was all to the benefit of the men hidden beneath a thick tarpaulin in the wagon bed. Robin leaned over the side to pop out another rivet with the tip of his dagger, then ducked under the tarp at the front. The expected clang tore another aggravated growl out of the driver's mouth. Stilling the horses, he dropped into the mud for the fourth time. He bent to kick the hub back into place, cursing like a Bretagn sailor. This time, the soldiers kept their eyes on the road. They preferred to ignore the angry little man and his problems when so much already weighed upon their overtaxed sensibilities.

The driver had been guarding his wagon whilst they'd been burning, dismembering, and decapitating their friends. His bellyaching only made them march faster toward the textile wagon a few paces ahead. That driver, at least, kept his thoughts and complaints to himself. Therefore, no one noticed when the driver's grousing suddenly ceased. They didn't turn around to hear him pop his axle into place, nor to mark how long it took for his whip to crack, or his horses to plod forward. They didn't glance backward to note that he'd somehow grown nearly two feet taller or several handspans wider, either. Therefore, they didn't hear a thing as Robin cut the nearest guards' throats. The bulk were too far ahead to detect the clatter of armor clanging off the rocks, as their comrades' corpses were flung over the side. In fact, they didn't turn around once until the horses were breathing down their necks. Ben cracked the whip and lashed the reins with ruthless determination, steering the horses and their weighty burden down the road at a breakneck pace. Men were trampled or violently shoved into the valley below.

Having hauled himself into the driver's seat, Robin took the reins from Ben with a maniacal grin. Clapping him on the back, Ben leapt onto the lead horse's back and severed its tether with a quick swipe of his sword. In a panic, men corralled into each other to avoid being flattened, knocked off the hillside, or cut in half by the massive sword they saw swinging right and left with abandon. That sword decapitated the driver of the lead wagon in one go, then gutted a handful of guards all scrambling to escape. Kicking the headless driver out of his seat, Ben cracked the reins like a madman, setting the forward wagon on a frantic downward course.

By the time Damek's officers looked back to see what all the commotion was about, the wagon and its spooked horses had already trampled or dislodged a dozen or more men. A surprised corpsman squeaked a belated warning to Damek's lead group. Just then, one of the stampeding horses stumbled under its own hooves. It went down with a terrible shriek, bowling into its fellows. The wagon flipped end over end, tossing sharp spears, arrows, and paraffin into the air. At gravity's mercy, Lord Bishop's men had nowhere left to run.

THE PRINCE

n.e. ꝼ08
oj, ꝺoꝛ oꝛꝛas
samhain

D amek's head whipped around just in time to avoid the spear-
tip that came sailing toward him from higher up the road. His
honor guard rounded the last high corner when the artillery
wagon upended, slinging metal, wood, iron nails, lanterns, and other
heavy supplies into his men. Soldiers screamed as they were tossed over
the ledge, impaled, bludgeoned, or crushed beneath the runaway wagon.

For the third time that night, the sickly-sweet scent of blood choked
the air. Driving right as far as he could without tipping himself over
the last incline, Damek spurred his charger's flank hard. Banking into
the final turn in the path, he shouted for his men to follow suit to level
ground. He reached the bottom first. Cunningham and Sergeant Douglas
wedged their mounts between him and the soldiers rushing to escape
calamity.

Shifting Una's dead weight to his left arm, Damek drew his sword
with his right.

"Cavalry, to me!" His eyes widened at the bloodbath behind them.
There were another fifteen men down, at least. He couldn't get a fix on
the rear wagon, but the remains of his artillery were scattered all over the
hillside, smearing human and animal gore in their wake. Those few who
managed to dodge the catastrophe were running or riding down the last

slope as if the dead still snapped at their heels. Many flung their weapons aside in haste to evade the tangle of limbs, steel, and splintering wood tearing toward them. Damek absorbed all of this with a caustic frown. At this point, nothing could shock him. Watching dead men drag their own corpses after the living... he might be permanently impervious to surprise.

He'd missed no detail of the horrors to which he and his men had been subjected since they ascended this cursed hill, yet his emotions were weaker, duller. Damek felt as if he'd been hovering outside of his own body, an impassive observer in all that had transpired. Not even the weight of the prize he'd fought so hard to gain, resting safe in the cradle of his arms, could move him. Perhaps, this was shock, some reflexive dampening of emotion as a result of all he'd been forced into on Una's account. Thus, when he noticed an odd silver shape speeding toward him like a vicious steel-tipped wind, he mustered only an impatient aggravation. *What now?*

As the figure neared, Damek got a good look at a face full of inhuman concentration and impartial disdain. He'd seen it before, glowering from a stained-glass window over his uncle's throne— the very relief that commemorated the murder of his great-grandfather. Heat rose up Damek's throat at the sight. *You!*— he wanted to scream over his men. He *knew* this man, even if he'd only seen him immortalized in glass or imagined him falling under his sword in childhood fancies. He didn't need to witness the disciplined precision of each measured sword-stroke to know that he was facing the greatest swordsman in Innisfail. This bastard *was* the infamous Crown Prince, Kaer Yin Adair. There he was, the very man Damek had longed to meet his entire life, cutting through his men like chaff. The how and why no longer mattered. Cunningham belched the command to form a vanguard before Damek's mount. Douglas stiffened beside him; meaty fingers gripped his sword until the knuckles bled.

"Reason," he breathed. "That's—"

"Never-mind him now," Major Cunningham sneered. "He'll come no further. Lances up!"

The vanguard of mounted men and shields deflected their panicked infantry like a massive plow. Damek didn't mind their breach of discipline. All he could see was that whirling sword barreling through man and beast alike. When it reached the bottom of the hill, it dipped and came up red again and again. Hardened spearmen and heavy infantrymen carrying spears and pikes shoved against Damek's line of horseflesh, desperate to escape that vengeful maelstrom.

"Company, drop shields!" Cunningham barked. Damek's honor guard slammed their steel-capped shields into the earth before the warhorses, resting their lances and swords over the top lip. Damek's surviving infantrymen dashed behind their makeshift wall. The prince halted some feet away, his bloody sword arced over his shoulder in a high guard.

"Archers, get your shite together back there!" Douglas bellowed. A handful of yeomen unslung their longbows from their backs, then dropped into firing positions. Damek was aware of all this, if impassively. He couldn't tear his attention from the blood-streaked figure who stood astride an unbroken line of corpses at the bottom of the rise. The prince didn't appear winded. Despite the simmering rage in his gut, Damek could only smile. So, *this* was what a legend looked like. He couldn't say he was disappointed.

"Nock!" called Douglas, while Cunningham shouted abuse at the vanguard.

Kaer Yin Adair didn't move a muscle. His piercing silver eyes met Damek's without an ounce of fear. He knew a few shields and arrows weren't enough to stop him. Damek knew it too. He couldn't help the tingle of excitement that trickled down his spine at the thought.

"Damek Bishop." The prince's voice managed to resonate without rising. "Let Una go, and you'll leave here alive. I give you my word."

"Is he mad?" guffawed Douglas, incredulous. Cunningham said nothing, merely kept an eye trained on the speaker, his fist poised to give the next command. Damek threw back his head and laughed. He couldn't help it. Perhaps the prince's comment was funny because Damek understood it was no idle boast? If any one man could take down a dozen mounted knights with a single sword, Damek believed the Kaer Yin Adair he'd read so much about certainly could. Hadn't he just cut through as many men on his way down? More? Damek couldn't stop laughing. After quite a while, he was forced to cram a knuckle into his mouth to still the fit.

Cunningham spared him a worried glance. "My Lord?"

Damek shook himself, pulling Una close. "She's not your property, Dannan! She's my blood, you know. If you think I'd leave her behind in this place, you're sorely mistaken."

Kaer Yin didn't blink. "Nor is she your plaything. Considering that she's spent near a month fleeing from you and your men, I'd say her preference is plain. Hand her over. I won't ask again."

Douglas raised an arm to order the archers to fire, but Damek caught his wrist. "Don't. He'll be over our makeshift wall and through your arrows before they ever hit the ground. We won't beat him that way."

"But My Lord—"

"Don't you know who that man is, Gilbert?"

Douglas didn't, but Cunningham nodded. "*I* do."

"Good," said Damek, looping his reins around his forearm. His horse danced impatiently beneath him. "I want you to take Una to Martin, Wallace. Ride like the wind. Let nothing stop you, no matter what comes out of those trees at you."

"Respectfully, Lord Bishop... no," spat Cunningham.

"*What* did you say?"

"Beggin' your pardon, but you're wasting time arguing with me."

"Wallace, I'll suffer no man in my regiment to fight my battles for me," Damek said. This was a fight he'd longed for since childhood. He'd be damned if the glory he craved would be snatched away so easily. How many chances would he get to slay the Crown Prince of Innisfail in single combat?

"You *will* go. That's an order."

Cunningham's brow furrowed. "Get her home safely, My Lord. That's what our men died for, isn't it?"

Damek covered his shame with gritted teeth.

484

There was an argument he couldn't foil. His men would take the night's slaughter as a selfish whim if he tried. They were here for Una. He had no rebuttal. *"Damn you—"*

"Then get the hells out of here." Cunningham didn't wait for Damek's reply as he turned to the men. "Nothing gets past this line! D'ye hear? Douglas, escort his Lordship to the city!"

"Aye, Major," Douglas replied with audible relief. Cunningham lowered his fist, and a cascade of arrows converged at the center of the road. The prince wasn't there to receive them. He dashed forward and leapt over Cunningham's wall of shields. His longsword dealt death from every conceivable direction. Damek had time to suck in a breath at the unimaginable feat of speed just as Douglas' sabre slapped into his mount's haunches. Mouth agape, Damek was forced to grip Una tight as the scene shrank behind him. His last glimpse of Wallace was of his sabre catching the prince's longsword mid-stroke.

He launched into a valiant counterattack. Cunningham was a crack swordsman, one of the best in Bethany. He wouldn't make it easy for the Adair, no matter how unnaturally gifted the big blond bastard was. Even so, Damek knew the match was unequal. He'd never seen anyone move like him before, as if the wind obeyed him, and gravity was merely another servant at the prince's beck and call. Damek didn't feel concern for his friend, nor pride in the courage and skill of one of his best warriors.

He felt... *envy.*

As Wallace's sabre slid down that monstrous silver longsword; as the prince ducked under his next thrust; as Wallace grunted, stepping sideways to bring his sabre around for another strike, and another, and another— all of which the prince batted away as easily as he might a child's sparring stick— Damek seethed, his regret keener than any blade.

One day, he vowed silently. *One day*, my *sword will be there.* He and Una were soon at full gallop, and Damek could no longer see them. He faced forward, his heart heavy. *One day soon, you'll meet your match, Kaer Yin Adair. Once Una is safe, I'll be back for you...*

THE SOUTHER WAS GOOD. VERY good. Ben had it within himself to give credit, when due. The major hadn't mastered the high guard and lacked the footwork necessary to maintain a steady rhythm, but he didn't want for strength. Wild as his thrusts were, and defensive his parries, he kept Ben on his back foot more than he was eager to admit. A few loyal pikemen remained to cover their lord's escape. They hovered near, waiting to strike at Ben wherever there was an opening. Without ado, Ben killed two and hamstrung a third, whose screams rent the pre-dawn air with chilling intensity. Ben met the Souther's next barrage with several glancing thrusts, before he leaned in with a closed fist and cracked his opponent in the face. The major staggered; his nose had imploded like a smashed melon. Ben switched Nemain to his left hand, intent to ram it through the Souther's kidney, but the fellow rolled out of Ben's grip to the ground. His serrated sabre bit deep into Ben's shin. Hissing in surprised pain, Ben fell onto his rump, his sword skittering into the trees at the edge of the road. Wasting no time, the major clawed himself up Ben's legs like a limb over deep water, attempting to drive his dagger through Ben's heart.

Ben caught his arm and held him aloft, though the effort cost him dearly. The wound in his chest hadn't fully healed. Fresh blood seeped through the gaping hole in his once snow-white cuirass. Grunting, the major pressed down with the total weight of his body while jabbing his gauntleted elbow repeatedly into the wound. Livid stars flashed behind Ben's eyes, but he held on. Summoning every ounce of strength he had left, he twisted sideways. The motion displaced the Souther's weight far enough to draw his blade into his shoulder. Ben gasped as the tip dragged against bone. Sucking in a deep breath, Ben pounded his forehead into his assailant's broken nose. Dazed, the major splashed into the mud on his back. Ben rolled with him, wrenched the dagger from his own flesh, and shoved it to the hilt through the major's eye. The Souther's body jerked; limbs twitched, then stilled forever. He'd been a tough bastard. Ben was impressed, if angry.

Breathing hard, he got to his feet, stumbling just a bit. The remaining pikemen circled, eying him like a wounded boar. He spat blood beside the major's corpse, brandishing his hard-won blade.

486

"Come on then," he goaded.

With a cry, the first jumped forward, his pike aimed at Ben's gut. Ben grasped the pikeman's forearm, then stepped in close enough to carve out the fellow's Adam's apple. The next took a slice out of Ben's thigh, but he barely felt the blade sink into the meat above his knee. Instead, he spun the spear he'd stolen over his shoulder, and cast it through the eager fool's midsection. The pikeman slumped forward, impaling himself further as he sank down its shaft. Ben retrieved Nemain from the roadside and used her length to keep himself upright. He was huffing now, and furious. Despite the blood spattered over his face and armor, his eyes were hard with determined ire. Rather than meet his comrades' fate, the last pikeman threw down his spear and ran.

Ben's eyes drifted to a small cadre of battered archers a few paces up the road. One got off a single shot. Directed from a shaking arm, it went wide, bouncing harmlessly off a tree trunk and landing somewhere in the leaves. Ben was on the archer before his finger left the string. His head followed his misfired arrow into the woods. Ben killed another contender with a backward slash that nearly cleaved his victim's shoulders from his body, and the next, he nearly cut in half at the pelvis. Pulling Nemain free for anyone else impatient to die, Ben heard Robin's voice from somewhere behind him.

"Ben! Watch yer arse!"

An arrow caught him in the side. Its tip sailed between the ribs under his arm. His back struck a tree trunk with a solid thwack. Groaning, Ben pried the missile free and searched for its source. The archer dropped his bow and held his hands up as if he hadn't meant to release his string. Reaching for the major's dagger, Ben flipped it up by the tip, and threw it straight into the archer's open mouth. When Robin arrived on the scene, the remaining archers took a last look at their murderous target and fled. Robin caught Ben under the arm before he fell. With a curse, he heaved him upright by the waist. Pausing to marvel at the river of corpses lining the road, Robin's eyes stretched wide.

"*Siora*. Ben... remind me to never get on yer bad side again. There must be... I can't even count 'em all."

Ben tore a wad of cloth from his tunic, then undid his belt to strap it in place over the wound on his leg.

"Bishop can't be far ahead. The mud's too deep. I need a horse, and every blade you have on you."

Robin gaped, mesmerized by the carnage all around them. "How did ye even manage all this? Great Ancestor, but yer a monster…"

"There's no time," Ben pointed at the horses wandering the road ahead, deprived of their riders. "It's not over yet. I need your help."

"Ye can't mean to go after him now? Yer bleedin' all over yerself as it is."

"Robin!"

Throwing up his hands, Robin picked his way over the dead toward the abandoned mounts.

"All right, all right! If any o'these bastards stands up and takes a bite outta me, I'll haunt ye for eternity, singin' every song ye loathe until ye hack yer ears off at the root."

"So MUCH FOR OUR SWIFT retreat," Douglas grumbled beside Damek. From his saddle, he kicked out at the infantrymen working to shore up the mud. "Put your backs into it, damn you! Or do you want to die in this bloody wood with the rest of your mates?"

Damek paid no attention. He stared behind them. He'd marched up that hill with *sixty* men. Now, fewer than a dozen remained to guard him and his prize. Una rested motionless in his arms, her cheek pressed into his breastplate. She was more beautiful than he remembered, by far. Her golden-brown skin, the curls he knew would gleam when they were clean and coiffed once more, and that generous mouth that drove him to distraction in their youth, lush with ripening maturity. She was worth every dead man. He wouldn't deny it. If he had to do this all over again, he would doubtless make the same choice.

Yet… *he loathed her for it too.*

He hadn't realized it was possible to hate and love with equal intensity. Damn her eyes. He hadn't expected her to leap into his arms with glee, but this... he'd lost over fifty men for her. Good men. Loyal men. Men that fought for her honor with as much zeal as him. Yet, he knew it wouldn't matter to her in the least.

Damek swallowed as a burst of hatred flared in his gut. Those men lost their lives to save her, but she wouldn't see it that way. He despised her for it. To her, *they* were the enemy— her own people. Her father's bannermen. She'd spent over forty lives for her pride. Damek thought he might choke the life out of her for such cruel treachery, such undeserved disdain. What had happened to the girl he knew all those years ago? The absolute kindness she showed to all creatures, great or small! The love that shone from her soft brown eyes when she'd looked at him? The warmth of her tender embrace?

Una made a small sound in her throat. A thin trickle of blood slid down his breastplate from her nose. Snapped alert, he realized he'd been crushing her. Hands shaking, he wiped the red smear away with a conflicted tenderness that only made him angrier. He wasn't sure he'd ever forgive her for the horrors of this night. Perhaps Aoife was right? Maybe she *would* serve him better dead? He thought about it. He was tempted to wrap his fingers around her throat. He could declare that she'd been afflicted by the dead, as so many of their fellows had been. No one would gainsay his word. He could suffocate her right now, and no one would stop him. In her sleep, her dark brows knit together in unconscious pain. Her full mauve lips trembled. Before he knew it, his fingers wound through her hair and smoothed her cheeks. He cursed himself for his weakness—his pathetic attachment to the past.

She deserved to die for what she'd wrought this night. If only he had the strength to do it!

If only he didn't need her.

If only he did not *love* her.

A sharp, ululating shriek pierced the riotous haze of his thoughts. Another answered. Dozens more followed. The roadside came alive with ear-splitting, guttural, animalistic cries. Douglas spurred his mount around to guard Damek's back. His eyes weren't on the trees or the road ahead. He pointed behind them with the tip of his sabre.

"My Lord!" Douglas shouted in alarm. The men had no idea which way was safest to turn. They crowded around Damek's charger like the last bit of wood floating up from a wreck. "That elf lord is a devil!"

Damek's brows rose in surprise... and not the least amount of competitive elation. "He's neither. He's Kaer Yin Adair, Douglas. I imagine we each seek the same goal."

The prince's stolen horse wound through the trees opposite like a half-mad dervish. Damek had but a moment to grin. The prince wasn't alone in the wood. Hundreds of twisted shapes dropped from the highest boughs, surging toward every moving thing within reach. Damek's men broke ranks. They clattered up the road as fast as their armored legs could carry them.

"*Reason*, what now?" Douglas groaned as the yelping horde descended upon their battered cavalcade.

Damek said, "Goblins. Drawn by the slaughter, no doubt."

"I fucking *hate* the North," declared Douglas, as the pool of snarling imps swirled around them. His mount reared when a humanoid shape barreled into its chest, rotting teeth snapping in delighted bloodlust. Douglas severed its misshapen head from its sleek grey body. "Company, hold your bloody line!"

Damek hacked left and right of his saddle, slashing at anything brave enough to reach for Una. He lost sight of the prince, who must have been swept into this undulating wave of reeking, grasping, goblins, same as everyone. They swarmed the road like wasps. There was little he could do but fight. In mere moments, a wire-thin arm coiled around Damek's waist, while another dug its claws into his arm to pry Una loose. A goblin with carrion breath leaned in to chew her throat out, but Damek's sabre exploded through its hideous skull, spilling its gnarled yellow teeth over the ground like coins.

"Douglas! Get the shieldmen down here!" he bellowed, but to no avail. His sergeant was as imperiled as he.

490

A sudden glancing blow to the back of his head disoriented Damek long enough for a pair of sharp grey claws to rip Una from his grip.

"No!" he raged. Knowing he'd never catch them on horseback, Damek dismounted and pounded through the mud after them. Something had already taken a bite of her upper arm, leaving a brilliant trail of bright red blood through the woods on his right. He carved a wide path through milling grey flesh in his haste to retrieve her. One squirming thing jumped onto his back, sinking its razor teeth deep into the meat at his shoulder blade. With a sharp cry, he reached behind to tear it off by its jagged jaws. While it spat and scratched, he smashed its skull in with his boot heel. Una, still unconscious, was dragged away again. Damek couldn't get there as swiftly as he needed to. They were everywhere. "Una!" He yelled at the top of his lungs and redoubled his efforts with every atom he had to spare. They swarmed him, clawing and biting.

He would never reach her in time.

All at once, a tremor ran through each writhing beast. The goblins raised their warped heads, sniffing the air like frightened rabbits. He saw Kaer Yin then, striding from the forest like a wraith. Damek's guts roiled with hatred and frustrated longing. He was so close! The victory he'd longed for all of his life was at hand. Though, it wasn't his sword that cut through these beasts like water through a sieve.

It wasn't *Damek* who the Dor Sidhe rats took one look at and covered their slimy faces in fear. It wasn't *Damek*'s hands that plucked Una from the ground, nor held her in his arms like some priceless artifact. Damek ground his molars in envious loathing. The prince was wounded too, but everywhere his eyes drifted, goblins shrank back.

Ard Tiarne! they wailed, fleeing as if in despair of his very presence. Damek's men recovered themselves as best they were able with their numbers reduced to ten.

Douglas had managed to keep his mount and his sabre, despite the scratches covering his face. "My Lord! They're leaving. Let's get out of here!"

Damek didn't hear him. He was already moving for the prince. He clutched his sabre in a quaking fist. Goblins fled into the woods with abandon, yipping in retreat. The prince didn't see him coming, for the mass of grey bodies shoving past him. Damek's shoulder caught him square in the spine. He tipped forward, dumping Una like a sack of kindling at his feet. Kaer Yin Adair reeled; his leg and ribs bled freely over his once pretty armor. Damek didn't spare him a moment to recover. He kicked Kaer Yin in the face on his way past, jerking Una upright by the elbow. Douglas waited at the corpse-strewn roadside, ready with a fresh mount and a reaching hand. Damek flung Una face-down over Douglas' saddle.

"Get her to Martin! Go!" He slapped the sergeant's charger on the rump. Ducking low in the saddle, Douglas spurred his steed to a gallop.

Damek watched until Una was well out of sight. Drawing a deep breath, he turned to catch the prince's first thrust with a backhanded parry. Kaer Yin skidded sideways from the impact, but the blow didn't bow him in the least. He righted himself, then came again. Soon enough, Damek broke out in a sweat. It took everything he had to dodge each lightning quick attack. Up, around, up, down came his blade. Damek would backpedal, and the prince would slide his foot forward. Without pause, he used his own body weight as a fulcrum for the unending vertical and horizontal pendulums his blade etched between them. Its edge forged a wall that was nigh impenetrable. Damek knew he wasn't going to beat him in a fair fight. Never. Not like this. After five minutes of losing ground, he limped into the road, gasping. He wasn't good enough to beat the Adair. Not yet. Furious with himself, Damek spat a long low curse. Following, the prince swung his sword back up into his high guard. *Neithana*, Damek knew. The Dannan Art, which took lifetimes to master.

Kaer Yin Adair was *unbeatable*. He was so far above Damek's current level, his former hubris seemed laughable.

Very well, Damek thought. *Any victory is better than none.*

Just as he reached toward his saddle for his crossbow, something bright sailed out of the trees from the east. The arrow plowed straight into his hand— pinning it to his own chest. His howl of pain startled the

492

prince enough to look behind him for its source. While he was distracted, Damek took the cue. Using his uninjured hand, he launched himself up into his saddle. Noting the unmistakable swish of several fired arrows, he tucked himself low over the reins to escape the next volley. His groom, and any other waiting soldiers, fell into the mud, arrows sunk into each of their skulls with perfect accuracy.

Damek didn't need to hear the horns blowing throughout the clearing to know he must get out of there fast. These were not Eirean horns. Not Tairnganese. Not Taran. These were Dannan horns. *Daoine Sidhe* horns. The prince's own people had come for him. Damek peeked over his shoulder before he made it out of range. White and red flags swirled into view. A host of scarlet-tipped arrows soared into the brightening sky. Damek smashed himself tight over his charger's sweating neck. He hung on for dear life as he kicked the beast into a slavering gallop. He didn't look back again. He might not have killed the one man he wanted to above all others, and he may have lost his first match with the deadliest swordsman in Innisfail... but he'd beat him, all the same. Damek had won this round. He got what he came for, no matter the cost.

I beat you, princeling. He allowed himself to smirk through the pain. *I beat you, nonetheless.* Una was his, and the North with her.

⚔ ⚔

Aoife tumbled into the ravine, the last of her magic spent. An empty, feeble husk, she crawled forward on her knees, groping for somewhere dry to hide. Her body sang with pain. Every nerve, every vein, every muscle— was a stinging, burning wreck. She had *failed*. She'd failed Vanna Nema... *twice more.* All the pain she felt now would pale in comparison to the symphony of morbid delights that awaited her in Tairngare. Aoife longed to dig herself a hole and bury herself deep within it, never to emerge again. She wished she had the power of Transmutation. Then, she might transform herself into a salmon, a fox, an insect— it didn't matter. She would do *anything* to escape the fate she knew she'd earned by failing to kill one simpering, Milesian girl.

493

Aoife knew there was no safe harbor anywhere. If she became a salmon, Nema would become the bear that ate her whole. If she became a fox, Nema would become the wolf that dragged her from her den. If she became an insect, Nema would become the fish that leapt from the river to swallow her in one gulp. Everywhere, anywhere, any way she ran, Nema would follow and exact her vengeance. Nema did not tolerate failure in her disciples... even less, in her own grandchildren. There was no hope. Aoife could feel the pull of the geis in her blood, even now. Nema would exact her due.

Aoife dozed for a time. She cowered beneath a knoll, shivering in the chill Samhain air. When she awoke, the sun beckoned from the east— a spotlight, searching for Aoife in the dark. Helpless against it, she dragged herself toward that beacon. She might crawl all the way to Tairngare, just to be torn apart for her own miserable failure.

Forgive me grandmother, she pleaded with that immutable sunlight. *The girl lives. The prince is yet free... and your grandson has the means to make himself a king at your expense.* The sun held no warmth in its cold brilliance. No sympathy. Neither would Nema, Aoife knew only too well.

THE SOUTHERNMOST STAR

n.e. ⊏08
OJ, ÒOR ORQS
bechany

Patrick sneezed his way down the corridor, wrapped head to toe in white bearskin. With each day dawning colder than the last, his old bones ached for warmth he doubted he'd ever feel again. His physicians had passed through his chambers so many times in the past week that his imminent expiration may as well be painted on his forehead.

Consumption, they told him.

Six months past, they'd warned of a growth blooming in his gut like a weed, its tendrils slithering deep into his blood, sapping the remnants of his strength. Now, this. The malignancy had spread to his lungs, throat, liver... and soon, his heart. Patrick's physicians declared he would likely be dead long before that happened. The lungs would do the job much faster than the stomach, throat, or liver. *Months,* they'd told him. *Less,* if he didn't take to his bed now.

Dying was a bothersome business. Untidy. Inconvenient. He couldn't afford to sit back and let the sharks circle his corpse for the final feast—not yet. He had things to see to: a country to run, a kingdom to forge, a daughter to marry off, a war to plan, and an heir to crown. Patrick was too damned busy to play invalid. There was much left to do! His legacy was on the line. He was the last Eirean lord who could trace his bloodline to Eber Finn, the first Milesian High King: the hero who cut the hand from King Nuada of the Tuatha De Dannan. The very man that sent the Sidhe scurrying into the Otherworld in the first place. In Patrick's blood walked giants: Fionn Mac Cumhail, Cu Chulainn, and Brian Boru. His ancestors *were* Eire. Men who faced the Sidhe time and again and emerged victorious.

Patrick had far too much to live up to, to die now.

His grandfather's chapel lay at the southernmost tip of the fortress, facing a roaring Dor Oras sea. Duch Kevin had it built more to honor Innish heritage than as a place for prayer and contemplation. The old ways had died out well before Kevin's time. New gods sprang from the soil after the Transition, taking root the breadth and length of Innisfail. The cult of the Ancestor in Tairngare, with its alchemical Mother Goddess Siora, was undoubtedly the strongest faith remaining in Eire.

Above the eastern arch, *Siora* was represented by a winged dragon bearing the sun in her talons. Astride the Southern lintel with its tall glass doors, two converged circles signified *Reason*: the only God of any importance in Bethany. Striding into the knave, he stepped over the beautifully rendered symbols on the floor—*the Cross, the Scimitar,* the ancient Hebrew character for law— *Elohim.*

Behind him, over the northern lintel, The World Tree reached toward three shining stars that winked with diamonds the size of eggs. On the West wall, the fulcrum and anvil— *Innovation.* Entering this chapel, one was meant to stride over the old gods and be swept into the future, toward the True South: *Reason.*

The point was to be awed by the might of human potential. A smug bit of architectural theater on his grandfather's part, but effective, all the same. One *could* imagine the scope of human existence as a romp through myth and superstition. Patrick never much cared for the lesson. He found the chapel crass, its symbols meaningless, and its uses impractical as they were pompous. To his mind, humanity *was* its history, no matter how punitive, servile, self-aggrandizing, or absurd. Men could no more sever ties with the stories that sculpted them than they could move about without skin.

The most human trait that Patrick could conceive of was the ability to learn from one's failings. Humans could imagine worlds far outside of their collective experience, strive toward goals most creatures could scarcely conceive. No other animal on earth could boast of a human being's potential. The Sidhe, by comparison, suffered for their stability. They were too long-lived, detached, and selective. In the bosom of immortality, there was little change and less urgency. Mortals thrived because they knew *want*... they could endeavor to greater heights because they understood *fear* and *need*. That was why Patrick couldn't allow himself to die, not with his final victory so near. He was going to teach the immortals why humans had held the biological advantage for thousands of years. Lost in his musings, Patrick shambled past the last row of dusty pews and hobbled up the steps toward the southern promenade. He was well-armed against any impertinence his caller meant to throw at him tonight. Her immortality be damned.

To Patrick's mind, his very humanity made *him* superior.

His guest may pontificate all she liked.

Outside, the ocean roiled. Crashing waves sent frigid spray dozens of feet over the cliffs below. He pried open a latticed door coated with salt, tasting the ether of a storm on the air.

His visitor approached from the far balustrade, mindful of the ice coating the paving stones. She sniffed, tucking her hands deep within her ermine-lined muffler.

"About time. Your thoughts are as loud as that racket down there. I despise the sea, you realize. It stinks of dead things."

He leaned against the open door, huffing, "You'll have to forgive me, madam. I'm dying, apparently."

Liadan turned, her violet and green eyes narrowed in the ochre perfection of her skin. "Do you suppose I find that a reasonable excuse? My time is more valuable than you can possibly comprehend."

"Yet... here you are. I wonder, Lady MacNemed, that you'd bother to come so far south, if my message was a mere inconvenience?"

"Perhaps I wished to hear the explanation from your own wormy lips?"

He let the insult slide. "My daughter is coming home, no thanks to you."

"Is that all you meant to say? I wish you joy of her."

"You've tried to kill her at least three times in the last two months, or so I'm told. Odd, considering that you went well out of your way to ensure her birth, education, and rise through the Cloister's ranks." Patrick crossed his arms with some effort. "As I recall, it was *you* who arranged for Arrin's capture those many years ago... begged me to take her, if I'm not mistaken?"

"You *are*. I never beg."

"You might say, you planned every step of Una's life from birth on. I'm merely curious why you'd wish to undo all of that hard work, those years of careful plotting, just as she became useful to me?"

She gave him a cold smile. "I needn't explain myself to you, mortal. Long before your cursed forebears set foot in this land, my people ruled here. The Children of Danu were our enemies thousands of years before you or your infuriating offspring were conceived."

"All utterly irrelevant. Do you think that hive of self-important women and soft boys in Tairngare stands a chance against my army?" He made a rude sound. "When we're done with the Red City, I think we'll march on Armagh next. The High King will keep, for now."

"You wouldn't *dare*."

"I absolutely would, dear lady. We had a deal, and you've broken it. I want to know why, before I decide what revenge suits me best."

"I suspect you decided days ago, Patrick. Let's not pretend either of us is a fool." She pulled her heavy fur cloak tight around her shoulders.

"Make no further attempts on my daughter's life."

"She could undo everything we've worked to achieve."

"... ah. You fear her? That *is* interesting."

"I'm wary of anything I cannot control, as you can attest. She is... unnerving. Dangerous. Her gifts are unnatural, and entirely without precedent. I fear you'll never be able to take her to heel."

498

"That is for Damek to decide."

Her eyes flashed. "You shan't wed that abomination to a son of Falan Mac Nemed!"

"I'll do whatever I damned well please, Liadan."

Patrick possessed a standing army some five-thousand strong in the South alone, not to mention the troops scattered throughout the midlands. He held forts bursting with soldiers in Swansea, Kernow, and the isles ringing Bretagne. With a word, he could muster a force of twenty thousand. While Liadan Mac Nemed, the Dowager Queen of Armagh, boasted her own impressive Fir Bolg combatants, she had half his numbers, and they both knew it.

"My sister's son will be King of Eire and my daughter will reign beside him as queen, or I *will* destroy you. Living or dead, I vow it. If you wish to crown your son Ard Ri, back off. This is my last warning. Please assure yourself of my profound sincerity."

She was quiet for a time, observing him from beneath lowered lashes. As beautiful as she still was, he found the weight of her ancient eyes unbearable. She'd been a woman of middle years when she'd led her people up the hill at Tara to partake of the Dagda's brew. Time stopped for her then, eons before Patrick was born. He imagined, to her, mortals like himself were fleeting as grass in winter. Though they were allied against a common enemy, he could never trust her; nor she, him. No matter. Patrick had his own reasons for this tremulous alliance, didn't he? Plans within plans, the pair of them. A pity he wouldn't live to see her suffer the loss she so richly deserved.

"If Falan is to take and hold the throne, he needs my nephew to prop it up for him. Never forget that, Liadan. Perhaps once the Dannans have been pushed into the West from whence they came, you'll have your chance to purge Innisfail of Mil's bloodline. Who knows? *Who cares?* Without my men, my daughter, and my nephew, Falan Mac Nemed will be king of the wind, and nothing more."

She exhaled, slowly. "Very well. I'll allow your spawn to live, so long as she devotes herself to my great-grandson, and remains out of sight. In return, I demand that you formally declare Damek your heir. No more grandstanding with your zealotous brother or his inferior children."

Patrick chuckled. *If only she knew.* He let no trace of his triumph reveal itself on his face. "Done. Your hand on it, My Lady?"

She wrinkled her nose, unamused. "I hope you realize, any agreement forged between us is valid only so long as you draw breath. I can smell the taint in your blood, Patrick. You aren't long for this realm."

"For your sake, it had better be a long time coming. I shudder to imagine what will become of Armagh if my people are able to imagine a world without the Sidhe. How far did your people ever come, Liadan? What marvels have you wrought, frontiers have you explored, mysteries have you solved? Have you ever set a foot anywhere else?" he laughed. "You believe you have some divine right to rule over men, simply because you cannot die. I say that is your greatest weakness and, in the end, it will be your undoing."

She spun on her heel. Her scarlet robes swirled beneath her cloak like blood. "Yours is unfailing arrogance. Your impermanence and short-sighted greed are laughable. We, as always, will *outlast* you."

Patrick shrugged. "Perhaps. Perhaps not. Have a safe trip back to the Cloister, madam Nema. I doubt we'll meet again."

"Die well, Donahugh." Liadan stalked from the chapel, her back straight as a prow. Patrick at last allowed himself to cough, wiping the blood it produced against his sleeve. He couldn't stop smiling. He was in a fine mood. For that vaunted old schemer to travel so far in the midst of an engineered revolt against the Cloister, meant only one thing— she came because she was *afraid*. Without Patrick, she was running thin on reliable Eirean allies. Damek was no pawn. Liadan would learn that fact, very soon. *Nine hells*, he'd raised that boy to be a bloody pain in the arse, hadn't he?

Patrick almost pitied the whole Mac Nemed Clan, for they had no idea what they were in for. Though he longed to watch Damek cast the arrogant Sidhe from their self-appointed throne, Patrick could go to his rest confident the best was still to come. He'd unleashed a final weapon: one with the potential to burn through the Sidhe like a forest fire. The very same insidious force that banished them to the Otherworld before the Transition. That which had wiped them from living memory for a time, like a half-remembered nightmare. This weapon was *faith*. Its arbiter, the most charming, focused, and singularly arrogant man he'd ever encountered— Henry Fitz Donahugh. Patrick's laughter rang throughout the chapel as he took his leave. His attendant closed the heavy iron doors behind him. The torches in the hall cast an ever-thinning stream of light over the symbols on the floor, until it winked out altogether, shrouding their majesty and mystery in a patient, protective darkness.

Kaer Yin rested against a rowan with his tunic open to the waist, while Rian cursed over his bleeding torso. The sun was out and shining over the river. Its incandescent rays spread reassuring warmth over his closed eyelids. He felt its heat all the way to his toes. Now that Dor Oras had arrived, this brief glimpse of sunlight might be the last in Innisfail until Imbolc. He sighed. Six months of dark and cold to come, yet he didn't mind so much, now. Something larger and more pressing took up every inch of free space in his mind. Rian snorted, and he cracked an eye. Her face was tear-streaked, filthy, and much thinner than he remembered. She was angry too. Her cheeks had gone red as an autumn apple. Shredding scraps of linen out of whatever anyone could scavenge for her, she refused to look him in the eye.

Well, at least he knew where her ire was directed.

"Pull him up, if you please?" Shar Lianor hovered close, as if waiting to do her bidding. His pristine white cuirass creaked as he moved.

Kaer Yin was jerked upright by a pair of too large, too strong hands. He yelped. "That hurts, damn it!"

Shar dipped his fair head, silver chains jingling in his ears. "Forgive me, *Mo Flaith*. The lady must see to your wounds." The ghost of a smirk tugged at the corners of Shar's mouth, though his eyes were tactfully trained on his feet.

Rian wrapped torn bits of fabric around Kaer Yin's torso. She tied several makeshift bandages in place over his chest, shoulder, and ribs.

Whatever she'd doused his wounds with smelled strongly of peat, ground nettles, and something fouler, which he fervently refused to investigate.

"If her *ladyship* would be kind enough not to break my ribs in the process, I'd appreciate it."

Her nostrils flared. "I'm sorry, does this hurt?" She knew it did.

He glared back at her.

"Now, now, lass," cooed Robin from his right side. He passed Kaer Yin his bone flask full of miraculous uishge. "We know he's a charmer, but ye needn't bother to kill him to mark yer snit. He's half-killed hisself for ye as it is."

That shut her mouth with an audible snap. She bent back to her work, silently fuming. Shar set Kaer Yin against the tree trunk when she was done. He visibly fought the urge to grin. Kaer Yin was happy to see him, even if he couldn't show it. He hurt too damned much to crack a smile for the young Sidhe's benefit. Rian stole a veiled upward glance at Kaer Yin's face.

"What now? Am I breathing too hard?" he scowled.

She flushed. "No. I... ah, that is... thank you, Ben."

His head swiveled toward her. "Forgive me, *what was that?*"

"You heard me."

"One more time?"

"Fine, fine. Thank you for saving my life," she mumbled.

Well. How about that? "Thank Una, Rian. Not me."

"Don't tell me you're discovering humility now? How... annoying."

"You're welcome, Rian."

"You don't deserve her, you realize?"

"Trust me, *I know*."

Nearby stood a tall figure in white and crimson. The eight gold chains dangling from his ears chimed when he shook his head at one of his scouts. He waved the fellow away, then turned. He had familiar violet eyes and flaming red hair shot with silver blond streaks which he kept tied back at the temples, as all Dannan nobles wore it.

"Yin," he said, his tone bland. "They're already marching South. They left the city burning behind them."

Kaer Yin exchanged a long look with Robin. "Get me a horse."

"Now wait a minute, Ben," Robin objected.

"Absolutely *not!*" interrupted Rian.

"*Mo flaith*, I don't think," began Shar.

"We could take the game trails, and—" Gerrod piped in.

The redhead's answering sneer trumped each response. "Why? So you can beat him to death with your one good leg? Should I have this girl saw it off for you so you might wield it as a club?"

Kaer Yin growled, "I am your Ard Tiarne! You'll do it or—"

"You going to hop along after me too? Quick, protect me, Shar. I *quake* with fear for my life."

"You know these scratches won't stop me. I *demand* a horse, Tam Lin. I have places to be, and no time to—"

The redhead crammed a finger in his ear. "Bah. I'm your cousin, not your slave. The only place you're headed is the nearest bed. You there," he ignored Kaer Yin and rounded sharply on Robin. "You're from Rosweal; I take it?"

"Aye?"

"My men hold many of your fellow citizens at the crossroads outside Donaghmore. Are you their Headman? This Gramble character?"

"I am." Robin crossed his arms.

"Unfortunately, your little town is the nearest with reasonable shelter. My men have already put out the blaze. I'm sorry to say, you lost quite a lot of real estate at the South End."

"Figured. Wasn't the best neighborhood anyway."

Tam Lin had no idea what to say to that. "*Quite.* Well, we'll have to beg your hospitality for a few days, if that would suit you fair?"

"Why not take him straight to his father, at Bri Leith?" Rian asked, wiping her hands dry on the underside of her homespun skirts.

Tam Lin's eyes cut sideways at her, as if he couldn't imagine why such a lowly creature should have the nerve to address him without invitation. "For reasons you needn't worry your pretty head over, sweetheart."

Gerrod sucked in a breath. He grasped her shoulder to keep her from launching upward, but it was a near thing. She stilled when Kaer Yin's hand caught hers.

"I know he's an arrogant bastard, Rian... but he *is* the Prince of Connaught. You can't kill him for cheek."

She settled back onto her haunches, her expression dripping ice. "No, but I can slap his face, and will, if he ever speaks to me like that again."

Tam Lin wandered closer to get a better look at her. Gerrod positioned himself between them, embarrassed but standing firm. There was no telling what Rian might do, if Gerrod let him pass. The Sidhe lord quirked a brow at the lad's bravado. Tam Lin not only towered over Gerrod by at least four handspans, he was also half-again as wide.

"What charming company you keep, Yin. Are all Milesian women in Eire like this one? Brash?"

"Only the good ones," Kaer Yin said.

Tam Lin batted Gerrod away as if parting a flimsy curtain. "What's your name then, girl?"

She chewed at the inside of her cheek. "Drop dead."

Tam Lin's men laughed with him. "Rather mouthy, aren't you?"

"Lin," Kaer Yin warned. "You're being a bore."

"Am I?"

"Yeah, ye are," answered Robin, tapping his dagger.

Shar dispelled the tension by retrieving a skin from his saddle. "More water, *Mo Flaith*? This is from the spring at Aislin Bres."

Kaer Yin shook Robin's flask. "Got something better."

Tam Lin pried his gaze from Rian's burning face. "Yin, I know your geis is broken, but that doesn't mean all is forgiven in Bri Leith. I meant to spare you until you were well again."

"I know."

"If you wish to go home first, I'll gladly escort you. Though, I can't promise you'll be pleased by your reception."

"I know that too, Lin," sighed Kaer Yin.

Tam Lin crouched beside him, grinning. "My father has no quarrel with you. Come to Connaught for a time! We'll hunt the hills of Sligo, as we did in our youth, and climb the pass at Donegal. There'll be wine and feasting *for years* in honor of your return. Surely my uncle's anger will wane in time and you'll take your proper place soon enough?"

If only he'd made such an offer a year ago, hells, four weeks ago, Kaer Yin would have leapt at the chance to return to Aes Sidhe. No longer an outsider. No longer forbidden the wilds of his homeland, or the hearths of his kin. Still, the homecoming would be bittersweet at best. He'd be unwelcomed in his family's *tuath* until Midhir deemed him worthy by edict. Kaer Yin might've slain the beast that jailed him but that had been a technical victory, at best. As far as Midhir was concerned, Kaer Yin remained an exile. A month before, he might not have minded. He might've leapt at Tam Lin's offered hospitality and considered it his due. Not so now. He knew *better*. Midhir hadn't banished him to Eire merely to be rid of a disobedient, dishonorable son. Finally, Kaer Yin comprehended his father's compassionate mind.

His father had exiled him to find Una.

Kaer Yin Adair, the ruthless Crown Prince of Innisfail, son of the Ard Ri, Midhir Mac Nuada— once loathed the Sons of Mil with every fiber in his being. He'd disdained them as *lesser* creatures: the unhappy children of a downtrodden god. Kaer Yin dealt with them when ordered to, meted justice where it was warranted. Otherwise, he held nothing but contempt for their meager lives. Their woes, joys, and loves were once alien and inscrutable, as the cold blackness between the stars. They were insignificant as autumn leaves; impermanent as a passing cloud. Despite these sentiments, Kaer Yin had meant to rule over them one day. His would have been a reign of condescension, cruelty, and inequality.

Midhir sent his only son to Eire to alter his perspective. Kaer Yin was meant to walk amongst the Sons of Mil: to fear, hunger, thirst, rage, laugh, cry, and strive alongside them. Midhir wished for his heir to know mortals, to feel the power and purpose in their lives. He intended that Kaer Yin share their hearths and friendships; for him to respect them, as Midhir respected them… to love them, as he loved them— as any noble king should. Midhir wanted to make him *their* king. A real king. A *great* king. Kaer Yin understood everything now, as if he could read his father's intentions on the wind. He wondered how he'd ever believed himself anything but a fool. Nearly a thousand years of life… and Kaer Yin had never actually felt *alive* before this moment.

"I thank you for your offer, cousin," Kaer Yin smiled. "But I'm afraid I must decline."

Tam Lin blanched. "Why on earth would you *want* to stay?"

"I have my reasons."

Tam Lin gawped at him, as if unsure what sort of lunatic he was looking at. "Girl. Give him something to clear his head. He's raving."

"May I slap him now, Ben?" inquired Rian, sweetly.

"Surely they know your name, Yin," Tam Lin ignored her comment. Again. "Why won't they use it?"

"Go ahead Rian, but he'll enjoy it," sighed Kaer Yin, patting her hand. He should keep his cousin away from the faerie for a while, for Tam Lin's own safety. "He loves a challenge. Best to pretend he's an overlarge tree, and skirt around him."

Her nose wrinkled. "Ugh. Duly noted."

Robin doffed his cap to scratch his head. "Ben, ye should go home while ye can. Isn't that what you want? What ye've wanted all this while?"

"… It was."

Robin ogled Kaer Yin for several breaths. All of a sudden, he tossed back his head on a hoot of laughter.

"Oh, aye? 'Not like that', then eh?"

"Hang yourself, Robin."

"What in the hells are all of you on about?" demanded Tam Lin. "Shar? Do you have any idea what this nonsense pertains to?"

Shar spread his hands. No help there.

"Tam Lin O'Ruiadh," Kaer Yin said.

"*Ard Tiarne*," Tam Lin mocked, in return.

"I ask that you and your Blood Eagles escort me South to Bethany, as soon as my wounds allow."

"… You've gone daft," scoffed Tam Lin.

"Donahugh's nephew took something from me. I want it back. Will you help me or not?"

On the spot and at a disadvantage for explanation, Tam Lin paced a bit. "Tell me, what could be so bloody important?"

"A woman," Rian answered for Kaer Yin, failing to hide a knowing smirk. "One *far* too good for him."

Kaer Yin squirmed. "Afraid she's right, Lin. Now, are you going to give me the men, or would you rather go home and hunt the same boar you always hunt? Raid the same boring *raths* you always raid? Hm?"

"*A woman?*" Tam Lin's voice cracked. His men all found something very interesting to observe in the trees around them. "You *have* gone mad."

"If I told you she was a princess and her father is Patrick Donahugh himself, would that change your mind?"

"Yin, you're barking."

"Better yet," Kaer Yin said, holding up a finger. "Her grandmother is the Doma of Tairngare, and in the Red City, she's wanted for a heretic by Parliament. Any interest yet?"

"Did she cast a spell on you? Bash in your brains with something heavy?"

"All right," Kaer Yin chuckled. "What if I told you she's the future Princess of Innisfail? How would that hold you?"

"The… *what?*"

"Think the boy's in love, ye dolt," Robin guffawed; his craggy cheeks shook with mirth. "Ye want me to spell it?"

Rian made a face. "She'd be mad to take you."

"Aye, she would at that," agreed Robin. Kaer Yin rolled a bandaged shoulder.

"What are you two on about? I'm a bloody prize." He gave a hacking cough and spat. "I'll keep asking. As many times as it takes."

Rian shook her head. "Poor Una."

"What am I listening to right now? Yin, have your brains melted inside your skull?" Tam Lin held his hands up.

Robin patted Kaer Yin's good arm with an exaggerated wink. "I'll try to talk ye up, but I'm afraid I can't make ye smarter or more dashin'. She'll have to be satisfied that yer daddy is rich."

Kaer Yin shot Robin a doleful glare, while Tam Lin sputtered. "Take your time, Lin. I can see you need it. Rian, would you be overly put out if I asked you to help me to the river?"

She blinked a stray tear away, wiping her nose on her sleeve. "You'll wet your bandages, and I'll kill you."

Kaer Yin crossed his heart. "My solemn vow only to wade."

"Fine," she sniffed. "Gerry, would you mind giving me a hand? And, oh—" Without ado, Shar Lianor hooked an arm under Kaer Yin's opposite shoulder while Gerrod helped Rian bear up his left side. She gave the Dannan soldier the briefest smile. "Erm, thank you. I might ask you both to help me drown him if he splashes that bandage on his thigh."

"I'm not going to!" protested Kaer Yin as they shuffled past Tam Lin's thunderstruck expression. Robin sidled up to him as the argument moved to the river's edge. "You gods-damned nag! I only want to wade, all right?" continued Kaer Yin. "I haven't been allowed in this cursed river for nearly—"

"You're already knee-deep! Take your boots off! I *swear to Siora...*"

"Rian, we can always wrap 'em again. I'll do it meself," placated Gerrod. He winked at Kaer Yin. "Swear."

"Stay out of this, Gerry!" Rian said.

"*The Princess of Innisfail?*" Tam Lin mumbled, his cheeks wan, "A *Milesian woman?*"

Robin took a long pull from his flask and handed it to the Prince of Connaught. Tam Lin stared at it like it might be a bubbling cauldron full of poison. Perhaps, in a way, it was; the best kind.

"Ye look like ye need this more'n me, yer highness."

Tam Lin grimaced as the warm amber liquid sailed down his gullet. "*A Milesian woman?*" he repeated, dumbfounded.

"Aye, and a bloody terrifying one, ye ask me," Robin's laughter rasped in his throat, "but a finer one, I've never seen. Brave. Smart. Good for him, I think."

Tam Lin took another drink. "*The Duch's* daughter?"

"Well, nobody's perfect, I expect, but that ain't what matters. I've known Ben a long time, and I must admit, she's the makin' of him. None o'us would be here now if not for her."

"My uncle won't approve of her. None of my people will." Tam Lin watched his cousin argue with Rian while she helped him out of his boots. Shar held him up so he might stroll into the current. Once there, the erstwhile Crown Prince closed his eyes and raised his chin to the setting sun— a free man at last. Encouraged, Kaer Yin waded too far toward the center, splashing his bandaged thigh to the skin. Rian's infuriated screech shattered the idyllic scene. Gerrod moved to intercept her lunge for Kaer Yin's ear, nearly dousing her in his haste to prevent her from murdering her patient.

"I said I was sorry, you harridan!" Kaer Yin used Shar as a massive, affable shield.

Rian was livid. "You *will* be when I start stitching!"

"I wouldn't be too sure of that, milord," said Robin to Tam Lin, gesturing to the fracas. Gerrod lost his footing and dragged Rian bodily into the icy, slogging current. He came up first, shying away as she rose from the riverbed like a vengeful sea goddess. Laughing, every man fled her boiling wrath. "Seems to me this mighta been what his majesty intended, all along."

Tam Lin blew air over his lower lip. "Don't be absurd. Have you ever been outside of Eire? These wilds? What does a woodsman like yourself know about anything?"

"Well, when ye put it like that, not much, I 'spose," Robin conceded. "But some things I can see, plain as me own nose. For one, I probably know Ben better than ye do."

"Is that so?"

"It is." Robin clapped him on the back, hard as he would any man in his acquaintance. Tam Lin was too surprised to conceal his flinch. "Come on. I'll show ye where we stashed the rest o'our uishge and tell ye all about it over a few drams."

The Prince of Connaught held up the bone flask. "Is it as good as this?"

"Better," Robin promised, leading the way.

EPILOGUE

n.e. 508
03, ÒOR ORAS
navan

N avan Village was a smoking scar in a wasteland of skinny charred sticks. The air was heavy with smoke and the sharp tang of blood. Eva heard the wailing long before she passed through the Slanic Gate from the east end of the High Road. There weren't many people around, save those keening outside the ruins of their homes and businesses. She did not stop to ask what had happened. No need. They'd passed the Corsairs on the road. Their faces were smudged with blood and soot as they limped back to Tairngare, their few remaining mounts burdened by ill-gotten gains. Mel recognized one of their officers, Lieutenant Camur Hamma, from the Citadel Guard. The Corsairs had been in quite the fight from the looks of them, and Hamma must have taken command from a fallen captain. He didn't appear pleased by his new rank in the least. He wouldn't be, would he? Knowing very well, he was marching home to announce his failure to Alta Nema. Eva and company passed them, disguised and unnoticed. Opening her Spark like a tap, she listened to their hearts' anger, hatred, fear, and despair. She pitied them, despite the crimes they'd committed in their rage.

The Corsairs lost the Moura Domina in Rosweal.

Along with nearly seventy men.

Eva suppressed the relief that surged through her at the news. These men, frustrated by their defeat in Rosweal, took revenge on every town they passed in retreat. Navan ahead had taken the brunt of that rage. Eva stymied her disgust at the disturbing images she prized from each of their depraved minds. Punishment was not her purpose, as much as she longed to mete the justice they so richly deserved. Knowing what awaited them in Tairngare, Eva had to be satisfied. Most of them would hang from the outer walls by nightfall tomorrow, including fine Lieutenant Hamma. That was not to say that she didn't leave each of them a special gift to mull over for the remainder of their march. Like a rotting tooth, the specter of their bodies swinging from a chain thirty feet from the ground gnawed its way into their subconscious like a persistent rat. She'd utter no prayers for their loss.

In Navan, the devastation was so much worse than she imagined it would be. Using all the Spark she could muster, she soothed the survivors as much as she was able. Their minds were a dark jumble of pain, shock, and anguish. Through their memories, she watched the Corsairs ride into town from the Rose Gate in the west, battered, impotent, and furious. The soldiers sought an easy target: someone to blame, someone to still the quaking fear in their souls.

They did to Navan what they could not do to Rosweal. The villagers in this small, inoffensive hamlet paid the price for the Corsairs' ineffectual cowardice. Women were savaged and slaughtered before their children. Husbands, fathers, and brothers were dragged through muddied lanes behind the Corsairs' horses. Some were slashed, bludgeoned, or cut down for attempting to protect their wives, mothers, and daughters. Some fled in time. Many died in their burning homes. Most lay broken in the streets, unseeing eyes filling with rainwater as they gasped their last. Mel, for one, hadn't seen horrors like this since the previous war. It was unconscionable: treacherous and unnecessary. He was unashamed to weep openly before his men. That fellow soldiers from their own city could do something like this made it unbearable. None of them were prepared. *Tairnganese* men did this. Men from the grand, *enlightened* city they loved enough to die for. Eva shoved a fist into her mouth to stall a bubbling scream. She did not have the right to mourn with these people, did she? Navan reeked of death and despair. She doubted that a single soul in this town would ever again trust anyone from the Red City.

Eva's heart broke a little more with every step she took.

They stopped under the charred awning of a tavern to rest—an illegible sign with the barest hint of two crossed arrows crumpled to charcoal beneath her booted foot. The structure was a husk of blackened beams and smoking timbers. Tugging at her Spark to search for survivors, Eva was led down the alley on her right, toward its stables. Mel Carra ordered his men to wait as he followed at a sedate, respectful pace.

This stable withstood most of the flames, owing in no small part to its heavy stone walls. Only half of the roof was burned away, which left the northernmost end largely intact. She followed her Spark through to the rear. A filthy boy covered in poorly tied bandages lay beside a dying mare in the hay. He whispered meaningless words of comfort as he stroked her mane with all the love he could muster. Softly, Eva approached. Mel waited just shy of the entrance, covering the lower half of his face with a large, strong hand. Mel Carra had five children of his own at home. This was too much for him. The mare had a broken spear shaft embedded in her lovely brown throat. She fought the fluid that filled her lungs with a valiant effort, but it wouldn't be long now.

The boy's father was dead. He had no one now to care for him. Eva crouched, reaching into him with her Spark. She saw the night's events through his eyes; saw Hamma and his men rush through his father's door. Saw them cut the old man's throat for a cask of ale. She watched them chase the lad into the stables; watched the mare, *Vixen*, charge the soldiers to protect him. The violence was… she couldn't look any longer. She forced her Spark down deep. Her fingers sought the curve of one narrow shoulder.

"There now, lad. She's gone," Eva crooned. Wet tears slid down her cheeks. He looked up, his face a swollen mass of welts and purpling bruises.

"Who're ye?"

She pushed back her black hood. "A friend."

He clutched at the silent muscles of Vixen's throat. "She tried to save me."

"I know. She was a brave girl, wasn't she?"

"She were me mam's."

Eva gently pulled him upward, tucking the top of his head into the crook of her arm. "Hush now. She's with Siora in the Land of the Undying— the wind in her mane, a blue sky stretching forever over her proud head. I vow it."

The boy's body shook with hacking sobs. His mind lay open to her like a bubbling fountain. There, in his recent memories, she caught a glimpse of a face she longed to see. *Una.* Una had been here. This boy's father had risked his own life and livelihood to help her and her companions. Eva took a deep breath. The knowledge would keep for now. The boy had too many wounds inside. He didn't have long. If she had her queen's gift, she might have been able to stitch him back together with her Spark. Fuse veins, join bones and cartilage, perhaps even shore the seeping organs around his pancreas. Alas, Eva's gifts were different. She could only hold him and direct his mind to all the fantastic, beautiful places he imagined. She heard him gasp with delight and felt him relax in her hands.

"I... I see Vixen! Ye were right! She's there, waitin' for me..."

Eva wiped her face with the back of a shaking hand. "What adventures you'll have together, but not yet. Your father is waiting in the hall with your supper. Do you see him? He's just there, waving."

"Da," his voice trailed off. "I fought so hard. Ye'd be so proud o'me—"

Eva sat in silence for what felt like hours. She wrapped the boy in a discarded tarpaulin and tucked him in beside his beloved friend. A slow simmering rage swallowed the consumptive sadness in her blood. She couldn't break down now. She had work to do.

"How long 'till Rosweal?"

514

"A day and a night if we keep to the road. Four, maybe, if we don't," Mel answered, absently stroking the daggers concealed beneath his Mercher's cloak. The disguise would not bear intense scrutiny, but it had served them well enough for the last few days. "The roads should be largely empty now this lot has burned their way through every town."

"Don't worry. They won't live through the week."

"Aye," he swiped at his own tear-stained face. "It'll have to do."

"I know where Una is. This boy and his father helped her. She travels with two companions. A man and a girl."

"That's good, by Siora. I'd rather the queen not be on her own out here."

"Me too," Eva sighed. "She's in Rosweal, Mel— as you suspected. Though, I'm not sure if they've moved on already."

"Well, there's only one way to know for sure."

GLOSSARY

A

- *Aenghus Mac Og-* (Aynn-guss-mack-Oh-ge) Dannan god of the Western Sea, love and poetry. Comparable to the Greek god Dionysus.
- *Aes Sidhe-* (Ayess-Shee) "Land of the ever-living', or 'Land of the Sidhe'. Northernmost region of Innisfail, home of the Immortal High King, and his people. Comprised of two major tribes; the Tuatha De Dannan, in Bri Leith and the Fir Bolg in Armagh.
- *Agrea-* (Ah-gray-ah) The Agriculturists Guild in Tairngare, run directly by the House of Commons in Tairnganese Parliament.
- *Alta-* (All-tah) A priestess second in rank to the Doma, in the Cloister of the Eternal Flame, in Tairngare.
- *Amer Gin Gluingel-* (Ahmer-genn-glonn-gall) "Amer the White kneed". A son of Mil Espanga, bard, druid and magician. Helped his brother Eber Finn, conquer Innisfail, and defeat the Tuatha De Dannan.
- *Aoife-* (Eee-Fah) "Radiant one".
- *Ard Ri-* (Ardh- Ree) "Highest King".
- *Ard Tuaithe-* (Ardh-too-ah-hee) "Highest Landsman". A common way to address a Sidhe noble. "Tuaithe", simply means 'countryside'.
- *Ard Tiarne-* (Ardh-tee-arh-nah) "Highest Lord, or Prince". A title reserved for the Crown Prince of Innisfail.
- *Armagh-* (Arr-mah) Capital of the Kingdom of Ulster, and seat of the ancient Kings of the Fir Bolg. As the Fir Bolg's power has waned over the centuries, the Kingdom of Ulster is less than one-third its size in ancient times. Ruled by the Mac Nemed Clan (House of the Black Bull).

B

- *Badh-* (Bae-ve) Sidhe goddess of discord, disharmony and dread. Pestilence and famine are also her domain. One of three divine sisters. SEE MORRIGAN AND MACHA. Her herald is the crow.

- *Ban-* (Bahn) "White", "Light" or "Bright". As in "Ban Lug"— or the Month of Midsummer (formerly August).

- *Ban Sidhe-* (Bahn-shee) "White Spirit" or "Good Folk". A term reserved for the higher classification of Sidhe (or Immortal Ones). The Tuatha De Dannan and Fir Bolg, belong to this class, on whole. See *DAOINE SIDHE*, for nobility.

- *Bel-* (Ball) The Sidhe sun god. Considered a male figure, but otherwise one of the few non-personified deities in the Sidhe pantheon, save for Samn, his mate.

- *Beltane-* (Ball-tinna) A festival celebrated on the first of the Month "Ban-Bela" (Bahn-balla), formerly 'May'. A celebration for seeding crops, full spring, and fertility.

- *Bethany-* (Beth-ahn-nee) The Southernmost Kingdom in Innisfail, and second-most powerful city in Eire. Ruled by the Donahugh Clan, under their line of ancestral Duchs. Seat of Duch Patrick Donahugh, fervent enemy of Aes Sidhe. Sometimes called the 'Machine City', for their use of cannons and other siege devices in warfare.

- *Bodhran-* (Bode-ran) A circular frame drum made from animal hide and polished wood. The Sidhe carry bodhrans into battle.

- *Bov Mac Nuada Dearg-* (Bove- mack- new-ah-dah-derrck) King of Connaught, and former High King of the Tuatha De Dannan, in pre-Celtic times. Known as 'Bov the Red', for his famous temper, and rash behavior. Rules from his capital at Croghan. Brother to the High King, Midhir.

- *Breccan-* (Breck-ahn) "Freckled one".

- *Brehon-* (Breh-honn) "Teacher" or "Knowing One". Brehons are the highest ranking magic users in Innisfail. They are considered 'holy men', for the ability to commune with both spirits and nature itself. Their advice is sought by Sidhe leaders before any major commitment, such as war, marriage, treaties, or policy making. They are as feared as they are respected, for to incur a Brehon's wroth is to endure all manner of travesties. It is illegal to harm a Brehon, and they are immune to Common Law. A Brehon may gainsay even the High King, without fear of repercussion.

- *Bretagne-* (Breh-tan-ee) A peninsula jutting into the Southern sea, from the old kingdom of Francia. A major sea power in its own right, and one of the few remaining kingdoms free of Innish over-rule.

- *Brida-* (Bree-dah) The Sidhe goddess of the dawn. The Dagda named one of his own daughters for her, who died in ancient times. The horse, is her herald— speed and strength, are her creed.

- *Bri Leith-* (Bree-leyth) "Highest Realm", or "Foremost Hall". Capital of Aes Sidhe, and home of the High King, Midhir. Ruled by the Adair Clan (House of the White Stag).
- *Bru Na Boinne-* (Broo-nah-boyne) A valley of ancient hillforts at the Northern border of Eire, along the river Boyne (*Boinne,* in old Innish). The passage tombs of Newgrange, Dowth, and Knowth— gird the river from the North, in Aes Sidhe. The passage tombs are older even than the Sidhe, having been built many thousands of years before the Invasion Cycles of Innish history. The Sidhe call these first peoples 'Fomorian', or sometimes 'Stone People'; for the complex network of standing stones, passage tombs, dolmens, and hillforts they left behind. Considered the holiest site in Innisfail, by the Sidhe.

C

- *Clare-* (Clayre) A sea province along the South-Western Coast of Eire. Ruled by Lord Damek Bishop.
- *Connaught-* (Cuhn-aught) Westernmost kingdom in Aes Sidhe. Ruled by King Bov, 'The Red'.
- *Croghan-* (Crew-Hahn) Capital of the Kingdom of Connaught, and seat of Bov Dearg, and the Marshal of the West. Ruled by the Dearg Clan (The House of the Red Eagle).
- *Cu Chulainn-* (Cu-hoo-linn) An ancient Innish hero, and champion of a Milesian King of Eire.
- *Crom Dagda-* (Cruhm- dagh-dah) The 'good father'. First King of the Tuatha De Dannan, and also a Skysinger of unimaginable power. Sacrificed his own eye to save Nuada's life after the battle at Magh Tuiredh, against the formidable Fomorian King, Balor. And years later, sacrificed his own life to save his people from the onslaught of the Milesians, after Nuada's death. He is honored at Cromnasa, each midwinter. Opened a path into the Otherworld with his own sacrifice, which granted all Sidhe tribes everlasting life.
- *Cromnasa-* (Cruhm-nah-sa) "Festival of Crom" or "Crom's Feast". Celebration of the Dagda's sacrifice for the Immortality of the Sidhe. Midwinter festival, celebrated on the Longest Night of the year.
- *Cymru-* (Kim-ree) An ancient Kingdom at the Easternmost reaches of Innisfail, having once been called 'Wales', before The Transition. A mineral rich country, for its mountains and hills are filled with precious ores. In the West of the Kingdom, their major export is wine, which is grown largely in the South, toward the capital at Swansea. Cymru is a Tairnganese colony but pays homage and tithes to Aes Sidhe. Over the Cyrmian mountains in the far east of the Kingdom, lies a region known as the 'Wastes', for its inhospitable, uninhabitable, and arid landscape.
- *Cymrian-* (Kim-ree-ahn) One who dwells in Cymru.

D

- *Dagda*- SEE CROM DAGDA, under 'C'.

- *Danu*- (Day-new) The goddess of the earth, in pre-Innish Europe. The patron goddess of the Tuatha de Dannan, who claim to be descended from her and her mate Donn, the god of death.

- *Daoine Sidhe*- (Doone-Shee) A term reserved for the upper echelons of Ban Sidhe society. The nobles and royalty of Aes Sidhe.

- *Dearg*- (Derckk) "The Red".

- *Damek Bishop, Lord of Clare*- (Dahm-eck) Alis Donahugh's illegitimate son, fathered by an unknown Sidhe lord. Adopted by Duch Patrick Donahugh after his mother's death. An accomplished soldier and statesman. Commander of Bethany's armed forces.

- *Dian Cecht*- (Diahn-caysht) Sidhe ancestor god, son of the Dagda. Forged Nuada's Golden Hand, after the battle at Maigh Turiedh. The Sidhe consider him the father of healing.

- *Diarmid Mac Nuada Dubh*- (Derr-mett-mack-nu-ah-dah-duvv) King of Tech Duinn, and Lord of the *Oiche Ard Fad*. Called *Fiachra Ri*, by the Sidhe- or Raven King, in Eire. A Skysinger, like his father Crom Dagda; and Brehon of the Tuatha De Dannan. He is the only member of his house, as he rules a kingdom of the dead. All lesser Sidhe call him 'King', including the Lu Sidhe, and Dor Sidhe- which would unleash themselves upon mortal kind, did he not guard the gates of the Otherworld with a firm hand. Brother to Midhir, the High King. An ambitious, mercurial man, whose loyalty can never truly be counted upon. Also known as "Diarmid, The Black". Servant of Donn- the god of the dead; and Donn's daughter, Morrigan.

- *Doma*- The title of the High Priestess of the Cloister of the Eternal Flame, in Tairngare. The theocratic and secular ruler of Tairngare. Holds a seat on the High King's Council, and the highest-ranking official in Eire. Currently held by Drem Moura.

- *Donn*- "Dark One", the Sidhe god of the dead. Mate of Danu, goddess of the earth. Donn is the only god the Sidhe and Milesians shared before the Invasions. Donn, was also the name of one of Mil Espagna's seven sons. He died after cursing his brother Ir. Diarmid as a Skysinger and Brehon, is his servant.

- *Dor*- (Door) "Black" or "Darkest", see also 'dorchas'. As in "Dor Samna" (Door-Sawa), or the Month of Winter's Birth (formerly, October).

- *Dor Sidhe*- (Door-shee) "Darkest Spirits", or "Evil Folk". A term to describe the darker denizens of the Otherworld. Unnatural beasts and spirits that harm and hunt mortals for food or sport. They only exist within the Otherworld, or sometimes on the fringes of the border with Aes Sidhe- where the veil between worlds is thinnest. Often roam wild in Eire on Samhain, when the veil vanishes altogether, once a year. Goblins, selkies, pookas, trolls, ghasts, giants, and gnomes- all belong to this classification.

- *Drem Moura-* (Drehm-More-Ah) The High Priestess of Siora, the Ancestor; in the Cloister of the Eternal Flame at Tairngare. Head of the wealthiest and most influential family in Eire, and most powerful woman on the continent. Not well-loved by the common people, for her frequent attempts to crown members of her own family Queen of the Commons; in order to shore up absolute power for the Moura Clan. Mother of Arrin Moura, and grandmother to Una.

- *Donahugh-* (Donnah-hew) The ruling clan of Bethany, and the greater South of Innisfail.

- *Dubh-* (Duvv) "Black".

- *Duch-* (Duke) A lord second only to a king in rank— but far removed from a High King, who rules over all lesser kings and lords equally.

- *Dumnain-* A village in the lower Midlands of Eire, which was destroyed by the Crown Prince Kaer Yin Adair, during the war with Bethany in '84. The site of one of the bloodiest battles in Innish history, and the very place Duch Donahugh lost his right to a seat on the High King's Council, in exchange for his life. Due to this battle, the Kingdom of Bethany pays the highest tithes and taxes in Innisfail, in reparation for the horrors inflicted on the Eirean people for Bethany's warmongering. Also, the site where the High King's son was exiled from Aes Sidhe for war crimes, after the extreme measures he took to safeguard his own troops.

Є

- *Eber Finn-* (Everr-Feen) A Milesian King, son of the King Mil Espagna. The first 'celtic' king of Innisfail.

- *Eire-* (Ay-err) The Milesian (mortal) region of Innisfail. It borders Aes Sidhe at the Boyne in the Midlands and ends at the Bretagn Straits in the far South. Straddles the Straits of Mannanan in the East. Cities like Tairngare and Ten Bells have colonies in Cymru and Kernow (formerly Wales, and Cornwall).

- *Emain Macha-* (Aavvinn-mash-ah) A holy hillfort, in the Kingdom of Ulster.

- *Eochaid Mac Nemed-* (Yoh-hee- mack- nehm-ehd) Ancient King of the Fir Bolg. Slain by Nuada, king of the Tuatha De Dannan for his throne and the right to rule in Innisfail. Married to his cousin Liadan, by their Fomorian Grandfather, Balor. Was a just ruler, and fearsome warrior.

- *Eri Mac Midhir Bres-* (Ayre-ee-mack-med-heer-bray) Daughter of Midhir and Etain, Princess of Innisfail, and Queen of Scotia. Married to Jan Fir Bres, King of Scotia; and Lord of Skye.

- *Eriu-* (Ayr-yoo) One of the Dagda's daughters, for which Eire was named. Died in ancient times.

F

- *Faerie-* (Fare-ee) "Doomed One", or "Touched by Doom". A racial slur for those of half-Sidhe blood. Also used to denigrate people born with deformities, mental disorders, or those whom suffer from depression or madness. It is believed that the blood of the Sidhe is a curse for mortal kind, and often leaves its progeny unnaturally lovely, but usually deficient in every other area. Faeries (whether real or slandered) are largely reviled in Eire.
- *Fainne-* (Feene) The literal gold standard, upon which all Innish currency is based. Also called "Crowns", or "Royals".
- *Falan-* (Fahl-ahn) The given name of two members of the Armagh royal family, Falan the Elder, and Falan the Younger, respectively. An ancient Bolgish name.
- *Fiachra Ri-* (Fee-ah-cruh-ree) "Raven King". Refers to Diarmid Mac Nuada Dubh, the King of *Tech Duinn*— or the Land of the Dead.
- *Fir Bolg-* (Feer-Bolck) A tribe of Sidhe warriors, descended from the ancient warrior Nemed. They fought with the Fomorians for several generations, and were expelled for a time to Southern Europe, where they were enslaved by the Greek tribes in Macedon. Forced to carry bags of stone up and down ladders into mines, before their escape back to Innisfail, they became known as the "Bag Men". Close cousins of the Tuatha De Dannan from their mutual ancestor, Nemed- but dark complected, where the Dannans are fair. Sometimes called, "dark elves" for this trait. Their last stronghold in Innisfail is the city of Armagh, ruled by the Mac Nemed Clan.
- *Fodla-* (Fole-ah) One of Crom Dagda's wives.
- *Fomorians-* (Fov-or-ee-ahns) Ancient people whom lived in Innisfail before the first invasions. Worshipped dark gods of earth and stone, harvest and reaping, until a Comet known as Lug of the Long Arm came sailing out of the west, bringing calamity, and famine. They began to build stone circles and passage tombs to mark the heavens after this, to honor their new god. Defeated by the Fir Bolg in ancient times. The Tuatha De Dannan revere them as wise ancestors and keep their holy places sacred. They also adopted several of the Fomorian gods, like Lug of the Long Arm, Bel the sun god, and Samn the moon goddess. Also known as the "Stone People".

G

- *Geis-* (Gay-ehss) "Unbreakable Vow". A curse, taboo, or restriction placed upon an individual of power, to restrict their actions. In a Dannan warrior's case, it is an obligation one cannot break, without great personal sacrifice.

H

- *Hamish-* (Hay-mesh) A soldier from Bethany.
- *Herne-* (Hurrn) The White Stag, or God of the Forest. The patron god of House Adair.

522

I

- *Imbolg-* (Em-bolk) A festival in high winter, to summon spring. Celebrated on the first day of the Month of Blinding White, "Dor Imba" (Formerly February).
- *Innisfail-* (Enn-ess-fay-ehl) "Land of Destiny". A small continent at the rim of the Northern Ice Flows, comprising much of what was once Ireland, Scotland, Wales, and Cornwall. Much of what was England has largely become tundra, or inhospitable wastes; due to catastrophic climate change, and trace human corruptions of the land. In many places, the soil is either frozen under two feet of ice, or simply too toxic from long-forgotten nuclear reactors that have leached radiation into the soil. Innisfail is the last bastion of relative habitable land in what was Europe. Parts of Northern France, Spain and Portugal, are similarly liveable- but not as biodiverse. This biodiversity and ecological prosperity are due in large part, to the Sidhe, whom have reclaimed dominance over the land.

J

- *Jan Fir Bres-* (Yahn-feer-bray) King of Scotia, and Lord of Skye. Descended from the Half-Fomorian king Bres, whom married one of the Dagda's daughters, and emigrated to Skye. Second cousin to the High King and married to his daughter Eri.

K

- *Kaer Yin Mac Midhir Adair-* (Kayer-eeann-mack-med-eehr-ah-dare) The *Ard Tuiathe* of the *Tuatha De Dannan*, and Crown Prince of Innisfail. Son of Midhir and Etain, he was the first Dannan to be born in Innisfail after The Transition. Grand Marshal of the Wild Hunt, and Commander of Aes Sidhe's standing armies. Slayed Kevin Donahugh in single combat, during the first Bethonair War, and ended the war of '84, at Dumnain with another victory over the Donahugh Clan. Prince of Eire, and Cymru. A cold, unfeeling character, who values martial might over all other virtues.

L

- *Libella-* Tairngare's elite class of nobles. To be a member of the Libella, and its House in Parliament, one must hold a Patent of Maternas, which must be traced back at least three generations, in the Cloister of the Eternal Flame. Also, refers to the House of Nobles in Parliament.
- *Libellum-* (Ly-bell-uhm) Founded by the Tairnganese aristocractic class. The Educator's Guild in Tairngare, also a collection of schools, in which all Tairnganese citizens (even those whom live in the Colonies) may study free, although to earn a degree in any field, one must pass a series of aptitude tests before and after each school term,

to assure the student is devoted to his or her craft. The schooling might be free, but each school requires a sizeable donation from the family to ensure employment afterward. Most students who are not from Aristocratic families, often take secondary education in the Agrea for agriculture, or buy into the Merchanta to apprentice for a trade. The Libellum educates all children not accepted in the Cloister, until the age of 16, when the more expensive secondary education begins. Usually specializing in Law, Engineering, Rhetoric, or Medicine.

- *Liadan Mac Nemed* (formerly, Mac Balor) (Lee-ah-dann-mack-neh-mehd) Queen of the Fir Bolg in ancient times, and Dowager Queen of Armagh, after The Transition.
- *Lir* (Leer) A Sidhe ancestor god. His children were changed into swans by his second wife and were forced to languish in these forms for hundreds of years.
- *Lug-* (Lew) Lug of the Long Arm, was a Fomorian sky deity that the Dannans appropriated when they conquered Innisfail in ancient times. He is represented as a traveling god, who comes only once every eighty years or so— sometimes bringing fortune, and others, calamity. The Sidhe pray to him for luck and guidance. Often considered the God of Law, and Chance.
- *Lugnasa-* (Lew-nah-sah) Festival of the sky god Lug; to curry Lug's blessings upon the Harvest, and to guard the living from the coming starving season. Lugnasa is the time of year in which the Sidhe's major policies, treaties or major martial and agricultural matters are decided. Trials are held during Lugnasa, children are named, and funerals are held. Property may change hands or be gifted at Lugnasa. Celebrated at the start of Ban Lug, or 'The Month of The Bright Sky' (formerly, August 1).
- *Lu Sidhe-* (Lew-shee) Less powerful, wise, or long-lived denizens of the Otherworld. Some share blood with the Ban Sidhe, but many are simply spirits or other mischievous creatures who assume a human-like shape. Often, faeries and other halfbloods are classified as Lu Sidhe. Such as: Slyphs, satyrs, Pixies, Niskies, Dryads, Nymphs and Brownies.

M

- *Mac-* (Mack) "Son of", or "Daughter of".
- *Macha-* (Mah-sha) Sidhe goddess of strategy, ambition, and courage. She is associated with sovereignty. One of three divine sisters. See also: Badh and Morrigan. Her herald is the eagle.
- *Maeve-* (Mae-ve) Sidhe goddess of wisdom, magic, and mystery. Her herald is the Owl. SEE BABH, the goddess of discord, strife, and pestilence.
- *Magh Tuiredh-* (Moy-teer-ah) Site of two ancient battles, the first of which was waged on the Fir Bolg by the Tuatha De Dannan. The Dannans took control of Innisfail at the end but granted the Fir Bolg their own corner of the land to rule— Ulster. The second battle was fought between the resurgent Fomorians, where Nuada of the Golden Arm was killed.

- *Manipulation-* A form of magic studied by the *Siorai* acolytes of the Cloister of the Eternal Flame, in Tairngare. Using one's own body energy (or Spark*)*, one can force particles to join or separate, and even build unnatural chains which change an objects trajectory, composition, or shape.
- *Mannanan Mac Lir-* Sidhe god of the Eastern Sea. Son of the god Lir.
- *Merchanta-* (Merr-cant-ah) The Merchant's Guild of Tairngare, run directly by the House of Commons in Parliament.
- *Midhir Mac Nuada-* (Mehd-eer-mack-nu-ah-dah) *Ard Ri* of the Tuatha De Dannan, and High King of Innisfail. Brought his people out of the Otherworld at the end of the Third Age of Man- also known as The Transition. Conquered the surviving mortals and brought them firmly under unified Sidhe overrule. A kind and compassionate ruler, if distracted and detached.
- *Mil Espagna-* An ancient 'celtic' king, hailing from the Iberian plateau. Forced to search for a new home when climate, war, and famine struck his people; they came to Innisfail— a lush, green, fertile land— in such numbers and with far superior weapons than anything the Sidhe could muster. His victories forced the Sidhe into the Otherworld and began the long period of Gallic rule. To the present, all Sidhe refer to mortal men and women as 'Milesians'
- *Morrigan-* (More-ah-gahn) Sidhe goddess of war, bloodlust, fury and pride. One of three divine sisters. (Equivalent to the Greek Fates). Her herald is the raven.

N

- *Navan-* (Nah-vahn) A small town on the river Boyne, at the border with Aes Sidhe.
- *Nemain-* (Neh-mayne) Sidhe goddess of the waterways and springs. It was said that her beauty drove men to madness for desire of her, but her kiss was poison and tortuous death. Kaer Yin's longsword is named for her. Her sister Niamh is the goddess of purity and love.
- *Nemed-* King of the first Innish invaders, in ancient times. Mortal grandson of the earth goddess Danu, and her mate, Donn— the god of death. Their daughter Brida took a mortal lover, from the tribe of Abraham. An accomplished sailor and adventurer, Nemed led his sea-faring tribe around the Mediterranean before a storm swept them out into the ocean, to Innisfail. Nemed fought the Fomorians for almost thirty years, before his death. His people divided and fled in separate directions. One half went South and were enslaved in Macedon; the Fir Bolg. The others took their ships far into the north and west, battling gods and monsters, until they returned with 300 ships, to oust their cousins from Innisfail- The Tuatha De Dannan.
- *Niall-* (Nay-all) A Dannan warrior, in Tam Lin's retinue.
- *Niamh-* (Neh-ve) Sidhe goddess of purity and love. Dwells in the waterways and springs, with her corrupted sister, Nemain.
- *Norther-* One whom dwells in Northern Eire.
- *Nova-* An initiate of the Cloister of the Eternal Flame, in Tairngare.

O

- *Oiche Ar Fad*- (Eesha-arh-fah) The Otherworld. A realm that exists just below the mortal. The Sidhe retreated to this realm for thousands of years, until the Milesians nearly purged themselves from the world. Only the Sidhe may come and go from this realm unmolested. To humankind, it holds mainly horror, forgetfulness, or death.

P

- *Porter*- A game of cards and two-sided dice.
- *Prima*- (Preema) A tertiate acolyte of the Cloister of the Eternal Flame, in Tairngare.

R

- *Ri*- (Ree) A king, or high lord.
- *Ruiadh*- (Roo-ah) "Red".

S

- *Samn*- (Sow) Sidhe goddess of the moon. Bel, god of the sun, is her mate.
- *Samhain*- (Sow-ahn) Festival of the moon, and the onset of winter. Celebrated (or mourned, considering perspective) at the end of the Month of Oncoming Night or Winter, or "Dor Samna". Samhain is the passage of life into death, and of autumn to winter. It is the one night of the year, in which the dead and all manner of Otherworld creatures may wander free of its borders— to trouble, torment, or comfort the living.
- *Scota*- (Skoh-tah) "Fierce One". The Queen of the Milesians in ancient times. Wife of Mil Espagna. Died fighting on the beach during the first Milesian invasion. Her son Amer Gin, who led his own men across the sea of Mannanan, named the land east of Skye after her (formerly Scotland).
- *Secunda*- (Seh-koon-dah) An intermediate in the Cloister of the Eternal Flame, in Tairngare.
- *Shannon*- The longest, widest river in Innisfail.
- *Sidhe*- (Shee) "Ever-Living", Describes the Immortals who dwell or dwealt in the Otherworld. Some are powerful and human-like, the Ban Sidhe; and some merely aspire to take human form— or never wish to.
- *Siora*- Patron goddess of Tairngare, also known as the 'Ancestor'. A goddess of unity, knowledge, and feminine power.

526

- *Siorai*- Acolytes of the Cloister of the Eternal Flame. Considered witches, by most of the peoples of Innisfail.
- *Souther*- One who dwells in Southern Eire.
- *Spark*- The life-force, or energy within one's body, that can be harnessed to manipulate the actions and properties of an object's compositional particles.

T

- *Tara*- (Tare-ah) A midling-sized town in Eire, south of the Boyne. In ancient times, it was a hillfort, fortress and castle— belonging to the High Kings of old Eire. Site of the *Lia Fail*, or "Stone of Destiny", before which all Kings of Eire were crowned. Now, it is a hub of the Merchanta— or Merchant's Guild, in Tainrgare.
- *Tairngare*- (Tare-ehn-gare) A matriarchal city in the Northeast of Eire, at the mouth of the Boyne (formerly Drogheda). A city run by a religious order of women, and a Parliament elected from noble families and commoners. Founded by a woman named Siora, a former prostitute who had magical abilities she shared only with the women who swore their supreme loyalty to the nameless earth goddess she claimed to have been born of. She vanished after the women took over the city. They call her the 'Ancestor'.
- *Tech Duinn*- (Teck-Doon) "House of Donn", or "Realm of Donn". The god of death in pre-Innish Europe, also the mate of Danu, goddess of the earth. His realm is the land of the dead, and all whom share his blood (Such as the Tuath De Dannan, Fir Bolg, and Milesians alike), must come to his realm after death. In the Otherworld, Diarmid is the king of Tech Duinn, and Donn's servant. All whom are given the god of death's name, are said to be cursed, or bring misfortune to their families. Such as the son of Mil, whom was angered by his brother Ir's rowing abilities, and cursed him, causing the oar to snap and both boys to die. The realm of Tech Duinn is a peaceful but solemn one within the otherworld, and only once a year on Samhain, are the dead given reprieve to wander outside its confines.
- *Tir Na Nog*- (Teer-nah-noge) "Land of the Undying Ones". The realm of the Sidhe gods. Only great heroes or those with divine blood, may enter when they die. All else must go to Tech Duinn
- *Tir Falias*- A Sidhe city in the Otherworld.
- *Transition*- SEE TUATHA DE DANNAN.
- *Tuatha De Dannan (or Tuatha De Danaan, or De Danann)*- (Too-ah-ha-day-dahn-ahn) "Children of Danu". A half-divine tribe of warriors descended from the demi-god and adventurer Nemed. Unlike their Fir Bolg cousins, the Tuatha De fled Innisfail in ships, toward the north and west. They traveled from Isle to Isle, fighting monsters, hostile tribes, and brushing elbows with the gods. When they returned to Innisfail in ancient times, they defeated the Fir Bolg for supremacy over the land; then defeated the Fomorians, the old Fir Bolg enemy. They ruled in peace for many seasons, until they were defeated by the crafty Milesians from the Iberian Peninsula. Their greatest Brehon, Crom Dagda, sacrificed his life to the god

of death— Donn, to give all those whom shared the Dagda's blood immortality, and a piece of the Otherworld to rule. They remained there for thousands of years, vowing to return when the rule of Mil's spawn failed. In N.E. 1, when the Milesians were fast becoming extinct, the Dannans came back to reconquer what was stolen from them in ancient times. This is known as the 'Transition'.

U

- *Uishge-* (Whisk-ey) "Water of Life". An ancient, amber colored spirit.
- *Ulster-* (Ull-Sterr) Kingdom in the north of Aes Sidhe, its capital is Armagh. Ruled by the remaining Fir Bolg nobility, the Mac Nemed Clan. Has been one of the chief Innish kingdoms since ancient times.
- *Una Moura Donahugh-* (Ooh-nah-more-ah-donnah-hew) "Bright One". Prima of the Cloister of the Eternal Flame. Reigning Domina of House Moura, and proposed Queen of the Commons, in Parliament. Studying to ascend to Alta Prima, and being groomed to succeed Drem as Doma. Daughter of Arrin Moura and Patrick Donahugh.

V

- *Vanna Nema-* (Vah-nah-Nee-mah) Alta Prima, Mistress of the House of Commons in Parliament, and second-in-command to the Doma.

DRAMATIS PERSONAE

eire-

TAIRNGARE

- *Drem Moura*- Doma, high priestess of the Cloister of the Eternal Flame. Highest ranking noble in Tairngare. Represents all of Eire in the High King's Council.
- *Vanna Nema*- Alta Prima, Mistress of the House of Commons in Parliament, and second-in-command to the Doma.
- *Arrin Moura*- (Deceased) Former Alta Prima of the Cloister of the Eternal Flame. Former Queen of the Commons, appointed by the Doma, her mother. Taken from a market by Duch Patrick and made Duchess of Bethany, against her will. Committed suicide in *N.E. 487*, when her daughter was but two years old.
- *Una Moura Donahugh*- Prima of the Cloister of the Eternal Flame. Reigning Domina of House Moura, and proposed Queen of the Commons, in Parliament. Studying to ascend to Alta Prima, and being groomed to succeed Drem as Doma. Daughter of Arrin Moura and Patrick Donahugh.
- *Aoife Sona*- Prima of the Cloister of the Eternal Flame. Servant of Vanna Nema. Rumored to hold Fir Bolg blood.
- *Eva Alvra*- Member of the Libella, and Domina of House Alvra. Servant of the Doma, and former Prima of the Cloister of the Eternal Flame.
- *Pors Yma*- High ranking member of the Libella. A staunch opponent of the House of Commons.
- *Mel Carra*- Member of the Mercher's Guild, and highest-ranking member of the House of Commons. Ardent supporter of Vanna Nema.
- *Fawa Gan*- Steward, to Vanna Nema

BETHANY

- *Duch Patrick Donahugh*- Ruler of the South. Ardent opponent of the High King in Aes Sidhe. Instigator of two wars, which cost him many men and most of his fortune— as well as his seat on the High King's Council. Chafes under Sidhe rule, and plots to take the throne for himself. Kidnapped Una's mother from a market in broad daylight and forced her into a loveless marriage of convenience. Una's father; he means to conquer all of Eire, and rule in her name.

- *AlisDonahugh*- (Deceased) Kidnapped by an unknown Sidhe lord in *N.E. 474*, returned home several months later, heavy with child and mad. After the child was born, she threw herself from the north parapet. Some say, her death prompted the battle at Dumnain, ten years later.

- *Henry Fitz Donahugh*- Patrick's illegitimate half-brother. Attempted to overthrow Patrick after his failure at Dumnain. Banished to the wastes of Cmyru, for nearly twenty years. A fervent Kneeler.

- *Damek Bishop, Lord of Clare*- Alis' illegitimate son, fathered by an unknown Sidhe lord. Adopted by Patrick after his mother's death. Accomplished soldier and statesman. Views himself as Patrick's rightful heir, and plots to conquer the whole of Eire to force his uncle to legitimize his claim to the throne. Commander of Bethany's armed forces.

- *Martin O'Reardan*- Lord Marshal at Arms, of Bethany. Damek's self-appointed right-hand man, and protector. Damek reveres him as a father figure and close confidant.

- *Wallace Cunningham*- Major of Bethany's Steel Corps (formerly, Captain, (Heavy Cavalry). An accomplished tracker, and talented swordsman.

- *Killian*- A lieutenant

- *Hamish*- A corporal

- *Douglas*- A sergeant

- *Dawes*- A corporal

- *Blane*- A ranger

ROSWEAL

- *Barb Dormer*- Madam of the tavern and pleasure house, *The Hart and Hare*. A former Nova in the Cloister of the Eternal Flame. Mistress of the Greenmakers' Guild. Aims to be the Town Headwoman, and dreams of modernizing their backwater town.

- *Robin Gramble*- A poacher, and town crime boss. Master of the Greenmakers' Guild, answers only to Barb, his undeclared mistress. Well-respected by his men, and greatly feared by his enemies.

- *Ben Maeden*- A drifter, and sometime poacher. Mysterious origins, and curious loyalties. Fond of drink, dicing, and women.

- *Matt Gilcannon*- A bootlegger, distiller of illegal spirits, and whoremaster. Owner of the *Black Corset*. A bordello of ill-repute. Fond of using the sons of his whores to do his dirty work. Desirous of destroying the Greenmakers' monopoly on trade, and opening new revenue streams outside of the North.

- *Solomon Trant*- A brewer and tavernkeeper, in the Greenmakers' Quarter. Member of the Greenmakers' Guild.

- *Samuel Trant-* A butcher, tanner and crime underboss. Brother to Solomon Trant, but not a member of the Greenmakers' Guild.
- *Gerrod Twomey-* A competent woodsman, and member of the Greenmakers' Guild, despite his youth and optimism.
- *Colm-* Tavernkeeper at the *Hart and Hare*, member of the Greenmakers' Guild. Barb's right-hand man.
- *Seamus-* A tracker and woodsman. A member of the Greenmakers' Guild.
- *Dabney-* Barb's dimwitted bodyguard.
- *Dean-* A bouncer at the *Hart and Hare*, and sometime hired thug.
- *Paul-* A hired thug, sometime member of the Greenmakers' Guild.
- *Rose-* A prostitute at the *Hart and Hare*, from a disgraced Tairnganese noble family. Soft-spoken and loyal.
- *Violet-* A prostitute from the Midlands.
- *Tansy-* A prostitute.
- *Vick-* One of Matt Gilcannon's street toughs.

Ferndale

- *Arthur Guinness-* (Deceased) Physician. Once a triage doctor for the Tairnganese forces in the war of '84.
- *Aednat Guinness-* (Deceased) His wife. Sidhe half-blood.
- *Rian Guinness-* Took over her father's practice after his death. Reviled by all whom seek her out for her faerie blood. Methodical, practical and intelligent- if not overly friendly.

aes sidhe-

Bri Leith

(House of the White Stag)

- *Nuada of the Golden Arm-* (Deceased) Ancient ancestor of the House Adair (White Stag). Son of the Dagda, and King of the *Tuatha De Dannan*. Defeated the armies of Balor the One-Eyed, King of the Fomorians. Defeated the Fir Bolg King, Eochaid Mac Nemed in single combat for the title of *Ard Ri*. Slain by Eber Finn, son of Mil Espagna- a mortal man.
- *Crom Dagda-* The 'good father'. First King of the *Tuatha De Dannan*, and also a Skysinger of unimaginable power. Sacrificed his own eye to save Nuada's life after

531

the battle at Magh Tuiredh, against the formidable Fomorian King, Balor. Years later, sacrificed his own life to save his people from the onslaught of the Milesians, after Nuada's death. He is honored at Cromnasa, each midwinter.

- *Midhir Mac Crom-* Ard Ri of the *Tuatha De Dannan*, and High King of Innisfail. Brought his people out of the Otherworld at the end of the Third Age of Man- also known as The Transition. Conquered the surviving mortals, then brought them firmly under unified Sidhe overrule. A kind and compassionate ruler, if distracted and detached.

- *Etain-* (Deceased) Midhir's Queen. Died in childbirth, or some say, retreated to *Tir Na Nog* on the other side of *Tech Duinn;* to await her beloved in peace. Long believed to be the daughter of the sun god Bel, and Danu, the earth goddess. Midhir's winning of her hand, is its own tale.

- *Kaer Yin Mac Midhir Adair-* The *Ard Tiarne* of the *Tuatha De Dannan*, and Crown Prince of Innisfail. Son of Midhir and Etain, he was the first Dannan to be born in Innisfail after The Transition. Grand Marshal of the Wild Hunt, and Commander of Aes Sidhe's standing armies. Killed Kevin Donahugh in single combat, during the first Bethonair War, in (408), and ended the war of '84, at Dumnain with another victory over the Donahugh Clan. Prince of Eire, and Cymru. A cold, unfeeling character, who values martial might over all other virtues.

- *Eri Mac Midhir Bres-* Daughter of Midhir and Etain, Princess of Innisfail, and Queen of Scotia. Married to Jan Fir Bres, King of Scotia; and Lord of Skye.

- *Fionn-* Lord Protector of Aes Sidhe, and Midhir's sworn Sword.

- *Ysirdra-* High Priestess of Danu, and trusted advisor to the High King.

CROGHAN

(House of the Red Eagle)

- *Bov Mac Crom Dearg-* Son of Nuada of the Golden Arm, and King of Connaught. Called Bov 'The Red', by his people, for his fiery hair and disposition. Some call him the 'Red Boar of Connaught', behind his back- for his stubborn pride, short temper, and devotion to the hunt. A peerless warrior in battle, but too hotheaded to make much of a commander. Brother of Midhir, the High King.

- *Grainne Mac Eochaid-* Bov's Queen. A Former Fir Bolg princess, daughter of Eochaid Mac Nemed, and his wife, Liadan Mac Nemed- also, his first cousin. She was married into the *Tuatha De Dannan* as part of a peace treaty with Armagh, after Nuada slew Ecohaid, and took his throne. She and Bov have a stormy relationship.

- *Tam Lin Mac Bov Dearg-* Prince of Connaught, and Marshal of the West. Son of Bov and Grainne, making him the only living Dannan prince who is also half Fir-Bolg. Beloved nephew of the *Ard Ri,* Midhi— and Commander of Croghan's Blood Eagles; an elite fighting force, second only to Bri Leith's Wild Hunt *(An Fiach Fian).* Favorite cousin and trusted friend of Kaer Yin Adair.

- *Shar Lianor-* Tam Lin's First Lieutenant, and right-hand man.
- *Niall-* A Blood Eagle
- *Oisin-* A Blood Eagle

TECH DUINN

(House of the Raven)

- *Diarmid Mac Crom Dubh-* King of Tech Duinn, and Lord of the *Oiche Ard Fad*. Called *Fiachra Ri*, by the Sidhe- or Raven King, in Eire. A Skysinger, like his grandfather Crom Dagda; and a Brehon of the Tuatha De Dannan. He is the only member of his house, as he rules a kingdom of the dead. All lesser Sidhe call him 'King', including the Lu Sidhe*,* and Dor Sidhe- which would unleash themselves upon mortal kind, did he not guard the gates of the Otherworld with a firm hand. Brother to Midhir, the High King. An ambitious, mercurial man, whose loyalty can never truly be counted upon.

ARMAGH

(House of the Black Bull)

- *Eochaid Mac Nemed-* (Deceased) Ancient King of the Fir Bolg. Slain by Nuada, king of the *Tuatha De Dannan* for his throne, and the right to rule in Innisfail. Married to his cousin Liadan, by their Fomorian Grandfather, Balor. Was a just ruler, and fearsome warrior.
- *Liadan Mac Nemed-* Queen of the Fir Bolg in ancient times, and Dowager Queen of Armagh, after The Transition.
- *Falan (the elder) Mac Eochaid-* King of the Fir Bolg, and lord of the ancient city of Armagh. A notorious philanderer and by all accounts, a terribly irresponsible ruler. Often wanders the *raths* of his Sworn Shields, to seduce their wives and avail themselves of their forced hospitality.
- *Falan (the younger) Mac Nemed-* (Deceased) Prince of Armagh, and former Marshal of the North. Despised his father so much, he took his grandfather's surname. Believed to have been the mightiest warrior in Armagh, and the greatest swordsmen in Innisfail— until he was defeated by Kaer Yin Adair at a tourney, years before his death. Slain at Dumnain, by a nameless Milesian soldier from Bethany.
- *Grainne Mac Nemed-* Princess of Armagh, and daughter of Falan the Elder and his third wife, Taliu. Half-sister to Falan the Younger, and an astute pupil of the Dowager Queen. Named for her aunt Grainne, whom married Bove Dearg in ancient times.

Author's Note

october 2020
(02, Dor samna)
sunny florida

The Sons of Mil is the culmination of over twenty years' work. Born in the glitter-drenched annals of 80's fantasy books, comics, and feature films… it wasn't long before it took on a life of its own. From a tender age, I'd scribble nonsense tales from 'Innisfail' in crayon and read them aloud to my grandmother.

Years later, I knew it was the story I *had* to tell, no matter what.

As a complete work, it's lived four lives already. The first of these began in hastily scratched notebooks, written in lackadaisical cursive. Kaer Yin had a name, an occupation, and a terrible attitude— even then. That version was first copyrighted way back in 1998. Back then, I thought no one would ever take a silly book about 'elves,' swords, and magic seriously. TSOM's second version was drafted and edited shortly after The Lord of The Ring's release in 2001. Boy, I'd been wrong about people not enjoying elves and swords. This time, I'd gotten somewhat tech savvy (had a myspace page and everything, ya'll!) and learned how to type and properly format. Around 2003, with a completed TSOM, I queried agents and publishers like crazy. Lo and behold, my little fantasy had attracted an agent. I was a serious, for REALS writer! But oh wait— she *hated* my ending, loathed half of my characters, and wanted me to change everything I loved so much about this world I'd created. I mean…

535

what did *she* know? — I was a 'for really-real' writer! I knew what I was doing. Right? Nope.

Lost my contract for being a 23-year-old prat.

Having loved and lost, TSOM was shelved for a couple of years until I decided to give it another go-round. Into the interwebs went I! In 2007-08 I joined a popular online writing community, sharing bits and pieces of TSOM with (I believed) other like-minded writers. My work was promptly stolen, altered, and redistributed by another member of this community. This person achieved runaway success with content they neither conceptualized nor understood. I was heartbroken. Feeling betrayed and utterly disillusioned with writing at large... I gave up for YEARS. Then, in 2017, mourning the penultimate season of Game of Thrones... I was cleaning out my old filing cabinet when I came across my first copyrights. I promptly dug up my old notebooks, downloaded my old files, and pulled up my bootstraps. *The Sons of Mil* is, was, and had *always* been *my* story to tell. I refused to go out like a punk.

The result? Version number four, which you are holding now.

Kaer Yin lives again, as he was always *meant* to.

This book could never have made it so far without the love and support of many wonderful people. First and foremost, my father... for being the writer, I aim to live up to. Obi-Dawn, for teaching me how to be a good person, and believing in me, even when I didn't deserve it. Dianne, for being the guiding star in my life. Jessica and Bev, for constantly encouraging me to keep going; despite the world's demands; jobs, bills, illness, divorce, or distance.... and most of all, My Nana... whose heritage and brilliant storytelling were the foundation of this book.

All of my love.

L.M. Riviere
www.lmriviere.com
FB: LMRiviereAuthor
T: @LM_Riviere
I: @lmrfoto2

About the Text

This series leans heavily on Irish Gaelic. As a student of the language, I have done my level best to include the appropriate usage of every term and phrase, from syntax to punctuation. That said, I am not entirely fluent, and there are bound to be mistakes in the text.

Additionally, most of the terms I use were derived from the most archaic forms, as the characters and place names are meant to reflect a time period and etymology that precedes written alphabet by at least a thousand years. In that order, there are bound to be minor variations in spelling and pronunciation. Some terms I changed to suit myself and the rolling language I hear in my head when my characters speak... and I daresay, that is my prerogative in a fantasy novel.

For example, there a few obvious 'me-isms', like the use of '*Tuatha Dé Dannan*', which is historically spelled '*Danaan*', or '*Danann*'. I elected to place a hard focus on the interior 'n' to aid its pronunciation for non-Gaelic speakers.

If there are any mistakes or unbearable abuses of the language that distract from the text, please keep in mind that this story exists in a (semi) fictional continent a thousand years from now. A few liberties were taken.

CPSIA information can be obtained
at www.ICGtesting.com
Printed in the USA
LVHW081731031122
732316LV00015B/814

9 781914 152078